'The undisp[...]
of crime writing'

Erwin James

MARTINA
COLE

Author of 23 novels – and counting…

15 No. 1 bestsellers

4 screen adaptations

3 stage shows

Over 15 million copies sold across the world

Celebrating 25 years of record-breaking bestsellers

Stay in touch for film and TV news,
book releases and more…

🐦 @MartinaCole
f /OfficialMartinaCole
www.martinacole.co.uk

'The stuff of legend. It's vicious, nasty...
and utterly compelling' *Mirror* on **FACELESS**

'Her gripping plots pack a mean emotional punch'
Mail on Sunday on **THE RUNAWAY**

'A blinding good read'
Ray Winstone on **THE KNOW**

'Intensely readable'
Guardian on **FACELESS**

THIS IS WHAT THEY SAY

'Right from the start, she has enjoyed
unqualified approval for her distinctive
and powerfully written fiction'
The Times on **BROKEN**

'An extraordinarily powerful piece of family drama'
Daily Mirror on **THE BUSINESS**

'The acknowledged mistress of the insanely
readable gangster thriller, Cole has delivered
another addictive tale of men of violence and the
women who love them...brutally compelling'
Sunday Mirror on **GET EVEN**

'We always get excited when a Martina Cole novel drops on our desk, and she continues to maintain her reputation as one of the best fiction authors around with this gritty and unforgettable story of a family immersed in a world of violence and revenge. Spectacular' 5 ★★★★★
Closer on **THE LIFE**

'Martina tells it like it really is and her unique, honest and compassionate style shines through'
Sun on **THE TAKE**

ABOUT MARTINA COLE...

'The queen of crime'
Woman & Home on **HARD GIRLS**

'Dark and dangerous'
Sunday Mirror

'Thrilling, shocking and exceptionally written, you'll get lost in this gritty novel, which proves there really is only one Martina Cole'
Closer on **REVENGE**

'The undisputed queen of British crime thrillers'
Heat on **GET EVEN**

*Martina Cole's No. 1 bestsellers – at time of press she has
spent more weeks at No. 1 than any other author

MARTINA COLE

THE LADYKILLER

HEADLINE

Copyright © 1993 Martina Cole

The right of Martina Cole to be identified as the Author
of the Work has been asserted by her in accordance with the
Copyright, Designs and Patents Act 1988.

First published in 1993
by HEADLINE BOOK PUBLISHING

First published in paperback in 1993
by HEADLINE BOOK PUBLISHING

This edition published in paperback in 2017 by
HEADLINE PUBLISHING GROUP

9

Apart from any use permitted under UK copyright law, this publication
may only be reproduced, stored, or transmitted, in any form, or by any
means, with prior permission in writing of the publishers or, in the case of
reprographic production, in accordance with the terms of licences issued
by the Copyright Licensing Agency.

All characters in this publication are fictitious and any resemblance to real
persons, living or dead, is purely coincidental.

Cataloguing in Publication Data is available from the British Library

ISBN 978 0 7553 7213 3

Typeset in Galliard by Avon DataSet Ltd,
Bidford-on-Avon, Warwickshire

Printed and bound in Great Britain by Clays Ltd, St Ives plc

Headline's policy is to use papers that are natural, renewable and recyclable
products and made from wood grown in well-managed forests and other
controlled sources. The logging and manufacturing processes are expected to
conform to the environmental regulations of the country of origin.

HEADLINE PUBLISHING GROUP
An Hachette UK Company
Carmelite House
50 Victoria Embankment
London, EC4Y 0DZ

www.headline.co.uk
www.hachette.co.uk

I dedicate this book to
Les and Christopher

I would like to thank my agent, Darley Anderson, for his faith, his trust and most of all his friendship.

Many thanks to Sergeant Steven Bolger of the Windermere Police Department, Florida, for all his help while I researched this book.

And a little thanks to Julie, for typing and typing and typing.

And a special thanks to my husband and son, they know what for.

Book One

Of all the griefs that harass the distress'd
Sure the most bitter is a scornful jest;
Fate never wounds more deep the gen'rous heart,
Than when a blockhead's insult points the dart
                                   – Samuel Johnson, 1709–84

I have chosen thee in the furnace of affliction
                                   – Isaiah, 48:10

Prologue

'All I asked you to do was take off your muddy shoes. For Christ's sake, George, are you thick or something? Can't you even take in the most simple thing?'

Elaine Markham looked at her husband's expressionless face and fought down an urge to slam her fist into it. She could feel herself gritting her teeth and made a conscious effort to relax. Once more her eyes went to the wet mud all over her kitchen floor.

Sighing heavily, she took out the floor cloth from underneath the kitchen sink, slammed the cupboard door shut and began to fill a plastic bowl with water. George Markham watched his wife as she sprinkled some Flash into the water. Sitting down on one of the kitchen chairs, he began to remove his gardening shoes, careful not to let any more mud or dirt fall on the pristine floor.

Elaine turned from the sink with the bowl of water and shrieked at him: 'Can't you do that on a piece of newspaper? Are you so stupid you can't even think of doing a simple thing like that?'

George stared at his wife for a few seconds, chewing on his bottom lip.

'I'm sorry, Elaine.' His voice was low and bewildered. The sound of it made his wife screw her eyes up tight.

Pulling off his shoes, George went to the kitchen door and dropped them outside. Shutting the door carefully, he turned back to his wife.

'Give me that, Elaine. I'll clean up the mess.' He smiled at her sadly, causing her breathing to become laboured. She shook her head in irritation.

'No. You'll only make it worse. By God, George, no wonder you can't get on at work. It's a wonder they even allow you to go there every day.' She put the bowl of steaming water on the floor and knelt down. As she began washing the floor she was still complaining.

'Honestly, you're enough to drive a person up the bloody wall. You can't do anything . . . *anything* . . . without ballsing it up in some way. Look at last week . . .'

George watched his wife's ample buttocks moving under her apron as she worked and talked. The rolls of fat around her hips were shuddering alarmingly as she scrubbed at the floor. In his mind's eye, he saw himself getting up from his seat and kicking her as hard as he could in the rump, sending her and the bowl of water flying. The fantasy made him smile to himself.

'What are you grinning at?' He brought himself back to the present with difficulty and focused on Elaine's face. She was staring at him over her shoulder, her bright green eye-shadow and ruby red lips lurid in the glare from the strip light.

'Nothing . . . Nothing, love.' He sounded confused.

'Just piss off, George. Out of my sight.'

He continued to stare at his wife. He watched as her strong arms and hands wrung out the floor cloth, her fingers squeezing until every last drop of water was gone. He wished he was squeezing Elaine's neck. Instead he went towards the back door.

'Where are you going now?' Her voice was high and querulous.

George stared at her.

'I still have some things to do in the shed.'

Elaine rolled her eyes to the ceiling.

'Well, why on earth did you come in in the first place? Messing up the floor, causing all this.' She spread her arms in a gesture of wonderment.

'I just wanted a cup of tea. But I can see that you're busy . . .'

He made a hasty exit from the kitchen and pulled on his gardening shoes again outside the back door. Elaine stared at the closed door for a few seconds. As always after she had 'been at' George, as she termed it to herself, she felt guilty. Guilty and flat. He was just so useless. Over the years, his placid acceptance of their way of life had driven her mad. Sighing, she carried on washing the floor.

Inside his shed, George bolted the wooden door and leant against it for a few moments, the sweat cold on his forehead. Licking his lips, he closed his eyes and began to breathe deeply.

One of these days Elaine was going to get a shock. She was going to open her mouth once too often. He could feel the hammering of his heart against his ribs and placed his hand over it as if to quell the movement.

He turned from the door and walked to the opposite end of his shed. Pulling a pile of gardening magazines from an old school desk, he opened the top. Inside the desk were a couple of scruffy jumpers – his gardening jumpers. Taking these out, he smiled. Underneath them were his books. His *real* books, with real women in them. Women who did not nag and chide and want. Women who just lay passively and smiled. Whatever you might do to them.

He picked up the top book. On the cover was a young girl of about twenty. Her arms were tied behind her back and she had a leather collar around her neck. Her long golden blond hair lay across her shoulders and partially obscured her breasts. A man's hand was pulling her head backwards, his hairy maleness messing up the girl's lovely locks. She was smiling.

George stared at the picture for a while. His small, even teeth just showed beneath his lips in a slight smile. Licking his lips again, he sat in his chair. He opened the magazine slowly as if for the first time, wanting to savour the pleasure of every picture.

He looked at the girl in front of him, a different girl this time. Oriental-looking, with tiny pointed breasts and a curtain of black hair. She was on all fours; the leather strap around her neck was attached to her feet. If she struggled against it, you could see that she would choke to death. A man was behind her. He wore a black leather mask and was about to plunge his erect penis into the girl's anus. Her back was arched and she was looking at the camera, a smile of beatific pleasure plastered across her face.

George sighed with contentment. He slowly looked through the magazine, pausing here and there to hold the book away from him, to see the pictures from a different angle. He could feel the familiar sense of excitement building up inside. He pushed his hand into the crease of the chair. He felt around for a second, then his hand found what he was looking for. He drew out an army knife, then, placing the magazine carefully across his knees, he pulled the knife out from its cover. It was a large knife with a seven-inch serrated blade. He turned it around in the sunshine that was streaming through the window, watching it glinting. He looked down at the girl in the centrefold of the magazine. Her face was looking up at him in a mixture of agony and ecstasy as a hooded man ejaculated into her face, the semen running down her chin and on to her breasts.

Carefully and precisely, George began to dismember her. He drew the knife across her throat, slitting the paper. Then he began to tear at her breasts and vagina. All the time she watched him. Smiling at him. Encouraging him. He could feel his erection building, could feel the cold sweat under his arms and across his back. He began to hack at the magazine, pushing the knife into the paper. He heard the rush in his ears as if he was swimming underwater and then the graceful, almost euphoric waves of the orgasm as it reached its crescendo.

George lay back in the comfortable old chair, his breathing coming in small gasps, his heartbeat gradually returning to normal. He closed his eyes and gradually the sounds and sights of the day came back to him.

He could hear his neighbour's strimmer outside his shed. Could hear the children next door playing in their paddling pool. Their high-pitched baby laughter drifted into his consciousness. A bead of salty sweat dripped into his eyes and he blinked it away. He shook his head slowly and looked down at his lap. That was when he saw the blood.

He blinked rapidly for a few seconds. The girl was covered in blood. The body that he had slashed to pieces was slowly being stained crimson. George stared.

He pushed the magazine from him, every nerve in his body vibrating with shock.

He had cut himself! He stared down at the gash on his thigh. It was pumping blood everywhere. He jumped from his seat in a panic. The knife had slit his jeans and pierced his own flesh!

He must tell Elaine. Get her to take him to the hospital. He went to the shed door in a blind panic.

Then he remembered the books.

Holding the injured leg with one hand, he gathered the magazines from the floor. He thrust them into the child's desk with the others. Bundling the jumpers on top, he shut the lid. He could feel the blood running down his leg.

He picked up the pile of gardening magazines and threw them on top of the desk. Blood was everywhere now.

Pulling the bolt from across the top of the shed door he burst out into the sunlight. The sound of splashing and shrieking coming over the larch lap fence assaulted his ears. George ran up the path to the back door and thrust it open.

Elaine was preparing the vegetables for dinner. She turned towards him in dismay. He stood before her, covered in blood.

'I – I've cut myself, Elaine.' He was nearly crying.

'Oh my God, George!' She grabbed a tea towel and would it round his leg, pulling it tight. 'Come on. I'll drive you to the hospital.'

George lay in a cubicle of the Accident and Emergency department of Grangely Hospital. He felt sick. A young nurse was trying to remove his trousers.

'Please, Mr Markham. I must take them off.' Her voice was young and husky.

'No! No, you mustn't. Cut the trouser leg off or something.'

George and the nurse stared at one another. Then both looked towards the curtain as it was pulled back. The young nurse breathed a sigh of relief. It was the Charge Nurse, Joey Denellan.

'What's the matter, Nurse?' His voice held the false jocularity peculiar to male nurses.

'Mr Markham won't let me remove his trousers.'

The man smiled at George. 'Bit of a shy one, are you? Well, never mind. I'll do it for you.'

The nurse left and before George could protest the young man was pulling off his jeans. George tried to grab the waistband but the boy was too strong. They were off.

George swallowed deeply and turned his head away from the boy's face.

Joey Denellan stared at the wounded leg with an expert eye. Deep, but it had not affected any main arteries. His eyes flicked over the man before him and stopped dead. No wonder the old boy was so against Jenny pulling his trousers off. The stains were very recent and still sticky. What had he been up to that could have got him such a large gash in his leg? He shrugged. Theirs was not to reason why.

'What kind of knife was it?' Joey was careful to keep his voice light.

'Oh, a Swiss army knife.' George's voice was small and the younger man felt sorry for him.

'Well, it will need a few stitches in, but don't worry. You didn't sever anything important. Would you like me to see if I can find you some clean pants?'

George heard the 'man to man' inflection in the other's voice. He nodded. 'Please. I . . .'

'Righty ho then. I'll be back in a minute. The doctor will be here soon, OK?'

'Thank you. Thank you very much. Would you . . . keep my wife away, please?'

George's eyes were pleading and Joey nodded slowly.

'OK. Don't worry.' He walked from the cubicle and went out to the reception area.

'Mrs Markham?' He looked around the assembled people and was not surprised to see the fat woman with the dyed red hair and bright green track suit stand up and walk towards him. He had somehow known that this would be the poor bloke's wife.

'Is he all right? My God, only George could cut himself while sitting in a bloody shed. Honestly, Doctor . . .'

'Nurse. I'm a nurse.'

As Elaine went to speak again he interrupted her.

'We're going to stitch your husband after the doctor has seen him. If you would like to get yourself a coffee or something, there's a machine at the end of that corridor.' He pointed to the swing doors to the right.

Elaine knew when she was being shut up and her eyes took on the steely glint usually reserved for George. Turning away, she walked towards the swing doors and pushed them open with such force they crashed against the walls.

Joey Denellan watched her. No wonder the poor old sod looked so downtrodden. Being married to her must be like being married to Attila the Hun. Still Joey was puzzled. How did the old boy get the gash on his leg? What had she said? In a garden shed. How did that account for the semen, which it definitely was, in his underpants? He heard someone call him.

'Joey, an RTA on the M25.'

'How many involved?' He walked towards the reception desk.

'Four. Estimated time of arrival seven minutes.'

'OK. Call Crash.'

Joey began to make arrangements to receive the casualties from the road accident. George Markham was pushed from his mind.

*

'Are you coming, George?' Peter Renshaw's deep boom-ing voice seemed to bounce off the walls of the office and hit George in the face.

'Coming where?' He peered at Renshaw.

'To the do, Georgie. The bloody leaving do – for Jonesy.'

'Oh, yes. Jonesy's leaving do. Of course, of course. Yes, I'll be going.'

'Good on you. Got him a strippergram, the lot! Tell you what, Georgie, it will be a great do. Bl-oody great!'

Peter Renshaw had a habit of stressing some words by chopping them in two to get his point across. It drove George up the wall.

Renshaw was a salesman for the clothing company for which George worked. He towered over George in height and it was obvious he liked this. Peter Renshaw was in his early thirties and from what everyone could gather, he earned a lot of money. He was the number one salesman. He liked George for some strange reason and always made sure he was invited to any dos that were on the agenda.

'I arranged the strippergram meself, Georgie boy. Biggest set of Bristols this side of the water. Can't wait to see old Jonesy's face.'

George smiled.

Old Jonesy ... Howard Jones was younger than George himself. About forty-five was Howard Jones. George was fifty-one. He shuddered inwardly. Fifty-one. His life was nearly over. Peter Renshaw's voice was still booming on.

'It's all arranged. The Pig and Whistle first. Twenty quid whip-round by the way. Then on to that new night-club – what's it called? The Platinum Blonde, that's it. Watch all the little birds stru-tting their stuff. Be a right laugh!'

George carried on smiling.

'Well, I'll let you get on then. Got a hot piece of pussy down in accounts who's just dy-ing for it. See you Friday then?'

George nodded. 'Yes. See you on Friday, Peter.'

He watched the man walk from his office. Old Jonesy . . . He supposed they called him Old Markham. He looked at his watch. It was five thirty-five. He got out of his chair and, putting on his jacket, made his way out of the building.

Kortone Separates was a thriving firm, even in the recession. George worked in the book-keeping department of accounts.

He left the small corridor and went to the stairway that led to the car park. He never used the lifts. As he walked down the stairs he saw Miss Pearson kneeling on the floor picking up some papers. She was young, only about eighteen, and had worked for Kortone's for a year. George had never spoken to her. She had left three buttons undone and from the landing above her George could see the swelling of her bosom as she stretched out her arms to gather the papers.

He stared down at her. The creamy flesh was firm and inviting. The girl looked up at him. He saw the heavily made-up face and forced himself to move down the stairs. He bent down and retrieved some papers, handing them to her silently.

'Thank you, Mr Markham.'

She knew his name! George felt an enormous surge of pleasure over this little fact.

'You're welcome.' He stood up and looked down at her again. Then the door above opened and Peter Renshaw's voice boomed down to them.

'There you are! I've been looking everywhere for you.

You sly old fox, George. Might have known you'd be where the pretty girls are!'

Miss Pearson looked at Peter and gave a broad smile. George watched her face closely.

'Oh, Peter.' Her voice was husky and breathless. 'I waited for you but . . .'

George was aware of Peter Renshaw's footsteps on the stairs, bringing him closer. He quickly picked up the rest of the papers from the floor and handed them to Miss Pearson.

George walked away from them, certain that he would not be noticed. He was right. Neither of them said a word to him. He walked out of the building and unlocked his car, an A-reg Orion. He sat in the driving seat, waiting.

The couple finally left the building and walked towards Peter's car, Renshaw's arm draped across the girl's shoulder, one hand squeezing her breast. Miss Pearson giggled and pushed it away.

Another slut. Another whore. What had Peter said? Dying for it? George closed his eyes and savoured the picture his words had conjured up.

He visualised Miss Pearson, her body open to him, her legs sprawled apart, tied to the legs of a bed. Her hands tied behind her back, her heavily made-up face smiling at him as he approached her. She was begging for it. Begging and pleading with him . . .

'Mr Markham?' George's eyes flew open.

'Are you all right? You look very white.'

George stared at the man looking in at the window of his car. It was the car park attendant.

'Yes, thank you.' George smiled timidly. 'I felt a bit tired, that's all.'

The man made a salute and straightened up.

George watched him walk away, his heart hammering

in his ears. He tried to get the picture back in his mind but it was no good. Trembling, he started up his car and drove into Grantley town centre. The books he had ordered were due in today. He smiled, enjoying the late summer sunshine and the exquisite feeling of anticipation.

It crossed his mind briefly that his 'hobby' was now becoming an obsession, but he thrust the thought aside. His leg was still sore and he rubbed it absentmindedly as he drove.

It was the end of September 1989.

Chapter One

Elaine Markham looked at her husband as he watched the television. His shiny balding head was nodding up and down as if he was agreeing with everything that the newscaster said.

'Oh, for Christ's sake, George! Stop agreeing with the TV.'

He turned in his chair to face her, a hurt expression on his face. Elaine closed her eyes. She could feel her hands clenching into fists and made herself relax.

'Shall I make you a cup of Ovaltine, dear?' George asked in his soft voice.

'Yes, you do that.'

George went out to the impossibly clean kitchen and set about making the bedtime drinks. He put on the pan of milk and then, opening one of the kitchen cabinets, took out Elaine's sleeping pills. Carefully grinding one between two spoons, he placed the powder in the cup with the sugar. Smiling, he poured steaming milk into the cup and stirred it vigorously. Then, removing two more of the sleeping pills, he took the Ovaltine and the pills into Elaine.

'Here you are, dear. I brought your pills in for you as well.' She took the drink and pills from him.

'Thanks, George. Look, I know I go on at times . . .' Her voice trailed off.

'I don't take the slightest bit of notice, Elaine. I know that I – well, that I irritate you is the word, I suppose?'

George smiled at her, the sad smile that always made her want to rip him to shreds.

She put the sleeping pills into her mouth and washed them down with the Ovaltine, burning her lips.

George was still smiling.

'This tastes bitter.'

He raised his eyebrows and took a sip of his own drink.

'Well, mine is fine, dear. Maybe it's the aftertaste of the pills?'

'Could be. I think I'll take my drink up with me.' She pulled herself from her seat with difficulty.

'Night, Elaine. Sleep well.'

She stared at her husband.

'If I slept well, George, I wouldn't be taking sleeping tablets.'

'It's just an expression, dear. That's all.'

Was it her imagination or was George different lately? Although she could not pinpoint what had changed, she had the distinct feeling that the balance between them was shifting slightly. Looking at her husband now, she would swear on a stack of bibles that he was laughing at her.

'Good night then, dear,' he said again.

She tried to smile at her husband.

'Yes. Good night, George.'

She walked from the room and his gaze followed her. As she made her way up the stairs to their room, the feeling of uneasiness came over her once more. It was the beginning of December and George had been 'wrong' somehow for the last couple of months. Nothing she could put her finger on exactly, but subtle little differences. He had taken to going out in the evenings for walks, for instance. He was only gone an hour or so but . . .

She pulled off the candlewick dressing gown and sat on the edge of the bed. He had never once, in twenty-seven years of marriage, gone out walking anywhere. In fact, it was his pet hate.

She took off her sheepskin-lined slippers and rubbed at the corn on her foot. Her legs were fat like the rest of her and were disfigured by varicose veins. She stared at them and shrugged.

She sat against the pillows, picked up her latest Mills and Boon and read while the pills took effect and she finished her Ovaltine.

The words were becoming blurred. She blinked her eyes, trying to focus. The pills were working quicker and quicker lately.

Finally she gave up. Turning off the bedside lamp, she settled down to sleep.

Ten minutes later, George popped his head around the bedroom door and grunted in satisfaction as he heard his wife's heavy snores.

George slipped out of the house. He had on his heaviest overcoat as the night air was cold and damp. In the street light he looked no different from anyone else who walked the streets late at night. He pulled on the cheesecutter hat he had recently purchased and began his prowling.

He felt a freedom he had not experienced for twenty years in this new pastime. He walked the length and breadth of Grantley. Silently and diligently he walked. Tonight he had decided to walk by the flats that were on the other side of town. Taking a deep breath, he began his lonely trek.

As he walked, he kept a vigilant eye out for open curtains and movement. He walked to the end of Bychester Terrace and turned right. Peabody Street took him on to a dirt road that led round the perimeter of Grantley. No busy traffic, only a lone car containing a courting couple here and there. George was outside the flats in Beacham Rise within fifteen minutes.

Stationing himself under a large cherry tree opposite the small block he waited. It was eleven fifteen before he saw anything, and as usual it was the woman who lived on the second floor. The flats were what was termed 'low rise', only three storeys high. George had been here many times in the last eight weeks and it was always the woman on the second floor who provided his show. Where he was standing, under the cherry tree, was a small hill, part of the council landscaping plan, which gave him the perfect vantage point to see into the woman's flat. Taking the small opera glasses from his pocket, he watched.

Leonora Davidson yawned cavernously. She stretched her hands above her head and pulled up her thick black hair. She was dead tired. She would have to stop all the overtime, it was killing her.

She unbuttoned her blouse slowly, letting it fall from her rounded shoulders on to the floor. She unhooked her bra and let her breasts fall free, rubbing them furiously as the itching started. Lifting one breast with her hand, she looked into the mirror of her dressing table. A thick red line marked the tender flesh. She sighed. She would have to get herself some decent bras.

She cupped her breasts in her hands and pushed them up, as if weighing them. She had definitely put on weight. Then she unzipped her skirt and let it fall to the floor. Stepping out of it, she kicked it away from her.

Leonora looked at her body in the mirror. Not bad for her age. A bit saggy these days but everyone lost the war with gravity eventually. She automatically held her stomach in, then let it out. Sod it! There was no one to admire her any more. Why bother?

Yawning again, wider this time, she went to her dressing stool and picked up her nightie, a wincyette affair that kept her warm if nothing else. After one last stretch, she turned out the light and climbed into bed.

George stood under the cherry tree entranced. When the light went off in the bedroom, he mumbled a curse under his breath and pushed the opera glasses back into his overcoat pocket. He was sweating. Taking a handkerchief out of his trouser pocket, he mopped his forehead.

Stupid bitch! What he would not give to be in that flat now. He would show her what it was all about, by Christ! Standing around naked. Inviting people to look at her. The slut! In his heightened excitement George was unaware of the two youths who had been watching him watching her.

'What you doin'?' The voice caused him to swivel around on the balls of his feet.

'I . . . I beg your pardon?' His voice squeaked with surprise. Two youths stood there, one wearing a long leather coat and with straggly brown hair. The other was wearing a large sheepskin and was what George knew was called a skinhead.

'You heard, you old ponce. What was you doin' watching Mrs Davidson getting undressed? You a nonce?'

The boy in the leather coat stepped towards him, a menacing look on his face.

'Got any money?' This from the skinhead. George smelt a distinct odour of glue and vomit.

He stared at them, nonplussed.

The youth in the leather coat lurched towards him and he stepped back nimbly.

'If you two don't go away I will call for assistance.'

The leather-coated boy mimicked him.

'"If you two don't go away I will call for assistance." Well, we –' he pointed to his friend and himself – 'might just call the Filth ourselves. You're a fucking peeping Tom, ain't ya? So just give us your dosh and you can go. Quietly.'

The skinhead heaved and George watched in revulsion as a stream of vomit ejaculated from the boy's mouth. It landed just by his shoes, splashing them. The odour wafted into his nostrils as the sick steamed in the freezing night air.

The leather-coated boy laughed uproariously at his friend, who was now hanging on to the cherry tree for support.

Fumbling inside his coat, George pulled out two five-pound notes and handed them to the boy. Leather coat took them from him and pushed them into the pocket of his jeans.

'Come on, Trev. Let's trounce the bastard.'

Trevor was not capable of letting go of the cherry tree and so the leather-coated boy launched himself at George alone. He held up his arms in self-defence as the first blows hit him in the face and head. He could feel himself being pushed down to the ground and the knowledge that he would end up lying in the skinhead's vomit was all that kept him upright. He felt the cold sting as the boy's fist came into contact with his face. Then he was rolling down the small hill, the leather-coated boy kicking him.

'Oi! What's all the racket about out there?' A man's deep voice echoed across the road and the boy looked up in its direction. A light was on on the third floor and a

20

large man in a string vest was leaning out of a window, shaking his fist. Lights were going on all over the flats. George heard the two boys stumbling away while he lay on the cold ground, gasping for air.

Leonora Davidson heard the shouting and leapt from her bed. She pulled on her dressing gown and slippers and looked out of her bedroom window. She saw the body of a man lying at the bottom of the small rise, underneath the lamp post. She could see the two youths running away. One of them, in a leather coat, was dragging his friend along. She gritted her teeth. No one was safe these days. It was obvious the poor man had been mugged! She walked from her flat, picking up her door keys as she went, and ran down to where a small crowd had gathered around the injured man.

'What happened, Fred?' Her breath steamed in the cold night air. She shivered.

'Little buggers want slaughtering. Mugged this poor old bastard as he walked by!'

George still lay on the ground, quite enjoying all the attention.

'Oh, you poor thing.' Leonora's voice was filled with pity. 'I called the police. They'll be here in a minute.'

George's ears flapped at the word 'police'. He was up off the ground and brushing himself down in record time.

'Really, there's no need for the police. They'll never catch them anyway. And I'm in a hurry.'

He began to walk away from the small gathering.

'But if you saw them you could give a description like.' Fred's voice was cajoling.

George was shaking his bald head. He was aware that he had lost his hat somewhere along the line. He looked around for it frantically.

21

Leonora walked over to him.

'You've had a terrible shock. Shall I make you a nice cup of tea?'

George could not believe what she was saying. She was inviting him into her home. If it had not been for her he would not be in this condition. The stupid whore!

'It's perfectly all right. I just want to get home.'

His voice held its usual meekness and he saw her smile at him pityingly.

A police car sped around the corner of the flats and screeched to a halt by the little crowd. George put his hand over his face in dismay. This was all he needed.

'All right, all right. Calm down. What happened?'

Everyone started talking at once.

Sergeant Harris's voice boomed out and George guessed it would wake up any of the residents who were not already up.

Sergeant Harris looked at Leonora.

'What happened, love?'

'This poor man was mugged. Right here.' She pointed to George who was trying to creep away.

The sergeant looked at him, bewildered.

'Where are you going?'

'I . . . I really must get home. My wife will be worried . . .'

Harris smiled at him. In shock, he thought to himself.

'Come on, sir. Come to the station and we can get this all sorted out in no time.'

'NO!' George was amazed at the sound of his own voice. 'I . . . I . . . Oh, leave me alone!'

Harris stared at him stonily. 'We're only trying to help, sir.'

'You know you won't catch them. I just want to go home and forget about it.'

He began to walk away as quickly as he could.

The small crowd stared after his retreating back. Sergeant Harris nodded at PC Downes and they got back into their Panda car and followed him.

'Get in, sir. The least we can do is give you a lift.'

George got into the car, his heart in his boots.

'Well I never, Fred! That poor man was in shock, I reckon.'

'You're right there, Leonora love. Poor old git. Not safe to walk the sodding streets these days . . .'

'That's the truth, Fred. I even get worried in me flat, with all the doors locked. You hear so much about rape and violence, it makes your blood run cold. Then to see that poor old man getting beaten up like that . . .' She left the sentence unfinished.

Sergeant Harris kept up a stream of chatter all the way to George's house.

'Look, sir. If you change your mind just pop into the station.'

'I will, Officer. At the moment all I want is to get home. This is the house.'

The Panda car pulled up outside George's home and he made a hasty retreat. Once inside he pulled off his overcoat and hung it on the banister, then went up to the bathroom. His face was slightly swollen but not too much. He breathed a sigh of relief.

He went back downstairs and checked his overcoat. It was covered in vomit. He cursed silently and set about cleaning it.

Fifty minutes later, there was no evidence of his escapade whatsoever. He made himself a cup of tea, and carrying it into the front room went to the lead light cupboard that housed the brandy and poured a generous measure into the cup. He sat on the settee and drank it gratefully.

When he had finished he felt better, and getting up from the sofa went up to his wife's room and popped his head around the door. Her snoring was loud and heavy. He smiled to himself. Three Mogadons to knock the old bag out, but it was worth it.

Sneaking downstairs, he went to the hall cupboard. Opening it, he pulled up the carpet and folded it back. Then, using the screwdriver he left there for this express purpose, he prised up one of the floorboards. There, staring up at him, was his Mandy!

He picked up the video almost lovingly, afterwards replacing the floorboard and the carpet. He took the video into the lounge. Pouring himself another measure of Three Barrels brandy into his dirty cup, he watched the film. As he did, he felt the tension and pain of the last few hours leave his body. As Mandy was assaulted over and over by a motley crew of degenerates, George Markham finally relaxed.

Visions of Mrs Davidson cupping her breasts kept coming into his thoughts. Her furious rubbing of them. He watched Mandy take a man's penis into her semen-smeared mouth and suddenly her face was Mrs Davidson's, the man was him. He felt his breathing getting heavier.

One good thing had come out of the evening: at least he knew her name now.

The next day, George did not go to work. His face was swollen and he told Elaine that he had an abscess on his tooth. She dutifully rang his office and then left to go to her own job.

She worked in a large supermarket in Grantley town. She was a 'checkout girl' and hated it.

Left alone, George had an idea.

Dressing himself meticulously, he got into his car and drove to London. As he admired the Essex countryside (even in the cold and wet it looked magnificent) George made his plans. After the fiasco of the night before, he decided that he should get himself kitted out properly.

He turned on Essex Radio and sang along to the Carpenters as he drove. Lighthearted and gay, he made his way to London's West End.

George walked nervously into the shop in Soho. It was his first time in a sex shop; he'd always sent for his books and videos by post. But once inside he felt strangely at ease.

Behind the counter was a man of about his age who smiled at him as he browsed around the shop. The only disappointment was that the books and videos were tame. Tame and boring. He picked up a leather mask and took it to the counter.

'Eighty-five quid, please, guv.'

George meticulously counted out the money. It would be his Christmas present to himself. He felt almost jovial.

'You into bondage?'

George nodded shyly. 'Yes.' He smiled his secret smile that just showed his teeth. 'Yes, I am.'

'Was you after the hard porn like? Only if you was, I think I can help you . . .'

George picked up the carrier bag with the mask in and smiled again. Wider this time.

'I've got snuff movies here for two hundred quid a throw.'

George was perplexed. 'Snuff movies?'

The man saw his confusion and pulled him to one side to explain.

'Look, they're films with birds in . . . getting the business

25

like. But they ain't pretend, see? It's really happening to them. That's why they're called "snuff" or "stuff" movies.'

The man could see that George was still unsure. He sighed. He had been in this game for thirty years, man and boy. He knew a nonce when he saw one, and he would swear on his granddaughter's head that this bloke was one. A prize nonce.

'Look, it's the Yanks who thought them up. They kidnap some bird. Tie her up. Rape her and all that, you know . . . And her screams and moans are real, get it? Real. It's true. I've got a new lot in and they are well dawdy, I can tell you. There's one where the bird is actually dead and they still fuck the arse off her. Going like hot cakes they are.'

George's eyes were gleaming.

'How much did you say they were?'

'Two hundred smackers, mate. And cheap at the price. I can tell yer.'

'Can I pay by Barclaycard? Only I haven't got any more cash, you see.'

''Course you can, guv. We take everything here. Even American Express. Just as long as you have some other form of identification, we're cooking with gas.'

The man smiled and George smiled back. He felt as if he had found a true friend.

'If I was to give you a ring every now and then to see what was in stock, so to speak . . .'

The man patted his shoulder.

''Course you can, my old cocker. I'll save you anything a bit near the mark. How's that?' The man knew a policeman from thirty paces and was patting himself on the back. This bloke was a right prat.

'Oh, thank you so much. Where I live . . .' He spread his hands helplessly.

'I know what you mean. People don't understand us real men, do they?'

The shopkeeper was busy taking the credit card from George before he had time to change his mind.

'No, they don't.'

He left ten minutes later, with his mask and his new film, both in a plain brown carrier bag clutched in his sweaty hand.

Looking around him at the faces and sounds of Soho, George Markham felt as if he had finally come home.

When Elaine opened the front door after her day at work, George had the dinner on and a pot of tea waiting for her.

'Sit yourself down, my love, you must be tired out. I've made us a nice bit of steak and chips.'

Elaine stared at her husband as if she had never seen him before. He seemed almost happy.

'Thank you, George. I must say I'm glad you bothered to cook. I didn't feel like it one bit.'

He chucked her under the chin as he placed a cup of steaming tea in front of her.

'For you, my precious, anything!'

He grinned at her, and Elaine grinned back.

There was definitely something odd here. The last time George had chucked her under the chin had been over twenty years ago, when they had still been happy. She sipped her tea and tried to shake off her suspicions. That had been before they'd had to move. Before everything had started going wrong.

Elaine drank her tea, watching George as he cooked.

She shook her head. There was no doubt about it: he was happy.

But why?

Chapter Two

George sat at his desk, blind to the ledgers in front of him. All he could see was the movie that he had purchased from the sex shop in Soho. Ever since he had watched it, he'd had a sense of unreality. Sometimes it frightened him, like the night before when he had been sitting with Elaine watching a programme about Giant Pandas. He had sat, sipping his tea, watching the film – and then he had just gone. Gone away in his mind to the other film. He was *in* the other film. He was the star. He was in complete control.

He had been brought back to reality by Elaine's voice. It could crack glass and sour milk, all in one fell swoop. But his aberration had scared him. Because lately he could not control his thoughts at all. They ran away with him any time of the day or night.

He shook himself mentally and told himself to get on with the job in hand. He stared once more at the sales ledger in front of him.

'Mr Markham, have you five minutes to spare?'

The voice of Josephine Denham broke into his thoughts. He turned in his seat to see her standing in the doorway, smiling at him.

'Of course, Mrs Denham.' His voice was soft and polite.

Josephine Denham turned and walked back to her office. George Markham gave her the creeps and she did not know why. He was always polite. Chillingly polite. He never took days off for no reason, he always kept himself to himself, never took long lunches or tried to engage her in banter, like some of the other male employees. All in all he was a model worker. Yet she had to admit to herself there was something about his soft, pudgy body and watery grey eyes that gave her the willies. She sat at her desk and observed the little man in front of her.

'Please, take a seat.'

She watched George take the material of his trousers between his thumb and forefinger and pull it up before sitting down. Even this action irritated her. She saw his funny little smile, that just showed his teeth, and felt even more annoyed. George on the other hand was surreptitiously looking at Josephine's enormous breasts. He could see the rise and fall of every breath she took.

As far as he was concerned, Josephine Denham had a chest of Olympian standards.

She saw his smile widen, and forced herself to grin back.

'I am sorry to have to call you in, George. You've always been a good worker . . .'

He was more alert now. The smile had gone.

'I'm afraid that in these difficult times . . . with the recession . . . well, we're going to have to let some of the staff go. You will be paid redundancy money, of course.'

George felt as if someone had burst his own private bubble of happiness.

'I see.' But he didn't see. He didn't see at all. He had been with this firm for fifteen years.

'How many will be going?'

Josephine Denham took a deep breath. He may as well know now as later.

'Five. Johnson, Mathers, Davids and Pelham. Not forgetting your good self, of course.'

George stared at her. His expressionless face seemed to be drinking her in. She shuddered.

'I see.' So all the older men were to go. The young so-called dynamos were all staying. George felt an urge to leap from his chair and slap the supercilious bitch with her painted face, her dyed blond hair, her fat, wobbling breasts. The dirty stinking slut! The dirty whore! He hoped she died screaming of cancer. He hoped they sliced her breasts inch by inch. He hoped . . .

'Are you all right, Mr Markham?' Josephine Denham was nervous. He had sat staring at her for over five minutes. No expression on his face, nothing. He knew and she knew that he was finished. No other firm would take him at fifty-one. He just did not have what it took. He had no charisma, no personality. George Markham had nothing going for him at all.

'I really am dreadfully sorry, George.' She said his name timidly. Unsure of herself.

He looked at her before turning towards the door. 'You will be.'

His voice was muffled and Josephine could not hear him. 'Sorry, I didn't quite . . .'

George turned to face her and smiled again.

'I said, you will be.'

Was he being sarcastic? She watched as he shuffled from her office, his shoulders even more rounded and dejected-looking than when he had come in.

She breathed a sigh of relief. At least she had got that out of the way.

She picked up her cigarettes and lit one. For some unknown reason she was shaking. She grinned to herself. Imagine being nervous of a little runt like George Markham! But her uneasiness stayed with her all day.

George went back to his desk and sat silent and still until lunchtime. His mind was whirling underneath his calm exterior. He got into the little pub, the Fox Revived, at five past twelve and ordered himself a large brandy.

The barmaid was about forty-five with long bleached blond hair and enormous false eyelashes. Her tiny, empty breasts were visible through her cheesecloth top. George looked at her in disgust.

Another slut. They were all fucking sluts. He put his hand to his mouth, shocked at even thinking such a word.

'That'll be one pound ninety, please.' The barmaid's voice had a nasal twang as she tried to speak in a refined manner.

'Thank you very much, dear. Please have one yourself.'

She answered his tiny smile with a wide one of her own, showing big tobacco-stained teeth.

George handed her the five-pound note and waited for his change. Then, taking his drink, he went to a small corner table and sipped his brandy.

Elaine would go stark staring mad when he told her. It would be another thing to hold against him. Oh, Elaine was good at collecting grudges. She collected grudges like other women collected hats or shoes. She still hadn't forgiven him for that other business. She never mentioned it, oh no, but he knew that it was there between them, like a silent ghost. He took a gulp of his drink, the rawness of the cheap brandy burning his throat.

It was not his fault. He had hardly known what was happening. One minute they had been smiling and laughing and the next the girl had been screaming. Oh, that scream! It had gone right through his skull and into his brain. The silly little bitch. Surely she had known what was going to happen?

'Hello there, Georgie boy!'

Peter Renshaw stood in front of him, positively beaming with good humour and camaraderie. George felt his heart sink to his boots. This was all he needed, that bloody numbskull Renshaw twittering on.

'Hello, Peter. Can I get you a drink?'

'No. It's my shout, Georgie. Not every day I see you in my little love nest!'

George watched him click his fingers at the blonde monstrosity behind the bar and wink at her.

'Vivienne, my cherub. Bring me a G and T with ice and a slice, and whatever my good friend here is drinking. Oh, and not forgetting one for your lovely self.'

George watched the woman preening as she smiled her assent. Peter sat down beside George and whispered: 'She's been round the turf a few times, but she can warm a man's cockles when the fancy takes her.'

George wrinkled his nose in disgust and Peter laughed.

'Listen, Georgie boy, a bit of advice, man to man.' He nudged George in the ribs. 'You don't look at the mantel-piece when you're stoking the fire. Know what I mean?'

George smiled for lack of anything else to do. He wished that Renshaw would have a massive heart attack and die if that was what it took to keep him quiet.

'If you say so, Peter.'

'Pete! Pete, for God's sake, Georgie boy. No one calls me Peter, not even my old mum, God bless her.'

Vivienne brought their drinks to the table and George saw her tickle Peter's neck with her fingers as she walked away. Bloody dirty filthy slag!

'What you staring at, Georgie? Fancy a quick bonk with her, do you?' Leaning back in his seat, Peter went to call the woman back.

George, mortified at what Peter meant to do, dragged the man's head round by grabbing the collar of his sheepskin coat.

'NO! Peter . . . I mean, Pete.' He calmed his voice. 'I was just thinking, that's all. I had a bit of bad news today.'

'So they told you then?'

George looked at him, perplexed.

'Told me what?' Peter could not detect the edge to George's voice.

'That they was "outing" you. It's been common knowledge for months.'

George was dumbstruck. So everyone knew? Everyone but him. Everyone had been looking at him and laughing at him. Oh, yes, laughing at him. Laughing up their bloody sleeves at him!

Peter watched the amazed expression on George's face turn to one of virulent anger. It shocked even him. He'd thought that George had known. Everyone else had. Sorry now, he put his hand on George's arm.

'Hey, I'm sorry, old man. Christ, I thought you knew. I really thought you knew.'

George took a deep breath.

'No, Pete. I didn't know. I really didn't.'

George's voice was his own once more. Quiet and polite. 'I never even guessed.'

'Come on, Georgie boy. Best thing that could happen really. I mean, what are you – fifty-eight? Fifty-nine?'

'I'm fifty-one, Peter. Fifty-one.'

'Oh. Well, never mind anyway. Get an early pension. Live a little. See the kids.'

'I have no children, Peter. Elaine and I never . . .'

'Oh.'

Peter was finding it increasingly difficult to find things to say. He himself had a wife, four children and a string of mistresses and one-night stands the length and breadth of the country. People like George amazed and intrigued him. How could you live fifty-one years and have nothing to look forward to? He saw himself in years to come, when he was a bit long in the tooth for affairs and fumbling encounters, living with his wife and watching his grand-children grow up. With hundreds of happy memories to see him through the twilight years.

'Come on, Georgie boy, drink up. Think of the great leaving do we'll have for you! There, that'll cheer you up.' He snapped his fingers at the barmaid again. 'Another round here, Viv, if you please.'

The pub was beginning to fill up and George watched Peter greet friends and acquaintances. He nodded hello at different introductions and all the time his mind was in a turmoil.

What the hell was Elaine going to say?

Elaine sat in the canteen at work and stirred her coffee listlessly.

George was not right, yet she had to admit he had been a lot better to live with these last few weeks. He had been lighthearted. Like before all the trouble.

She pushed the unpleasant thoughts from her mind. George had paid his debt to society. He had a clean slate. They had built themselves a new life of sorts. After twenty years, maybe it was time to let go of the past.

'Oh, Elaine, I hate Fridays, don't you?'

Margaret Forrester sat down at Elaine's table and slipped off her shoes.

'My feet will end up in the *Guinness Book Of Records*

one of these days. The most swollen feet in the world.'

Elaine laughed at her friend.

'Why do you insist on wearing those heels? Get yourself a pair of comfortable flats.'

'No. My legs are me only vanity. I won't let them go till I have to.'

Elaine shook her head. 'Shall I get you a coffee?'

'Oh, yes please, Elaine. And a bowl of cold water if they've got one.'

Elaine got her friend a coffee and they sat together chatting.

'So where you off to on holiday then?'

Elaine shrugged.

'Probably Bournemouth again.'

'Oh, sod off, Elaine. No one goes to Bournemouth these days unless they go in a wheelchair. Why don't you come to Spain with me and the girls? Sun, sand, sea, sex . . .'

Margaret did a little dance in her chair.

'I can't wait to get there! Last year we was in this hotel, right on the seafront, and next door was only a bloody parrot sanctuary. All bloody night the sodding things screeched. And you know Caroline from frozen foods? She threw all our shoes at them one night. Pissed out of our heads we was. We had to go and ask for them back the next day. It was a scream!'

Elaine smiled.

'I don't know, Margaret. George . . .'

'Oh, balls to George! It's only a hundred and twenty quid for the fortnight, full board. I know it's in March and it's not that hot. But, oh dear me, do we have a good time! Please come.'

For the first time in her life Elaine felt a surge of pleasure in doing the unexpected. George was quite capable of looking after himself.

Margaret put her hand on Elaine's arm.

'Come on, girl. Let your hair down before it's too late.'

Elaine ran her tongue slowly over her teeth, then bit her lip. Margaret could see the indecision on her friend's face.

'All right then . . . I'll go!'

Elaine began to laugh in excitement.

'We'll go and book it after work. That way you can't change your mind.'

'George will have a fit when I tell him.'

'Let him! My old man did the first time, but as I said to him: "You only live once".'

'That's the truth.'

Elaine bit her lip again. This time in excitement. Two whole weeks without George! Bliss . . .

Elaine heard the front door shut and squared her shoulders as if waiting to begin a fight. But George wouldn't fight. George never fought about anything.

He would give her his wounded soldier look, his baffled schoolboy look, or his 'What have I done to deserve this?' look. She carried on mashing the potatoes. George entered the kitchen. Summoning every resource she had, Elaine put a smile on her face and looked at her husband.

'Hello, George. Sit yourself down, the meal's nearly ready.'

She saw George's right eyebrow rise and forced herself to carry on mashing.

He sat in his usual seat at the table. The white Formica table that they had bought from MFI aeons ago. When white Formica tables had been important to them.

'Have a good day?' She was determined to be friendly.

Oh yes, Elaine, George thought, I had a great day. I

was called into Mrs Denham's office and all but kicked out of the firm on my arse. He put the back of his hand over his mouth. He must stop swearing to himself. One day he would forget and swear at Elaine.

'Not bad, love. You?' His voice was low and flat.

She put the mashed potato on the plates next to the pork chops. George watched her as she patted it into shape with her fingers. Then she began to ladle out the peas.

'I had quite a good day actually, George.'

He allowed himself another lift of the eyebrow. Well, well, well. That was a turn up for the book. Elaine enjoying herself at work . . . If she was to be believed, she ran the whole store single-handed from her till.

'That's good, dear.'

Elaine was pouring the gravy and had to stifle an urge to pour it over George's bald head.

'That's nice, dear. That's good, dear. Hell's bells, George! I'm your wife. You don't have to be polite to your own wife.'

George could see the confusion in her face as she looked at him. Elaine was such a difficult woman. He could just imagine the reaction if he told her that she bored the arse off him. That her voice went through his head like a marauding migraine. That he wished she were dead so he could claim the insurance money.

Elaine put his dinner in front of him.

She was still talking, but George was on the special auto pilot he reserved for Elaine's chatter about work.

'Anyway, when they asked me . . . I mean, one of the girls had dropped out you see . . . I thought: Why not? I'd love to go to Spain.'

George was in the process of eating a piece of tough pork chop when he realised what she was saying.

'Spain? Did you say Spain?' Elaine heard the incredulity in his voice and it annoyed her. What did he think then? That she was not the Spain sort?

'Yes, I said Spain, George. You know, where the Spanish people live.'

'And you're going? You . . . to Spain?'

Elaine put down her knife and fork, balancing them on the side of her plate.

'Just what's that supposed to mean?'

George opened his mouth to answer but Elaine was in full flood by then.

'I suppose you think of Spain as full of page three girls and blond Adonises? Well, let me tell you, George, the girls at work have a bloody good time there, mate. A bloody good time. And just for once in my life –' she poked herself in the chest with her thumb – 'I am going to join in with the real world. I am going to have fun. Have a laugh. I'm not too old to enjoy myself.

'Let's face it, if I waited for you to show me a good time, I'd be six feet under.'

George watched her face as she spoke. Her features were bunched like a screwed-up handkerchief and for one dreadful moment he imagined her topless on the beach.

Then he started to laugh. He laughed until the tears ran from his eyes and he had an attack of coughing. He laughed while Elaine slapped him on the back to stop him choking. Finally he was too weak to laugh any more and slowly his breathing returned to normal.

She was staring down at him, bewildered.

'I am sorry, Elaine. Sorry for laughing. It's just that you gave me a shock. I mean, you've never wanted to go before, have you? And now out of the blue . . . You go, Elaine. You go and enjoy yourself. I can just see you with a lovely tan. It will do you the world of good.'

She was nonplussed. She had a sneaking feeling that George was taking the piss.

He read her mind and spoke again.

'I laughed because after all these years you can still surprise me.'

Elaine relaxed.

'Shall I open a bottle of wine, dear? To celebrate?'

'Yes, George. Do that. You do that.'

She sat back at the table and resumed her meal. She was too hard on George, that was the trouble. He was pleased that she was going off to enjoy herself. He didn't begrudge her a little time away from him. She made up her mind to be more friendly, try and understand him a bit better. A short while later they clinked glasses.

'To Spain, my dear.'

'To Spain.'

They finished their meal in peace, and George left Elaine finishing the bottle of wine while he went for a walk.

George walked the streets for twenty minutes, his hands deep in his pockets and his head burrowed into the neck of his overcoat. He liked the winter months, liked the anonymity the dark nights created. He made his way to Motherwell Street and walked slowly along the lines of houses.

How the hell was he going to break the news to Elaine about his redundancy? From what he could gather from Renshaw, he would be out on his ear in February. He shuddered. He had calmed her tonight but that wouldn't last long. He closed his eyes briefly, pondering his problem. His redundancy would only make her more convinced that he was an all round loser.

*

Geraldine O'Leary smiled at herself in her mirror. Still not satisfied with her make-up, she applied more fuchsia pink lipstick. Opening her mouth wide, she spread it liberally then rubbed her lips together. She smiled at herself again, satisfied. Picking up her hairbrush, she began to pull it through her long brown hair, the electricity crackling as she did so.

Mick O'Leary watched his wife from the bed. Even after twelve years she could still excite him. At thirty-four she was the mother of his three children and did not look much older than the day he'd married her. He gazed at her as she slipped on her bra and pants. Their eyes met and they smiled, an intimate smile.

'I wish you wouldn't go tonight, Gerry.'

'I don't want to go, Mick. But if I stay home I'll regret it next week, you know that. Fifteen quid is fifteen quid. And Christmas will be here soon . . .' Her voice trailed off.

Mick sighed. Getting off the bed, he pulled on his trousers.

'I suppose you're right. You're not wearing that blouse, are you?'

Geraldine looked down at the blouse she was buttoning up. 'Why? What's wrong with it?'

'You can see your bra through it.'

'Oh, Mick! You're crazy . . .'

'Well, I don't like the thought of men looking at my wife.'

'Women come in the wine bar as well, you know.' She pursed her lips at him and he laughed.

'Not as good-looking as you though, girl.'

Geraldine smiled and slipped on a black skirt. Then she stepped into her high-heeled shoes and sprayed herself liberally with perfume.

Checking her make-up one last time, she left the

41

bedroom with her husband and they went downstairs.

Sophie, Donald and Grania, aged three, five and ten respectively, looked up as they came into the lounge.

'See you all later, and be good for Daddy.'

Sophie, in pink pyjamas, put out her arms for a cuddle and Geraldine picked her up, smelling the babyness of her and cuddling the little girl to her chest.

'You be good, madam.' She looked over at her husband who had sat down and picked up the TV section of the paper.

'Don't let her play you up. Eight o'clock is bedtime for the three of you.'

Grania and Donald groaned.

'I mean it. Or no sweets tomorrow.'

She placed Sophie on the couch with her brother and sister and pulled on her coat. As she buttoned it up she gave her orders.

'There's some chicken left in the fridge, Mick, if you fancy a sandwich, and I got you in some beers. Oh, and before I forget, I've left my Avon order by the phone. The girl will be calling around tonight.'

'You just get yourself off, Gerry. I'll sort out this end. See you later, love.'

She kissed him on the mouth.

'Be careful, Gerry, and don't take any lip. Right?'

Geraldine looked down at her husband's face and grinned. 'Right. 'Bye, kids.'

She kissed them all in turn and went from the house. The cold wind hit her in the face as she shut her front door and began walking the half mile to the wine bar where she worked. As she walked, she made Christmas lists in her head. She had already got most of the stuff for the two eldest. Grania had a bike which was at this minute hidden in her mother-in-law's shed and Donald had an Atari game. She was deliberating whether to get Sophie a kiddies' kitchen set or a doll's pram when she turned into Vauxhall Drive.

She instinctively pulled her coat tighter around her. She hated this bit. The road was wide and pitted, banked on the left-hand side by woods. She had played in the woods many times as a child and knew every inch of them. Yet still they gave her the creeps. It was so dark, and only a couple of the houses were now lived in. The others had been demolished to make way for a new development that had never been built. Many years ago this had been the 'good' end of town. Now it flanked the woods on one side and the council estate on the other and the large Victorian dwellings were gradually being razed to the ground.

Her heels clattered on the uneven pavement as she walked and the sound comforted her. She could see the end of the road ahead and relaxed.

Silly cow! she chided herself. Frightened of shadows!

She began to walk faster, the lights at the end of the road like beacons drawing her towards them.

George had been standing in the entrance of the woods for about fifteen minutes. He looked at the luminous dial on his watch. Here she came. Right on time. It was a quarter past seven.

He swallowed and flexed fingers that were now encased in white cotton gloves.

As Geraldine passed him he stepped out from his hiding place and grabbed her hair. The long brown hair that was her best feature.

As she opened her mouth to scream, George grabbed her under the jaw and began dragging her into the woods. As she kicked out to free herself she lost one of her shoes. She was terrified.

43

George was puffing and panting; she was bigger than he'd thought. He dragged her along with difficulty, her muffled cries annoying him. He still had a good hold on her hair and jaw. Pulling her sideways with all his strength, he threw her down.

Geraldine hit the ground with such force it winded her. She lay in the dirt, stunned for a moment. But only a moment. George saw her pull herself to her hands and knees, and as she tried to rise he kicked her as hard as he could in the stomach, sending her reeling back on to the ground.

Geraldine was holding her stomach with both hands when she saw the man kneeling beside her. Gathering up every ounce of strength she had left she rolled away from him, trying to get to her feet.

George watched the woman rolling away again and tutted. She was getting on his nerves now. Picking up a piece of wood which lay close to hand he brought it back over his head and slammed it down on her skull. He watched her crumple and sighed with relief. He sat quietly beside her for a few moments until he got his breath back and his heart stopped hammering in his ears. Then, pulling out his handkerchief, he wiped his forehead clean of sweat.

Happier now, he looked at the woman. She was lying on her back with her head turned away from him and he smiled to himself. Good! He didn't want her watching him. Going to her, he began to unbutton her coat. George decided he liked her coat and opened it up gently. Then, humming to himself, he began to pull off her skirt. No tights on, and in this weather as well! He tutted to himself again. Her limbs felt heavy as he undid her blouse and laid it back neatly with her coat. Still humming, he looked down at her bra. In the dimness he could just make out a piece of plastic. He fiddled about with it for a second and then her breasts seemed to burst out of it into his hands. She had been wearing a front fastening bra – she must have known what was going to happen! George caressed her breasts. He was feeling a deep tenderness towards the woman now. Then he used the knife to cut off her panties.

While he carried out his ministrations he felt the excitement building up within him. And such was his feeling of ecstatic happiness as he pulled her legs open, he had to stifle the cry that had gathered in his throat.

This was what she wanted. This was what they all wanted.

It was when George lay across her, spent and replete, that he found out why she had not moved at all during his little 'game'.

The lump of wood, so convenient, had contained a six-inch nail. It had been forced through her skull and into her brain.

George looked at her and tutted once more.

It was her own fault. All her own fault. Women always caused trouble. They were just so bloody stupid . . . Stupid fucking bitches! Bringing his fist back he smashed it into her face as hard as he could.

Mick O'Leary looked at the policewoman's face in disbelief. He had been up all night and thought that maybe his mind was playing tricks on him.

'What did you say?'

The WPC had never felt so bad in all her life. She saw the three children huddled together on the settee. Their father's fear had communicated itself to them. She could have cried herself.

'Your wife was found an hour ago, Mr O'Leary. She's been murdered.'

The WPC watched the man's face crumple before her eyes, and put her arm around his shoulders.

'Not my Gerry . . . Not my lovely Gerry. Please tell me that it's not true? Please?'

Mick O'Leary's voice broke as he spoke the last word and he put his hands to his face, the tears bursting through his fingers like a dam.

'Dad! Don't cry, Daddy!'

Ten-year-old Grania pulled her younger brother and sister into her arms. She had never seen her daddy cry before.

'I want my mum. When's my mummy coming home?'

At the same moment as Mick O'Leary was being told that his world had been ripped apart, George Markham was cooking his wife a nice breakfast.

Elaine walked into the kitchen, the smell of eggs and bacon making her mouth water.

'Oh, George, I would have done that.'

He actually laughed.

'I wanted to do it for you, my love. I do love you, you know, Elaine.'

'Do you, George?'

For some unknown reason his saying that he loved her depressed her more than anything else he could have done.

George held out her chair for her and she sat down at the table.

'Eat that up, my dear.'

Elaine stared at the eggs, bacon and tomatoes, and her appetite came back.

George watched her eat.

That's why you're so fat, Elaine, he thought, because you're a greedy bitch.

46

'Now then, my dear, what's it to be? Tea or coffee?' His voice was as polite as ever.

But George had a secret. A very important and exciting secret that he would not tell to a living soul.

He ate his own breakfast. For some reason he had a ravenous appetite this morning.

Chapter Three

Elaine sat at her till in the supermarket. Every customer who had passed through the large glass doors today had had only one thing on their minds: the rape and murder of Geraldine O'Leary. Since the body had been found, Grantley had been buzzing with news, views and assumptions. While tills crashed around her and people packed their shopping Elaine chatted to a customer, a woman who had known the victim.

'It makes me go all funny, just thinking about it.' The woman paused to force a large packet of cornflakes into her shopping bag.

'I mean, poor Gerry, she had three of the most gorgeous children you're ever likely to see. And she was happily married.' She nodded her head sagely. 'And how many can say that in this day and age?'

'You're right there. So who found her then?'

The woman rearranged her silk scarf. In the heat of the supermarket it was beginning to make her head itch.

'It was a young kid. He was on his way to deliver the papers. Well, he used the cut through from Vauxhall Drive and there she was . . . dead as a bleeding doornail!' She shook her head again.

'I bet this will just be the start. You mark my words. This is just the start.'

Elain grimaced and totalled her till.

'Seventeen pounds and eighty-five pence, please.'

The woman opened her purse and took out a twenty-pound note. 'Bleeding daylight robbery, if you ask me. I ain't even got the makings of a dinner here!'

Elaine smiled in sympathy but her mind was still with Geraldine O'Leary. Poor woman, to die like that. She shuddered.

Giving the woman her change, she went on to the next customer.

The whole of Grantley was appalled and shocked at the rape and murder. Every woman knew that it could easily have been her and they were all frightened.

Frightened and excited. Because nothing like this had ever happened in Grantley before.

Detective Inspector Kate Burrows looked down at the body and winced.

Detective Sergeant Willis watched her surreptitiously, smiling slightly as he watched her blanch.

Who, he wondered, in their right mind, would give a female copper a rape and murder? Women were too emotional for this type of thing.

He looked Kate up and down on the sly. Not a bad-looking bird for her age. Bit flat-chested to his mind, but she had good legs and nice eyes. Deep brown eyes that matched her hair exactly.

Willis dragged his mind back to the present as the pathologist spoke again.

'The nail entered the head here.' He pointed to

Geraldine's temple. 'On the left-hand side, where it entered the brain. I would say that death was instantaneous. We found traces of semen on her thighs and breasts, which is unusual in these cases. Only a small amount was inside the vagina.'

The man rubbed his eyes with the forefinger and thumb of his right hand.

'The blow to the face was administered after she had died. As you can see, he crushed the nose. She has several broken ribs. I would hazard a guess that she had been kicked. Kicked very hard as one of the ribs broke and punctured a lung.'

He shook his head. 'A very brutal attack. Very calculated. She has scratches and particles of dirt on her knees. My guess is that she put up a fairly good fight.'

'Any skin under the nails? Anything else for us to go on?' Kate's voice was low and subdued.

He shook his head. 'Nothing, I'm afraid. Of course we can get a DNA reading from the semen . . .' His voice trailed off. He shrugged. 'Maybe some traces of hair or fibre will turn up off her clothes. I'll let you know.' The pathologist began combing Geraldine's pubic hair slowly and carefully, his mind back on his job. Kate turned away from the woman's rapidly greying body.

'Thanks.'

She walked from the mortuary and Willis followed her. Neither spoke until they were back in the canteen at Grantley Police Station sipping cups of coffee.

'Look, don't let it get to you, love. These things happen.'

Kate stared at the younger man, frowning in concentration. She took a deep breath.

'How dare you?' Her voice was low and filled with rage. Willis was shocked. 'How dare you patronise me like

51

that? Just who the hell do you think you are? "These things happen"! Is that what you honestly believe?'

Her voice was incredulous. 'Do you think that Mrs Geraldine O'Leary is standing in heaven thinking: These things happen. Do you think her husband and children are just shrugging their shoulders thinking: These things happen!'

Her voice was beginning to rise and Willis looked around him in embarrassment.

'These things don't just happen, boy.' She stressed the last word. 'Out there somewhere is a murdering rapist. Do you understand the enormity of that? Do you? Well, DO YOU?'

Willis sat rigid in his seat, crimson with shame. Everyone in the room had gone quiet and was sitting watching them.

'It means that for the majority of women normal living will now be curtailed at four-thirty when it gets dark. It means that women who live alone or whose husbands work nights will be sitting uneasily in their own homes. It means that even locked in a car driving along they will not feel safe. It means that parents with young daughters will be sick with apprehension until they return from school, work, wherever they may have been. The list is bloody endless! How dare you sit there and tell me these things happen?

'And one last thing, while we're getting ourselves sorted out. I am a Detective Inspector. I am your boss. So in future you address me as such. In the six months I have been here there has been a general lack of respect, and as from today your lackadaisical attitude stops.'

Getting up from her seat, Kate stormed from the canteen, leaving a hush behind her.

Willis sighed heavily and one of his friends, DS Spencer, went to his table.

'So the vixen's got claws, has she? Flash bitch! If she'd spoken to me like that I'd have punched her in the mouth.'

A female voice from a nearby table said, 'Very macho, Spencer. Sure you ain't the rapist? I hear the victim had a broken nose.'

'Get stuffed!' Spencer went back to his cronies and sat down.

'Bloody women. Whoever it was who let them in the force in the first place wants psychiatric help. As for that Burrows . . . Uppity cow!'

'She's been put in charge of the murder and rape, so you'd best get used to it.'

Spencer looked at the speaker. 'Well, let's see how well she does, shall we? Personally she gets on my wick.'

'Maybe that's what's wrong with you, Spencer. She *won't* be getting on your wick.'

Everyone laughed.

Spencer picked up his cup of tea and with his free hand shoved his middle finger under the other man's nose.

'Spin on it, Fisher.'

Fisher grinned.

'Only if you ask me nicely!' He fluttered his eyelashes suggestively.

Spencer drank his tea down. Bloody women. It would take a rape to bring out their true colours. He wouldn't mind but the silly bitch O'Leary had probably been asking for it.

Kate Burrows sat in her office and tried to calm down. She admitted that she had been hard on Willis, but he got on her nerves. Most of the plain clothes at Grantley CID got on her nerves. She rubbed her hand over her face. She had been on the receiving end of discrimination since she had joined the force, it was an occupational hazard. But this lot here . . .

She turned her attention to the file in front of her. She wanted every bit of information imprinted on her brain. As in most of the cases she worked on, she wanted to be more knowledgeable than her male counterparts. She began to read.

A little while later there was a tap on her door.

'Come in.'

The door opened and Willis walked into the room.

'Yes?' Her voice was clipped.

Willis nodded. 'Ma'am, Superintendent Ratchette would like to see you, if you're not too busy.'

'Thank you, Willis.'

She watched him turn and walk meekly from the room. Mentally, Kate licked her finger and chalked one up to herself.

'You wanted to see me, sir?'

Superintendent Ratchette smiled at her as she entered his office.

'Sit down, Kate. I suppose you know that we have had the nationals on to us already?'

She grimaced. 'I didn't know, but I guessed it wouldn't take long.'

'Well, as usual they're making a nuisance of themselves. We must try and contain this as much as possible. Hopefully this is just a one-off thing. It's all we need, especially with Christmas not two weeks away.' Superintendent Ratchette's voice was tired and Kate felt sorry for him.

'Well, at the moment, sir, there's not that much to go on. We're hoping that forensic will show something up. I've already arranged the door-to-door, it's within a mile radius. The usual thing. Every male from fourteen to sixty-five will be interviewed – their make of car checked, where they work, where they were between six thirty p.m. and seven a.m. Oh, and before I forget, I've made DS Dawkins the office manager. She's good.'

Superintendent Ratchette raised a bushy grey eyebrow. 'I bet that went down well, didn't it?'

'Not really.' Kate laughed ruefully. 'Two women on a big case. Makes male CID eyes red just thinking about it!'

Ratchette laughed out loud. He liked Kate Burrows.

'Well, whatever you think, Kate, it's your case. If you could just keep me informed of any developments, as and when they occur?'

'Of course, sir. But I don't like the feel of this one. Geraldine O'Leary worked at Rudys wine bar, but from what I can gather she was not a woman who encouraged men, although she was good-looking and would obviously attract them. We're checking out all the customers anyway. Most are local men. Her husband was babysitting last night and a woman called Conroy called around at seven-thirty to collect an Avon order and stayed chatting till gone eight when Geraldine O'Leary's mother came round to drop off some Christmas presents. There's no way it's the husband. His alibi is watertight.'

Ratchette nodded at her.

'Looks like you've got your work cut out for you.'

Kate stifled a yawn. It had been a long day and it still wasn't over.

'I have a feeling this is going to be a tough one, sir, a very tough one.'

George walked into his house and was grateful for the warmth of the central heating. He was freezing. Under his arm he had the local paper. He could hear Elaine clattering around as she cooked. Taking off his overcoat, he hung it up in the hall cupboard and silently entered the kitchen.

Elaine turned from the sink and jumped.

'Oh, George! You gave me a start. I didn't hear you come in!'

She waved her hand in front of her face as if cooling herself down.

He smiled.

'Sorry, dear.' He sat at the table and looked at the paper. He smiled wider. Across the front page in large black letters was one word: MURDER.

Settling himself into his chair, George began to read. This morning the body of a woman had been found in Grantley Woods. She had been raped and murdered . . . He felt the familiar excitement flow through his veins. The victim was a Mrs Geraldine O'Leary, a thirty-two-year-old mother of three.

The poor children! The poor, poor children. Shaking his head, he began to read again.

Elaine placed a cup of tea by his hand and he looked up at her.

'Isn't it terrible, George? That poor woman. Those poor little children losing their mother like that, and just before Christmas as well.' George was surprised at the emotion in Elaine's voice.

'It's all we've talked about at work. I mean, no woman's safe, is she?'

George tutted and shook his head. 'You be careful, Elaine.' He pointed a finger at her. 'Promise me you'll get a taxi home from work? I don't want you standing at bus stops in the dark.'

She stared at her husband and then smiled.

'Oh, George! You old silly.'

Despite herself Elaine felt an enormous surge of pleasure at his concern. Getting taxis home from work!

Well, she would, because as George said it wasn't safe for her to be standing at bus stops in the dark.

She started to dish up the dinner.

Later in the evening, the sex murder was reported on Thames News. Elaine shook her head sadly. But George smiled. His secret smile that just showed his teeth.

Kate finally arrived home at eleven fifteen. She pulled into her drive and decided that she just couldn't be bothered to park the car in the garage. She was too tired. Getting out of the car she locked it, stifling a large yawn.

The front door was opened as she approached it and a woman of indeterminate age practically pulled her into the hallway.

'Get yourself in now, love, you must be frozen. I've got your dinner in the oven keeping warm.'

Kate smiled to herself. Her mother still thought she was eighteen.

'Where's Lizzy?'

'Oh, she's in the bath, she'll be down soon. I heard about the terrible goings on today. Scandalous, bloody scandalous! Was it the husband?'

Kate followed her mother through the lounge and into the kitchen, where on a small breakfast bar her knife and fork were laid out. She sat on the stool gratefully and accepted a cup of steaming coffee.

'It wasn't the husband, Mum.'

Evelyn O'Dowd wasn't listening which did not disturb Kate. Her mother never listened to anyone or anything.

'It's usually the husband or some other relative . . .'

Evelyn opened the oven and Kate felt her mouth water as the tantalising aroma of a good beef casserole wafted towards her.

'Be careful of that plate now, it's roasting.'

'Thanks, Mum, this is just what I needed.'

'I've made soda bread to go with it.'

Evelyn O'Dowd was tiny and thin, like a little bird. She had black eyes that darted continually and never settled on anything. She wore black all the time which accentuated her thinness. She still looked after her forty-year-old daughter as if she was ten. Kate loved her.

As she broke off a piece of bread her mother sat opposite her with a cup of coffee and the ever present cigarette. Taking a large draw on it, she blew smoke across the breakfast bar and smiled.

'What a feather this one will be in your cap – when you finally solve it, of course. Which you will, I'm sure of that.' It was said with absolute certainty.

'Well, we're doing the best we can, it's early days yet, Mum.'

Kate ate the food with an enthusiasm that pleased her mother no end.

'If only your father could have lived to see you, he'd have died of happiness!'

Kate grinned to herself. Her mother's Irish sayings were not only unintelligible most of the time, they were often highly amusing – though Evelyn didn't always think so.

Declan O'Dowd had been a London docker and had made sure his two children received a good education. Kate's elder brother now lived in Australia to where he had emigrated to twenty years before. He was a civil engineer and had a wife and five children whom Kate and her mother had never seen in the flesh. Kate had made her career in the police force. Declan O'Dowd had died a happy man shortly after she had passed out from Hendon.

Kate's mother had come to live with her shortly after

Lizzy, her daughter, had been born. Danny Burrows, Kate's husband, had left her when Lizzy was three months old. He showed up periodically over the years, turned everyone's world upside down and then disappeared again. Kate was secretly dreading this Christmas because he was due on one of his flying visits. Lizzy adored her father, which made it hard for Kate to keep everything on an even keel.

She heard her daughter patter into the room in her slippers.

'Hello, Mum. I heard about the murder. Me and Gran watched it on the news.'

'Hello, baby, come and give us a kiss.'

Lizzy went to her mother and put her arms around her. At sixteen she was exquisite. Sometimes the beauty of her own daughter made Kate frightened. Lizzy had the O'Dowd darkness, like her mother and grandmother, but she also had porcelain white skin and startling violet eyes. She looked sixteen going on twenty-five. Unlike her mother she was full-chested, already a thirty-six B and still growing by the looks of her. She was as tall as her mother but far more graceful. One thing she had not inherited from Kate was brains. Though shrewd enough in her own way, she was no scholar, had no interest in anything academic. She worked now in the local Boots, filling shelves and waiting for the magical day they trained her for the tills. That was the height of her ambition and Kate accepted this.

'How was your day then, love?'

'Not bad, Mum, the usual. With the Christmas rush, we just don't stop. I never even had my coffee break today. Mr Williams the manager said I was doing very well indeed, though.'

She put on a very posh voice for the last part and Kate

and Evelyn laughed. Kate broke off some more soda bread and mopped up the gravy on her plate.

'Shall I run you a nice bath, Mum? I got some bath crystals from the Body Shop last week. It's the aromatherapy range. They're lavender and supposed to make you relax.'

'That would be gorgeous. Today has been pretty hectic.'

Lizzy went from the room and Kate and her mother smiled at one another.

'Sure, she's a good girl, Katie. That fellow's been ringing her again. I think it's love.'

Kate lit herself a cigarette from her mother's pack and pushed her plate away from her.

'Well, she's young, the boys are bound to be after her.'

'True, Katie, but I worry about her. I don't think she realises the effect she has on them, you know.'

'That's part of her charm, I think. We'll keep an eye on her.'

'That we will. Now you smoke your fag while I clear this lot away. You'll need all the sleep you can get, I'm thinking.'

Kate grinned again. Her mother was not happy unless she was looking after someone. Over the last sixteen years, Kate did not know what she would have done without her.

Going up to the bathroom a little while later, she lay in the steaming and fragrant water. She had been working for sixteen hours non-stop. She had seen a woman practically dismembered on a mortuary slab, had set up an incident room, and had organised over thirty policemen and women for the door to door inquiry. She had at her fingertips information about anyone and everyone.

Yet her mother still made her feel like a child. And after a day like this, it felt good.

*

George lay in bed with Elaine. He listened to her deep snores and smiled into the darkness. Every time he thought of Geraldine O'Leary he felt great.

Once more he replayed in his mind what he had done. He took himself through the act step by step, congratulating himself on his cleverness.

Then he frowned.

Into his mind's eye came pictures of his mother. He wiped his hand across his face in the darkness as if that would erase them. He saw his mother as she had been when he was a child. Her bright red hair, naturally red not dyed like Elaine's, was shining in the sunlight. Her sea green eyes were sparkling mischievously, and George could see himself smiling back at her. He could see the room: the cast-iron fireplace with the dried flowers in the hearth, the Victorian prints on the flock wallpaper and the black leather Chesterfield. He could also see the pipe and the bag and the china bowl.

George tried to shut out the images but they were too strong. He lay in bed and watched.

'Come to Mummy, Georgie boy.' Her voice was a caress. She held out her arms to the little boy in front of her. In the distance Georgie could hear the sounds of the anti-aircraft fire. He stood silently in front of her.

She spoke again, her voice harder this time.

'I said, come to Mummy, Georgie.'

The little boy looked at the doorway and his mother laughed.

'Come in, kids!' Her voice was loud.

George looked at the doorway with frightened eyes. He watched his elder sister and brother come into the room.

'Lie on the floor, Georgie boy.'

The child shook his head and began to edge his way

backwards. He watched his mother's red-lipsticked mouth twist into an ugly shape.

'Don't annoy Mummy, Georgie. Just lie on the floor.'

The child watched the others make a semicircle around him. His elder brother Joseph was so close he could smell the odour of bull's eyes coming from him.

He closed his eyes at the inevitable. She had already given them the sweets. They would want this over with as quickly as possible. He felt the familiar sensation of ice water in his bowels as the older children pulled him to the ground. He felt a surge of hatred for his mother as his shorts and underpants were pulled off. He felt the contained violence from the others as they held him, face down on the floor.

He began to cry. Slowly at first, then violently, painfully, as his mother began pushing the rubber piping into his rectum. He tried to fight but it was useless. He felt the warmth of the soapy water hitting his bowels and then he felt the sick, wrenching feeling as they emptied. He winced as she ripped the rubber tubing from inside him. Then it was all over.

He lay on the floor looking up into his mother's smiling face. The sweat was standing out on his forehead, and he felt the waves of nausea washing over him.

Then he saw his mother's heavily made-up face approaching his own, felt the coolness of her lips as they sucked at his mouth.

'That feels better, doesn't it, Georgie boy?'

Lying on the floor of the parlour, weak and sick, he nodded at her. Fighting back the words.

Then his mother picked him up in her arms tenderly and took him to his bed. He felt the coolness of the sheets that smelt of Lux soap flakes and then the red pain in his behind.

He saw her smile again.

'You're Mummy's little soldier, what are you?'

The child watched her through tear-filled lashes and sighed, sending a shudder through his thin little body.

'I'm Mummy's little soldier.'

Then he was pulled up from the bed and held against her ample bosom while she rained kisses all over his face and neck.

George watched it all as if it was a film. He closed his eyes to shut out the sight. But his mother just would not go away.

She never went away.

It was Saturday and George was alone in the house. After carefully washing up the breakfast things and putting them away, he made himself a pot of tea. While it brewed on the kitchen table he walked down the garden to his shed and brought back his scrapbooks.

Sitting at the kitchen table, he settled himself down and opened the first book. He felt the anticipation course through his veins as he looked at the familiar pictures and smiled.

Soon he would have his own album of death with pictures of his victims instead of Peter Sutcliffe's. He had already started it.

George took a sip of his tea and began to read, though he knew the words off by heart. After a while he glanced at his watch. It was nearly lunchtime. He had hours yet until Elaine came home from work. He decided to watch his video. He clenched his fists tightly with sheer elation at his good luck.

No Elaine. No noise. No company.

Putting the scrapbooks back in the shed, he locked up the house, closed the front-room curtains, unplugged the phone and put on his new film.

As the pictures flickered before him, George finally relaxed.

The girl on the video looked just like Geraldine O'Leary and the most violent of the men looked just like him.

This was what they wanted. This was what they all wanted. Walking around, covered in make-up and perfume. Even the very young girls. He knew all about them.

In his agitation George started to blink rapidly.

He had seen films of school girls. The real life ones were as bad. Learning to be sluts, every last one of them. Oh, he had watched them, walking to school. He began to nod his head. Bare-legged, some of them. With bouncing bosoms, emphasised by their school uniforms. Oh, he knew all about women. Dying for it, the majority of them. Just dying for it. Well, he would show a few of them before he was much older. Oh, yes. He would show them.

The girl on the television screen was dead.

George cleared his mind. This was the best bit.

He smiled.

Detective Sergeant Amanda Dawkins brought Kate a cup of coffee.

'Thanks. I could do with this.'

The other woman smiled. 'You look beat.'

Kate nodded. 'I feel terrible. I didn't have a very good night and today isn't much better.'

Amanda sat down opposite her.

'Well, we're gradually collating all the door-to-door info. The thing with this type of inquiry is that everyone with a grudge against their neighbour tries to implicate them.'

'I know. The thing is that for every five hundred screwball accusations, there are normally one or two that are worth following up.'

'Drink your coffee, ma'am. Before it gets cold.'

She grinned.

'Call me Kate. I only threw my weight around yesterday because I am getting heartsick of this lot.'

She waved her arm in the direction of the male CID staff.

'Bloody load of know-alls they are. Well, I'm going to make myself felt and heard from now on. I tried the friendly, tactful approach and it didn't work.'

Amanda grinned, showing crooked white teeth.

'This lot have never had a woman in charge of them before. It's galling for them, to say the least.'

Kate sipped her coffee.

'Shall I tell you something, Amanda?'

The girl nodded, a slight frown on her face at the other's tone of voice.

'I don't give a toss what they think. If they give me any more hag, they're off the case. I would appreciate it if you would be so kind as to set the rumour flying. Know what I mean?'

Amanda giggled.

'I know exactly what you mean, ma'am.'

'Kate.'

'Sorry, Kate.'

'That's better. Now then, let's get this show on the road because I have a feeling that this murder was only for starters. Whoever did it is getting ready for the main performance, and I want to find him before he does any more harm.'

Kate's serious intention communicated itself to the younger woman. Amanda nodded at her boss, glad that she was going to be working with her and not one of the male officers.

DS Spencer was watching the two women. He sighed.

Nudging his friend DS Willis, he poked his head in their direction, a frown on his ruddy face.

'Looks like the Dolly Sisters are getting better acquainted.' His voice was disgusted.

Willis shook his head in exasperation.

'Oh, give it a rest, for Christ's sake. She's in charge and that's that. Let's just put all our combined experience together and find the bloody nutter who's on the loose.'

Spencer's face closed up.

'Oh, yeah, of course. I suppose your experience with shoplifters and vandals will be invaluable, won't it?'

Willis coloured slightly. He had not been a DS for long and this was his first big case. No one else had mentioned this fact except Spencer. But what more could he expect from the man? He was the most ignorant, bigoted and self-opinionated officer in the whole of the division.

'Well, thanks for the little reminder, Spencer. All this new empathy policing should be just up your street, I reckon. Since we're obviously looking for a complete and utter pratt, we can all just follow your line of thinking, can't we?'

Spencer looked as if he had been slapped across the face. 'You cheeky little bastard!'

Willis grinned. 'And you're a miserable old bastard. Know your trouble, Spencer? You never got further than DS, did you? Well, if you listened to yourself sometimes, you might find out why.'

Willis walked away, leaving Spencer open-mouthed with astonishment and rage. But against his will a phrase sprung to mind which he could not ignore: The truth hurts.

How many times had he said that to other people?

Too many.

He forced his mind back to the case, looking at the

blown-up photograph of Geraldine O'Leary on the wall.

It was one of the pictures taken in the morgue. Her greying face with the splintered nose was pinned up beside another smaller photograph taken a few months previously by her husband. In it Geraldine was laughing, her eyes crinkled at the corners. She looked what she was: a beautiful young wife.

Spencer shrugged. Willis was right about one thing. The man who murdered her had to be caught, and fast. Before he struck again.

Chapter Four

1948

The two small boys walked fast. Driving rain was pelting into their faces. The smaller of the two had red-rimmed eyes and had obviously been crying. A large clap of thunder boomed overhead, followed by a flash of lightning that lit up the sky.

'Come on, George, for Christ's sake.' The bigger boy began to drag his brother along by his coat sleeve. As they turned into a small cul-de-sac George tried to pull away.

'I'm not going in there. I mean it.'

Joseph sighed loudly and faced his brother. He did not like the job he had been given. In his heart of hearts he couldn't blame Georgie for running off, but their mother's word was law. He looked into the terrified little face before him.

'Look, Georgie, the sooner you get in there, the sooner it will be over. Now come on.'

He resumed dragging him along the pavement until they came to the house they both lived in. In the dark stormy light it looked sinister. The brickwork was stained black and the front door, even with its polished brass knocker, looked dingy. Joseph pulled his brother up the garden path and banged the knocker hard. The door was opened almost immediately by a mousy-haired girl of fifteen. She looked at her youngest brother with tenderness.

'She's a bit quieter now, George. Hurry up out of your wet things.'

They walked into the hallway and he pulled off his wet coat slowly. His heart was hammering in his chest. The house always seemed to smell of cabbage; the odour hung on the air, making him feel sick. It mingled with the smell of beeswax polish, and the heaviness of it burned his quivering nose.

'Is he gone?' Joseph's voice was a whisper.

The girl shook her head.

'You go on upstairs, I'll take Georgie in.' The brother and sister looked into each other's eyes. Joseph turned away, unable to face his sister any longer. He forced himself to smile at the little boy beside him.

'I'll wait upstairs for you. Micky Finnigan gave me some comics yesterday. You can read them after me if you like.'

Georgie nodded and swallowed deeply. His grey eyes seemed to have taken possession of his whole face.

'Pull your socks up, Georgie.' He did as he was told. Clumsily he dragged the thick woollen garments up his shins. The three stood stock still as they heard a movement from the front room. Then Joseph ran lightly up the stairs as if the devil was after him. George felt his hands begin to tremble as the front-room door opened and a harsh light fell across him.

'So you're back home, are you?' His mother's voice was hard and low. She held the door open for him and at a little push from his sister he walked through. His mother's fist hit him in the back of his head and sent him careering into the room.

'Mum . . . Mum! Don't hit him, Mum!'

Nancy Markham turned to her daughter. 'Get upstairs now, before I give you more of the same.'

George lay on the cold lino, terrified. He watched as his mother knelt beside him and pushed her face close to his.

'Run away from your mummy, would you, Georgie boy?' She entwined her fingers in his hair and pulled his head towards her.

'Where was you running off to this time?'

The child's trembling communicated itself to her. She brought her red-stained lips back over her teeth and then, closing her eyes, began to lay into him. His skinny little body was unable to cushion the ferocious punching and he lay with his hands covering his head.

Upstairs Joseph lay listening to the muffled sounds of his brother's beating. His mother's foul-mouthed shouting reaching a crescendo.

Nancy stood up, her breathing laboured. 'Now you go and apologise, Georgie boy.'

The child was sobbing, every so often gulping large draughts of air into his aching lungs. His nose had a thin trickle of blood running from it. He stood up unsteadily, grabbing the table for support.

'You heard me, boy!' She slapped the child hard across the face. He stumbled from the front room and through the connecting door to the kitchen.

He felt his mother stand close behind him and looked into the big man's face.

'Don't you worry, Bert, I've given him such a larruping he won't be so quick with his tongue in the future.'

The man looked at George with tiny dark eyes. The boy

could smell the rancid odour of stale sweat and swallowed down the urge to vomit. The man's belly was quivering as he moved to make himself more comfortable in his seat. His string vest was stained with tea and food. George tried to concentrate on the man's red-veined, bloated face.

'He ain't saying much, Nance. What's the matter, you little bastard? Cat got your tongue?'

George bit on his lip for a second.

'I'm very sorry . . . I'm sorry.'

Nancy Markham put her face so close to her son's he could smell her breath. 'You know what else to say, Georgie boy.'

He swallowed and took another deep breath. 'I'm sorry . . . Dad.' The last word was barely audible.

'Speak up, lad.'

'I'm . . . sorry, Dad.'

The man saw the hatred in the child's eyes. It was unmistakable. For one second he felt frightened, then pulling himself together he grinned, showing tobacco-stained teeth. This little runt was no more than five stone! He screwed up his eyes and made himself look as ferocious as possible, wanting to intimidate the child.

'You remember to call me that, boy.' He poked his finger at George. Then he looked at Nancy and bellowed: 'Where's me fucking tea, woman? Get this little shit out of me sight and get yourself sorted!'

Nancy pushed George out of her way and stood in front of the man.

'Don't you talk to me like that, Bert Higgins . . .'

He pulled his enormous bulk from the chair and brought his fist back.

'You want a right-hander, Nance, or what? You might be able to sort out little kids but don't ever think you can order me around!'

George watched his mother's face as she battled with herself as to whether to carry on fighting or whether to retreat. As usual her fighting temper came to the fore and George bolted from the room as her hand went to the teapot on the table and she flung it at Bert.

George took the stairs two at a time, his injuries forgotten in the panic to get away from them. He rushed into the bedroom he shared with Joseph, straight for his sister's arms. He began to sob again as he heard the crashing from below. Edith caressed the short-cropped head, wincing every time a loud crash thundered up from below. She saw Joseph lying on the bed staring at the ceiling and felt a sense of futility.

'Oh, please God, make them kill one another. Please make them both die.'

Her anguished voice was muffled with tears. Since Bert Higgins had moved into the house eighteen months earlier their lives had been even more disrupted than usual. Nancy had found in him a bully who was even more violent than she was. They had been alternately loved to death or beaten within an inch of their lives ever since they could remember. But since the advent of Bert, things had gradually grown worse. Their mother had never been stable; now she was positively deranged. Her main outlet for her frustrations was George. Edith did her best to keep him from her mother's rages but lately it was getting more and more difficult. Bert drank, her mother drank, and the children, mainly George, took the brunt of it. Edith had been given the task of cleaning the house. Nancy Markham had pretensions to respectability, even blind drunk.

All three stood rooted to the spot as they heard their mother running across the front room and out into the hall. Her heavy footfalls on the stairs were followed by Bert's.

'Talk to me like that, would you, you slut? You bloody big fat slut!'

'Take your filthy hands off of me, Bert Higgins, I'm warning you now.'

They listened to the scuffle on the stairs and then heard a thud and all went quiet. The three looked at each other in consternation.

'Nancy? Nance?' Bert's voice was low and filled with fear.

Edith pushed George from her and ran from the room.

'Oh my God!' She ran down the stairs and pushed Bert roughly away. Her mother was lying sprawled on the stairs, her head bleeding profusely from the temple.

'I never meant it, she fell and hit her head.'

Edith ignored the man and examined her mother. It was a flesh wound. As she peered at it, Nancy's eyes opened and she pushed the girl away from her.

'Get away out of it, you.' Joseph and George stood at the top of the stairs dumbstruck.

Nancy put her hand to her head and brought the fingers away blood-stained.

'You bastard! I'm bleeding.'

'Look, Nancy, I'm sorry. Honestly, darlin', I wouldn't hurt you for the world, you know that. I could cut me hands off.'

Edith walked slowly up the stairs. She knew she wasn't needed any more. It was the same thing over and over again. No worries about Georgie who would be bruised for a week or ten days, and who would get another hiding between times. No concern for Joseph who was getting iller and iller with his nerves each week. Not a thought for Edith who had to keep everyone together. Let's just worry about Mummy and her bloody head. A bloody head she asked for, to all intents and purposes.

'Come on, you two.' She pushed the two boys into the bedroom and closed the door.

A while later the three heard Bert and their mother enter their own bedroom and the squeaking of the bed springs and loud groans that heralded their making up.

Chapter Five

23 December 1989

Mandy Kelly pulled her coat tighter across her breasts. It was freezing. Her toes in her flat-heeled boots had already gone numb. She would murder Kevin when he finally arrived. She looked at her watch again. It was eight fifteen, he was a quarter of an hour late. She stood by the light of the phone box and stamped her feet. She wouldn't mind but he had her car, and if she got a taxi her father would guess immediately what had happened and then all hell would break loose. Plus it was Saturday night and they were supposed to be going out to eat with her father and his new girlfriend. Well, she had to be honest, she wasn't worried about missing that so much, but her father would be upset. Sod Kevin! He always did this to her.

She pushed her hands deeper into the pockets of her sheepskin. The cold night air was burning her lungs with every breath she took. The street was deserted except for the occasional car. Everyone was either putting the finishing touches to their trees after a hectic day's shopping, or ensconced somewhere warm with a drink or a meal. The world was at the quiet empty stage that seemed to suspend the laws of time until Christmas Day came. She pulled her long blond hair from inside the collar of her sheepskin. The air was damp and her hair was lank around her face.

Oh God, it was so cold.

She watched a dark blue Orion drive past her slowly and stared after it uneasily. She was sure that it had driven past once before. She shrugged. No need to worry, Kevin would be here soon. She smiled to herself. Her orange lipstick was smudged where she kept rubbing her lips together. Her father would be waiting for them, they were supposed to leave at nine. If Kevin didn't hurry up she wouldn't even have time to change.

She carried on watching the road, hoping against hope that Kevin would drive along in her white Mercedes sports and take her home.

Sometimes she wondered what exactly it was Kevin liked about her. Whether it was the fact that her father was Patrick Kelly, or whether it was her car, or whether it was in fact her he liked. She tried not to dwell on thoughts like these as they upset her. Like her father's girlfriends who were getting younger and younger by the month. She looked at her watch again. Eight twenty-five. Oh, sod Kevin! She wasn't going to stand here all night.

She went into the phone box and picked up the phone. It was dead.

That was all she needed. Pulling her coat tighter around her she began to walk down the road, still keeping her eye out for Kevin and her car. The car that she never got the chance to drive any more.

She saw a set of headlights coming towards her and her heart leapt into her mouth. Please let it be Kevin!

It was the dark blue Orion and it stopped beside her.

*

'Come on, Kevin. Have one more drink.'

'Nah. I'd better get going. Mandy will be doing her nut.'

Jonny Barker laughed out loud and looked at the crowd of men around him.

'He's well and truly pussy whipped, ain't he, boys?'

Everyone laughed, none more so than Kevin Cosgrove himself. 'Nah, I've got to, lads. I'm half an hour late as it is.'

Garry Aldridge clapped Kevin on the back. He was as drunk as a lord.

'I'll tell you sommick, mate, since that murder I won't let my bird go nowhere unless she's in a cab or a crowd.'

Kevin looked at his friend's open face and for the first time worried about Mandy. She was a pain in the arse in a lot of respects, but he would not like anything to happen to her. Not just because he cared about her, though that was part of it, but because her father was what was known as a Bad Man. A very Bad Man indeed.

Putting his pint of lager on the bar, he said his goodbyes and made his way hastily to the car.

Opening the door, he climbed into the luxurious smell of leather and musk perfume. Mandy's perfume.

He loved this car. He envied Mandy her father's money, but admired her more because she still went to work. She was a beautician. In a few months her father was going to buy her her own shop.

He drove into Portaby Road and scanned the kerb looking for Mandy. She was nowhere to be seen. He had arranged to meet her here because it was quiet, and there would not be much chance of anyone who knew her father seeing her standing around waiting. If Patrick Kelly knew that his daughter did not really have the use of her own car he would go mad. He had bought her a car every year since she had passed her test at seventeen. Always a brand new car and always a very expensive one. Kevin knew for a fact that this Mercedes had cost well over forty thousand pounds. That was why he loved driving it. He loved the feel of being in something that was pure class. He turned around at the bottom of Portaby Road and began to drive back up it slowly. Mandy was definitely not here.

Kevin gripped the steering wheel tightly. That meant only one thing: she had gone home without him and without her car. He felt his heart sink as he began to drive to the outskirts of Grantley where Patrick Kelly lived with Mandy in a large rambling house.

Kelly would be furious. Though Kevin would never admit it outright to her or to anyone else for that matter, he admitted it to himself: Patrick Kelly frightened him out of his skin. He frightened anyone who had even half a brain.

Kevin drove slowly. All the excitement he usually felt at driving the car was gone now. It had been replaced by fear.

Bugger that bloody Mandy! Why didn't she just wait like he'd told her?

Patrick Kelly poured himself a brandy in a large snifter and sat back in his chair. He looked at his new girlfriend Tiffany and hid the glimmer of annoyance that swept through his features as he watched her, watching herself, in the full-length mirror opposite her chair.

Tiffany was nineteen, three years younger than his daughter, and she was built like Jayne Mansfield. Kelly liked his women voluptuous. He allowed himself a slight smile. Tiffany would not even know who Jayne Mansfield was. She was what he commonly termed as thick as two short planks. But that was all right because he didn't particularly want to talk to her. Just go to bed with her.

The large Christmas tree in the corner twinkled with lights and he glanced at it for a few seconds, then his eyes strayed once more to the photograph of his late wife, Renée, on the mantelpiece. Suddenly he was engulfed in sadness. He shrugged silently inside his Armani suit. A memory of another Christmas came to his mind, he could see Renée holding Mandy in her arms in their little bedsit, the bathroom was full of steam and the smell of camphor. Mandy, just turned one, had croup and both he and Renée had sat in the damp little bathroom all night with her.

He missed Renée, missed her every day of his life. They had worked together to build up their businesses, she was the real brains behind the repo business, not him. He had always been the muscle, the hard man. He had collected outstanding debts from villains, men who had done a robbery and then tried to 'tuck up' the other men with them.

Kelly had a knack of finding people, of making people tell him their whereabouts – he still had it to this day, despite his large house, his hand-made suits and his aura of semi-respectability. Deep down in his boots he knew that he was still an East End urchin, still got a thrill from his illegal dealings. Even though these days he mixed with the highest in the land for one reason or another, he knew that inside, he would always be Patrick Kelly from the East End. The years of living in coldwater bedsits, rat-infested tenements and watching his mother work herself into the ground would never be far from his thoughts, and as far as he was concerned, that was how it should be. He was honest enough to admit to himself that it was his dead wife's business acumen that he could thank for his respectable way of life these days. It had been Renée who had somehow managed to get them their first respectable client. Without her, he would still be pretty well off, but the chances were he'd have been sent down by a judge years before. He had learnt from her, and now he missed her. He had respected her, loved her and built a life with her for their only child.

Suddenly, Tiffany annoyed him more than ever. He did not want her sitting there, with her tight dress and professionally tanned legs, he wanted Renée. With her blond hair swept up as it had always been and her tiny frame encased in a nice black dress that screamed of class, to him anyway. She had dressed quietly, had a quiet demeanor that he had loved. He looked at the tree again and felt the sting of tears. Christmas was always an emotional time. It was a time to think of absent loved ones, a bitter-sweet remembering. Ten years he had mourned her, taking on the responsibility for his daughter, a daughter who had all her mother's zest for life, even if she had taken up with that geek of a boyfriend. He looked like he was a bit Stoke on Trent, but Mandy had assured him he was straight as a die. Patrick still had his doubts.

The silence was beginning to get on his nerves: Tiffany was a girl of few words. Even in bed she lay back with a serious expression while he did the business, then she got up silently and washed herself over the bidet before getting back into bed and going straight to sleep. It was like shagging a blow-up doll. The only time she showed any emotion was when she was admiring herself in the mirror. The telephone jangled into the stillness of the room and Kelly jumped in his chair. He went to the table and picked the phone up thinking it might be Mandy.

It was Bill Doon.

'Pat, I've been to see the bloke and he's skint. He's blown the bloody lot on the horses. His wife never even managed to get a bit out of him for Christmas, the ponce.'

'What did you do, Bill?'

'That's why I'm ringing you, shall I give him a hiding or what?'

Patrick closed his eyes for a second and then gritted his teeth.

'Now you work for me don't you, Bill?' His voice low and patient as if he was talking to a child.

'Yeah.' Bill's voice was puzzled.

'And I pay you a good piece of wedge to collect outstanding debts for me don't I?'

'Yeah.'

'Then go and break his fucking arms. Jesus wept, I might as well go and do the fucking job meself.'

'All right, Pat, keep your hair on. He's got six kids sitting in that flat with him.'

'Then take him out of the flat, you prat, and as it's Christmas you can give him a dig near a casualty department, how's that?' He slammed the phone down. After a couple of seconds he picked it up again and pressed 4. The phone was answered by Kelly's right-hand man, Willy Gabney.

'What do you want, Pat?'

'I want you to make up a goodie bag, Willy, and drop it round Bob Mason's place. He won't be home for Christmas.'

'Okey doke. Mandy back yet?'

'Not a bleeding sign of her. That ponce Kevin's probably still tarting himself up!'

He put down the phone and poured himself another large brandy. The ormolu clock on the mantelpiece showed ten to nine. Where the hell was Mandy? He had booked the table for nine thirty.

Kelly sat back in his chair and fingered a piece of paper in his breast pocket. It was the deeds to a small hairdressing salon and beauty parlour, his gift to his daughter for Christmas. He allowed himself a small smile.

Mandy would be over the moon.

He sipped his brandy in the silence once more. Tiffany, he noticed, was still watching herself in the mirror.

George Markham was smiling at the girl in his car. Her eye was already beginning to swell where he had punched her. It was her own fault for trying to fight him. Here he was trying his hardest to be friendly and nice and all she could do was sulk! He had driven to a piece of wasteground and now they were both watching each other warily.

Mandy was terrified. Since the man had stopped and asked directions, everything had gone wrong. She had walked to his car and the next thing she had known she was being dragged bodily into the car. She had kicked and screamed and no one had come to help her. She could feel a throbbing above her right eye, and it hurt her ribs every time she took a breath. As he had dragged her across his lap by her hair she had scraped her knees and thighs on the metal of the car. They had driven away fast and she had attempted to open the door and jump but he had held on to her hair, making it impossible. She would have landed under the wheels of the car.

Oh, please, please. Someone, anyone, help her!

George liked the look of her, he decided. The only thing he did not like was the orange lipstick. He hated orange lipstick. Mandy saw him scowl at her and her heart lurched. She inched her way round, her arm behind her back. She was going to open the car door and run for it. Run as hard as she could.

George read her mind.

Taking a length of rope from the glove compartment, he grabbed her hands.

Mandy began to fight, her long false nails flying

dangerously close to his face. Sighing heavily, George punched her with all his might. He hit her on the cheekbone and heard the high cracking sound as it broke beneath his knuckles.

The girl slumped back on to the seat dazed, the red hot pain in her face making her quiet and subdued. The man was mad. Suddenly Mandy knew that with stunning clarity. If she didn't play along he would kill her. Maybe he would kill her anyway. She lay back in the seat crying quietly. Wishing her dad was here. George tied her hands together as if she was going to say her prayers.

'Please let me go.' Her voice was low and surprisingly gentle and childlike.

George felt magnanimous, even happy at the humility of the request. She learnt fast, he would say that much for her. Rubbing his hands together, he leaned over her and took a carrier bag off the back seat. He pulled out the black leather mask he had purchased in the sex shop.

Mandy was in a state of fear so acute she was rooted to the seat. Her eyes opened wide as she saw the man putting the mask on. He even turned on the interior light of the car, and pulled the mirror above the windscreen towards him so he could fit the mask on properly.

It crossed George's mind that she had seen his face clearly already, but he could hardly drive around Grantley with the mask on, could he? He felt the fear coming from the girl and was gratified. It was all working out even better than he'd expected.

Getting out of the car, he slipped off his 'good' overcoat, as Elaine called his Burberry. Folding it carefully, he laid it across the back seat. It was freezing cold and George shivered. Then he walked round to the passenger side and, opening the door, dragged Mandy out. Pulling her along by her coat, George led her to an old shed that had been standing empty for years. He opened the door and pushed her inside.

Mandy landed on the dirty floor, and was in too much pain to care. She watched as the man took two candles from his suit pocket and lit them.

George smiled. That was better. Going to Mandy, he untied her hands.

'Take off your coat.'

She lay on the floor staring up at him. A thin line of blood was seeping from her nose and rolling down the side of her face.

'I said, take off your fucking coat!'

George put his hand over his mouth. But the swearing seemed to do the trick because she pulled herself up slowly.

He felt the stirring of excitement and then grabbed the front of her sheepskin and tore it from her body. As he dragged it from her arms she seemed to spin over and George heard a heavy thud as she landed back on the floor.

He shook his head. Another one! Out in this weather in a little jumper and skirt. Still, at least she had the sense to wear tights. Thick tights.

He could see the fear in her eyes and he grinned.

Mandy watched the man lay her coat on the dirt floor. She tried to gather her wits about her and glanced around the shed. There were no windows, only the door, and he was wedging a piece of wood under that. Lying about on the floor were numerous pieces of wood and metal. Just to the right of her was a crowbar. She would await her opportunity and then make a grab for it. She swivelled her eyes back to George. Her face was so sore, she was having difficulty swallowing. She watched as the man came back to her.

'Lie on the coat, dear, or you'll get a cold.'

His voice was muffled inside the mask and he could feel the warmth of his breath against the leather.

George liked wearing the mask, it made him feel different. He had wanted one of these masks since he'd read Donald Neilson had worn one to murder Lesley Whittle.

Mandy dragged herself on to her sheepskin. Her whole body was aching now. Especially her face and knees. She looked down at her legs and saw the blood seeping through the holes in her tights. She felt panic welling up inside her and fought it down. She had to keep a clear head. She had to get hold of that crowbar. She pushed her hair from her face and George watched her through the mask's eyeholes. It was a very feminine gesture, a graceful gesture, and George felt an enormous lump in his throat as he looked at her.

His mother had possessed a grace of movement just like that, a feline quality that had set her apart from other women. He smiled into the mask with tenderness.

'What's your name, dear?'

Mandy didn't reply. Just stared at the mask.

George tutted to himself. She was getting difficult again. Women were always the same. You tried to be nice to them, to help them even, but were they grateful? Were they?

He began to breathe heavily and the mask grew even hotter. He was beginning to sweat now and it was all her fault. He kicked her on the leg, a savage kick that brought the tears back into her eyes.

'I asked you your name, you little slut!'

'It's Mandy . . . Mandy Kelly.'

Her name was Mandy! His favourite name! The name of the girl in his video . . . Mandy.

He watched her tiny pointed breasts that poked

through her jumper as if surprised to be there and felt an aching in his loins.

He knelt in front of her.

He wished he did not have to wear gloves. He clenched and unclenched his hands in anticipation.

Then she kicked him. He felt the sting as her boot came into contact with his chest. In a split second, she had rolled away from him, across the dirt floor, eyeing a lump of metal!

The dirty stinking bitch was trying to grab a weapon! But George beat her to it. He jumped up and ran to her. As her hand curled around the crowbar he stamped on it with his heel. She screamed, loudly and piercingly.

George picked up the crowbar and before he knew what was happening he had broken open her head. He threw down the crowbar. It made a dull and hollow thud as it hit the dirt floor.

Now look what you made me do, he thought.

It was all her own fault. They were all the bloody same. Troublemakers the lot of them.

Dragging the girl's body back to the sheepskin, he dumped her on to it and arranged her limbs so that she was open to him. He was sweating like a pig now, even in the extreme cold. It was the mask.

George sat back on his heels and looked at her for a long moment.

Then he began to take off her clothes.

'Well, I'm starving.' Tiffany's voice was like a spoilt child's.

Patrick Kelly turned from the telephone and bellowed at her: 'Then fuck off, love. Go on. FUCK OFF!'

Slamming the phone back in its cradle, Patrick Kelly stormed over to where Tiffany was sitting. Kevin saw her flinch. Kelly picked her up bodily and half dragged, half ran her from the room. He threw her from him as they entered the large hall.

'Get your coat. Get a cab. Get out of my sight, Tiffany, or I'll punch your stupid face in.'

She rubbed her arm.

'Oh, come on, Pat. You know I didn't mean it.' Her voice was low and pleading and Kelly felt a moment's pity for the girl.

He breathed out heavily, suddenly feeling deflated. Where the hell was Mandy? It was gone eleven now. He picked up the phone in the hall and dialled a number.

'Jimmy? Drive the car around the front. Tiffany's going home.'

Kelly saw her lips tighten. He replaced the receiver.

'So when will I be seeing you then?' Tiffany was slightly mollified by the fact he was sending her home in one of his cars and not a taxi.

'You won't, love. Not now. Not ever.' His voice was low and hard.

'I beg your pardon?'

'You heard. Here's Jimmy with the car. Get your coat and go.'

She watched him walk back into the lounge and shut the door. Bloody cheek! No one, but no one, dumped her without a by your leave. She had a good mind to give him a piece of her mind.

Luckily for Tiffany, she didn't have one.

Kevin sat in the armchair. Neither man said a word as they heard the crunch of the wheels on the gravelled drive. Kelly poured himself another drink. He did not bother to offer one to Kevin.

'Well then, I've tried all her mates. All me relatives. Everyone. Are you sure she ain't got another bloke who she could be out with?'

Kevin bridled despite himself.

'Of course I am. She's not that sort of girl.'

Kelly nodded at him as if agreeing.

'One thing I want to get straight in me mind. Why did you have her car? And if you had it, how was she going to get home?'

Kevin's heart was beating a tattoo in his chest. He had been waiting for these questions all night.

He licked his lips nervously.

'Well.' He cleared his throat. 'She said to me to use her car today to pick up some things like I said I would . . .' His voice trailed off.

Kelly walked to his chair and stared down at him.

'Yeah? Go on.'

'I arranged to pick her up from the phone box in Portaby Road. Only when I got there – I was a bit late like – she wasn't there.' Kevin could see Kelly's slate grey eyes hardening by the second. 'So I come here, thinking she'd got a cab or something.'

'What time was you supposed to pick her up then?'

'Eight o'clock.'

'And what time did you finally get there?'

'About twenty to nine.' Kevin's voice was so low Kelly couldn't hear it.

'What time? Speak up, lad, for Christ's sake.'

'About twenty to nine.'

Kelly's face screwed up in abject disbelief.

'What do you want for Christmas, son? A Rolex or fucking Big Ben hung round your neck, eh? You left my baby standing outside a phone box for forty minutes in this weather!'

Throwing the brandy glass to the floor Patrick Kelly delivered a stinging blow to the younger man's ear, knocking him off the chair.

'You ponce! You little ponce! My Mandy could be fucking dead because of you. Start saying your prayers, boy, because if I don't locate my baby soon, you'll be dead. Do you hear me!'

Kevin wiped his running nose with the back of his hand. He was absolutely terrified.

'Y-Y-Yes. I'm sorry . . .'

'You're sorry, are you? You've been driving round in my Mandy's car for weeks. Oh, I know all about it, sonny boy. I've had you watched. Now I don't doubt you've heard some stories about me. About my businesses up West, and the heavies that work for me. Well, you take all you've heard and times it by ten and you'll get a little inkling of what you are so desperate to marry into. I make the Godfather look like Little Red Riding Hood. You remember that, boy, because if anything, anything at all, has happened to my little girl, you'll be deader than an Egyptian mummy!'

Kelly's face was contorted with rage. He had the same sick feeling inside him he had had the day Renée had died. It was like history repeating itself.

She had been killed driving home from her mother's in West Ham. She had been over two hours late and he had known deep in his heart that something had happened. Her Mini that she loved so much she had named it Jason had been hit by a lorry on the A13, outside the Henry Ford public house. But his Mandy wouldn't be in a car accident, because this pratt in front of him had her bloody car!

He went to the phone and picked it up. He dialled a number and turned back to face Kevin, who had pulled himself off the floor and was now sitting back in the armchair crying.

'Bloody real, ain't it? Patrick Kelly, the most feared man in London, phoning the Old Bill!'

*

Kate was at home putting the finishing touches to the Christmas tree with Lizzy. As her daughter put the old fairy on the top, she remembered when Lizzy had made it. She had been only five at the time and every year since, the pieces of cardboard and tattered lace had graced the top of the tree.

'That looks lovely.'

Lizzy stepped back to admire her handiwork. 'Not bad. I'm really looking forward to Christmas this year, Mum.'

'So am I, love.'

As she spoke there was a loud banging on her front door. Lizzy ran from the room and a few seconds later there was a loud squealing. Kate closed her eyes briefly. The wandering hero had returned, as per usual. Her mother walked from the kitchen and looked at Kate, her eyebrows raised.

'It's himself?'

'It is.'

'Well, it makes her happy anyway.'

Kate plastered a smile on her face as her daughter tugged her father into the room. Kate was aware of the chaos of the room and grinned, this time genuinely. Gone were the days when she took trouble for Danny.

'Hello, Dan, long time no see.'

He looked great, as usual. He was tall, blond and deeply tanned. Kate wondered, not for the first time, why men looked better as they got older. He was hugging his daughter to him with real affection.

'Hello, Kate old girl.'

'Not so much of the old, Dan, if you don't mind.'

They looked at each other over their daughter's head.

'Oh, Mum, Dad's laden down with gear. Presents for all of us.'

Kate saw the question in Dan's eyes and sighed inwardly. He had his suitcase with him which meant he wanted to stay 'for a while'. Over the years he had done this to her a few times. It meant that the current recipient of his affections had either caught him out with her best friend or just caught him out in general.

Evelyn walked into the room and Dan immediately embraced her, lifting her off the floor as he kissed her.

'Evelyn, you never change!' For once he was being truthful. She looked the same at seventy as she had at sixty.

Evelyn waited until he put her down and then said, 'Neither do you, Dan.' They looked at each other, the animosity between them almost tangible. 'I see you've got your case with you this time?'

It was a question and Dan avoided her eyes, turning instead to his daughter.

'I thought I'd spend some time with my girl. Now how about a cup of tea for a cold traveller?'

Lizzy skipped from the room to the kitchen, her grandmother following her. Dan looked at Kate. His deep blue eyes were sparkling.

'You look great.'

'So do you. How's things?'

She picked up a couple of Christmas tree decorations and began to hang them precariously from the branches.

'All right, I suppose. Look, Kate, can I stay, just for the holidays?' His tone was wistful and Kate, with her back to him, afforded herself a little smile.

'Of course you can, Dan, provided you don't mind the settee?'

'I'm quite used to it now, Kate.'

'I'm sure you are.'

The silence between them was heavy. Kate made herself relax. She put up with Dan's invasions for Lizzy's sake, knowing that the girl enjoyed them. Dan was a wastrel, a lazy good for nothing – and his daughter adored every bone in his body.

Kate had never attempted to put her daughter wise about her father. Instead she allowed him to come into their lives when it suited him and then gritted her teeth and smiled until he breezed out again. Kate could even sympathise with Lizzy; once upon a time he had had the same effect on her. She was living for the day when Lizzy found out her father's shortcomings herself. Then she would pick up the pieces and breathe a sigh of relief.

Lizzy came back in the room with a mug of steaming tea. Dan had ensconced himself on the sofa and Kate watched from the easy chair as Lizzy gave him the mug, careful not to let one drop fall on to her father's natty outfit. She would bet her last pound that every bit of money he had was already spent. His presents would be large and as expensive as possible. Now he wanted somewhere to recuperate and relax that did not cost anything. Kate knew he was mugging her off and it annoyed her.

'So how's Anthea?'

'Oh, she's fine, fine. Got her boys home for Christmas, so I thought I'd come and see my poppet.' He ruffled Lizzy's hair as he spoke and she smiled at him.

Kate felt an urge to be sick but fought it down bravely. 'When's she expecting you back?' It came out sweetly but Dan and Evelyn, who had walked into the room, both knew it was a loaded question. He was saved from answering by Lizzy.

'Oh, Mum! He's only just got here and you want to know when he's going?'

The phone rang and Kate went out to the hall to answer it, glad of the respite.

'Hello, DI Burrows speaking.'

'Kate? Ratchette here. Bit of bother, I'm afraid. Could you sort it out for me, please?'

'What's up, sir?'

'It seems that one of the town's leading citizens has mislaid his daughter.'

'Who?'

'Patrick Kelly.' Ratchette's voice was flat. 'I've had the Chief Constable on to me. It seems the girl went missing at eight this evening. The boyfriend was supposed to pick her up from Portaby Road and when he got there she was nowhere to be seen. She's not a girl to go off without telling anyone apparently, so the Chief Constable himself wants the matter thoroughly investigated.'

Kate could hear the annoyance in Ratchette's voice.

'I'll go and see him, don't worry. It's probably nothing. How old is the girl, by the way?'

'Twenty-two. I think she had a row with the boyfriend and is holed up at a friend's but the boy's too frightened to tell the father.'

Kate laughed softly.

'Well, you can't really blame him for that, can you? Patrick Kelly isn't exactly a calm and caring individual.'

'No, Kate, he's not. But he's very friendly with the Chief Constable. At least, that's how it seems to me anyway.'

'Don't worry, I'll sort it out.'

'Thanks, Kate. Give the girls my best, won't you?'

'Of course. I'll let you know what happens, sir.'

The line went dead in her hand.

She walked into the living room and smiled her best smile.

'I've got to go in, I'm afraid. A girl's gone missing.'

'Oh no . . . Who?' Lizzy's face was concerned.

'No one you know. Look, I'll be as quick as I can, all right?'

'Mum's on the murder-rape, Dad, she's in charge.'

'Really, Kate?'

'Yes. Look, you lot catch up and I'll be back soon.'

She went from the room and pulled on her coat quickly. Evelyn followed her out with Lizzy.

'I hope the girl turns up, Mum.'

'I think she will, love, don't worry.'

'You make sure you ring me as you're coming home and I'll have something hot for you when you come in. Wrap up now, it's bitter cold out there.'

'Mum, I'm forty years old, you know.' This was said playfully.

'You don't look that old, Mum. You only look about thirty-eight.'

'Thanks a million, Lizzy, I feel much better!'

'You don't mind Dad staying really, do you?'

Kate looked into the lovely face and felt a twinge of guilt. 'No, of course not.'

Lizzy kissed her and went back into the living room. Kate and her mother looked at each other for a few seconds.

'She's growing up at last, Kate.'

'So it would seem. See you later, Mum.' She kissed the tiny woman in front of her.

Evelyn held her daughter's arm. 'You be careful out there now, with a maniac on the loose. I'll sort out his lordship if he starts his antics.'

''Bye, Mum.'

Picking up her car keys Kate went out into the cold night air. She felt a strange sense of relief to be out in her car. As she pulled away her mind was once more full of the investigation. They were nowhere near solving the case. It had not been planned but was a spontaneous act. Geraldine O'Leary had been murdered by a random killer.

Those were the worst kind of cases. In almost eighty-five per cent of murders the killer was known to the victim, the percentage was even higher in rape cases. She honestly believed that whoever had murdered Geraldine O'Leary had not known who their victim was going to be. But even knowing this brought her no nearer to solving the case; quite the opposite in fact, it made everything harder, much harder. The door to door had not been much use, though there were a few leads they were following up. A sighting of a dark coloured car in Vauxhall Drive at about six fifty-five. They did not know the make, only that it was a saloon. It was like looking for the proverbial needle in a haystack. She turned right at the crossroads that led to the outskirts of Grantley and Patrick Kelly's house. She did not need to find out his address. In Grantley, everyone knew where Patrick Kelly lived.

Especially the police.

Kate felt a flicker of annoyance, even though this call had got her out of the house and away from Dan. If Frederick Flowers was so worried on Patrick Kelly's behalf, why the hell didn't he come out here and investigate the matter himself? Normally a person had to be missing for over twenty-four hours before the police were interested, especially when it was a grown woman. It was different with children, but this Mandy Kelly was twenty-two, for Christ's sake. She pulled into the sweeping gravelled drive and stopped in front of the large Georgian house, set in three acres of parkland. It was lit up like Battersea Power Station. Seems that massage parlours and repossessions paid well and earned friends in high places as well. Kelly's electric bill came to more than her mortgage by the looks of things.

The entire house was floodlit and even the trees had lights in them. You'd have no chance of creeping up to

Patrick Kelly's door without being seen. Nursing her resentment she walked up to the front door and rang the bell.

One of the first things Kate noticed was that the house was decorated in superb taste. Not what she expected at all. She looked around, impressed despite herself. Obviously Kelly's money ran to interior designers. She followed Kelly into the drawing room and took a seat on the chesterfield. The room was beautiful, with the original ceiling roses and cornices; the walls were lined with books, everything from leather-bound volumes to garish paperbacks. It was predominantly silver grey with dusky pink carpets and curtains. It was a room designed by a woman, Kate was certain. It had a woman's feel for colour and space. Men tended to put things in the first place available and just leave them there. Women thought a room out, knew how a room would look at its best. Women, Kate had observed, took time with details. Small details that could make a room like this.

Despite its immense size, it was a homely room and obviously well lived in. A sleek black cat lay asleep before the fire. Her eyes rested on Kevin Cosgrove, who sat whitefaced and subdued. Kate guessed, rightly, that he was the boyfriend, and that he had been having a hard time from Kelly.

She took the Scotch Kelly offered and sipped it gratefully. This was the last thing she had wanted tonight. Even with Dan, the long lost father's return, this was still not what she needed. The Scotch was good and she savoured it for a second before she looked at Kelly directly.

'What makes you think that your daughter's gone missing? She could be at a friend's, anything.'

Patrick stared at Kate as if seeing her for the first time. 'What did you say your name was?'

'Detective Inspector Burrows.'

Kelly put his tongue between his lips and stared at her for a long moment as if committing her to memory. The action and the tone of voice were not lost on Kate and she felt her temper rising. He was trying to tell her she was here at Flowers's express command and she had better take this seriously. Kate fought down the urge to confront him. Instead she broke his gaze by putting her drink on the small occasional table beside her and rooting around in her bag for her notebook and cigarettes. It was going to be a long evening.

As she put a cigarette in her mouth, Kevin Cosgrove gave her a light, his hands shaking. Kate put her hand over his and held her cigarette to the flame. His eyes held a warning and he shook his head imperceptibly.

Kate breathed in the cigarette smoke and sat back, crossing her legs.

Kelly watched her from his chair and approved of her. She had a bit of spunk and he liked that. Providing she didn't 'come it' with him, she was a woman he'd want in his corner if the time came. He looked into her eyes as she spoke.

'Why are you so worried about your daughter, Mr Kelly?' As she spoke, Kate realised that the man really was worried. This was not an over-anxious father throwing his weight around, this was a genuinely worried man.

'This prat here was supposed to pick my daughter up at eight.' He flicked his head at Kevin, who kept his eyes firmly on the carpet. 'He had her motor, her car. He went to pick her up and she wasn't there. I've rung her mates, her aunt, the fucking manageress of the shop where she works, I've rung everyone in Grantley and I can't find her. This is no girlish prank, Ms Burrows. My baby is definitely on the missing list. Now then, what are you going to do about it?'

Kate took another drag on her cigarette and met the dark blue eyes full on.

'Has Mandy ever gone missing like this before?'

Kelly shook his head. 'Nope. Never. Me and Mandy are like that.' He crossed two of his fingers together. He licked his lips and took a large gulp of brandy.

Kate pushed her hair off her face and watched Kelly. He was handsome all right. In other circumstances she would have given him a second glance. This was the first time she had seen him in person. Oh, she'd seen pictures of him, everyone had. But in the flesh, he had a presence. He was a man who was all there, was alive. He crackled with energy and vitality. Now, seeing his concern for his daughter, Kate felt a stirring of pity for him.

'Have you and Mandy had an argument, Kevin?' She looked at the boy; his face was ashen and he still stared at the carpet as he shook his head dismally. With one bound, Kelly was out of his chair and had dragged the unfortunate boy from his seat. Holding him up by the hair he pushed him towards Kate and shouted.

'Tell her anything she wants to know, boy, I'm warning you. If Mandy turns up here and her story differs from yours I'll snap your bastard neck for you.'

Kate jumped up and separated the two men.

'Mr Kelly, please! This is not doing anyone any good. Now calm down, will you? Can't you see you're frightening the life out of him? How can you expect him to tell you the truth when he's so obviously terrified of you?'

Her words crept into Patrick's brain. It was after eleven now and Mandy had still not been in touch. He could feel a panic inside him like the day Renée died. When she hadn't been home at five thirty, he had known, deep in his gut, that she'd never walk in again. He felt the same now.

He forced down the panic and went back to his seat. His haunted expression tore at Kate's heart. If it was her Lizzy, so soon after the murder of Geraldine O'Leary . . . she shuddered.

Kevin Cosgrove was crying silently. Kate led him back to his chair and, without asking, poured them all another drink. Patrick took the glass from her and drained it, his handsome face haggard.

'You don't know my Mandy, she wouldn't stay out without letting me know. No way.' The last was said with the finality of a father who knows his child.

Kate glanced at the clock on the mantelpiece; it was nearly eleven thirty.

Patrick saw her looking and exploded again.

'Want to get home, do you? Am I boring you or something?'

As he opened his mouth to speak again, Kate held up her hand for silence.

'No, Mr Kelly, you're not boring me, you're annoying me. Until you calm down and speak rationally, we will get nowhere. Now, if you don't mind, I'm going to ask you some simple questions. If you could just bring yourself to answer them, we might start getting somewhere.'

Kelly's eyes were like slits. The cheeky mare, she was talking to him as if he was a naughty little kid. He felt a surge of annoyance and something else as well. Admiration. She was not intimidated by him and he was glad. If his Mandy had gone missing, then this woman would find her. The cold fear that had engulfed his body for the last two hours gradually let go its hold.

'I'm sorry, Ms Burrows.' He emphasised the Ms.

Kate looked at him and smiled slightly. 'That's all right, Mr Kelly. I have a daughter too. I can imagine what you're going through.'

'Can you?' It was a question they both knew she could not answer.

'Right, Kevin, what were your exact arrangements with Mandy?'

As Kate questioned the boy, Kelly watched her from his seat. Even in his agitated state he could see she was an attractive woman. What he really liked about her though, was her sass. He did like a woman with a bit of spunk in her. Mandy's mother had had that. She was as quiet as a church mouse till you set her off, then you'd better watch out. This Ms Burrows was interesting. She was taking his mind off his child for a few minutes and for that, he was grateful.

Kate felt his attention and shrugged it off. She wanted to get her job done and get back home. This house was too fraught for her liking.

'Listen you.' Caroline's voice had a smile in it. 'I am not having it off in an old shed.'

Barry laughed with her.

'Well, there's one thing for certain, girl. My wife and your husband ain't gonna let us use their beds, so it's the back of the motor, or the shed. I've got a sleeping bag in me boot. We'll be as snug as two bugs in a rug!'

Caroline screeched with laughter again.

'What's the time?'

Barry stared bleary-eyed at his watch.

'Half-past twelve.'

'My old man ain't expecting me in till after two. He thinks I'm doing an extra shift.'

'So what's it to be then? Out here in the motor or in the shed?'

'You've done this before, ain't you?'

Barry nodded.

'Yeah. I've got a sleeping bag, a bottle of wine and a couple of plastic glasses. All waiting for you, my darling.'

'Oh . . . go on then. But you're sure no one comes round this way at night, ain't ya?'

'Yes! Now help me lug all the stuff in.'

They got out of the car. Caroline carried the wine and the glasses. Barry carried a large sleeping bag. Caroline pushed open the shed door. As she walked in she stumbled over something and screamed with fright.

'Here, hold up, girl. You'll have the Old Bill here if you're not careful.'

Dumping the sleeping bag on to the floor, Barry flicked his lighter into life.

He heard the real scream that came from Caroline this time and was hard pressed not to follow it with one of his own.

On the floor in a pool of blood lay a young girl. She was nearly naked.

The lighter burnt his fingers and he pulled his thumb off the fuel button. In the darkness Caroline began to panic and Barry pulled her from the shed. He held her to him tightly.

'Calm down . . . Calm down!'

He could hear her teeth chattering and guessed she was in shock.

He took her back to his car, turned the engine on and put on the heater. Then, taking his torch from the glove compartment, he went back to the shed. His mind was in a turmoil. He stepped gingerly inside and shone the torch on to the girl's body. Her head was stuck to the floor where the blood had dried on to her hair and the dirt. He knelt down beside the body and put his fingers to the main artery in her neck.

She was alive! Surely not?

He felt again with trembling fingers. He was positive there was a faint heartbeat. He jumped up quickly and, opening the sleeping bag, covered her with it. Must keep her warm. Must keep her warm. Don't move her. Bless her little heart. Let her live, God. Oh, let her live!

Running from the shed, he jumped into his car and drove as fast as he could to a phone box.

Within fifteen minutes Mandy Kelly was on her way to Grantley Hospital and Caroline and Barry were explaining their embarrassing story to the police, who promised that neither of their spouses would be informed of the circumstances that heralded the finding of the girl.

In the pocket of the sheepskin the police found a purse. It contained Mandy Kelly's credit cards.

A positive ID had been established.

Kate was listening to Kelly talk about his wife and daughter. Kevin had gone upstairs to lie down and, without his presence, Kelly seemed to relax a little. Kate knew that he was blaming the boy for whatever had happened to Mandy. Kate still thought there was a good chance Mandy would turn up any minute. She'd probably had an argument with Kevin and stormed off, possibly because he'd taken her car again. Kate could not begin to comprehend the wealth that enabled a man to give his daughter a fifty thousand pound car for her twenty-first birthday. She thought of the sovereign earrings she had bought Lizzy for Christmas, the struggle she had had to find the money for them, and shook her head. The funny thing was that Kelly, back to his old self now, was an interesting and articulate man. He spoke of his wife and child with a love that was almost tangible. He was telling her a story now about his first months of fatherhood.

'Anyway, there I was, all on me own with Mandy, a

baby like.' He smiled. 'Well, she wanted her dinner. She was crying her eyes out. Do you remember those big glass bottles in the sixties? I picked one up out of the hot water to check it on me arm and I dropped it. It shattered all over the kitchen floor. Well, that was it then. We only had the one bottle and I was beginning to panic when I saw the sauce bottle on the table. I put Mandy in her pram, she slept in a pram then, because we couldn't afford a cot, see. And I washed out the sauce bottle and sterilised it with boiling water, then I made a feed up and put the teat on the top and fed her.'

Kate laughed with him, picturing the scene in her mind.

'Well, Renée came home like, laden down with the shopping, took one look and went through the roof.'

It was the sort of thing she could see him doing. He was resourceful. She had been on the point of leaving when he had persuaded her to have another drink. She had guessed that he was frightened of being alone at this time, that he needed another human being. She had stayed out of pity and now she was glad. He was a good talker, a great storyteller and even though she knew what he was capable of, she liked him. She trusted him, too, though why this should be so after his earlier performance she had no idea. Kelly was a hard man, but he had an Achilles heel. Mandy Kelly.

Already, Kate felt as if she knew the girl. And if all her father said was true, she was most definitely not a girl to go off without letting him know. Kelly was the kind of father who would demand to know his daughter's whereabouts. It was as much a part of him as his swearing.

'I'm sorry about carrying on earlier, but I've been out of me mind.' His voice was low. Kate knew it had taken a lot for him to give her an apology.

'I understand, Mr Kelly.'

As if of one mind, they both looked at the clock; it was just after half past twelve.

'Where the hell can she be? When she walks in, I'll slap her from one end of this room to the other, I take oath on that. I've never raised me hand to her before but I will tonight, by Christ.'

Kate put her hand over his. 'Calm down, hitting her won't solve anything.'

'No, but it might make me feel better.'

The phone rang and Kelly rushed to answer it.

'Mandy?'

Kate saw his face dissolve from hope to fear in the space of seconds. He held the phone out towards her and said, 'It's for you.'

'Burrows here.'

Patrick Kelly watched her face blanch and in that moment he knew that something had happened to his only child. He clenched his fists so tightly the nails dug into the skin of his palms, drawing blood.

Kate put down the phone and looked at him fully.

'We've found your daughter, Mr Kelly. It seems she's been attacked.'

Kelly stared at the woman in front of him, confusion and pain flitting across his face.

'Attacked? My Mandy?'

His voice sounded like a little boy's, full of hurt and disbelief.

Kate nodded. 'She's in Grantley Hospital and they're operating on her. She's in a bad way.'

Patrick Kelly felt the wetness in his eyes and did not care. He felt as if his world had just come to an end. He swallowed hard. When he finally spoke it was in a low croak.

106

'Is she gonna die?'

Kate put her hand on his arm gently.

'I think we'd better go to the hospital, don't you?'

As she sat beside him on the way, Kate felt that she had received an insight into Patrick Kelly. He had his Achilles heel, just like everyone else.

All her problems seemed small in comparison to what the man beside her was going through.

They drove in silence.

George was still sitting in his lounge. It was just past one. He could hear the regular thud-thud of the music from a party a few houses down. He took a long drink of his Ovaltine. It was stone cold and he grimaced.

Elaine had gone to bed earlier and he had told her he was feeling overtired. She knew that when he got like that he could not sleep. She had been happy to leave him downstairs.

He smiled to himself ruefully, laid his head back on the chair and savoured once more the events of earlier in the evening.

She was a very silly girl. Well, he had shown her. Oh, yes, he had shown her all right. The little slut! Hanging around at night, in deserted streets. Well, he had put a stop to her gallop. Oh, yes. It might just make a few of the women of Grantley sit up and take notice of him.

They'd all be talking about him again tomorrow. Oh, he knew what would be said. Elaine, the hungry hippo, would fill him in on all the local gossip. He smiled to himself at the comparision.

In his mind's eye he saw the girl as she had been when he had left her. Legs akimbo. He grinned. He knew all her secret places now. She had seen his face. That was a mistake, he realised it now. He should have put on the mask first.

He wondered vaguely if the girl had been found yet. Mandy . . . He liked that name very much.

The party was in full swing now and George could hear one of the records blaring out.

He liked people to enjoy themselves.

As the strains of 'Blue Velvet' wafted towards him he smiled again. In his mind he saw all the young girls dancing with men. He pictured tight dresses and straining busts against white silk.

Oh, they were all the same. Every last one of them.

It would be Christmas Day soon. He was glad, because he needed a holiday. It had been a hectic few months.

As they reached the hospital Kelly asked Kate to tell him all she knew. She explained that Mandy had been found with horrific head injuries and that they were operating on her. She did not elaborate. It was not the right time.

Together, they walked into Grantley Casualty Department and Kate explained who they were to the receptionist. Like most hospital receptionists, this one was a breed apart. She pulled her glasses down an almost non-existent nose and surveyed Kelly and Kate over the top of them. Her thin hair was scraped back from her face in a bun so tight her eyes had taken on a Chinese appearance. Kate could see her in a kaftan and clogs and had to stifle a bubble of laughter.

'Name of patient again please.'

'Mandy Kelly. I am Detective Insp . . .'

The woman held up a chubby finger in reproof. 'One question at a time please.'

Patrick watched the performance with a darkening face. The woman was tapping Mandy's name laboriously into her computer.

'And how was she brought here?'

'I beg your pardon?' Kate was losing patience now.

'How was she brought here? By ambulance, in a car . . .'

Kelly pushed Kate out of the way. He peered into the glasses that separated him from the receptionist.

'She came by fucking bus. There was her, with her head smashed in. Two ambulance men and a fucking dirty great stretcher. Even you couldn't have missed them walking through here. Now shut your trap and tell me where my daughter is or you'll be going in to see the doctor yourself!'

The woman's mouth puckered into a small O and a nurse, hearing the exchange, hurried out from the cubicle area.

'Mr Kelly?'

Patrick nodded. Kate could see the tension in his shoulders and back. It was as if someone had stuffed a metal pole inside his coat to hold him up.

'Where's my daughter? I want to see my daughter.'

'She's still in theatre. If you'd like to follow me, I'll take you to the waiting room.'

Kelly and Kate followed the young girl.

'How is she?'

'I'm sorry, Mr Kelly, I really don't know, a doctor will see you soon.'

Kate followed Kelly up two flights of stairs and into a tiny waiting room off the ITU. She thanked the nurse, who offered to bring them coffee.

'I knew this had happened, I knew it. I had a feeling in me bones.'

Kate didn't answer. Amanda Dawkins walked into the tiny room and Kate motioned with her head that they should go outside, closing the door quietly on Kelly.

'How is she?'

'Bad, Kate. Really bad. Half her head's gone. It's obvious

it's the same man who attacked Geraldine O'Leary. She's been raped. Buggered as well I think. She's in a terrible state. Even the doctors were amazed at how she's hanging on to life.'

Kate pursed her lips. Kelly would go berserk if anything happened to his daughter. He was wound up like a watch spring now. She nodded at Amanda.

'Look, do me a favour. Keep everyone away from Kelly for a while. I'll stay with him. Get someone out to interview Kevin Cosgrove. He's at Kelly's house. OK?'

'Will do. Anything else?'

'Not until we know more.'

As Amanda walked away Kate called after her. 'There is one more thing: ring my house and leave a message on the answerphone. Tell them I'll be there as soon as possible, OK?'

Amanda nodded and Kate went back in to Kelly.

'What's happening?' His voice was flat, dead.

'Nothing at the moment.'

'Is Flowers here?'

Kate was startled.

'Of course not.'

Kelly got up and began pacing the room. 'Then get him here, tell him I personally request his presence. You can also find out who's the quack on my daughter's case and then find out who's the best quack for her kind of complaint. I don't care who the man is or how much he costs, just get him.'

Kate felt her mettle rise again. All her sympathy for Kelly evaporated out of the little window and she pulled herself up to her full height.

'With respect, Mr Kelly, I am not a secretary. If you want Frederick Flowers, or another doctor, I suggest you get them yourself.'

Kelly looked at her with a stunned expression on his face. He was used to people jumping when he told them to jump. He was used to pure unadulterated agreement with everything he said and did. He stared into Kate's face and she could see the battle raging inside him. His hand clenched into a fist and Kate knew it was taking all his willpower not to slap her a stinging blow.

What she'd said was tantamount to mutiny.

He bit his lip, his chest heaving. He pointed a finger at her, waving it up and down in front of her face.

'If I don't do something I'll explode, and if I explode here you will never see the like again as long as you live. I just *can't* sit here and wait. I have to do *something*.'

It was said simply and sincerely and Kate felt the power of him then, knew the depth of fear inside him and felt petty. Petty and nasty and childish. The man was trying to cope with his grief as best he could. He needed to be moving, doing, as if the act of movement would take away his fears. Would at least postpone them. If he was doing something he wouldn't feel so useless. Kate swallowed hard.

'I'll arrange for a phone for you.'

As she walked past him he grabbed her arm. She looked first at his hand, the fingers digging into her arm, and then up into his face. She saw the terrible knowledge in his eyes and then he crumpled. It was as if someone had punctured him – he just crumpled before her eyes and instinctively she put her arm around him. He clung to her.

'If she dies I have nothing, nothing.'

She steered him back to the chair and he put his head into his hands. Harsh racking sobs burst from inside his chest, exploding as they hit the air.

The nurse walked in with the coffee and Kate took the tray and hustled her out.

She gave him his coffee and lit a cigarette for him, placing it between his lips.

'It's the bastard who murdered that barmaid, ain't it?'

Kate knew it had taken a lot for him to admit his real fears.

She nodded. 'We think so.'

'Has she been raped?'

Kate nodded again.

He sipped his coffee and a calm descended on him. He knew the worst now. Nothing else could be this bad.

'You realise he's a dead man, don't you? Even if she lives. He's a dead man.'

Kate sipped her own coffee.

There was nothing to be said.

Chapter Six

Patrick Kelly drove home from the hospital at eight in the morning. He looked terrible and he knew it. His mouth tasted foul from instant coffee and cheap cigarettes. And he was fuming.

His daughter was lying between life and death, raped and beaten nearly to death. He felt the tightening around his heart and for one horrible second thought he was going to have a heart attack. He tried to control his breathing.

When he had seen her, his baby, lying in intensive care, full of tubes and drips and bandages, he had felt a red rage behind his eyes the like of which he had never experienced. Some piece of filth had taken his child – his child! – and forced himself on her.

She had been buggered, that was the worst of it all. His child had been buggered by some piece of scum.

Well, that piece of scum had better start saying his prayers, because Kelly was going to find him – find him and rip him to shreds.

He screeched to a halt in his driveway and as he ran towards it the front door was opened by Willy Gabney.

Without speaking to the man, he rushed through the entrance lobby, the large tiled hall, and up the curved staircase, taking the steps three at a time. By the time he got to the bedroom where Kevin Cosgrove lay asleep, his chest and lungs were burning with every breath.

He threw open the bedroom door and it crashed against a bureau, sending an antique jug and bowl crashing to the floor. Before Kevin had even opened his eyes properly, Patrick Kelly was on him. Dragging the boy by the hair he pulled him from the bed, shaking him like a terrier with a bone. He began to rain punches on Kevin's body, kicking him and screaming at him at the top of his voice.

Kevin curled himself up into a tight ball, taking all that Patrick Kelly doled out to him. Frightened out of his life, he felt the savageness of the attack but was powerless to put a stop to it. Dragging him up by his shoulders, Patrick Kelly drew his head back and brought his forehead down on to Kevin's face with all his might. The force of the blow stunned them both. Kelly let Kevin drop to the floor, the boy's whimpering barely penetrating his rage.

Gabney, who had followed his boss up the stairs, stood in the doorway, his face neutral. The violence of the attack affected him not one iota. He was only surprised that Kelly had acted out the whole thing himself. It was precisely what Gabney himself was paid to do.

Kelly stared at the crumpled figure on the floor below him. He pointed, his finger shaking.

'My Mandy was raped and half murdered last night, you fucking ponce! Some piece of shite buggered my baby! Do you hear what I'm telling you, wanker?'

Kevin stared up, bemused. Mandy, raped?

Kelly brought back his leg and kicked Kevin in the knees as hard as he could.

'She's in a coma. She could be a vegetable because of you. But I promise you this, dickhead, whatever happens to my baby, happens to you! Remember that. Keep it stamped in your mind.'

He was so exhausted by his exertions he could barely talk, every few seconds gasping for breath. 'You're dead meat, boy. Dead meat.'

He leant against the dressing table until his breathing returned to normal. Then he nodded at Willy. 'Get all the lads here NOW. I don't care if it is Christmas Eve, I don't care if they're at their mother's death bed, get them here pronto!'

Gabney hurried away. When Patrick Kelly was annoyed, it was best to do exactly what he said.

Kelly stared down at the crumpled heap on the floor. Crimson stains were appearing as if by magic on the Axminster carpet. Gathering up the spittle in his mouth, he bent over the prostrate form and spat into his face.

'Get up, Cosgrove, and piss off out of my house. You get yourself a sherbet dab and all, because my Mandy's car stays here. Get it?'

Kate had been busy all day with the new development. There was no doubt in anyone's mind that it was the same man who had murdered Geraldine O'Leary. She had been shocked to see the severity of the beating the girl had taken. All the fingers of one hand were broken, as if stamped on, and a large chunk of her head had been literally hacked from the skull. Even the doctors agreed that the girl should by rights be dead. But she was a fighter, like her father.

In spite of everything Kate knew about Patrick Kelly, she still could not help liking him. He was arrogant, self-opinionated and a bit of a male chauvinist. That much was evident even to an inexperienced observer. He had obviously ruled his daughter's life. A life that she was hanging on to by a thread. But after he had calmed down, she had seen another side to him. Inside the hospital she had witnessed the depth of his grief. Even with his bombast and his violent temper, Kate had felt an affinity with him. Anyone who had to witness the destruction of a child would feel the same.

She remembered when, years before, Lizzy had gone missing for an afternoon. Everyone had told her not to worry, that she was probably playing and had forgotten the time and Kate had felt the same rage inside her. Being a policewoman, she knew exactly what could have befallen her daughter. She had seen it enough times. She had wanted to slap the supercilious smiles off the faces around her. Lizzy had been found in the local woods setting up camp with a boy from two streets away. Kate had given her the one and only good hiding of her life. Not so much because she had gone missing but because of the fear she had caused her mother. Kate had sensed that same feeling in Kelly in the night.

She had stayed with him until Mandy had come out of theatre. During the long vigil he had talked again about his daughter and his dead wife. As if the very action of talking about her would somehow keep Mandy alive. It was this gentleness that attracted Kate to him. His more sinister reputation was overshadowed by his grief for his child.

Kelly had come up the hard way and Kate wondered if events in his childhood had made him what he was. Socialisation, the social workers called it. Kate had her own opinion. She thought that Kelly was a man who would have made something of himself whatever class he was born in: he had an inbred cunning, a need to achieve by whatever means he could. And she sensed that he wanted those achievements not so much for himself but for his wife and his child. He had worked to give Mandy everything, a fifty thousand pound car and a hairdressing salon and beauty parlour. She would love to be able to hand those to Lizzy on a plate. Wouldn't all parents? No, Patrick Kelly's reputation as a hard man was only true to an extent. Deep inside he was no different to anyone else; he just earned his money in unconventional ways.

When he had finally been able to see his daughter Kate had felt his anguish. It was obvious that Mandy was not going to live; she was so badly brain damaged, it would be kinder to let her die. But she was hanging on and Kate knew that Kelly would find it very difficult to accept that she was going to die. He felt pure willpower could pull her through.

Kate sighed. When she had finally left him to go home and grab a quick shower and a change of clothes before coming to work, she had felt as if she was abandoning him. As she'd walked from the ITU, she'd felt his eyes burning into her back. Now, at her desk, she admitted to herself that she found Patrick Kelly attractive. He was one hell of a good-looking man. She chastised herself. Your trouble, Kate Burrows, is you haven't had a man for too long. You should get yourself laid. Do you the world of good.

She smiled.

She had only ever had one man in her life and she was divorced from him. Shows how much Kelly affected me, she thought. I haven't thought about sex for years.

No, that was a lie. She'd thought about it, just never done anything about it.

She was glad when DS Spencer broke into her thoughts.

'So, ma'am, what's the next step?'

Kate sighed.

'Well, as far as I can see, we just keep interviewing. I want you to find out if any of the door-to-door had a dark-coloured Orion car. One was reported seen on the waste ground last night.'

Spencer looked at the ceiling.

'Look, ma'am, the man who reported that was not exactly a reliable witness . . . know what I mean . . .'

Kate chewed the inside of her mouth for a few seconds before answering.

'I am well aware that the man is a tinker, a pike, a gypo – whatever you want to call him, Spencer. I am also aware that they are camped not five hundred yards from the waste ground itself. Whether the man was drugged, drunk or both is not the issue here, Spencer. I want every lead followed up. And you can tell Willis that I'll be down to interview Fred Barkis myself in about . . .' she glanced at her watch . . . 'fifteen minutes, OK?'

'Yes, ma'am.' Spencer failed to keep the irritation out of his voice.

Kate studied the file in front of her. Fred Barkis was a known flasher. He had also acquired a dark green Mark One Cortina, and a dark car had been reported by three different people cruising around by Vauxhall Drive on the night that Geraldine O'Leary died.

Kate stared at the wall opposite her and tapped her pen on her chin. Fred Barkis was harmless, she would lay money on it. For a start he was not violent-natured. All her years of policing had proved to her that the most mild-mannered men could be animals beneath the skin, but by the same token she had also learnt that ninety-five per cent of policing was working from hunches. And she had a hunch that Fred Barkis was not the man they were after. Still, he had to be eliminated.

That was the trouble with Spencer and his ilk, she had seen it so many times: get a suspect and dress up the evidence to suit yourself. Well, she had never worked like that and she was not going to start now. How many times had she seen witnesses' statements that had been doctored? Too many. She could understand that at times the job could be stressful – like now, when they had one woman dead and another fighting for her life and literally nothing to go on – but that did not excuse using a 'live one', as a pressured suspect was called. Barkis fit the bill, but in reality they could not tie him in to both cases and they now knew from the DNA samples that they were looking for one man. Anyway, Barkis had given samples of blood, urine and semen without a murmur. No, he was not their man, he was a common or garden sex pest which was a far cry from a fully fledged sex murderer.

The most annoying thing was that the local paper had nicknamed the rapist the 'Grantley Ripper'. Whoever he was, he was local, Kate was sure of that, very sure; and she was also sure that when he read his 'nickname' he would feel pleased. The criminal psychologist had already begun his profile of the man, and certain things shone through. He was a misogynist. He also had a job or a home life that allowed him free rein to roam the streets.

The misogynist part of it Kate had already worked out for herself; the ferocity of the attacks had told her as much. There seemed to be no motive of any kind; there rarely was in such cases. He was a sick man.

What they had to try and find out now was something that tied the two attacks together in some way. Kate frowned. Could he have a job that had brought him into contact with the two women? But one worked in a wine bar and one in a beauty salon. No matter how hard she thought she could not tie them together.

119

Even as all the evidence was being collated, there was nothing. Not one single thing that gave even a hint of who or what the murderer was. He had worn gloves on both occasions. The fibres from the body of Geraldine O'Leary had belonged to a family of wool that was used in literally hundreds of thousands of jumpers, coats, and other garments.

Kate felt the steel band of a headache tighten over her eyes and rubbed them with her finger and thumb, pressing on the closed lids as if the action would conjure up something she or one of the other officers had missed.

Finally she stood up and made her way to the interview room. Alongside the photos of Geraldine O'Leary there were now two more. In one Mandy Kelly was smiling, long blond hair framing her tiny heart-shaped face. In the other she was lying in a hospital bed, her lovely hair shaved from her head. Deep gouges showed up in burgundy and black where her skull had been smashed. Both eyes were swollen and her nose was broken beyond recognition. Kate sighed. All around her the incident room was a hive of activity. Amanda Dawkins had tapped into the DVLC's computer and was finding out the name and address of every person in Grantley and the surrounding areas who owned either a dark green saloon car or a dark blue Orion.

The tapping of the typewriters and the constant buzz of voices in the smoke-filled room had not given Kate the headache, it was the stress of this case.

Picking up a file from Amanda's desk, she walked from the room.

Patrick Kelly lit a Dunhill cigarette with his gold lighter and exhaled noisily. By the time he had showered and changed, six men had arrived at his house. Now they were sitting in his morning room, uneasily awaiting their orders.

Kelly looked at the lighter for a long moment. Mandy had given it to him for his forty-second birthday. Every time he thought of Mandy he felt panic rise in his breast. If she died . . . Oh God in heaven! If she died he had nothing. Nothing in the world.

For the first time, his thirst for money had become a secondary thing. He realised he would cheerfully give up everything he possessed to have his daughter back as she had been the last time he had seen her.

Happy and smiling and alive. Bursting with youth and vitality . . .

He heard a discreet cough and snapped his eyes from the lighter in his hands to the assembled men.

'I suppose you all know what's happened?'

At his words they started to murmur condolences. Kelly held up his hand for silence.

'I want this bastard caught, and I want him caught as fast as possible. I would not wish what has happened to me and mine on my worst enemy.' He paused while he pulled himself together. 'As you are all aware, the Chief Constable is a very dear and treasured friend of mine. He has assured me on the phone today that any information I want is open to me.

'I don't have a lot of faith in the Old Bill's methods of catching criminals. After all, they've never caught me, have they? I want all of you to drop everything you are doing and find this cretin. And find him fast! I want him dead. As soon as is possible, I want him dead.

'Now, later on today I am having some files delivered here. They will contain the name of every nonce in the South East of England. I want you lot –' Kelly gestured to the men with a sweep of his arm – 'to get yourself up individual armies. I don't care how much it costs, or who the men are, as long as they are reliable. I want every shirt

121

lifter and pervert rousted and trounced as soon as possible.'

He looked around as his words sunk in.

'At the moment a skirt is on the case, a DI Burrows – a very nice woman by the way. You *do not* give her any grief, right? But you give as much grief as you like to the other officers! I want them questioned one by one, and anything that they even think is a bit dodgy you find it out, then take it from there. The wedge for the bloke who finds the wanker is two hundred and fifty thousand pounds, tax free. Now, any questions?'

The six men stared at Kelly with a mixture of sorrow at what had happened to his daughter and joy at the prospect of a quarter of a million pounds.

No one spoke and he nodded at them.

'OK, lads. Report here with whatever you get. If you find him then I want him first, right? Now then, let's all have a drink while we get our heads together.'

Kelly walked through to his bar and a fleeting picture of Kate Burrows came into his mind. She was a fighter – he liked people who stood up to him. He allowed himself a brief smile. He wouldn't give her any grief. He thought there was a good chance she would find the bloke before he did. She was a good-looking piece as well, even in his trouble he had noticed that. No, he wouldn't hurt Kate Burrows. He had a feeling that they were going to see more of each other. She'd sat with him through the worst hours of his life. He felt that he owed her something for that at least.

Once his Mandy was home from hospital and he could concentrate better, he'd make a point of seeing Kate, thanking her.

He would not allow himself to admit that Mandy might not come home.

It was like tempting fate.

*

Dan sat with his mother-in-law and smiled to himself. Even though he knew that Evelyn couldn't stand him, he still had a grudging respect for her. Looking round the warm kitchen, he felt, not for the first time, that he had been a fool to leave Kate. That he had dumped her with a small baby sometimes gave his conscience a nasty twinge. Since then he had had his fill of women. They liked him. He knew that, and relied on it to keep a roof over his head and a pretty good standard of living. At forty-six, though, it was beginning to pall. Anthea had not been very nice to him at their final parting. In fact she had pointed out his age in rather a derogatory fashion. She could talk, the bitch! She was on the wrong side of fifty, not that she'd ever admit it. Still, the jibe had stung.

What really hurt, though, was the fact that she was holidaying in the Canaries for Christmas and he should have been with her. Instead he had had to throw himself on Kate's mercy. Good old Kate. He knew he was all right with her because of Lizzy. She would do anything for their daughter. He grinned ruefully. Even put up with him. What was worrying him, though, was what he was going to do after the holidays. For the first time he was not going from one home to another.

Evelyn took the turkey out of the oven and basted it. The smell was absolutely delicious. Suddenly Dan knew without a moment's doubt that the only course he had left to him was to stay in this house. Somehow he had to get Kate back on his side. She had wanted him for years after he had left. He had seen the naked longing in her face when he had turned up, ostensibly to visit his daughter. He had slipped back into her bed and then, when the time was right, slipped back out of it. He knew that she would not put up with that these days. She had told him once

123

that he was her Achilles heel, but not any more. He would enjoy the chase all the more. Before she knew it she would be eating out of his hand. At least he hoped so anyway.

Kate had changed over the years. She had made a life for herself, had a good career in the police force. She wasn't waiting there open-armed any more, but she would still put up with him for Lizzy's sake and on that he could build.

He looked at Evelyn and closed his eyes. He'd have to get around her as well.

His mother-in-law put the kettle on for one of her endless cups of coffee.

'You're quiet, Dan.'

'Just thinking, Eve, that's all.'

'Well, don't strain yourself, son.'

He grinned.

'I was thinking about Lizzy, actually.'

He watched Evelyn's face light up with interest. Her granddaughter was the reason for her existence.

'What about her?'

He had her interest and crossed his fingers. 'I feel bad you know, Eve, that I never really saw her grow up.'

She snorted. 'Well, you wouldn't, would you? Always skedaddling off somewhere. You were a fool, you know, Dan. My Kate was a good wife and mother. I watched her die inside when you first left her.'

She pulled two mugs from their hooks on the wall and slammed them on to the worktop. 'She worked like a frigging Trojan to give that child a decent upbringing. You never even gave a few pounds here and there to help her out.'

Danny's face was a mask of regret. This was not how he wanted the conversation to go. He wanted an ally, he didn't want recriminations.

'When I came here she was in a terrible state, but she got back to work and she's done very well for herself, so you leave her alone, Daniel Burrows. I can see through you as if you was made of glass, my boy, always could.

'Now, let's have a coffee before that child gets in. It's cold enough to cut the legs from you out there.'

Danny had the grace to redden. Evelyn knew him so very well. But ever the optimist he decided to wait a while then try again. There wasn't a woman alive he couldn't charm if he put his mind to it. He was absolutely certain of that.

'Merry Christmas, George!'

Elaine smiled at him. Since booking her holiday and going out two nights a week with the girls from work, even life with him had begun to be bearable.

'Merry Christmas, dear.' He dutifully kissed his wife's cheek.

George waited for Elaine to go back to her cooking before he curled his lip with contempt. The house stank of Christmas. Of turkey and mince pies.

'Joseph and Lily will be here soon. Lily's bringing one of her sherry trifles with her. I hope your mother won't be a nuisance this year . . .'

George felt his heart sink down to his boots. It was the same every year. His elder brother Joseph and his wife came for dinner. The brothers rang each other every New Year and Easter, and every Christmas Joseph and Lily came to dinner. Other than that, they had nothing to do with each other. George wished he had the guts to pick up the phone and tell them to go to hell. He wouldn't though. He never did.

He started fidgeting with his knife and fork. He didn't want any breakfast now. The thought of seeing his mother had made him feel ill.

He saw her once a year, at Christmas. She lived with

Joseph and Lily. Or, more precisely, they lived with her. Joseph might have worked all his life and bought his own house, but from the day his mother had moved in with them, it had become hers. She ruled the roost.

The only good thing about Elaine was the fact that she gave his mother short shrift. When she was told that Mother wanted to live with them, she had put her foot down firmly. Refusing even to discuss the situation. It was the one and only time in his life that George had been glad he had married her.

Elaine brought his scrambled eggs to him and he smiled his thanks. He noticed that she looked nice. He looked at her for a long moment and, noticing his look, she laughed. Picking up her own breakfast, she walked to the table and sat down.

'So you finally noticed, then!'

George stared at her, more puzzled than ever.

'I've lost a stone, George. I'm down to eleven and a half now. If I carry on like this I shall be about nine and a half for my holidays!' She laughed gaily.

'Well, you certainly look much better, dear.'

'Thanks. Haven't you noticed that I've been dieting at all?'

Her voice was half happy and half sad. George realised that she had been waiting for him to notice before mentioning it.

'Well, I had an idea, but I didn't like to ask outright . . .' He was stumbling for the right words and Elaine dropped her eyes.

After all their years of marriage, there was not an ounce of closeness between them. Since her first night out with the girls, she had discovered a whole new world. A world where George did not exist for her. A world where she could forget about him, just for a while.

*

Joseph Markham was at screaming point. Lily had gone into one of her painfully long silences, interspersed with black looks that she threw across the car at him at every set of traffic lights. Behind, Nancy Markham stared at the back of their heads. Her heavily lipsticked mouth was set in a grim line.

Nancy Markham was big. Her body, which in her young days could bring a grown man to his knees on first sight of it, bulged over the back seat of the car. Her dyed hair, now a vivid burgundy, was shampooed and set like a bloody halo around her face that now sported numerous chins. The only thing about her that were still young-looking and alert were her eyes.

They were still a startling green colour, except that the once pristine whites were now bloodshot and tinged with yellow. She held her large handbag across her chest like a weapon, her fat pudgy hands gripping the handles so tightly her knuckles were a livid white.

'Mind that lorry!' Nancy's voice, naturally loud, was now set at a depth that could melt concrete.

'Mother, the lorry is on the other side of the road. Please, let me drive. I have been doing it for over forty years . . .'

Nancy Markham interrupted him as if he had not spoken a word. 'You're like your father, God rest him. Always in a hurry, never taking his time. You'll have a heart attack and die, you mark my words. Be careful of the motorbike!'

Her voice rose on the last few words. Joseph took a deep breath to stem the beating of his heart. If he had a heart attack it would be because of the woman sitting in the back seat!

She had driven his father to his and she would drive

127

Joseph into having one. He knew that as surely as he knew that she would outlive the lot of them. Look at her! Eighty-one and still going strong. He shook his head as he drove. Please God George would take the brunt of her today, give him and Lily a bit of peace for a few hours. His own two children would not come near his house unless they absolutely had to, thanks to their grandmother's presence.

Nancy's voice broke into his thoughts again.

'Did you see that maniac? My God!' She swept her arms out in a gesture of hopelessness and knocked Lily's Lady Diana hat over her eyes. 'He must have been driving at two hundred miles an hour.'

Lily straightened her hat and turned to face her mother-in-law.

'Cars can't go that fast, Nancy. We're only doing forty-five, so all the others look fast to us.'

Joseph was aware that his wife was talking between gritted teeth.

'Joseph! Slow the car down. Forty-five miles an hour. Oy! If God had wanted us to travel that fast he'd have given us legs like a cheetah!'

Joseph carried on driving. He knew that his mother played up her Jewish ancestry to annoy Lily. Sometimes her performance as the Jewish mama was so good he felt like videoing her in action and sending it to BT to use on their adverts. It was a far cry from when he was a child and her Jewishness could never be mentioned, even in passing. Their given name had been Markowitz, but his father had anglicised it shortly after his marriage. In the East End of London then, Jews were classed lower than the Irish. At least the Irish were Catholics. Now, though, his mother revelled in her Jewish ancestry, not because of any love for her religion but because she knew it annoyed Lily who was a Christian Scientist.

He saw the signs for Grantley and heaved a sigh of relief. Soon they would be at George's.

Kate got in just in time for Christmas dinner. She took off her coat in the hall and listened to the sound of laughter coming from the kitchen. Dan must be on top form today. He was a born raconteur. Kate could see him in her mind's eye sitting up at the breakfast bar, with Lizzy hanging on every word, looking for all the world as if he was in an expensive restaurant.

She shook herself. For all his faults Dan loved his daughter, she was sure of that much. But sometimes, seeing him brought it all back. All the pain and heartache he had caused her. Especially today, when she felt low, when she had so much going on with the murder inquiry and had to be lighthearted and gay because it was Christmas.

She walked into the warmth of the lounge and through the door to the kitchen. Dan's back was to her but Lizzy and her mother were facing her. Both were laughing out loud. Seeing her daughter, in her best dress, her dark hair brushed to a shine, eyes alight with happiness, brought a lump to Kate's throat. If she ever had to go through what Patrick Kelly had, she would die, she thought.

'Come away in, Katie, I've got your dinner nice and warm here.' Evelyn was off her chair and going to the oven.

'I'll do it, Mum, you sit back down.'

Evelyn waved a hand at her. 'You sit yourself down, young lady, and have a glass of the excellent wine Dan brought. I've nearly finished me own dinner anyway.'

Kate sat beside Dan and he smiled at her.

'Merry Christmas, Kate.'

His voice was low and while Evelyn was getting the

dinner from the oven he brushed her lips with his. Lizzy giggled. Kate was stunned. She expected a lot from Dan, none of it good, but that was the last thing she had anticipated. And the worse part of all was she had felt a shiver inside her as he had done it. She forced a smile on her face and grinned at her daughter.

'Merry Christmas, love.'

'Merry Christmas, Mum. How was it today?' Her face was concerned.

'Oh, not too bad, we're getting there.' She deliberately kept her voice light. Dan had unnerved her and she had a sneaking suspicion he had guessed the fact. He was looking at her now, a smile playing around his lips.

Evelyn put a large dinner in front of her and Kate felt her appetite return.

'Oh, Mum, that looks great. I'm starving.'

'Dad was just telling us about when he was in Egypt.'

Kate took a mouthful of turkey and nodded.

Evelyn sat back at the table and winked at her daughter. Kate noticed the flushed cheeks and guessed she had been on the whiskey, or 'Holy Water' as her mother referred to it. Dan poured Kate a glass of wine and she sipped it.

'Tell Mum about the Valley of the Kings, Dad.'

'Your mother's not interested in all that.'

'Oh, but I am, Dan. You carry on with your story.'

Dan was where he wanted to be. He had an attentive audience and he loved it. He would try and impress Kate with his worldliness. She might deal with rapists and murderers and the lowest of the low, but he was an adventurer, a traveller, and that beat policing hands down!

'Well, we got to Luxor. It was something else, you know, the Nile. I mean, it was just a thrill to be there. To be walking along the banks. Well, you get a boat and cross over to the Valley of the Kings . . .'

'And Queens.' Kate spoke through a mouthful of food.

'Well, yes, and the Valley of the Queens. We went into Tutankhamen's burial chamber. You would have loved it, Lizzy. The paintings on the ceilings . . .'

Kate let Dan go on. She felt like asking him why he hadn't taken her with him; Lizzy would have loved it and Anthea's boys had gone, she knew that for a fact. While Dan was describing the delights of Egypt, Kate drank her wine and carried on eating. She had heard it all before. Oh, not Egypt, but other places – all described in detail in the same sing-song voice. Kate closed her eyes and berated herself.

Dan's kiss had affected her more than she liked to admit. She had been without a man for far too long, that was her trouble. There were plenty of men at work who had asked her out over the years, but they had nearly all been married. The few who had been divorced only wanted to talk about cases, with a bit of sex thrown in, and that had never appealed to Kate. One thing she had learnt in the police force: male police officers could be the biggest whores going but a policewoman, especially one in a senior position, had to be above reproach.

'What's the matter, Mum?' Lizzy's voice was concerned.

'Oh, just thinking, poppet. That's all.'

Dan put his arm around her shoulders and hugged her to him. 'You leave that old job behind you now, Kate. You've got your family around you.'

She pushed his arm from her shoulders and looked into his face.

'I've always had my family, Dan, thank you very much.'

The atmosphere at the table turned chilly. Kate carried on eating her dinner.

'She's always like this, Dad, with the big cases.' Lizzy's voice was placating and Kate felt mean for what she had done.

'I think she does a grand job. How's the young girl who was attacked?' asked Evelyn.

'In a very bad way, Mum. She took an awful beating.'

'I've seen Mandy Kelly about. She's really pretty, with long blond hair. Her dad's a right one, always in trouble with the police.'

'No, he is not!' Kate's voice came out louder than she intended and she bit her lip.

'He's been under suspicion but he's never actually been charged with anything. He's never even had a parking ticket, young lady, so just you get your facts right!' Her voice was jocular now and Lizzy relaxed.

'Well, Joanie's mum said he owns massage parlours and places like that.'

'And massage parlours and places like that are perfectly legal, love.'

'More's the bloody pity.' Evelyn's voice was disgusted.

'Well, that's the law for you. He's done nothing wrong!'

'I think men who live off women like that should be shot.' Dan's voice was low and hard.

Kate felt an urge to laugh.

'There's other ways for men to live off women than by putting them on the game, you should know that, Dan.' Kate sipped her wine so she wouldn't have to look at his face.

Dan pushed his chair away from the table and went into the lounge. Kate saw Lizzy bite her lip, her face a mass of confusion. But Dan was back almost immediately with a packet of cigarettes. 'Let's open our presents, shall we?'

'Oh yes, let's. We've been waiting for you, Mum.'

Kate placed her knife and fork on her plate and followed everyone into the lounge.

Dan gave Lizzy a large package which she opened slowly, taking off the paper carefully. Everything in their house was saved. Kate knew it was annoying Dan, who would have ripped the paper off regardless, and allowed herself a tiny smile from her seat by the fire. She heard Lizzy's intake of breath as she took out a sheepskin flying jacket. It was the latest fashion, and for some unknown reason this annoyed Kate even more. Trust Dan to know exactly what a sixteen-year-old girl would want for Christmas! Lizzy threw herself into her father's arms and hugged him.

'Oh, Dad, it's great, just what I wanted! Wait till Joanie sees this!'

Evelyn passed over Kate's present and once more the slow ritual of opening began. Kate sat back in the chair watching her daughter with glee. As Lizzy took out the tiny box Kate caught her daughter's eye.

'Is it what I think, Mum?'

'Open it and see.'

Lizzy reverently opened the box and squealed with delight. She threw her arms around her mother.

'Oh, thank you! Thank you! I thought they'd be too expensive!' She held up the sovereign earrings for all to see.

'Come on, love, now open mine.'

Evelyn pushed a package into her hands and Lizzy opened it excitedly.

'Oh, Gran!'

Evelyn laughed as Lizzy brought out a pair of Reebok bumpers.

'I knew you wanted them so I thought I'd get them.'

'Oh, Mum!' Kate knew they cost over eighty pounds and shook her head at her mother. 'You shouldn't have spent that much!'

'You only live once and money's for the spending, I'm thinking.'

'Hear, hear.' Dan's voice was wistful. 'Now then, you two, here's your presents.' He gave Kate and Evelyn small packages.

'Oh, you shouldn't have, Dan, I never got you anything.'

Kate opened her present to find a bottle of Joy, her favourite perfume. Evelyn had a bottle of Chanel No. 5.

'Now isn't that grand? I've never had a bottle of real French perfume before. Thanks, Dan.'

'You're welcome. All women should be cosseted at some time, Eve, that's my motto.'

Kate felt an urge to ask him how many he had cosseted over the years, but bit it back and instead smiled at him.

'Thanks, Dan, it's lovely.'

'Still your favourite, I hope?'

'Yes, it's still my favourite.'

Kate watched as Lizzy shoved a present into her father's hands. Then she went to the kitchen and poured herself out a glass of wine.

She stared at the perfume in her hands and sighed.

Oh Dan, she thought, why did you have to do this?

It brought back too many memories and she wasn't fit to cope with them today. She had too much on her mind. She didn't need to be reminded of how lonely she was.

Not today.

George watched his mother demolish a dinner large enough for two men. He smiled to himself. She could certainly put her food away. Gone were the days when her figure was the most important thing in her life.

'Pass me the salt, someone.'

Nancy held out her hand and Joseph thrust the salt cellar into it. She belched loudly, holding her hand to her chest as if forcing her wind out. Lily and Elaine both pursed their lips in disgust.

'Better out than in, eh, Georgie boy?'

'Yes, Mother.' He smiled at her.

Nancy poked her finger at him, a nasty light in her eyes. 'Don't eat too much stuffing now, you know it gives you constipation.'

George blanched.

'Really, Nancy! We don't want to discuss George's digestion at the dinner table!' Elaine's voice was high. She could never understand her mother-in-law's preoccupation with George's bowels.

Nancy swivelled her huge bulk in her seat to see Elaine better.

'George is a martyr to constipation. When he was a child it plagued him. Why, the hospital showed me how to give him enemas. Before that I had to give him what was called in those days a "manual". I had to push my fingers . . .'

'Oh, for God's sake! We're eating!' Lilian pushed her plate away from her roughly. 'Can we just for once . . . for one year at least . . . give George's bloody bowels a rest!'

Nancy sniffed loudly and turned back to her food. 'You know your trouble, Lilian?' She shovelled a large forkful of vegetables into her mouth. 'You're too namby-pamby for your own good. Eighty-one years I've lived because I've always watched my bowels. They are the most important part of the body. They get rid of all the bad . . .'

'Please, Mother.' Joseph's voice was strained. 'As Lily says, let's leave talk of bowels till later on, shall we? Now then, George, how's work going?' Joseph beamed across the table at his brother.

'Fine.' Oh, yes, Joseph, my work's going so well they're going to kick me out soon. I can't afford a nice Daimler

Sovereign like you. But you know that, don't you? That's why you ask me the same question every time I see you. Why Lily goes on and on about your large detached house. Well, it was your large detached house that lumbered you with Mother, wasn't it?

'George? Lily's talking to you.' Elaine's voice broke into his thoughts.

'He was always the same, Elaine, even as a child. Always in a world of his own. Always a dreamer, was my Georgie. That's why he never got on like the others. Look at Edith, out in America. Her Joss is a surgeon. Living the life of Riley them two. Off to the Bahamas every few months. It does a mother's heart good to know that at least some of her children did well.'

Her voice was reproaching George with every word she spoke.

'Edith always enjoyed travelling, Mother. Do you remember when she ran off to Brighton with the travelling salesman?'

Elaine felt the tension she had created and was actually enjoying it. Edith's foray down to Brighton was never mentioned. Neither was the child she gave up for adoption a year afterwards.

Nancy pushed her plate away from her, her heavily powdered face looking more wrinkled than ever with the deepness of her frown.

'Only you, Elaine, would bring up something to break my heart. Joseph, George, help me into the lounge. I want to be alone.'

'I'm sure Elaine didn't mean anything by it, Mother.'

'Shut up, George, and help an old woman to a comfortable seat.'

George and Joseph both rushed to their mother's side, helping her heave her bulk from the chair. She leant on

136

their arms as she slowly trekked from the kitchen to the lounge. Elaine and Lilian watched the three leave the kitchen. As soon as the door shut behind them Lilian whispered: 'The woman is like a waking nightmare.'

'I heard that, Lily! I may be old but I'm not deaf!'

Nancy's voice seemed to drill through the wooden kitchen door.

Elaine put her hand over her mouth to stifle a high laugh.

'She has ears like an elephant, Elaine, you don't know what it's like.'

'I can imagine, thank you very much, and before you ask the answer's no. Both George and I work and she can't be left on her own all day.'

Lily sighed.

It was worth a try, even if you already knew the answer.

In the lounge George and Joseph had set their mother on the settee, packing cushions all around her.

'Joseph, you go back to your dinner. I want to speak to George in private.'

Joseph left the room as quickly as possible. He was nearly sixty years old. He had his own prosperous business. Yet his mother could reduce him to an eight year old in a few sentences. When Joseph left, Nancy patted a tiny expanse of seat beside her.

'Sit with your mama, Georgie boy.'

He sat beside her warily.

Nancy looked into her son's face for a few moments.

'The years haven't been kind to you, my boy, have they? No. You know this yourself.'

George could smell her perfume. It was lily of the valley. The scent brought back his childhood. The terraced house in Bow, the war, his father's death, his mother's endless stream of men friends. His 'uncles' as he had had to call them. George could not remember his father and knew that there was something not right about his death.

After the war his mother had packed up what was left of their home and moved them all to East Ham where she had made a niche for herself.

Nancy Markham had been a formidable person all her life. She ruled her children. When she said do something, you did it or took the consequences. Like Edith's baby. She had wanted to keep the child. It had broken her heart when she had had to give him up. But, as always, Mother knew best.

Nancy was still talking, her voice low and caressing as she enumerated every failure in his life.

George knew that his mother did not like him, though she swore that she loved him. As he watched her ruby red lips opening and shutting he had a vision of himself getting up from the settee, going out to the hall and getting his Swiss army knife from beneath the floorboards in the hall cupboard. He could see the fear in his mother's face as she realised that he was going to plunge it into her fat body. Over and over again. Slashing and ripping at her fat breasts and overhanging stomach . . .

'George boy, you're sweating! Are you feeling all right?'

He smiled at her. His secret smile. 'Yes, Mother, I'm fine. Absolutely fine. Never felt better, in fact.'

For the first time ever, Nancy Markham felt as if her son had the upper hand. And like Elaine before her, she didn't like it one bit.

Patrick Kelly sat at his daughter's bedside in Grantley Hospital. The bruising on her face was beginning to fade, but still she lay in a deep coma. The doctors had opened a little window in her skull because her brain had swollen so much they had to relieve the pressure on it.

He held on to her hand. Christmas had no meaning for him now. The big dinner he had planned, and the present giving, were all far from his mind.

Earlier in the day he had attended Mass in the hospital chapel. It was the first time in over twenty years. He'd prayed to God to save his daughter. Make her be as she was before she was attacked. Even as he prayed he knew he was a hypocrite.

While he sat in the chapel, paid muscle was looking for the perpetrator of the horrific deed. He gritted his teeth.

If it took him the rest of his life and every penny of his considerable fortune, he would find the bastard. And when he did, when he confronted him, he would exact his payment, which was death. A long slow death.

Putting Mandy's hand to his mouth, he kissed it softly.

Chapter Seven

Christmas 1948

George lay in bed staring up at the ceiling. He pulled the blankets over his shoulders and rubbed his frozen ears with his hands, breathing into his palms every so often to warm them. His whole body was numb with cold. The sash windows had iced up inside, reflecting weird murals on the walls with the breaking dawn. He poked his head out of the blankets once more as he heard a noise from his mother's room. He let his breath out slowly, carefully, watching it spiral like cigarette smoke in the cold dimness. He strained his ears to listen. Nothing. Gradually he relaxed. Then he heard the dull thud of footsteps on the linoleum. He squeezed his eyes shut as hard as he could. Maybe it was Mother going to the toilet? Or Edith? But the footsteps stopped outside his door.

He hunched himself lower down in the bed. The inadequate bedding barely covered him – one sheet, one blanket, and an old overcoat.

He closed his eyes and tried to feign unconsciousness, his mouth quivering with apprehension. He listened as the door creaked open slowly and someone came into the room. George's nose quivered as he smelt the heavy mustiness of the man. It was a mixture of sweat and beer. He was terrified. The man moved towards the bed purposefully, treading only on the boards he knew would not creak.

'Georgie? You awake?'

The child lay there unmoving. His heart was beating so loud and fast surely the man could hear it?

He closed his eyes even tighter, then felt the warm breath on his neck. George's head was tucked beneath the blanket and overcoat, and he instinctively brought his knees up to his chest until he was in a foetal position.

A large warm hand entered the bed and George felt the roughness of the skin as it began slowly to caress his buttocks. Then the bed was sinking with the weight of the man, and against his will the child was rolling into his heavy stomach.

At least he was warm.

Then the blankets were pulled over both their heads and George was being dragged down, down, into the fantasy world that was his only escape from this life.

Later the man crept from the bed, and George could finally sleep the sleep of the exhausted. His eyelashes still glistening with the silent tears, he lay there in the warm space the man vacated.

He slept then.

Bert Higgins slipped back into bed with Nancy Markham and was just settling himself when she spoke.

'How was Georgie tonight, Bert?'

He froze beside her.

'Oh, I know all about your little visits to him in the middle of the night.'

Nancy was enjoying the fear she was creating. She finally had something over him and she liked that. She liked that very much.

She laughed derisively.

'I can just imagine what your friends would say if they knew you liked little boys, Bert.'

He turned over in bed and grabbed her throat with an iron hand.

'What you going to do about it, Nance?'

She laughed again, no trace of fear in her voice.

'Who, me? I'm not going to do anything, Bert. You know me – each to his own. The only thing I want from you is more money.'

Bert let go of her and lit the candle by the bed. He lay on his back, staring at the ceiling.

'You mean . . . you're not going to stop me?'

His voice was incredulous.

'Why should I? Providing we can come to a financial arrangement, I'm not bothered about it.'

Bert smiled in the candlelight.

'You'd do anything for money, wouldn't you?'

Nancy lit a cigarette and blew the smoke out. Then she turned to him full on.

'That's about the strength of it, yes.'

'Fair enough then, Nance. How much?'

'An extra fiver a week should do it.'

Bert considered this for a few minutes.

'I can go to three quid.'

'It's five or the deal's off.'

'All right then. But what about us?'

Nancy stubbed out her cigarette, then blew out the candle.

'Us? We carry on as usual. Good night.'

'Good night, Nancy.'

She was asleep in minutes. Bert, though, lay awake for a while pondering the situation. Nancy Markham had sold her son to him for a measly five pounds a week.

George came home to find Bert slumped on the settee, snoring loudly. When Bert turned over on the settee to make himself more comfortable, George smiled to himself. A little smile that barely showed his teeth.

He could smell the alcohol fumes with every breath Bert took and guessed, rightly, that he had passed out at some point in the evening. That's why his mother had left him there.

George walked closer and stared down at the man. He had spilt a glass of whisky over himself. The smell was strong and the glass still beside him. It was trapped between his body and the back of the settee.

George picked up the bottle of Black and White whisky and gently poured the last of it along the back of the settee. He was feeling acutely excited.

He placed the bottle back on the table and then picked up a box of matches. With shaking hands, he lit one. He stood watching the burning match in fascination until it got down to his fingertips. Then the burning sensation made him throw it from him. He watched, sucking his finger, as it ignited the whisky. In the semi-darkness he saw a tiny blue flame slowly lick its way along the back of the settee, gathering momentum as it went. A sticky burning smell emanated from it. George watched as Bert, still snoring heavily, began to breathe in the black smoke.

It wasn't until Bert's clothes caught fire that George felt a shiver of apprehension. He watched as the trouser material began to curl up and melt, his excitement growing stronger as Bert did nothing to help himself.

Then all at once the settee was a fireball. It just seemed

to burst into big red and yellow flames that snaked over the arms and on to the floor.

George stepped back towards the door, the heat from the flames touching his aching face.

Then he heard an almighty roar. The flames were standing up and coming towards him.

He backed out quickly into the hallway, his woollen socks making him slip and slide in his haste. The terrible agonising roar came from the flames again. The man was stumbling round the room in panic. George saw Bert grab the brocade curtains and watched in fascination as the flames began to creep up them as well. Suddenly, everywhere was pandemonium. Edith was behind him and her screams brought George back to himself. He watched as she pulled the tablecloth off the kitchen table and ran back into the front room and tried to put out the flames on Bert with it. He was lying on the floor and Edith was patting at the flames.

'Go and get some help, George, for goodness' sake. Hurry UP!'

He snapped into action and collided with Joseph who came careering down the stairs at the noise.

'Bloody hell!' Joseph's voice was incredulous.

Then he was out of the front door and running up the garden path in his pyjamas. George turned back to the scene in the front room.

Edith's nightdress was burning, the hem was beginning to glow blue, and he ran into the room and pulled on his sister's arm.

'Your nightie! Edie, your nightie!' She allowed him to stamp it out with his woollen socks.

'What the hell's going on here?'

Nancy's voice was loud. She stood in the doorway blinking rapidly.

The room was blazing now and Edith pushed George towards the door.

'Mum . . . help me pull him outside. For God's sake, the whole place is gonna go up.'

Nancy threw George out of the front door. He stood in the rain, his feet beginning to freeze, while Nancy and Edith dragged Bert's bulk from the house. Thick black smoke was coming from the front door and the smell of burning was everywhere. Little flakes of grey ash were trying to rise up with the smoke but the rain was forcing them down on to the pavement and eventually into the sewers.

Lights were now on all over the little cul-de-sac and people were coming from their houses in fear and excitement. George felt Mrs Marshall put a heavy coat around his shoulders and pull him from the garden. Her slender arms were gentle as she propelled him towards her own house. He watched the proceedings from her lovely warm front room. He stared out of the lead light window and across the road with a feeling of unreality.

The clamour of the fire engines made him start. The firemen were clearing everyone away from the burning house. Bert was taken from the garden on a stretcher, a blanket covering his face.

George was elated. Bert was dead. He was dead. Bert Higgins was dead. He turned to Mrs Marshall and she mistook the light in the boy's eyes for unshed tears. She pulled him into her sweet-smelling embrace and kissed the top of his head gently.

'Poor little mite, aren't you?'

He had never felt so powerful. He had rid the world of Bert Higgins.

Mrs Marshall put him from her and looked into his face. 'Shall I make you some nice sweet tea?' She placed him gently on her settee and went out to her kitchen.

Joseph walked into the room and sat beside George. His face was ashen.

'Mum's gone to the hospital with Bert. Edith's gone with her. We're to stay here until they come back.'

George slipped his hand into his brother's, and Joseph squeezed it tightly.

'Mrs Marshall's making some tea, Joseph, do you want some?'

The next day George and Joseph raked through the ruined house. They managed to salvage quite a bit of stuff and piled it carefully in the front garden. Edith and Nancy came home from the hospital in the afternoon.

Nancy went straight into Mrs Marshall's, Edith came for the boys.

'Bert's dead. Mum was sedated and I had to stay there with her. Are you two all right?'

'Where are we going to go?'

Edith shrugged.

'I don't know. But don't worry, things will turn out all right, they always do somehow.' Her voice was tired and George felt a great sadness for her.

'Mrs Marshall made us eggs and bacon this morning. She might make you some if you ask her nicely.'

Edith smiled at him wanly.

'I'm not very hungry.'

George shrugged and resumed his searching.

'Do they know how the fire started, Edie?'

'Well, as far as I can gather, they think Bert fell asleep with a lighted cigarette. I know he was a pig, but to die like that . . . His face was twisted up in torment, it was terrible. Skin was burnt off the bone in some places. He died in agony, Joey, mortal agony.'

Joseph put his arm around his sister.

George had heard everything and smiled to himself. Then he began to giggle out loud.

He ran out into the road, and holding out his arms began to spin round and round like a whirling dervish, until he fell, dizzy and exhilarated, on to the pavement.

He lay there in the wet, his mind reeling. He had a secret.

Edith knelt beside him and he smiled up at her. His secret smile that just showed his teeth.

Chapter Eight

Kate went for a bath at seven thirty. She put plenty of bubble bath in the water and lay back, letting the hot water seep into her bones. Her long hair was pinned on top of her head and her face scrubbed free of make-up. She closed her eyes tightly. She was really feeling this case.

Earlier Lizzy had tried on all her finery and Kate had watched her twirling around the tiny lounge and suddenly felt as if a hand had gripped her heart. Supposing this man, this murderer, took her daughter and did to her what he had done to Mandy Kelly and Geraldine O'Leary? She pushed the thoughts from her mind. Nothing was going to happen to Lizzy. Kate would make sure of that. With luck Mandy Kelly would recover. She was a fighter, that much was evident.

Kate pushed her shoulders under the water. Her skin had erupted in goose pimples and it wasn't because of the cold. She closed her eyes again. She had fought hammer and tongs to get Christmas Day off, and all Lizzy had time for was her father.

Dan did look well, though. After dinner one of Lizzy's friends had come round. Joanie of the acne and the braying laugh. Kate chastised herself. What on earth was the matter with her? Poor Joanie was a nice girl. But the worshipful look she had given Dan had annoyed her. It wasn't fair the way Dan affected women . . .

She heard the bathroom door open and smiled. Lizzy with a nice glass of wine, or better still a cup of coffee. She opened one eye and sat up in the bath with shock, water going everywhere.

'What do you want?' Her voice was a loud whisper.

She crossed her arms across her breasts.

'I brought you a glass of wine and a cigarette, that's all, Kate. Don't worry, I'm not going to rape you.' Dan's voice was normal and she felt a fool. He placed a glass of wine in her hand and, wiping her free hand on a towel, as if she was a child, he gave her the lit cigarette.

'You looked done in so I thought I'd try and help you relax.'

Kate settled back in the water, glad now of the concealing bubbles. Dan sat on the toilet seat and laughed.

'I don't know why you're going all modest. I do know what you look like undressed, remember.'

'What are the others doing?' She was having difficulty keeping her voice light.

'They're watching James Bond, my dear. I taped it for them last night. How's the case going?'

His voice was conversational and friendly. Kate was taken back, over the years, to when they had bathed together. When it had been good between them, before Lizzy had been born.

'Not very well, actually. We haven't even got a suspect.'

'I admire you, you know, Kate. The way you've built yourself a career.'

'It's called working, Dan, you should try it some time.'

He smiled, showing his perfect teeth.

'Put the claws away, Kate. I know what you think of me but I've changed, you know. I realised a long time ago that I needed to grow up, and believe me when I say I'm working on it.'

Kate took a gulp of the wine and a long draw on her cigarette. This close, Dan made her feel uncomfortable. He slipped to the floor and knelt by the side of the bath.

'What are you doing?' Kate's voice was suspicious. Her hands were full and she didn't trust Danny Burrows one bit.

'I'm not doing anything. I was just going to wash your back, that's all.'

'I don't want my back washed, thank you very much. Now if you don't mind, Dan, I want to get out.'

She sat up again in the water, looking around for somewhere to dump the cigarette and wine. Dan took them from her.

'Look, Kate, all I'm trying to do is make myself useful, that's all. While I'm here . . .'

She didn't let him finish. 'While you're here, Dan, I'd appreciate it if you left me alone. We don't lock doors in this house and I'd hate to have to start now.'

'Can't you even try and be friendly?'

His blue eyes were puzzled and for a few seconds Kate felt sorry for him. Dan honestly didn't know what was going on. To him, if you wanted something you took it. He never realised how much he had hurt her in the past. How many times had she taken him back over the years, only to come home from work to find he had gone again? No note, nothing. Just her mother's pitying face. Too many times having to tell Lizzy that Daddy had gone again. That he worked away, a long, long way away, that's why he didn't write very often or call.

As he traced his fingers along her arm, she felt a

response inside her. She still wanted Dan sexually, she admitted that, but she'd deny herself that satisfaction before she let him scramble her brains all over again.

'You're the only woman I ever really loved, you know, Kate. Whatever you might think of me, that at least is the truth.'

She stood up and pulled a towel from the rail, wrapping it around herself. The funny thing was, she knew it was true. Dan chased excitement. A new woman to him was as necessary as water to everyone else. If she had been able to accept that, then they would never have parted. But Kate wanted someone one hundred percent. And that sort of commitment was beyond Danny Burrows.

'Leave me alone, Dan. I mean it. You had your chance and you blew it. I have no intention of going through all that rigmarole again. I stopped wanting you a long time ago. Now, if you don't mind, I want to get myself sorted out.'

He gave her one of his winning smiles.

'Well, you can't blame me for trying, Katie, you're still a very attractive woman.'

You should know about attractive women, Dan. Christ himself knows you've had enough of them.

After he'd left she felt flat and cheated, because she hadn't been with a man since Dan had left her for the last time, five years earlier.

Though he didn't know it, he was the only man she had ever slept with in her whole life.

She picked up the wine from the window sill where he had placed it, and drained the glass. Her hands were shaking, and it wasn't with fright.

Sometimes, when they'd had a bad domestic, there would be a woman battered black and blue. The man would have a restraining order placed on him, the woman would be taken to hospital. Then Kate would hear that the woman had gone back to her husband, wanted the charges dropped, and the others would say what a fool the wife was. But Kate had sympathised. Some were like the little girl with the curl. When they were good they were very, very good, but when they were bad they were bastards. There were other ways of battering women too, ways that did not involve physical violence, and Kate sometimes thought that the mental battering was worse.

Unless, of course, you were dealing with the Grantley rapist. With a husband or boyfriend at least you had an inkling of what you were up against.

With him, you were on your own.

Kate's thoughts strayed to Patrick Kelly, keeping a lonely vigil by his daughter's hospital bed. She dried between her legs and felt the stirrings there. Kelly brought out feelings she had forced down for years. She closed her eyes to stop the pictures that were invading her brain. She was tired and lonely and Patrick Kelly had affected her for all the right reasons – he was an attractive man. Dan, on the other hand, affected her for all the wrong reasons. Namely, because he was here now, and she knew exactly how their lovemaking would be.

She hoped that Kelly's daughter pulled through, she really did. He had such faith in himself, he had such a strong belief that Mandy would open her eyes and look at him as though she had just had a nap. Kate wanted that for him too.

Of course, Patrick Kelly kept invading her thoughts because of his daughter's terrible predicament. She forced that thought into her head and held on to it. It was just pity.

But she knew she was lying to herself.

She fancied Patrick Kelly with all her heart and soul. He was the first man she had fancied for over five years.

She heard Dan's voice coming up from the lounge and Lizzy's laughter. After all, he had given her Lizzy. For that reason alone she would forgive him an awful lot. But their days of bedding down together were over.

Patrick Kelly looked at his watch. It was just after seven. He realised that he had not eaten for over twenty-four hours. Putting his daughter's hand gently back on the bed, he walked from the intensive care unit. In the small waiting room he lit a cigarette and took a hip flask from the pocket of his jacket. The brandy burnt his empty belly. He was unshaven and unkempt.

The young PC who had been staying at the hospital, in case Mandy awoke and said anything, came into the room.

Patrick watched him as he sat down. He was only a kid. Twenty at the most.

'The nurses are turning her and that.'

His voice was apologetic. Patrick felt an enormous surge of sympathy for the boy. Christmas night and he was stuck here waiting for a half-dead girl to say a couple of words when he would much rather be at a party or something.

He offered the boy his hip flask.

'Go on, son, have a shot.'

The PC took the flask and had a few sips, coughing as the liquid hit the back of his throat.

'Merry Christmas, son.' Patrick's voice was sad and flat.

'She'll pull through, sir. It's amazing what they can do now.'

The boy was talking for effect. They both knew that.

Suddenly they heard the frenzied high-pitched bleeping of the monitors attached to Mandy. They stamped on their cigarettes and ran from the room.

Mandy's bed was surrounded by nurses and doctors.

The sister pulled Patrick away from the scene as they tried to save his daughter's life.

Finally, everything was quiet and all that could be heard was the low buzzing sound of the heart monitor. Then that was unplugged and all there was was a deathly silence.

'I want to use the toilet again. George, Joseph, help me to the toilet.'

They helped their mother heave her huge bulk from the settee. This was the sixth time they had toileted her since she had been in the house.

As they walked her from the room Elaine glanced at the clock. Eight thirty. They would be leaving soon, thank God.

'So how's Betty these days, Lily?'

'Fine. She's a buyer for a big fashion store as you know. She's doing very well. Of course, we don't see as much of her as we'd like . . .' She left the sentence unfinished but even without the words being said, Elaine knew why. Nancy was hated by her grandchildren.

Nancy sat on the toilet. Her two sons stood outside the door, puffing and panting. Getting Nancy Markham up the stairs was a major event. Both the men were aware that she could walk perfectly well, yet like everything in their lives that had to do with their mother, they studiously avoided mentioning it.

George could see the blue tinge around Joseph's mouth. His mother would put him into an early grave.

'I'm ready!' Nancy's voice broke through the air like a thunderbolt. The two men opened the bathroom door. The smell of faeces was overpowering.

'You can wipe, George. Joseph did it last time, and made a bloody awful job of it.' She held a warning finger up. 'Do it properly or there will be hell to pay!'

Nancy stood, forcing all her considerable weight on to

her sons' arms, before deliberately letting herself drop to her knees. Joseph and George were dragged to the ground with her.

'Fuck this!' Joseph's voice reverberated around the tiny bathroom. George looked at his brother, amazed.

Joseph had sworn in front of their mother!

Nancy had been on all fours on the floor. Before she had time to think what she was doing she was standing up of her own accord and staring down at her eldest son, hands on ample hips.

'What did you just say?'

George pulled himself from the floor and sat on the edge of the bath, giggling nervously. He was enjoying himself. Joseph lay on the floor. His arm was killing him where his mother's weight had nearly wrenched it out of its socket.

'What's going on up there? What's all the crashing about?'

Elaine's voice, which could outshout Nancy Markham's on her better days, carried up the stairs and into the bathroom. George heard the thud of her slippers coming upstairs.

'I said, what did you say Joseph Markowitz? Answer me!'

Elaine stared into the bathroom in bewilderment. She saw her mother-in-law prod Joseph's thigh with her foot.

'I'm sorry, Mother. It just slipped out.'

Nancy, realising that she was standing up of her own accord, held her chest, her eyes rolling up into her head.

'Oh, George, help me. I'm going to faint . . .'

As she crashed to the floor once more, Joseph did a roll that would have made a paratrooper proud; Elaine watched the whole charade with wide eyes.

'Listen here, George Markham, this is the last time! Do

you hear me?' Elaine's voice had risen fifteen decibels louder than usual.

'Next year, we are going away for Christmas. Now pick your bloody mother up and get her out of my house. I've had enough!'

Nancy's and Joseph's mouths both opened simultaneously, but snapped shut as they looked at George. He was still sitting on the edge of the bath and laughing his head off, tears running down his face, which he wiped now and then with the back of his hand.

Lily, who had come up to see what all the noise was about, stared around her in amazement. Her mother had warned her about marrying into the Markham family and she had been right.

They were funny. Not funny ha-ha, but funny peculiar.

When Kate received the call saying that Mandy Kelly had died, she drove straight to the hospital. Now she had two murders to contend with. When she saw Patrick Kelly, she was shocked. That he had taken the death badly was hardly surprising, but he looked positively old. Old and haggard.

She went to him. He was still holding his daughter's body in his arms and the doctors and nurses could not persuade him to leave the bedside. The body had to be put on ice, and soon. Kate motioned for everyone to move away and went to him.

'I'm really very sorry, Mr Kelly. I can assure you that we shall do all that we can to find the man responsible.'

Her gentle voice broke in on him. He looked at her with red-rimmed eyes.

'She was only twenty-two, just a baby. Just a kid, that's all. I'd bought her a shop, you know.' His voice caught and he sniffed loudly. 'A lovely little shop. She would have done well and all, she wasn't a silly girl. She had a good brain, did my Mandy.' He bit his lip hard. 'What will I do without her?' The plaintive note in his voice went straight to Kate's heart.

'She was all I had.'

Kate put her arm around his shoulders and he cried into her jacket. She stroked his hair. Patrick Kelly was a Repoman. The best in the business, it was said. He would repossess anything, from a car, to a crane, to a large yacht. He had been nicknamed 'The Snatchman' by friends and enemies alike. That his business was not strictly legal Kate was aware, he owned sex shops, massage parlours and many other businesses. Yet, as he was now, broken hearted, Kate felt an enormous affection for him. Whatever he may be, he had been a loving father and husband and at this moment in time, Kate envied his wife the love he had borne her.

'Come on, Mr Kelly, let's get you home, shall we? There's nothing you can do here now.'

She pulled him away from his daughter's body. As he let go of Mandy he slipped his arm around Kate's waist and she held him tightly while he cried, his shoulders heaving beneath his expensive crumpled suit.

When he was spent she walked him from the room, motioning with her head to DS Willis, who had met her at the hospital, to finish off there. She would take Patrick Kelly home.

Willis watched her leave and felt a spark of respect for his boss. Patrick Kelly was notorious, a villain and a thug, yet DI Kate Burrows had him eating out of her hand. One of the advantages of being a female, he supposed.

Outside the hospital, Kelly's driver was waiting for him in his Rolls-Royce Corniche. Kate helped Patrick into the back, relieved that she did not have to drive him home. As she went to shut the door, his voice stayed her.

'Please, come home with me . . . I need to talk to someone.'

His voice was wretched, and Kate hesitated only a moment before climbing into the car beside him. Maybe he would inadvertently give her some clues. People often did, without even realising that what they said had a bearing on the case in hand.

He grabbed her hand and held on to it tightly. Kate looked at his strong profile as they drove to his house. He was staring out of the window at the cold deserted streets, his hard chiselled face set, despite his grief. His dark hair, though untidy, looked manly and strong to Kate. Like Patrick Kelly did. He glanced at her; his violet blue eyes held a depth of gratitude that she knew he would never be able to convey in words.

She squeezed back.

Lizzy sat with her father and grandmother watching the end of the James Bond film. As the credits began to roll she stretched in her chair.

'That was great! I love Sean Connery. Can I have a glass of Babycham, Gran?'

Evelyn looked at her.

'Oh, all right then, but just one mind!'

'Thanks, Gran.' She skipped across the room to the drinks cabinet.

Dan watched her, a smile on his face. She had really grown up since the last time he had seen her. She had the long-legged coltish look peculiar to sixteen-year-old girls. Her breasts were heavy though; she took after his side of the family in that respect. But facially she was all her mother. She was just like Kate had been when they had first met. From the long silky dark hair to the perfect white teeth. She even had Kate's distinctive nose.

159

She walked back to her seat with her drink and sipped it. 'Mmmm, lovely.'

'It's a shame your mother had to go out tonight.'

Lizzy shrugged. 'It's her job. Mum really has to work hard to keep us all, doesn't she, Gran?'

'That she does, child.

'Oh, I know that, but it doesn't seem fair, her having to shoot off on Christmas night.' Dan kept his voice deliberately light.

'You get used to it after a while, Dad. I can't remember the last birthday when she was home early enough for the party! Still, Gran's always here.'

Dan nodded and sipped at his brandy.

Evelyn stood up. 'Who fancies a turkey sandwich?'

Both Dan and Lizzy nodded assent and she went to the kitchen. Dan squeezed his daughter's hand. 'You're a good girl you know, Liz. A lot of girls would hate a mother who was never there when they wanted her.'

She bit her lip and thought hard. 'She's there when I really want her, Dad. Don't you worry about that. When's Anthea back?'

The question took him by surprise.

'Oh . . . Anthea and I are not really together any more.'

Lizzy took a large gulp of her Babycham and put the glass on the little coffee table.

'I'm glad, Dad. I never liked her very much.'

'You didn't really know her.' His voice was strained.

'No, but when I used to ring up, she'd be very off-hand with me. I felt as if I was intruding or something.'

'That was just Anthea's way. She didn't mean anything. How do you get on with your mother's . . . er . . . friends?'

'Boyfriends, you mean? She never has any. I know she gets asked out on dates, but she never goes. My friend's dad wanted to go out with her, and she said no.'

'Your friend's dad!' Dan's voice was scandalised.

'Oh, don't worry, her mum's been dead for ages. Oh, that sounds terrible, but you know what I mean.'

'Yeah, I know what you mean.'

They smiled at one another.

'Oh, Dad, it's great to have you here like this.'

'It's great to be here, love.'

If it rested with him, he'd be here for a long time to come. He was convinced that his Katie still held a torch for him, and he'd do everything he could to get that torch blazing again.

The first part of the plan was getting his mother-in-law on his side. He'd start working on that straight away.

Kate and Patrick sat on the large settee in Patrick's lounge; both were drinking coffee. Patrick had been talking about himself for over an hour and Kate let him.

All the stories about him, true and imagined, had not prepared her for the almost brutal attractiveness that he had in abundance. His dark brown hair, just beginning to grey at the temples, gave him a distinguished air and softened his rugged features. Dark-skinned and full lipped, he had eyes that were a deep penetrating blue, and from the way he moved Kate could see that he had looked after himself well over the years. Only a slight paunch belied his age. He was a very attractive man. Too attractive, in fact, for his own good. And Kate had a sneaking suspicion that under other circumstances he would deliberately make her aware of the fact.

Patrick Kelly loved women. But he had only really loved two with all his heart and soul. His wife, Renée, and his daughter, Mandy. Mandy who was lying now in a mortuary, waiting to be dissected by the pathologist's scalpel.

Kate closed her eyes. Patrick's voice was a low drone in her ears. All this unhappiness and confusion pouring out of him like a dam.

Patrick rose from his seat and picked up a bottle of brandy. He brought it back together with two Waterford crystal glasses. Like everything else in the house, they were of the best quality, but as he poured out two generous measures, Kate was made aware that money meant very little when you had no one to share it with.

'My old mum used to take in washing, you know. Me dad had had it on his toes years before, leaving me and my four sisters. My mother worked like a black to give us a decent life, but she was held back, like we all were then, by lack of education and decent jobs.

'I found my old man a few years ago. He'd only gone as far as North London. He'd shacked up with some old bird who was on the game. She kept him in the style he had rapidly grown accustomed to. He'd been a good-looking bloke in his day. I went to see him and told him I was his son, like. He just smiled and asked me if I had any money. He never even asked after my mum or my sisters. Not even casually.

'But I told him. I told him Mum died of a massive stroke, that she'd been riddled with rheumatism from years of washing other people's dirty clothes, but he wasn't even interested . . .'

Kate saw him drop his head on to his chest.

'All those years my old mum had been waiting for him to come home, and he never even thought about her.'

'What did you do?' Kate's voice was low.

'I smacked him. Punched him all around his little bedsit. An old man, and I kicked him in . . . me own father. Then, as I left, I gave him fifty quid. Threw it on the bed. I told him that was all he would ever get from me.

I can still see him crawling over the bed. His face was bleeding but he grabbed that money like a dog with a bone. I hated him then.

'I came home and I looked at my Mandy and I patted myself on the back. Oh, yes, I thought, my child will never know pain like that. But she ended up knowing a worse pain than I could ever have given her. A much worse pain.'

He sniffed loudly. 'Well, whoever this pervert is, I'm gonna catch him. I've already got blokes sniffing about, and when I do find him . . .' He left the sentence unfinished.

'You're much better off letting us find him, Mr Kelly.'

Patrick laughed at her. A hard bitter sound.

'You must be smoking, as the youngsters say. Do you honestly think I'll let the social workers and the bleeding hearts get their poncey hands on him? Do you? Do you think I'll allow him to go to some nice top security hospital, where he can roam the grounds freely and have a television and video in his room? Where he can con his way out in a couple of years and end up working in a children's home or something?

'No way, darlin'. I intend to see he pays dearly for the death of my girl and for that other woman. She had three little kids, for fuck's sake. Be honest, do you really think he is entitled to a life while my child is rotting underground? No way.'

Kate hung her head because part of her grudgingly agreed with what Kelly was saying. It was all right being high-principled, saying if you resorted to violence you were only bringing yourself down to an animal's level. But what Patrick Kelly said struck a chord with her. She had a daughter of her own. But on the other hand, she'd dedicated her life to the idea that justice should only be done through the proper channels.

She would find the Grantley rapist and when she did she would put him away. That was the law, and that's what she was paid to do. She could understand his temper, his wish to destroy the man, it was natural for him to feel like that. But although she might sympathise, she would never agree.

You could not fight violence with violence. This man, whoever he was, was sick. Sick in the mind. He needed to be taken away from society. And when she found him – not if, when – he would be put away for good.

There were always two sides to any coin. When Kelly calmed down he would see that much for himself.

At least, she hoped so. She could hear Kelly's deep breathing and she sighed gently, reminding herself that he had lost his most precious possession.

'What's the time?' Kelly asked finally.

'A quarter to twelve.'

He looked at her sadly. 'I'm sorry. I've kept you from your own family, tonight of all nights.'

'Don't be sorry, Mr Kelly.'

His face was close to her and Kate felt an absurd fluttering sensation inside her. As if she had just run a long race and was breathless. 'I am working, you know.'

Patrick Kelly stared into Kate's brown eyes. The sadness there gave them an added beauty. He felt as if the whole mystery of woman was hiding in their depths.

Kate was in Grantley Police Station by one fifteen. Kelly had put his car at her disposal and she had let the driver take her to Grantley Hospital, where she had picked up her own car. The less people knew about her and Patrick Kelly the better. Yet, she reasoned with herself, what was there to know? She had comforted him in his hour of need, that was all. But Kate knew that it was more than that. On her side at least. She pushed the thought from her mind, annoyed with herself. He was a bereaved man, that was all.

Inside the incident room Amanda, Willis and Superintendent Ratchette were all working.

'I've been with Kelly, he's pretty cut up. I never thought I would ever say this, but I feel sorry for the man.'

'Well, Kate, we have no new developments, except that the car, the dark blue Orion that was seen on the waste ground, was also seen driving near Portaby Road earlier in the evening. A woman walking her dog said it made a U-turn near her and that's why she remembered it. First thing in the morning we're going to be interviewing these people.'

'Right. I'll see to it.'

Ratchette raised an eyebrow. 'Let one of the youngsters do their share. It's Boxing Day. You've earned your rest.'

Kate shook her head violently. 'No, I'll do it, sir. I want this bastard caught.'

Willis and Dawkins both looked at her curiously. She hardly ever swore.

'Amanda, would you get me a coffee, please? Black with lots of sugar. Willis, you can start filling me in on what's been happening here today.'

He picked up the file he had been working on and brought it over to Kate.

Ratchette watched her closely. She'd been drinking, that much was evident, but there was something else . . . something he could not quite put his finger on. Well, it would all come out in the wash as his wife was fond of saying.

Chapter Nine

George and Elaine had taken their Boxing Day constitutional in Grantley Woods. As they drove past Vauxhall Drive, George smiled to himself. He wondered fleetingly what Elaine would do if she knew that he was the 'Grantley Ripper'.

At the moment though all she was interested in was her holiday with the girls, and her two nights out a week. George knew that she was a bit nonplussed at his eagerness for her to have her own social life. She thought it was an act of selflessness on his part. She could not have been more wrong.

On the nights that Elaine went out with her friends, he went out on the prowl. He liked the word. Prowler, prowling, prowl. It was similar to prowess, another of his favourites. While Elaine was out gallivanting, he could do his prowling in peace and watch his videos without interruption. He had talked her into ringing him when she wanted to come home so that he could pick her up, make sure she was safe.

He grinned to himself. All he really wanted to know was when she would be arriving so he could clear away.

Her absences had done wonders for their marriage. Now, when they were in, they managed a sort of truce. He didn't annoy her and she shut her almighty trap. He wished she had done it years ago.

Bugger Elaine! He grinned again. No chance. She wouldn't even let him have what she termed normal sex.

'George, what are you thinking about?'

Elaine watched him sceptically. She hated his long silences. He parked the car outside their house and smiled at her.

'I was just thinking how lucky I am to have a wife like you.'

Elaine leant back in the car seat to get a better look at him. 'Really, George?'

'Really. You've been a good wife, Elaine.'

'Oh. Well, thanks.'

They got out of the car and George noted that she did not return the compliment.

Elaine walked up the garden path and he followed her. As she opened the front door the phone began to ring and she rushed to answer it.

George slipped off his Burberry and hung it up in the hall cupboard.

'It's your sister Edith from America!'

George took the phone.

'Hello, Edith!' There was genuine affection in his voice. He had always been close to her. Both had taken the brunt of their mother's tongue and had a natural affinity.

'Hello, Georgie. I just had to ring you – Merry Christmas!'

'And to you, dear, and Joss. How are the children?'

Elaine smiled at George's happiness. God knew the man had little enough from his family, and she had always liked Edith herself. She had the same manner as George, a sad kind of demeanour that on a woman was attractive while on a man like George it was annoying. Elaine went into the kitchen and made two Irish coffees. What the hell? It was Christmas. When George had finished on the phone he came in to her, beaming.

'She sends you her love and wants us to go over and stay with them.'

Edith asked them over every year. Elaine bit her lip for a second, her round face thoughtful.

'Let's go over next year, shall we, George? We could easily afford it, and you and Edith have always been close. It would be a great holiday for us.'

George caught her excitement. 'Yes, let's. Oh, Elaine, let's.' He looked into her eager face and almost loved her.

'Right then, George, I'll see to it after the holidays! Now, I'm going in to watch the film. Are you coming?'

'In a little while, my love. I'll drink my coffee out here, I think, make some plans.'

'Okey doke.' She left the kitchen, beaming.

George sat at the white Formica table and smiled. Then he remembered the redundancy. He clenched his fists. Elaine still did not know that he was going to lose his job. The redundancy money would be quite a bit but that was not the same as having a wage coming in.

He brightened. He could take the redundancy money and put it in a separate account! Then he felt discouraged again. Where could he go all day? No, Elaine would find out. She always found out. There was nothing for it but to tell her the truth.

They would go out to Florida and see Edith, though. He was determined on that.

He remembered Edith as she had been when a girl. She had been exquisite. Not too tall, and she had developed early. She had the same mousy brown hair as George himself, except on her it looked right. It had a slight curl in it that made her look soft somehow. She had porcelain white skin that showed the blue veins perfectly, especially on the swell of her breasts. She had fine grey eyes that were heavy lidded, giving her a sensual look, a tiny rosebud mouth and soft round pink cheeks. His mother had always hated Edith.

Then one day she had gone away. Only George knew that she had run off to Brighton with a salesman, but his mother had guessed as much and beaten her daughter's whereabouts out of him with a belt. He had told on his sister, poor Edith. The scene when Nancy had turned up at the Shangri-La guest house must have been terrible. As always his mother had had the upper hand. Edith had been pregnant and alone, the salesman abandoning her when she had told him her condition.

How his mother had made her pay! Oh, how. She had taken a delight in reproaching Edith at every opportunity. The mother who swore to everyone that she loved her children!

Edith had lost weight while other pregnant women bloomed. She had looked like a spectre; all the fight and vitality were gradually sucked from her. Then, when she had finally gone into labour, Edith had been left to birth alone in her bedroom with only their mother's reprimanding voice to help her along. George had sat outside and listened.

'All children come into the world in pain, Edith, but none as painfully as a bastard child.'

He clenched his teeth. He had only been thirteen then, but had wanted to burst into the room and strike his mother to the ground. The groans and cries of his sister had broken his heart. He sat up all night and into the next day until he heard a soft mewling sound like a kitten and knew that the child had been safely delivered after all that pain.

Edith had loved the boy. Loved him with all her heart and soul, thinking in her ignorance that her mother would allow her to keep him because adoption had never been mentioned. Believing in her heart of hearts that Nancy would soften towards her and the child once it arrived and made a niche in her heart. But it was not to be. When the boy was two months old they had come to take him away. A big woman from an adoption agency, with hard steely blue eyes and cherries in her hat, and a smaller woman, kinder, with watery eyes and a big grey folder. Edith had screamed, pleaded and begged on her knees but her mother would not relent. She had enjoyed it.

In the end, the big woman with the cherries in her hat had dragged the now screaming child from his mother's arms, pulling poor Edith along with her for a few steps until she had dropped sobbing on to the linoleum. Then it was all over. Edith's son was gone from the house and from her life. And she had been left bereft, broken-hearted. The next day George had seen his mother forcing her to drink a cup of cold tea full of Epsom salts to help her get rid of the milk in her breasts. He had finally hated Nancy on that day. When Edith had met Joss Campbell a few years later he had been so glad for her, because Joss was older than Edith and was more than a match for Nancy. When his mother had told him, as she always told any man interested in Edith, about the bastard child, he had just smiled. Smiled and said he would have her under any circumstances. George had loved Joss for that one sentence alone.

Yes, he would go and see Edith. Even if it took every penny of his redundancy money. He was fifty-one now and Edith fifty-five. Life was drawing on, and he wanted to see her before it was too late.

He drank his now cold coffee and was grateful for the whisky that Elaine had put in it.

Somewhere in the world was a man, a thirty-eight-year-old man, who was probably married with children of his own. Who, because of his grandmother's warped mind, would never know the kind and gentle woman who had borne him.

George washed up his cup and saucer carefully and placed them in the plastic drainer. Then he joined Elaine to watch the film. But thoughts of Edith stayed with him all that evening.

Kate glanced at her watch. It was five forty-five. She had been interviewing people since nine that morning and was tired. She sat in her car and turned the heater on while she wrote her comments on a piece of paper. The man she had just interviewed, a Mr Liam Groves, had not been too happy to be interviewed on Boxing Day. He was not at all impressed by her explanation that it was just to eliminate him from their inquiries. In fact, he had told her in no uncertain terms to go forth and multiply. Only not in the biblical words!

She finished her notes and looked at the list of suspects. Peter Bordez, Geoffrey Carter, John Cranmer . . . the list still had over fifty names on it. She decided to call it a day.

Placing the file on the passenger seat, she started up her car. The little Fiat pulled away quickly and Kate put on the radio. 'I Saw Mommy Kissing Santa Claus' blared out. Frowning, she turned it off. She was not into Christmas this year. Maybe next year she would be able to enjoy it.

Dan had taken Lizzy and her mother to a pantomime of all things. Which left her free, on Boxing Day, to get on with her work. She gripped the steering wheel until her knuckles were white. She scanned the houses in the streets, looking at the Christmas trees in gaily lit windows, the decorations that were hanging from ceilings. She knew that behind a similar door somewhere, the Grantley Ripper was sitting by his fireside, stuffed full of Christmas goodies. He could have children sitting at his feet. His wife might even be sparing a thought for the murdered women's families, never guessing that the man she was married to had been the perpetrator.

Kate wished she was at the pantomime. Wished that she was laughing and joking and shouting out 'Behind you' and 'Oh no you don't' to the dame on the stage of the theatre. She wished she was anywhere but Grantley at this moment.

Dan was doing his utmost to be helpful and she appreciated it. At least this Christmas she didn't have to feel guilty because Lizzy didn't have either of her parents with her. Oh, her mother was good, she worshipped her grandchild, but sometimes Kate felt a twinge of guilt at the amount of time she herself spent away from Lizzy. It was a joke really, because if she was one of the male officers then she would not have given it a second thought. But being a woman, she had to juggle her home life and her police work with expert precision. She consoled herself with the fact that her daughter understood. And Lizzy, bless her, really did.

She knew how important Kate's job was. How it kept the roof over their heads as well as helping the community. How many times had Kate snuck into a school hall, late for some school event, her male driver beside her cringing with embarrassment at the childish antics on stage. But she knew that Lizzy appreciated her turning up, and that her reputation as a DI had not suffered because of her being a mother. On the contrary, male CID officers admired her. Well, if she was honest with herself, only the older ones.

She was finished today, though. She'd had enough. This inquiry was getting to her. What she wouldn't give for a nice warm lap to rest her head in. She didn't go as far as to say a nice warm man to slip into bed with, but that was not far from her mind. Dan's arrival had aroused all her dormant sexuality. Sex with him had always been good. It had been wonderful in fact. The trouble was, Dan liked it so much he tended to spread it around and that was no good to Kate. No good at all.

She stopped at the crossroads that took her towards her house and, instead of going right, as she normally would, went left towards the outskirts of Grantley. To the large eighteenth-century house that belonged to Patrick Kelly.

She decided that she would drop in and see how he was.

Patrick Kelly sat on his daughter's bed. She was all around him. The bedroom smelled of her musky perfume; on the floor by the bed was her diary. On the dressing table inside the large bay window all her cosmetics and lotions stood vacantly, as if they knew they would never be used again. There, all alone, stood a large framed photograph of himself, Renée and Mandy. They were all laughing. It had been taken in Marbella, just before Renée's death. Now they were both gone. He turned his head at a slight tap on the door. It was Willy.

'That detective bird's downstairs, I shoved her in the drawing room.'

'Thanks, Willy, I'm just coming. Get cook to make up a tray of coffee will you?'

The man nodded and left the room. Standing up slowly, Patrick walked from the room. He walked down the staircase, his shoulders bowed as if by a great weight, and Kate saw him pull himself erect. He walked towards her with his hands outstretched, and she clasped them warmly before she thought about what she was doing.

'Ms Burrows. Very nice to see you.'

Kate smiled. 'I was passing and I thought I'd just pop in and see how you were.'

Both knew it was a lie. No one was 'just passing' Patrick Kelly's house.

'That was very kind of you. I've ordered some coffee.'

Kate followed him into the morning room. A roaring fire was in the grate and the room was pleasantly warm. It was like going back a hundred years. Kelly sat on the settee beside her and smiled sadly.

'Actually, I'm glad of the company. My sister's no good at times like this. I've told her I'll see her at the funeral, though I suppose it won't be for a while. But I need company. My friends, or people I call friends, aren't really close. I never realised until now that in fact I have very few people I can trust. Only my daughter, and my wife when she was alive.'

Kate looked into his haggard face, so different from Dan's blond smoothness.

'I see so much unhappiness in my work, it's hard sometimes just to switch off.'

They sat together on the settee.

'What about your family? Won't they be wondering where you are on Boxing Day?'

'My daughter's sixteen, and today my ex-husband has taken her and my mother to a pantomime.' She saw the flicker of pain cross his face as she spoke of Lizzy and guessed that he was thinking of his own daughter. She hurried on, 'So I have a couple of hours to myself.'

Patrick Kelly heard the underlying loneliness in her voice and knew instinctively that they were two of a kind. Loners who worked and worked, and at the end of the day had nothing except their families. And when the families were no more, they had nothing at all to show for their efforts.

'Have you eaten today?'

Kate shook her head. 'Not since this morning.'

'Then why not have lunch with me? I could do with the company and Mrs Manners has still got enough turkey to feed the third world and the poor Albanians. Unless you have to get back of course.'

'That sounds lovely. I'd love to have lunch with you, Mr Kelly.'

'Patrick . . . The name's Patrick. Right then, I'll go and sort it out.'

Kate felt inordinately pleased at his offer, even though she was astute enough to know that it came from a desire for any company, rather than hers specifically. She was still thrilled to be there.

She self-consciously fiddled with her hair, tidied up her clothes. She wished she had worn her new suit, but she consoled herself that at the moment he didn't care what she looked like.

Willy brought in the coffee and smiled at her. Kate smiled back but inside she shuddered. The man looked like something from a bad nightmare. Half of one ear was missing, and his nose had obviously been broken more than a few times. He grinned at her from a toothless mouth.

'Shall I pour for you, love?'

Kate shook her head.

'I'll do it, thank you.'

Willy looked relieved and left the room.

Patrick Kelly returned. Lunch would be ready in twenty minutes. Leaving Kate with her coffee, he slipped into the library to use the phone.

Dimitrios Brunos, a London Greek, was one of the best 'minders' in the West End. He was also one of the most violent.

'Mr Kelly, how are you?' His voice was solicitous.

'Listen to me carefully and pass on what I say to all the others. My Mandy is dead and I'm upping the ante. There's half a mil' for whoever finds the ponce, right?'

Patrick heard a sharp intake of breath and smiled grimly. That should get some results.

'Also, I'll be looking for the slag personally, so I reckon between us we should find him. Whoever gives me his name gets the money, OK?'

'Yes. Please accept my most sincere condolences. Your daughter was a . . .'

'Yeah, yeah. All right, Dimitrios. I ain't got that far myself yet. Just let the others know the score.'

Patrick put down the receiver and closed his eyes tightly. He was going to hound the slag into the ground. He would find him and pay him out if it was the last thing he ever did. Pulling himself upright, he squared his shoulders. First thing tomorrow he was going to phone the Chief Constable to request copies of everything the Old Bill found out. Patrick intended to get to the suspects first.

He went back in to Kate and sat beside her. Even though she was an Old Bill, a Filth, he trusted her somehow. She had the same quietness and serenity his Renée had had.

Patrick liked her.

George and Elaine had opened a bottle of wine. She was tipsy and they were watching a comedy film on TV. The curtains were pulled and the lamplight gave a cosy glow to the room. In fairness, George thought, Elaine was an exemplary housewife. Never in all their years together had he lacked an ironed shirt or clean underwear. His suits always went to the cleaner's on time, and his meals were always cooked for him. Admittedly, Elaine's cooking often left a lot to be desired, but she was at least conscientious. A good woman.

His mother, whatever her faults – and they were legion – had been the same in the housewifely stakes. Hate her or love her, the children were always well fed. She made sure they were the best dressed, the cleanest, the brainiest. Her house was the best furnished and kept spic and span. She had been proud of her Nottingham lace curtains, her wooden beds . . .

George jumped.

Elaine had placed her arm around his neck. He looked at her from the corner of his eye. She was resting her head on his shoulder.

Oh God!

'Give us a kiss, George.' Her voice was low and slurred.

He concentrated on the television screen. Bette Midler and Danny DeVito were fighting it out. *Ruthless People* the film was called. Ruthless People? He was the ruthless one. Hadn't he proved it?

'Come on, George, give us a kiss.' Elaine pulled his face round and planted a wet, sticky mouth on his own.

George kissed her. He didn't know what else to do. For the first time in over sixteen years, Elaine showed some signs of interest in him! He shuddered.

'I've had a lovely day, George. A lovely day. And next year we will finally have a good year. Three hundred and sixty-five days of happiness. I'm going on holiday with you, to Florida to see our Edith. And I'm going to Spain with the girls.' Elaine was having trouble forming the words now and George guessed that if he kept quiet she would fall asleep. He put his arm around her with difficulty and held her close to him. She snuggled into him and closed her eyes.

Please God make her go to sleep.

His prayer was answered. Within moments the wine, the heat and the excitement of the day caught up with her and she began to snore softly into his thick cable-knit cardigan.

George breathed a sigh of relief.

He would do many things to keep her happy, but sex was not one of them.

Picking up the remote control, he turned the TV on to video. Mandy appeared on the screen. He had set the video up earlier in the evening while Elaine was making supper. He had been waiting for her to go to bed. Now he turned the sound down and watched the action on the screen. The element of risk gave it an added excitement.

So Mandy went through her nightly ritual and Elaine snored and George was happy, his finger poised over the TV button on the remote control.

In a funny way he wished that Elaine would open her eyes, but she was blind drunk and slept. And George just sat and watched.

Kate had enjoyed her late lunch with Patrick Kelly very much. They had opened up to each other. Now she sat with her own family and listened to their account of the pantomime.

'Oh, Mum, it was really funny. You should have seen the dame! He was hilarious. Joanie was there with her brothers. They sat with us and we had the greatest time.'

'Considering you didn't really want to go.' Evelyn's voice was jocular. '"I'm too old for pantomimes, I'm an adult." And when we got there she was shouting louder than anyone!'

'I'm sorry I missed it.'

'Dad was really funny, he made jokes all through it. I wish you could have been there, Mum.'

'So do I, Lizzy. It sounds great.'

'Oh, it was. Dad's gone up for a bath.' Lizzy looked at the kitchen clock and squealed. 'Oh my God, if I don't get a move on I'm going to be late.'

'Where you off to then?'

'Oh, me and Joanie are going to a party tonight.' She twisted her hair around her fingers. 'I'm sure I mentioned it.'

'You never said anything to me.'

'Or me.' Evelyn's voice was low.

'Well, it's been arranged absolutely ages and Joanie is coming round for me at seven thirty. I really must go, Mum.'

Kate and Evelyn exchanged glances.

'Well, I don't remember you telling us anything about it. Where is this party?'

'It's near Joanie's house, in the next street. I don't know the number.'

'I see.'

'Oh, Mum, don't say it like that. I must go! I want to go.' Lizzy's voice was high and near to tears.

'No one has said you can't go . . . yet.'

Dan walked into the kitchen in his dressing gown.

'What's all this racket then?'

Lizzy ran to him and he put his arm around her.

'I want to go to a party and Mum won't let me. Everyone will be there.'

'Your mother never said you can't go, Lizzy. That's not fair.'

'Oh, Gran, I want to go so much. And between you, you'll talk me out of it!'

'We will not! All your mother wants to know is where it is and who'll be there!'

'I'll take her and pick her up, how's that?'

Everyone looked at Dan. Lizzy kissed him on the cheek.

'That's settled then, I'll go and get ready. Blimey, Mum, sometimes your job really goes to your head. I'm not a suspect, you know!'

Her voice was happy once more and Kate watched her run from the room.

'Thanks, Dan. Thanks a bundle.'

He opened his arms wide. 'What have I done? All I said was I'd take her and pick her up. There's no harm in that, Kate.' He counted off on his fingers. 'First, we'll know where it is. And secondly, we'll be able to sort out a reasonable time for getting her home. Third, I'll have a quick look at who's there. I can't see there's any problem.'

He walked from the room and Kate felt an urge to jump on his back and tear his hair out. Not five minutes in the house and he was already countermanding her. Lizzy would be allowed to get away with blue murder while her father was around, it was always the same, then when he swanned off again, it would be left to Kate to pick up the pieces and get back some kind of equilibrium.

She sighed heavily.

'He's right, you know, Kate. She's not a child any more.'

'Oh, Mum, don't you jump on the bandwagon. She's so grown up that she shouted herself hoarse through a bloody pantomime not two hours ago. I saw a girl not much older than her battered and dying in a hospital bed, not twenty-four hours since. There's a bloody maniac on the loose and you tell me that she's grown up!'

Evelyn put her hand on her daughter's arm. 'That's not all that's bothering you, is it? Now is it? It's Dan taking the reins from your hands that's brought all this on. Well, listen to me and listen good. It won't last – it never does. But you can't stop that child from living a normal life. She'll be with Joanie and her other friends, Dan's picking her up. So swallow your pride and don't make an enemy of your own child.'

'I'll be glad when he goes. And first thing in the New Year he will be going. That, Mum, is a promise!'

'He only wants to see the child enjoy herself with her friends.'

Kate sighed noisily.

'Don't you start taking his side, Mum. It's bad enough Lizzy thinks the sun shines out of his . . .'

'Kate!' Evelyn stopped her flow of words. 'You should listen to yourself, young lady.'

She sat at the breakfast bar and lit herself a cigarette. It wasn't the time to remind her mother that she was forty. Her lovely afternoon had been spoiled. She would have let Lizzy go to the party eventually, she rarely denied the girl anything. But to have the decision taken out of her hands like that was irritating and downright unfair.

But Kate knew when enough was enough so she kept her peace.

Dan dropped Joanie and Lizzy off at a respectable-looking semi-detached house and after a quick kiss on his daughter's cheek drove away, pleased with the way he had handled everything. It would do Kate good to realise that he could be responsible too.

Lizzy went into the party with Joanie and was immediately surrounded by a crowd of boys. She was wearing a short black skirt and a tiny scrap of a top that emphasised her heavy breasts. Joanie stood by her side as she laughed and chatted with the guys. She was a different girl to the one her mother and grandmother knew.

'So come on then, has anyone got any puff?'

A tall thin boy with straggly hair passed her a joint and Lizzy took it from him, inhaling the fragrant mixture deeply.

'Mmm, smells like Sensimelle!' She took a large draw and held the smoke in her lungs for about ten seconds before letting it out.

Her breasts quivered and gathered the attention of every male in the vicinity.

'I have been dying for a toke all day. Where's Angela and Marianne?'

'They won't be here till later. They're trying to score a few Es over in Grays.'

Lizzy's eyes lit up. 'Oh, great. I have to be home for half-past one! There's plenty of time for fun yet.'

Everyone burst out laughing and Joanie smiled uneasily. Since they had got in with this crowd, she had not felt very happy. They were too forward for her, but Lizzy loved them. She thrived on all the attention and excitement. Joanie tagged along with her, as she always had done.

An hour later Lizzy was against the wall in the back garden with an eighteen-year-old boy named Joey Meeson. He had pulled the band of material that passed for a skirt up around her waist and was tugging at the top of her tights.

'Not here!' Her voice was scandalised.

Joey looked down at her and grinned.

'You really must learn to get into the swing of things, Lizzy.'

She pulled her skirt down and blinked rapidly. The

cannabis and the vodka she had consumed were making her feel light-headed.

'Is it true that your mum's a Filth?'

Lizzy giggled. 'You could call her that. She's a Detective Inspector.'

'Really? That's wild.'

'Actually, she's all right.'

'What would she say if she knew what we'd been doing tonight?' His voice was genuinely interested.

'Probably go ape shit.'

They both laughed and then Joey kissed her again. Softer this time. 'Talking of shit, how about I skin up again? This time in the bedroom?' His voice was low and husky and Lizzy was lost. He was the best-looking boy she had ever seen in her life.

'That would be fine.'

'Come on then.' He pulled her by the hand through the crowded kitchen and hall and over the bodies on the stairs.

Inside the bedroom, Lizzy found out what Joey's idea of a good time was.

And Joey found out that Lizzy, the daughter of a policewoman, was not as innocent as he had first thought.

Chapter Ten

New Year's Eve

'Are you sure you're going to be all right on your own, George?' Elaine's voice was concerned but deep inside she hoped he would not decide to go to the party. The last few days he had been getting on her nerves. George fit and well could get you down, but George ill was a nightmare.

'You go to the party, dear, and give everyone my best. I'm really much too ill to go tonight.'

She breathed a sigh of relief.

'Well, if you're sure?'

George smiled wanly. 'You go and have a good time. I've got a good book, a flask of soup and my tablets.'

She kissed him on the cheek.

'See you then. I might be late.' She giggled.

George nodded. In her new dress, a fitted emerald green sparkly affair with huge padded shoulders, George thought she looked like a cross between a Christmas tree and an American footballer. 'You look lovely, Elaine. You'll have all the men wanting to dance with you.'

'Oh, George. You old silly!' Elaine giggled again, a

schoolgirl going on her first date. She dropped her clutch bag and George frowned as she strained to pick it up. Not an American footballer – a sumo wrestler. God, she was bad enough in her shell suits.

A taxi hooted outside and Elaine rushed from the room, leaving a scent of Estée Lauder and face powder.

''Bye, George.'

He listened to the thud of her feet on the stairs and the satisfying slam of the front door as it crashed behind her.

She was gone.

He was alone.

Hallelujah!

George lay with bated breath until he heard the taxi turn at the end of the street, then jumped from the bed.

'Look, Mr Kelly, it's New Year's Eve. We always get lots of punters in on New Year's Eve. She's a good kid . . .'

Kelly stared hard at the woman in front of him. Violet Mapping had been running this massage parlour for five years. She was one of the hardest Toms he had ever met in his life, and he had met a few, but she had one vice: she was a dyke and liked the young girls. But this young girl was not working in his massage parlour until she was qualified.

'Listen, Vi, get the girl a certificate and she can work here till the cows come home. Till then, no way.'

'Oh, Mr Kelly, you know and I know that that piece of paper is a bloody con.'

'I don't care what you know, Violet. Once she's done a course in massage and has her certificate she can work here. Until then, no.'

Violet saw the man's face harden and decided it was better to give way on this occasion. Everyone knew about Mandy, it was common knowledge on the streets. It was best not to annoy him now.

She sighed.

'If you say so, Mr Kelly.'

'Good girl, Vi, you know it makes sense. Now then, if you get any weird ones in I want you to cop the names and addresses – the lot. Then I want you to pass them on to me.'

Violet snorted with laughter.

'They're all fucking weird, that's why they come here!'

Kelly shook his head in annoyance.

'You know what I mean. If one wants something a bit outlandish like, or gets violent with the girls, I want to know. OK? You're one of the best "lifters" in the game, Vi. You can lift a wallet better than anyone I've ever known. Only after you've lifted it, Violet, you put it back, comprenez?'

She narrowed her hard blue eyes.

'I give up lifting years ago, Mr Kelly, you should know that.'

The two eyed each other for a few seconds.

'Just make sure the wallet goes back into the pocket, Vi, or there'll be hell to pay. Now get back on reception. By the way, before I forget, how old is that little black bird out there?'

Violet pulled her mouth down at the corners and shrugged her skinny shoulders.

'I dunno.'

Patrick Kelly stood up.

'You don't know? Well, judging by the looks of her I'd put her at about fifteen, Vi, so get rid of her. Fuck me, I pay you to run this gaff. I might as well run the bastard place meself!'

'All right, all right, no need to get your knickers in a twist. I'll sort it, OK?'

'Good.'

'I'm sorry about your Mandy, Pat, heart sorry. We all are.' Her voice was soft now. She had been working for, and fighting with, Patrick Kelly for years. He was a good boss. Fair but hard. His daughter had been his life. Everyone knew that.

He dropped his eyes.

'Thanks, Vi.'

'Right then, face ache, I'd better go and give my little friend the bad news.' Her voice was once more loud and aggressive.

'You do that, girl, and once she's got her certificate, she can work her little arse off.'

'I'll get her a bent one off Vinny Marcenello.'

'You get it where you like, love, but she don't work till she's got it. I mean that, Vi.'

'I know that, don't I!' Her voice was shrill again. She walked from the office.

Kelly carried on looking over the books but his heart wasn't in it. Finally he got up from his desk and walked out into the foyer of the massage parlour. All around the walls were plushly upholstered seats. Girls and women of every colour, creed, shape and size were sprawled all over them. They all sat up straight as Patrick walked among them.

He nodded at them absentmindedly. Then turning to the left he walked through a door to the back of the parlour. That was where the cubicles were. He walked silently along the thickly carpeted floor until he came to the last cubicle. He listened.

A childish voice wafted from behind the thin curtain.

'Do you require any extras, sir?'

'How much will it rush me?'

'Well, hand relief is fifteen quid, a blow job's twenty, and the full bifta is forty-five quid.'

Patrick heard the man laugh.

'Gis the full bifta, girl.'

Patrick shook his head and turned to walk back to the foyer. For some reason the childish voice had upset him. He knew the girl. She was only seventeen and looked about twelve. She was blonde, like his Mandy, except unlike Mandy she had never had a chance in life. He walked out of the tiny corridor, through the foyer and out to his car.

Don't start getting soft now, boy, he told himself. Tomming is the oldest profession in the world. If they didn't work for you they'd only work for someone else.

He climbed into the back of his Rolls and tapped on the window. Willy's voice came over the intercom.

'Where to, Pat?'

'Forest Gate this time. I want to see how Juliet's getting on.'

The car purred away and Kelly relaxed in his seat.

Yet the childish voice was still repeating in his head.

'Stop the car!'

'Do what?' The car screeched to a halt in the middle of the road. Patrick Kelly jumped out and ran back into the massage parlour.

'Oi, Vi. In the office quick sharp.'

Violet followed him in.

'Yeah? What?' Her voice was belligerent once more.

'That little blonde bird, what's her name?'

'Marlene?'

'Yeah, Marlene. Well, she's giving the punter the full bifta.'

'So what?'

'Well, I want it stopped. From now on there's no full sex in here, right. The Old Bill can't touch us if the girls don't cock their legs over.'

Violet looked at Patrick as if he had gone mad.

'You feeling all the bleeding ticket? We won't get any girls working here if we do something like that. Gordon Bennett, if you had the choice between a mouthful of spunk or a pratfull, what would you rather have?'

Kelly's face screwed up. 'Don't be so disgusting, Vi!'

She opened her arms wide.

'I'm only stating facts, mate. We won't get a Tom in here with them rules, and you know it. Our clientele will go down quicker than free beer on a beano!'

Kelly felt sick.

'Why don't you go home and have a nice rest, Pat? It's all the worry you've had, it's turned your head.'

He felt a fool.

'Maybe you're right, Vi.'

'Listen.' Violet's voice was soft. 'We ain't social workers, mate, we're in business. Them girls out there are gonna flash their clout no matter what anyone does. It's the only thing they know how to do. So leave them to it.'

'Oh, I don't know, Vi, there's some fucking nonces about. Look what happened to my Mandy.'

'Well, let me tell you something. Them perverts, they pick on the nice innocent girls. They don't want no Tom. They like a struggle. Same as them posh blokes what come here – they all want to be caned. I'm telling you, Pat, we go out the back, into the garden and cut a swish from that bleeding forsythia bush, then come back in and beat the buggers' arses black and blue. Now if they didn't pay us they'd only pay the Paki down the road.'

Kelly nodded at her. He was very tired all of a sudden. 'Maybe you're right, Vi.'

As he walked back out into the foyer, the girls automatically straightened again as he passed them. Out on the pavement, an elderly woman with a small sausage dog gave him a filthy look. He sighed again.

That put the tin lid on it as far as Patrick Kelly was concerned. The old bird thought *he* was a nonce. The Rolls was parked outside once more and he climbed in.

'Forest Gate, guv?'

'No. Home, I think, Willy.'

'Okey doke.'

Kelly watched the people in the cold grey streets. It was New Year's Eve and he had arranged to spend it with Kate.

He settled into the seat once more. Sod the Toms. He had enough on his mind.

'Oh, Mum! Why must I always have you and Dad on my back? All the girls in my class are going. I'll be the only one who doesn't! I'll never live it down!'

Louise Butler stamped her foot.

Her mother Doreen grinned. She had a mind of her own did Louise. She glanced at her husband.

'What do you think, Ron, shall we let her go?'

Louise breathed a sigh of relief. If her mum was asking her dad then she was going. Mum had more or less said yes. Before her father answered she had thrown herself into her mother's arms.

'Thanks, Mum. Oh, thanks.'

'Hurry up and get changed then. I'll run you over there.' Ron's voice was jovial.

Louise looked at him with a mock stern expression.

'I am ready, if you don't mind!'

They all laughed. In her designer tracksuit of vivid mauve and gold, her Reebok bumpers and man's leather flying jacket, she looked the complete opposite of her parents' idea of dressed up. But she was a hardcore acid fan, from her backcombed sixties hairstyle to the sovereign earrings in her ears.

'Well, I've been reading about these waves.'

'It's raves, Dad. Raves.'

'Waves, raves . . . whatever. You be careful. Don't take no drugs or anything now, will you?'

Louise rolled her violet eyes.

'As if I would. I'm not stupid, you know.'

'We worry about you, love, that's all.'

'I know that, Mum. Come on, Dad, or we'll be late. Don't take me right to the party, drop me off at Sam's. We want to make our way there together, OK?'

'Oh, all right then.'

After kissing her mother, Louise followed her father from the house. Five minutes later she was outside Sam's.

'Now where is this rave again?'

'Just up the road from here at Woodham Woods. About seven miles away. Stop worrying, Dad, we'll be fine.'

'Well, you remember that I want you in by one at the latest.'

'OK. See you later, Dad.'

She kissed her father and got out of the car. She watched him drive off before walking up the path to Sam's house. She rang the bell.

'Hello, Mrs Jensen, is Sam here?'

'No, dear. She left about ten minutes ago. With Georgina, Tracey and Patricia. I think it was them, anyway, she's got so many friends. Well, they came round for her in a blue car . . .'

'Oh. All right then. Sorry to have bothered you.'

Louise walked up the path, her heart dragging in the dirt. That bloody bitch Sam had gone ahead knowing that Louise was coming round. The two-faced cow! Well, she would have to go home and get her dad to run her to the rave. But if he did he would see that it was in an old barn, and not at all legal, and then he would make her come home.

What was she going to do?

She smiled to herself. She would thumb a ride. Might even get a lift off some blokes. That would show Sam and her lot, wouldn't it?

She pulled her long dark hair from inside her flying jacket and began to walk to the outskirts of Grantley.

She'd show them.

Lizzy was dressed and ready to go. She took one last look at herself in the wardrobe mirror before she pulled on the sheepskin that her father had bought her for Christmas. Licking her lips to gloss them, she walked to her mother's bedroom.

'Oh, Mum, you look scrumptious.'

Kate smoothed down the deep red pure new wool dress that hugged her figure, and smiled at her daughter.

'Thanks, love.' She looked at herself in the mirror, knowing that she looked good. Her hair had been washed in a coconut shampoo and gleamed under the light. She was sporting a pair of gold hoop earrings, and her face was skilfully made up.

'Now what time will you be back from Joanie's tomorrow?'

'About lunchtime, I suppose. Don't worry about me, you just enjoy yourself.'

'I will.' Kate looked into her daughter's eyes. 'You look beautiful you know, Liz. Show me what you're wearing.'

'Oh, I just shoved on my black suit. After all, the party is at Joanie's house.' She pouted her red-lipsticked lips and Kate laughed. Joanie's family were what Lizzy would call 'lame'.

'I hope you enjoy yourself.'

'Oh, I will, Mum. You just concentrate on yourself.'

Lizzy eyed her mother critically. 'Wear the red lipstick,

it will look better with that dress than the coral. You're dark enough to get away with it.'

Kate laughed. 'Okey doke.' She began to tissue off her lipstick.

'What's Dad going to do tonight?'

Kate shrugged. 'I've no idea, love. Gran's off to Doris's. I should imagine your father's going out as well.'

'Well, didn't you even ask him?'

Kate stopped in her tracks as she applied red lipstick. 'Why should I do that?' She locked eyes with her daughter in the mirror. 'We're divorced, Lizzy, my life's my own, and your father's life is his own.'

Lizzy looked sad. 'I wish you two could get it together.'

Kate turned and held her daughter's face in her hands. 'I wished that for a long time, Lizzy, but your father has a different approach to life.' She was stumbling for the right words. She wanted to make Dan sound as good as possible and after some of the stunts he'd played on her in the past that was difficult.

'Your father is his own man, he lives his own life. And so do I.'

Lizzy stared at her mother and Kate could see her trying to comprehend what was being said.

'I'd better go or I'll be late.'

'Hang on a sec and I'll drop you at Joanie's.'

'It's OK, I called a cab. You go to your party, Mum, just forget about me for once! I'm a big girl now.'

'Well, Happy New Year then.'

Kate kissed her.

'Happy New Year, Mum.'

She rushed from the room at the sound of the taxi honking and Kate watched her go with a pang of regret. Picking up her handbag from the bed, she walked slowly from the room.

'You look a picture Katie.'

Evelyn was dressed up to the nines. She had on a bright green crimplene suit and a dark green hat. Her feet were encased in fur-lined ankle boots and she had a large brown handbag at her side.

'Will you drop me round Doris's?'

''Course I will. Are many people going?'

'About twenty I think. This'll be the first New Year we haven't seen in together, just the three of us.'

'I know that, but Lizzy's right, she is growing up however much we don't like it.'

'Where's your party again?'

'Oh, just one of the guys from the station. It's at his house.' Kate hated lying, but she wasn't ready to tell anyone about her feelings for Patrick.

'Where's Dan?'

'He's in the front room, you go and see him and I'll get me coat.'

Kate went into the front room. Dan was sitting on the settee watching television. He looked at her as she came in. She watched, with some satisfaction, the widening of his eyes. He gave a low whistle. 'You look lovely, Kate, really lovely.' He sounded sincere.

'Thanks, Dan. Did you see Lizzy before she went?'

'Yeah.' He ran his hands through his thick hair, a familiar gesture. 'Why don't you let me take you out, Kate?' His voice was small. 'You look much too good for a bunch of old policemen.'

'Haven't you made any arrangements?' She raised her eyebrows.

'Well, no. I was going to take you out – you never go out on New Year's Eve.' The petulant note was back in his voice.

'Well, I do now.' She heard her mother's feet on the stairs and smiled.

'Happy New Year.'

'Happy New Year, Kate.'

He watched her go from the room and felt an urge to drag her back. For the first time ever Kate was in charge and Dan was not sure how to act. In the past it had been her coming to him. There was a man involved this time or his name was not Danny Burrows. Kate was dressed for a date, not a party. He would make it his business to find out who it was.

As the front door closed he pulled himself from the sofa and watched her drive away. Then, when she turned the corner, he went out to the hall and picked up the phone. He dialled and after a few rings a female voice answered.

Dan had a motto in life: Always have a back-up plan.

In the car Evelyn kept up a stream of chatter.

'You really do look lovely, you know. It's a long time since I saw you looking so well. If I didn't know better I'd think there was a man on the horizon.'

'Oh, don't be silly, Mum. If there was a man on the horizon, you'd be the first to know.'

'Well, maybe the man himself don't know yet.'

'What on earth are you talking about?'

Evelyn smiled vaguely. 'Oh, nothing, nothing. Stop here, Kate.'

She pulled over to the kerb and turned off the engine. 'Happy New Year, Mum.'

'Happy New Year, love. And listen – if for some reason you want to spend the night with a friend, maybe you'll want to drink and then you won't be able to drive . . . you know . . . don't worry about Lizzy because I'll be home soon, should anything come up.'

She got out of the car and walked up Doris's path, her back ramrod straight.

Kate started the car and smiled to herself. Her mother was shrewd.

She began to drive to the outskirts of Grantley. She was looking forward to seeing Patrick Kelly.

George was wrapped up warm. Although he was not as ill as he had made out to Elaine, he still felt a bit under the weather. George always liked to look after himself. He was obsessed with his health. He had the car heater on and the whirring as it blew out hot air was beginning to annoy him. He snapped on the radio.

The sound of Mozart's Horn Concerto filled the car and he relaxed. That was more like it. He drove out of Grantley and along the road that led to the village of Woodham. He often drove out this way first; there was a small lay-by that was usually filled with cars with courting couples in them. Their steamed up windows excited George.

He put his foot on the accelerator and clipped his headlights. He felt free, free and happy. Later on he would drive back into Grantley and go and watch the flats. He began to hum along with the music. His usually dead grey eyes were sparkling. His bushy black brows, liberally sprinkled with grey, moved up and down in time to the music. His cheesecutter hat hid the balding patch on his head.

Then he saw her. In front of him were two other cars, which was unusual for this road. Normally it was dead. But it was New Year's Eve, and all the roads were busy tonight. George had no idea about the rave that was just beginning in Woodham Woods.

The girl had her thumb out. He saw the car in front of him slow down and slowed with it. The girl walked towards the car and it pulled away quickly, leaving her standing with her hands on her hips by the side of the road. George drove past her and into the first lay-by. Taking the carrier bag from the back seat he slipped on the mask. He felt the adrenaline begin to course through his veins, and smiled. Adjusting the holes so that he could see properly, he turned around in the road and drove back towards her.

His heart nearly stopped. A car was parked up beside her. George drove past and felt a terrible anger replace his elation.

The slut! He drove along the road, and turned again.

Louise stared into the dark interior of the XR3. There were three boys in the back and two in the front. They were obviously drunk.

'Come on, darlin'. Jump in the motor, we'll be there in no time.'

Louise was not sure.

One of the boys in the back wound down his window and spat on to the roadside.

'Look, hurry up, will ya? I'm fucking freezing me bollocks off!'

The blond youth who was driving leant across the front seat. 'Look, get in.'

Louise was frightened.

'No . . . No, it's all right. I'll walk.'

'Let the silly bitch walk then. Come on, I want a drink.'

'You stupid cow!'

The car screeched away and Louise watched its tail lights disappear into the distance.

They were drunk, or drugged, maybe both. She did not like walking along the dark road, but she was not getting into a car with five blokes! No way.

She pulled her leather flying jacket tighter around her.

No, she would walk and find Sam and the others. She began to hurry, sorry now that she had not gone home, because all of a sudden the thought of missing out on a rave didn't seem that bad. But if she had missed this one, she would be the laughing stock of her class. She wished she was sixteen. She wished she was at hairdressing college. She wished she was at home in bed!

Another car came up behind her and she heard it slow down. Oh, please don't let it be another car full of drunks! Let it be some dreamy boy of about seventeen with his hair cut in 'curtains' and some really nice gear, then she could show off to Sam and the others!

She turned as the car drew to a halt.

The passenger door opened and she walked hesitantly towards it. The dirt path she was on was flanked on the left by a steep bank. The bank sloped down about ten feet, into a large ploughed field. Bending, she looked into the car.

As soon as her mind registered what it had seen she jumped away from the car door, a scream issuing from her that cut through the night air.

Inside the car was a man in a black leather mask.

Nowhere in her wildest nightmares had she ever imagined anything like this! She stumbled backwards. Too late she remembered about the steep bank behind her and stepped into thin air. Landing with a thud on the dirty slope, her brand new Reeboks scrabbled in the dirt a couple of times before she finally pulled herself up.

There in front of her was the masked man! She dodged around him and ran into the road as he made a grab for her. In his hands she saw something glint and realised it was a knife. She felt her bowels loosen as she realised fully what was happening. She was dazzled by a set of headlights as a Volkswagen Golf swerved to avoid her, music blaring out of the open windows. She stood helplessly in the road as it shot past. With it went her hopes.

The man was standing on the grass verge watching her. On the other side of the road was another field. She bit her lip, weighing up in her confused mind where to run. It was dark, so dark and lonely.

She backed away from the man slowly, trying desperately to think of an escape. She saw him begin to walk towards her. In the distance she heard another car, and putting up her arms began to run towards it, waving and shouting.

Terry Miller had dropped a tab of Ecstasy at six that evening. He was buzzing, really buzzing. Beside him his brother Charlie was tripping out of his head. They had driven around for over an hour trying to find the rave that everyone was going on about. Inside the car the sounds of Technotronic screamed out so loudly that they could hardly hear themselves think. When Terry saw the girl in his headlights he snorted with laughter.

'Look, Charlie, she must be well stoned!'

He grinned, trying to clear his mind.

'Look at the geezer with her. Wild, man. Look at his headgear.'

They drove past the two figures and Terry sounded his horn that played the first few bars of the Star Spangled Banner.

'Wicked! Did you see that bloke, man. Really wicked.'

Louise Butler watched her potential saviours drive away, their horn blaring out into the dark night. She began to cry. Looking around her as if she thought someone was going to run out of the field behind her and save her, she saw that the man was much nearer.

Turning, she began to run. Before she had taken five steps she hit the chain link fencing that was invisible in the darkness. She felt the fence give a little and then it literally threw her back into the arms of the man with the mask.

As his arms tightened around her all the fight left her body. Fear took over and she went limp. Her shoulders were racked with sobs.

Oh please, please God, help me!

George half carried, half dragged her back to the car. Inside the mask he was smiling. His secret smile that just exposed his teeth.

Kate had had one glass of wine with dinner and was now enjoying an armagnac. Patrick smiled across the table at her. It was the second time that Kate had had dinner at his house, and he was finding that he liked her being around. She took his mind off Mandy, and that was strange considering she was on his daughter's case.

He had no illusions about the police. He had been dealing with them on and off all his life. But Kate was the first plain clothes police officer he had ever dealt with on a personal basis. Oh, he had greased a few of the Old Bill's palms over the years, such as the Chief Constable's, but they were both in the Masons. Kate was the first member of the Force he had met socially because he wanted to. Because he enjoyed her company.

She looked good enough to eat tonight. Red suited her. Her dark hair shone in the light from the candles. She looked softer somehow. More appealing. After all his empty-headed bimbos, he found he liked having a woman around him who demanded a bit of respect.

In fairness to the young girls who had come and gone over the years, he had deliberately picked well-stacked, dim-witted types whose only claim to fame was the fact that they were a good lay. He had not wanted to have to trouble himself making conversation. What on earth did a man on the wrong side of forty have to say to an eighteen year old? Nothing, that's what.

But Kate, she was a different kettle of fish altogether. They discussed everything under the sun. And she wasn't one of those pushy birds either, who wore their intelligence like a pair of boxing gloves, willing to punch a point home. Oh, no. Kate would listen to his opinions then give hers, quietly and fairly. He liked her. He knew that she was not making much headway with finding the nonce, but in fairness neither was he. The bloke was obviously a chancer. Kate had explained all that to him. He never left any clues. But she would not give up. One day he would make a mistake, then she would have him.

Only what Kate didn't know was that when that break came, Patrick would also be after the bloke. And when he was finished with him there would be nothing left. Nothing recognisable anyway.

'So you don't have anything to go on, really?' he asked.

Kate shook her head and he watched her hair ripple with the movement.

'We're gradually eliminating people from the inquiry but it takes time. We're still interviewing all men with dark-coloured Orions. We should be finished with that in the next ten days. I myself will be interviewing from tomorrow along with Spencer and Willis.'

'I see.' His voice was gentle.

'We will get him, Patrick, eventually. Normally when a murder is committed, or a rape, the person is known to us.' Kate smiled ruefully. 'I think I've said all this before!'

'You have. Come on, let's change the subject.' He nearly burst out laughing and Kate looked at him quizzically.

'I nearly said, "How's work"! My head's up my Khyber these days. Come on, let's adjourn to the drawing room, shall we?' His voice mimicked that of an aristocrat and Kate laughed. He was a character.

In the drawing room they sat together on the large settee. Patrick had brought the brandy decanter and two glasses.

'This is a lovely house – eighteenth century, isn't it?'

Patrick nodded.

'Yeah, I picked it up for a song about twelve years ago. Seventy grand I paid for it, and that was the national debt then I can tell you. It was a ruin.' He waved his hand. 'Cost me nigh on that again to restore it back to its original beauty, but it was worth it. Renée loved it and so did Mandy. Now though – well, it's empty without them. What's a house without a woman in it?'

Kate instinctively grasped his hand.

He stared into the dark depths of her eyes. She really was lovely, with a mature quality he had grown unused to in a woman.

Suddenly he wanted her wholeheartedly. He wanted to feel her arms around him. He wanted her to love him. He wanted, needed, a woman's loving. A woman's, not a girl's. A real woman's loving.

Kate read the expression in his eyes and parted her full lips to speak. Then he kissed her – a long slow kiss that set her tingling right down to her toes. And Kate kissed him back, caught up in feelings that had nothing to do with background or career or anything except pure sensation.

He wanted her. She could feel the want and the need in him. She felt him pushing her backwards on the overstuffed settee and she let him. She lay back gladly.

This was what she had been waiting for since she had first met him though she had never admitted it to herself until now. Dan was not even in the running any more. She wanted Patrick Kelly.

She felt his big rough hand running along her body outside her new dress. Felt the tingle as he found the skin of her thighs. Then everything was forgotten except the moment. He pulled away from her and looked into her face, his expression soft and serious at the same time.

'Will you stay the night, Kate?' His voice was husky. She loved him for having the consideration to stop now. For wanting to make sure she knew what she was doing.

She nodded.

Picking her up as if she were a doll, he placed her on to unsteady feet.

She followed him up the large curved staircase and decided that even if this was for one night only, she would be happy. Even one night with Patrick Kelly was better than none at all.

Inside the bedroom she stared around her in awe at the sheer scale and opulence of the room.

Patrick was slowly taking off his clothes and Kate felt scared for a moment. She was not a young girl any more. She was forty years old.

Patrick walked to her and pulled her red wool dress over her head, exposing her tiny naked breasts that had never really needed a brassiere, and her lower body, encased in black tights. As she pulled her head free she looked at his face fearfully.

He smiled.

'You're lovely, Kate. Really lovely.'

And she believed that she was, then.

He pulled her to the bed. Finally naked, they gazed at one another in the muted light from the lamps placed either side of the bed.

In all her years with Dan she had never had this

abandoned feeling. Had never felt the exquisite excitement that she felt at this moment. Had never experienced a hunger the like of which was eating at her now.

In the back of her mind she knew that the situation should never have got this far. The man was a villain. Patrick Kelly was a bad one, a robber, a violent repoman. 'The Snatchman' was his nickname. But at this moment Kate could not have cared less if he was a mass murderer.

She wanted him.

She had him.

She kissed him.

She would worry later. Much later.

Patrick Kelly kissed her back, then caressed her breasts, biting the nipples gently, pulling them up with his lips, until they were like tiny pyramids in his mouth. The wetness of his tongue as it slipped over them made Kate arch her back with delight.

Kelly was an experienced lover and Kate was glad. It had been so long for her she was like a dam waiting to burst. She felt his hand move gently down her body, caressing her thighs, then she felt the heat and the moistness as he slipped a finger inside her. She groaned. She could feel Patrick's erection digging into the side of her leg, his excitement making her more breathless by the second. He played with her tiny button, running his thumb over it lightly, until she tried to pull his hand away. Her whole body was trembling. She opened her legs wider, feeling her juices trickling out on to his fingers. Then he was moving down her body, his dark head moving slowly away from her and as he moved he kissed her skin, the little biting kisses that she was beginning to love so much.

When his mouth engulfed her sex she held in a long breath. She was going to come. She felt the waves begin to wash over her, and as each wave began, Patrick licked and sucked her, gently pushing a finger inside her simultaneously. Kate had never experienced such ecstasy in her life.

When, finally, the tremors stopped, she looked down the bed at his smiling shiny face.

'Oh, Patrick . . .'

She watched him climb from the bed and put on his dressing gown. His member was still swollen and purple.

'Where are you going?' Kate's voice was husky and bewildered.

'There's only one thing to do after an experience like that.'

'What's that?'

'That is to go down to my wine cellar and get a bottle of nice cold vintage champagne. After a couple of glasses I think you'll be ready for round two.'

He kissed her on the mouth and she tasted herself on his lips. As he walked from the room she hugged herself. Already, she wanted him to hurry back.

Patrick walked down the stairs in a daze. She was so juicy. He had never experienced anything like it before. It was as if he had opened her up in some way. It had taken all his willpower not to plunge himself inside her there and then.

But instinctively he knew that she needed gentle loving, the hard, penetrating loving would come later. Tonight she needed a long soft loving, and he was the man to give it to her.

He could not believe his luck. Who'd have thought she'd be so sexy? He got the champagne and two glasses and went back up the stairs. He smiled to himself as he realised he was practically running. It was a long time since he had been like this.

Too long.

*

Louise Butler was sobbing hard. In fact she was getting on George's nerves.

'Shut up!' His voice cut into her, sending shivers through her body.

'I . . . I want to go . . . go . . . home. Please.' She drew the last word out on a whine.

George gritted his teeth. The mask was hot again. His white cotton gloves stood out like beacons on the steering wheel. He glanced at her. She had drawn her lips back over her teeth while she cried, rocking herself backwards and forwards in the seat. Long strands of snot were hanging from her nose.

George shuddered.

Trust a woman to make a mountain out of a molehill! Anyone would think he was going to murder her. He was completely oblivious of the Swiss army knife clutched hotly in his hand, which caught the moonlight as he steered the car and drew Louise's eyes like a magnet.

He was the Grantley Ripper. He was the man everyone was talking about. He was going to kill her. She knew that as surely as she knew she would never get to the rave in Woodham Woods.

She cried harder, feeling a wave of sickness wash over her.

George drove to a large quarry near Woodham. He parked the car by the side of the deserted road and dragged Louise out of the passenger seat. The ground was hard beneath her feet and she stumbled, falling heavily on to the frosty ground. George dragged her upright by her hair.

'You are annoying me, young lady.'

He pulled her through a hole in the fencing. In the distance Louise could hear the music from the rave and every now and then a shrill cry broke the night. She was crying desperately, all the fight had left her body. She could only wait and see what was going to happen.

George pulled her towards a large hole that was blacker than the night around it. Giving her a final shove, he pushed her inside. Louise cried out as she felt her body tumbling down into the blackness. She felt her legs being pushed up over her head and heard the crack as her ankle hit a lump of granite. Her tracksuit and flying jacket dragged on the ground as she slid and bumped down into the blackness. She lay at the bottom, winded and in pain. She heard the man in the mask sliding down slowly and knew she should try and make a run for it but her ankle was already swelling inside her Reebok. Her hands and face were skinned from the descent, the gravel sticking to the skin and stinging.

She lay there in the pitch black. She had a pain in her chest that was not due to the fall, it was fear. Pure, naked fear.

George scrambled down to her. The mask was hot and he loved it. Loved the feel of it and the smell of it. He also loved the fear that was emanating from this girl. Thumbing lifts! My God, asking for trouble, just asking for it. Well, she had got it now, by Christ. She had well and truly got it now.

George felt the rage roar in his head. A red hot rage that made his hands tremble. Pulling a torch from his pocket he played the beam across her prostrate form. He frowned. She was unconscious. He sighed heavily, then taking back his heavily booted foot he kicked her in the chest, sending her skidding across the gravel. Still she did not move.

George sighed again. The mask was making his head itch.

Still she did not move.

George knelt on the gravel, and taking the knife more

firmly in his hand he stabbed her in the stomach. As the knife entered her she seemed to try to double up, but it was only a reflex action. George was puzzled. He pulled the heavy leather of her flying jacket from her arm and tried to find a pulse. There was none. She was dead. George was fuming. How dare she die on him? How dare she just die like that! He pushed the knife into her calf, through the thin material of her shellsuit and the soft plump skin, hitting the bone.

George sat on his haunches, biting his lip inside the mask. He pulled it off and felt the cold air bite into his hot skin, his scanty hair standing up and waving gently in the breeze. George spat into the dirt and pulled the knife out of the girl's leg, then he began to undress her.

He carefully pulled down the bottom of her tracksuit and cut off her panties. He opened the flying jacket and folded it then unzipped the tracksuit top. He was surprised to find that she was very big-breasted. He cut the white lycra bra so that her breasts sprang free.

He had placed the torch on a small mound of dirt and the light shone on to Louise Butler's cold and lifeless skin.

George cheered up. He glanced at his watch. He had hours before he had to get home. He began to hum.

In the distance the rave had really got underway. The music was blaring and the partygoers were dancing. It was New Year's Eve. Everyone was waiting for twelve o'clock, for 1990 to begin.

Everyone except Louise Butler.

'Happy New Year, Kate.' Patrick's voice was soft.

'Happy New Year, Patrick. I hope it's a good one for you, I really do.'

He smiled sadly. 'Well, I've got to be honest, girl, I ain't looking forward to it.'

Kate felt a great sadness for the man lying beside her. While they had made love she knew that, for a short time anyway, he had forgotten the events of the previous week. It had crossed her mind that he was using her, but wasn't she using him? He was only the second man she had ever slept with. In forty years, she had had two men. In this day and age it was laughable! Only she wasn't laughing.

Kate had surprised herself with the intensity of her response. She had never known any other man but Dan, but after tonight she was more than aware of what she had been missing all these years. Dan made love like he did everything else: with only himself in mind. Patrick Kelly, whom Dan would look on as an ill-educated lout, had actually spent time on her enjoyment. Oh, and she had enjoyed it! More than she had ever thought possible. The earth-shattering orgasms that she had read about were not a con, they were there just waiting for her to experience them. She snuggled into Patrick's hard body, enjoying the feel of him.

'I bet this would go down like a lead balloon if it was known in Grantley Police Station. The DI knocking off a local villain!' His voice was jocular and Kate found herself laughing with him.

'Knocking off? Thank you very much, Mr Kelly!'

Patrick held her tightly.

'That's just a figure of speech. You're a good woman, Kate.'

She put her face to his and kissed him. Let the outside world hang. At this moment all she was interested in was him. She would worry about the rights and wrongs of the situation in the morning. As she felt his hands travel across her body, she closed her eyes and with them her mind.

'Oh, Happy New Year!'

*

Elaine had been kissed until her lips were sore and her lipstick just a faded memory. She had not enjoyed herself so much in all her married life. Normally when they were invited to a party George never wanted to go. Elaine had therefore always declined. Since her newfound freedom, however, she had decided that she would get as much out of life as she could. With or if possible without George. And tonight had been her watershed. She had been danced off her feet and had loved every second of it.

She looked around the crowded room for her best friend, Margaret Forrester, and smiled as she saw her sitting on her husband's lap. Elaine wished she could have a marriage like that. Where everything was just plain and simple, laughing and joking the norm. Her face fell as she thought about her life with George. Still, they were going to Florida and she was going to Spain, so at least this year she had something to look forward to. And this party looked as if it could go on for hours yet!

'Would you like to dance?' Elaine turned to face the man who had spoken. He was about fifty-five and fat, but jolly with it. She had already danced with him three times. Someone had put on a Roy Orbison album and she slipped into the man's arms to the strains of 'Crying'. She loved Roy Orbison, and she loved all the attention.

'I'm ever so sorry, but I've forgotten your name.'

The man grinned, showing pristine but ill-fitting dentures. 'It's Hector . . . Hector Henderson. And you're the lovely Elaine.'

She felt a tingle going down her spine that could have been romance or could just as well have been the drink. Whatever it was, she liked it.

George was pushed from her mind as they took to the tiny space allocated for dancing in Margaret Forrester's front room.

*

Joey Meeson watched as Lizzy danced, her body undulating to the thumping rhythm of the acid house music. About an hour earlier they had each dropped an Ecstasy tab. He could feel himself 'coming up' now. Everything around him had taken on a rosy hue and he felt excitement in his guts. Lizzy's hair was flying around her head as she danced faster and faster. Since he had been going with her he had been having a great time. No one would think her mother was an Old Bill. Lizzy wanted to try everything and she did it in style.

Joanie also watched her. Joanie was cold and fed up. She glanced at her watch and sighed. She was supposed to be sleeping at Lizzy's house tonight and Lizzy was supposed to be staying over at hers. That meant they had to stay out all night whether she liked it or not. Lately Lizzy was getting on her nerves. All she was interested in was getting out and getting laid.

A black boy with extensions on his hair walked over to her and asked her to dance. Joanie bucked up. Maybe tonight wouldn't be such a cop-out after all . . .

Lizzy went over to Joey and put her hand on his arm.

'Enjoying yourself, Liz?'

'Oh, it's great. Really great. Look at the lights!'

To Lizzy, with her heightened awareness, the lights were a swimming halo of blues and red.

'How about we go to my car for a while?'

Lizzy giggled. 'OK.'

She was so far gone that Joey had to help her walk across the field to where he had parked. As they made their way through the throng of people, boys and girls laughed and joked with them. One boy, dressed like a refugee from Woodstock, was spinning around in circles. His hair was braided with flowers and he smoked a large joint. Lizzy and Joey laughed at him. The further they got from the rave the more bodies they had to step over. Some were making out; others were just tripping out of their skulls, lost in their own world.

Joey opened the Sierra and they both got in the back. He kissed her hard, pushing his tongue down her throat.

'Happy New Year, Lizzy.'

She looked up, trying to focus on his brown eyes.

'Happy New Year, Joey.' He slipped his hand up her top and she giggled.

'One moment, please, I've got a New Year's present for you.'

'What's that?' Joey was smiling in the darkness.

Then he felt his trousers being undone and her dark head slipped down on to his lap.

'Oh, Lizzy. Happy New Year.'

She was wild all right, and he loved it.

George decided to bury the girl's body in the gravel. Let them look for this one. Let the police earn their bloody money for once. He covered her over and ran the torch around the dirt, checking that he had not left any incriminating clues. Then he walked backwards, scraping the gravel with the side of his boot. He was certainly not going to do their job for them. Oh, no.

He scrambled up the side of the quarry to his car. The heavy thump of acid house music was everywhere. George frowned as he put his mask neatly in the brown carrier bag before driving home.

The youngsters today were like animals. What sort of parents would allow their daughter out until this time of night? There was no decency in the world any more. The family was a thing of the past. In this self-righteous mood he drove home.

Well, he would make them all sit up and take notice. 1990 was going to be his year. He would make all the parents and husbands in Grantley frightened. Then they might take a bit more care instead of allowing young girls to roam the streets like common prostitutes!

A man had to be in charge. It was a man's duty. And George Markham had never shirked his duty.

He was back home, showered, changed and in bed by eleven forty-five. Elaine tripped in at four thirty and George was well and truly asleep. She felt a moment's remorse as she looked down at his sleeping face. Then she thought of Hector and smiled. Hector Henderson. She said the name to herself a few times, enjoying the feeling it created. A good strong name. Hector Henderson. He had given her his phone number!

She giggled into her pillow, clenching her fists in excitement. She would ring him in the week.

Finally, Elaine slept.

Chapter Eleven

'How long has she been missing?'

'Since last night. Her mother's going out of her mind with worry, and I can't say I blame her, can you? They've tried all her friends. Her father had dropped her off at her best friend's house . . .'

Kate listened attentively to Amanda Dawkins.

'And she's never stayed out before? Has she got a boyfriend?'

'No to both questions, Kate. The girl seems to be the perfect daughter. Always rang if she was going to be late, always let them know exactly where she was. I get the impression from this friend, Samantha Jewson, that Louise was looked down on because of it. I think this Samantha fancies herself as a bit of a girl, know what I mean?'

'Well, we'll get the cars to keep an eye out for her, but I have an awful feeling in my gut that she is not coming home. Not alive, anyway.

'Listen, let the papers know about it, ask if any of the readers can remember seeing her. After she was at Samantha Jewson's house, she seems to have disappeared. Someone must have seen her. What's happening with the door-to-door? Anything suspicious in that department?'

'Not really, there are eighty uniforms on the job. Each has been allocated a certain number of streets, but like everything else it takes time. We had a couple of suspicious characters but their alibis are watertight. Oh, before I forget, we've received all the names of sex pests, perverts and fully fledged rapists. We're trying to locate each and every one of them. Most of the uniforms and CID from all over the county are offering to work in their spare time.'

'We could do with them as well. Right then, I think the best thing we can do now is try and calm Louise Butler's parents. If she was at a rave, how come we haven't had anything from the patrol cars about it?'

Amanda breathed out heavily.

'There were no patrol cars there.'

Kate looked aghast.

'You're joking! On the news this morning it said that over eight hundred kids turned up!'

'I know. There's more than one red face in the mobile division this morning, believe me. The old man was like a raving lunatic, apparently.'

'And can you blame him? Jesus wept! If we're not careful we'll have the heavy mob down here offering to hold our hands!

'Well, I'd better get in to see Ratchette. Do me a favour would you? Find me a decent cup of coffee.'

Amanda nodded.

Kate made her way to the Superintendent's office, her mind whirling. No mobile units at a rave? It was bloody laughable. The barn where it was held was owned by a local farmer, John Ellis, and if Kate knew anything about it, he had known exactly what was going on. He would sell his own mother for a profit. She knocked on Ratchette's door.

'Hello, sir.'

'Ah, Kate. Bad business this. What do you think?'

'In all honesty, sir, I don't think Louise Butler's coming home. It's just a case of looking for the body really. Once we ascertain her movements, we'll know more. Someone somewhere must have seen her.'

'True. Now listen carefully. I've had the big boys on to me today. They're sending a Chief Inspector over to work with you. I must stress that it's to work *with* you, OK? He's a good man, you've probably heard of him. Caitlin.'

Kate groaned. Oh, please, not Kenneth Caitlin!

Ratchette saw her face and snapped at her: 'Look, Kate, whether you like it or not, the man's coming. You are a Detective Inspector, I am a Superintendent. You take your orders from me and I take mine from the Chief Constable. Just try and work with him. Whatever his reputation, he gets results.'

Kate looked at the floor. Her heart had sunk down into her shoes.

'All right?' Ratchette's voice was still hard.

'Yes, sir.'

'Good. Now before he arrives, have you any thoughts on this that you want to talk to me about?'

'Actually, yes. In 1984 at Enderby in Leicester two young girls were raped and murdered. There was nothing to go on at all. The police took blood samples from just about every male in the vicinity. The only thing we've got here is the DNA of the murderer. I think, if nothing else, we should try and eliminate as many men as possible by DNA testing in the area.'

Ratchette's wrinkled face was incredulous.

'You're joking. Do you know how much that would cost?'

'A little over half a million pounds. I know it will be

expensive, but for Christ's sake we're dealing with a maniac.'

'You realise that some men won't allow us to take their blood?'

'Then they will immediately be under suspicion.'

Ratchette shook his head.

'I don't know, Kate. This is something I shall have to discuss with the Chief Constable. It's already going out on this month's *Crimewatch*. Hopefully someone will have their memory jogged. The man isn't invisible, he must have been seen.'

'Well, up till now, sir, he's done a pretty good job of eluding us.'

'Leave it with me. Caitlin will be here in about an hour. Make him welcome, won't you?'

The fact that the Superintendent could not look her in the eye was not lost on Kate.

'Of course, sir. Now if there's nothing else?'

When he didn't answer, she rose from her seat and walked from the room, giving the door a satisfying slam as she closed it. Bloody Caitlin! Bloody hell!

Elaine had a hangover and the shrill ringing of the telephone made her head ache even more. She heard George pick it up.

They did not get many phone calls and any other time she would have rushed out into the hall to see who it was. Today though she just wanted to curl up and die. Her mouth felt as dry as a bone and her eyes were closed against the intrusive light. She wished George would hurry up with her cup of tea.

'Hello?' His voice was quiet. Who could be ringing them? The only people to phone were Joseph and Lily, and now and again a friend of Elaine's from work.

'Hello? Mr Markham?' The voice was rough and coarse.

'Speaking.' George was bewildered.

'This is Anthony Jones from Sexplosion in Soho. You asked me to give you a ring like.'

George felt his heart begin to beat a tattoo against his ribs. He dropped his voice.

'I said I would ring you. How did you get my number?'

He heard the man laugh.

'You paid by Barclaycard, remember? I got your address from your driving licence – you gave it as further proof of your identity. I got your number from inquiries like. Listen, mate, I wouldn't drop you in it. If your wife had answered I would have given her a load of old cods. Said I was selling double glazing or something. So calm down, for Gawd's sake.'

'What do you want?'

'What do you think? I've got some new films in and they are *hot*.'

Despite his fear, George felt a tiny shiver of excitement.

'These are from Thailand, and you know what those chinky birds are like, don't ya?' The man chuckled and the action caused him to start coughing. George held the phone away from his ear as the man's phlegmy voice carried on: 'This new film makes the last one I sold you look like Noddy and Big Ears in Toytown!'

'How much?'

'Three hundred smackers.'

The man was aware that George was a bit too quiet at the other end of the phone and hurried on, 'But to you, two-fifty, being as how you're a regular customer like.'

'Well . . .'

'They won't last long, mate, these type never do.'

George was in a quandary. He wanted the film desperately, but he had already had to hide one Barclaycard statement. He racked his brains.

'Look, mate, if it's too much . . .' The other man's voice was placating and wistful. Suddenly George was frightened that the man would think him mean.

'I'll take it!'

'When can you get in?'

'First thing tomorrow.'

'See you then.'

The phone went dead. George replaced the receiver and went back to the kitchen. He reboiled the kettle for Elaine's tea.

The phone call had frightened him. George felt exposed. He poured the water into the teapot. He would get the film. He would draw the money out of the bank this time. Elaine might notice it was gone but then again she might not. He would cross that bridge when he came to it. Chinese women . . . He liked Chinese women. They knew their place all right.

'GEORGE!' He winced as Elaine's voice drilled through him.

'Who was that on the phone?'

George poured out her tea and took it in to her.

'Just a friend from work. Peter Renshaw. He wished you all the best, dear.'

Elaine took the tea.

'Oh. Do I know him then?'

'I don't think so, dear. But I often chat about you to him. Would you like a biscuit with your tea?'

'I'd love one, but with my diet and that . . .' She grinned at him, a girlish look on her face.

George grinned back. If she was waiting for him to say that she didn't need to diet she had a long wait.

Elaine felt the grin slip from her face. Her head was still pounding. She sipped her tea.

Imagine old George getting a phone call from a friend. Wonders would never cease.

*

Patrick Kelly was in his main offices in Barking. Normally on New Year's Day he would be at home with Mandy. Mrs Manners would cook a large early dinner and they would sit and chat about the coming year. Now all he had to look forward to was burying her. And in a funny sort of way he *was* looking forward to that. At least then he would know that she was not lying on ice in a bloody mortuary. He lit himself a cigarette with his gold lighter. He grasped it tightly in his hand. On the front of it was the inscription: *To Dad, Love Mandy – xxxx*. It was all he had of her now.

A sharp knock at the door brought him back to earth.

'Come in.'

Two large men entered. They were brothers, Marcus and David Tully. There was only ten months between them and they looked like twins. Both had skinhead haircuts and both wore identical grey tracksuits that hugged their large beer bellies. Both wore large chunky gold jewellery. Marcus, the elder, was the first to speak.

'So where to, guv?'

'I want you two to make your way up North, to Huddersfield. There's a brand new Jag and a few bits of plant up there that need to be repossessed as quickly as possible. Take shooters with you, I think you'll need them. The bloke don't want to give them back, that's how come we got involved. There's good bunce for you both as soon as the stuff's delivered back here. OK?'

The two men nodded.

'You'll need to take a couple of drivers with you. Take young Sonny and Declan, they're pretty good, and that new bloke ... What's his name? Dodson. Here's the address, and I'll see you sometime tomorrow with the stuff.'

'What's the plant then?'

221

'Two large earthmovers. The details are outside on the duty rosta. Select numbering, the works. The Jag has got private plates on it.'

'Okey doke, guv. See yer tomorrer then.'

'Try not to use the guns this time. Just frighten the bloke.'

'We'll only use them to wound, guv. We know what we're doing.'

'Be careful, that's all I ask. Now get on your way.'

The two men left the office. Patrick shook his head. They were two of the biggest lunatics he had ever met, and he had met a few in his time. Still, they got the difficult jobs done and that was the main thing.

He pressed the button on his intercom.

'Bring me in a cuppa, Debbie, will you?'

'All right, Mr Kelly.'

He carried on working until Debbie brought him in a cup of tea. She smiled at him, placing the cup on his desk in such a way that he got a glimpse of a fairly considerable pair of breasts.

'Thanks, love.'

'Anything else?' It was a loaded question and Kelly knew it.

No, thank you.' He smiled at her crestfallen countenance. Before he had met Kate Burrows, she had been on his list of 'things to do'. He had put her down as Tiffany's successor. Now he just wished she would leave him alone.

'Off you go then, Debbie.'

She stamped from the room. Physically she had a lot more to offer than Kate, but for some unknown reason he really fancied the policewoman. There was something about her. When he was with her, buried inside her, Mandy, Renée and everything else was gone from his mind.

For that he was supremely thankful.

*

Kate heard Caitlin before she saw him. Since the news had spread about him working on the case, the whole of the station had been in a state of excitement. She groaned inwardly. He was like something from a *Boy's Own* comic. A real macho man. She stayed seated until the excitement wore off. Caitlin's loud Irish accent boomed over everyone's heads.

'Sure Jesus, would you let a man get some air here!'

Everyone was greeting him. He was a living legend. Poor old Fabian and Spilsbury weren't even in the running where Caitlin was concerned. He made Sherlock Holmes look amateurish! Kate saw his bulky form moving towards her desk. She had worked with him once before, when she had been a Detective Sergeant. After she had been introduced to him he had sent her to get him a cup of coffee, but not before patting her behind. He had solved the case with a male DS and a DC. Or that was how it had looked on the final report. Kate fixed a smile on her face.

'Katie! How are you?' His voice sounded genuinely pleased to see her. She stood up and held out her hand.

'Chief Inspector Caitlin.'

He looked old. Kate was shocked. The man looked positively ancient. His head was nearly bald, his full mouth had that loose-lipped look peculiar to ageing men, and his startling green eyes were now watery-looking. The lids were wrinkled above them like old venetian blinds.

'You don't look a day older than the last time I worked with you.' The Irish burr was more pronounced than she remembered. 'I've been hearing great things about you, great things.'

Kate smiled.

Caitlin pulled up a chair and sat down opposite her.

'As we'll be working together, I thought we could share a desk. Make it more personal.'

Kate felt the smile freeze on her face. The smell of Teacher's and cheap cigars wafted across the confined space and she cringed inwardly.

Caitlin settled himself in the chair.

'Now what's this I hear about this madman driving an Irish Ford?'

Kate's heavy brows knitted together.

'I'm sorry? An Irish Ford?'

'An O'Ryan . . . Orion.'

Kate burst out laughing, causing many pairs of eyes to focus on her. Caitlin laughed with her. He leant across the desk in a confidential manner, scanning the room shrewdly. He tapped his nose.

'You can call me Kenny.' He nodded at her and Kate realised with growing dismay that the man was drunk. She forced the smile back on to her face.

'Whatever you say. Now shall I fill you in on all that I have?'

Caitlin leaned back in his chair. Opening his coat, he took out his handkerchief and blew his nose loudly.

'You do that, Katie. The sooner this bastard's caught the better.'

Well, they agreed on that much anyway. Taking a deep breath, Kate started to talk.

Chapter Twelve

2 January

George had left for work at his usual time of eight fifteen. By ten thirty-five he was walking into Sexplosion. Anthony Jones was behind the counter and George smiled at him tremulously. The shopkeeper gave a large toothy grin.

'Hello, cocker! Happy New Year.' He was full of good-humoured camaraderie.

'Happy New Year. Er, I have the necessary.'

'Good, good.' Tony Jones lifted the serving hatch and invited George through to the back of the shop. He looked around him hesitantly before walking through. There were quite a few customers even this early in the morning. Tony Jones shouted to a dark-haired boy of about eighteen.

'Emmanuel, watch the shop, I've got some business to attend to.' In the back of the shop he whispered to George: 'He's as queer as a nine-bob note, but he's a good little worker. Right then, look at this!'

He rubbed his hands together in anticipation and pressed the play button on a video that stood on a small table. On the television screen above it a young Chinese girl appeared. Her face was a mask of fear.

'Sit yourself down, mate, I'll make us a cuppa.' George sat down and watched the flickering images in front of him. In the dirty little office, he felt the first stirrings of excitement.

An hour later he left with the film tucked firmly under his arm, and a phone number and address in his pocket. He got into his car and began to drive aimlessly around London. It was a dark overcast day; the people milling around all looked grey. Grey and dirty.

George found himself in Paddington and smiled. He rooted around in his coat pocket until he found the address that Tony Jones had given him. He parked his car off Warwick Avenue and, locking it up, began his search. He walked along the Harrow Road until he found the small turning he wanted. He walked into Chippenham Road, scanning the house numbers. When he arrived at the right house he checked the number carefully against his piece of paper. He walked to the front door and looked at the array of bells there.

All the bells had little cards above them.

Flat one: Suzie, French model.

Flat two: Sexy Sadie, full correction.

Flat three: Imogen, Swedish masseuse.

Flat four: Carol, schoolgirl temptress.

Flat five: Beatrice, for naughty boys.

He wanted flat six: Sure enough there it was.

Flat six: Tippy – submission my speciality.

George rang the bell.

'Yeah, what?' George was startled. Hardly a submissive voice! He cleared his throat noisily.

'Er . . . Tony sent me. Tony Jones.'

Suddenly the voice changed.

'Oh, I'm so sorry, sir. You caught me offguard there.' George heard a throaty laugh. 'Bit early for me, love, but come up anyway.'

There was a whirring noise and the door clicked. George opened it cautiously. His cheesecutter hat and Burberry overcoat gave him the look of a working class spiv. His hard little grey eyes were moist with anticipation. He had drawn out three hundred pounds earlier. Two hundred and fifty had gone on the video that was now tucked away securely in his car. He still had fifty left. He'd decided to treat himself. If all that Tony Jones said was true, this Tippy was just what he needed.

He wrinkled his nose in distaste at the acrid smell of the place. The narrow hallway was littered with old newspapers and circulars. It was dark and dingy. George pressed the lightswitch on the wall by the stairs and a muted light came from above. He began to mount the uncarpeted stairs. The wallpaper was long gone from the walls, and here and there in places were rust-coloured stains that looked like blood. He began to hurry.

Inside her room, Tippy, real name Bertha Knott, was hurrying around trying to tidy up. The night before had been a hectic one with seven punters. One after the other. It was always the same in the holiday season. She picked up her discarded clothes and threw them into a small bureau, scratched and marked by years of neglect. 'She practically threw the overflowing ashtray and empty vodka bottle into the tiny kitchenette, the cigarette butts flying across the work surface and into the sink. Bollocks! Sod that bloody Tony Jones! Imagine sending her a punter at this time of day. No brass worth her salt was even up before twelve thirty!

She heard the timid knock on her door and sighed. She hoped this bloke wasn't too rough. She was sore as it was.

She pulled the grubby negligee around her bony body and opened the door, a wide professional smile on her face.

George looked at the woman, dismayed. She was absolutely horrible. She had dyed black hair that looked like cotton wool dipped in liquid boot polish, her face was thin and feral-looking, and through the flimsy see-through negligee George could see that under her arms was enough hair to make a pair of identical wigs.

'Come in then, cocker.' Her voice was jovial. 'Would you like a cuppa or a drink?' George walked into the room. He watched the woman's scrawny buttocks disappear behind a curtain and looked around him, heartsore. The room was filthy, the large double bed taking up most of the space. It had black sheets on it, and George was not sure if that was their original colour or just the result of years of use. The cord carpet on the floor was covered in cigarette burns. Around the iron fireplace there were hundreds of them. Obviously the men who had used this room over the years had tried to flick their cigarettes into the hearth from the bed, and the majority had missed. One large overstuffed chair stood under the window covered in items of apparel: stockings, suspenders and other types of underwear.

Tippy came back with two relatively clean glasses full of vodka and tonic. George took his for want of something else to do. Tippy placed hers on the old bureau. Picking up the underwear from the chair, she dumped it on the floor.

'You have a sit down, luv, and I'll go and get myself ready. Sorry about the mess but you caught me on the hop like. I'll only be ten minutes. She disappeared through a door that George had not noticed before and called over her shoulder, 'Take your coat off and get comfy.'

He stood with the drink in his hand, deciding whether

or not to make a run for it. Elaine's houseproud ways got on his nerves but he would rather them than this dirty cat's way of living. He walked to the chair and looked through the grubby net curtain. The street below was busy. George watched the people rushing about their business and just for a second he wondered what he was doing here. It was a disappointment. George did not class his pastimes as dirty in any sense. He had never thought that prostitutes and squalor went hand in hand. He had always imagined them as they were depicted in the media – beautiful young girls who loved their job and lived like queens. Reality was different and George did not like reality.

He had just turned from the window, intent on leaving, when the woman walked back into the room. She looked completely different! She saw George's mouth drop open and smiled. She had her hair in two pigtails. Her eyes were made up with heavy black eyeliner, her mouth was a deep red rosebud. She had discarded the dirty wrapper she had been wearing and had on long silky black stockings and suspenders, a black peephole bra and crutchless panties. An overpowering smell of Freesia perfume hung around her like a cloud. She grinned at George.

'Now this is more like it, isn't it?' Her voice had taken on a husky, girlish tone and he was gratified. All his earlier thoughts flew from his head. She looked like the women of his younger days who had adorned the packs of nude playing cards. Who had gazed up at him from his adolescent girlie mags. In short, she looked like a whore.

Her high-heeled shoes showed off her long thin legs to advantage. Her breasts were tiny and pert, the pink aureoles just hardening in the cold air of the room.

'You haven't taken off your coat. Shall Tippy take it off

229

for you?' She slipped it from his shoulders, folding it up and placing it carefully on the chair. George faced her, his eyes shining once more.

Tippy pouted.

'Tippy wants her money first. Twenty quid for the works, anal sex is an extra tenner.'

George nodded, and handed over the notes.

'Good. Well, I'm ready when you are, lover boy.'

She watched George pulling off his clothes and grinned again. They were all the same. Stupid buggers. She gritted her teeth. Oh, please, let him be a quick finisher. She wasn't in the mood for a long day's screwing.

She lay down on the dirty bed. Even through her perfume she could still detect the sour smell of the sheets. As George loomed over her, she was planning in her mind when to take the sheets to the launderette, and whether or not to pay for a service wash. She hoped he noticed the Durex she had strategically placed in the top of one of her stockings. He looked greener than the proverbial grass to her. Maybe she should have told him fifty quid. He looked as if he could afford it.

Well, she consoled herself, his type normally came back, and she liked that. If she got another regular customer it would keep her off the streets for a bit. King's Cross was not what it had been in her day. What with the runaways and the young druggies . . .

Tippy felt George bite her nipple painfully and suppressed a cry.

Another bloody nasty bastard. She sighed heavily. Here I go again. She pulled herself up on the bed and, kneeling in such a way that George could see her breasts to their best advantage, took his phallus into her mouth.

After a couple of minutes an idea occurred to her. She lifted her head and looked into the man's face.

'For another tenner, you can tie me up if you like.'

She got off the bed and, opening the bureau, took out a set of handcuffs and some leather-look rope.

George nodded and Tippy brought them to the bed and handed them to him.

As George tied her up she thought: Oh, well, in for a penny.

Even Tippy was amazed when she heard George actually humming while he worked. Finally, with the prostitute spreadeagled on the bed, her arms and legs stretched wide, he was happy.

This was submission. She would not fight him, she would just lie there and accept whatever he did.

Getting off the bed, he went to his coat. He took his white cotton gloves from the pocket and slipped them on. Tippy watched him, half bored already. But when she saw what he was taking out of the inside pocket of the overcoat, she felt faint with fright. It was a large knife in a leather holder. As he pulled it slowly free it caught the weak January sunshine and Tippy strained against the bonds that held her.

''Ere, what you doing with that?'

George walked to the bed and smiled. 'Don't worry, I won't hurt you, my dear.'

Kneeling over her lower body, his belly hanging on to her knees, he began gently to cut off her panties.

Tippy was breathing heavily, her face white under the black eyeliner and heavy foundation.

Her mind was reeling. The bloke was a fucking nutter and she had let him tie her up!

'Look, you're not gonna hurt me, are you? Promise.'

'I promise. Now shut up!'

George's voice had taken on a harsh inflection. Tippy shut up.

Suddenly, the mild-mannered little man didn't look green any more – he looked positively dangerous. Especially with that smile of his, that smile that just showed his teeth. Tippy closed her eyes tightly.

Just wait until she saw that Tony Jones. The ponce! Sending her a candidate for Broadmoor. Tippy lay back and prepared herself for the worst afternoon of her life.

'So, sir, what do you think?'

Kenneth Caitlin lit himself a cigar, blowing the smoke out in huge puffs that swirled around his bald head.

'From what I can see, Katie, this man is either very careful or has been very lucky. Very lucky indeed. There's nothing at the scenes of the crimes. Nothing on the bodies, except of course as you pointed out his genetic fingerprint. There is absolutely nothing else to go on at all.' He grinned at her. 'This is just up my street, by Christ. I'll find the bastard though.' He poked his finger at her. 'You just watch.'

Kate's voice was sarcastic. 'So what do you suggest we do now?'

'Well, the uniforms are out in force looking for the Butler girl. I think she's dead though. This man has never hidden the bodies before, has he? So obviously if he's hidden this one, he's playing a whole new ball game. But I'll tell you something now, Katie. They all bugger themselves up in the end. Look at the Yorkshire Ripper.'

Kate was annoyed. Caitlin was getting on her nerves.

'The Yorkshire Ripper killed thirteen women, sir, and was finally caught during a routine inquiry. Otherwise there's no knowing just how many more he would have killed. What we have here is a chancer. The psychological profile is of a man who hates women, that much we already know. A man who has a job that could possibly have brought him into contact with the victims, though I don't think so myself. If the women knew him, there would be someone else who knows him as well in the same capacity. The psychologist also says he's likely to be married. That narrows the field down a bit, if it's correct. He also has a knowledge of the area so is obviously a local man. Other than the dark-coloured car seen at the scene of the second murder, and a dark green car seen at the first, we have nothing whatsoever to go on.'

Caitlin watched her. Women were always so emotional. They took their cases personally.

'Well, I'm appearing on Crimewatch this week. Maybe something will come of that. Someone who's not from the area could have been driving through and seen something.'

'Yeah, and pigs might fly.' Kate's voice was bitter.

Caitlin took another puff on his cigar.

'Pigs can fly already, or so the druggies think when they see the police helicopters.'

Kate closed her eyes. The man thought everything was a big joke. She stood and picked up her jacket from the back of her chair.

'Where you off to?'

'I'm going to see how the search is going on.'

'Leave that to the uniforms, they'll let us know soon enough if they find something. It's bitter cold out.'

As Kate opened her mouth to answer, the phone on her desk rang. She picked it up.

'I'll be straight down.'

Caitlin heard the excitement in her voice.

'Who was that?'

'I think we may have a breakthrough. Come on.'

*

233

Geoffrey Winbush walked hesitantly into Grantley Police Station. The desk sergeant smiled at him.

'What can I do for you, son?'

'It's about the disappearance of Louise Butler. I think I may be able to help like. I think I saw her.'

The desk sergeant was all business now. Opening the security door, he led the boy through to an interview room.

'What's your name and address, son?'

'Geoffrey Winbush, 122 Tenerby Road.'

The sergeant wrote it all down.

'Well, sit yourself down. There'll be someone to see you in a minute.'

Leaving the boy sitting at the table, he went back to his desk and phoned up to Kate. Sergeant Mathers hoped that the boy could shed some light on the case.

Kate walked into the interview room followed by Caitlin. Her first thought was that the witness was a good-looking boy. He was blond with deep-set brown eyes which looked troubled at this moment, and he was well dressed. He looked about twenty. His shoulders were wide and even though he was sitting, Kate saw he was a large boy. She smiled at him.

'I'm Detective Inspector Burrows and this is Chief Inspector Caitlin. I understand you have some information about Louise Butler?'

Kate sat opposite him and Caitlin leant against the wall of the room, his cigar smouldering in his mouth.

The boy looked at them nervously.

'Well, I didn't know her personally but the other night like, I think it was her that we seen on the Woodham Road.'

'We?' This from Caitlin.

The boy nodded.

'Yeah, me and me mates. We was going to the rave –

me, me brother Ricky, and three others: Tommy Rigby, Dean Chalmers and Mick Thomas.'

He swallowed heavily and Kate felt sorry for him.

'Go on.'

'Well, as we was driving along, we saw this bird, walking by the roadside. She was on her own like. Anyway, I stopped and offered her a lift. But she wouldn't get in. I'm sure it was her though.'

'Why wouldn't she get in? Did she say she was waiting for someone? Did she mention what she was doing on that road on her own?'

'No, nothing. Mick Thomas was pissed out of his head. He slagged her off.' His voice broke. 'We all did. We left her there, on that road. We left her there to die. We drove on to the rave and left her walking, thumbing a lift.'

'Thumbing a lift? Was she definitely thumbing a lift?'

The boy nodded.

Caitlin's voice made him jump as he bellowed across the room: 'You left a young girl to walk along a dark road at night? You slagged her off, as you put it, and left her there? Have you any sisters, young man?'

'Yes, sir, two.'

Caitlin had the cigar clamped between his teeth. He removed it before saying venomously, 'Well, I hope if they're ever in Louise Butler's position, they're treated better than you treated that girl. Now then, names and addressess of the other boys. Pronoto. I can't be bothered to waste me breath on yer.'

Kate closed her eyes. Caitlin was right, of course. The boys should never have left her there. But by the same token, the girl should have had more sense than to walk along a road like that in the dark. But that bloody Caitlin, he had to throw his weight around. He had to make himself heard.

And the worst of it all was, Kate was the one who had to listen to the old sod!

She smiled at the white-faced boy.

'Shall I get us some coffee and then you can make your statement?'

'Please.' He began to cry. 'We never thought that she'd be murdered. We'd had a drink . . .'

'So you were drunk-driving on top of everything else? And how the thunder do you know she was murdered? We have no body that I know of.'

The boy looked at Kate beseechingly. She got up from her seat and manhandled Caitlin from the room. Outside she whispered, 'Don't you think he feels bad enough without you on his back?'

Caitlin shrugged his shoulders and buttoned up his wrinkled suit jacket. He blew cigar smoke in her face.

'No, actually, Katie . . . I don't. I think he's an arsehole.'

With that, he went back inside the interview room and she clenched her fists.

If he called her Katie once more she would be getting arrested herself. For grievous bodily harm.

She went to organise the coffee.

Kate pulled into her drive. She was tired. Winbush hadn't really been any help. Caitlin had put the fear of Christ up him and, consequently, he had been loath to say too much. Kate had arranged to go to his house and see him herself. The trouble with Caitlin was he still behaved as if it was the old days, when everyone wanted to help out the police. He should come back down to earth with everyone else. Since the West Midlands business and now all this about false evidence everywhere you looked, the police popularity poll was down to minus two.

She let herself into her house. The smell of meat assailed her nostrils and she followed the smell into the kitchen. Her mother was turning lamb chops under the grill.

'Hello, Kate, get yourself seated and I'll make you a coffee.'

Dan got up from the breakfast bar. 'I'll do it, Eve, would you like one?'

Evelyn shook her head.

'Oh, by the way, Katie, you had a call. Said his name was Pat and could you call him back.'

Kate felt her heart freeze in her chest. She could feel Dan's eyes boring into her face.

'Thanks, Mum.' She lit a cigarette for something to do. Patrick calling here. She felt herself go hot all over.

'So who's this Pat then?' Kate detected a hint of jealousy in Dan's voice.

'None of your business, Dan, actually.' He stared at her and Kate dropped her eyes. 'He's a friend of mine if you must know.'

'I see. Where did you meet him then?'

Evelyn watched the two of them with a little smile on her face. Dan's questions were annoying Kate and if he wasn't careful he just might end up on the receiving end of her tongue. She placed the chops under the grill once more and the only sound in the kitchen was the lamb fat spitting.

'I said, where did you meet him?' Dan's voice rose.

Kate put down her coffee cup and looked at her exhusband.

'What the bloody hell has that got to do with you?'

'It's got a lot to do with me. My daughter . . .'

'Oh of course, your daughter. Well it's a pity you didn't think of your daughter when you were whoring your way around the world, isn't it? The poor little mare wasn't even in the running then was she? WAS SHE?'

Dan stared at Kate in bewilderment. He realised that he'd opened up a can of worms.

'All I'm saying is, Kate . . .'

'You know your trouble, Dan? You don't know when you're well off. I don't like to remind you of this, but if it wasn't for me, you'd be in a bedsit somewhere now, living off the DHSS. I allow you to stay in my home because of Lizzy, but I warn you now, Dan, if you try and interfere in my life, I'll have you out the front door so fast you'll burn a hole in the carpet. Do I make myself clear?'

Dan's face was scarlet and for a fleeting second Kate felt ashamed of herself.

'Perfectly.'

He went from the kitchen quietly.

Kate let her breath out and put her head in her hands.

'He asked for that, Katie. Don't you go feeling bad now.'

'Oh Mum. I shouldn't have said it. I shouldn't have said any of it. But he annoys me so much.'

'Let me get you another coffee. Who is this Pat, by the way, or am I going to get my head bitten off as well?'

'He's a man I met during the course of my work.'

'Is that the one you spent the New Year with?'

Kate looked at her mother sharply and seeing the mischievous look on her face she grinned.

'It is actually.'

Evelyn held out her arms wide. 'You're a grown woman, Kate, you do whatever you want. Personally I think it's about time you had a bit of life.'

Kate smiled. She felt it was about time too, but Patrick Kelly was dangerous for her. For her career. He was a danger to everything, but knowing that, admitting it to herself did no good. She wanted him desperately. He gave her so much pleasure when she was with him and she had been lonely for so long. So very, very long. After the New Year, she could no more give him up now than she could cut off her own hands.

She had only been mad at Dan, because he had brought up Patrick's name when she wanted him to be a secret.

But it wouldn't be a secret for long.

She lit another cigarette. What would she do when the secret was out?

She would cross that bridge when she came to it. Everything people said about Kelly was supposition, nothing against him had ever been proved and in this country you were innocent until proven guilty. The thought had a hollow ring to it.

Kate felt she was tumbling headlong into something that she was not strong enough to fight.

But fight it she would.

If the time came.

Chapter Thirteen

Sexplosion was just getting busy when Tony Jones saw Tippy walk through the door. He smiled at her.

'Bloody hell, girl, you don't half look rough.'

Tippy's face was drawn and white.

'I want to talk to you Tony, *now*!'

He was puzzled. 'All right, girl, come through to my office.'

He looked around the shop for Emmanuel, who was trying to pick up an elderly man in a smart business suit.

'Emmanuel, get behind this bloody counter now! Come through, Tippy love.' He opened the serving hatch and she limped through.

In the dingy back room, the Tom sat down on the ramshackle chair. Tony watched her warily. There was something wrong here. He hoped she didn't have AIDS or something. She did look ill, and Tippy looked rough at the best of times. All the birds who worked the submission trade did.

'Got any booze, Tone?'

He opened a small cupboard in an old sideboard and took out of a bottle of Gordon's gin.

'I ain't got nothing to go with it. Will you drink it straight?'

Tippy nodded. 'I'd drink of a cup of cold piss at this moment in time, Tony, if it blotted out the world. I've never felt so bad in all my life.'

Tony poured her out a generous measure into a half pint glass. 'Here you are, girl, get your laughing gear around that.'

Tippy took a long drink. Tony noticed that her hands were shaking. He bit his bottom lip in consternation.

'Look, I ain't being funny, love, but I ain't got all day.'

She looked at him with hooded eyes.

'That punter you sent me yesterday . . . he was weird, Tone, really weird.'

Tony relaxed. Was that all?

'They're all weird, girl . . .'

She interrupted him.

'No, not normal weird. He was a nutter, Tony. A bloody nutter.'

Tony pictured mild-mannered George. He liked a bit of old bluey, and admittedly they were a bit near the mark, but that aside he seemed a nice, quiet, polite man.

'You're just feeling low, Tippy. All brasses feel like that at holiday times . . .'

She laughed scornfully.

'Listen, Tone, I've been on the game for eighteen years, woman and girl, and I've had some strange ones in my time, but never anyone like this. Look . . .'

She stood up and lifted her skirt. She heard Tony's intake of breath.

'Stone me, Tip, he done that?'

She nodded, big tears welling in her eyes. 'They're all over me. On me tits, arse, the lot.'

Tony stared at the criss-cross cuts all over Tippy's

thighs. Some were superficial and some looked deep. All were scabbed over. Purple and black bruises abounded.

'I've been pissing blood all night, Tony. He shoved something up inside me.' Her voice broke. 'He tied me up and he had a knife. He kept holding it at me throat and threatening me . . .'

She began to cry in earnest and Tony, for the first time in his life, felt emotion for a working girl. He took her in his arms and cuddled her.

'All right, Tippy. Calm down, love.'

'How am I gonna work while I'm like this, Tone? I'll be out of action for weeks. And supposing he comes back? He knows where I live, he knows I won't go to the Old Bill.' Her face was grimy with tears and Tony set her gently on the chair.

'Listen, Tippy, I'll give you enough to tide you over. And I'll have a talk with the bloke, all right? Make sure he leaves you alone in future. OK?'

'Promise.'

'I promise. Now how about I take you to a doctor I know in Swiss Cottage. Payment on the nose and no questions asked. How's that?'

Tippy nodded, wiping her streaming face with her hands.

'I'll just go and tell Emmanuel to mind the shop and we'll be on our way.'

Tony Jones walked from the room. Who would have thought it? A polite little bloke like that with a tiger in his tank? Tony shook his head in wonderment. He'd have to sort George out in a delicate way. He didn't want to lose a regular customer. He'd just warn him off Tippy by saying she'd got herself a big coon for a boyfriend. There was nothing like a big coon or a dose of clap to get rid of a punter.

He shook his head again. Poor old Tippy. She'd be scarred for life.

Terry Miller picked up the *Grantley Times*. He had just made himself a cup of coffee and sat in his mum's kitchen smoking a cigarette. There were six Miller children, ranging in age from nineteen to seven. Terry was eighteen and his brother Charlie nineteen. To sit in relative peace and quiet in the Miller house was a very rare occurrence and Terry was enjoying it. That was until he saw what was on the front page.

It was a picture of Louise Butler and Terry recognised her at once as the girl who had run out in front of his car on the night of the rave. The girl who was being chased by the bloke in the weird headgear. He had had to swerve to avoid them. He read the article and frowned. They believed she had been murdered by the Grantley Ripper although as yet no body had turned up. He ran his hands through his hair. Should he go to the police?

If he went to them he would have to admit that he left her there. That he was high as a kite on Ecstasy and had thought they were larking about!

He screwed up the paper and threw it on the kitchen table.

He knew what he would do. He would talk it over with Charlie when he got in from work.

Terry relaxed a bit now that he had made a decision. Charlie would know what to do. He always did.

The search for Louise Butler had been going on for over two days. Police had covered every piece of waste ground, undergrowth, field, wood. Even the quarry.

Nothing.

Kate Burrows and Kenneth Caitlin were getting worried. If something didn't break, and soon, they would be back to square one. Frogmen had dragged the local river. Every shed and garage and outbuilding had been searched. Louise Butler had disappeared off the face of the earth.

Every sex pest and rapist had been interviewed and their whereabouts checked out.

Still nothing.

The Grantley Ripper looked set for a long reign of terror.

Kate sat in her office staring at the files in front of her. She rubbed her eyes with her finger and thumb of her right hand. She was bone tired. Caitlin was off at the BBC studios, he was appearing on Crimewatch later in the evening. He had walked in and taken over and the marvel man had come up with nothing. Kate looked around her at the busy incident room.

Phones were ringing, computer screens were displaying information, and still there was nothing to go on. She thought again of the Leicester murders. If they could get even some of the men in Grantley to take the blood test they would be halfway home. Because if only three thousand of the potential five thousand male suspects took the test, that was three thousand they could eliminate. There was also the chance that the man himself would go for the test. If they sent haematologists around local firms and offices then men would be honour bound to take the blood test when they saw their colleagues taking it. A subtle form of coercion.

But no one in authority would even countenance the idea. Money. It all came down to bloody money.

Kate chewed on her bottom lip. There must be something she had missed.

Even Geoffrey Winbush's statement only told them that Louise had been on the Woodham Road. Surely someone else must have seen her? She was a good-looking girl, dressed in a purple and gold tracksuit and man's flying jacket. She would not be easy to miss. Eight hundred youngsters had been at that rave. Someone must have noticed her.

Kate stared back at the files in front of her.

The people who owned dark-coloured Orions were still being interviewed. Nothing yet. There were only a few names left on the list from the DVLC. Maybe the man had lived in Grantley at one time and now lived somewhere else? That idea had occurred to her before now, but a gut feeling told her that he was still living locally. And if he was, the best way to catch him was through blood testing. Back to square one.

Her phone rang and she picked it up.

'Hello. DI Kate Burrows here.'

'Hello, Kate.'

She felt her heart miss a beat. It was Patrick Kelly. 'Are we still on for tonight?'

'Oh, yes, of course. I can't promise what time I'll be there, I'll have to ring you as I'm leaving work. We're pretty snowed under . . .'

'Nothing yet then?' His voice was flat.

'No, nothing concrete.'

'I'll see you later then. 'Bye.'

''Bye.' Kate replaced the receiver and smiled. She was getting to like Patrick Kelly. Getting to like him a lot. Yet the sensible part of her was telling her to grow up. She was a policewoman and he was a . . .

He was a what?

He was a nice man, that's what he was, and when she left this station her life was her own!

She picked up the file and began to read again. She was being paid to find this murderer, and find him she would!

Charlie Miller came in from work at six fifteen. The house was, as usual, in pandemonium by then. All the children were in, and their Irish ancestry made loud arguing the norm. Like most children from big families, they had learnt to outshout one another at an early age. Charlie went straight up to the room that he shared with Terry and put on a Fine Young Cannibals tape. He was in the middle of getting underssed as his brother walked in with the paper.

'All right, Tel?'

He shook his head and sat on the bottom of the bunk beds.

'No, actually, I ain't.'

Charlie frowned and stopped in the middle of taking off his shirt. Terry did look bad. He sat beside him.

'What's the matter, bruv? You got aggravation?' His voice was low. Even though there was only a year between the two boys, Charlie looked on Terry as his little brother.

'It's about that bird who went missing . . . Louise Butler. Look.'

He opened the paper and Charlie glanced at it. Terry watched his brother's face.

'It's that bird from the other night! The one with the weird bloke in the mask!'

Terry nodded.

'I reckon we should go to the police. Tell them we saw her.' Charlie shook his head vigorously.

'Not on your bleeding nelly, mate. I ain't going nowhere near them. And neither are you!'

'But, Charlie . . .'

He pulled off his shirt and threw it into the corner of the tiny room.

'No buts, Tel . . . Leave it!'

Terry knew by the sound of his brother's voice that he had to do as he was told. Charlie didn't like people disagreeing with him.

Terry ground his teeth in consternation. The girl was missing. She could still be alive.

Charlie looked at his brother and sighed. Terry was such a soft touch. He pulled off his work jeans and threw them on to the little pile in the corner. He hunkered down and looked into his brother's face.

'Listen, Tel, I'm sorry about that bird and all. It's that Ripper bloke they're all going on about. But for all that, I ain't putting my . . . or your . . . face in the frame. Get it?'

Terry nodded.

'Good. Now don't let me hear any more about it. Besides, we was out of our nuts. What the hell could we tell them that would do any good?'

With that, Charlie picked up his deodorant and shampoo and went to have his bath, leaving Terry sitting on the bed, his mind in a turmoil. Fine Young Cannibals were singing 'Johnny Come Home' and listening to the words made Terry feel like crying. He wished Louise Butler would come back home and be safe, then he could stop thinking about her.

Turning off the tape, he lay on the bottom bunk and crossed his arms under his head.

They had nearly run her over. If the Grantley Ripper had got her, as the papers seemed to think, he wished now that they had. At least her end would have been short and quick.

*

Elaine and George were sitting in their lounge watching *South East at Six* when the story of Louise Butler's disappearance came on the air. As her photograph appeared on the screen, Elaine shook her head.

'Oh, George, isn't it terrible?'

Louise was in her school uniform and looked very young. Quite unlike the girl of the previous Saturday.

'Yes, dear. That's all they've talked about at work, you know.'

'Same with us. Her mother uses my supermarket. How must she be feeling? It must be like a nightmare. This is the third one, isn't it? I was reading in the *Sun* today that the other girl, what's her name, her father is a London gangster!'

'Mandy Kelly.'

'That's it, Mandy Kelly. Imagine you remembering her name like that.'

George felt a tightening around his heart. It was fear.

'Oh, it stuck in my mind, that's all.'

Was Elaine looking at him oddly?

'Would you like a nice cuppa, dear?'

Before she could answer there was a loud banging on the front door.

'Goodness me, who on earth can that be?' Elaine's voice was high. People knocking at the door was a very unusual event in this household. She stood up quickly to answer it.

George remained seated. He was still trying to recover from his earlier slip. He looked even more surprised when Elaine walked into the lounge with two men.

'George, this is Detective Sergeant Willis and PC Hemmings. They want to have a word with you.' Elaine's voice was quavering.

'Can I make you two gentlemen a cup of tea or coffee?'

Willis smiled. 'Tea would be lovely, madam.'

George sat in his seat, stunned.

They knew it was him! They had come for him!

'Please sit down. Would you like fresh tea, George?'

He could feel his head moving up and down of its own accord. He was aware of Elaine leaving the room. His eyes were glued to the two men now sitting on his couch. He could feel his breathing quicken and strove desperately to control it.

'I'm sorry to trouble you, sir, but we are questioning everyone in Grantley with a dark blue saloon car. It's just so we can eliminate people from our inquiries.'

Eliminate. Eliminate. Eliminate. They didn't know. They *didn't* know. George smiled.

Outside the lounge door Elaine relaxed as well. Walking to the kitchen, she filled the electric kettle, her heart hammering in her chest.

George would never do anything like that. What had made her think that he would? She was too hard on him.

It was just the shock of seeing two policemen on her doorstep. It was like the other time. The terrible time. Then a thought occurred to her. Would they bring that up now? All these years later?

She set about making a pot of tea.

George would never do anything like that again. Never. Not in a million years.

In the lounge, Willis and Hemmings were listening to George's account of where he had been on the nights of the murders and the disappearance.

'I was in bed with terrible flu. My wife can vouch for that, officers. May I ask you a question?'

'Certainly.'

'If one of you is a police constable, surely he should be in uniform?'

250

Willis smiled.

'On these kind of cases, sir, we try to be as informal as possible. We recruit uniformed officers into plain clothes so that people like yourself, who are being eliminated, won't feel under pressure. From neighbours etcetera.'

'How very thoughtful of you.'

Elaine came into the room with the tea. Her big-boned body felt clumsy and she placed the tray on the coffee table with a loud clatter.

Willis watched her surreptitiously. She was a bundle of nerves. She began to pour the tea and when she had finally finished and sat down felt as if she had run the London Marathon. She tried to calm herself.

Willis spoke directly to her.

'Now, madam, on the second of December, 1989, which was a Saturday, I understand that your husband was home with you all evening?'

Elaine nodded.

'He very rarely goes out in the evenings.'

'I see. Now on the twenty-third of December, which was a Saturday, he was home with you then, as well?'

'Yes.'

'And on New Year's Eve, you were home together?'

'Yes. No. Actually, he was in bed with very bad flu. I went to a party at my friend's alone. George was much too ill to leave the house.'

Elaine was aware that she was babbling.

Willis and Hemmings were both staring at her. Even her red hair seemed to be trembling.

Willis smiled and closed his notebook.

'That will be all. I am very sorry to bother you, but I'm sure you understand.'

'Of course.' George was more his old self now. He could feel a giggle in his throat, just waiting to explode.

They were fools. Utter fools. He swallowed hard. The giggle was nearly at the roof of his mouth.

'Would you gentlemen like another cup of tea?'

Hemmings was about to say yes when Willis declined. George smiled at the younger man. Hemmings smiled back. Elaine watched them. Was it her imagination or was George laughing at them all? More and more lately she had the feeling that George was different somehow. Now all this. Eliminating him from their inquiries.

'Have you found the other girl yet? The one who's missing?'

'Louise Butler? No, not yet. We're hoping against hope that she's gone off with a friend or a boyfriend and will get in touch with her parents. But every day that goes by makes it less likely.'

George tutted. 'How terrible. This man, whoever he is, must be very clever. I mean, three women murdered and no clues. That's if the other young lady has been murdered, of course.'

'He'll make a mistake, sir. They always do.'

'Quite.' George smiled. They always did, did they? Well, not this one, Mr Clever Clogs policeman. Not this one.

'He must be some kind of animal.' Elaine's voice was low and throaty. 'Those poor girls. No woman's safe any more.'

Hemmings nodded at Elaine, thinking, Well, you are. Any man who'd try and attack you would have to be mad!

Willis stood up and held out his hand to George who shook it warmly.

'Thanks for all your help, sir.'

'You're welcome. Any time.'

Hemmings nodded and Elaine pulled herself from her chair and saw them to the door.

'Thanks for the tea, madam.'

'That's OK. Goodbye.'

She closed the front door and leant against it, her heart beating fast once more. What was wrong with her? Why did she feel so worried?

George walked out into the hall.

'All right, dear? You look dreadful.'

'I'm fine, George. But it was like before. You know . . .' Her voice trailed off.

He put his arm around her.

'Now then, Elaine, there's nothing to worry about. It was all a terrible misunderstanding. Anyway that was a long time ago and I paid my debt to society.'

He led her back into the lounge and steered her to her chair. 'Now you stop worrying, my love. Just because I have a dark blue saloon car . . . well, does that make me a murderer?'

She shook her head.

'Of course not, George. I'm sorry.'

'There now, you're chasing ghosts again, Elaine. It's always been there between us, hasn't it?'

George's voice was soft.

She couldn't look at him in the face. After twenty years this was the first time George had ever referred to what had happened. And he was right, it had always been between them. Because it had always been in the back of her mind, from the moment she got up in the morning until she went to bed at night. Even then, sometimes, it strayed into her dreams.

'I'm sorry, Elaine. Really I am. I wish with all my heart that I could go back and change that time, but I can't, I just can't.'

George watched Elaine's guilty expression and felt the laughter threatening again.

'I know that, George. It was just seeing them, standing on the doorstep like that.'

'I know, my love, I understand. I know that you've never forgiven me for what happened, and I don't blame you, darling. I appreciate the way you stood by me. Really I do.' He took her plump hand in his and repressed a shudder. 'I love you, Elaine, I always have.'

She wiped her eyes with the back of her hand, knowing in her heart that it was an excuse to curtail the physical contact with him.

'I'm just an old silly, George. I'll make another cuppa.'

George moved so she could get out of the chair. He watched the material of her shell suit strain to the limit as she bent over the coffee table and picked up the tray of cups and saucers. She must have gone off her diet over Christmas.

When she left the room he sat back in his seat and grinned. They were all bloody fools! Every last one of them. And he was cleverer than a bag of monkeys, as his mother used to say, and would outwit them all. Starting with that fat bitch out in the kitchen.

Elaine was making the tea. She felt an urge to smash the teapot against the wall. The night of Mandy Kelly's murder George had been out on one of his walks. She pushed the thought from her mind. The other night she'd been in with him. On New Year's Eve he had been ill. Very ill. She was just paranoid, that's what was wrong with her. She wished the time would go faster until her holiday in Spain so she could go away, leave George and just enjoy herself. She poured the water over the tea bags and felt the tears again.

For all George's faults he was not a murderer. He was not a killer.

She had to believe that.

She had to.

Roll on Friday. She was seeing Hector Henderson, and more and more as the days went on found that she needed him, his simplicity and his jolliness. Most of all his kindness.

Willis and Hemmings discussed George and Elaine on their way to the next address.

'He seemed OK, but that woman! She was a bundle of nerves.'

Willis shrugged.

'We affect some people like that. Make them nervous. People like her never have the Old Bill round, see. When they do, it throws them like. He was a nice bloke though. Very polite and well spoken.'

Hemmings nodded.

'I wish a few more people were like them. Afford us a bit of respect now and again. I went round a house the other week – the kid had been caught shoplifting and the father wanted to fight me. Like it was all my fault.'

Willis grinned.

'I know what you mean. Everyone's on our case these days.'

'Don't I blinking know it!'

Evelyn and Dan sat at the breakfast bar. Evelyn lit herself a cigarette.

'I think you should find yourself somewhere, Dan. After all you've been here over a fortnight. Kate's a kind woman but I think there's a chance you just might wear out that welcome of yours.' She sipped her coffee and watched him over the rim of the cup.

'Has she said anything? I mean, about me going?'

Evelyn took a deep breath. 'Let's just say I think she's had enough.'

Dan picked up her pack of cigarettes and lit himself one. Evelyn snatched the packet from his hand and put it in the pocket of her apron.

'Surely things aren't that bad? You've got the money for your own cigarettes, haven't you?'

Dan raised his eyebrows and tried to decide whether or not to confide in her. Anthea had always paid the bills. They had lived a life of pleasure. Dan had not had a proper job for over ten years. Oh, he talked about deals and the market, but it was all for effect.

Dan realised with growing dismay that at forty-six he was qualified for nothing. It was a frightening prospect.

'Listen to me, Dan, I'm only trying to help you. Kate can't abide wasters, you know that as well as I do. You were an insurance salesman once, why can't you go back to that? They must be crying out for men like you. Good-looking eejits who could charm the birds off the trees.'

Dan, for once, had the grace to look away. How could he explain to the old woman sitting opposite him that he wore a five thousand pound watch? His suits were the best that money, Anthea's money, could buy. That he had not had to think about paying a bill or buying food for God knows how long. How could he explain that Kate was his last chance? Because Kate, for all her faults real and imagined, was the only person ever to take him at face value.

He glanced at his Rolex and closed his eyes. Then, taking a deep breath, he began to talk, the words tumbling out of him as he finally admitted the truth.

'Look, Eve, I'm the wrong side of forty. I don't know if I could even get a job as a junior salesman. What would I be looking at? Ten grand a year? Fifteen top whack. That wouldn't even pay for my clothes . . .'

The self-pitying tone of his voice was not lost on Evelyn and she snapped at him.

'If you could hear yourself! Like a big ninny sitting there bemoaning your fate. If you'd let your heart rule your head instead of your winkle, you wouldn't be in this state!'

Dan stared at her in shock.

'Oh, I've seen plenty like you in me life, Danny Burrows, only the majority of them were women. What you've got to do now is get yourself together. Get a life, as Lizzy is always saying. Take your jewellery and pawn it, get yourself a place to live, and then get yourself a job. It's what everyone has to do at some time – it's called taking responsibility for yourself.

'Do you know, all those years I watched my Kate yearn for you, it used to amaze me. How could such an intelligent and articulate woman want a bloody waster like you? You're no good to man or beast. By Christ, Dan, how you've lasted as long as you have amazes me on its own!'

The atmosphere in the tiny kitchen was charged. Dan felt an urge to take back his fist and slam it into the old woman's teeth. But he knew he wouldn't, because he was too much of a coward. Anthea knew it, which was why she did what she did to him. She told him what to wear and eat, when to sleep or make love to her. In short, she had called the shots and Dan had let her. In all the years he had not had one really happy day because Anthea was always the boss. What she said went. They travelled extensively, but he had to pander to her every whim. If she decided that they had had enough of sightseeing or whatever, then they had had enough. The woman sitting in front of him was right, he had to take responsibility for himself. Because there was no Anthea to do it for him now.

'I know what you're saying is right, Eve, but I'm not sure I'm man enough to do what you suggest.'

She slipped the cigarettes from her pocket and gave him one. 'Listen, Dan, Kate's sick of seeing you on that settee. Get yourself somewhere to live and gain her respect again. Get a job, sort out your life. If you really want her back, that's the only way to get her.'

'What about the man she's been seeing?'

'What man?' Evelyn sounded puzzled.

'Oh, come on, Eve. There's a man in the pipeline or my name's not Danny Burrows.'

'Well, if there is it's the first one I ever knew of.'

God forgive me for lying, she thought. She knew as sure as eggs was eggs that Kate, bless her, had finally caught herself a man. A mysterious man, she admitted, because she couldn't get anything out of her daughter about him, but a man all the same.

'You get yourself fixed with somewhere to live and then start your campaign to get Kate. Life has a funny way of sorting itself out. I've learnt that much over the years.'

He smiled at her. A genuine smile. Danny had never liked Kate's mother because he had always known she didn't like him. That she could see through him as if he was glass.

'Thanks, Eve. It's meant a lot to me to have us talk like this.'

Evelyn grasped his hand and smiled.

'I'm only trying to help you, son.'

She had the grace to look down at her wedding ring, a worn gold band. She couldn't look him in the face any more. All she really wanted was to see him out of the house.

For all their chatting about him and Kate and Mystery Man, he had not mentioned his daughter once.

That was typical of bloody Danny Burrows.

*

Lizzy pushed her fingers through her long hair and yawned. Joey lay beside her smiling. Both were naked. Lizzy looked around the room and blinked.

'This place is a right dump.'

Joey laughed out loud. 'Of course it is, it's a squat.'

The walls were daubed with splashes of paint, and here and there large eyes were drawn, with daggers sticking out of them.

'Who did the decorating, Joey?'

'Oh, some bloke called Nipper. He fancies himself as a gutter poet and artist.'

'Well, my advice to him would be, don't give up the day job.'

The sour smell of the sheets was wafting up to her nose and she grimaced. 'Why don't you skin up?'

'All right then.'

Joey sat cross-legged on the bed and proceeded to build a joint. Lizzy watched him languidly. She liked Joey a lot. He was exciting. He knew all the places to go and all the people to know. She had bunked off work all this week, Joanie had rung in and said she had flu, and every day had been spent like this. Lazing around in someone's flat or car, just getting right out of it. Her mother was becoming suspicious at the amount of time she spent in her room, but Lizzie had told her everyone liked to be on their own at times.

Her mother was a pain in the ass. Always wanting to know where she was and what she was doing. Who she was with and what they had done. Her gran wasn't much better. Lizzy's butter-wouldn't-melt-in-her-mouth image had kept her in good stead the last few years, but soon she wanted to break away. Go her own way and enjoy life. If her father got himself a place she'd go and live with him.

She was like him in a lot of ways. He liked the good life, lived to enjoy himself. Her mother lived life in a vacuum. Waiting for things to happen instead of making them happen. That was the secret.

Joey lit the joint and drew on it deeply, passing it to Lizzy. She took the smoke down deep into her lungs and held it there for a while before letting it out slowly.

'That's the way to do it.' She sounded like Mr Punch and Joey grinned at her.

He had never met anyone like her before. Lizzy Burrows was game for anything and everything. He watched her sit up and flick the ash on to the floor. She was not in the least self-conscious of her body. He grabbed a breast and squeezed it. His rough hand had dirt under the nails. Lizzy pushed it away. All she wanted now was to get really stoned and lie back on the mattress thinking good thoughts. She did this all the time at home, listening to Sinead O'Connor or Pink Floyd.

She passed the joint back to Joey and lay back. He took a toke on it and, putting his mouth over hers, breathed the smoke down into her lungs. She laughed and kissed him back. From one of the other rooms came the harsh sounds of Guns N' Roses, the heavy guitar making the walls vibrate.

'Oh, shit! Stud's back already. Come on, let's get dressed and shoot off.'

Lizzy pulled the dirty sheet over her breasts and laughed.

'Why?'

'Because Stud's like an accident waiting to happen, that's why.'

'Oh, fuck off, Joey! I'm just nicely stoned. I don't want to move yet.'

Joey sighed and scratched his greasy head.

'Look, how about we go and score a bit of Wiz or something?'

'All right, but only if we can come back here. Deal?'

'You've got a deal. Now get dressed before all the bikers come in here.' Joey was genuinely worried. The bikers were a good crowd but could get a bit out of hand. He didn't fancy Lizzy's chances much if they decided they all wanted a bit of the action. It wouldn't be the first time.

Lizzy pulled on her underwear and jeans. As she was pulling her T-shirt over her head the door opened.

A large man with a long ginger beard and straggly blond hair stood there. He had a beer belly that hung over the top of his filthy jeans. His sweat shirt had a death's head printed on it.

'Hello, Joey, who's this?' The voice was deep and had a drawl to it that Lizzy didn't like.

'This is Lizzy . . . Lizzy Burrows. Lizzy, JoJo Downey. He runs the squat.'

Lizzy picked up Joey's fear from his voice.

'Hello.' Her voice was small.

JoJo frowned at them both through little squinting eyes, then his face broke out into a toothless smile and he grinned at them. This was more frightening than his frown.

'Come and have a drink with us, you two.' The music was once more blaring out and Lizzy slipped on her boots and followed Joey and JoJo from the room. In the lounge she saw about fifteen people, mostly men. Two girls sat with them. Both had dyed black hair and wore the female biker battledress, the uniform black leather miniskirt, black lycra top and short bumfreezer denim jacket. They had on the heavy black mascara and purple lipstick of female bikers. Both smiled at Lizzy and she smiled back. It was easier now that she was dressed.

'Sit down, love, and have a drink.' JoJo motioned to the girls on the broken-down couch to move over, and they hastily made way for Lizzy. She sat between them. Joey sat on the floor with the others. His joint was taken from his hand by a man in his forties with a studded leather jacket flung across his lap.

It was when Lizzy was sipping her cider that she realised what the man with the leather jacket was doing. He was burning something in a small crucible, watching it bubble. Then, placing it gently on the jacket, he took a syringe from off the floor and began to draw the liquid up into it. He caught Lizzy's eye as she watched and winked at her.

The music was turned down at the request of a fat man who was actually trying to sleep through all the noise. Lizzy saw that Joey was once more skinning up and quailed inside. All she wanted to do was get out of here. Get out and never come back.

But Joey was relaxed again. The two girls either side of Lizzy were both chatting together about their children. As they spoke a little girl of about two stumbled into the room. Her nappy was so wet it was falling down her legs. The girl on the right of Lizzy held out her arms and the child tottered towards her. The heavily sodden nappy slipped down her legs and she just stepped out of it, much to the amusement of the assembled people. The stench of urine was added to the other rancid smells of the room. Lizzy looked over the child's head to where the man on the floor was jacking up. The needle slipped into his blue-veined arm and he closed his eyes while he felt the first rush. He opened his eyes and looked straight at her.

'Wanna go?'

Lizzy shook her head.

'Well, stop fucking staring at me then!'

She bit her lip and the man laughed.

The joint that Joey had rolled was passed to her and she drew on it gratefully. The girl beside her took it and puffed over the child's head.

Joey smiled at Lizzy and she relaxed. The cannabis was working at last. Someone got up and put on a Pink Floyd album. 'The Great Gig In The Sky' filled the room, the woman's haunting voice soothing Lizzy. This was better, this was music she knew, and somehow the room didn't feel so menacing. The man on the floor who had jacked up grinned at her and she found herself grinning back. Then Jojo offered her a tab of LSD. She took the proffered tiny scrap of blotting paper and wiped it on to her tongue. Joey did the same. An hour later she was floating somewhere between reality and the fifth dimension. She was having a great time. Somehow more children seemed to have arrived from the bedrooms in the flat. The music, although still loud, was not blaring and someone had even made sandwiches, which were being passed around along with a cider and vodka mixture. Joey was now lying tripping out of his head on the floor.

Then there was a loud knocking on the door.

One of the girls got up to answer it and two well-dressed women came into the room.

JoJo stood up and took them out to the kitchen. Joey watched from his vantage point on the floor as they did the deal. Three thousand tabs of Ecstasy were handed over for a thick wad of notes.

Joey relaxed, happy in the knowledge that for the next few weeks at least, the place wouldn't run dry of drugs. It was just as the two women were leaving that the pandemonium started. Police seemed to be crawling everywhere.

Lizzy was so far gone by this time that she just smiled at them as they took her out to the meat wagon.

*

Kate and Caitlin were both going over 'suspect' evidence. This involved taking apart any statements made by known offenders and seeing if they could pinpoint a flaw somewhere along the line. As yet they had got precisely nowhere.

Caitlin yawned loudly.

'There's nothing here, Katie, you know that and I know that. This man, whoever he is, isn't your normal nutter. He's one of the new breed.'

Kate smiled despite herself. 'New breed?'

'Sure isn't that what I just said? I've noticed over the years that the violent attacks are changing subtly. If you go back to the fifties and sixties, there were a few killers around like this one. But their attacks, bad as they were – well, they weren't as violent as now. Look at this man we have here. He batters the girls to death. Now most rapists get off on their domination of the woman. The struggling, the fear, the knowledge that they are committing the worst violation a woman can experience. This chappie here, though, he seems to want them still. As still as death, in fact. It's almost if he wants the ultimate submission. As if the woman's acquiescing, if you like. Giving him permission.'

Kate stared at Caitlin's ruddy face and nodded. 'I think I understand you. But even knowing that, we're still as far from finding him as we are from the Holy Grail.' Her voice was flat.

'Oh, we'll find him, don't you fret. It's just when. That's the bastard of it all. When. He'll make a mistake. They always do.'

The phone on their desk rang and Kate picked it up. Caitlin watched her face register astonishment.

'I'll be right there.'

'What is it, Katie? Another one?' Caitlin's voice held disbelief.

'Oh, no, it's not another murder. But it could bloody well end up as one.'

Picking up her bag she rushed from the incident room, leaving him staring after her.

Chapter Fourteen

Kate slammed into her house, banging the front door behind her. Dan and Evelyn heard her stamping up the stairs and both followed her. They found her in Lizzy's bedroom, systematically tearing the room apart.

'What the hell's going on here, Kate?' Dan's voice was incredulous.

She was pulling underwear from a drawer and searching every piece as she picked it up.

'Lizzy is at this moment in Grantley Police Station on a charge of possession of cannabis.' Her voice was thick with fury.

'What!' Evelyn held her hand to her heart. 'Are you sure?'

'Oh, I'm sure all right. I know what my own daughter looks like.'

She pulled the drawer from its hole and examined the underneath. There, taped to the bottom, was a small plastic bag of amphetamines. Kate ripped it off and shoved it in the pocket of her jacket.

'Look, Kate, relax for a second and tell us what happened. There must be some mistake.'

'There's no mistake, Dan. I thought that as well, until

I saw her. I was called from the incident room by the desk sergeant who recognised her. She was in a squat in Tillingdon Place. Yes, Tillingdon Place, the biggest dump in Grantley, and she was tripping out of her head.'

'No.' Evelyn felt sick inside.

'Yes, Mum. Now will you two just get out? I must find out what she's got, what's going on. I got the duty doctor to give her a blood test, for my eyes only. I could break her bloody neck!'

'Listen, Kate, maybe someone took her there and gave her the drugs . . .'

'Oh, don't you think I thought of that? Well, don't you?' She rounded on Dan. 'I went into the cell and she told me to fuck off out of it. Those were her exact words. She was shouting and swearing at everyone. I have never been so humiliated in all my life. Miss Goody Two Shoes hasn't been to work for a week apparently. I went round to Joanie's and she told me everything. Lizzy wasn't at Joanie's on New Year's Eve, she was at that bloody rave! She's nothing but a lying, scheming little bitch!'

She burst into tears. Evelyn went to her and put her arm around her shoulders.

'I'll make us all a cup of coffee, shall I? Dry your eyes, Katie, crying won't solve anything.'

'I did everything I possibly could for that girl. We treated her well, tried to bring her up decently. Why has she done this to us? To herself? It's as if I never knew her.'

Evelyn kissed the top of her head.

'Sure there's plenty of people must have said the same thing after a visit from you, love. You bring your children up, you do your best, but in the end they go their own way.'

'I could cheerfully kill her, Mum, for this. From what I can gather from Joanie, she's been taking drugs since her last year at school. No wonder she didn't want to stay on and make something of herself.' Kate clenched her fists. 'If she was here now I'd tear her apart. What a foolish, foolish girl!'

Dan walked from the room, his head reeling.

Lizzy on drugs? His Lizzy? He sat at the top of the stairs as the news sank in. A little while later Kate's sobs had subsided and Evelyn pushed past him to make her daughter a coffee. Inside the bedroom Kate began once more to search the room. She had just found Lizzy's birth control pills when Dan came back in.

'Look, Dan, she's on the pill. Another first for Madam Lizzy. When she gets home I'm going to slaughter her.'

'It's because of you, Kate. You were never there for her. You should have dedicated yourself to bringing up your child . . .'

Dan's trite speech was what she needed to bring herself down from her temper. She turned to face him. Her voice was deadly calm as she spoke.

'You *dare* to tell me what I should have done, Danny Burrows? You dare to tell me about my child?' She poked herself in the chest. 'Yes, my child. Never yours, Dan. You were never here for her. My mother and I brought her up and she brought herself this low. Where that girl is concerned I have nothing on my conscience. Nothing.'

But Kate knew that no matter how many times she told herself that, she would always blame herself. Always.

She began to pull all her daughter's clothes from the wardrobe, searching the pockets as she went.

'Look at you, you'd think you were at a suspect's house instead of your daughter's bedroom. You haven't even tried to hear her side of it.' Dan's voice was disgusted. He turned and walked from the room.

Kate followed him on to the landing and shouted: 'You're another one. You can take your stuff and get out.

I've had enough of freeloaders. She's like you, Dan, that's the trouble. She looks like an angel and she's a slut . . .'

She heard him slam the front-room door and went back into the bedroom. The Paddington Bear wallpaper that had been on the walls for years was mocking her. On a shelf over the bed were Lizzy's dolls from childhood. Picking up the Tiny Tears she grasped it to herself, cuddling the cold plastic head to her face.

Oh, Lizzy, Lizzy, when did it all start to go wrong? How could she not have noticed what was going on under her nose? What had come over her child?

She licked the salty tears from her lips and, taking a tissue from the box by the bed, blew her nose loudly.

Placing the doll on her lap she pulled the legs off. Kate knew everywhere there was to look for drugs. It was her job, after all.

Patrick answered the door himself and smiled in delight as he saw Kate on his doorstep.

'Hello, love. Come in.'

She stepped into the hallway.

As Patrick walked her through to the lounge he frowned. She did not look like a happy woman. When she was seated on the sofa with a glass of brandy, he spoke.

'What's up, Kate? You look terrible. Is it something about the case?'

She sipped the brandy. 'No. Nothing to do with that.'

Then it all tumbled out. Patrick sat beside her, unsure if what he was hearing was true. When she had finished, he sighed heavily.

'Sounds to me like your daughter needs a good kick up the arse, if you'll pardon the expression.'

'I'm sorry to bring my troubles here but I really didn't know where else to go.'

Patrick grasped her hand. 'Listen, Kate, if ever you need me, I'll be there. All right?' He meant it. Seeing her like this made her more human somehow. It was gratifying to know that she could feel the same as him. That she had the same troubles, worries and hopes that he had. It made her more a person and less a policewoman.

Kate ran her hands through her long hair and sniffed. 'It was just the way she acted when I went in the cell. You know, as if I was the enemy or something.'

'At the moment, Kate love, you are the enemy. She probably feels ashamed of herself.'

'I know what you're saying, but she was drugged out of her head, Patrick. She was nicked in a filthy squat with a load of known druggies. The boy who took her there was called Joey something or other. He already has a record as long as my arm and he's only eighteen. I tried to kid myself that someone took her and dragged her there, you know the scenario. But after talking to her best friend, I realise that my daughter is nothing but a little slut.'

Patrick slapped her knee sharply. 'Hey, hey, you listen to me now, Katie, that's your child you're talking about. I wouldn't care if my Mandy was flashing her clout on the Old Kent Road if it meant having her back! You're being too hard on her. She's sixteen. Christ Almighty, didn't you ever do anything wrong at sixteen?

'Kids today have too many choices in front of them. Drugs are part and parcel of their everyday life. That's why they go to these raves. In our youth, the sixties and early seventies, we had the same thing, only we were the generation who were going to change the world. Remember Sergeant Pepper and all the other drug music? What you've got to do now is try and build some bridges with her. Try and get her back on an even keel.'

Kate stared up into his face. What he was saying made

271

sense in some respects but she would never, ever forgive Lizzy for the charade of the last eighteen months. She had thought her daughter was pure and good, and she had been gratified by that. Seeing the lowest of the low on a daily basis made you glad your child was normal. Was safe. Was secure. To find out that she was a drug user was like finding out your twin was a murderer. It was unbelievable. To see that child lying in a cell out of her head on drugs was like having a knife twisted somewhere in your bowels.

Kelly watched the changing expressions on her face and guessed what she was thinking.

'I feel I've failed Lizzy, Pat. Failed her dreadfully. I put my work before everything. I could have got a nine to five job but I never wanted one. I wanted to be a police-woman. I suppose you, of all people, find that hard to believe.'

Patrick shrugged. 'Look Katie, your job is your business, I admit that until I met you I didn't have a lot of time for the police. But that's history. I am a hundred per cent legal these days.'

'All the same though, Pat, what I'm doing with you is not really any different to what Lizzy did with the drugs. We both want something we shouldn't really have.'

Patrick stared into Kate's eyes, his expression soft.

'Drugs destroy people, Kate. I don't. I resent you implying that. I've never intentionally hurt a woman in my life. If you feel that you are in any way compromising yourself with me, then I think we should both say our goodbyes now, before it becomes even harder.'

Kate returned his gaze. He was offering her an out and she respected him for that. While another part of her, the female part of her, resented the way he was willing just to end what they had.

'I'll miss you though, Kate, you've kept me together

body and soul since I lost Mandy. I've come to rely on you very much. I'd even go so far as to say I'm falling in love. But what you said has a ring of truth. All I can say in my defence is that I have nothing now in my life that I would need to hide from you.'

'What about the future?'

He smiled. 'Who knows what the future has in store for us?

Kate looked away from him and concentrated on the ormolu clock on the mantelpiece, its ticking the only other sound in the room. She bit her lip. So much had happened in the last few months. Her life would never be the same again. Her relationship with Lizzy was over. It would be different now between them. Lizzy would need a firm hand after this. All the trust was gone. The one person whom Kate had always seen as constant and good had been shown up in a dark light. It scared her. How could you not know that about your child? On the other hand, the man she had been wary of seeing, who had a bad reputation, who in her right mind she should never have got involved with, had turned out to be a good man underneath. A good and kind man, whose reputation was only believed by the people who didn't really know him.

'I don't want to finish with you, Kate.'

His voice was soft and low.

'I don't want to stop seeing you either, Pat.'

She wasn't sure she could stop now, even if she wanted to.

'When is she home?'

'Tomorrow, I could have taken her tonight, you know, being a DI. But I didn't trust myself, Pat, I thought I might harm her if she was with me while I felt like this.'

'Why did you come to me?' It was a low whisper.

'Because I trust you, I suppose.'

He smiled and pulled her to her feet. 'Come on.'

'Where are we going?'

'I'm going to run you a nice bath, Katie, and I'm going to soap your body personally, every nook and cranny. Then I am going to lay you on my bed and stroke every care and worry from your mind. Then when madam gets home tomorrow, you'll be in a fit frame of mind to see her and get this sorted out once and for all.'

He pulled Kate to the bottom of the staircase and she dragged her hand from his.

'Oh, Pat, what am I going to do? What with the case and everything, and now all this with Lizzy . . .' Her voice trailed off and Patrick took her hand once more.

'Just you bear in mind that you've got me now, Kate, and you'll have me for as long as you want me. I'm here for you whenever you need someone.'

It was said simply and sincerely and Kate followed him up the stairs gladly. For the first time in years she had someone she could rely on. It was a heady feeling.

'After the bath, we can have a good old chat. That's what you really need, you know. Someone who's not too close to the source of the problem.'

Kate followed him up the stairs. She had left Dan packing and her mother had retired to her bedroom. Kate had felt she could not stay in that house a moment longer. She had found cannabis as well as amphetamines in her daughter's room. What Patrick said made sense. She needed a real shoulder to cry on.

It was not until much later, after her bath and with Patrick snoring softly beside her, that she realised the implications of her visit to Patrick Kelly.

The irony of it all was not lost on her. But she leant up on her elbow and looked down into his face and knew the truth of it.

She was falling hopelessly in love with the man. And it felt good. Very, very good.

She pictured Lizzy as a small child. Her white socks and sandals pristine on her little feet. Her Holly Hobby dress ironed to crisp perfection. Her long dark hair brushed like burnished jet. It was her first day at school. Kate had been so proud of her. What had happened to make her daughter take drugs? When had Lizzy grown away from her?

She felt the anguished tears of motherhood blur her vision and blinked them away. She was done with crying. Patrick was right, she must build bridges now with Lizzy. Try and make some good come out of all this badness.

Patrick turned over and his arm settled across her stomach. It felt good, it felt right. She felt safe.

Kissing the dark head beside her, she settled down. Not to sleep, that was a long way away, but to think and plan. The initial shock and fury were gradually disappearing; now she needed a plan of action and would concentrate her energies on that.

Somewhere, at some time, she had missed some vital step with Lizzy. It was up to her to rectify that as best she could. And rectify it she would.

Snuggling into Patrick, she closed her eyes and let the memories drift in front of her closed lids.

The only thing she forgot to wonder was how Lizzy was going to feel about everything.

It was a mistake she would soon regret.

Kate felt the eyes of the desk sergeant boring into the back of her head as she signed the papers for her daughter's release. She made her way to the cells with a heavy heart. The fact that Lizzy had been nicked was the talk of the station, she knew that. She passed Amanda Dawkins who smiled at her sympathetically. Kate looked away. As the cell was unlocked she held her breath. Lizzy was sitting cross-legged on a mattress on the floor. Her make-up was smeared over her face and her hair was a mass of tangles. She looked defiantly into her mother's face as the door opened.

'So you've come then?'

Kate swallowed deeply. 'Get up, Lizzy.'

The girl pulled herself from the mattress and stood with one hand on her hip, in an aggressive pose. The duty officer shook his head in wonder. If she was his daughter he'd give her a smack she wouldn't forget in a hurry.

'Come on, get your things, we're going home.' Kate's voice was low. She turned to the duty officer, a man called Higgins. He was nearly fifty and Kate could see the pity in his eyes.

'Has she eaten?'

'Not a thing, love, but we made her drink the orange juice. It brings them down you know, the Vitamin C.'

'Yeah, I know. Come on, let's get out of here.'

'I want Dad to come and get me.' This was said through gritted teeth.

'He can't come so you'll have to make do with me. Now come on, Liz, I'm not in the mood for games.'

Lizzy sneered, then sat back down again. 'I'll just have to wait for Dad then, won't I?'

'You're coming home with me now, Lizzy.'

She grinned annoyingly. 'I'm going to do whatever I want, Mum. I'm through with you and Gran always telling me what you want, what you expect me to be . . .'

Kate felt herself reddening. She tried desperately to control her voice.

'We can talk about this at home, Lizzy. This is neither the time nor the place.'

'Really? Funny that, because you seem to spend enough

time here. I'd have thought this was the place for you, Mum, more than anywhere else.'

'I'm telling you for the last time, Liz, get up and let's go home. We can talk this through, make some sense out of it.'

Lizzy laughed out loud, her mouth wide with mirth. 'That's about right for you, isn't it? Let's analyse everything. Let's find the hidden meaning in everything. Oh, fuck off, Mum. You sound like a bad play!'

Kate spoke between clenched teeth to the duty officer. 'Would you leave us alone, please?'

The man had been so embarrassed he had been pretending to study the graffiti on the cell walls. He rushed from the cell, shutting the door behind him. He liked Kate Burrows a lot. She was a nice woman, a good DI; to see her shamed like that was terrible.

Mother and daughter stared at one another and Kate was aware that it was now a battle of nerves between them. For some reason Lizzy was enjoying this. She was not contrite or sorry or any of the things she should have been. In fact, it seemed as if she was actually enjoying it. Where, oh where, was the daughter of two days ago? Where was the girl with the ready smile and the laughing face? It was as if she was seeing a stranger, a stranger with her daughter's face and body. A body that had been well used, judging by the diary she had found.

'What's all this really about, Lizzy? Come on, tell me.'

She stood up and walked to the back of the cell. Her hair was in her eyes and she brushed it away impatiently.

'I want Dad.'

'Well, your dad isn't here, I am. And if necessary, Lizzy, I am going to take you out of here by force.'

She laughed again.

'I'd like to see you try!'

It was said in a tone of such contempt that Kate felt something inside her break. She walked across the room and, grabbing her daughter's long hair, yanked her towards the cell door. It took every bit of strength that she possessed.

Lizzy, though, was not having any of it. She brought her fist round and punched her mother in the shoulder. Kate felt the blow, and swinging Lizzy round to face her, slapped her hard across the face, sending the girl flying to the corner of the cell.

Both were breathing heavily.

'Get up, Lizzy, now, before I really lose my rag! Get up, I said!' The last sentence echoed around the small cell.

Kate walked towards her daughter and Lizzy scrambled to her feet.

'You are coming home with me now, and if you so much as open that foul mouth of yours, I'll beat you within an inch of your life.'

Something in her mother's voice told Lizzy that she meant it. Kate grabbed the shoulder of her daughter's tee-shirt and dragged her to the cell door. She banged on it with her free hand and it was opened by Higgins. Kate then marched the girl along the cell row, through the desk sergeant's office and out of the building to the car park. She threw Lizzy in the car. Getting into the driver's seat, she started the engine.

'You'd better have a good reason for all this, Lizzy, because I want to know exactly what's going on with you.'

With that she drove out of the station and home. Neither of them said a word more.

Evelyn desperately wanted to clean up Lizzy's room for her but Kate had forbidden her to touch it. She sat on the bed looking at the utter chaos around her. Pictures of

Lizzy as a child were everywhere. She shook her head. If anyone had told her that her granddaughter was on drugs she would have laughed in their face.

'Not my Lizzy,' she would have said. But now the truth was facing her and it was like gall. That beautiful girl was ruining her life, was breaking her family apart – for drugs.

From what Kate had told her Lizzy had been on amphetamines for a couple of years. She shook her head. Standing up, she looked around the familiar room. How many times had she come to tuck Lizzy in when she had been small? Kissed the soft skin of her face? Brushed the long hair till it gleamed?

She walked to the window and looked out into the dull afternoon light. That was when she saw the diary. It was a girl's diary, with birds and flowers painted on a pale green silk background. Evelyn opened it up idly and began to read.

She was still reading when Kate and Lizzy arrived. Kate had to pull the girl from the car and practically drag her up the garden path to the house. Opening the door, she pushed her daughter inside.

Lizzy walked into the front room and through to the kitchen where she began to make herself a cup of coffee as if nothing had happened. Kate pulled her coat off and put it on the banisters. She followed her daughter through to the kitchen.

'Right then, I want to know everything that's been happening. I want to know where you got the drugs, who from, and who you took them with.'

Lizzy poured milk into her cup.

'That, Mother, is none of your business.'

Kate pushed her hands through her hair.

'I'm not going to argue all day, Lizzy, I mean it. I want some answers and I want them now.'

Lizzy faced her mother and crossed her arms over her breasts. 'That's you all over that is. "I want some answers and I want them now." Who the hell do you think you're talking to? I'm your daughter not a bloody suspect.'

'That, madam, is just where you're wrong. As far as I'm concerned at this particular moment in time you're both those things. You are suspected of dealing in drugs, Lizzy. You were at a known dealer's house, so where exactly does that leave you? I found drugs in your bedroom. I also found your diary. So I know I'm not dealing with Snow White here.'

Lizzy turned to the kettle and poured boiling water into the mug.

'I don't need this at the moment, Mum, I've had a terrible night. Maybe later I might feel like discussing it.'

Kate watched in amazement as Lizzy stirred her coffee. Her long fingers gripped the spoon so tightly her knuckles were white. Kate looked at the womanly figure in the jeans and T-shirt. She wasn't even wearing a bra. The T-shirt was stained and crumpled. Her hair was like rats tails and she just stood there making herself a cup of coffee. Not for the first time in the last twenty-four hours Kate wondered what on earth had happened to her child.

Evelyn had been in the front room listening to the exchange. Now she walked into the kitchen as Lizzy sat at the breakfast bar and threw the diary in front of her.

'I have seen a lot of things in my life, Elizabeth Burrows, but I never thought to see this. I felt sick to my stomach reading that filth.' Evelyn's voice was hard and cold.

Lizzy picked up the diary and looked at her grandmother.

'You shouldn't have read it, Gran.' Her voice was small. Her grandmother was important to her.

'Don't you call me Gran! Don't you ever call me that again. That you could do those things with boys and then write about them . . . It's disgusting!'

'It's real life, remember that? You must have been young once.' Lizzy felt her voice rising and tried desperately to control it. 'My life is my own now, I'm nearly seventeen years old. If I want to sleep with boys I like, then that's my business. *Mine*. Not yours or Mum's or anyone's. Mine!'

Evelyn gave her a look of contempt. 'That's all you're interested in, isn't it? You know, it's funny but over the years I can always remember you saying: me, my, mine. I want, I think, I, I, I. Never a real thought for anyone else. We all fell in with what you wanted, we all bent over backwards to do what you wanted. Never a thought for ourselves. You're nothing but a conniving, scheming, little bitch!'

'Mum!'

'Oh, don't "Mum" me, Kate. That diary says it all. I make you feel suffocated, do I, with my loving? My cuddling annoys you. Well, don't worry, Lizzy, because I never want to touch you again as long as I live.'

With that Evelyn walked from the room, her shoulders stooped.

Lizzy put her head in her hands.

'Why did this have to happen? Why did you have to let her read that?' She threw the diary on to the breakfast bar and Kate could hear the tears in her voice.

'I think you should ask yourself why you wrote it, Lizzy, and why you did those things? That's the important issue here now, not what we think.'

Tears were pouring down the girl's face and every maternal instinct in Kate's body told her to comfort her child. But the descriptions in the diary were there in the forefront of her mind and they stopped her. To picture your daughter with two boys in the back of a transit van is not exactly conducive to maternal solicitude. It caused a wide gap, a void that Kate was sure would always be between them.

'Why can't you just let me live my life how I want to?'

'Because you're set on a course of self-destruction, that's why, Lizzy.'

'I didn't mean the things I said about you and Gran in the diary. I was just a bit stoned at the time and it all poured out . . . I love Gran, I always have.'

Kate sat opposite her and sighed.

'It's not just what you wrote that hurts us, Lizzy, it's the way you've been living a lie all this time.'

'I had to live a lie! If you knew what I was doing you'd have moved heaven and earth to stop me. It's my life, Mum, my life.'

Kate lit a cigarette. Lizzy leant across the table and took one from her packet.

'Yes, I smoke as well. You know everything else, you might as well know that.'

Kate shook out her match and Lizzy took the box from her hand. The touch of her daughter's warm skin on her own was like an electric shock.

She watched Lizzy light her cigarette. Her fingers were stained with dirt, her nail varnish chipped. Her lips were cracked and dry. She looked like a girl who had been tripping all night. She also looked very young and unsure of herself, but Kate knew that was just an illusion. How many times had she pulled in young girls over the years? 'Tarts' was how she had described them in her own mind. Little tarts with too much make-up and too much to say for themselves. Now, here was the truth of her life in front of her. Her daughter had been sleeping with boys, and men since she was fourteen. Kate couldn't even justify it by saying it was a boy Lizzy loved, whom her daughter had been with for a long time and so sex was a natural progression. From what she had read in the diary, it seemed any boy with a pleasing face and the latest clothes was in for a good time. Kate closed her eyes tightly.

'Where's Dad?'

'He's gone, Lizzy. I don't know where.'

'Figures. You never cared about him anyway.'

'Listen, you! I let him stay here because of you. If it had been left to me I would have put him out on the street long ago. Turning up here as and when it suited him. I thought you needed a father, even a lousy father. A father who loved you was better than no father at all.'

Lizzy laughed softly.

'I never had a father. I never really had a mother either, did I?'

Kate took a long pull on her cigarette and sighed.

What the hell had happened to her life?

Evelyn lay on her bed and stared at the ceiling. The shock of what she had read was just wearing off. In place of her anger was sorrow. Sorrow for her daughter. Not for her granddaughter, but for Kate. She had battled against all the odds to give that girl everything she could possibly want. Evelyn had watched Kate over the years putting her own life on hold for Lizzy, and for what? What?

She admitted to herself that she had been partly to blame. She had spoiled the child rotten. But what else could she have done? Who would have thought that that bright articulate girl would turn out like this? That the little girl who had sat on her granny's knee and smiled and laughed, would grow up to give herself to anyone and everyone who asked her? Hadn't she tried to instil morals into the girl? Not for the first time she missed her husband dreadfully. He would have known what to do. She wiped her eyes with the back of her hand.

Lizzy had never known the love of a father, a real father. Kate used to wait in the hallway, sitting patiently on the stairs, listening for her father's boots to clump up the tiny pathway. Then, as he opened the door, she'd be picked up in a big hug. Kate had known the security of love, as a child and as an adult. It was the advent of Dan that had changed her. When he had left her with a tiny baby, she had hardened her heart somehow. Oh, she loved Lizzy with all her being, Evelyn knew that, but she had also channelled her energy into her work. On reflection, Evelyn wondered now if this was such a good thing. If Kate had maybe married again and given Lizzy a father figure . . .

She shook herself mentally. 'What's bred in the bone comes out in the blood.' How many times had she said that to people? Lizzy was like her father. She used people for her own ends. Dan had been the same. He was still the same. He had packed his bags and disappeared, as he always had, at the first sign of trouble. He said he couldn't cope with aggravation. Those were his exact words. Well, he generally caused any aggravation that was floating around, but he would never admit it.

She heard the bedroom door open and put her hands over her eyes to shield the glare from the landing light.

'I've brought you a cup of coffee, Mum.'

Kate set the cup down on the dresser by the bed.

'How are you feeling?'

Evelyn had closed her eyes. She felt the springs in the bed shift as Kate sat beside her. They clasped hands.

'I don't know how I feel, to tell you the truth. Now the shock's wearing off, I keep trying to make excuses for her.'

She heard Kate sigh.

'I know what you mean.'

'Oh, Katie, that we would ever see the day . . .' Her voice broke.

'I know. Believe me, I know what you're feeling. The worst of it all to me is that I never guessed anything. Me a policewoman, a DI, never saw what was in front of my face.'

'That's because you trusted her.' Evelyn's voice was so filled with despair that Kate felt rage again. Rage at her daughter, not just for what she had done but for all the unhappiness she had caused her grandmother. Evelyn was of a different era, a different breed. She had been a virgin when she married, had stayed faithful all her married life. Even when she had been widowed young, she had never wanted another man. Kate had envied her mother her nice clean life. Now Lizzy had taken all that her grandmother held dear and dragged it through the dirt.

For that Kate would find it hard to forgive her.

The two women sat together in silent despair. Then the phone rang.

Kate answered it and went back in to her mother.

'Frederick Flowers wants to see me. No prizes for guessing why.' Her voice was trembling now.

The Chief Constable had been quite nice, Kate conceded. He had asked her what was happening and she told him as truthfully as possible. The possession charge had been dropped because her daughter had only had a small amount on her. Not enough to be a dealer, only enough for what the police termed 'personal use'.

Kate drove home in a stupor. She knew that this would be a black cloud hanging over her for the rest of her working life. But that wasn't the issue here. The real crux of the matter was finding out why her daughter felt the need to take drugs. Why she lied and cheated. What the hell was going on in the child's mind.

She pulled into her drive and sat looking at the house. It was early evening and the day had been too long. Far too long and far too fraught. She rubbed the back of her neck with a gloved hand. She had to walk into work tomorrow and face her colleagues. It was the talking point of the station, she would lay money on that.

Groaning slightly, she got out of the car. Inside the house, all was quiet. Kate went to the kitchen and turned on the light. She put the kettle on for a cup of coffee. Preparing three cups she went upstairs to her mother's room. She opened the door slightly and listened. All she could hear were soft snores. She shut the door gently then went to her daughter's room.

She opened the door and went inside. Lizzy lay in bed, with just her head showing. Kate tiptoed to her and looked down. Her long dark hair fanned out across the pillow. In the light from the streetlamp Kate could see the long dark lashes against her daughter's cheekbones. Lizzy really was lovely. She had so much going for her, why had she felt the urge to destroy herself? Because as far as Kate was concerned, that was all people who took drugs wanted to do.

She felt a tear squeeze itself from the corner of her eye. Turning away, she looked at the familiar little room: the dolls, the make-up scattered over the dressing table, the books, haphazardly placed on their shelf. She had attempted to clean up at least.

Then Kate saw the piece of paper. Walking the few steps to the dressing table, she picked it up. Words registered in her mind, but she just could not comprehend them. She read the piece of paper again and again.

Sorry, Mum . . . Sorry, Mum. Tell Gran I love her . . . Tell Gran . . .

She dragged her eyes from the paper to the bed and the deathly whiteness of Lizzy's skin made her spring into action. She dragged back the covers and stared. Even in the dim light she could see the blood. Somewhere in her mind she registered the fact it was still pumping.

Picking up a hand towel from a nearby chair, she wrapped both of Lizzy's wrists tightly. Her fingers were suddenly stiff, she couldn't control them. The hammering of her heart in her ears was like a drum beating.

She ran into her bedroom to phone an ambulance. She registered the blood on the white telephone. It was Lizzy's blood. Lizzy's. She answered the telephonist's questions calmly and rationally, she had no idea how. It was the policewoman in her taking over.

Please hurry. Oh God, please hurry. She was not sure whether she was speaking out loud. She put down the phone and rushed back in to Lizzy.

Oh God, please let her be all right. I'll do anything you want if you let her be all right. I'll go to Mass every day of my life . . .

Like many another before, she was trying to bargain with God for her child's life.

Then, somewhere in the stillness, she heard the ambulance siren.

It wasn't until she was stumbling from the room that she saw her mother. Evelyn stood in her bedroom doorway, her face ashen.

Kate couldn't look at her. She went in the ambulance with Lizzy.

Of all the things she had expected from life, the events of the last twenty-four hours had not been remotely near them. If someone had told her what was going to happen she would have laughed in their face.

Now, in the middle of the biggest case she had ever worked on, she had problems of a much larger scale and Kate was aware that her life would never be the same again.

Kate sat in the hospital waiting room. The young doctor was smiling at her. She noticed that his hair had scissor marks in it, as if it had just been dry cut. He had a day's growth of beard covering a weak chin.

'Well, we've stitched her, Mrs Burrows. The cuts were quite deep, but not really life threatening as such. She cut lengthwise along the arm and missed the main arteries. She was unconscious because she had taken some sleeping pills. But she's awake now, though groggy.'

'Can I see her?'

'Of course. She'll stay here tonight and the psychiatrist will see her tomorrow.'

'Psychiatrist?' Kate's voice was small.

'It's standard procedure after a suicide attempt. Don't worry, everything will be all right.'

Kate swallowed the trite remark. He was only trying to make her feel better.

She stood up and stubbed out her cigarette. It had in fact gone out minutes before but she hadn't noticed.

'Can I go and see her then?'

'Of course. Try not to keep her too long. Sleep's the best thing for her now. Sleep is a great healer.'

Kate felt an urge to tell him to get stuffed. But she didn't. Instead she gave him a tight smile.

'Thank you.' Slipping past him she went into her daughter's ward. Lizzy had the curtains pulled around her bed and Kate stepped towards them gingerly.

She saw Lizzy's eyes open and tried hard to smile.

'I'm sorry, Mum. I really am sorry.'

'Oh, Lizzy!' All the pain and anguish inside her rose like a tidal wave and enveloped her.

Mother and daughter cried together.

'Everything will be all right, Lizzy, I promise you. We'll work this out, I swear. We'll work this out.'

'Oh, Mum, I wish Gran hadn't seen my diary.'

Kate could hear the little hiccoughing sounds in her voice.

'We'll make it right between us. You just concentrate on getting better.'

A nurse rustled into the tiny space. Kate could smell Pears soap and the smell brought back memories of when she had been younger. When Lizzy had been a baby.

'I think you'd best get yourself off home now. She really does need her sleep.'

Kate nodded. Kissing Lizzy on the lips, she pushed back her hair from her face and tried valiantly to smile.

'I'll be here in the morning, OK?'

Lizzy nodded and closed her eyes. Kate walked from the ward. As she pushed open the swing doors to the corridor, Patrick walked towards her.

'Oh, Kate, I'm so sorry.' He put out his arms and she walked into them. Feeling the strength of him, the security he offered. He pulled her to him, stroking her hair and kissing her forehead. At the display of sympathy she was undone. She sobbed into his cashmere overcoat, smelling the peculiar odour of him, Old Spice and cigar smoke.

As he accompanied her out of the hospital and towards his car, it did not occur to Kate to ask how he knew where she was. How he knew what had happened.

She was just glad to see him.

Chapter Fifteen

Evelyn heard a car pull up and poked her head through the heavy curtains of the front room. She sniffed loudly. It was a big expensive car, must be someone for one of the neighbours. Then as she looked she saw Kate getting out of the back. She frowned. Too much had happened today for anything else really to surprise her. She saw the man emerge from the car and as they both turned towards the house she quickly shut the curtain.

She sat back on the settee until she heard Kate's key in the lock. She couldn't summon up her usual boisterous welcome for her daughter. She heard Kate speaking then a man's voice, a deep, dark brown voice. Wiping her eyes once more with a sodden hanky, Evelyn waited for them to come into the room.

Patrick helped Kate with her coat then shrugged off his overcoat. He slung them on the banister in a casual manner. Somehow this little act pleased Kate. Her home was not very grand and she knew it. But Patrick was acting as if he lived her kind of life, which indeed he had once. Only, from his beginnings, Kate's home would probably have been something to aspire to.

Patrick followed her into the front room, his eyes taking in her home. He noticed everything, from the good but worn carpets to the books that abounded in the room. It looked comfortable and warm. He saw a tiny woman sitting on the settee, dressed all in black. She had a remarkable face, one that denoted a quick intellect and a kind heart. He warmed to her immediately.

'Mum, this is a friend of mine, Patrick Kelly. He brought me home from the hospital.'

Evelyn inclined her head. She noted the breadth of his shoulders, the long legs and dark good looks, and decided Kate had better taste than she'd given her credit for. Then the name registered. It was the man they had been talking about at Christmas dinner. Evelyn pushed the thoughts from her mind. With a name like Kelly, he must have some Irish in him so he couldn't be all bad.

'How do you do?'

Patrick smiled at her, and she found herself smiling back.

'The child?' She stared into her daughter's drawn face.

'She's fine, Mum, or at least as fine as she could be in the circumstances. The cuts weren't deep enough to really harm her. I found her just in time. She's to see a psychiatrist in the morning.'

Patrick sat on a chair by the fire and Kate turned to him. 'Can I get you a drink? I've got some Scotch somewhere.' She went to the drinks cabinet and opened the door. She poured out three large whiskies.

When everyone had their drink Kate sat beside her mother. Patrick looked at them. They were like two peas in a pod, both with the same high cheekbones and widow's peak. Both had a slightly Roman nose. Individually, all their features were beautiful, but altogether they just missed being wholly lovely. Instead they had what was termed attractive faces. Women who looked better as they got older. Kate certainly looked all right to him.

Evelyn broke the silence.

'So she's to see a head man, is she? Well, I think it's for the best, Kate. There's something drastically wrong with the child.'

She nodded, her eyes on the floor. Patrick's heart went out to her.

'You're the man who lost your daughter, aren't you?' Evelyn asked.

'Yes.'

'Tragic to lose a child like that.'

He looked into the old woman's face, saw the sympathy there and the understanding.

'My son went to Australia, you know. I've not seen him for twenty years. It's like he died. I hear from him regularly but it's not the same as holding them to you. Watching them grow and turn into whatever they become. He's a big grown man now and all I have are photographs to chart his years. It's not like seeing for yourself.'

Her little speech touched Patrick to the core. He felt the empathy between them. Knew that she had warmed to him, that she wanted to ease his grief, and for a dangerous few seconds he thought he would cry. He swallowed the lump that had come to his throat and downed his whisky.

'Are you family Irish, Mr Kelly?' Evelyn had to keep talking, had to stop thinking about Lizzy.

'Yes, My father was a Dublin man and my mother was from Cork. I was born in Glasnevin. I came over here when I was two.'

'Jesus save us, I know Glasnevin well! Is your mother still alive?'

Patrick shook his head. 'No, I'm afraid not. She was a wonderful woman.'

'I bet you have some great memories of her?'

He smiled again.

'Yes, I do.'

He saw his mother in his mind's eye, her arms red to the elbows from doing other people's washing and ironing, her knees permanently swollen from scrubbing floors. But he also saw the tiny smile she had, that serene look when she came home from six o'clock Mass every morning. Her pressing a shilling in his hand every birthday, no matter how hard up they were. Oranges at Christmas and a small toy. Oh, he had fond memories all right.

Kate watched her mother and Patrick as if in a trance. She could see that if the circumstances of their meeting had been happier they would have had a good drink of her mother's secret stash of Bushmill's and reminisced all night. She was glad Patrick was here. He was like a big dependable rock, taking both their troubled minds off Lizzy. But her daughter had to be helped and that was what scared Kate.

Getting up she went to the cabinet to replenish their glasses and found that the Bell's bottle was nearly empty. Seeing this Evelyn got up from her seat and said, 'I'll go and get me Bushmill's.'

She went from the room and Patrick smiled at Kate. 'Try and relax. Lizzy's in the best place for her at the moment. Tomorrow's time enough to worry.'

'I feel so bloody useless. How could all that have gone on under my nose?'

Patrick grasped her hand and pulled her to him.

She stared into his eyes.

'Look, Kate, you're not the only person this has happened to. Every parent says this at some time. I remember when I found out Mandy was sleeping with that geek Kevin, I felt like throttling the pair of them. But it's something that's happened and you can't make it unhappen. No matter how much you might want to. I told you, build some bridges now. Let some good come out of this.'

Oh, he sounded so right, but deep inside Kate she felt she had failed Lizzy somehow.

Evelyn bustled back into the room with her Irish whiskey. 'I call this my Holy Water, it's as good as a tonic. My cousin from Coleraine sends it to me, may God bless her and keep her. It's the mountain water that gives it the taste. You know her name's actually Katie Daly. It's true.'

Patrick laughed.

'Katie Daly' had been one of his mother's favourite songs. It was about a girl who made poteen, an illegal Irish whiskey, and the troops who came to arrest her.

Evelyn poured everyone out a generous measure. Kate sipped the liquid and felt the burn as it hit her throat. 'Tomorrow, when she sees the head man, I'll go with you, Kate, and we'll try and sort this business out. We'll make it all right, you'll see.'

'But to cut her wrists like that, Mum. She was more worried about you reading the diary than anything else.'

'And so she should have been, the ungrateful little villain!'

Patrick sipped his drink. This was getting personal.

'I think I better go soon, I know you have a lot to talk about.'

Kate nodded. The driver was sitting outside waiting and suddenly she remembered him.

'Oh, your poor Willy must be freezing!'

'I beg your pardon, Kate Burrows?'

Despite herself she laughed at her mother's scandalised face.

'That's his driver, Mum. Willy's his name. He's waiting outside for Patrick.'

'Oh I see. Well, bring him in. We don't stand on ceremony in this house.'

Patrick drank up quickly. Somehow he didn't think Kate's mother was quite ready for Willy yet.

'No, I've intruded long enough. I just wanted to make sure that Kate got home OK.' He stood up and the two women stood with him. He shook Evelyn's hand. 'It was a pleasure to meet you, Mrs . . .'

'O'Dowd. Evelyn O'Dowd.'

He smiled at her again. 'Mrs O'Dowd, I hope we meet again, in more pleasant circumstances.'

'So do I, son.'

Kate went out to the hall with him and Patrick kissed her gently. 'You stop worrying now, Kate, and if you need anything, anything at all, you just ring me. OK?'

Kate nodded, too full of unshed tears to answer.

She watched him walk down the path and get into his Rolls-Royce. When the car was out of sight she shut the door and went back into the warmth of the lounge.

'Well, you're a dark horse and no mistake.'

'Oh, Mum, he's just a friend.'

Kate sat down and picked up her drink again.

'Just a friend is he? Well, if you want my advice, I'd say make him more than a friend, if you get my meaning. Men like that don't grow on trees.'

'He owns massage parlours, Mum.'

Evelyn O'Dowd had her own set of principles, which she changed and updated depending on the situation.

'Well, we can't all be policemen can we? He's a good kind man by the looks of him. You take my advice and grab him quick, then you can show him what he's doing wrong.'

Kate sipped her drink.

'If the Chief Constable knew that I was seeing Patrick, all hell would break loose.'

Kate didn't know that the Chief Constable knew all about her and Kelly. Patrick Kelly and Frederick Flowers went back a long way. They were much closer than anyone knew – except the two of them, and they certainly wouldn't be telling anyone.

Evelyn bridled in her chair.

'Well, in that case you just refer him to me, young lady. What you do when you're out of that station is none of his business.'

If Kate hadn't had so much on her mind she would have laughed at her mother's scandalised voice.

'It's not like that, Mum, and you know it. Patrick's a nice man, you're right there, but he is also just on the verge of being a criminal.'

'I'm on the verge of being one meself, child, if I had the name of that person who gave Lizzy the drugs I'd scalp the face off them.'

Both women were silent.

'Listen to me, Katie. If you like this man, and you're happy seeing him, then you do what you want. No matter what your Chief Constable or Dan, or me or Lizzy or even King Street Charlie feels. You only live once. Live your life how you want. Before you know it you'll be old. Old as me. And when you get to my age you get a different perspective on life. Suddenly, every day seems just that little bit shorter. You feel the ache coming in your bones. You know that the best, most fruitful part of your life is over. I read once that when people get old and go senile, they go back to a time in their life when they were useful. To when they had young children, and a husband coming home from work. Meals to prepare. Maybe a little job as

297

well. I could understand them wanting to escape back to a time when they were "needed". Maybe because my days of being needed are nearly over.'

Kate slipped off her chair and knelt in front of her mother.

'I'll always need you, Mam.' At the word mam, Evelyn pulled her daughter into her arms, memories flooding back to her. Kate and her brother had both called her mam as children.

'Well, Kate, I'll be here for you for as long as you want me. The same for Lizzy, God love her. I could cheerfully cut the legs from her, but I'll always love her. Mary Ann that she is.'

Doctor Plumfield surveyed Kate and Evelyn as they sat in front of him. Kate had asked for another day of leave to try and get her family affairs sorted out. It had been granted grudgingly and she knew she was on thin ice as far as her superiors were concerned. Sympathetic they may be, but at the end of the day she was a DI and should put her work first. Particularly a murder investigation.

Lizzy's attempted suicide had been whispered around the station by now, she was sure.

Plumfield was young, and Kate thought he looked more like a social worker than a psychiatrist. He wore a pair of faded blue jeans and a rugby shirt. His hair was thinning on top but he had a small ponytail at the back. His fingers were tobacco-stained as he fiddled with a biro.

He sat back in his chair and sighed. Kate felt like a little girl who has been caught cheating in her exams.

'Your daughter, Mrs Burrows, is a very confused and unhappy girl.'

She listened attentively, all the while thinking, Tell me something I don't know.

Plumfield continued talking in a nasal voice and she decided that he must be a demon to live with. He did not address people as equals but spoke down to them.

'Lizzy has manifested signs of severe depression, and I feel that her drug taking and other behavioural patterns need close attention. To a child, Mrs Burrows, a slap is as good as a cuddle. After all, they are both forms of attention.'

'So you think that Lizzy needs more attention?'

Plumfield held up his hand. 'I am still talking, Mrs Burrows.'

Kate rolled her eyes to the ceiling. This man just could not be real!

'I can see you are used to being in charge.' He pointed a finger at her. 'You are not at the station now.'

He smiled to take the edge off his words and suddenly it hit Kate: he was a Bill hater. Kate had come across them all her working life, from the solicitors who tried to get off known offenders to the social workers who stood up in courts of law and gave character references for people who should have been locked up once and for all.

He was going to lay all the blame at her door.

Kate bit her lip and let the man speak.

'Your daughter –' this was said like an accusation – 'has agreed to go into a psychiatric hospital for a while, where we can assess her properly. She will travel there later this afternoon from here. She'll be in Warley Hospital.'

Evelyn watched his loose-lipped face and felt her mettle rise. 'Excuse me, Doctor Plumtree . . .'

'It's Plumfield.'

'Doctor Plumfield then. I think you've got an awful cheek! This is my granddaughter that you're talking about. Now I don't like your attitude, young man. Just tell us when she's going, what's going to happen to her, and how long we can expect her to be there.'

Doctor Plumfield shook his head as if he was dealing with two recalcitrant children. Kate put her hand on her mother's arm.

'Your daughter will be there as long as it takes to help her, Mrs Burrows. She is rebelling against something. What, we're not sure of yet.' He looked at Kate as he said this and the message was quite clear to her. 'This destructive behaviour needs to be looked at. If you wish to see her you may do so, but I must stress that you should try not to upset her in any way.'

Kate stood up.

'Thank you very much, Doctor Plumfield. Before we go – will you be treating her at Warley?'

'No, I won't.'

Kate smiled then.

'Well, at least we have that to be thankful for. Come on, Mum, let's go and see Lizzy.'

They left Doctor Plumfield sitting shaking his head. As they walked through the hospital to Lizzy's ward, Evelyn kept up a stream of abuse.

'The cheek of that one! To try and insinuate that we had done something wrong. I'd have liked to have cut the face off of him with a few choice words. And what's Lizzy been saying to him, I'd like to know?'

As always when she was very angry, Evelyn's voice was a thick Irish brogue.

Kate let it all go in one ear and out the other.

They finally arrived at Lizzy's ward. She was sitting up in bed listening to the radio on the headphones. Her face was washed and her hair brushed. In the hospital gown she seemed very young. She looked at her mother and grandmother and smiled tremulously. Pulling the headphones from her ears she put out her arms, and Kate hugged her.

'Oh, Mum . . . Gran . . . I'm so glad you're here!'

Evelyn pushed Kate gently out of the way and hugged her granddaughter. Lizzy began to cry.

'Now, now, whist now. Everything's going to be all right.'

Kate sat on the bed and watched them.

'They want me to go to a mental hospital, Mum.'

'How do you feel about that?'

Lizzy shook her head. 'I don't know. They seem to think that I'm a bit touched . . .'

Evelyn broke in, 'Now don't call it that. All you need is a bit of a rest, time to sort out your thoughts.'

'I don't know what's wrong with me, though!'

Lizzy was on the verge of hysteria. Kate grasped her daughter's hand.

'Well, they'll find that out in Warley. A sui—. . . what you did, is a very frightening thing, Liz. You must try and find out why you did it.'

'I know why I did it! It was because of Nan reading the diary, that's all.'

'Why did you take the drugs?'

'Oh, everyone takes drugs nowadays. I'm not an addict, Mum. I don't take heroin or anything like that.'

'But from what I read in the diary you take them often, every day. Amphetamines, cannabis, Ecstasy. What I can't understand is how this all went on under my nose.'

Lizzy lay back in the bed. 'Sometimes, Mum, when I was stoned, I would come and chat to you when you got in. You never even guessed because the amphetamines just make you chatty. They make you high, happy.'

'And you're not happy without them?'

Lizzy stared down at the bandages on her wrists.

'Not very often.'

'But why?' Kate's voice rose and the girl in the next bed stared at them all.

'I just don't know, Mum. I don't know. I think about death all the time.'

Kate stared at the white-tiled floor. How could a sixteen-year-old girl think about death? Her life was just starting.

'Where's Dad?'

'I don't know.'

'He hasn't even tried to find out how I am, has he?' Her voice was flat.

'He'll be in touch, Lizzy, he thinks the world of you.'

'Yeah, of course he does.' Her voice was bitter and Kate and Evelyn exchanged worried glances.

Life had a funny way of catching up with you, thought Kate. Just when you thought you had it all figured out, it threw you a curve like this.

Doctor Plumfield was right about one thing. Lizzy should go to Warley Hospital.

She needed help, professional help, and Kate was honest enough to admit that it couldn't come from her or her mother.

Patrick was standing outside a house in Barking. Three of his best men were with him. It was twenty to twelve and he had arrived ten minutes earlier. This was one of the jobs that he hated. They were to evict a couple and their three children from a rented house. Patrick had been called in when the man had threatened his team with a baseball bat. In normal circumstances the men would just have forced their way in and relieved him of the weapon. But the police had been called so everything had to be done by the book. The man was watching them from a bedroom window, the bat visible.

A young PC went to the letter box and began shouting through it.

'Come on, Mr Travers, this is silly. If you come down here we can talk about it.'

He stepped away from the letter box and looked up towards the window. Mr Travers, a plasterer, who had lost his house when he had been made bankrupt, opened the window slowly. He poked out a grizzled head.

'Fuck off, the lot of you. I paid that bastard and he knows I paid him.'

The constable tried again. He lifted the letter box.

'The man you rented the house from has never paid the mortgage. It is the building society who's evicting you, Mr Travers, not your landlord. If you'll just come down we'll try and get this sorted out.'

He looked through the letter box. He could see a woman holding a young baby standing at the end of the hall. She looked haggard. Her clothes were crumpled and she had no shoes on. He noticed that her feet were filthy. She shook her head at him in a gesture of bewilderment.

'We paid him the other day. We paid him four hundred quid, a month's rent. We've been here for six months. We ain't got nowhere to go.'

Two little girls, twins, walked from one of the downstairs rooms and went to her. The constable sighed heavily. He shut the letter box and went back to the little crowd on the pavement.

'Poor bastards. This is happening more and more. Someone buys a house, gets a mortgage and then rents it out to poor gits like them. They take the four hundred a month or whatever for as long as they can, then when the place gets repossessed they've had it on their toes. Nowhere to be seen. Some of these blokes have eight or nine houses on the go. They make a fortune.'

Patrick nodded. Mortgage scams were as old as the hills. He hated these jobs.

'Let me have a go.'

The constable shrugged. 'I'm getting on to Social Services. They might find them a bed and breakfast or something.'

Patrick nodded and went up to the front door.

He bellowed through the letter box: 'My name's Patrick Kelly and I have been asked to repossess this property. I am a court bailiff. Now, Mr Travers, you have your wife and children in there with you, and they are probably frightened out of their lives. Come down and we'll try and get something sorted.'

Ben Travers stood in the bedroom. He knew who Patrick Kelly was, everyone knew who Patrick Kelly was. He was a legend in his own lifetime.

Travers looked around the squalid room. Their so-called furnished accommodation had consisted of two old beds that had come from a second-hand shop, a broken-down settee, and a gas cooker that had probably been used all through the war. He looked around the room and felt the frustration and anger building up inside him. He had come to this, with a wife and three kids to support.

Every penny he'd saved had gone to getting the key money for this house, over a thousand pounds, and then the four hundred a month rent. They'd had to get away from Louise's mother! They had lived with her for three months before they got this place, and it had been three months too long as far as he was concerned. Two years earlier he'd had a privatised council house in East Ham, a nice little business and his family. Now it had come to this, the repomen at the door for the second time. He caressed the baseball bat, then holding it down by his side slowly walked down the uncarpeted stairs.

His wife was crying quietly and he looked at her sadly. 'I'm sorry, Lou.'

'Just let them in, Ben, let's get this over with.'

He nodded and went to the front door. As he opened it Patrick Kelly walked inside. He shut the front door on all the onlookers.

'Mr Travers? I am really very sorry about this, but the eviction notice has been granted. I know that the bloke who tucked you up will get off with it scot free. By the way, do you have a name for him at all? Maybe I could find him and recoup some of your money?'

Ben Travers nodded.

'It's Micky Danby. I trusted the ponce. He was only round last week to collect the month's rent. He never told us nothing. We signed a year's lease on this place but it ain't worth the paper it's written on. What the fuck we gonna do now?'

Patrick opened his coat and took out his wallet. He pulled out three fifty-pound notes.

'Take this to tide you over. Get a B & B or something. This is my card. Leave a message with my secretary about where you are and I'll see about recouping some of your losses. Micky Danby is a prat and I owe him a few scores meself.'

The man took the money. 'Thanks, Mr Kelly. I'll pay you back one day.' His voice was shaky.

'Give me the baseball bat and we'll get this over with.' Patrick inclined his head to the woman watching him. 'How about a nice cuppa, love, while we get this sorted out?'

The woman nodded, glad of something to do.

Patrick opened the front door and smiled at everyone. 'Everything's OK, officers, you can go now.'

'Fair enough. I've radioed in for the Social Services, they'll find them some alternative accommodation. See you, Mr Kelly.'

The PC got in his car and drove off. Patrick followed

Ben Travers into his front room. It was nearly bare except for an old portable TV and a sixties-style PVC settee. He sat on it with the two little girls and gave them a big smile. He'd wait until the Social came, see what the score was. He looked at Ben Travers. He looked a big strong man.

'Working?'

'Only on the lump, here and there. The building game's fucked at the moment. They're laying down the footings for houses and then just leaving them. It's a bloody joke.'

Patrick nodded.

'Ever thought of doing this job?'

Ben Travers frowned. 'What, being a bailiff you mean?'

'Yeah, why not? It's good steady work.'

'Never thought about it.'

'Well, see one of my blokes and they'll tell you what you'll need. I'd take you on. I'm always after decent blokes with a bit of savvy.'

'I'll do that, Mr Kelly, I'll do that.'

Patrick smiled at the woman as she brought in the tea.

'Thanks, love.' He gestured around the room.

'Not worth four hundred sovs a month this.'

The woman grimaced. 'The fucking Ritz it ain't. If I could get my hands on that Micky Danby now, I'd break his sodding neck.'

Patrick looked at Ben Travers.

'Do you think she might want a job and all?' Ben Travers burst out laughing. It was a laugh he didn't think he had in him.

Patrick sipped his tea.

Since Mandy had died, he'd gone soft, he admitted that. Knowing grief as he did, he wanted to spare as many people as possible the experience. Except the Grantley Ripper. That was one man he wanted people to grieve for.

When that bastard was dead, maybe he would start living a proper life, a life that he hoped would include Kate Burrows.

Kate was beginning to mean a lot to him. He thought about her constantly. The day she had come to his house to talk about her daughter's problem he had felt much closer to her. He knew that she was a DI and a bloody good one, by all accounts. He knew that they came from two different worlds, but still nothing would deter him.

When she'd said she was worried about her superiors, he'd felt like telling her that he had her superiors right where he wanted them, but he couldn't. Kate would not stand for anything like that, she was too straight. That's what he liked about her. From the first night he had met her, when she had stood up to him in his own house, he had been attracted to her. She was one of the few people who had no fear of him, even her Chief Constable would be shocked if he heard the way she argued with him sometimes.

Kate was a woman in every sense of the word, and she was a woman who would not give herself to a man lightly. When they had gone to bed together on New Year's Eve it had been like a revelation to him. Never before, not even with Renée, had he felt such a force of love in him. She confided afterwards that it was the first sexual contact she'd had in over five years. She had only ever had one man before in her life. To Patrick that statement had put her above everyone. She was clean and decent and he wanted her on any terms.

He wondered how her daughter was. How Kate was coping with the day.

He found himself thinking about her all the time.

Despite all his heartbreak, it was a pleasant feeling.

*

Kate and Evelyn took Lizzy to Warley themselves. They had stopped off at home and packed a case for her and then they had stayed to help her settle in. The funny thing was that Lizzy seemed glad to be going. At least everyone there seemed very nice, they had welcomed Lizzy and made her feel secure and wanted. She was sharing a room with a girl called Anita, an ex heroin addict. Anita was small and blonde and full of life; she seemed to hit it off with Lizzy straight away.

Lizzy had made Kate promise not to let on she was a policewoman. Kate had been reluctant to agree, but she saw the sense of it. In a unit where most of the people were drug abusers it would not exactly endear Lizzy to them to have a mother who was a 'Filth'.

Lizzy's white, drawn features haunted her. She watched her mother and daughter talking together and felt a deep hurt, as if she had somehow been the cause of it all. She had lain awake the night before, thinking, If only I'd made Dan stay. But he had not wanted to stay. She had not made Dan go, he had practically run out of her life. Bag and baggage. Lizzy had adored her father and he had only ever let her down. Kate had prided herself on never doing so, but maybe she had failed?

As they left the hospital, Evelyn grabbed her hand to cross the road to get to the car park. Kate closed her eyes tightly. Her mother still helped her across the road. It was laughable really.

She dropped Evelyn off at home and then made her way into work. She had to see Ratchette and try and undo some of the damage that had been done there. As much as she loved Lizzy, and as much as she wanted to help her, without her job they would all be up a creek without a paddle.

Something Lizzy often forgot.

As Kate and her mother left the hospital, Dan was making his way in. It was just as well they missed each other. Kate wasn't in the right mood for him. But his presence made Lizzy happy.

Ratchette and Kate faced one another. He had offered her coffee and now the two of them sat sipping it.

'Are you sure everything's OK, Kate? If you need compassionate leave . . .'

She shook her head. 'No, I don't. Lizzy is being very well looked after and I shall be back at work tomorrow.'

'Well,' Ratchette drew the word out between his teeth, 'this is a very stressful case, Kate. As I'm sure you're aware, we need people on it who will give it one hundred percent . . .'

As she opened her mouth to speak there was a knock on the door.

'Come in.'

Caitlin bowled into the office.

'Hello there, Katie! How's your poor daughter?' He beamed at them. 'I'm glad that I caught you. When are you back? Because I've been keeping a record of everything that's been happening for you, you know, so you won't have missed anything.'

'I'll be back tomorrow.'

'That's grand, just grand. I hope everything works out with the girl.'

'Did you want anything, Kenny?' Ratchette's voice was loud.

Caitlin poked himself in the chest. 'Who me? Not at all. I just heard that Katie here was in so I came to see when she'd be back on duty, that's all. See you tomorrow then.'

He smiled at her and gave her a little wink. Then, as he was walking out the door, he slapped his forehead hard and turned back to face them. 'Have you finished here, Kate?'

She looked at Ratchette who nodded his head.

'Yes, sir.'

'Then come with me and pick up the latest reports. Very interesting they are as well.'

She put down her coffee cup and, nodding at Ratchette, followed Caitlin from the office. Once outside he linked arms with her and took her to the little pub that the station staff used. It was called the Swan and was always busy. He bought two large whiskies and, sitting Kate in the corner, drank to her daughter's health.

'Thanks, Kenny.'

He waved his hand at her. 'Sure I know what you're going through. I remember when one of my girls had an abortion, I was like a maniac for days after. You need your work at the moment to keep you sane and normal!'

'I thought you were Catholic?'

'Oh, I am, we all are, but you see she was only fourteen at the time. It was terrible, absolutely terrible. Now how's the child really?'

Kate found herself opening up to him. She told him everything.

'Them drugs is the scourge of parents. But just keep a good eye on her and keep her out of draughts. A blanket for disease, draughts are.'

Kate smiled to herself. He meant well.

'What's been happening with the case then?'

'Sweet FA to be honest, Kate. I gave Ratchette a load of old fanny just now. Hopefully, something will break soon. We're still following up on all the nonces and suspected nonces but it's a piss in the ocean, there's so many of them.'

'Thanks a lot, Kenny, for standing by me like that.'

Caitlin laughed. 'Where else am I going to get such a good-looking DI? Normally I get a big sweaty drunkard who smells like a year-old jockstrap. Anyway, one of me is enough on any case!'

Kate grinned. You found friends and allies in the most unlikely places.

'What about Louise Butler?'

'Nothing. We're treating it as a murder obviously, but if her body doesn't turn up soon . . .' He left the sentence unfinished.

Kate stood up. 'Same again?'

'That's what I like about this women's lib, it's cheaper to take a lady out these days!'

Kate went up to the bar. She glanced at the large clock on the wall. It was six thirty. She'd have a half of lager and make her way home. She was seeing Patrick at eight, and wanted to ring round and see if she could find Dan first. She had a few words to say to him which he wasn't going to like.

She was quite looking forward to it.

Chapter Sixteen

George stood in his bedroom, perplexed. His face settled into a deep frown. He knew, in fact he was absolutely sure, that his tiepin had been in the top drawer of the dressing table. Now it was nowhere to be seen. He lifted the drawer out and placed it on the bed. He began to rummage through it again.

Nothing.

He bit his cheek in consternation. There was only one place it could be. He had searched his bedroom thoroughly so he must have lost it on New Year's Eve. He began to sweat. When Elaine had left that night he had dressed quickly. He could not remember whether he had put a tie on at all, but the logical side of him said that he must have. He put the drawer back and absentmindedly tidied it.

There was only one thing for it: he would have to go back and see if it was on the body. Thank God he had had the sense to bury this one! The devil looked after his own – another of his mother's sayings that proved once more to George that she was always right.

He looked at his watch. It was six fifty-five. Elaine was

off out with the girls tonight, he would go as soon as she left. He straightened the bedcover so it was nice and smooth, he hated untidiness of any kind, and walked from the bedroom. On the landing he could hear Elaine, in the bath, singing 'I Could Have Danced All Night'. He grimaced. Elaine's singing was like everything else about her: terrible. As he walked down the stairs she reached a high-pitched crescendo and George felt his shoulders disappearing into the back of his neck. Elaine's voice grated on him.

She grated on him.

At eight forty-five, George was standing over the makeshift grave of Louise Butler. He had brought his large torch with him. Setting it on the ground, he began to disinter the girl. George was puffing and panting, his gardening gloves making the removal of the stones difficult. He had not realised he had buried her so deeply. He squatted for a second to get his breath.

That's when he noticed the smell. An awful smell of rotting meat. George heaved, his face in the torchlight looking green-tinged and old. Standing up, he took his handkerchief from his pocket and tied it across his nose and mouth. Steeling himself, he began once more to pull at the stones and dirt.

He felt something soft and sighed with satisfaction. At last!

He felt along the small stones and, locating a hand, pulled it from the debris. Then he began to clear away the dirt from around the body, flicking it from the girl's face fastidiously. Leaning out of the hole, he grabbed at the torch and shone it down on the corpse.

George tutted.

After eight days of death, Louise was bloated. Her

semi-naked body was twisted grotesquely in the earth. Her lovely hair was caked with dirt and the eyes that were staring at George were a milky white. Her mouth was open in a perfect O, and George cleaned the dirt out of it with his gloved finger, like a midwife with a newborn baby. He searched through the dirt as he poked it from her mouth, rubbing it between finger and thumb.

No tiepin.

He began to unearth the rest of Louise Butler, searching her meticulously, the horror gone now as self-preservation took precedence over everything. He searched everywhere, even between her legs and buttocks. Her skin was spongy and when he tried to turn the body over, it came away in his hands, ragged pieces of skin sticking to his gardening gloves.

George tutted again. This time in temper. The bloody little slut! She could get him in trouble!

He looked at his watch. It was nine thirty-seven. He had been searching for over an hour. He had been through the dirt and all over the bitch's body and the tiepin was nowhere to be seen!

Standing up, he began to brush himself down. The damp weather had made the dirt sticky and George was aware that he would have to leave soon, to be clean and ready for Elaine coming in.

Then, his temper getting the better of him, he began to kick at Louise, enjoying the feel of the soft flesh beneath his boots. He kicked at her until he was tired. His eyes were hurting and he closed them for a few seconds. When he opened them he sighed loudly.

Louise Butler's face was a pulp.

George took off his gloves and pushed them into the pocket of his coat. He bent down and, feeling a delicious tenderness take the place of his temper, arranged the remains of her hair lovingly around her face, brushing away a centipede that was trying to get back inside the warmth of her ear cavity.

Satisfied she looked all right, George picked up his torch and made his way back to his car. He had parked it about a quarter of a mile away and walked to it, dirty and bedraggled and in a daze.

Where the hell was that tiepin?

Louise Butler was fully exposed to view. Her rifled body looked milky in the moonlight.

Elaine sat in the restaurant with Hector Henderson. She smiled at him happily. Hector smiled back, displaying his erratic teeth. Elaine didn't care if they clicked now and again when he spoke, or the fact he had to hold his hand over his mouth while he pushed them back into position with his tongue. As far as Elaine was concerned, the big, fat, jolly man opposite was her own personal Rudolph Valentino.

'I hope everything's all right for you, Elaine?'

'Oh, it is, Hector, it's lovely.'

He beamed at her. His heavy face was glistening with a fine film of perspiration as he leant forward awkwardly in his chair and poured her another glass of Chianti.

'I'll be drunk!' Elaine's voice was girlish and in the subdued lighting she looked much younger than usual. She caught a glimpse of herself in the large mirror on the opposite wall and was pleased with herself. Her diet had taken off quite a few unwanted curves. She actually looked quite well. Not exactly thin, she was big-boned and knew it, but at least she didn't look so chunky.

Sitting in this restaurant, with Hector telling her all she wanted to hear, she felt quite light-hearted and gay. They had been to this restaurant twice before. It was through the Dartford tunnel and so was officially in Kent. They came here because there was no likelihood of seeing anyone that they knew. Now it had become their restaurant. Elaine loved Italian food and had practically starved herself for three days in order to enjoy a small helping of lasagne.

Hector watched Elaine tuck into her dinner. He liked a woman with an appetite. He approved of her size and shape, liked big women – he was a big man – and tonight he was going to get inside Elaine's tights if it was the last thing he did. He felt a stirring of excitement at the thought of it. Her breasts, he could see, were absolutely enormous. Being a regular subscriber to *Bra Busters*, he was automatically excited by this. He closed his eyes and savoured the picture of them loosed from their confines and lying in his open palms . . .

'Would you like a dessert, Elaine?'

She grinned girlishly again. 'I shouldn't really. My weight . . .'

Hector put up his hand to quieten her. 'You have the voluptuous figure of maturity, and that's just how I like my women.'

Elaine felt like swooning across the table. She wasn't too sure about the maturity bit, but the rest was like music to her ears. Hector took her hands in his and kissed each palm in turn.

'If only you were truly mine. But you belong to another man and I can but worship from afar instead of drinking from the fountainhead.'

Elaine listened to him with fascination.

A waiter nearby bit his lip to stop a laugh escaping. Elaine had no inkling of that though. Hector brought back the old longings she had repressed for so long. He made her feel feminine and desirable. He gave her the romance that she craved so desperately. He was, in short, her knight in shining armour.

It was then she decided to sleep with him. He could drink her fountain dry if he liked.

Kate was sitting, listening to some music, which was turned on low so as not to disturb her mother who had retired to bed at nine, an hour earlier. She was listening to Billy Paul singing 'Me and Mrs Jones', relaxing to the music and trying to think rationally about Lizzy. She had showered earlier and now sat in an old cotton dressing gown, her hair spread across her shoulders to dry naturally, her face wiped clean of make-up, shining with Ponds cold cream in the firelight. As the record ended she shifted position slightly on the settee and tucked her feet up underneath her. She needed this quiet time, without even her mother with her. She felt at times that she did not have enough time alone, except in bed. As Sad Cafe began to sing 'Every Day Hurts', she heard a knock on her front door. She glanced at the clock on the mantelpiece. It was past ten. Who could be knocking at this time? Dragging herself from her seat she went out to the hall. Through the glass of the front door she saw the unmistakable figure of Dan.

That was all she needed.

Squaring her shoulders, she opened the door. He pushed past her, his face set in a deep frown, and walked into the living room.

'Why don't you just come on in, Dan?' She kept her voice low. She didn't want her mother down here.

She went into the lounge where he was pouring himself a brandy. This lent her anger an added edge. Who the hell did he think he was? He charged in here without a by your leave and acted like it was his house or something.

He faced her and took a deep drink of the brandy, then

pointed his finger at her menacingly. She watched it stabbing the air as he spoke, adding emphasis to his words.

'What's this I hear that you're seeing a bloody wide boy? Our daughter's in hospital – a hospital for the sick in the head, I might add – and you're running round with Grantley's answer to the bloody Godfather!'

Kate suppressed a smile. So that was what really rankled. He knew she was seeing someone. I don't want you, but I'm damned if anyone else will have you.

'I'll thank you to keep your voice down, if you don't mind. My mother is in bed. As for my private life, that's why it's called a private life – it's sod all to do with you who I see, when I see them or what I do with them. Now finish your drink and go. I've had a very trying day and it's not getting any better.'

'I'm not going anywhere until I get to the bottom of this!'

Kate was exasperated. 'The bottom of what, for goodness sake? I'm a big girl now, Dan. What I do is no business of yours.'

'It is when it affects my daughter.'

This was said so low as to be virtually inaudible. Kate raised one eyebrow.

'What did you say?' Her voice was dangerously low and Dan should have heeded the warning in it.

'You heard.'

She walked towards him, and he watched the bottom of her dressing gown flapping open as she walked. She'd always had good legs.

'Listen, you, I've put up with you for Lizzy – but I warn you now, Dan, leave me alone! I mean it. You just keep out of my face.'

Dan laughed.

'My God, you're even talking like a gangster! You're

warning me? You're the one who's making a slut of herself. No wonder Lizzy turned out like she did, with you as an example!'

The record came to an end and the sound as Kate slapped his face was like a gunshot in the quiet of the room. Dan put down his glass. Kate could see he was trembling with temper. But she felt no fear. One thing in Dan's favour, he would never raise his hand to a woman. Oh, he might break their heart, use them, abuse their trust, but he fancied himself a gentleman so would stop short of slapping her.

'If you really cared about Lizzy, Dan, you would have seen more of her over the years. You would have tried to make her feel loved, secure and wanted. Lizzy is like she is because you drifted in and out of her life, building up her fragile hopes and then dashing them. I was to blame in as much as I let you. I let you come here and use us between women and homes. I thought it was good for her to see you.

'But I tell you, Danny boy, if she asks me anything about you from now on she won't get the nice rosy edited version, she'll get the truth. I'll tell her just what a tosser you really are!'

Dan put both palms on Kate's chest and pushed her backwards with all his strength. She landed, winded, on the settee.

His face was twisted with rage but he kept his voice low.

'And what about you then? What about marvellous Kate the Wonder Woman? You're a ball breaker, Kate, that's why I left you. You always wanted to own me. I always had to be what *you* wanted.

'Well, listen and listen good. I always thought of you as a good woman but when I was told by an old friend you were on your back for Patrick Kelly, I finally saw you for

what you really are! You'll not drag my daughter down
with you. When she comes out of hospital, I'm going to
ask her to come to my flat with me. And when I tell her
about Patrick Kelly, I think she'll come without a
backward glance.'

Kate sat up, stunned.

'I don't believe what I'm hearing.'

'And what have your superiors got to say about it, eh?
I'd like to know what they think about a DI running
around with a bloody villain.'

Suddenly Kate had had enough.

'I think you'd better go before we both say anything
else we'll regret. Lizzy is coming home to me for a short
time. I've written to my brother in Australia to see if he
will take her and my mother for an extended holiday. I
think a change of environment and some sun will do her
the world of good. What Lizzy needs now is an uncom-
plicated way of life, time to put all that's happened behind
her. If you try and shove a spanner in the works, Dan, I'll
dog you until the end of your days. I mean it. You'll not
ruin that child's chance of getting well, I won't allow it.

'I'll tell you what's wrong with you, shall I? You're
jealous because you think I'm having an affair, a
relationship. Good old Kate, who always waited for you in
the past, has now got herself a man.

'And believe me, Dan, he's more man than you'll ever
be, in bed and out of it!'

The words were said in temper, in hurt, but the look on
Dan's face told her the effect that they'd had on him. Dan
thought he was a gifted lover, a woman's man; he lived his
life for the pleasures of the flesh. Now his last hope of
regaining a normal family life had turned sour on him.
Kate felt a sneaking triumph at the way she had finally put
him down, as he had put her down for so long.

'So you're sleeping with him then? It's true?'

All the fight seemed to have seeped out of him. In the space of a few seconds Kate saw his body sag, saw the paunch that he tried so valiantly to hold in, saw the puffiness under his eyes from too much booze and too many late nights, saw the slackness of his jaw that was finally denoting his age. Kate saw him as he really was and it was the end of the line for both of them.

Years before Dan could conquer Kate all over again with a few sweet words, a few practised caresses. He realised now, with stunning clarity, that he had played tonight's scenario all wrong.

Kate had finally and unequivocally grown up. Up and away from him. Bluster and bombast would not work now because she wasn't frightened of what he thought any more. The worst thing of all was the fact that she had never looked more beautiful or desirable to him, with her cheeks flaming and her long silky hair strewn around her shoulders.

He wanted to throw himself on top of her, felt an urge to take her there and then on the settee as he had in the past. Kate had never resisted when he'd touched her then. She would yield and abandon herself to him then everything would be fine, everything would be roses – until he felt the wanderlust again. The need for new pastures, for new faces, for a different life.

Kate heard a tap on the window and looked at him. Who could that be?

He walked across the room and peeked out of the curtain. He turned back to face her and she saw the fear in his eyes.

'Who is it? It's not someone from the hospital?' Her voice was filled with fear for Lizzy. It was nearly ten thirty, who would be tapping on her window now?

'It's your boyfriend, come for a late night legover by the look of things.'

It took a few seconds for the words to sink in. Patrick? Here? She pulled herself from the settee and went out to the hallway. Dan pulled her back.

'Don't open the door, Kate, please. I'll do anything you want – we can get married again, anything – but please don't answer the door to him. If you do it will always be between us.'

Kate searched his blue eyes with her own dark ones. She saw the wanting in him, knew that this time she had the upper hand, what she had craved all her life with him – and it meant nothing. Patrick Kelly was nearby and he was what she wanted, for however long it might last.

Kate had never loved lightly, she had always loved one hundred per cent, and now Dan knew, looking into her eyes, that her allegiance to him had gone for good. He wasn't really surprised when she pulled her arm free and, straightening her dressing gown, walked to the front door. With those few steps she finally severed any remaining ties between them.

Patrick stood on the doorstep perplexed. He had seen the light from the front room and wondered what was keeping Kate. He was sorry now that he had come round so late, but he had felt an overwhelming urge to see her. He had been sitting in his house alone, and Mandy had invaded his thoughts as she always did when he had nothing else to occupy him, and suddenly the urge to see Kate was so strong it was almost tangible. Taking his BMW he had driven himself to her house. Now it did not seem like a very good idea.

He saw her slim form walking down the hall and felt a surge of pleasure. As she opened the door he smiled at her crookedly.

'I know it's late but I saw your lights on . . .' His voice trailed off.

Kate had never been so glad to see anyone in her life.

'Come in, it's freezing.' He followed her down the hall and into the lounge. Kate was not surprised to find it was empty. She had heard the back door close as she opened the door to Patrick. Dan was a lot of things but brave was not one of them.

'How about a drink? Tea, coffee, a brandy?' She saw Dan's glass where he had left it on the coffee table. It was still half full.

'Coffee will be fine, I'm driving myself tonight. Where's your mother?'

'She's in bed. I gave her a sleeping pill. All this with Lizzy has really hit her hard.' Kate was amazed at how normal she sounded.

'How's Lizzy?'

'Better. She seems to be thriving on being somewhere different. I know that sounds crazy but from what her doctor said, hospital can often be a stress-free environment. It gives people time to gather their thoughts, make decisions without any outside pressure. I only hope it works for Lizzy.'

She walked out to the kitchen and put the kettle on. The only light out there was from the tube lighting under the worktops. She left the overhead lights off. Patrick followed her out and slipped off his coat. He could see her body through the thin dressing gown and felt a stirring within him. Going to her, he slipped his arms around her waist.

Turning, Kate put her arms around his neck and pulled his face down to hers. Suddenly, she wanted him desperately. He was dangerous to her, she knew that. He lived his life taking what he wanted. He was a rogue, a villain, but he was also the most exciting man she had ever come across. She could ruin her career with this association, but at this moment she did not care.

He was there, he wanted her, and, oh God, how she wanted him. After the set-to with Dan, she wanted to be held, to be loved, to feel wanted and desirable.

He undid the belt of her dressing gown and rubbed her breasts gently. Kate moaned in his ear. After tasting the delights of Patrick Kelly, you found yourself willing to run risks.

She abandoned herself to him, unaware that Dan was watching them through the kitchen window. As he saw his wife, as he still thought of Kate, put her long legs around Patrick Kelly's waist, he felt pure hatred.

And now he had something to use against her. He would go and see the Chief Constable. See what he thought about the situation. He crept away from the window.

But he was already learning one thing: the prospect of revenge was not sweet at all. It left a bitter aftertaste.

Elaine and Hector Henderson had enjoyed themselves thoroughly and she tiptoed into the house at twelve thirty. As she heaved her substantial bulk up the stairs, George spoke to her from the darkness and she screamed at the top of her considerable voice.

'Oh, George! You bloody fool! You nearly gave me a sodding heart attack!'

He clicked on the hallway light and saw a red and flustered Elaine sitting on the bottom stair, her hands over her heart. The wild red hair that she had backcombed earlier looked as if it had been set on end by an electric shock.

'Sorry, my love. You're very late.'

'What were you doing sitting in the dark, waiting for

me to come in? Are you checking up on me, George Markham?'

Elaine's voice was dangerously low. Like most guilty partners, she found attack the best form of defence.

George looked at her long and hard. Surely she didn't think he was jealous? By God, who would touch her, for Christ's sake?

'Of course I'm not checking up on you. I had one of my headaches, that's all.'

Elaine squinted at him suspiciously, her old cantankerous self battling it out with the newer, more self-confident and laidback Elaine. As she stared at her husband it suddenly occurred to her that she didn't even hate him any more. She didn't feel anything at all, and wasn't sure that wasn't worse. At least while you were hating you were feeling something.

'Shall I make you a nice hot drink, dear, and bring it up to you?'

'OK, George.' Elaine mounted the stairs. She was tired. George always made her feel tired and depressed. Thank God she had Hector.

When George brought her up a cup of Ovaltine a little while later, Elaine was sitting at the dressing table in her corset, taking off a pair of stockings. George placed the Ovaltine on the bedside table and watched her, surprised at just how much weight she had lost. Her legs were getting quite shapely! As she peeled off the stockings and waggled her toes George noticed some tiny red marks on her neck. His mouth set in a grim line. Elaine lifted her arms and unclasped her gold locket, the action causing her enormous breasts to rise up in the heavily underwired bra she wore. She moved naturally, as if after years of having her husband take no notice of her she was invisible to him. She glanced at him and jolted as she saw him watching her.

'What's the matter now, George?' Her voice was clipped and demanded no reply.

He just carried on staring. She opened the jewellery box that held her few treasures and dropped the necklace into it.

'Oh, by the way, George, here's your tiepin. I nearly hoovered it up.' She picked up a ring box from inside her underwear drawer and threw it to him. 'I don't know what possessed me to put it in my drawer. I meant to give it to you yesterday but I forgot.'

George caught the box and opened it. There was his tiepin. He grinned his widest grin. Going to Elaine, he put his arms around her and kissed the top of her head.

'Here, steady on, George.' She pushed him off in disgust but he was too happy to notice.

He had the tiepin.

It was not lost.

There were no clues.

He was free as a bird.

Kate awoke to a feeling of lazy euphoria that seemed to have started somewhere in her legs and had, during the course of the night, washed through her entire body. She could smell Patrick Kelly on her and pulled the covers back over her head and breathed in the scent of him deeply.

Emerging once more, she noticed that it was light. Her bedroom curtains were open about two inches and she saw the weak dawn and felt it was invading her privacy. She glanced at the alarm clock. Six fifteen. She could lie for a while in total silence and think about the night before. Not about Dan, he was gone from her now as surely as if he was dead, but about Patrick. Patrick Kelly . . . even his name gave her a thrill.

He was here, or at least she felt that he was, and at this moment that was enough for her.

She had lived in a vacuum. Now, at forty, she was finally finding out what life was all about. The love side of it anyway.

If she could just get Lizzy back to her old self life would be nearly perfect. She didn't dare think completely perfect, because she knew that was too tall an order for anyone. But nearly perfect suited her right down to the ground.

The phone beside her bed rang.

'Hello?'

'Kate, this is Amanda. Louise Butler's body has turned up.'

She took a deep breath. 'Where?'

'In the old quarry. Look, I don't want to say too much over the phone. You can't miss the place, it's full of Panda cars. I'll see you soon.'

Kate put down the receiver and leapt from her bed. As she showered her mind was cleared of everything but the task ahead. As always when on a case, once she had some-thing to work on it took priority over everything. Her mind was blank now of Patrick, Lizzy, Dan. She thought only of Louise Butler. As she walked downstairs ready for work her mother was standing at the bottom with a cup of coffee for her and a lighted cigarette.

'Five minutes won't kill you, Katie. What's up?'

She took the coffee gratefully and took a deep puff on the cigarette. Coughing hard, she gulped some more coffee down.

'Louise Butler's body has been found.'

'Heaven help the poor child! Are you fit for all this?'

'As fit as I'll ever be.'

Kate gave her back the cup and pulled on her coat, the cigarette between her teeth, the smoke curling up into her eyes making her squint. She kissed her mother and went towards the door.

'Tell Lizzy I'll get in this evening, will you? I can't promise I'll be there this afternoon, but I'll try.'

'All right, love. You get off, and drive carefully.'

Kate kissed her again and went from the house. It was a chilly morning and she pulled the collar of her coat up around her neck.

She drove to the site of the discovery with a feeling of trepidation mixed with excitement. Please God let there be some kind of clue! To Kate's mind it wasn't a lot to ask.

She arrived at the quarry before Caitlin and slithered down the loose-stoned rise that led to the murder scene. When she got there she wished she'd stayed in bed.

The girl's body was covered. When they pulled the canvas away Kate felt a sickening lurch in her guts.

DS Spencer watched her and rolled his eyes.

'He must have come back and dug her up!'

Spencer looked at his superior with raised eyebrows.

'Dug her up, ma'am?' His voice was sceptical. 'Looks more like an animal had her to me.'

'I can see you'd think that at first, but look at the way the dirt's been smoothed around her, the way her hair has been arranged. No, our man came back and disinterred her for some reason. Cover her up, Spencer. Where's the pathologist?'

'In the jam sandwich over there, ma'am.'

Kate walked to the large police car and climbed into the back seat. 'So what's the gen so far? Am I right in thinking that our man's been back and dug her up?'

'Well, well, you are on top form this morning, Kate! I would say that she has been recently disinterred, yes. The facial injuries were inflicted after death, I'd lay money on that one.'

Kate was stunned.

'You mean he came back, dug her up and then attacked her again?'

'Spot on. Quite a nice chap you're looking for, I don't envy you. Ah, here's Caitlin, looking a bit the worse for wear. Never was at his best first thing in the morning, was our Kenny.'

Kate watched as Caitlin slid heavily down the stony incline to Louise Butler's body.

'One other thing, Katie, the girl was stripped naked last night. He usually leaves the clothes on them, cutting off the underwear. I couldn't find any evidence of recent sexual activity, but by the marks on the skin of her buttocks I would hazard a guess they were pulled apart recently, and quite savagely at that. Obviously, I'll know more after the PM. I'll have the report ready as soon as I can.

'I hate the stinkers, Kate, especially when they're young girls. She's higher than a damn pheasant at the moment. I'll be tasting formaldehyde with my dinner for days.'

Kate looked at the man beside her and bit her tongue. Nodding, she got out of the car and made her way carefully to where Caitlin was looking at the body. Higher than a damn pheasant! That was a fifteen-year-old girl he was talking about. She hoped against hope that she never became that cavalier about her job.

'Hello there, Katie darling.' Caitlin's Irish brogue drifted over to her on the cold wind. 'The fucker dug her up, the dirty bastard!'

Kate was gratified at the distress in his voice. If even hard-nosed coppers like Caitlin could still be moved, there was hope for her yet.

'Well, sir, he saved us a job, didn't he?' Spencer's nasal twang caused Kate, Caitlin and the uniforms to stare at him.

'Oh, yes, son, he did that all right.' Caitlin's voice was sarcastic. 'Shame all the perverts don't bury their victims and then dig them up later on. Save a fortune on inquiry charges that would. You stupid eejit . . . Get away out of me sight, before I give you a dig!'

Kate flicked her head at Spencer and he walked back to his police car, shamefaced. Kate felt sorry for him in a sense; she knew what he meant: at least the body had turned up, even if it was in this grisly fashion. Poor Mr and Mrs Butler.

'The pathologist thinks he attacked her again last night. Whether or not it was sexual he doesn't yet know. He thinks the face was beaten recently, but he could find no evidence of a sexual assault.'

'Probably wanked over her. That wouldn't leave anything.'

'I'm not so sure. Look at the way her hair has been arranged, the way the dirt's been smoothed around her. I think he was searching her. We know he's a nutter, and we know he's a sexual deviant.'

Kate knelt by the girl's body, repressing a shudder at the rancid smell. 'Suppose he thought he'd left some evidence on the body? What, I don't know. He could have come back, dug her up, searched her. Then when he didn't find what he wanted, or maybe even when he did, he attacked her. It's got a kind of twisted logic to it.'

Caitlin nodded. 'Sure you always was a clever girl, Katie. I think you're probably right. But this man has finally made his biggest mistake . . . He's wound me up, Kate. He's pushed me too far this time. When we find him – and we will – I'm going to beat his fucking brains in!'

Caitlin looked towards the uniforms and shouted: 'Where's the bloody undertakers? Get this child covered up and into a body bag.'

Kate stood up. In the grey light of day Caitlin looked terrible. His haggard face with its grey stubble seemed to have sagged overnight. For all his faults, and they were legion, at that moment Kate almost loved him.

'Come on, come back to the station with me and let forensic finish their work here.'

She took his arm and pulled him away gently. 'We'll go and get some hot coffee inside us.'

Both noticed she didn't mention breakfast.

Ronald Butler walked into the mortuary at Grantley Hospital, Kate beside him. The mortuary assistant pulled the white sheet from Louise's body and Ronald Butler stared down at the remains of his daughter. Kate looked away. Out of the corner of the eye she saw the man's hand go up to his mouth.

'Is this your daughter, sir?' Her voice was low. The formal identification had to be made.

He nodded and then bent double. The mortuary assistant quickly covered Louise up and both he and Kate rushed to Butler. He was now holding his chest tightly, and as he collapsed on to the floor Kate shouted: 'Get the bloody Crash team now. He's having a heart attack!'

When the assistant had run off she loosened the man's shirt and tie.

Ronald Butler was grey and a thin film of sweat shone all over his face and neck. His lips were blue. Kate knelt over his body and felt his neck for a pulse. It was barely noticeable. Entwining the fingers of both hands she pushed down hard on his chest, just to the left of his heart.

Oh, please God, let them hurry!

As if her prayers had been answered, she heard the clanging of the Crash trolley bursting through the plastic doors.

Kate carried on the heart massage until the Crash team took over and a few minutes later was gratified to hear Ronald Butler breathing relatively normally. She waited until he had been put on a trolley to be taken to the CCU. As he was being taken out of the mortuary to Cardiac Care Unit, he grasped Kate's hand.

'Would you tell my wife . . . please, tell her not to worry . . .'

'Of course I will.' Kate felt the burning inside her own chest. It was not physical pain but hatred and had been building up inside her all day.

'Louise was our life, you see. We hoped . . . we hoped she would walk back in the house. You know.' He squeezed his eyes shut to stem the tears. 'That she was still alive somewhere. Anywhere.'

Kate felt the man's agony as if it were a tangible thing. As the trolley was pushed away, she knelt down and retrieved the handbag that she had thrown to the floor as he collapsed. Standing, she went once more to Louise Butler's body and pulled the sheet away from her face.

Fifteen. Loved and wanted. Her whole life ahead of her. And now she had been reduced to a bloody pulp.

Swallowing hard, Kate left the mortuary. She had decided to be in on the post mortem and now she would go to the Pathologist's office and wait for the remains of Louise Butler to be laid on the mortuary blocks and then systematically cut to pieces.

Ronald Butler had made Kate feel the futility of all their investigations. His daughter was dead, Mandy Kelly was dead, and Geraldine O'Leary was dead. Three women raped and murdered in less than seven weeks.

They had to find him before he struck again, and they had nothing to go on. Nothing at all. Every avenue they pursued hit a dead end. Every lead went nowhere. This man was either very clever or very lucky. Or else had a mixture of the two.

She was still dwelling on it when the post mortem started. Kate had been given a small white mask to wear and when the pathologist cut Louise Butler from the breastbone to the navel she was glad of it. The stench of the gasses was appalling.

Kate watched everything through heavily lidded eyes. The burning was back in her breast. Stronger this time.

She brooded on what kind of man raped, murdered and buried a young girl, then went back and dug her up and mutilated her again?

He had to be caught.

Chapter Seventeen

Kate was feeling depressed. She'd just had the news that both Geraldine O'Leary's and Mandy Kelly's bodies could be released for burial. She decided to tell the families herself. She was not looking forward to it.

She drove towards the O'Learys' house with a feeling of trepidation. She parked just down the road and sat for a few minutes, watching the house itself. The nets were pristine white. Obviously either Mick O'Leary was a good housekeeper or he had someone helping him. Probably Geraldine's mother; Kate had met her on one occasion and had had the impression that she was a capable woman. Taking a deep breath, she got out of the car and locked it. She walked slowly to the front door and rang the bell.

The door was answered by Kathleen Peterson, Geraldine's mother, who had the youngest child, Sophie, in her arms. Kate could see Geraldine in the child: the same long, brown hair and almond-shaped, hazel eyes. She smiled.

'I don't know if you remember me? I'm Detective Inspector Burrows . . .'

'Oh, come in, love. Come in.'

The woman moved from the doorway so Kate could enter the tiny hall.

'Come through.' She walked through a doorway to her left and Kate followed her into the lounge. On the carpet toys were lying about everywhere. The television was on and Mick O'Leary was sitting in the armchair by the fire, staring at the screen. Kate was shocked at the sight of him. He was hunched in his chair like an old man, it was obvious he had not shaved for days and his clothes looked a crumpled mess.

Kathleen Peterson caught Kate's eye and shrugged her shoulders. She motioned for Kate to follow her through to the kitchenette.

Putting Sophie down on the floor, she closed the kitchen door quietly behind her. 'Sit yourself down. Would you like a coffee? Tea?

'Coffee would be fine, thanks, no sugar.'

While Kathleen put the kettle on, Kate watched the child. She stood on the floor exactly where her grandmother had left her. She watched avidly every move her granny made, her eyes darting restlessly around the kitchen to wherever Kathleen was. Kate smiled at the child, but Sophie just glanced at her and then carried on watching her granny.

When Kathleen had put the coffee in front of Kate, she sat at the small table and pulled the waiting child on to her lap. Sophie curled into her granny's bosom and popped a thumb into her mouth, shifting herself around for a few seconds before she was fully comfortable. Kathleen swept the hair back from the child's face and then looked at Kate.

'She's taken it hard, the young one. They all have.'

Kate couldn't answer.

'Have you any news about . . . about the man?'

Kate shook her head.

'I'm here about Geraldine. Her body can now be released for burial.'

The woman sipped at her own coffee and placed the cup back into the saucer with trembling hands.

'Thank God! I think that if we . . . well, if we could bury her like . . . it wouldn't seem so bad. The thought of her . . .'

'I know. Believe me, I know. Please don't distress yourself.'

'It's funny,' Kathleen's voice had taken on a confiding tone, 'I used to think that nothing really bad could happen to us. I'd see things on the news – like Suzy Lamplugh and murders and rapes – all sorts really. I'd think, How terrible, and then I'd go and cook my dinner or get ready for bingo and it would be out of my mind, you know? It's amazing how little you really care until it happens to your own family. Oh, I would feel distressed for the victims and their family, but not really for any length of time . . . Now it's with me every waking moment. I feel as if she's near me sometimes, I feel her presence.'

Kate sat and let the woman unburden herself. She guessed rightly that she was the first person to cross the doorstep for weeks. After the initial shock wears off, people seem to give victims' families a wide berth. Maybe they really do think people want to be left alone, or maybe they are frightened of getting too caught up. As if that kind of bad luck is catching.

'I was shopping the other day in town and I met a girl who went to school with Geraldine. She had her children with her, two boys. Lovely little things. She said hello and we chatted for a while, and I thought after, Why couldn't it have been you? Why did it have to be my Gerry?

'I felt terrible later. Just terrible to wish on her and hers what we were going through. I mean, you can see for yourself how Mick is. He lives on tranquillisers. How could you wish that on somebody? It's wicked.

'But deep down inside I wish it had been anyone but my child. The older children are back at school but very withdrawn, and this little mite here – she doesn't know if she's coming or going. Keeps wanting to know when her mammy will be coming home. Maybe once she's buried we'll all come to terms with it a bit more. Say goodbye like. You know?'

Kate nodded, unable to swallow the large lump in the back of her throat. She took a gulp of coffee to try and right herself.

'Well, if you get in touch with the undertakers, they can collect Geraldine's remains.'

'Remains.' Kathleen smiled. 'My Gerry's gone, love, all that remains is memories. Memories and children. I used to look forward to being a granny. You know the jokes about having the children when you want, but being able to give them back? Now I have them all the time and I don't really think I'm up to it. But these things are sent to try us or so they say. Would you like another coffee?'

'No thank you. I have to be on my way.'

'Have you any idea who it was who did it? I mean, my Gerry was the first of three, and people seem to think he's going to strike again. Do you think you'll catch him?'

'We'll catch him, I can promise you that.'

Kate's voice was hard and strong and Kathleen Peterson believed her.

Sophie scrambled off her granny's lap. Going to the back door she urinated on the mat, her thumb still tucked firmly in her mouth. Kate saw Kathleen's eyes roll up in dismay.

'Now, Sophie, you know that's naughty.' She looked at Kate. 'This is the latest thing with her. It's funny though, she's as dry as a bone at night. Come on, madam, let's get those wet knickers and socks off you. Though if you keep this up I'll make you wear them all day, see how you like that.'

As Kathleen went to the child, Kate stood up. 'I really must go now, Mrs Peterson. I hope everything works out all right.'

'So do I, love. So do I.'

'I'll see myself out. Goodbye.'

''Bye, lass, and thanks for coming to tell us. It's a load off of me mind.'

Kate left the kitchen and walked through the lounge. Mick O'Leary was still watching the flickering screen. He did not even know that Kate was there.

She left feeling worse than she had before.

Patrick Kelly was in the West End. He owned massage parlours the length and breadth of London and surrounding areas. Today he was in Soho, supposedly checking the books, but in effect just showing his face. It paid in this business always to be on top of everything. If the girls ever thought they could tuck you up, they would.

While he sat in the makeshift office his mind was on his daughter. The account books lay open in front of him so that if anyone came in, it looked official.

He was startled by a knock on the office door. It was opened almost immediately by a tall thin woman who strode purposefully into the room.

'All right, Pat? Everything shipshape and Bristol fashion?'

Kelly nodded. Juliette Kingsley had worked for him for years and like all his top girls – that is, the women who ran the parlours – she was a trusted friend.

'I want to ask you a favour, Pat, if you don't mind?' She

sat in a chair opposite the desk and, leaning over, took a cigarette from the box on the desk.

'What is it, Ju? Trouble?'

'Sort of. Nothing to do with this place. Remember my youngest son, Owen?'

Patrick scanned his mind and came up with a picture of a tall, blond-haired, good-looking boy. Not unlike his mother.

'Yeah. What about him?'

Juliette ran her hands through her short blond hair and Patrick was surprised to see that she was agitated.

'You know Jimmy McDougall, the pimp?'

He nodded, frowning now.

'What about him?'

'He's got my boy up the 'Dilly. I can't find him, Pat, and I'm worried out of me bleeding mind. He's only twelve, as big as he is. Well, I heard a whisper on the street that McDougall had him. I know I ain't exactly lived the life of a virgin, I don't deny it, but all my kids have done well, you know that. My eldest girl is a secretary, my eldest boy is at university, my Owen was doing well at school.

'He's my baby, Pat, my little surprise I call him. I mean, I was nearly forty-one when I had him. I can't eat, I can't sleep with worry at what he's getting into . . .'

Patrick looked at her. She looked terrible – Juliette never had looked that good. But she'd been one of the best Toms in the business in her day. Bought and paid for her own house and kept her husband in the life of Riley until the ponce drank himself to death. Patrick liked her, respected her.

'I want you to have a word with McDougall for me. I know it's a cheek . . .'

He felt a rage inside him and was glad to have somewhere to channel the hatred that was slowly building up in him day by day. McDougall was a scumbag in his opinion. Anyone who lived off the earnings of young boys was a scumbag. Homosexuals bothered Kelly not one iota as long as they were consenting adults. It was the men who slept with children that disgusted him, whether they were young boys or young girls. There was a fortune to be made from youth. Extreme youth. But Kelly would have none of it.

'Don't you worry, Ju. Owen will be home within twenty-four hours. Now go and get yourself a stiff drink and let me deal with it.'

Juliette's hard face relaxed. 'Thanks, Pat. If you only knew what I've been going through.'

'I have a pretty good idea, you know, Juliette.'

'Of course. I'm sorry, Pat. What with Owen and everything . . .'

'You leave it with me, girl, and just bide your time. How long has he been gone?'

'Nearly a fortnight. I've told the school that he's been ill with flu. I didn't know what else to say.'

'How did he get involved with McDougall in the first place?'

'Well, from what I can gather, a friend of his from school went on the trot about a year ago. Poor little sod had a terrible time of it at home. Didn't get on with the mum's boyfriend. You get the picture, I'm sure. Anyway, he rang my Owen up and told him what a great life he was having and Owen went to see him and I ain't seen hide nor hair of him since.'

'Well, stop worrying. If he's with McDougall he'll be home, quick smart.'

Juliette stood up and left the room.

Patrick picked up the phone and dialled. He was looking forward to sorting out McDougall.

*

Tony Jones was chatting with Emmanuel at Sexplosion when Patrick Kelly and three large men walked into the shop.

'All right, Jonesy?' Kelly's voice was not friendly and Tony was aware of it.

'Hello, Mr Kelly, how can I help you?'

'I want to know where I can find Jimmy McDougall. Now. This second.'

Tony Jones was squirming in his shoes. Jimmy McDougall was not a man to fall out with, but then again neither was Patrick Kelly. Of the two he decided he was more frightened of Kelly. He looked at Emmanuel.

'What are you staring at, you great big fairy? Get out the back and sort the videos or something. And keep your big trap shut about what you've heard here tonight.'

Emmanuel did not need to be told twice. He literally ran from the shop.

'What day is it today? Tuesday . . . He'll be at his safe house by King's Cross Station. I'll write down the address.'

He went to the counter and hurriedly wrote a few lines on a piece of paper. Kelly took it from him and glanced at it.

'Do you know something, Jonesy? I used to like you once but now I find you disgust me. Flogging all this crap is one thing, but to be an active participant in this kind of filth . . .' Kelly waved the paper at him and shrugged. Then, spitting on the shop floor, he turned and left, his men following.

Jones breathed a deep sigh of relief. It crossed his mind to phone McDougall and warn him, but after weighing up the pros and cons of such an act in his mind, he decided against it. McDougall could do with being knocked down a few pegs and Patrick Kelly was just the man to do it.

*

Owen was sitting on a large settee watching a video. The glamour of his new life had already worn off. There was nothing to do but watch videos, drink alcohol and smoke cigarettes, and the novelty of all that was long gone. Plus the big man, Jimmy, who had been so friendly at first, had twice come into his room and made him do things. Things that made him feel sick. That was when he realised he was a virtual prisoner.

Last night he had been taken out to King's Cross Station. There, his friend Joseph had walked up to completely strange men and asked them if they wanted 'the business'. All the time this had been going on, Jimmy had stood with Owen, holding him tightly by the arm. He had never been so frightened in his life. Joseph was doing what was called 'clowning'. Picking up a punter and offering him a 'chicken'. Chicken was the term for the younger boys. If they were under the age of ten then they were termed 'spring chickens' and were worth a fortune.

Jimmy was a bit concerned about Owen's height at first, but one feel of his face, so smooth and silky, was proof to any discerning punter that he was indeed a chicken. As luck would have it, Owen had been violently sick and Jimmy had taken him home and given him a good hiding for being so stupid. In Owen's mind this was preferable to doing with one of those men what Jimmy had made him do. Now, with a black eye and bruised body, he was safe for a while. It hadn't taken him long to suss that much out.

Sylvester Stallone was stitching himself up on screen and with the resilience of a child Owen watched avidly. *First Blood* was his favourite video and Sylvester Stallone his favourite actor. He didn't like the other videos that Jimmy liked to watch. Joseph was in some of them. Joseph and Jimmy and other boys. Some of them were really young. Like the little boy Jimmy kept in the bedroom whom no one was allowed to see. He cried all the time so they had to turn the television up loud to drown him out. Then every so often Jimmy would bring back a man who would go in there with him and then the crying would be terrible for days after.

Owen had glimpsed him only once. He was about five years old, half caste with enormous brown eyes. But he had seen him in the videos that Jimmy watched. Joseph said that when they made the videos Jimmy gave them whisky and pills and it made them all laugh. But Owen didn't think he would laugh. He just wanted his mum. His mum and his old bedroom. He had only come up here for a couple of days. Now it was two weeks and he was scared. He was sick of pizza and Kentucky Fried Chicken. He was sick of it all. Especially Joseph and Jimmy.

'You're not watching that crap again, are you?' Jimmy's loud voice brought Owen out of his reverie.

Jimmy walked over. His cumbersome body rippled with fat. He had on nothing but a pair of grubby underpants. Owen instinctively pulled the flimsy pyjama jacket he was wearing tightly around his body. He was not allowed to wear his own clothes.

Jimmy sat heavily on the broken-down settee. He patted the cushion beside him.

'Come and sit beside me, let me look at that eye. You shouldn't have annoyed me, you know, Owen. I don't like hurting my boys. I just want to look after them, that's all.' McDougall's voice had the sing-song quality that Owen was beginning to loathe, along with everything else about the man. He was aware that Jimmy was trying to talk him into doing what he wanted.

'Come on, Owen, you know it makes sense. Think of

all the money you'd have if you just played along with me . . . I give Joseph ten pounds a day to spend on what he likes. And how many twelve year olds do you know on money like that, eh? Answer me that then. Over seventy quid a week I give him sometimes. And all me other boys. I've got loads of boys you know . . . all ages and sizes.' Jimmy's voice had taken on a threatening inflection. It was a veiled threat but not wasted on Owen all the same.

'Some of my bigger boys are very nasty, you know, Owen, and if they thought that someone, especially someone young and green, was taking the piss they would be very annoyed. 'Cos they love me, you see.'

Owen was half relieved and half scared when a discreet tap came on the front door. Happy because it took Jimmy away from him, and scared in case it was some of the bigger boys that he'd just been talking about. Jimmy leapt off the sofa and pulled on a reasonably clean pair of trousers from the floor. Then, smoothing his hair with his hands, he went to the front door.

Owen heard mumbled voices and then Jimmy walked back into the room with a man in a black suit. He was carrying a briefcase and he smiled at Owen. He felt his heart sink.

'The boy's in here, sir. I keep the door locked because you know what children are like. Always prying into things that don't concern them.' Jimmy spoke as if he was a benevolent father and smiled at the visitor. He smiled back and Owen felt the sickness again. The man was going in to the little boy in the bedroom.

The house where they were had once been a large, imposing residence, now it was a mismatch of flats and bedsits. It still had the communal front door and as they were on the ground floor, their front door came into their lounge. The rooms that were once the morning room and the dining room were now bedrooms. All the windows were barred, as they had been since the houses were built. Jimmy also had the basement flat. He had set-ups like this all over London. Once Owen was established and trustworthy, he would be relocated to one of the other safe houses.

He watched Jimmy unlock the bedroom and the man with the briefcase walked inside. A couple of minutes later Jimmy came out and went to the kitchenette. Owen watched him carry through a bottle of pills and a glass of whisky. Owen could hear the little boy's cries through the door and put his hands over his ears.

He wished more than ever that his mum was here. She would know what to do.

She would sort out Jimmy.

She would take him home.

Owen realised that his video had ended and the television screen was blank. He stared at it, trying to hold back the tears. If they were going to do to the little boy what Jimmy had done to him, he would be in a lot of pain.

Owen felt sick again.

Then there came another knock on the door. This time it was loud and aggressive and Owen was convinced that it was the bigger boys that Jimmy had been talking about. He felt himself hunch into the settee.

Jimmy came out of the bedroom and called out: 'All right, all right, I'm coming. About bleeding time and all.'

He opened the door and Owen was amazed when he tried to slam it shut immediately, pushing on it with all his might. Then whoever was outside got the better of him because the door was pushed open so hard that Jimmy went sprawling on the floor and the door banged against the wall loudly.

Four large men were standing over him and one of

them, a dark man in a light brown overcoat, kicked him hard in the kidneys. Then he faced the boy.

'You're Owen, aren't you?'

He nodded.

'I'm here because your mum's been worried out of her head, son. Now you come with me and I'll take you home. OK?'

Owen stood up on trembling legs. He was trying hard to pull the pyjama jacket down so it would cover his naked genitals. He saw the man in the brown overcoat frown.

'Where's your kacks, son? Go and put them on. We'll wait here for you, all right?'

Owen nodded and went to the bedroom he had been using with Joseph and Jimmy. He began to pull his clothes on as quick as possible, glad of the unfamiliar feel. He went back into the lounge and pulled on his bumpers. Jimmy was still on the floor and one of the men, a large shaven-headed character with gaps in his teeth, was grinning at him. He was holding a large screwdriver to Jimmy's throat.

'Tell them that I never hurt you, son. Tell them that, will you?'

Jimmy's voice was frightened and then Owen remembered the boy in the bedroom. It was very quiet in there now. Too quiet.

'Hey, Mister. There's another boy in there.' He pointed to the door. 'He's only a little mite. There's a man in there with him.'

Patrick's face seemed to harden and he opened the door. On the bed was the man in the suit and the little boy. The man had his hand over the little boy's mouth. His trousers were undone and his shirt, so nicely pressed and ironed was hanging over his flaccid penis.

'Fuck me, Mr Kelly, what's going down here?' This

from one of the other large men, a hard case called Dicky Brewster. He walked into the room and punched the man in the suit as hard as he could. The little boy, realising his mouth was free, began to scream in fear. His large brown eyes were opened to their utmost and snot and tears were raining down his face into his mouth. Dicky Brewster picked up a corner of the grubby bedsheet and wiped the boy's nose and eyes gently, his great hands seeming to cover the child's whole head.

Patrick and the other men watched him, fascinated. All were shocked and appalled at what they had stumbled on. It was worse than even they had expected. Dicky wrapped the child in a blanket and picked him up, trying his hardest, in his rough-handed way, to be kind. Kelly flicked his head to the other man with him.

'Take the boys and go down to my car, Dicky. You, go with him.'

The men nodded and left the flat with the children. The little boy's sobs were subsiding now, but Patrick waited until they were gone before he walked into the bedroom. Then he began systematically to kick the suited man in the head, chest, anywhere he could. The rage inside him was white hot now and it needed to be spent. Finally, the man lay still and Patrick Kelly didn't care if he was dead. Breathing hard he went back into the lounge.

'You're a fucking piece of shite, McDougall, and I am personally going to see that you never get to ply your filthy trade in this city again.' He nodded at the man with the shaved head.

'You know what to do, Tim. Do it.'

Jimmy McDougall was terrified, and his terror gave him an added strength. He fought as hard as he could to get away from the man but Patrick Kelly kicked him in the head, a stunning blow. Then Tim pushed the screwdriver into Jimmy's ear, banging down on it hard with the palm of his hand.

Jimmy was still and silent.

Tim wiped his hands on his jeans and both he and Kelly walked from the flat.

They were disgusted.

Not at their own violence, but at what they both knew had been going on in there. It just didn't fit in with their code of right and wrong.

In Kelly's mind, a man had to do many things, such as dole out a hiding to the likes of McDougall. Anyone who lived off the proceeds of children, whether it was putting them on the streets or dealing in child pornography, was classed as a nonce or a beast. It was quite reasonable and just to maim or harm them permanently. That was right to Kelly. Just like robbing a bank was considered gainful employment. It grieved them that a rapist often got a lesser prison sentence than a bank robber. It was the old, old story. Property had more value than people. Kelly might own massage parlours and be a repoman, but he would never raise his hand to a woman or a child. The men in the car with him felt the same.

There were just some things you did not do, and these were some of them. You could break a man's arm or a leg for the payment of an overdue debt, but this was right and fair. When the man borrowed the money he knew what the penalty for not paying would be, and he generally took his punishment like a man. That was how Kelly had always lived his life. How he had survived in life. His first business had been founded on a two thousand pound loan from one of the biggest villains ever to walk the earth. Kelly had paid back the loan and the interest with it. He had showed the man the respect due to him, and now, all these years later, the man was a trusted friend.

Kelly was the old-style villain and proud of it. He had no time for the youngsters who went steaming through the trains or who took it into their heads to go and run a stolen Range Rover through an electrical shop. Ram Raiding they called it. That was a mug's game. He blamed society for these people. He did not put himself on a par with them. He saw himself and his colleagues as businessmen. Men who did a job that had to be done. Like the job they had done tonight.

When he found the Grantley Ripper, and he would find him, he was sure of that, he would pay back his daughter's debt one hundredfold. He would exact his payment painfully and with the minimum of fuss. In Kelly's mind it was expected of him. If you didn't look out for your own then who would?

He shook his head at what the world was coming to.

Inside Kelly's car, Owen sat as still as death. Relieved to be out of the flat, but still not sure if he was out of danger. Now the relief had worn off he was wondering if he had walked into more trouble.

'We're going to take you home, son, to your mum. But first we've got to drop the little fellow off. All right?'

Owen nodded warily.

'Give me the phone, Tim.'

Kelly dialled a number and the deep voice of a Chief Inspector friend of his came on the line. He outlined the situation in as few words as possible, then smiled and switched the phone off.

'We're taking him to Charing Cross Hospital, they'll be expecting him. Come on then. Let's get our arses in gear.'

He smiled at Owen.

'When was the last time you two had a bath? You smell like a couple of paraffin lamps.'

'They look like a pair of tramps and all, guv.'

This from Dicky, who was feeling happier now they were taking the boy somewhere.

They all chatted amiably until they'd dropped the little boy off. Kelly wondered briefly what would become of him. At four or five he wasn't a runaway, more likely sold to Jimmy by his mother or father. It was surprising what people would do for a couple of ounces of heroin.

Owen was delivered to his mother's house and Juliette cried her eyes out as she hugged her son to her, thanking Patrick and the other men profusely until Dicky's face was as red as a beetroot in embarrassment.

Later on, Patrick drove home and his heart felt lighter than it had since Mandy's death.

He was seeing Kate the following night and couldn't wait. He had observed Owen's happiness at the attention from his mother who had hugged and kissed and shouted and berated him in her joy to see him home in one piece. It crossed Kelly's mind that twelve, twenty, forty or eighty, everybody needed someone to care for, and to care for them. He wished he still had his Mandy.

If only they could find a clue to the villain responsible for her death.

Patrick Kelly didn't realise he had spoken that very day to the man who had George's full name, address and phone number.

Later that evening Patrick had a call from his police contact.

McDougall would live, though he would walk as if he had been on a roundabout for the rest of his life.

Kelly smiled to himself. It was a job well done.

Now all he wanted was his daughter's murderer and then he could settle down to some kind of a normal life.

*

Kate watched Patrick's face closely, her heart going out to him. 'I tried to get in touch with you yesterday, but I just couldn't locate you anywhere. I wanted to tell you myself.'

'I know that, Kate.' He pulled her towards him and kissed the top of her head.

'In a way I'm relieved, but in another way it makes it all seem real somehow. Sometimes I wake up in the night and I think it was all a big mistake, and if I get out of bed I'll walk into her room and she'll be there. Fast asleep, her arm draped across her eyes. That's how she slept even as a small child. But I suppose I'll get over all that eventually. The wishful thinking. I'll make the arrangements first thing in the morning. What's happening with the O'Leary family?'

'I told the mother yesterday, the husband is taking it all very badly . . .'

'I mean, how are they off for dosh? Money?'

Kate was surprised.

'I don't really know, they aren't rolling in it. They were buying their council house so I expect her death has paid off the mortgage. He's not working though, and as she worked at the wine bar for extra money for Christmas I shouldn't think he earns that much anyway. Especially with three children.'

Kate saw Patrick's jaw clench. She knew it was the motherless children that affected him the most.

'I'll send my brief round to see the mother. I'll pay for the funeral for them. I'll pay for the Butler girl's as well when the time comes.'

Kate was silent. She didn't like to say that maybe the Butlers wouldn't want him to pay for something so personal, but she knew it was a salve to him. In his mind he was making amends and actually doing something.

More than anything, she knew Patrick Kelly was only happy when he was sorting out things. She knew that in his own way he was trying to take the responsibility from other people, trying to make things easier for them.

She wasn't really sure if this was a good thing. After all, he wasn't God.

'Do you want to go out, Kate?'

'Not really, Pat, but it's up to you.'

He hugged her close again. 'Good. I've had Mrs Manners make up a nice bit of dinner for us. We'll eat in and have an early night. What do you think?'

He tried to smile at her, but Kate was aware that his heart wasn't in it. But she would go along with him; she had a feeling that he needed her tonight for more than the usual reasons. Even if they didn't make love, she knew that having someone beside him through the night would mean a lot to him.

'That sounds great. I could do with an early night, I had a hard day myself.'

'Good. I'll go and make the arrangements.'

As he left the room, Kate could not help but notice the slump to his shoulders and felt a rush of love for him. She sat back in the settee and sighed. She wasn't sure if it was a good thing or a bad thing. But she knew that she liked the feeling.

George was watching Elaine. Since the night of the tiepin and his euphoric relief at finding it, the marks on his wife's neck had been bothering him. He watched her shove a Ryvita with a scraping of low fat cheese on it into her mouth. She was definitely a lot thinner and, he admitted to himself grudgingly, getting quite attractive for her age. She had toned down her eye make-up, and had taken to putting kohl pencil on the inside of her bottom lashes.

This small act had opened up her eyes and given them a mysterious look. He gritted his teeth.

They were all the same, women. He knew, without a shadow of a doubt, that Elaine, that slob Elaine, was having an affair. Was lifting her skirts in the back of someone's car and sitting on someone's erect . . .

'George! Are you all right?' Elaine's voice was sharp.

The picture in George's mind evaporated and he dragged himself back to reality.

'Of course I am, dear.' His voice was his usual mild and humble one.

'Well, stop staring at me, it gives me the creeps.'

George stood up from his seat and felt dizzy as a picture rose into his mind once more. This time, he was standing over Elaine with his Swiss army knife raised above his head . . .

'I think I'll go for a walk, dear, I don't feel very well. I need to clear my head.'

'But *Taggart*'s on in a minute.'

Taggart was George's favourite programme. But tonight he had to get out of his house and away from Elaine before he exploded.

'I won't be long, dear. Tape it for me.'

Elaine turned her gaze back to the television. George knew that within seconds he would be forgotten. She would be thinking of her fancy man. He hurried from the room, grabbing his hat and coat, and left the house. As he walked down the road he pulled his gloves from his pocket and put them on. He felt a rage inside him. A blinding rage. How dare she? He didn't want her, he had not wanted her for years, but she was still his wife. His *wife*. He had married her and given her his name. He had raised her from the gutter to be his wife. But, like them all, she was a conniving cunt.

He saw Elaine again in his mind, taking off her clothes as she had been the night he had seen the marks on her neck. He saw her then in the back of a car, with a faceless man touching all her secret places. And Elaine liked it! She liked it, the slut!

George was walking faster and faster, his shoes clattering on the pavement. Elaine was like his mother. Oh, they pretended to be good women, but deep down they were whores. Like Eve, they betrayed you. You gave them your all and they took it. They took it and they smiled and they simpered – and all the time they were laughing at you. Laughing their fat ugly heads off.

George's breathing was laboured.

He stopped and looked around him. He was outside the block of council flats where he'd been mugged. He crossed the road and strode purposefully up the incline and under his tree. He watched the second floor, cursing Elaine because in his haste to get away from her he had forgotten his opera glasses.

Leonora Davidson was watching *Taggart*, unaware that not twenty yards away the Grantley Ripper was watching her bedroom window. She snuggled into her chair, a mug of coffee on a small table beside her and her cigarettes on the arm of her chair. She was content.

George watched the window for ten minutes. Nothing. He glanced at his watch. It was ten to ten.

He began to walk towards the block, his eyes scanning the street and the windows of the flats for movement.

Leonora heard a knock at her front door and tutted. 'Taggart' was just about to unmask the killer. She got up from her chair and went out into her tiny hall.

'Who is it?' Her voice was loud and impatient.

'Is that Mrs Davidson?'

Leonora frowned. She didn't know the voice.

'Who wants to know?'

'I'm the man who got mugged, you came out to help me.' George's voice was quiet and meek.

Leonora's eyebrows went up.

'Oh, yes, I remember.'

She opened the front door, pulling back two large bolts and taking off the chain before opening it.

George stood there smiling.

'I'm sorry to come so late but I work rather unsocial hours, you see. I just wanted to thank you properly for all your help that night. I really don't know what I would have done without you.'

Upstairs, he heard a door opening and began to panic.

'May I come inside for a moment? I won't keep you long, I promise.' He could hear footsteps on the landing above. Whoever it was would see him. They would see his face and know he had been here.

Leonora stepped back and George walked into her hall, pushing the door shut behind him. He smiled at her. His little smile that just showed his teeth. He had observed her for weeks and knew that there was no man in the house. She always went to bed alone.

Leonora smiled back. Now she knew who he was, she was happier. You couldn't be too careful when you lived alone. 'Will you come through to the lounge? I was just having a coffee, would you like one?' Her open face was like balm to George.

'If it's no trouble . . . I don't want to put you out.'

He followed her into her lounge.

'Sit down and I'll get you your coffee. Do you take milk and sugar?'

George nodded. 'Oh, you're watching *Taggart*, I love that programme myself. My wife's taping it for me.'

'Well, sit down, Mr . . .'

'Markham. George Markham.'

'Well, sit down, Mr Markham, I won't be a second.'

George sat down on the sofa, an old PVC affair that had obviously seen better days. He noticed that the room was clean and tidy if very old fashioned. It needed decorating. He undid his coat. He gazed at the television screen smiling to himself. Leonora came back with the coffee and gave it to him.

'So how are you now? I tell you, Mr Markham, this place is getting worse. The youngsters seem to be taking over. I don't leave the house now of a night, unless I have to. What with the muggers and the Grantley Ripper, a woman isn't safe any more.'

George sipped his coffee.

'You're absolutely right. I tell my wife that she has to be very careful. Very careful indeed.' His face clouded.

Leonora lit herself a cigarette.

'Did you go to the police station? Did they find out who did it?'

'Oh, no. It's a waste of time, the police can't catch anyone these days. Or so it seems anyway.'

Leonora nodded, not sure what to say.

'Are you divorced?'

'Yes. Ten years now.' She smiled sadly.

George watched her drink her coffee. Her hair was mousy brown and her eyes a watery blue. Around her mouth she had deep grooves. Not an attractive woman, he thought. His eyes dropped to her breasts. George liked her breasts. He had seen them many times.

He put his coffee on the table.

'May I use your toilet, please?'

'Of course. It's the second door on the right, in the hall. You have to pull the chain hard or it won't flush.'

He stood up.

'Thank you.'

He walked out to the hall and went into the kitchen. Opening the drawers slowly and quietly, he found her knives and taking out a large breadknife, he slipped it into the belt of his trousers, covering it with his coat. He walked back into the lounge.

He smiled at the woman.

She smiled back.

Then he walked towards her slowly. He started to talk. 'This ornament, may I ask you where you got it?' He picked up a large vase, about sixteen inches high, made from cut glass. It was on the mantelpiece, over the gas fire. He turned back to Leonora with it in his hands.

'Oh, that was my mother's.' She leant forward in her chair that was pulled up near the fire, her hands outstretched as if to take the vase from him. As she opened her mouth to speak again, her face froze.

George lifted the vase above his head and the action pulled his coat open. Leonora saw the breadknife in his belt and the heavy vase descending towards her at the same time. She felt the scream rise in her throat, but George was too quick.

He brought the vase down with all his might on to her forehead. He was amazed that the force of the blow did not break the vase. It had not even broken the skin on her forehead, though a lump the size of an egg was slowly appearing.

She was out cold.

George sat on the sofa and watched her for a few minutes. She lay sprawled across the chair. The skirt and jumper she was wearing were both bunched up and looked uncomfortable.

George got up from his seat and placed the vase back where he had found it, arranging it precisely. Then he tidied Leonora up, pulling her skirt and jumper down so she looked more natural. Then, taking the breadknife from the belt of his trousers, he placed it by her chair. He took off his overcoat and folded it up neatly on the settee.

Satisfied with his work, he once more retrieved his knife and began the process of cutting her jumper from the neck to the navel. As usual, he laid it open tidily and began on her bra.

Leonora's arms were hanging over the sides of the chair and her head was lying on her shoulder, slightly bent. By the time George began to hack at her skirt, she had begun to stir. He tutted and, walking out to the hall, picked up a tartan scarf from the coat rack. Going back to Leonora he pulled her head forward roughly by the hair, causing her to groan. He placed the scarf around her neck and pushed her head back.

Then he began his task. Crossing the scarf over her naked breasts, he picked up each end, wrapping the woolly material around his hands to get a good grip. He began to pull his arms outwards. He watched the tartan material stretch and stretch until eventually it cut into her neck.

George was whistling a little tune through his front teeth. All the tension was gone now. He felt himself relax.

George was back on top.

Chapter Eighteen

Elaine heard George's key in the door and glanced at the clock. It was twenty past twelve. She listened to him humming as he took off his coat and hung it up. Her nerves were jangling and she swallowed deeply as he walked into the lounge. His face was animated. The dead grey eyes seemed to be twinkling as he looked at her.

'Hello, dear, can I make you a drink? I'm having one, I'm parched.'

'Where have you been, George?' Elaine's voice was flat.

She could sense George's surprise even though his face was calm.

'Why, I've been out walking, dear, where on earth would I go?'

'So you've been walking for over three hours, have you?'

Elaine could feel his confusion. She realised that he was unaware how long he had been out of the house.

'I . . . I was just walking, that's all. I often walk, you know that.'

Elaine still sat staring at him, her eyes hard and steely. She ran her tongue over her lips before she spoke.

George's eyes were glued to her, watching every nuance.

'In all the years we've been married, George Markham, I can count on one hand the times you went out walking alone. Now all of a sudden you're never in the house. I want to know where you go. And I'm warning you, George, you lie to me and there will be murder done in this house tonight.'

He stared at her for a few seconds and then he felt it: the high-pitched giggle that came from his stomach and gradually worked its way up to his throat. He tried valiantly to calm himself, swallowing heavily, but to no avail.

He burst into nervous, high-pitched laughter. Like a child who laughs out of sheer terror when being told off by his teacher. In his mind was one word: murder.

He had already committed one murder tonight. Elaine would murder the murderer. Every time he thought of it it sent him into gales of hysterical laughter. Where had the time gone? Where the hell had the time gone?

'George?' Elaine was standing now. His laughter was frightening her. 'For Christ's sake, George, calm down.'

He had dropped on to his knees, his hand holding his stomach. Tears were rolling down his face.

He was heaving with mirth. A strange sinister mirth. Elaine stood and watched him until he was quiet.

When George was finally capable of movement, he pulled his handkerchief from his pocket and blew his nose vigorously before he pulled himself on to the nearest chair. The laughter was all gone now, only fear of discovery remained. His knife-sharp brain was ticking away as he watched his wife. Did Elaine guess?

'There's something not right, George, I know it. All this walking, being gone for hours – is not like you. I have to drag you from the house normally even to go shopping.' She sat down heavily in the other chair.

'I want to know exactly what's going on.' Her voice brooked no argument, but deep inside she did not want to know. She did not want to believe what the rational part of her was dreading.

George sat quietly, twisting the handkerchief between his fingers. He needed something that would throw Elaine off the scent completely. Then it jumped into his mind and he grabbed at it like a drowning man a straw. He looked at her, gathering every ounce of sorrowfulness he could muster into his lacklustre grey eyes.

'I have a terrible problem, Elaine. I've been going out of my mind with worry about how to tell you. Something dreadful has happened.'

She felt her throat go dry. Please God in heaven, don't let George tell me . . . I don't want to know. I just don't want to know.

'I've been made redundant, Elaine.'

He watched her eyes screw up into tiny slits. 'I beg your pardon?'

'I've . . . I've been made redundant. They told me a while ago. There's five of us going in all. Streamlining, they call it. I just couldn't tell you, dear. I felt as if I had failed you again. I've been walking the streets in a daze. I'd look at you, my love, watching television, and I just couldn't tell you.'

Elaine was stunned.

'I see.'

George could hardly suppress the laughter. He was a sly old fox. He was as clever as a bag of monkeys. He could talk his way out of anything. He was the man.

'I'm so sorry, dear. I know you'll think it's another failure on my part. I always wanted to give you the best, you know I did. Things just never worked out right, no matter how hard I tried.'

Elaine sat very still. Her face was closed to George through years of habit. One tiny part of her felt that she should go to him, put her arms around him and commiserate with him. But she could not. Years of avoiding physical contact with him had made such a simple act impossible.

Poor George had received the ultimate insult. At fifty-one he was on the scrap heap. He would never work again and she, his wife, was relieved that that was all that was wrong. That he was not a murderer. That he was not a rapist. She knew she shouldn't have thought such terrible things about him, but after what had happened before . . .

She pushed the thought from her mind. She would not think about that now. She had a duty to George if nothing else.

'I'm sorry, but we'll get by somehow. I expect the redundancy money will be quite a bit. The house is paid for. I'm working. We'll get by.'

He smiled at her sadly.

'That's why I said at Christmas that we would go to see Edith in Florida. I knew I would have the redundancy money and I wanted you to have something to look forward to, you see. I wanted at least to have given you that. A trip to America with no expense spared. The trip of a lifetime.'

George was warming to his theme. He had killed two birds with one stone. He knew what Elaine had thought and she had been right. Oh, so right. But he, George Markham, had sneaked in and extricated himself from a very dangerous situation. Because if push ever came to shove, he would cut Elaine's throat without a second thought. Now he had told her the thing that he was most scared of and instead of the recriminations and the upset, he had her sympathy. He had told her about the redundancy. He was on top.

'I don't know whether a trip to America would be a good idea now, George, what with losing your job like that.'

'We're going, Elaine. We are going. I want to give you that. God knows, I've never made you happy and I always wanted to, you know.'

Elaine stared into his lifeless grey eyes. The faint gleam had gone now and he was once more the George she knew.

'Would you like a cup of tea?'

Elaine nodded at him.

George got up from his seat and went to the kitchen. The clock said five past one. He had better hurry and get to bed or he would be tired in the morning. He was humming again as he put the kettle on.

Dorothy Smith knocked on Leonora's door as usual. They travelled to work together. Her fat face, under a dark brown wig, was homely and friendly. When her knock was not answered, she frowned. She banged on the door again, harder this time. Still no answer.

Surely Leonora had not gone already? They had travelled to work together for over two years and they were on the ten till six shift. She looked at her watch. Nine thirty-five. She was early, so where was Leonora? Maybe she'd popped up to the shops. She sat on the flight of stairs that led down to the first floor and ground level, her heavy bag on her knees. She smoked a cigarette and checked her watch again. Nearly ten to ten. Leonora was cutting it a bit fine, they'd be late. She ground the cigarette stub with her boot. Then she heard footsteps coming up the stairs. She stood up, a half smile on her face to greet her friend, but it was Leonora's next-door neighbour.

'Hello, love. Have you seen Leonora this morning?'

The other woman shrugged. 'No.'

'I wonder what could have happened to her? I've been waiting here for ages.'

'Maybe she overslept?'

The woman was opening her front door.

'No. I banged the door down.'

'Sure it's not her day off?'

'We always have the same days off. I don't like it. If Leonora was called away sudden like, she would have rung me. She knows I come out of me way to walk to work with her.'

The neighbour put her shopping bags down heavily in her hall and pulled the keys from the door.

'I've got a key. She gave it to me when she got locked out that time. Just in case it happened again. Cost her over forty quid to get all new locks. Bloody scandalous, I say.'

Dorothy nodded in agreement.

'Do you think we should let ourselves in like? In case she's had an accident or she's ill or something.'

'I'll knock one more time.'

Neither woman liked the thought of letting themselves into Leonora's house unless they had to.

Dorothy banged on the front door again, the sound echoing through the block of flats.

Nothing.

She opened the letter box and called through it. Then listened in case Leonora was in bed ill or something.

She straightened up.

'The telly's on.'

The neighbour slowly opened the front door. Inside, the hall was quite dark. All the doors in the flat led off it and as they were closed there was no light from the windows. Dorothy switched on the light. Both sniffed and stared at one another. There was a slightly pungent smell beneath the heavier smell of lavender polish. The two women felt uneasy as they walked to Leonora's bedroom. Dorothy opened the door.

'The bed's made.' Her voice was puzzled.

Leonora's neighbour stood by the front door. She had a terrible feeling.

The door to the lounge was shut tight, and Dorothy felt a prickle of apprehension as she put her hand on the handle. She walked into the lounge.

The gas fire was on full and the television was showing a children's puppet programme. Her mind registered these facts. Her eyes, though, were on her friend.

Dorothy just stood and stared at the remains of Leonora Davidson.

Finally, after what seemed an eternity, she screamed – a high-pitched, animal scream that bounced around the tiny room, filling it with her fear and outrage.

As a parting shot, George had stuck the breadknife through Leonora's left eye socket.

Her naked legs were sprawled in front of the fire, and had been gradually singed during the course of the night. Somewhere in the back of her mind Dorothy realised that that was the funny smell.

Burnt meat.

Caitlin and Kate were elated. The killer had once again changed tack. He had gone into someone's home. That meant one thing: the victim knew him.

The door-to-door was trying to establish not only people's whereabouts, but also whether or not they had seen anybody either in or near the block of flats.

Kate's elation soon dissipated when she saw the woman's body. What kind of man would do that to another human being?

'There's semen on the mouth, breasts, and in and around the vagina. I'd hazard a guess our man went on rather a spree last night. She's been buggered, I'd lay money on that one.' The pathologist shook his head.

Caitlin was staring at the woman as if committing her to memory. She still had the breadknife jutting from her eye, like a grotesque statue. At least someone had turned off the gas fire and opened the windows.

All around people were getting on with their jobs. Scenes of Crime were taking photographs. Taking fibres from the carpet and furniture. Picking up individual hairs. Taking samples of blood from the body, the chair and the carpet. Kate saw one pop the two coffee cups into plastic bags for fingerprinting and knew immediately that would get them nowhere. He always wore gloves. Always. He was as shrewd as they come.

Caitlin pulled his gaze from Leonora's body and his eyes burned into Kate's.

'There's got to be something this time. He's not the Invisible Man, for God's sake. Someone must have seen him.'

Kate wasn't sure who he was trying to convince.

'The two women who discovered the body are both in hospital. Shock.'

'Well, I should think they are, Katie. Look at what they stumbled on. But this time we've got him. I just know it. I feel it.'

She hoped that Caitlin was right.

'Are you coming with me to watch the post mortem?'

He nodded.

'Yes. I'll be there, Katie. I want to know everything.

Something is going to lead us to that bastard. I just know it.'

DS Spencer came into the tiny room and stared at Leonora's body. She was rapidly greying. He stared at her hard, like Caitlin before him.

'I expect the time of death will be difficult to determine. If the fire was on full all night it would delay rigor mortis.' Spencer's voice was smug.

'Once we get all the statements in we'll have an idea, don't you worry.'

Kate disliked Spencer, and knew that he knew that, and somehow it gave him an edge.

'You hang around here and book the body, Spencer. Sir, I'm going to see how the uniforms are doing on the door-to-door. I want to speak to a couple of the neighbours myself before I interview the two who found the body. Maybe one of them will know where her ex-husband is. From what I gather she had no children or immediate family. Do you want to come with me?'

'You go, Katie, I'll meet you at the hospital for the PM.'

'OK.'

She was glad to leave the flat. The picture of the woman's body was still in her mind.

At the first flat she visited, she was offered a cup of coffee and accepted gratefully. She needed something after the scene downstairs. The woman though, friendly as she was, knew nothing. Kate was sure of that within five minutes. She gave them a lead on the missing husband. He'd run off with Leonora's friend and was now living in Canada. Kate thanked the woman and left.

She walked to the door opposite and knocked. It was opened by a large man in a string vest. Fred Borrings brought Kate into his little flat and sat her down ceremoniously. It was obvious she had been expected.

'Now then, Miss . . .'

'DI Burrows, sir.' Kate smiled at him.

'I popped down the pub just before ten last night. You get to know all the sounds in the flats like. It becomes part of your hearing, if you get what I mean; I even know what time people pull their lavatories in the evening. I can time them.

'Anyway, I left here last night at about ten, and as I walked down the stairs I heard a door closing. It was Leonora's. I assumed she had a visitor, 'cos I remember thinking it was unusual. She very rarely had any visitors did Leonora. Very nice woman, you know, but always kept herself to herself. No men calling, if you get my drift. Some of the women in these flates! My God, it's like a knocking shop. But Leonora was a good woman.'

'She never had any men friends at all?'

'No. Used to work all the time. Scared of going out at night she was, because of the muggings around this area. We seem to get all the glue sniffers here, I don't know why. Have to step over the little sods some nights to get up the stairs. They come in the lobbies to get out of the cold, I expect. Poor Leonora. Wouldn't hurt a fly.'

'You didn't actually see anyone then?'

Fred shook his head. 'Nah. I know what I heard though. I wish I'd knocked now. I do sometimes. See if she wants a packet of fags or anything from the offie. I know she don't go out at night, see. Whoever went into her house knew her. When I knocked there on me way out she'd call out to me "Who is it?" or "Is that you, Fred?" You know the kind of thing. She never opened the door without establishing who was there first.

'That's what makes me think she knew him. I've been thinking about it all morning. When I heard all the hubbub going on I went down, see. Two bloody old biddies screaming their heads off. It was me who phoned you and the ambulance. I've been thinking about it ever since. Leonora knew her attacker, my girl, I'm convinced of it.'

Kate let the man talk. What he said made sense. If she lived alone, and was not the type to socialise very much, Leonora would be aware of the dangers. Women who had no social life were always more wary of people knocking on their doors than those who got about a bit.

'Did you notice any strange cars parked outside when you went to the . . . ?'

'I went to the Hoy and Helmet. And, no, I didn't see any unusual cars parked outside. My friend gave me a lift back at about eleven fifteen and I noticed that Leonora's lights were still on. I could see them through the chinks in the curtains. It's like I said before – you get to know everything about everyone. Living on top of one another like we do.'

'Have you ever seen Leonora with a man? Maybe a man from work who might have given her a lift home?'

'She always went to and from work with her friend Dorothy. I've never known either of them go to work alone. They even have the same days off.'

Kate smiled to take the edge off her next sentence.

'You seem to know an awful lot about Leonora Davidson, Mr Borrings.'

He watched her grimly.

'I happened to like her, missis. I liked her a lot. There's no law against that, is there? I'm trying to help you so you can find the person responsible. That's all. You can check out my story. Plenty of people saw me in the Hoy, I use the pub a lot.'

'That won't be necessary, Mr Borrings.' It would be checked out as a matter of course but Kate was too wise to mention this. 'It's just that normally people are undecided about a lot of things that they see or hear. You know, like after a bank robbery, every witness has the robber in a different coloured sweater with different coloured hair.'

'I understand exactly what you're getting at, missis.' His voice was hard. 'But I am not like that. I don't waste words. I say what I think and I think about what I say. Be a damn sight better world if more people were like it.'

'Quite. Well, I've taken up enough of your time, Mr Borrings. Thank you very much, you've been very helpful.'

The man stood up and nodded at her but his friendliness had gone. Kate knew that he was the kind who normally overpowered people. From the little she had gleaned about Leonora Davidson, he had probably overpowered her. He was like a child who knew the right answer, jumping around in his chair, hand up in the air, quivering with excitement. Only he was the child the teacher normally overlooked.

'I'm quite willing to identify the body formally, missis. Her ex-husband's in Canada or some such place.'

'Thank you. We'll let you know if that will be necessary.'

Kate took her leave and drove off to the hospital for the post mortem.

When she got there she first went in to see Dorothy Smith. She had been given an injection of Diazepam to calm her down. When Kate sat beside her she saw that the woman had a glazed look in her eyes. She smiled and Dorothy tried to focus.

'Hello, I'm Detective Inspector Burrows. I'd like to ask you a few questions if you feel up to it?'

Dorothy nodded her head.

'Are you sure you're OK? I can come back later.'

'No. No, I'll answer you. I'll have to eventually. It may as well be now while it's all still fresh in my mind.'

'Did Leonora ever mention any men friends at all? Not just boyfriends, I mean friends in general. Maybe a man at work who was taking undue interest in her?'

Dorothy shook her head.

'Never. She didn't like men much, you see. She kept herself to herself, she was that kind of woman. I've known her for over fifteen years and if she had a man friend I'd know about it. We told each other everything.' The woman's eyes spilled over with tears.

'She was good, was Leonora, she was kind and considerate. Why would anyone want to do that to her? Why?'

Kate was powerless to answer. Instead she placed her hand on the older woman's and squeezed it gently, letting her cry.

When she quietened, Kate spoke again. 'What about Fred Borrings?'

Dorothy pulled her hand from Kate's grasp.

'He used to look out for her, that was all. I think he would have liked to have been more than friends with her, you know, but Leonora . . .' Her voice chocked again. 'She didn't want anything like that. Her husband used to knock her around and she swore she'd never ever get involved again.'

Kate stared at the woman without seeing her.

Then how the hell did the man get inside her house? Maybe he was dressed as a workman, that was an old trick. Knock on a door and say you were from the gas or the electricity board and people automatically gave you entry to their homes. But surely someone would have noticed? She would have to wait and see what was said by the people interviewed. Once all the statements were collated they would have some idea to work from.

Someone must have seen something, however small. Those flats were a hive of activity. From glue sniffers to heroin addicts, that's where they congregated. Even their statements, however vague, could spark off a train of inquiry.

As the post mortem began Kate and Caitlin both had the same thought: once more the man had come and gone without being seen.

For the first time in years Kate crossed her fingers. She had a feeling that she'd need all the luck she could get.

Patrick heard about Leonora Davidson from his friend the Chief Constable. He was promised all the information they had about it within twenty-four hours. He was sitting in his drawing room contemplating the new event. However much he liked Kate – and he did like her, he liked her a lot – she was getting nowhere. Neither were the men he had employed, he had to admit. He closed his eyes and rubbed them hard.

If only he had something to go on. One little clue was all he needed. He knew that Kate was doing everything she could but this man was taking the piss now. He was sitting somewhere, laughing up his sleeve at them all, and Patrick Kelly was not a man who could stomach that. Every time he thought about it, it brought on a red hot rage.

He had picked out a white coffin for his daughter, with a deep red satin interior. The coffin was lead lined, airless and insect proof. The thought of his lovely child under the ground in the cold and the damp, with centipedes and other lifeforms crawling all over her face, in her mouth and through her long blond hair, made him feel sick. But the man who had put her there . . . now he was a different kettle of fish altogether. Patrick Kelly would see to it that he rotted away, that he died as horrifically as he had killed.

Kelly rubbed his eyes again. The strain was beginning to tell now. He knew he was dangerously close to exploding point. He glanced at the photograph of Mandy on the mantelpiece. It had been taken a few weeks before her death at the birthday party of one of her friends. The girl had had it enlarged and framed and sent it to him, a kindly act that had brought tears to his eyes. Whoever had taken the picture had caught Mandy with her head back, her eyes half closed, her teeth looking like perfect pearls as she laughed. It was one of those lucky photographs that occasionally get taken with a cheap snapper camera, and he loved it.

Willy tapped on the door softly before entering the room.

'It's Kevin Cosgrove, Pat, he wants to see you.' The big man's eyebrows lifted. 'Want me to smack him one and send him on his way?' Willy's voice was hopeful.

Kelly shook his head. 'No. Show him in.'

He felt the tightening inside his chest again. He wondered lately if he was getting some kind of heart trouble, but had dismissed the thought.

Kevin walked into the room. Even Kelly was shocked at the sight of him. He had lost weight and his usual pristine appearance was gone. His hair was unkempt and he needed a shave.

'Christ Almighty, you look like a paraffin lamp.'

Kevin stood uneasily in the doorway, his face white with fear. 'I came about Mandy's funeral, sir.'

Patrick knew that it had taken the boy a lot of courage to come to his house and in spite of himself was impressed. He knew men who were harder than granite who would not have had the front to walk into his home after what he had done to Cosgrove.

'What about her funeral?' His voice was soft.

Kevin looked around the room, fixing his eyes on a Japanese vase before answering.

'Well, I wanna go. Please.'

The last word was quiet and drawn out. A plea in itself.

He stared at the boy, battling it out in his mind.

'You can go, boy, but keep away from me and mine. I mean it, Kevin, I'll always blame you for what happened to her. Always. If you hadn't've left her there alone . . .' Patrick's voice trailed off, he could feel the tightening around his heart again. 'Go on, piss off. Before I lose me rag again. And remember what I said, Kevin. Keep well away from me, son. I don't know what I'd be capable of if I saw too much of you while I was burying her.'

Kevin hung his head and turning on his heel walked from the room, closing the door behind him. Patrick stared at the door for a long time. Finally, Willy came into the room with a pot of coffee. Placing the tray on the small Edwardian table by the sofa he poured out two cups, one for Kelly and one for himself. He laced them both liberally with brandy. Kelly watched the big man's clumsy attempt at being a butler and felt amused.

'I thought you could do with a bit of a natter, Pat. I don't think it's good to be on your own all the time. You need a bit of company now and then. Cheers.' He held up his coffee cup and sipped at it, burning his mouth.

'Bloody hell, is that Mrs Manners trying to weld my lips together or what?'

Patrick laughed loudly.

Willy was a tonic sometimes without even realising it.

'Have you heard any more, Pat?'

All the formality was gone now and the serious business of the day was about to begin. Kelly had an understanding with Willy. He allowed the man a free rein when it was necessary. They went back a long way.

'No. Nothing really. I'll have all the gen on the new murder by tomorrow.'

'That little ponce had some front, didn't he? Coming round here like that. I was going to give him a right-hander just for his sauce.'

Patrick waved his hand.

'Forget him. He'll get his comeuppance one day. If God don't see to it, then I will.'

'I've been thinking, Pat . . .'

Kelly closed his eyes. That was a turn up for the book, Willy thinking.

'You know that Old Bill bird you've been knocking . . . I mean, going out with?'

Kelly nodded, on the defensive now. 'What about her?' He wasn't in the mood for a lecture from Mr Charisma today.

'Well, I heard you two nattering one day. She was saying about how they took blood samples or something for DPP or something?'

'DNA. It's DNA. DPP means Director of Public Prosecutions. Anyway, what about it?'

Willy's round face looked puzzled. 'Then what's DNA mean?'

Patrick was getting agitated. 'How the fucking hell do I know? I'm not a scientist, am I?'

'All right, all right, Pat, keep your hair on.'

'Well, what are you trying to say?'

'She was saying that they could do that here, but it would cost too much money.'

'Do what?'

'To take the bloody blood tests. Stone me, Pat, don't you listen to nothing people say?'

Looking at Willy's open face it dawned on Kelly that for once he had a good idea.

Kate had told him, one night while they were having dinner, that DNA was a genetic fingerprint. Everyone knew that much from the papers. Until now he had not really understood the full meaning of what she'd been saying.

'Do me a favour, will you? Get on to the Chief Constable and tell him I want facts on all the cases ever solved by DNA. Remember that now – DNA not DPP. We'll be here all day otherwise with files of every poor bastard the Old Bill's ever fitted up.'

'I'll do it now, Pat.' Willy stood up and went to the door.

'And, Willy.' The man turned around. 'Thanks a lot. You've been a great help, I appreciate it.'

Willy grinned.

'DNA . . . DNA . . .' He was still saying it as he walked out of the door, as if terrified he would forget it.

Patrick picked up his coffee and sipped it, savouring the bite from the brandy.

Maybe he could get Kate's wish granted.

Maybe then they could all get somewhere.

Caitlin and Kate had the majority of the collated statements in front of them and both were feeling down. Not even a sniff of anything out of the ordinary.

The post mortem had revealed that although Leonora Davidson had been strangled by her attacker, the cause of death was most likely 'Vagal Inhibition'. In other words she had literally died of fright.

'Well, another murder and we have nothing to go on.

Bloody hell, someone must have seen something. It stands to reason.'

Caitlin nodded.

'There are clues here, it's just sorting out what could be viable. People see things and don't take in what they're seeing.' He poked the papers in front of him. 'One of these must have seen the man only they don't realise it yet. Either he's local and so they're used to seeing him, or he was walking nearby and they just passed him on the street. He *has* been seen, only he hasn't been tied in with it all yet. I think he's stopped using his car. So either he cabs it wherever he goes or it's all within walking distance.'

'He could have caught a bus.'

'There you are then, so he *has* been seen by people. If we could trace just one person who saw someone different on their bus coming home from work, whatever, we'd be in business.'

'Well, Spencer has been in touch with all the minicab firms and he's checking out all the people who got cabs between nine and twelve on the night of Leonora's murder. So far he's come up against malice, upset, aggravation – and nothing else.

'The murders are causing strife now. One murder is exciting, two is exciting, four means we aren't doing our job and every person interviewed now thinks their face is in the frame.'

'Sure they're all fecking eejits. Listen, I'll get Willis to go and see the bus drivers. You know, one of them might have seen something, or more precisely someone.'

Kate nodded.

'"Vagal Inhibition", I'd never heard of that before. It sounds tcrrible.'

'It make me sick to me stomach even to think about it.

Get yourself off, Katie. I'll stay on for a while here. You get some sleep.'

She got up, smoothing down her skirt.

'You've got good legs, you know, Kate.' Before she could retort he spoke again. 'How's the girl?'

'Lizzy? She's fine. I'm going to see her actually.'

'Well, she'll soon be back on her feet, God willing. Would you get me the files under W please, before you go?'

Kate went to the filing cabinet and opened the drawer. In the back was a bottle of Teacher's. She pulled it out and took it to Caitlin who picked it up.

'This country's a terrible place, you know. An Irishman drinking Scotch whisky.' He shook his head. 'Please God I'll find a shop that sells Bushmill's one day.'

'You sound like my mother.'

'Ah, sure she's a very astute woman!'

Kate picked up her bag and jacket. 'See you in the morning, Kenneth.'

'Kenny.'

Smiling, she made her way through the room, deliberately averting her eyes from the victims' photographs on the wall. She stopped at Amanda Dawkins' desk.

'Anything?'

Amanda shook her head. 'Nothing.'

Kate sighed. 'See you tomorrow.'

''Night.'

She drove to Warley Hospital. It was early evening and the traffic had just eased up so she had a straight drive. In twenty minutes she was there. As she stepped from the car and looked at the big old building she felt a lump in her throat. But Patrick was right when he said at least Lizzy was alive and kicking. If Kate had had to identify her as

Ronald Butler had had to identify his daughter, she did not know what she would have to do.

With the latest murder the pressure was really on. This man had to be caught, and fast. Extremely fast. It was said that unless a murderer was apprehended within three days, the likelihood of finding the person was minimal. Which was true, but this man committed murder after murder. He had tried it, liked it, and by all the signs was now unable to stop himself.

She walked along the corridor towards Lizzy's ward. She could hear Simply Red singing 'If You Don't Know Me By Now' and she smiled slightly. At least this was not the usual hospital environment. Here Lizzy could listen to music, wear her own clothes and there were trained staff to talk to her, listen to her problems.

Bracing herself and planting a smile on her face, Kate entered the ward. Lizzy was sitting at a table with two other girls. Kate went to her and kissed the top of her head.

'Hello, Mum!' Lizzy looked great. In the week she had been in here she already had made a marked improvement.

Kate sat down at the table and nodded to the two others. A large-boned dark girl got up. 'Can I get you a coffee?'

'Thanks, no sugar.'

'I heard about the murder, Mum, it's terrible. We were just talking about it.'

Kate didn't know what to say. Lizzy had asked her not to mention she was a policewoman. Now here she was blurting it out.

A blonde girl with large green eyes and a mass of permed hair shook her head.

'You must really get stressed out in your job like. I don't know how you can look at those dead bodies, man!'

Kate grinned. The girl was impressed!

'It's not very nice, I must admit, but someone has to do it.'

'My mum's worked on lots of murders, haven't you, Mum?'

Kate felt quite embarrassed. 'Well, not lots, a few. Murder is not as common as you might think.'

'Have you any idea who the Grantley Ripper is?'

Kate looked into the girl's green eyes. 'No. To be honest we have no idea. But we're working on it.'

The dark one brought her back a cup of coffee and the two girls left. Kate sensed they knew she and Lizzy wanted to be left alone.

'They call this quality time, Mum. When you have a visitor the others have to go away.'

'Why are they in here?' Kate sipped her coffee.

'Well, the dark girl is Andrea. She tried to kill herself because she had a lot of problems. She was studying for her A levels, and everything just got on top of her. She's really nice, you know.'

'What about the little blonde?'

'She's a nurse, Mum! It's hard to tell the difference, isn't it?'

Kate laughed. 'It is! Now then, how are you?'

Lizzy sighed, lifting her fringe as she exhaled.

'I feel much better. I saw the psychiatrist again today. He's really nice, Mum. He said that I was having a personality conflict. That I tried to be one thing when I wanted to be another. He said that my behaviour was caused by insecurity. I wanted to belong but I sort of rebelled against everything.'

'Do you think he's right?'

Lizzy looked into her mother's eyes and nodded.

'I am sorry, Mum, for what I did. When I knew that

Gran had read the diary, I just wanted to die. I know you love me, Mum, I love you and Gran too, but I've felt at times like I was second best, you know. Your job always took precedence over me. Dad was never really there. I know that he's a user. He uses me, I've known it for a long time, but I still love him. He's my dad.' Her eyes were pleading for understanding.

Kate nodded.

'My job came first because I needed the money, to be honest with you, Lizzy. Your father never once contributed to your keep. He left me with a mortgage, a child and a broken heart.' Kate smiled to take the edge off her words. 'I had to make some kind of life for us, I had to work. I went for promotions because it was more money. I bought the house we live in today, and I still have to pay the upkeep, your gran only gets a small pension . . .'

Kate grasped Lizzy's hand tightly across the table. 'I never meant to make you feel left out, Lizzy. You were my reason for working. I wanted you to have the best that I could provide. That's why I never had a personal life.'

'Dad's told me about your boyfriend.'

Kate felt coldness wrap itself around her heart, but when she looked at Lizzy, she saw that the girl was smiling.

'Don't look so stunned, Mum, I think it's great. I saw him once, that Patrick Kelly. He came to my school to give a donation. He's really good looking. Dark and brooding! That's my type, Mum, we have the same taste.'

Kate dropped her head on to her chest and bit her lip. After what she had read in Lizzy's diary, anyone seemed to be Lizzy's taste. Kate swallowed the thought. She had to stop making judgements or they'd never get back on an even keel.

'He's all right. I'm a bit old for a boyfriend though, don't you think? Let's say he's more of a . . . man friend.'

'As far as dad's concerned he's a boyfriend stroke lover. He's so jealous. Honestly Mum, you should have seen him, he was practically green!' Lizzy hooted with laughter, making the others in the room look at her and smile themselves.

'What did you say to him, Liz?'

Lizzy leant across the table and in one of her old gestures, that brought a lump to Kate's throat, she pushed her heavy hair off her face and grinned, for all the world looking like a schoolgirl. This girl-woman made Kate want to weep. She blinked away the burning tears.

'I told him it wasn't any of his bloody business.'

Kate's eyes widened.

'I bet that went down well, Liz!'

Lizzy laughed out loud. 'Like a lead balloon, Mum. I told him straight though,' Lizzy was serious again now, 'I said that was the trouble with this family, everyone did what was expected of them and never what they wanted to do!'

Kate stared at Lizzy in amazement. Her daughter sounded more grown up and intelligent than she had ever done before. 'I sent him away with a flea in his ear, I can tell you.'

'Oh, Lizzy!'

'Oh Lizzy nothing. If I'm to say what I really think, like the psychiatrist says I should, then I'm afraid that please or offend, I'm gonna say it!'

She stretched her arms out wide. 'I feel great, Mum. Really great, for the first time in ages. Joanie came in this morning and we had a long chat. She told me in no uncertain terms what a complete shit I've been and I had to agree with her. But I promised her, and I'm promising you now, I'll be better. I am going to be much better.'

'Lizzy, I love you, whatever you are, whatever you do.'

She smiled.

'I know that, Mum. Now tell me, what's this Patrick Kelly like?'

'He's just a friend. When his daughter was murdered we sort of – I don't know – we sort of made a friendship, I suppose.'

'Gran says he's lovely. That's because he's Irish. Do you remember when Boy George was on Top of the Pops and Gran went, "What on earth's that on the telly?" And I said, "That's Boy George, Gran, his real name is George O'Dowd. His family's Irish." And Gran listened to him for a while and then went, "Sure he's not that bad!"'

Kate laughed. 'Yes, I remember that.'

'So come on, Mum, what's he really like?' Lizzy's little face was earnest.

'He's a very kind man. Now that's enough of that, madam. You tell me about yourself. What's been happening here?'

Lizzy began telling her about her day and Kate listened, glad to drop the subject of Patrick.

But she admitted to herself that he strayed into her thoughts often. She relived their lovemaking in her mind at odd moments. He was exciting and potentially danger-ous, a lethal combination, but Kate didn't care. For the first time in her life she was being loved and she was thriving on it.

'Before I forget, Lizzy, how would you feel about going out to Australia?'

Her eyes widened. 'Really? You mean, go out to Uncle Pete?'

Kate nodded.

'Oh, Mum, that would be excellent.'

'Gran would go with you. I can't, because I can't get the time off work, but I thought you'd enjoy it. It would be a break. You'd have the sun, and see your cousins.'

Lizzy launched herself from her chair and wrapped her arms around her mother's body. Kate could feel the excitement in her.

She hugged her daughter back. Kate would have loved to have gone, but she just couldn't afford it. As it was she was going to get a bank loan to pay for Lizzy and Evelyn to go, for spending money and everything else. But she would willingly sell her soul if it meant making her daughter happy.

'Oh, Mum, you're so good to me!'

Kate kissed her soft, sweet-smelling hair.

'We'll find out when you're leaving here and then I'll book it. It'll give you something to look forward to.'

Lizzy skipped over to a small crowd by the record player and told them her good fortune. Kate felt lighter inside at seeing her daughter's happy face than she had for a long time.

At that moment Dan was sitting opposite Frederick Flowers. It was after seven and Flowers was surreptitiously trying to glance at his watch. Dan saw and it annoyed him.

'Well, what are you going to do about it?'

Dan's blond good looks had annoyed Flowers straight off. He had felt distaste for the man from the minute he had opened his mouth.

'Your ex-wife, Mr Burrows, is a senior officer. She is working on a case involving Mr Kelly's daughter.'

Dan broke in, 'But she's sleeping with the man!'

Flowers smiled annoyingly. 'I'm afraid I only have your word for that.' He stood up and held out his hand. 'I promise you I will look into your allegations personally.'

Dan stood up too and ignored the outstretched hand. He pointed a finger at the man in front of him.

'She's knocking him off, a known villain. Personally, I think that needs pretty close attention.'

Turning on his heel, Dan marched from the room. Flowers sat down and sighed.

He could just see himself ringing up Patrick Kelly and telling him to lay off Kate Burrows. Flowers and Kelly were hand in glove. They had been for a number of years.

He was surprised at Kate Burrows though, he admitted that to himself. She was a good officer, one of the best. He had not thought she would ever have got involved with Kelly. Well, that was female logic, he supposed.

But he could fully understand Kate Burrows wanting to get rid of that big handsome husband of hers. The man was a bully boy.

Getting up, he smoothed out the creases in his trousers. Home, that's where he wanted to be now. He walked from his office and closed the door, making a mental note to tell his secretary that Daniel Burrows was not to be given appointments to see him, no matter how urgent they sounded.

One set-to with him was quite enough.

Kate drove home, ate a hurried meal, bathed, changed and left the house in record time. She told her mother not to wait up for her, at which she got one of Evelyn's knowing smiles.

She drove up Patrick's drive at just before nine o'clock. Willy opened the door for her before she knocked and showed her into the lounge.

'Mr Kelly will be down shortly. Can I get you a drink?'

'I'll wait for Patrick if you don't mind.'

Willy smiled at her in his friendliest manner. He bowed and walked from the room.

Kate sat on the sofa and smiled to herself. She relaxed

back into the comfort of the chair. Like everything in the house it was beautiful and practical. She was so glad that Lizzy was feeling better. It was as if a lead weight had been lifted from her. The psychiatrist had said a lot of young-sters went through what Lizzy was going through; it was part and parcel of growing up in the modern world. It was he who had suggested that a change of environment might do her good. He said that her drug taking was not habitual, she was not psychologically hooked but used drugs as a means of escape. He also remarked that Lizzy's over-active sex life was not abnormal these days. Many young girls had had eight or nine sexual partners before they were twenty. It was a real sign of the times. He was more interested in whether she had used a condom.

We live and learn, thought Kate.

Patrick walked into the room. He was wearing a deep blue dressing gown.

'Were you having a bath?'

'No, I was building a bonfire!'

Kate laughed. He came to her and kissed her. She felt his lips touch hers gently and once more sensed his animal strength. He was like a drug, dangerously addictive.

'I've had Willy open a bottle of Barolo. How about a glass?'

Kate nodded and Patrick went from the room. She sat in the chair with her hands on the arms. Another thing she admired about Patrick – there were no televisions to be seen anywhere although she knew that the big oak cabinet along the wall beside her housed a thirty-two-inch state of the art flat screen TV. Kate was not a television watcher, but a reader. That was her chosen form of relaxation. Patrick was the same. In fact, they had a lot in common. One part of her was frightened by Patrick; she knew a lot about him, and not all of it good. But when she was with him, near him, she could forgive him anything. Anything at all. She knew that she made excuses for him to herself.

He came back into the room with the bottle and two crystal glasses. He poured them both a drink and sat on the floor by Kate's chair.

'This is lovely, Kate. It's good to have a woman about the house again.'

'What about Mrs Manners?'

Patrick sipped his wine.

'Mrs Manners is a great cook and a lovely old dear, but she don't exactly turn me on, know what I mean?'

She looked down into his rugged face and felt a tightening in her stomach.

She really wanted this man.

'How's it going with the case?' His voice was sombre now.

Kate felt her good mood begin to fade.

'I take it there's still nothing to go on?'

She shook her head.

'We're doing our best, but as I said before, Pat, with someone like this, well, it's a hard slog.'

Patrick knelt in front of her and sipped his wine. 'What was this thing you was going on about before? DNA.'

'Oh, genetic fingerprinting. That's just about all we have. The trouble is no one will authorise all the money it would cost to give over five thousand men a blood test. But it's been done before, in Enderby in Leicestershire. In eighty-three, I think it was.'

'Did it work?'

Kate nodded. 'Yes, it did actually.'

Both of them were quiet and Patrick sat back on the floor. They sipped their wine in silence. It was an amiable silence. This was another thing that attracted Kate to Patrick. She could sit with him without saying a word.

With Dan, if there had been a silence it was loaded. With Patrick it was natural. He stood up and took the glass from her. Pulling her from the chair he kissed her, long and hard.

'Come to bed with me, Kate, I really want you.'

She nodded slightly. Taking their glasses, they made their way up to his bedroom, where Patrick began slowly to undress her, caressing each part of her body as it became exposed to him. The first time he had done this to her, she had felt as if she was going to die from pleasure. That he had a wide experience of lovemaking bothered her not one bit. Kate had never been loved like this before. He made love to her at his leisure, keeping her in a state of anticipation that was both erotic and mind blowing. He brought her to orgasm first with his mouth before he entered her, then made love to her slowly, with long hard strokes, until she felt ready to come again. She had never experienced so much pleasure and happiness from the sex act. It would be very hard to give it up now.

Chapter Nineteen

1953

George's arms were tired. He hitched up the parcels further and grasped them tighter to his chest. He stood in the queue, his feet cold and sore. He needed new shoes desperately, these were far too small and they had a large hole in the sole that he covered with cardboard. It was now soggy and uncomfortable. He watched in annoyance as the old lady in front of him made a big performance of counting her change. He felt like dragging her away from the counter and kicking her from the shop. Instead he smiled at her as she moved and placed the parcels gratefully on the counter while the bespectacled woman weighed and stamped them.

Free from his burden, his hand went into his pocket where his wages sat snugly.

He grinned to himself. His first week's wages. He would treat himself to some new shoes. His final errand of the day done, he began the long walk home. From tomorrow he could take the bus to work. Unless . . . He shook his head to clear the bad thoughts away. He walked the busy streets confidently, like a boy who knew where he was going. Over the years, he had gradually found his way all over London – north, south and east. His mother moved so often he knew just about everywhere. Now they were in Ilford and he knew the place like the back of his hand.

Finally, after an hour's walking, he came to the house in Green Lanes. He was tired. Bone tired. One good thing about his mother, she always provided a good meal. He walked round the back and let himself into the kitchen, wiping his feet fastidiously on the mat by the back door.

'You're late!' Nancy's voice was annoyed. George nodded, aware that there was no appetising smell to greet him. He glanced at the cooker in consternation.

'It's no good looking like that, Georgie boy. Until I get me housekeeping we ain't got nothing to eat. I thought we'd have chippy tonight, to celebrate like.'

George took off his jacket and hung it on the back of the door on the hanger there for that express purpose. Nancy hated sloppiness.

'Well?' It was more a statement than a question.

George slipped his hand into his pocket and took out the wage packet. It was unopened. Nancy grabbed it greedily from his hand and ripped it open. She poured the coins out into her large red-varnished hand.

'Is this all?' Her green eyes narrowed as she looked at him. 'Thirty bob?'

George nodded again. 'I need new shoes.'

Nancy laughed. 'Don't we all?' She threw two half-crowns on the table. 'That's your cut, Georgie boy. Twenty-five shillings is for your housekeeping.'

She saw his face and went on the defensive. 'Listen here, you, I kept you all your life, it's about time you paid some of it back.'

As she spoke Jed McAnulty came into the kitchen. He had obviously been asleep. He looked at the money on the table and his face lit up. Nancy saw and turned on him. 'You needn't think you're getting any of this, 'cos you're not.'

George sighed and hastily picked up the two half-crowns. He couldn't have the shoes and bus it to work. He'd have to save up. His newfound freedom dissolved around his ears while Nancy and her boyfriend fought. George walked into the front room and sat on the settee. A little while later he heard the back door slam and his mother's high heels on the concrete pathway. Jed walked into the front room.

'She's gone to get the chips.' Jed sat on the chair by the fire and ran his plastic comb through his hair. 'I don't know why you don't get yourself a little place, Georgie. Don't give that old bat your dosh.'

He was silent, staring into the fire.

'Listen to me, son, she gets a fortune doing what she does. She don't need your money, she's taking it for spite. I've never known a woman like her in me life.'

George looked at the man calmly.

'You live off her, Jed. That's where all her money goes.'

Jed bit his lip and grinned.

'Me and your mother's got an arrangement. I supply her with the means to do her job, that's all. But all that aside, son, she's got a small fortune stashed, she don't need your money.'

George knew it was true. Knew that Jed was trying to help him. But as always his loyalty to his mother came to the forefront.

'All you men – the men she meets – you all take advantage of her.'

Jed grinned again. 'Listen, boy, your mother likes her

393

way of life. She's one of the only Toms . . . I mean, working women . . . I know who loves her job.'

George closed his eyes. Jed brought men to the house for Nancy and then sat drinking downstairs while she plied her trade upstairs. The last man Nancy had had was a big Irishman who had made George part of his arrangement. Jed, in fairness, never tried anything like that on. When Nancy had mentioned it he had gone mad, saying that she was unnatural. George had quite liked Jed after that. He seemed to have taken over where Edith had left off.

'Think about what I'm saying, son. You got a good little job, try and get yourself a room somewhere.'

Neither was aware that Nancy was standing in the kitchen listening to the conversation, having forgotten her own purse, which was stuffed full of money. Money that Jed knew about but couldn't find. She had come back to the house and heard everything. Her face set in a deep frown, she went out of the back door quietly and off to the chip shop.

George lay in bed listening to the quietness. He was tired out but couldn't sleep. Jed's words were echoing in his head. If he left home and got a room he could have a life of his own. He fantasised about having a little place with nice wallpaper and a record player. He saw it in his mind as if it was real. A clean candlewick bedspread on the double bed. A stack of records by the record player and an electric fire to keep him warm. Maybe a small wardrobe with nice clothes and shoes in it. And mats either side of the bed. In one corner of the room was a comfortable chair, with his favourite books on a coffee table alongside. He was so deep in his fantasy that he didn't hear his bedroom door open. When Nancy sat on the edge of his bed he was startled.

'Georgie boy?' Her voice was low and soft.

He didn't answer.

Nancy turned on the lamp by his bed and looked down at him, her face wreathed in smiles. She took a ten-shilling note from her dressing-gown pocket and placed it on the night table.

'That's for you, Georgie. Fifteen bob a week should be enough for your housekeeping. I don't like the thought of you walking to work like that, especially in this weather.'

George stared at her warily. She raised her hand and automatically he flinched. He heard her deep throaty chuckle, then felt her cool hands on his face as she caressed him. The hands moved down his body on to his chest, moving in circular motions that made his skin prickle. Against his will he felt the erection and pulled the sheets up over his stomach. Nancy pulled them down and grinned at him.

'You wouldn't leave your mummy, Georgie boy, would you?'

Her voice was husky and George could smell her perfume as she moved nearer.

He was willing her to go away. Begging her in his mind to leave him alone, but the habits of childhood are hard to break. He associated Nancy with excitement. He felt her fingers grasp his penis, and closed his eyes tight.

Nancy stroked him. Her eyes were brilliant in the candlelight. 'Mummy loves you, Georgie boy.'

He ejaculated, his thin body jerking frenziedly.

'And Georgie loves his mummy, doesn't he?'

She kissed him on the lips, pulling him towards her. Then, turning off the lamp she left the room as quietly and unobtrusively as she entered it.

George felt the stickiness on his thighs and suddenly the dam burst. He cried – hard, shuddering sobs that were as confused as his mind. He pushed his fists into his eyes to stem the tears. Because he hated her. He hated her so much. He hated the things she had done to him, he hated the way she made him feel and hated the way she touched him. It frightened him. But most frightening of all was that, as much as he hated her, he loved her.

He loved her so much.

Nancy lay beside Jed listening to the boy's sobs, and smiled. George was all she had and no one left her. At least, not until she was finished with them.

She slept. Jed turned over and broke wind loudly, sleeping contentedly, unaware that after his conversation with George, his days were numbered.

George awoke to a cooked breakfast and bussed it to work on a full stomach. In his half-hour lunch break he bought himself some new shoes. He went home on the bus to a cooked dinner.

Nancy made a big fuss of him. It wasn't until later in the evening he found out Jed had gone. If he had been a more worldly boy he might have realised what she was doing. Instead, as usual, he was grateful for the respite in her baiting of him.

The events of the night before were forced from his mind. Until the next time.

Chapter Twenty

Chief Constable Frederick Flowers was sitting in his office reading the latest reports on the Grantley Ripper. He was not happy with what he saw. It was the beginning of February and so far the man had got away with four murders. All murders were newsworthy, he conceded that, but sex murders like these seemed to grab the public interest and the daily papers made the most of this fact. His calls were now being screened because both the *Sun* and the *Star* were after something to pin on the police force. Flowers sat back in his seat.

After twenty-two years on the force he had seen many changes. He could remember when the police were respected, admired and feared – yes, feared. Now, if you grabbed a suspect by the arm the chances were his MP would shout out from the House of Commons: 'Police brutality'. Then, when something like this happened, everyone expected an arrest within twenty-four hours.

He frowned. If they did catch the man, the bleeding hearts would get him. By the time the psychologists and the social workers and every tin pot liberal with a BSc after their name had finished, the man would be found to be unfit to stand trial and would be put away in Broadmoor with a better style of living than he had ever been accustomed to. He had seen it too many times before. At the moment though, the papers and the public were after *his* blood, so Chummy had to be caught – and quick.

Flowers picked up the reports again, but his heart wasn't really in them. He had wanted to play golf today, like he did every Wednesday, but that was a no-no. All he needed was a picture of him on the course during a major investigation and the papers would finish him overnight. He was so deep in thought when his secretary buzzed him, he actually jumped in his seat.

He pressed the button on his intercom.

'What?'

Outside, Janet rolled her eyes to the ceiling. She did not like Frederick Flowers very much and his abrupt manner got on her nerves.

'There are two men downstairs to see you, sir, a Mr Kelly and a Mr Gabney. Shall I tell the desk sergeant to send them up?'

Frederick Flowers felt his mouth go dry and a wave of nausea washed over his body. Patrick Kelly, *here*? If someone saw them and put two and two together . . .

The logical part of his brain reminded him that Kelly had never been convicted of anything, that he had every right to be in a police station. But his gut told him it was dangerous to be professionally associated with Kelly at the station. They met socially, as many police and villains did – that was part and parcel of everyday life. They were masons, they were both members of the same clubs. They both socialised regularly with the local MP. But all the same, to have him here, in his office, in front of all his staff . . . Suppose he called him Freddie?

'Sir, can I send up Mr Kelly and Mr Gabney?'

'Oh yes, yes, Janet. Show them up please.'

The worst thing was, there was no way he could refuse to see him.

Flowers opened a drawer in his desk and took out a small packet of Settlers; he popped two into his mouth and chewed them noisily while he waited for Kelly.

Why couldn't he just see him at the club as usual? What was important enough to bring him here?

By the time Janet showed the two men into his office, Flowers had calmed down, but as she shut the door behind her the sourness returned to Flowers's face.

'Have you gone mad? Coming here like this? Do you realise I have got the press practically camped out on the doorstep? Why couldn't you have seen me as usual in the club?'

Kelly looked at the tall greying man in front of him. He guessed that he and Flowers were of an age. But dissatis-faction with his life had aged Flowers. He had a large paunch that he tried to hold in with a corset and he dyed his hair. All in all, Kelly thought that Flowers was a silly, vain man and he disliked him immensely.

His voice dripped ice.

'Are you taking the piss out of me?'

Flowers blinked rapidly as Kelly stared him out.

Patrick pointed a stiff finger at Flowers and enjoyed seeing the man flinch.

'In case it escaped your notice, Freddie,' he spoke the man's Christian name with contempt, 'my daughter was murdered recently. I know the news reached you like, 'cause I can remember mentioning it to you myself on several occasions.' The sarcasm was not lost on Flowers or Willy.

Patrick sat down and his minder followed suit. Flowers returned to his seat behind his desk. He had dropped a clanger and knew it. But he was relieved. If the press got wind of who Kelly was, then the fact that his daughter was one of the victims would cover up the fact that he and the Chief Constable met socially.

'I'm sorry, Patrick, but this place is literally under siege at the moment.'

'And you've missed your golf as well? My heart's breaking for you.'

Flowers did not like the fact that Kelly had hit the nail straight on the head but he swallowed the insult. Kelly was a formidable man and knew too much about Flowers and others ever to be made an enemy.

Janet came in with the coffee and left it on the desk. She smiled at Patrick briefly before leaving. Flowers poured it with a hand that was trembling slightly. Kelly always affected him like this.

'What can I do for you?'

'I have a proposition for you, Freddie me old son.'

Flowers looked perplexed. Surely Kelly wasn't here to talk business?

'What kind of proposition?'

'It's about the murderer. I think I know how we can catch the ponce.'

Flowers put down his coffee cup.

'Do you know who he is?' He knew that Patrick Kelly had a price on the man's head. In some circles it was common knowledge.

Patrick sipped his coffee slowly.

'No, I don't know. If I did then he'd be dead, Freddie. Deader than a week-old kipper. No. I don't know who he is, but I know how we can catch him. I need your help, though.'

'In what way?' Flowers was puzzled.

'In Leicester a few years ago every man in the vicinity

of a murder case was given a blood test. Which narrowed down the police's line of inquiry.'

Flowers put up his hand in a gesture of dismissal. 'It would cost too much money, Patrick. Plus there's no guarantee it would work. You don't know the whole of it. We'd have the NCCL after us, not to mention every other crackpot group. They'd say it was just an excuse to monitor people. That their DNA samples would be ready and available for investigation in every sex crime that occurred. That it was an infringement of their civil liberties. Oh, you don't know the half of it.'

Patrick finished his coffee and put his cup on the desk. 'Listen, Freddie, I couldn't give a monkey's bollock for any of this. It is going to be done, and I am going to pay for it. So just button your mutton for five minutes and listen to me. All right?'

Kelly's eyes were hard and Flowers felt the power of the man in front of him.

Patrick Kelly began to talk, slowly and deliberately. After five minutes he had Flowers in a state of fear so acute he could taste it. But after fifteen minutes he could see the sense of what Kelly was saying and relaxed. Two hours later they had reached an amicable arrangement. Patrick got up to leave.

'I had a man in here yesterday evening – Daniel Burrows.' Flowers waited a few seconds for the name to sink in before he started to talk again.

'He seems to think that I should reprimand his ex-wife because of an association with your good self.'

Flowers relaxed. There, it was out!

He watched Patrick's eyes, which were like pieces of flint. Finally, after what seemed an eternity, Kelly went from the room. Fifteen minutes later Flowers also left for the day. For the rest of the afternoon Patrick Kelly made numerous phone calls from home. By eight that evening he had spoken to the DPP, two prominent cabinet members and a host of other people. He phoned Flowers back at seven fifteen with the result of his efforts.

The next day Kate and Caitlin were both called into Ratchette's office. Kate was surprised to see the Chief Constable in there. When everyone was seated he spoke.

'I understand, Detective Inspector Burrows, that you are of the opinion that as all we have in the way of evidence is the genetic fingerprint of the murderer, we should set about taking blood samples of all males from fourteen to sixty-five in this area?'

Kate looked around at the three men.

'Yes, sir. I do believe that. If nothing else it would eliminate an awful lot of people.'

'But surely the killer would not be foolish enough to take the test?'

Kate shrugged.

'That's as may be, sir. But if only some people did, at least it would narrow the field of suspects. A majority of those would be eliminated through corroborated statements. That would leave . . .'

'All right, all right, we get the picture.' Flowers's voice was impatient.

The room went quiet. Kate saw Caitlin and Ratchette look at one another briefly. She knew then that something was going on.

Flowers took out a large white handkerchief and blew his nose loudly. He made a bit of a performance out of it and Kate sensed he was playing for time.

'You fill them in on the details, Ratchette. I have to get back.' With that, he walked from the room. Kate watched him leave in amazement.

'What on earth's going on here?' Her voice was plaintive.

Ratchette smiled at her. 'You got what you wanted, Kate. You got the blood and saliva testing.'

She sat back in her seat, stunned.

'My God!'

Caitlin laughed. 'It's all set up, Katie. I've never seen anything arranged so quickly since my daughter's wedding. The testing starts on Monday the twelfth of February.'

Kate turned to him.

'How come you knew? Why was the Chief Constable in such a foul mood? Just what's going on down here?'

Ratchette answered.

'Let's just say that your idea was put to the big boys and they liked it, Kate. The Chief Constable is against the expenditure, but this man has to be caught. There's a public outcry at the moment, and now the government is putting the funds at our disposal. So make the best of it. You never know when they may pull out again.'

'But how come you knew and I didn't?'

'Let's just say it was discussed first by your superiors, shall we?'

The message in Ratchette's voice was clear enough to Kate but she still wasn't happy about it. Though she was elated that the blood testing was going to happen she was not too sure about the mysterious way it had come about. But Ratchette's tone would brook no more questions. She changed tack.

'So how many mobile units are we getting? I think that if we take the units to all the big firms, men will be forced to take the test in front of their colleagues. We could catch our man out likc that.'

'First things first. We're getting eight different mobile

units. We'll concentrate on the bigger firms first. There's the Ford plant and the electronics factory for starters. We'll also set one up in the town centre. Every male in the age group will be sent letters and documentation that can be produced to prove they have had the test. The sixth form colleges etcetera will be done systematically, and pensioners and the unemployed will be approached by letter to visit one of the mobile units on specified days. It's all in hand. All we have to do now is begin the ground-work. It's going out on local radio and television today, so everyone will be aware of what is happening. Firms will be asked to notify us of people who have suddenly taken holidays or sick leave. I think that we've covered just about every angle. Anyone on the electoral register who does not take the test will be immediately under suspicion, until we can cancel them out.'

'Come on, Katie, it's ten past twelve. I'll buy you a drink and a sandwich.' Caitlin stood up and winked at Ratchette.

Kate stood up and stared into her superior's face.

'Thank you, sir.'

Ratchette smiled.

'Go and get some lunch, Kate. You'll be working like a beaver now, setting all this up with us and keeping your lines of inquiry open. It's going to be a hard old slog, you realise that?'

'Yeah.'

Kate and Caitlin left the room.

Ratchette sat down. Kate Burrows obviously did not realise it but she had a powerful ally in Patrick Kelly. A very powerful ally indeed.

Kate bit into a beef and tomato sandwich, surprised at how hungry she was. She watched Caitlin chatting up the barmaid as he ordered their drinks. She chewed the sandwich slowly, savouring the rich taste. There was something wrong but she did not know what. Caitlin ambled back to the table with her vodka and tonic and his pint of Guinness with whisky chaser.

'What's going on, Kenny?' Kate rarely called him by his first name so it gave the question an edge.

Caitlin sipped his Guinness before answering.

'Look, Katie, whether you realise it or not, you've made yourself a very influential friend, and it was this friend who pushed the issue with the Chief Constable.'

Kate stopped chewing and stared at Caitlin, dumbstruck.

Everybody knew. They all knew about her and Patrick Kelly.

'Don't look so shocked, now. The police force is a very small world, you know. Look at it this way – if a new man or woman comes to a division, within twenty-four hours everyone knows their past track record, their marital status, everything. It's just one of those things. Now then, the fella you're going around with is a big man in his own way, and it was natural it would come to the attention of people. I don't think that the uniforms know, but Ratchette knew, and I knew, and now the Chief Constable knows. I gather he had a visit from your friend yesterday, and apparently he has some even bigger friends of his own. Probably how he's kept out of clink for so long.'

Kate was looking into her glass, embarrassed. Caitlin felt a twinge of sympathy for her.

'Shall I tell you something? It's a thing I've always believed. Most people in the force could have gone one way or the other. Either become a villain – and I mean villain as in bank robber and such, nothing to do with perverts or nonces – or become a policeman. You need the inbred cunning to be a villain in order to catch one. That's why so many of them get on so well.

'Myself, I've nicked men I've had a great deal of respect for. I'm not talking about gas meter bandits or kiters. I'm talking about men who have masterminded some of the biggest bank robberies in the country. I admire them, Katie, even while I've tried to find them and lock them up. Everyone has dreams of winning the pools, whatever. These men set out to steal money that makes the average person in the street drool just thinking about it.

'Kelly now, he works within the law, and sometimes just outside it, but he's first and foremost a businessman. Only he's not a kosher businessman like, say – oh, I don't know – Henry Ford or someone of that ilk. He's part of the new breed, and for myself I admire him. Anyone who can get that eejit of a Chief Constable shitting in his pants has to have something good going for him.'

Kate smiled slightly but her brain was whirling.

Kelly had gone and made the Chief Constable 'see sense'. That is exactly how he would put it when she challenged him about it. In the little time she had known Patrick she had got to understand him so well. In Patrick's mind there was no black and white. Just Patrick Kelly's opinion. And that opinion was worth more to him than the crown jewels.

'Look at it this way, Kate, he got you what you wanted and – I admit now – what I wanted. This is the most difficult case I've ever worked on in my life. We've had four horrific murders and literally nothing to go on except for the bugger's car. And the witnesses can't even agree on the colour of that! Take this opportunity and use it, girl, it's like a gift from God.'

Kate sipped her drink and bit into her sandwich again. What Caitlin said made sense, she admitted that, but she was worried all the same. If her association was common knowledge . . .

'Look, Kenny, can I ask you something?'

Caitlin took a deep draught of his Guinness and wiped his mouth with the back of his hand.

'Ask away.'

'What's being said about me and Kelly? I really want to know.'

'What do you think? "Kate Burrows is having it off with a villain." The usual.' He watched Kate turn white and could have kicked himself.

'That was a joke, Katie, a bad joke I admit, but a joke all the same. What's really being said is this. Kate Burrows has been seeing Pat Kelly. Oh, Pat Kelly says the other person, isn't he the one with the repo business? Yes, that's him, says the first person. Lucky old Kelly is the general opinion. Christ, girl, most of the senior men have tried to get into your knickers at some time or another, that's common knowledge. That you're a respectable woman and a bloody good DI is also common knowledge. *You're* making more of this than anyone. Until Kelly is convicted of something, you're as safe as houses and let's face it, Katie, he's not liable to get caught out now is he? Everything he does is more or less above board. Why don't you relax? You're too hard on yourself.'

'I've fought tooth and nail to get where I am today, Kenny. You don't know the struggle it's been.'

'I don't, no. But, if you're as worried as you say then all you have to do is stop seeing him. Meself I think you'd be a fool. They used to call you the Mother Theresa of Enfield when we worked together before. You're doing nothing wrong, child. Has he ever compromised you?'

'No.'

'Has he ever asked you anything he shouldn't, like?'

'NO!'

'Then why all the drama and fuss? Jesus Christ, you women make your own crosses you know. And believe me it's a long old journey when you have to carry it. I know. Personally, I like Kelly. He's an astute businessman, a good friend, I should think and he's one handsome fucker. You do what you've got to do with him. As long as it doesn't interfere with your work, who cares? They'll be gossiping about someone else next week.'

Kate saw the sense in what Caitlin was saying. He was right. She wasn't doing anything wrong. And if Flowers hadn't said anything then there was obviously no problem.

She wanted to believe it. She had to believe it.

'You're right. I'm worrying about nothing.'

She picked up her glass and drained it.

Caitlin laughed softly and rose to get her another.

'That's the way to do it, girl.'

Kate lit a cigarette and drew the smoke deep into her lungs. She wished Patrick was with her, when he was near she had no doubts. No doubts at all. Then something occurred to her. How the hell did Kelly get them to agree to the blood testing? That's why Flowers was so annoyed with her. Everyone knew she had been rooting for it since the word go, and somehow Patrick had made it possible. Suddenly, Kate was annoyed, very annoyed and the most annoying thing was, she wasn't really sure why.

Elaine and George had finished their tea and were sitting in the lounge watching *Thames News*. Since George's announcement about his redundancy, they had been living under an amicable truce. The murder of Leonora Davidson was the talk of Grantley, and Elaine was well aware that it had happened on a night when George was out walking. A hundred times a day she told herself that it was coincidence, that on the nights of the other murders he had been indoors with her – except for New Year and she was confident that he had been too ill to leave his bed then.

When the newsreader mentioned the Grantley Ripper Elaine's ears pricked up. The screen went to an outside broadcast. Grantley Police Station was in the background as a young girl came on the screen. Elaine was watching George's reaction as the girl spoke.

'The Grantley Ripper case. It has been announced today that the police are going to take blood and saliva samples from all males in the area in the fourteen to sixty-five age group. This means that just over five thousand men and boys will be tested.

'Wide-scale testing has been done only once before in 1983 at Enderby in Leicestershire, after two rapes and murders. The police hope that testing will eliminate as many people as possible in the hunt for the Grantley Ripper. Mobile units will be going around factories and offices, school and unemployment offices. Any man who refuses the test will be under suspicion. We shall be updating you on what happens during the course of the investigation.'

Elaine looked again at George.

'I think it's a good thing, don't you, George?'

'You're absolutely right, my dear. Best thing that could happen if you ask me.'

For the life of him he was not sure how he managed to sound so normal. He was sweating.

'I mean, George, whoever this man is, he's a maniac, a sick maniac, and should be caught and locked away as soon as possible. Hanging's too good for him. I reckon he should be tortured like he tortured those women.'

George nodded absentmindedly. His mind was racing.

What was he going to do? He could not take the test. They'd be coming to his place of work. He would be forced to take it with his colleagues.

'Would you like me to make you a cuppa, George? I'm having one.'

'Yes, dear. That would be lovely.'

Elaine walked to the kitchen. Well, he seemed OK. It was her as usual. She was always down on George but couldn't seem to help it. He affected her like that.

Anyway, she reasoned, if he had had anything to worry about he would have shown it by now. George was like an open book to her. When she'd poured out the tea George walked into the kitchen and picked up his cup.

'I'm going down to the shed, dear, I want to sort out the bulbs for the spring planting. I won't be long.'

'All right then. Shall I call you when *EastEnders* comes on?'

'No. I won't bother tonight, I've too much to do.'

He walked from the kitchen and Elaine went into the lounge feeling a bit happier. If he was worried about anything he wouldn't be doing something so mundane as sorting out the spring bulbs.

George locked himself into his shed and put on the light. He placed a piece of material over the window and then put on the small Calor gas heater. The shed was soon warm and cosy. He sipped his tea, sitting on the old chair, and thought deeply about his predicament. He could see no way out. Finally he got up and moved the gardening catalogues from the desk, pulling out his books reverently. He finished his tea and settled himself into the chair with them on his lap.

He began idly to flick through them but tonight he felt nothing. Not even the semi-erection he usually got just from the act of having them near him. He looked through the pile and then picked out one of his favourites. He looked at the girl's face and tried to empty his mind of everything. Closing his eyes he pictured himself straddling her, his penis forcing its way into her mouth against her will. His breathing became heavier and he opened the flies of his trousers, pulling on his penis to try and force some life into it.

It was beginning to stir. Slowly he began to pull the foreskin back and forth, enjoying the sensation it created. Now he was pushing it into the girl's vagina, squeezing on her naked breasts, and she was begging him to stop. Pleading with him. He rubbed at himself, faster and harder, the sensations taking away all the worry and uncertainty. He was building up to an orgasm when Elaine began banging on the shed door.

'George . . . George! There's a phone call for you. Some bloke called Tony Jones.'

He felt the icy hand of fear on the back of his neck. He pulled his hands from his trousers as quickly as he could. The small space was hot and cloying from the Calor gas heater and he felt a moment's sickness as he realised what Elaine was saying.

'Are you listening to me, George?'

'I'm just coming, dear. I think I dozed off in the chair, looking at the gardening catalogues.'

Outside in the cold and dark Elaine rolled her eyes. 'Well, hurry up, it must be costing this bloke a fortune.'

George stood up and threw the magazines into the desk. It wasn't until he was halfway up the path that he remembered that his trousers were undone. He hurriedly zipped them up and pulled his jumper down over them. Tony Jones. What the hell did he want now? He walked through the kitchen and went to the phone in the hall.

'Hello?'

'Georgie? It's me, Tony Jones.'

'What do you want?' His voice was hard.

'Calm down, I told your wife I was a friend of yours. You have got friends, I take it?'

'What do you want, Tony?'

'I've got some new films in, Georgie, and I think you'll like them.'

'I'm a bit strapped for money at the moment.'

'Well, pop in and see me and I'll do you a deal. You're a good customer, Georgie, and I'd hate to lose you.' Tony's voice was friendly now.

'I'll try and get in over the weekend.'

'You wanna see these films, mate, they're hot. The birds in them! Tits like you've never seen before . . .'

George was already picturing it in his mind and Tony knew this. He knew exactly how to sell his merchandise.

'One bird's built like a fucking Amazon and she's loving it, Georgie. For all her shouts and protests. You can see her coming as you watch.'

George was feeling hot now. He wanted the films. He wanted them now.

'I'll be in tomorrow night after work, OK?'

'You know it makes sense.'

The line went dead. George replaced the receiver.

'Bring me in the paper, George.' Elaine's voice was at full throttle and he winced inwardly. He picked up the paper from the telephone table and took it into the lounge.

'Here you are, love.'

'Who was that then?'

'Oh, a friend from work about my leaving do.'

'Leaving do? For you?' Elaine's voice was incredulous.

'Yes, Elaine. For me.'

George was annoyed now. What with everything that

was happening, the last thing he needed was one of Elaine's little innuendos. Do her good to let her think he had friends. Might shut her up now and again.

'I know you find it hard to believe that people might like me, but they do!'

She was annoyed at his attitude. 'I'm sorry, George, but after fifteen years I'd have thought you might have mentioned these friends now and again.'

'When have you ever wanted to know, Elaine? Answer me that if you can. Just when have you ever wanted to know?'

With that he went back down to his shed. He was aware that he had dropped his guard with Elaine and was glad. Give her something to think about for a change. She took him for granted, always had. He locked himself into the shed and put the Calor gas fire on again.

Fifteen minutes later he was once more locked into his fantasy world.

George sat at his desk. He wished he had not bothered to come to work. The only topic of conversation was the blood testing. Peter Renshaw was making one of his lightning appearances. George wished it was time for one of his sales visits to Yorkshire, or better still Scotland. Peter's insistence on being his friend unnerved him. But hadn't he told Elaine last night that he had friends? George pondered this for a while. He watched Renshaw monopolising the conversation, his eyes scanning the small crowd around him as if he was trying to catch them out not listening to him.

George wondered if in fact he had any friends. It was the first time in years such a thought had occurred to him. As a child he had not had many, but that was his mother's fault. She had not encouraged her children to bring friends home. George unconsciously pursed his lips. He could never remember bringing anyone home. He could not remember one true friend. He began to feel sorry for himself. No friends. Fifty-one years old and no friends. No real friends. Even Elaine had friends. Big, fat, brash till girls who dressed like tarts and spent their life in bingo halls like mutton dressed as lamb. His mother had been right about Elaine. She'd said he would rue the day he married her, and he did. But Elaine had been so sweet once. Long ago. She was the only girl who had ever shown a spark of interest in him and he had been grateful. He grimaced. Grateful to her?

Now he could have any woman he wanted. He *did* have any woman he wanted. He let his mind stray to Leonora Davidson. He didn't feel any regret. She was alone, no husband or children to worry about her. Just a lonely woman. He had done her a favour really. Lately he hadn't liked thinking about Geraldine O'Leary. Her children had been in the local paper. Beautiful children, like their mother. Elaine said they had taken her husband away to a mental hospital. That he had had a nervous breakdown. He pushed the thought from his mind. He had more pressing things to think about.

'I say, Georgie . . . I'm talking to you!' Peter Renshaw's loud voice echoed across the room. George looked at him. 'Sorted out your leaving do, old matey. Friday week at the Fox Revived. We'll all meet there straight from work. I've got a surprise for you, old chap. A bl-oody big surprise.'

George smiled at him.

Josephine Denham walked into the office. As usual she looked immaculate. She was wearing large grey-framed glasses that gave her a look of intelligence and sophistication, and was carrying a sheaf of papers.

'Can I have your attention, please?'

Everyone stared at her.

'The mobile blood unit will be here on Thursday the twenty-second of this month. The office staff will be the first for testing then the factory and warehouse staff. If we do it on a rota basis it won't affect production too much. I've been talking to the police this morning and they say that they'll be giving out questionnaires nearer the time. Anyone who is not at work that day must account for their whereabouts to me personally. I will then pass on the message to the police. If anyone is against the taking of the test please feel free to come and see me, though personally I can't see why anyone would object.'

Her eyes scanned the small sea of faces and it was evident that anyone who refused would be immediately judged guilty, by her at least. When no one answered she turned on her heel and walked from the room, her footsteps ringing on the tiled floor as she walked away.

'I'd go and see her, but it wouldn't be to tell her about the blood testing, eh, chaps? I'd give her a portion of the pork sword anytime!'

The men laughed, even George, though his mind was whirling.

What the hell was he going to do?

He looked at his watch. It was eleven thirty. He got up from his seat and began to put on his jacket.

'Where you off to, George?' This from Carstairs, a man whom George had worked with for fifteen years and barely knew.

'I'm going down the pub for some lunch actually.'

'But it's only eleven thirty!'

George never left until twelve on the dot. 'I can tell the time, you know.' With that he walked from the office.

'Well I never!' Carstairs looked at the others.

Peter Renshaw picked up his sheepskin, slipped it on and followed George out of the office. He caught up with him in the Fox Revived.

George had walked into the warmth of the pub. He knew that Peter was behind him and tried to ignore him, hoping against hope that he would take the hint and leave him alone. But not Peter Renshaw. As George ordered his drink, Peter pushed in beside him and ordered his own, paying for the two. George sighed. Picking up his glass he took it to a small window table and sat down. Renshaw followed him.

'I say, Georgie, you all right?'

He sipped his half of bitter and nodded. Renshaw, he decided, was like a virus. You just had to put up with it until it decided to go.

'Look, George, I know that this redundancy has hit you hard, but in reality it's the best thing that could have happened to you. I mean, fifteen years' loyal service. You're looking at a good twenty-five thousand, aren't you?'

George's eyes widened. 'That much?'

'Yes, I was talking to Jones. He says that as it's not a voluntary redundancy, you'll all get a golden handshake. Like they did with the dockers and the car workers. They'll be paying you off, Georgie boy.'

'Twenty-five thousand pounds?'

Peter smiled now. 'That's a lot of dosh, Georgie. I reckon you should get the next round in!'

He smiled. This time it was his secret smile. He was feeling a bit better now. He had four more weeks at work. Then he could go where he wanted. Until then he had to avoid the blood testing.

But how?

*

Kate's phone rang and she picked it up. She was up to her eyes in statements, had been going over the same ground over and over again. There had to be something, something trivial, that they had missed.

'Hello, Burrows here.'

Patrick's voice crackled over the line and Kate felt her stomach tighten.

'What happened to you last night? I tried ringing but your phone was either unplugged or you were out on the razzle.'

His voice was playful, but Kate detected a note of uneasiness as well. Carefully hidden but there nonetheless.

She closed her eyes.

'I had some work to finish. I meant to ring you today but I'm up to my eyes here. I take it you know about the blood testing?' Her voice came out harder than she'd intended.

The phone went quiet.

'Can I see you later, Kate? I think we need to talk.'

She sighed. Caitlin was supposedly reading statements but she knew that his ears were on red alert.

'I'll ring you from home. When I finally arrive there.' She replaced the receiver without saying goodbye.

She looked at Caitlin who was now watching her openly. 'What are you staring at?' She sounded childish, petulant, and knew it.

'I don't know, it's not labelled.' Caitlin's voice was like a little boy's.

'Oh, sod off, Kenny.'

Caitlin laughed, then said seriously: 'Don't you be a fool now and bite the hand that feeds you. He did you a favour, girl, if you could only see it.'

Kate dropped her eyes and made a pretence of reading another statement.

What Caitlin said held the ring of truth but her pride was hurt. Kelly had managed what she had been trying to do for months without a murmur in response.

It galled her.

Patrick stared at the receiver in his hand.

She had put the phone down on him. She had actually put the phone down on him! He couldn't believe it.

He replaced the phone in its cradle, a flicker of annoyance on his handsome face. Who the bloody hell did Kate Burrows think she was? She had stood him up last night. Now she'd put the phone down on him, apart from all that sarcasm about the blood testing. He'd been under the impression that was what she wanted.

As he walked into the morning room Willy, who had been reading the paper, hastily got up from his seat.

'Comfortable were you? I hope I'm not interrupting anything?'

'Sorry, Pat, but I was just having five minutes off like.'

'Go and get the motor, Willy. If that's not too much trouble like, I'd hate to think I was overworking you . . .'

Willy rushed out, the paper rustling as he tried to fold it as he went.

Patrick smiled. His eyes strayed to the window and suddenly he was assailed with a memory of Renée. He could see her now, in his mind's eye. She'd had no qualms about slamming the phone down on him. She'd shout, 'Out there, mate,' pointing to the window, 'you might be a big man, but in this house you're only my husband. Get it?'

He laughed. She'd had so much spirit.

Maybe that's why he liked Kate so much.

Slamming the phone down on him, the cheeky cow!

Five minutes later he was in the back of the Rolls Royce on his way to his Manor Park parlour.

He grinned.

She'd actually put the phone down on him.

He couldn't believe it!

Maybelline Morgan was known for her large breasts and her larger mouth. She was now arguing violently with Violet Mapping over a customer.

'I always have him, Vi, and you bleeding well know it!'

Violet gritted her teeth. 'He didn't want you, Maybelline. He wanted the blonde girl and that's that.'

Maybelline's eyes were like pieces of flint. She wagged a deep red-varnished nail in Violet's face.

'Don't fucking push me, Vi. I need the dosh and you know it. You're not bumming me out now. I know that little bird's flashing her clout for you, that's why she's getting all the good punters.'

She pushed her finger roughly into Violet's chest. 'I'll take you out first, and then her. I'll rip you to fucking shreds . . .'

Violet knew that the argument was being listened to by the majority of the girls who were sitting outside the office door. If she didn't shut Maybelline up she would lose her authority. She grabbed at the other woman's hair, bringing her knee up into her stomach at the same time. Maybelline bent double. Still clutching her hair, Violet slammed her face into the corner of the heavy wooden desk. Maybelline dropped on to the carpeted floor, her eyebrow dripping blood.

Violet smiled at her nastily.

'Don't ever threaten me again. Now you can get your stuff and piss off.'

Maybelline pulled herself up with the help of the desk and faced Violet. Her long bony face framed by flame-coloured hair was twisted in hatred. Putting her hand into the pocket of her skirt she brought out a knife. The blade flicked into view and glinted in the fluorescent light.

Violet went white which was not lost on Maybelline. She rushed forward, slashing at her with the knife. Violet put her arms up to defend herself and felt the coldness of the steel as it bit into her skin just above the elbow, scraping on the bone with sickening ferocity. Maybelline brought the knife up and slashed at Violet again. This time she caught her on the side of the face. Both women were sticky with blood.

Violet made an effort to grab Maybelline's wrists. Using all her considerable strength, she managed to hold the other woman's arms apart.

Patrick Kelly and his minder walked into the massage parlour to a scene of pandemonium. Women and girls were clustered around the office door and Kelly could hear shouting and swearing coming from inside.

'What the hell's going on in here?'

The women parted like the Red Sea as they recognised his voice. The two men forced their way into the office.

'Bloody hell!' Patrick's voice was incredulous. Without speaking further he grabbed at Maybelline and Willy grabbed at Violet. After another struggle the women were separated. Patrick banged Maybelline's hand on the desk until she dropped the knife. Then he threw her from him and stepped on the knife. Willy let go of Violet gladly. 'What's going on here? You –' he pointed at Violet – 'what the fuck has happened here?'

Maybelline answered.

'She's picking the Toms, Mr Kelly, and we've all had enough. That little bird she's screwing has made over a thousand pound this week. Every decent punter that comes in gets her. Me and the other girls ain't made more than a couple of ton. If something ain't done we're going to the Paki down the road. At least he sees his girls all right.'

Patrick was dumbstruck. There was blood everywhere and the thought of HIV was not far from his mind.

'I want you two to go out to the kitchen and get cleaned up, then I want you both back in here and we'll try and sort it all out. You've got ten minutes. So get your arses in gear.'

The two women left his office and were immediately surrounded by the other girls. Willy shut the door and looked at his boss with raised eyebrows.

'I gotta be honest, Pat, that Maybelline's got a point, you know. I heard that Vi's mad about this little bird. Well, it was bound to happen, weren't it? Even the old lezzies must go funny as they get older.'

'Willy, shut up! I pay you to drive my car and do the minding. If I wanted a gossip I'd have employed Nigel Dempster, all right?'

Walking out of the office Patrick went to the kitchen. He tapped a young black girl on the shoulder.

'Do me a favour, Suzie, get a bucket and cloth and clean the office, would you, love? I'll bung you a score.'

'Yeah, all right, Mr Kelly.'

Ten minutes later Patrick was behind the desk and Maybelline and Violet were standing in front of him like recalcitrant schoolgirls.

'I'm telling you, Mr Kelly, unless we get a fair crack of the whip we'll have it on our toes. This ain't the only place to work, you know.'

'I've always looked after my girls. I resent the implication that I'm doing you down, Maybelline.'

Violet spoke. 'I was out of order, Pat. I admit it.'

Maybelline smiled at her and Kelly shook his head.

These women amazed him. One minute they were at each other's throats. The next they were best friends again.

'I don't like my girls carrying weapons. If I find out you've brought a knife or anything in again, Maybelline, there'll be trouble. Big trouble. Get it?'

'Yes, Mr Kelly.'

'Now then, Violet, I want you to get your priorities right in future because if anything like this happens again, I'm gonna out the lot of you. Now fuck off the pair of you and leave me alone.'

The two women left the room.

'Pour me out a brandy, Willy, a large one.'

Willy went to the drinks cabinet and opened it. He held up an empty bottle of Remy Martin.

'Only got Scotch left, I'm afraid.'

Patrick clenched his fists. 'That'll do.' He got up from the desk and went to the door. 'Violet!' His voice was so loud the girls jumped in their seats. Violet rushed from the kitchen, her face white.

'What, Mr Kelly?'

'Stop drinking my fucking booze! No wonder this place is like a madhouse. You're all either drunk or drugged!'

He slammed the office door.

He took the large Scotch from Willy and drank it straight down, handing the glass back for an immediate refill. Then, sitting at the desk, he opened the drawer and took out the ledgers. If Violet was skanking off the other girls to subsidise this little bird there was a good chance she was skanking off him too.

Bloody Violet! He would have laid money on her being the most dependable of all the girls working for him. They had been friends for years.

'Willy, go out and get me a bottle of Rémy Martin and give the bill to Violet. OK?'

Willy nodded and left the room. Patrick began to study the ledgers. The phone rang and he picked it up.

'Yeah? Kelly.'

'Pat, thank God you're there, I've been trying to trace you. You'd better get your arse over here, mate.'

'What is it, Karen?'

'Trouble, Pat. Big trouble.'

The phone went dead.

Kelly closed his eyes. If one more woman put the phone down on him today he would throw a paddy. He put the ledgers away and waited for Willy's return.

'Come on, you, we're off to Barking. Karen's been on the blower, there's hag over there.'

He walked from the office. As he passed Violet with the girls, he pointed at her.

'Don't touch me booze, and don't touch the ledgers, Vi.'

He went out to his car and began his journey to Barking. More bloody girl trouble, he supposed. Poxy Toms weren't worth the hag half the time.

The trouble was bigger than he had ever expected.

As he walked through the dark-glassed door of his massage parlour in Barking, Kelly was amazed to see the girls all white-faced and quiet. He walked into the office where Karen, the head girl, was drinking a large brandy.

'Is that my brandy you're drinking?'

'Oh, shut up, Pat. Come through.'

Karen's voice was trembling and he followed her without question.

Karen took him to the cubicle area, big tears rolling down her face as she pointed to a curtained booth.

'It's in there, Pat. I can't go in. I didn't know what to do. I ain't called the Old Bill, I just didn't know what to do!'

Her voice was wretched. Willy had followed them inside and now Patrick motioned to him to open the curtain. Against his will he felt a prickle of fear.

Willy pulled the curtain open and both he and Patrick stared in amazement. Lying on the table was a girl. Her long blond hair was nearly touching the floor and her eyes were closed. If not for the impossible angle of her neck you would think she was sleeping. She was semi-naked. Her tiny cropped top was still in place though her breasts jutted from under it where it had been pulled over them. Her lower body was exposed and her legs were wide apart.

'She's dead, Pat. I found her like it. The bloke must have walked out the front door.' Karen's voice broke again.

'What did he look like, Karen?' Patrick shook her roughly. 'Did you get a look at his boat?'

She shook her head. 'No. They all look the same to me.'

'Well, someone must have bloody seen him. Cover the poor little cow up, for Christ's sake.'

He went to the front of the parlour. All the girls were in different stages of shock.

'Did anyone see the bloke? Can anyone remember him?'

They shook their heads but an Asian girl spoke up.

'I think he was the old bloke who came in this afternoon. That's the last time I saw Gilly.'

'What time this afternoon?'

'At about one. One thirty.'

Patrick was stumped. He looked at his watch. 'Do you mean she's been lying there dead for over five hours? She's been lying there dead, and you lot were doing the fucking business, and not one of you noticed she was gone?'

All the women stared at him.

'What did he look like?'

The Asian girl thought. 'I don't know. About forty-eight, fifty. He had a beard . . .'

'No. I had him. That's Mr Jenkins. I have him every week.' A dark-haired girl looked at Patrick timidly. 'He's ever such a nice man, Mr Kelly, very polite.'

'I'll call the Old Bill.' Patrick's voice was quiet.

It was like his Mandy all over again, only this time it was his fault. Some piece of scum had taken that girl and murdered her, and it was his fault because he owned the place. He owned every brick and every cubicle and every girl who worked here.

He went to the office and rang the police. Then he sat in the chair and waited for them to arrive.

Chapter Twenty-One

Patrick finally got to Kate's at ten thirty. He pulled up outside her house and was gratified to see that the light was on in the lounge. He told Willy to take the car home and walked up the tiny path to her front door. He rang the bell. Kate was making herself a cheese sandwich in the kitchen. She went to the door licking her fingers clean.

'I rang you at eight, but Mrs Manners said you were out. I didn't expect to see you until tomorrow.'

He walked into the hall. 'I didn't know if you'd rung or not, to be honest; I haven't been home.' He followed Kate into the lounge.

'Take your coat off. Be quiet, my mum's in bed. I'm just making a sandwich, do you want one?'

'What is it?' Kelly hadn't eaten since lunchtime.

'Cheese or cheese?'

'Cheese it is then. I'll make the tea.'

He went to the kitchen and they both worked in silence for a while.

'You upset me, you know, Pat. With what you did. But I see now that whatever way we got the testing, it can only be for the best.'

Patrick had forgotten about it. He shrugged.

'Kate, you know I'm a repoman, don't you?'

His voice was quiet and serious and it made her look at him.

'Yes, why?'

'Did you know I owned massage parlours too?'

'Yes. I knew you had a vested interest. What's all this about?'

Suddenly she was not at all sure she wanted to hear any more. What was it Caitlin had said – Patrick Kelly was one of the new breed of businessmen? He worked within the law, just. Was he going to ask her to help him with something not quite legit?

'One of my girls was murdered earlier today. I don't know if you heard it on the news? In Barking. Her neck was broken. Snapped like a twig. I feel terrible, Kate, really terrible. She was twenty-one years old.

'From what I can gather she had on average five or six punters a day. She slept with all those different men every day. Do you know, it's weird, Kate, but it never occurred to me before. Those women were like animals to me. You're sorry if people ill treat them but you forget about them quickly . . .'

Kate watched him for a second. She picked up the plates of sandwiches and took them into the lounge, then she poured the tea and took that in too.

'Come and sit down, Pat, I think you need to get all this off your chest.'

He followed Kate through into the lounge. Sitting on the settee, he sipped his tea.

'What's really wrong, Pat? Is it the girl getting murdered or the fact that she was on your premises at the time?'

Kate had hit the proverbial nail on the head and Kelly

was shocked that she knew him so well after such a short time.

'A bit of both, I think, if I'm honest. You should have seen her, Kate, she could have been my Mandy lying there. I've been doing everything humanly possible to help catch this Ripper bloke and yet I've been catering to scum like him for years.'

'Well, Pat, women will always sell their bodies. From soft porn to hard porn to streetwalking, sex is one of the biggest moneyspinners in the world. The girl would maybe have done it anyway, if not for you then for someone else. Is that what you want to hear? Is that what you want me to say?'

Kate's voice was low but there was no mistaking her fury. Patrick looked into her face and for the first time he saw real anger. It unnerved him.

'I heard about that girl's death today, Pat, it was on the news. I didn't know you owned the massage parlour. But shall I tell you what went through my mind as I listened to the radio? I thought, I wonder who's the man making money off this girl's back. I knew it would be a man. Funny that, isn't it? I never dreamt it was you though. The man who paid for the blood testing of five thousand men to find the pervert who killed his daughter. Will you be paying for this inquiry, by the way?' Kate lifted her eyebrows at Kelly and he had the grace to look away.

'No, I didn't think so. If you've come here for tea and sympathy and somewhere to lick your wounds I'm afraid you came to the wrong place, Pat. I have nothing for you as far as that girl's concerned. You helped murder her as if you snapped her neck yourself. Any sympathy I have is for her family. I bet that never occurred to you either, did it? That all the women who work for you are someone's daughter or someone's mother. You don't have the monopoly on grief, Pat. Try and put yourself in her parents' position. At least when you found out about Mandy's death you didn't have the added trauma of finding out she met her death while plying her trade, fucking strange men.

'What's it you just said? "Those women were like animals to me." My God, Patrick Kelly, you've got some bloody front coming here!'

Patrick stared at her.

'Have you quite finished? If I'd wanted a bloody lecture I'd have gone to a university. I came here to try and sort out my head, that's all. I never harmed that girl, I never wanted anything to happen to her, to any of them . . .'

He was floundering and he knew it. Kate had stated the plain, ugly truth and his only form of defence was attack.

'You make me laugh sometimes, Mrs Highbrow Bloody Policewoman. Well, did it ever occur to you that some of them girls like their job? Did it? That if they didn't work for me they would work for someone else . . . Well, did it? DID IT?'

Kate shook her head sadly.

'I'm not seeing them though am I? I'm seeing you, Pat, and I don't care how much you rant and rave, I've nothing for you tonight. I've no sympathy for you, I'm sorry. If you want that I suggest you go and see the girl's parents. That might put it in perspective for you. Though after what happened to Mandy, I'd have thought you of all people would have understood what they're going through.'

Patrick felt the temper rising and he was honest enough to admit that it was not because of Kate's words, but because he felt ashamed. He could not admit that to her though.

'I'm bloody going. I should have known a bloody Old

Bill wouldn't be any good to me when the chips were down. Your trouble is you fancy yourself as some kind of bleeding saint, Kate. Well, listen to me. I don't need you or anyone else to point out my shortcomings. I've been aware of them for years. From the time I could understand what was going on around me. Yes, I wanted a bit of tea and sympathy, the same as you did when your daughter OD'd. And thanks a lot for nothing. I tell you something now, I don't need you. I don't need anyone really, I never did and I never will.'

As soon as he said the words he was sorry. He wanted to take Kate in his arms and love her, have her love him, but he couldn't.

Kate watched him walk from the room, and heard the front door slam.

They had needed to get all this out in the open. But she was sorry it had come about like this. His dealings with the massage parlours would always have been between them; now they both knew where they stood.

That poor girl was dead. Patrick was feeling guilty, whatever he said. But where had that got her?

Kate stared at her sandwich.

She didn't feel hungry any more.

Patrick walked out of Kate's and cursed silently. He had let Willy go and now he would have to phone for a taxi. He began to wander aimlessly, looking for a phone box. Like George he was finding solace in the darkness. He breathed the cold night air into his lungs and once more his mind was on Gillian Enderby. He saw her lying in the cubicle, her hair falling down over the table, nearly touching the floor. She was a sweet-looking girl. She didn't look like a prostitute, but then none of them did at first. He remembered a younger Violet — what a girl she had been!

He saw the lights of a call box and quickened his stride. Renée had never been happy about the prostitution. She would sit in for him on the repo side of the business but had flatly refused to have anything to do with the massage parlours. It was an unspoken agreement that they were never mentioned at home, even in passing.

He walked into the phone booth and after unsuccessfully trying to find a cab number rang up Willy and ordered him to pick him up. He knew better than to ask why his boss was ringing from a call box and not from Kate's.

Patrick stood outside the phone booth and stamped his feet. It was freezing. Kevin Cosgrove had supposedly been picking up Mandy from outside a phone booth. It had been vandalised, that's why she had begun to walk home. He pushed his hands deeper into the pockets of his overcoat. Gillian Enderby was at this moment on ice somewhere. Her parents were going through what he had gone through.

Later that night, as he lay in his bed, he wished that Kate was with him. He missed her. She was in her forties; she was dark when he had always had a preference for blondes; she was flat-chested and he had always liked his women to be well endowed; and to put the tin lid on it, she was a policewoman. In fact, she was the antithesis of everything he had ever said he wanted in a woman.

Yet he wanted her desperately.

Mandy and Gillian Enderby crawled once more into his troubled thoughts and finally he admitted defeat and got out of bed and went downstairs. He went to make himself a hot drink and took it back to bed after lacing it liberally with brandy.

Still he lay there, tossing and turning.

Kate, in her lonely bed, was doing exactly the same.

*

Willy was surprised to see Patrick up and dressed at six thirty and already on the telephone. He wondered briefly who he had got out of bed. After his own breakfast Patrick called him at seven fifteen and said he wanted to go to an address in East Ham. It was a council maisonette. Willy saw a man answer the door and then, after a brief exchange of words, saw Patrick go inside.

Curiouser and curiouser, he thought. Then he picked up his paper and began the process of looking at the semi-naked woman on page three once again.

Patrick introduced himself to Stan Enderby and the man invited him in. Enderby was about his own age but had not had the benefit of money. He looked older than his years, from the tobacco-stained fingers, the large beer belly and receding hairline to the impossibly thin roll-up clamped to the side of his mouth.

'The wife's upstairs, Mr Kelly. Took it bad, she has. Gilly was her pride and joy, you see. We never knew that she was . . . that she did what she did.'

Patrick followed him into a tiny front room that was sparsely furnished though very clean. He sat on the chair by the window and looked down briefly at his car.

'Would you like a cup of tea, or something stronger?' Stanley held up a bottle of cheap Tesco whisky and Patrick nodded his head in assent. He waited until the man gave him his glass.

'Thank you.'

Kelly knew that Enderby was at a loss. His reputation had as usual preceded him and inhibited a natural response. He'd have welcomed blame, anger. Anything but this passivity, this pretence that he was a welcome visitor. But he knew that Enderby was scared of him. In the past he had profited from his reputation, but at this moment if Enderby had slammed the glass of whisky into his face, he would have accepted it. Would have admired him even.

'I have come to offer you my condolences, Mr Enderby. I feel a sense of responsibility for what happened to your daughter and would be most grateful if you would allow me to pay for the funeral.'

'That's more than kind, Mr Kelly. We never expected anything . . .'

As he spoke, the front-room door opened and a tiny woman walked in. She was a faded blonde, and Kelly knew immediately this was Gillian's mother. They were like two peas in a pod.

'What do you want?' Her voice was aggressive.

Stanley Enderby looked at his wife in shock.

'This is Mr Kelly, Maureen.'

'Oh, shut up, Stan, for Gawd's sake.' She turned back to Patrick. 'I asked you a question, Kelly, what do you want?'

He dropped his eyes. He could see the accusation in her face. 'I came to offer my condolences, Mrs Enderby.'

'He's gonna pay for the funeral and that, ain't you, Mr Kelly?'

Stanley's voice was tight. He was not a man who could handle scenes of any kind. All his married life he had tried to avoid confrontations with his tiny but quick-tempered wife.

Maureen Enderby sneered. Her hard eyes slowly swept Patrick from his head to his toes.

'So Pat Kelly's coming around with his cheque book, is he, making everything better? I remember you when you didn't have a pot to piss in, you ponce! I remember your mother and your sisters when Gracie was moonlighting

434

down the bleeding docks. You learnt all about whoring at an early age, didn't you? Then you came and took my girl and put her on the fucking bash and now she's dead! Well, some pervert got your girl, didn't he? I'd call it poetic justice.'

Patrick's face was white now.

'I never put your daughter on the game, Mrs Enderby. I had no knowledge of her working there. I never know any of the girls.'

Maureen rushed at him and thumped him in the chest, her face contorted with grief.

'Well, you should have then! You should have known who they were. My daughter was a drug addict. I never knew that until today . . . I never knew it. She was sleeping with men to pay for her drugs. Drugs she probably bought from you!'

Patrick shook his head violently. 'I have never, ever sold drugs. Whatever else I may have done to you, real or imagined, I have never sold drugs!'

'No, Patrick Kelly.' Maureen's voice was quiet now. 'You just sold degradation, didn't you?'

She turned to her husband.

'Get this scum out of my house, Stan. Now!'

Patrick looked at the man in front of him and shook his head as if to say: I understand.

'Take your cheque book, Mr Kelly. I want none of your dirty money. I'll bury me own according to *my* purse, not yours.'

Patrick left the maisonette and Stanley followed him out on to the landing.

'I'm sorry, Mr Kelly, but it's what happened. It's turned her head like. She'll come round. We're potless, see. I ain't worked for four years. And now we ain't got Gilly's money coming in.'

435

Kelly nodded. 'I'll see that you get the money, Mr Enderby.'

'I think it would be best in notes like, we ain't got a bank account.' His voice trailed off and Patrick nodded again. He went down the stairs and got into his car. Out of the two of them he preferred the girl's mother. At least her grief was genuine. Gillian Enderby's father was capitalising on his daughter's death, which hardly seemed to bother him.

But it bothered Patrick Kelly.

It bothered him a lot.

Kate had arrived at the church early and sat alone at the back, enjoying the quietness and solitude. As a Roman Catholic, Mandy Kelly's body had been left in church overnight ready for the Requiem Mass in the morning. Her Aunt Grace was delegated to sit with the body while the soul departed for heaven. This was an old Irish tradition that was still kept alive by every new generation.

Kate knelt down and prayed for the first time in years. She had forgotten the feeling of peace and contentment an empty church could bring. She prayed for the soul of Mandy Kelly and all the murdered women and girls.

The funeral was at nine thirty, but the church had begun to fill up before nine. Kate watched from the back as various criminals and businessmen turned up. She was not too surprised when Chief Constable Frederick Flowers arrived with his wife. Or when the local MP and his wife also showed up. She did admit to a slight feeling of surprise when she noticed two prominent heads of the Serious Crime Squad. Both shook Patrick's hand and one of the men, known in the force as Mad Bill McCormack because of his unorthodox methods of obtaining arrests with a pickaxe handle, actually hugged him close. To Kate it was a real education and her naivety troubled her. She was a good detective, she knew her job, but this closeness between the criminal world and the police had never before been so blatantly thrust on her. Oh, she knew that it went on, but it seemed that the days when villains and police met only under cover of darkness were over. Now they met socially.

She pushed the thoughts from her mind. It was the funeral of Patrick's only child and she should be pleased for him that so many people had turned out to pay their respects. It helped some people when their departed were shown to be popular and cared for.

She watched Patrick scanning the church and finally his eyes found hers. She smiled at him briefly. His face immediately relaxed and for those few seconds she felt once more the pull he had on her.

After the Mass, as the mourners left the church and the body was taken to the grave, Patrick fell into step beside her. He held on to her arm lightly but firmly as if frightened she was going to run away. Kate glanced at him and saw the tears on his long dark lashes. She realised that he needed her, and more to the point, she needed him. She accompanied him to the graveside. As the priest began the final blessings she felt his grief as if it was a physical thing. His shoulders heaved and instinctively she grasped his hand tightly and he held on to her, pulling her to him. She knew that it was taking all his willpower not to break down there and then, in front of everybody. He was finally burying his beloved child and the full realisation of all that had happened had only just hit him.

Mandy was not coming home.

Not now, not ever.

Kate saw that she was buried beside her mother. Poor

Patrick. His whole life was now buried in two small plots of land.

Kate saw Patrick's sister watching her and dropped her gaze. Finally it was all over and people began to make their way back to their cars. Patrick stood at the graveside, oblivious of the offers of condolence. Kate stayed beside him and noticed Kevin Cosgrove standing apart from all the others. He waited until the grave was quiet and walked to it. On Mandy's coffin, now lying in the ground, waiting to be covered, he threw a single white rose. Then he walked away.

'Come on, Patrick, you'd best get yourself back home now.' She pulled him gently away.

'I can't go back to that house, Kate. I can't talk to all those people.'

'You must. Come on, I'll drive back with you. You have to face people. It's just the shock of what's happened hitting you.'

Patrick's sister Grace walked with them. She was about fifty, Kate judged, and looked well on it considering she had been up all night. Her hair was perfect as were her make-up and clothes. She was as fair as Patrick was dark.

'Come on, Pat. Let's get this over with. I don't believe we've met, dear. I'm Grace . . . Grace Kelly. I know what you're going to say but I'm used to it by now.

'Come on, Pat, the sooner we get this lot back, the sooner we can get shot of them. Old Auntie Ethel's pissed as a newt and if we're not careful she'll be taking bets on how many cartwheels it would take to go round the church.'

Kate saw Patrick relax. Grace Kelly was obviously a woman you listened to and nothing else. She kept up a running commentary all the way to the car.

'Look, Pat, I'll let you go with your sister. I must get back to work,' Kate said.

'I thought you were going to come to my house with me?'

'I was, but now that you have your sister, I really feel I must get back to work.'

'Will I see you tonight, Kate?' His voice was so lonely and wretched she could not have refused him even if she had wanted to.

'Yes, you'll see me tonight. You come to my house, Patrick.'

She had a feeling he was better off away from home for a few hours at least.

George walked into Sexplosion on the evening of Mandy's funeral. He was unaware of it, with more important things on his mind such as how he was going to get out of the blood testing. He had had the germ of an idea earlier in the day and now was about to sound out Tony Jones who was an integral part of it.

Tony smiled at him and took him through to the back room. George waited until the video was on before he spoke.

'Does this girl die?'

'Yeah. But they still do the business.' Tony's voice sounded bored.

'I should imagine that films like this are illegal? I mean, can't you get into trouble for stocking them?'

Tony Jones was alert now.

'You can get in trouble for buying them and all, mate.' His voice was annoyed.

George smiled.

'I appreciate that, Tony, it was just a query, that's all. Nothing to get worked up about.'

'Look, do you want the film or not?' George could hear

the aggression in the man's voice and knew that he was scared. He patted himself on the back.

'Any chance of a drink, Tony? I have a proposition to put to you . . .'

'What kind of proposition?'

'A very lucrative one.'

Tony Jones licked his lips and stared hard at George for a few seconds.

'What do you want? Beer or a short?'

George grinned. 'I think a short is in order tonight, Tony.'

He waited until they were both sitting down, sipping their drinks, before he spoke.

'I need someone to help me with something delicate. Someone who is completely trustworthy and in need of some money.'

'What for?' Tony Jones was intrigued.

'I need someone to take a blood test for me. They would have to pretend to be me, in fact.'

George saw Tony Jones's face drop. His mind was in a flutter. Blood test . . . blood test, where had he heard that? In the papers. He had read about it in the papers. George Markham came from Grantley in Essex! George Markham was the Grantley Ripper! George Markham had a half a million pound price on his head . . .

'Fucking hell!'

George felt a prickle of fear.

'You're the bastard Ripper, ain't you?'

George stared at the man and his fishy grey lifeless eyes sent a chill through Tony Jones. For the first time he was scared. He had let go his ace in his shock.

'What do you want from me?' His voice was quieter now. More controlled.

'I am willing to pay a substantial amount of money for

someone to take the blood test for me. If I was caught, you see, I would have to tell the police about my accomplice in all this.'

'Accomplice? What accomplice?' Tony's voice was puzzled.

'Why, you, of course.' George smiled again. 'If you hadn't introduced me to snuff movies, I would never have dreamt of murdering anybody.'

Tony's face blanched.

'That was nothing to do with me! I sell movies to loads of people and they don't go out murdering.' His voice was defensive. He had visions of Patrick Kelly hearing that the films that had triggered his daughter's murder had come from him. He'd had one run in with him already. He was hoping to use this knowledge to get back into his good books! Kelly would have his throat cut as soon as look at him else.

'How do you know that, Tony? How do you know that the men who buy your films aren't affected by them in the same way that I am? Death excites me, it excites a lot of people, that's why there's a demand for your films. I remember you saying they sold like hot cakes.'

He saw Tony's jaw tighten and played his trump card. 'I have left a diary of every time I visited your shop and what I bought here. I made it sound as if you were in on the whole thing. If you don't help me, Tony, and I get caught . . .' George left the sentence unfinished.

'I've a good mind to fucking kill you!'

'Oh, now don't be silly. If I died, all my personal effects would be seen, not only by my wife but by the police as well, I should think. And neither of us want that, do we now?'

Tony Jones saw his half a million pounds disappearing before his eyes. He watched George drink his whisky, taking little sips and then fastidiously wiping his mouth on his handkerchief, and a tiny spark of an idea entered his head. He was going to play George Markham back at his own game.

'How much can you pay?'

George grinned. This was more like it.

'One thousand pounds.'

Tony shook his head dismissively. 'Not enough. Two grand at least for criminal deception.'

'Criminal deception?'

'That means parading as someone else. Which is what I would be doing for you.'

'You'll do it yourself?'

'Of course. We're of an age. I'd need to know some personal things . . . the Old Bill are wily old fuckers when the fancy takes them. You find out what happens at the blood testing and let me know. I'll work it from there. I've not got a criminal record, believe it or not. Never even had a parking ticket. I'll be George Markham for two grand.'

George held out his hand but was not surprised when Tony did not shake it.

'Done.'

Tony stared at the man in front of him and thought, You will be.

George arrived home a little after eight. Elaine was sitting on the settee and called out to him as he came in the front door.

'I was getting worried about you, George.'

He took off his coat and placed it and the video he had bought in the hall cupboard. He went in to Elaine.

'Sorry I'm late, dear, we had a lot to do. I finish up in a few weeks and I have to pass over all the information to the man taking over my accounts.'

Elaine nodded.

'Come out to the kitchen, I kept your dinner warm.'

George sat at the table and as usual let Elaine chatter to him. He had noticed over the years that her chattering was a defence against the quietness that she hated. She kept up a constant stream of talk, seemingly unaware that George was not really listening.

Tonight he couldn't have listened even if he'd wanted to. He had more pressing things on his mind.

Caitlin was explaining the exact nature of the blood testing to the team in the incident room. Everyone was listening avidly as he spoke. Most were aware of the existence of genetic fingerprinting, anyone who read the papers was, but the actual task they had ahead of them was not really clear. Caitlin was hoping to enlighten them.

'The man we are looking for is blood type O, which is about fifty per cent of the population. Now this has been broken down again. Seventy-five per cent of the population is Rhesus B positive. The other twenty-five per cent being Rhesus D Negative. Well, I am pleased to say that the man we are looking for is Rhesus D. That means that we can eliminate the O group males of the Rhesus B positive blood group, thereby cutting down on the amount of men and man hours.

'At the actual blood testing, we shall be asking men for their mother's maiden name, their wife's and children's names, where they work, etcetera. We shall also take fingerprints and obviously they will sign the document saying they agreed to the blood testing and were put under no duress to take it. That should shut up the civil liberty eejits!'

People in the room began to titter. It was a bone of contention with everyone that the only lead they could follow was being criticised so much. On the one hand the public wanted the man caught and on the other they were making it as hard as possible to do it.

Caitlin lit a cigar. Clearing his throat noisily, he began to speak again.

'Now, you will all be given a set of instructions detailing exactly what you ask, where you are going, etcetera. You will be allocated men to help with any back-up inquiries and we want these carried out in as low key a way as possible. It seems that quite a few known sex offenders have been beaten up since this spate of murders and while I myself have no time for the perverts, they are not under suspicion so are entitled to our protection. Any inquiries we make must be polite and courteous. We are sitting on a potential bomb here and I don't want anyone . . .' he glanced at Spencer briefly 'especially you, buggering it up.

'Now then, most of you are thinking that the man responsible would have to be mad to agree to take the test. I think that too. But the police psychologist thinks that his ego would make him take it. That he gets his jollies as much from fooling us as from the actual attacks.' He stopped speaking and watched the sea of faces, letting all he said sink in. 'So if you get a particularly suspect individual I would like you to notify me. There's more than a few braggarts in this station alone.' He glanced once more at Spencer. 'So you know the type I'm looking for.'

Once more everyone laughed.

'Now then, are there any questions?'

Spencer's hand shot up before anyone's. Caitlin nodded at him.

'What I want to know is, are we getting more help? I mean, it's going to take ages to reinterview the new suspects . . .'

Caitlin held up a hand to silence him. 'We have more than enough man power – everyone is giving up free time from all over South East Essex. That could be social conscience but I think the double time from the Major Incident Fund is probably helping. Also the Specials come in handy at times like this for interviewing. There'll be more than enough men, don't worry about that.' He turned away from Spencer and looked at the faces before him. 'Now, any other questions?'

Before anyone could answer he turned away, saying, 'Good. Pick up your information sheets and let's get this show on the road.'

Kate smiled to herself. She had to hand it to him. He certainly knew how to run an incident room. He had answered straight off the most important question and now he wanted it all finished so the real work could begin. As much as he got on her nerves at times, Kate had to admire him. At least he got things moving.

Everyone was looking at their information sheets. It seemed that now they had a goal they were straining to get to work. It was always the same on these cases. Once a new line of inquiry opened up it renewed everyone's interest and enthusiasm.

Kate stared once more at the pictures of the dead women and girls. Her eyes lingered on Mandy Kelly and she thought of Patrick. Then she got on with the work in hand.

George came home from a particularly trying day at work. His leaving party was the talk of the office and he had felt like screaming at them all to go away and leave him alone. Somehow even some of the men from the warehouse had been roped in and George was annoyed. He had never spoken to one of them, even in passing. The last thing he wanted was to make conversation with a crowd of working-class bullies. All they were interested in was the stripper. Oh, he knew what they were after. Pity they didn't know about him, that would shut them all up. He didn't need sluts parading around semi-naked, he could have anyone he wanted. Whenever he wanted.

He closed his eyes tightly. Elaine as usual was chattering. Sometimes he wished he had the guts to slap her silly face, slap it till it stung and her big fat ears rang.

'George, are you listening to me?' Her strident voice bored through his skull like a newly sharpened axe.

'Of course I am, dear. I always listen to you.'

'Well, what do you think about what I said then?'

'I . . . I don't really know.' George was racking his brains to try and remember one item of gossip that might have entered his consciousness since Elaine started talking at him the moment he'd entered the house.

She sighed heavily and began to baste the roast potatoes. 'You haven't heard a word I've said, have you? I tell you my manager says they're thinking of cutting down on staff.'

George interrupted her.

'But they'd never get rid of you, Elaine.'

'Who said they were getting rid of me? Do you ever listen to me, George? My manager said that I stood a good chance of being put in as supervisor on the tills. Not before time, I might add. So even though they're cutting back on staff,' she poked herself in the chest, '*I* will still be employed. And at a better wage as well. And let's face it, George, now you've got the bum's rush from your job, a regular wage isn't to be sneezed at, is it?'

The last malicious twist of the knife made his breath come in shallow little gasps. So that was how she was going to play it, was it? Now the sympathy had worn off and the euphoria over the money, Elaine was going to become the one thing she'd always tried to be. The real head of the household. The major breadwinner.

George had visions of himself getting out of his chair and taking the large breadknife from the worktop and slitting Elaine's throat with it, cleanly and neatly, and laughing. Laughing his head off while he did it.

He stood up unsteadily.

'Where are you going?'

He ignored her and walked from the room, every nerve in his body taut. To George's mind this was the final insult. He walked up the stairs and went into the bedroom he shared with Elaine. There he lay on the bed and stared at the ceiling. He half expected her to come barrelling into the room demanding to know why he'd walked out on her, but she left him alone.

Down in the kitchen, it occurred to Elaine that she just might have gone too far.

George lay still until his breathing returned to normal and he watched as his whole life with Elaine floated in front of him. He saw her on their wedding day – he had been quite proud of her then. Proud that he actually had a wife. It was like a declaration to the world, as if he was shouting: 'See, someone wants me.' It had galled his mother that he had married. She wanted to keep him at home with her. Wanted to carry on 'looking after him', as she called it. She had called Elaine a red-headed whore. Well, his mother knew all about them, she had been one herself for most of her life. And in spite of everything their marriage had not been bad at first. Elaine had come to him a virgin and he had appreciated that fact. He had never tried it on with her because she was what George termed a 'good girl'. He knew that she would balk at anything other than a chaste kiss on the lips after an evening out.

Once married, though, Elaine had turned out to be quite a handful. She'd wanted sex much more often than he had. He had wanted to experiment, but Elaine wanted straight sex and no kissing. George could not keep up such a boring way of spending evenings and when she had become pregnant he had been secretly relieved.

It had been then that he had rediscovered his pornographic pastime. Before his marriage George had relied heavily on girlie magazines – or wank mags as he would call them to himself. He had built up a fantasy world of women who did whatever he bid them. He had thought that with the advent of marriage he would not need the fantasy world any more, but instead had found that he needed it more than ever.

At first, the fact that the magazines were in the house would excite him. The element of risking being caught out had always attracted George. He knew that if Elaine had found the magazines she would have blown her top and he relished that feeling. He had begun to frequent the porno movie theatres in Soho, and the bookshops that abounded there. This was in the days when the naked women had their photographs outside with strategically placed stars to just hide nipples and pubic hair. He had learned a lot from those French films, and from the blue films. That was when he had been introduced to the world of sadism and bondage.

The first time he had purchased a bondage magazine George had felt as if he had finally been let free. The pictures of the women, exquisite smiles on their faces as they were chained up and degraded, had struck a chord deep inside him. And that's when he made the terrible mistake.

He had been to an Electric Blue cinema and was travelling home on the train. They had been living in

Chatham in Kent at the time. They had bought an old house and gradually decorated it and made it into a home. George saw a girl on the train. She had long red-gold hair and it had attracted his attention because it had reminded him of his mother's when she was young. The girl had noticed him looking at her and had smiled at him. A carefree smile as if she was used to being admired.

As they had neared Chatham the train had begun to empty of people until there were only the two of them. George had been thinking about the film and the girl, and when he had touched her he had only wanted to feel her hair, just the soft springiness of it, that was all. But she had screamed, a loud piercing scream, and he had instinctively pushed his hand over her mouth. She had fallen sideways on the carriage seat and her jumper had risen up, showing an expanse of milky white skin. Then his other hand was pushing inside the jumper and he had felt the jutting breasts. He had experienced ecstasy then, wiping his mind clear of everything but the moment and the sensation. He had no recollection of ripping away her tights and panties, he had no recollection of beating her about the face and head, it had all been too nice. Too warm to be bad.

He had been caught as the train pulled into Chatham station. In his excitement he had not even realised what was happening.

And then there had been the police.

And the questioning.

And the arrest.

And Elaine. A heavily pregnant Elaine, who had been taken to hospital in shock when the police had knocked on the door and told her everything.

Elaine who had given birth to a stillborn son.

Elaine who had for some reason stood by him throughout the trial and had sold up and moved to Essex, so he would have a home to come home to. Elaine who had visited him in prison and written to him once a week.

Elaine who had never let him put it in the past because she hated him for it. Hated him for what he had done and for killing their child.

Elaine who had never referred to it again, except that one day a few weeks previously when the police had knocked on the door. Elaine whom he hated and loved. Oh, he loved her because she had been the mother of his child. The only thing he had ever really wanted in his life.

His son was dead. His marriage was dead.

Elaine was having an affair, he knew she was. He was so certain he could taste it. He could actually see her sometimes with a faceless man, in the back of a car. See her enormous breasts heaving with excitement. See her big fat behind being lowered on to some man's member. And it excited him. It made him want to watch them. It made him want to hide and see them doing it. It made him want to come inside his pants just thinking about it. His breathing was laboured now.

She wasn't so fussy now, was she? No more missionary position for Elaine nowadays. Not judging by the marks on her neck. He would like to put his hands around her neck and squeeze gently, till she expired.

Four women were dead. But it wasn't his fault. They had asked for it the same way that Elaine was asking for it and the girl on the train had asked for it. He had told the police that she had smiled at him, had led him on. But they didn't believe him.

They had believed her, and she was a whore. They were all whores.

And he had been locked up like a criminal! A common criminal. When all he had done was given her what she wanted. What they all wanted.

Then in the prison he had been beaten up by men who were no better than animals, and yet they put themselves above him!

But he had sat it out. He had won in the end because he had come out and had gone to Elaine and had got himself a job and had provided. He had been a good provider, until the redundancy.

What was it Peter Renshaw had said? Spend some time with the grandchildren . . .

The only time he spent time with grandchildren was when they were someone else's. George grinned to himself, thinking of Mandy Kelly, and knew that grandparents wouldn't approve of his games.

He lay on the bed and let the feelings of warmth Mandy Kelly had created wash over him. He was a bit sorry she was dead, because he had quite liked her. After all, Mandy was his favourite name.

Feeling better now, he gradually relaxed.

Downstairs Elaine was sitting at the kitchen table eating her dinner. She was seeing Hector later in the evening and she thanked God for that. Since he had come into her life she had felt as if a great weight had been lifted off her shoulders.

The great weight was George and all he entailed.

Kate was draining spaghetti while her mother put the finishing touches to the bolognaise sauce.

'Are you sure you don't mind him coming for dinner, Mum?'

Evelyn looked at her daughter. 'Now why should I mind that?' She turned off the gas under the pan and went to the breakfast bar to begin laying it. Kate put the spaghetti into a buttered Pyrex dish and went to give her a hand.

'Why is the table only set for two?'

'Because, Katie, I'm going to bingo with Doris tonight. I'll grab a bite to eat there.'

'Oh no you're not! He's making you leave your own home . . .'

Evelyn interrupted her. 'Did it ever occur to you that I might have wanted to go out more over the years, and didn't because I always had Lizzy to look after or had to wait for you coming home? No, I didn't think it had!'

Seeing the hurt look on Kate's face, Evelyn grinned at her. 'I didn't mean that really, Kate. I want you and this man to have a bit of time together, that's all. He's buried his only child today and I think he'll want you near him tonight. But for all that, if I wanted to stay in, I would. I'm going out with Doris because I want to go to bingo. I happen to like bingo so all in all this has worked out fine. Now, will you put the Parmesan on the table, please? I grated it earlier.'

Kate gave her a hug and Evelyn pulled her close. 'Don't you be hard on him now, you hear? He needs a bit of coddling tonight. Forget all the eejity talk about the blood testing and everything, he did you a favour you know.'

Kate nodded. She heard a knock at the door and went to answer it. Evelyn took off her apron and surveyed the little breakfast bar. It looked nice. She understood that Patrick's house was a huge posh affair with expensive carpets and a housekeeper and all manner of frippery! Well, as far as she was concerned her Katie's house was as good, if not better, because it had the added bonus of having herself, Katie and Lizzy living in it!

Thinking of Lizzy made her smile. She was looking forward to seeing Peter in Australia. She had been banjaxed with excitement over it, as her mother used to say.

Patrick walked into Katie's hall carrying a bottle of red wine. Kate took it from him and he slipped off his overcoat, placing it over the worn banister rail. He followed her through to the kitchen and Evelyn favoured him with one of her wide smiles.

'Come away in and sit yourself down. It's enough to cut the lugs from you out there tonight!'

Patrick grinned. He loved listening to Evelyn's voice, it was like listening to his own mother again. He missed the Southern Irish accent. It had a musical quality about it, even when spoken raucously.

Patrick took the corkscrew Kate handed to him, and opened the bottle of wine. He poured them all a glass. Evelyn took hers, and after a large gulp said, 'It must have been terrible for you today, Patrick. You just sit yourself down and get something hot inside you. Food always makes people feel better.'

Patrick looked down at his shoes.

Kate was making a salad. As she washed the vegetables, Evelyn kissed her on the cheek. 'I'm off then, Katie. Goodbye, Patrick, I'll probably see you later.'

'Let me run you round to Doris's, Mum.'

Evelyn held up her hand. 'I'm quite capable of going by shanks's pony, Kate. You get your food down you while it's hot.'

Patrick smiled at her and watched her putting on her coat, scarf, woollen hat and thermal boots. She had them all laid out in the front room. Giving them both another wave she left the house, a large leather bag clutched to her chest.

'She's a lovely woman, Kate, you're lucky to have her.'

'Don't I know it! Why don't you put some of the dishes on the breakfast bar, this salad's nearly ready.'

Patrick set about helping. As they worked they chatted

453

amiably about little things. The distraction of doing mundane everyday tasks took the edge off his misery. It had not occurred to him until today that he had not really grieved for his child because he had not really believed she was dead. It was only the lowering of her coffin into the earth that had brought it home to him. Finally and irrevocably.

Kate placed the garlic bread and salad on the laden surface and sat opposite him.

Patrick picked up his wine glass and held it in the air. 'To us?' It was more a question than a statement.

Kate picked up her own glass and touched it against his. 'To Mandy, may she rest in peace.'

'I'll drink to that.' Patrick sipped his wine, and then putting down his glass began to help himself from the dishes. He did not feel particularly hungry, the day had taken away any appetite he had. In fact, if he had not been going to see Kate, he would have got blind drunk.

'This is the first time I've eaten Greek salad with spaghetti bolognese, Kate.'

He shovelled a mouthful of salad in as he spoke.

'I know. But they complement each other. I think so anyway, and as we're in my house we'll eat as I think fit.'

The ice was melted completely now, and they chatted together as they ate. Nothing important or heavyweight, that type of thing could wait for the time being. Tonight was an interval. It was to be the night when Patrick's trouble and Kate's involvement in that trouble could be set aside. They were a couple of friends comforting each other.

Patrick ate. He watched as Kate sucked in a piece of spaghetti, and he smiled. He knew that when the pain was gone, he would always associate Kate with his Mandy. He would always think of them together, first Mandy and then

Kate. She was the one good thing that had come out of it all. He knew that if he had been left alone tonight he would have cracked. He needed company, but the company of someone he cared about, not a casual sexual encounter. If he had gone for that he would have felt he had cheapened his daughter's life. Trying to forget her and come to terms with her burial with a stranger, would have been like an insult.

After the meal, when they had taken the remainder of the wine into the lounge, their lovemaking began quietly. Kate allowed her clothes to be removed and lay on the floor with a tapestry cushion beneath her head, watching Patrick undress.

The thrill of watching him started as a heat, deep in her loins, and gradually engulfed her whole body. She saw that he was already aroused and was glad. She wanted no foreplay tonight. She wanted something hard, and sweet, and fast.

When Patrick collapsed on top of her ten minutes later, she felt the tension slipping out of both of them and held him to her breast, stroking his hair, while their heartbeats gradually returned to normal.

'Oh, Kate, I needed that.'

She kissed him on the mouth, gently at first and then hard, pushing her tongue between his lips.

'I know that, Pat. I'm glad you came to me.'

Kissing her breasts, he rolled from her and lit them both a cigarette. He lay back on the floor beside her and placed a large glass ashtray on her stomach.

'Oh, you! That's cold.'

Patrick smiled and lay back, putting one arm under his head. 'I ain't lain on a floor like this for years, have you?'

'Oh, we do this all the time at the station. You should see us some days in the canteen!'

Patrick laughed softly.

'You're crazy sometimes.'

'It's all this screwing.'

He glanced at her profile.

'I don't call what we do "screwing", Kate. I call it making love. There's a difference, you know.'

She turned her face slightly and looked into his eyes. 'You're very romantic, Patrick. What's brought all this on?'

But she knew what had brought it on, they both did. Losing his child had made him realise that happiness was there for the taking, and when you took it you had to grab it with both hands tightly, because you never knew when it was going to be taken away again.

Taking her cigarette he placed it in the ashtray with his own and put this on the hearth. He pulled her into his arms.

'I love you, Kate. I know we haven't known each other that long, but admit it – admit you feel the bond between us?'

Kate searched his eyes. All she could see was honesty and caring. She felt an absurd lump in her throat.

'Tell me you love me, Katie, make me happy.' It was a plea. Patrick needed words of love from her tonight; he needed to resolve the feelings that had been gradually welling up inside him since he'd first laid eyes on her. He knew, without a shadow of a doubt, that if he had met her under any other circumstances he would still have wanted her. It wasn't the fact that she had been there from the first, at the worst time of his life, that attracted him to her. It was the attraction of two kindred spirits they had here, heightened by the heartbreak each had experienced.

Kate was telling herself that it was the burial of his daughter that had brought all this on, that he was unhappy and needed someone, but inside her a little voice was whispering: 'He means it. It's written in his eyes.'

She knew that if she voiced what she had felt in her heart since the first time she saw him, there would be no going back. He was a repoman, a violent repoman. He had fingers in more than enough dubious enterprises. But for all that, for all she knew about him, real and imagined, she wanted him.

He could drag her down with him in an instant. Their association would jeopardise everything she had worked for and held dear. But even knowing this, she still wanted him. She had never wanted anyone so much in all her life.

'I love you, Patrick. I think.'

Her voice was low and husky, and he laughed.

'Only think? Well, I suppose that will have to do for the time being.'

Kate ran her fingers through his thick hair and traced the contours of his face with her fingertips, gradually travelling down, over his body and along his back muscles, to his rounded behind. He even felt strong. His skin felt warm and comforting on top of hers. He covered her naturally, as if he had been made specially to fit into the contours of her body. And as they kissed the shrill jangling of the phone broke their mood.

Kate pulled herself from the floor and padded out to the hall, dragging her blouse on as she went.

Patrick lay on the carpet and lit himself another cigarette. He felt at peace with himself, something he had not thought possible on this day of all days.

Kate came back into the lounge and sat beside him, her dark nipples showing through the thin silk of the blouse.

'That was my mother. She's decided to stay the night at Doris's.' She shook her head. 'She's about as subtle as a sledgehammer!'

Patrick smiled at her.

'She's a lovely person, Kate. Reminds me of me own mum. She had the same zest for life as Evelyn. It was overwork that killed her off, bless her. My one regret is she never lived long enough for me to give her a decent life. I'd have bought her a bingo hall of her very own.'

Kate laughed, knowing that he spoke the truth.

'I would have, Kate, you can laugh.'

'That's why I'm laughing, because I know you're speaking the truth. I can just see you doing it.'

They both grinned and then Kate took the cigarette from him and took a deep draw on it.

'Do you want to stay the night?'

Patrick grabbed her thigh and squeezed it.

'I'm not that kind of boy, miss.' He fluttered his eyelashes and she laughed again.

He watched her and knew that if it weren't for her, he would never have laughed again after today. Not really laughed.

She was as good as a tonic, as his mother used to say, and he did love her. He loved her very much.

Later on, in bed, they made love and she told him she loved him again.

In the dark and warmth of the night, with the musky smell of each other permeating their bodies, it did not seem wrong any more.

They talked till the early hours about Mandy and Lizzy, both exorcising their own particular ghosts. They had so much in common for two people who were, in outsiders' eyes, so different. He agreed with her about sending Lizzy to Australia. He said that he would have done the same with Mandy. Lizzy was a girl who felt things deeply – too deeply, he said – and Kate loved him for his understanding of her situation. He seemed to have guessed that Kate felt responsible for her daughter's troubles and tried, in his own way, to allay her fears. Finally, they fell asleep together, entwined, and stayed that way till the morning.

It was over breakfast that he told her his news.

'I sold the massage parlours, Kate. All of them. I sign the contracts in five days' time, and then they are nothing to do with me any more.'

Kate's eyes widened. 'You're joking?'

'No, I'm not. Since that girl was . . . What with my Mandy and everything, I don't want anything to do with it anymore.'

Kate put her hand on his and squeezed it gently. 'I'm glad, Pat.'

'It came home to me that the man who murdered my girl was like the man who murdered young Gillian Enderby – a pervert of some kind. Except my Mandy was dragged off the street and Gillian was like a baited trap, waiting to be sprung. I ain't silly enough to think that by selling the shops it won't happen again, there'll always be a demand for that type of thing, but at least now I know that I have no part in it.'

'I think Renée would have been pleased.'

Patrick smiled.

'Yeah. She would have. In a lot of ways you two are alike. Renée was small and blonde while you're tall and dark, but in your personalities you're similar. She had a brain, old Renée. She had more savvy than people gave her credit for.'

'You still miss her, don't you?'

He nodded. 'But not like before. The physical pain has gone now. When she died, I felt as if someone had chopped off one of my arms or legs. I feel like that now about Mandy. But with Renée I can remember her now without pain. It's a bitter-sweet memory.'

459

'I understand.'

'But I've got you now as well, and that helps me. It helps me a lot. If Renée could see me now I know she'd approve. She'd have liked you, Kate. You'd have liked her.'

Kate was not too sure about that but she kept her own counsel. Instead she poured him another coffee and smiled.

'Well, I think you did the right thing. I don't believe you would have been happy still owning those parlours, you know. Anyway, we start the blood testing in a couple of days and then we should start to get a result; if nothing else we can eliminate the large part of the male community, and that can only make our job easier.'

'Do you really think the blood testing will achieve something?'

Kate nodded. 'Yes, I do.'

Patrick sipped his coffee and then smiled back at her. He hoped so because he was footing the bill, but he would spend every penny of his considerable fortune to catch the man responsible for his daughter's death. It made no difference who got him first, himself or the police, because no matter where they locked him up, Patrick knew he could get to him. In fact, he had more chance of getting to him once he was in prison. There was more than one old lag who owed him a favour.

He did not say any of this to Kate though. Even though they were now real lovers, admitting their involvement, he saw no reason to disillusion her about his motives in helping to find the man they were after. He would cross that bridge when he came to it.

All he wanted was a name, and he would do the rest. If it lay with him Katie would never know what he had planned.

A little while later, under the shower with her, he felt a

twinge of guilt at keeping her in the dark. But it soon disappeared. Knowing Kate, she would fight for the man's right to a trial by jury, lecture on his rights as a human being. He admired her so much. He smiled to himself.

'What are you laughing at?'

'You.' His voice was jocular.

'Me!'

She looked outraged so he kissed her. Some things were better left unsaid.

Chapter Twenty-Two

Lizzy was packing her small case. She placed her bright green Kermit the frog slippers in last and pushed the lid down to fasten it. Her long hair was loose and trailed into her eyes. She pushed it from her face impatiently.

There, she'd done it! Picking up the case she placed it on the floor by her bed and, going to the coffee corner, made herself a large mug. She sat at the table sipping it.

Her two weeks in the hospital had been a turning point in her life. Every time she thought of cutting her wrists she felt a flush of humiliation. How could she have done that, not only to herself but to her mother and her grandmother? It was a last dramatic act, as if she was saying, 'Well, you know everything else about me, I might as well go out with a bang, not a whimper. Lay a bit of extra guilt on you all.'

Really she had done it because of her shame at her grandmother knowing about her diary.

The psychiatrist had explained to her about self-destructive behaviour. Lizzy had listened to the man, respecting his intelligence, knowing that he was trying to help her straighten herself out. And in two weeks she felt she had come a long way. One of the girls here had had a breakdown, and no one knew why. She had finally taken an overdose of aspirin and had nearly died. Her father was a respected lawyer and he had raised Cain every day his daughter had been in the ward. Finally the girl, a tiny redhead named Marietta, had admitted her father had been sexually abusing her since she was eight when her mother had died.

It was hearing this that had made Lizzy put her own life into perspective. She realised that she harboured all sorts of grudges against people. Against her mother for never being there when she really wanted her, for instance. When Kate had sneaked into school performances with her uniform on, she had wanted to die. She had wanted a mother like everyone else's. A warm human being who picked you up from school in a nice second-hand Volvo and made you your tea and spent her every waking hour with you. What she had was a woman working her way up a career ladder, with enough obstacles in her way to make Hercules balk at the task.

Deep inside Lizzy was proud of her mother. When people found out she was a detective they were impressed, and Lizzy had been jealous sometimes. She had inherited her mother's looks but not her quick brain. All in all Kate Burrows was a hard act to follow, and the worst of it all was that her mother accepted her for what she was; had never tried to force her to do anything against her wishes.

When they had spent time together, it had been good. Lizzy had loved being with her, getting the attention, but it only made it all the more lonely when her mother went back to work again, caught up in a big case. Lizzy felt then that she was shoved aside. That her mother used up all her energy on other people, other things, coming home sometimes hours after she had gone to bed. She would be half awake, waiting for the soft-footed padding of Kate's footsteps coming to her bed in the middle of the night. She would feel cool lips on her forehead and want to put her arms around the slender neck and tell her she missed her. But she never had. Her mother had smelt of Joy perfume and cigarette smoke, and the smell would bring tears to Lizzy's eyes.

She sipped the coffee again. It was only warm now, and she took the film of skin off the top with her finger and scraped it into the saucer.

Then her father had turned up periodically, upsetting the whole household with his presence. She had loved seeing him, had loved all the attention he gave her, the presents, the hugs and the cuddles. Then one morning she would get out of bed and he would be gone. Those were the days when he had come back and slept in her mum's bed. Her mother would be glowing with happiness – then off he went. He would take all the good things with him. Her mother would be hurt, Lizzy would be hurt, and her granny would be annoyed with them all.

She would hear her mother sobbing in the night and it would tear her apart. In her schoolgirl heart she would vow that if her father turned up again, she would not talk to him, would not let him use her any more. Then months later the vow would be forgotten when she would come in from school to find him ensconced in an armchair, a big smile on his handsome face, and his voice would be like a caress as he told her how she had grown, how beautiful she was, and how he was home for good now.

But it never lasted.

Then, lastly, there was her granny, the mainstay of her life. She loved that woman with every ounce of her being.

But deep inside herself she had always wondered why Gran had never done anything to make her mother stay home more often. Why she had sacrificed her own life for her daughter's and granddaughter's. And somewhere along the line Lizzy had started to think that her granny was a fool. That she was weak and foolish to spend her life looking after her grown-up daughter and grandchild. She got nothing out of it.

Lizzy had pondered these thoughts now for two weeks, and she was finally making some sense of them.

She wanted badly to go to Australia. She wanted to get away from the memory of what she had done, to herself and to her family. She wanted time to heal properly, without having to go over the same old ground, over and over again. When her mother looked at her with those big brown eyes, Lizzy could see how much she had hurt her, could see the barely concealed confusion in them, and it hurt her to know that she had put it there.

She had only been interested in how she felt, and what she wanted. She had never spared a thought for her mother and the struggle she had had trying to bring her up, buy their home, and keep them clothed and fed and warm.

It had been an illuminating time, this last two weeks. But it had also been a time of gentle healing.

She looked at the red lines on her wrists. Every time she saw them she would be reminded of what she had done. So would her mother and her grandmother.

It was best she went away to Australia, to give her mother a chance to get herself back together.

She finished the dregs of her coffee. Looking at the doorway opposite her, she felt her heart lurch. It was her father, with a bunch of flowers and that cringe-making smile he had.

She admitted to herself, for the first time, that her father actually irritated her.

The thought made her sad.

She took the flowers, dutifully admired them, and then sat and talked to him, avoiding any questions about her mother's private life. She was going home later and couldn't wait to get there.

She smiled at her father's little jokes and did not mention that she was being discharged as she knew he would insist on taking her home, there and then, and that was the last thing her mother needed now. Danny Burrows laying down the law according to him. She also noticed that his watch and gold jewellery were not in attendance. He'd obviously hocked them.

Lizzy had grown up all right.

Patrick stood with Willy, looking at the mound of dirt that was his child's grave. The flowers were still fresh and he rearranged them to cover up the earth completely. There had been over a hundred wreaths and he had sent them to Grantley Hospital to be torn apart and used in the wards. It had gratified him to see the number of people who had turned out for her. Even Mandy's teachers from school had come. And it wasn't just because of him – Mandy was a popular girl. He corrected himself. Had been a popular girl.

He heard Willy whistling between his teeth, and turned to look at him. He was reading Renée's gravestone. He looked at Pat and smiled.

'Do you remember that time Renée locked you out the house?'

Patrick frowned.

'When was that?'

'When you was first married – you had that bedsit in Ilford.'

Patrick smiled as he remembered. It had been their first home, when he was still trying to make his mark on the world. They had both been seventeen, two children playing at grown ups.

Willy carried on, 'It was Christmas Eve and me and you had been up the Ilford Palais, remember now? You got pissed out of your head and I had to take you home. Then, when I finally got you there, Renée had bolted the door and wouldn't let you in. You ended up kipping round my mum's.'

'Yeah, I remember. And the next day when I went home she threw me Christmas dinner at me.'

Both men laughed together, basking in the shared memories.

'She was a girl, old Renée. I really thought a lot of her, Pat.'

'Well, I've lost them both now.'

He walked away from the graves with a heavy heart. Willy slipped into step beside him.

'That Kate bird reminds me of Renée sometimes. I don't mean in her looks, but she's got the same air about her like.'

Patrick nodded. 'I know what you mean.'

'Is it serious like? The relationship?' Willy's voice trailed away. He knew he was on dangerous ground, but his natural nosiness overcame any fear.

Patrick stopped on the newly cut grass of Corbets Tey Cemetery and stared at his old friend.

'It's serious enough, Marjorie Proops. Happy now you know all the scandal?'

Willy jutted his chin. 'Well, you're me mate, ain't you? I just want to know that you're all right like.'

Patrick shook his head. Making a fist, he punched the air gently by Willy's face.

'We go back a long time. You know everything about me as I do about you. I know you just want to know how I am, and I'm all right, bearing up.'

Willy smiled. 'Well, that's all right then! Fancy coming for a beer in the Robin Hood? I ain't been in there for years. The Flying Bottle we used to call it when we was young, remember? We'd sit outside in the summer with Mandy in her pushchair and worry in case we saw someone we knew who'd tell Renée we'd taken the baby to a pub!'

Patrick nodded, smiling as he was assailed by a vivid memory.

Mandy in a white and pink organdie dress, her little fat legs wriggling with excitement every time Willy made a face at her.

For the first time it occurred to him that Willy must be feeling her loss almost as much as he was. She had been like his child as well. He had chronicled her growing up. Never missed a birthday or Christmas.

Patrick felt a lump in his throat and swallowed it down hard. He linked his arm through his minder's and Willy patted the gloved hand.

'I remember it well.'

Evelyn had made an Irish stew, a real Irish stew that was thick enough to stand the spoon up in it. She tasted it and added another dash of salt, stirring the mixture for a while. When the smell was just to her satisfaction she placed the suet dumpling on the top and put a large cover over the pan. Evelyn's Irish stews could last for anything up to a week. She added to them every day, different vegetables and different meats. The cereals and pulses gave a pungent thickness that made the final end of the stew into a thick broth.

Lizzy was home today and she wanted her to be welcomed with the smell of good hearty food.

Everything was ready. The soda bread was going in the oven the minute she heard the front door open, so they could have it nice and hot with melted butter. Her trifle was wobbling itself to death in the fridge and the little bottle of Bushmill's was snuggled into her apron pocket, where she could have a snifter without being seen.

She settled herself on the stool.

It would be grand to have Lizzy back home. There had been too much going on in the last few weeks, and Evelyn nearly admitted she was getting a bit old for it all.

Still, Kate looked better and that was good. Her child was dear to her heart and she was glad that Kate and Lizzy were finally coming to some kind of understanding of one another's ways. They were as alike as two peas physically, but temperamentally they were like chalk and cheese. She hated to admit that Lizzy had a lot of Dan's selfishness in her. But she blamed herself for that. She had doted on the child from day one.

She forced these thoughts from her mind. The child was coming home and she wanted everything to be lovely.

But she knew that what she had read in Lizzy's diary would stay with her for a long time.

She concentrated her thoughts on her son Peter and his wife Marlene. She was looking forward to seeing them. Seeing her other grandchildren for the first time. She took a deep drag on the cigarette and her thin body was racked by a fit of coughing. She'd have to knock these on the head, they'd be the end of her. She stabbed her cigarette out in the ashtray and heard the sound of Kate's key in the lock. Leaping from the stool, she put the soda bread in the oven and rushed out into the hall.

'Hello, me pets!' She hugged them both in turn, her

little dark eyes darting over her granddaughter with a critical glint in them.

She looked all right, a bit thinner, but a few good meals would remedy that.

'Hello, Gran.' Lizzy was shy all of a sudden. 'Is that an Irish stew I can smell?'

'It is, one of the best I ever made. I've done mashed swede to go with it. Now come along in and I'll get you both some.'

Fifteen minutes later they were all around the little breakfast bar enjoying the food when someone knocked on the front door. Kate stood up, wiping her mouth with a paper napkin.

'I'll get it.'

She went out to open the door. She could not help her face registering surprise when she saw who was there.

'Caitlin?'

He stood on the doorstep in his crumpled raincoat, a little smile on his face.

'I'm sorry to disturb you at home like this . . .'

'Come in. I'm sorry, I don't mean to be rude but it gave me a shock, seeing you standing there.' She took him through to the front room. 'Is it something to do with the case?' He could see the hopeful glimmer in her eyes and shook his head.

He could see the two women in the kitchen and smiled at them.

'Could I see you for a second alone, Kate?'

Something in his voice alerted her and going to the connecting door she closed it, apologising to her mother and daughter as she did so.

'What is it, Kenny?'

She had a feeling like a cold hand grabbing her neck. Something was up here, she knew it.

'It's Dan. He went to see Flowers about you and Kelly.'

Kate bit her lip. 'I see.'

'Well, Flowers wasn't interested, you know. So Dan took it one step further, Kate. He took it to the CIB.'

Kate felt as if someone had punched her in the stomach.

'I thought you ought to know. I found out through an old friend of mine, so no one at the station except me and you know about it, OK? It's not even definite that they'll investigate it, but just in case I thought you had a right to know. That ex-husband of yours is an Asshole with a capital A.'

Kate nodded. She couldn't have agreed more.

Evelyn opened the door, her face troubled.

'Is everything all right?'

'You must be Kate's mother. I'm Kenneth Caitlin.'

'A Kerry man by the sounds of it?'

He smiled at her and the little exchange gave Kate time to get her head together.

'Come through and have a drink, Kenny. This is my daughter Lizzy, and my mother's already introduced herself.'

'I'll be away home, Kate, I can see you're eating.'

'You'll do no such thing. Get that awful mac off and come and have a bit of stew, there's plenty.' Evelyn's voice brooked no argument. She had been intrigued by Kate's description of this man, and now she could judge for herself.

Caitlin had smelt the delicious aroma of the stew as he had walked up the garden path, and seeing the three faces smiling at him he hesitated only a second longer. Then he took off the mac and placed it on the sofa.

'If you twist my arm up me back, it does smell good!'

Kate was glad he stayed because he took over the main thrust of the conversation and she could think.

The Criminal Investigation Bureau.

Bugger Danny Burrows!

Patrick was sitting at the dining table just finishing his meal when Willy announced that he had a visitor. He wiped his mouth with an Irish linen napkin. When he heard the name of his visitor, his left eyebrow rose a fraction.

'Show him in here.' Willy nodded and left the room.

Now what would Peter Sinclair want visiting his house?

Sinclair walked into the room. He was small, wiry, and held out a perfectly manicured hand to Patrick. He stood up in greeting then offered Sinclair a seat, poured him a brandy and sat back in his own chair.

'To what do I owe this honour?'

'I had to come here, Patrick. It's about the piece of skirt you've been running around with.'

Immediately Sinclair knew he had said the wrong thing. Patrick's face hardened.

'And what piece of skirt might that be?' As if he didn't know.

'Detective Inspector Kate Burrows, of course.'

'Of course.' Patrick's voice was low and the menace in it was not lost on Sinclair.

'So, Peter, how's things at the Home Office? Lively by the sound of it. Actually doing some work, are you? Well, wonders will never cease, will they?'

Sinclair took a sip of his brandy.

'You've gone too far this time, the CIB are in on this. She's compromised herself. As much as I like you, Patrick, you're a known villain . . .'

He leant forward over the table. 'To be accurate, Peter, I'm an alleged villain. My brief would have kittens if he heard you talking like that.'

Sinclair grinned. 'Come on, Patrick, let's cut the crap. You're going with a senior police officer. The CIB are having kittens.'

'The police officer you're talking about is working on my daughter's case.'

'I know that, and I'm sorry about what happened to Mandy, Patrick. But Kate Burrows is another matter altogether. She's got an ex-husband who's kicking up a stink and threatening to go to the papers about this.'

Suddenly, it was as clear as a bell why Sinclair was here. They wanted him to sort out Burrows.

'Supposing I was to talk to this Danny Burrows, make him see the error of his ways, what then?'

Sinclair smiled.

'Provided he can be made to admit he was just trying to cause his wife embarrassment, everything will be fine.'

Patrick nodded and poured himself out some more brandy. 'Would you like a cigar?'

Sinclair smiled again, happier now that he had accomplished what he came to do.

'No, thanks, but I wouldn't mind a piece of that excellent Cheddar.'

'Help yourself. I've just got to make a phone call.'

He left the room.

Caitlin was in the middle of a very funny story, about a case he had been on as a PC, when the phone rang and Kate went out to the hall to answer it.

'Kate, it's me, Patrick. I must see you.'

'I wanted to see you, actually.'

He could tell, just by the inflection in her voice, that she also had had the bad news.

'I can get to you for seven thirty in the morning, how's that?'

'I'll come to you, Pat. Lizzy's home now.'

'Fair enough. I'll see you in the morning then.'

When Kate replaced the receiver she felt a shiver of apprehension go through her body.

It was going to be a choice between Patrick and her job and she wasn't too sure who would win.

She went back to the kitchen and sat through the punchline of Caitlin's story, but her laughter had a hollow ring to it.

Kate got up the next morning with a feeling of dread. She knew the CIB's reputation. She also knew that a female officer, consorting with a criminal – even an alleged criminal as Patrick liked to call himself – was just their cup of tea. They would crucify her.

A few years before she had been witness to one of their jobs. It concerned a detective sergeant with a taste for exotic holidays and even more exotic women. He had been on the take. Kate had had to stand by with the rest of her colleagues as the man was set up and routed.

It had not been a pretty sight. She had felt sorry for him because most officers used their status for something, whether it was the odd free meal or a few pounds extra for a hobby. She was not saying that she agreed with it, just that it went on, a perk of the job. The ones the CIB should be looking out for, to her mind, were the officers who raided a flat, found a couple of weights of cannabis and stashed half of it before they made the collar. The cannabis would make its way back on to the street and the officers would pocket the money. To her that was a crime, not going to a restaurant for a nice meal on your wedding anniversary and getting a bottle of decent champagne thrown in because you knew the owner ran an after hours card club.

Some laws were just made to be broken, and when you finally realised that, you became a much better officer. Why go after the silver plate when you could get the twenty-four carat gold? She wanted the criminals, the real lawbreakers, not the flotsam and jetsam that made up the majority of collars.

It was like when police visited convicted felons and said to them, 'We're going to go back to court and you're going to admit to another thirty burglaries. It won't affect the time you're doing, they'll be classed as TIC.' Taken into consideration. Which made the figures at the end of the year look great. On paper it looked as if they had solved more crimes than they really had. Except the perpetrators of the crimes the convicted man had put his hand up for were still getting off scot free. Case closed, thank you very much.

Kate drove to Patrick's house with a heavy heart. Her job was her life. At one time, it was all she had had, except for Lizzy.

Patrick gave her a cup of coffee and told her about Sinclair.

'Caitlin had already told me about it, an old friend of his had tipped him the wink.'

He looked at her. She seemed worried, her usual happy expression was strained.

'Well, I have a solution to our problem, but I thought I'd get your say so first.'

'What is it?' Kate's voice sounded hopeful and Kelly was glad about that because he wasn't at all sure how she was going to take what he had to say.

'Well, it's your husband who's shoved a spanner in the works, isn't it?'

Kate nodded, taking her cigarettes from her pocket.

Patrick lit one for her and continued. 'Well, if I was to

go and see him like, he might be encouraged to change his story, admit he was just trying to cause his ex-wife a bit of aggravation.'

Kate drew on the cigarette and looked into Patrick's eyes. 'You wouldn't hurt him?'

Patrick held out his arms in a gesture of denial. 'As if I would!'

Kate was tempted, sorely tempted, but a little part of her was not sure. She could be condoning an act of violence. Because for all Patrick's charade of being the big benevolent boyfriend, if he had to give Dan a slap to achieve his ends he wouldn't even give it a second thought.

'Let me think about it, Pat.'

'What's to think about? I go see him, give him the bad news and he shits himself and puts his hands up to the CIB. Sweet as a nut.'

'Have you got an answer for everything, Pat? A violent answer to everything?'

Her voice was flat and that was not wasted on him. 'Listen, Kate, we've got a lot going for us, and I don't want that geek of a husband . . .'

'Ex-husband, Pat.'

'All the better, ex-husband, to bugger it all up. Where there's a villain there'll always be an Old Bill. Our kind of partnership goes back to the start of skulduggery, my love. You know in your heart that you're not doing anything wrong. We are friends and lovers. I'm not asking you to tell me the secrets of the Serious Crime Squad. I'm not asking you to tap out on your little computer what they're trying to fit me up with next. We just enjoy each other's company.

'I love you, Kate, and I'm trying to help you that's all. I know that if you lost your job over me, we'd be finished for good. Because you'd always hold it against me.'

'We could finish it now.'

Patrick frowned. He was getting annoyed. He'd thought she felt a bit more for him than this.

'Well, that's entirely up to you, darlin'!'

Kate put her cigarette out and went to him. She sat on the arm of his chair and touched the lines of his face.

'I didn't really mean that, Pat, it was unfair.'

She could no more leave him now than she could walk past an injured child on the street. He was a part of her, a big part. But to keep him she had to let him do something that went against the grain.

'Let me think about it, please. Give me a couple of days?'

Patrick saw the confusion in her eyes and grasped her hand in his.

'I don't want to lose you, Katie. You've come to mean an awful lot to me.'

She kissed the top of his dark head.

'Same here.'

He pulled her on to his lap and kissed her hard. He wanted her to have something else to think about as well, just in case she forgot for a second what she would be giving up.

It was Friday 16 February 1990, and the blood testing had been going on for four days. The police were amazed at the response from the public. The men of Grantley seemed to be positively eager to have themselves eliminated from the inquiry. Thames News gave a report every day and even News at Ten had shown a film of the 'phenomenal' testing of a whole community.

There were already problems. The sheer magnitude of the task had caused a large backlog. The number of people taking the blood tests far exceeded the capacity of the people who carried out the testing of the blood. Still, even with this problem, Kate was happier than she had been for a long time. It was a chance to try and nail the man responsible and she was glad for that alone.

The fact that Leonora Davidson had been dead for two weeks now frightened her. She felt that with the closeness of the previous attacks the killer would be striking again soon.

The phone broke into her reverie and she answered it.

'DI Burrows here.'

'Kate? It's me, Dan.'

She had been expecting his call, and now that it had come she felt an overpowering rage. He had been visiting Lizzy when he knew Kate was gone from the house. Since his little escapade with the CIB he had been keeping a low profile where she was concerned.

'What can I do for you?'

Her voice was chillingly polite.

'I want to see you.'

'But I don't want to see you, Dan, not now, not ever. You went too far this time.'

The phone went quiet and Kate realised that she had let the cat out of the bag. She should not have let on she knew about what he had done. He would get in touch with the CIB and they'd know she was already on to them. It would damn her immediately.

'Dan? Are you still there?' The line was very quiet. Please God let him be there. Don't let him have gone. 'I think we should meet, talk this thing over.'

'I'll meet you tonight at the Bull in Bulphan, Kate. Eight o'clock.'

The line went dead and she felt herself exhale.

'You all right, Katie?' Caitlin smiled at her.

She nodded.

'I couldn't help overhearing your conversation – only your end, of course. If I was you now, from tomorrow I would carry out all other communication with him from a public pay phone. Know what I mean?'

Kate nodded again, and picking up her handbag from the floor she left the office.

So they were tapping her phones now. At work and also at home. It figured. She left the station and as she walked out wondered how many of her colleagues were in on this thing. Suddenly she was worried. Very worried indeed.

George had had a long bath and was sitting on the toilet, with the seat down, cutting his toenails when Elaine burst into the room.

'How long are you going to be? I'm off out in half an hour.'

'Not long, dear. Where are the girls taking you tonight?'

George smiled as he said 'girls', and pictured a crowd of big fat till girls drunk on Pernod and black, their raucous laughter escaping from heavily lipsticked mouths.

He stared straight into Elaine's face as she spoke and was grudgingly impressed with the way she lied so convincingly.

'Oh, I don't know yet, we don't decide till we get to the pub, bingo probably.'

She smiled back at him.

'I've run the bath for you anyway. Why don't you jump in it quickly? I won't be long now.'

Elaine hesitated for a few seconds and then slipping off her dressing gown dropped her eyes from his and put a foot gingerly into the water. She slowly climbed in and then relaxed gratefully into the hot steamy water. Her red hair was piled up on her head and George watched with morbid fascination as she closed her eyes and breathed regularly and deeply.

She looked dead.

She looked happy, dead.

Her breasts were rising and falling with each breath and the nipples had hardened at the sudden cold then heat. They were pointing up at the ceiling, big rosy tips that George suddenly longed to touch. The milky white skin that was once her best feature was jutting from the water in different places. Her pubic hair, that vivid red hair that had once driven him wild, was sparser now but still more luxuriant than most women's. He had seen a naked and relaxed Elaine many times since the New Year. He guessed that it was the man she was seeing who had given her a new lease of life.

George quite liked him, he thought. For making her happy. He could not make her happy.

'Are you staring at me again?'

The voice that could crack glass was back.

'I was just thinking how you would look on the beach in Spain, dear. You're looking ever so well, you know.'

Elaine squinted at him. Whenever George paid her a compliment she was never sure if he was really laughing at her.

George sat back on the toilet seat and grinned at her.

'Not long now until your hols. I bet you're looking forward to them? I know I would be if I was you.'

'Yes, I'm looking forward to them, George. What will you do while I'm away?'

By the tone of the question, George knew it had not occurred to her before and he grinned again.

'I thought I might arrange a little surprise for your homecoming.'

Elaine sat up in astonishment, causing the water to overflow on to the carpet.

'What kind of surprise?' Her voice was suspicious.

'Now if I told you that it wouldn't be a surprise, would it?'

'Oh, George! Tell me!'

He laughed good-naturedly.

'No! Wait and see. I think you deserve a surprise, Elaine. A nice surprise.'

She felt a lump in her throat. Why was George being so good to her all of a sudden?

He stood up.

'Get yourself washed and I'll put the towel on the radiator for you so it will be nice and warm when you get out. Shall I make you a drink? Brandy and coke? I made some ice yesterday. Get you in the mood for your night out with the girls.'

Elaine stared at him.

George raised his eyebrows. 'Brandy and coke, OK?'

Elaine nodded and watched him practically skip out of the bathroom.

She picked up the soap and began to wash herself all over. She stood up and soaped between her legs. Her mind went to Hector then. If only she was married to Hector. If only she had never stood by George.

She smiled to herself ruefully. If regrets were pennies she would be a millionairess by now.

Down in the kitchen, George was taking the ice cubes from their tray. He poured a generous measure of brandy into a tall tumbler and listened to the satisfying crackle as the ice cubes met the alcohol. Then he added a small dash of coke. He didn't want Elaine's amour to be disappointed, did he? Give her a few drinks and she'd be well away. George wondered idly who he could be.

He could follow her. He dismissed the idea, he wasn't really that interested. Whoever the man was, he got Elaine out of the house and that meant George could carry on his own business at his leisure. The thought of having something over Elaine appealed to him, but he might need her one day. Anyway, she deserved to enjoy herself. After all, he had his fun. Who was he to spoil things for her? And if it got serious and she left him, then he would help her pack her bag and kiss her goodbye.

He picked up the drinks and took them up to the bedroom. Elaine was drying herself when he came in. He gave her hers and raised his glass.

'Cheers. I thought I'd join you myself.'

'Cheers.' Elaine took a sip of her drink then grimaced and placed it on the dressing table. She pulled the towel around her tighter and tucked it in over her breasts.

'Did I tell you what happened today, George?' She sat on the stool by the dressing table.

'No.' He settled himself on the edge of the bed.

'Well, one of the fellows who deals with the deliveries went and took that test in the precinct . . .'

George's eyes gleamed. He was just going on to autopilot when her words penetrated his brain.

'Really! How thrilling! What happened?'

'Well, it seems it's a bit more complicated than people thought.'

'In what way?' He could feel a slight trembling in his hands and sipped his drink again. He almost loved her again. You could always depend on Elaine to find out what was going on.

'Well, they wanted to know his mother's full name, the address where he lived and phone number, plus his place of work and the phone number of that. The names of his children, then his post code! Oh, it was terrible, he said.

He was so nervous he nearly forgot his mother's maiden name!' She picked up her drink and took a swig. It wasn't often she had George's undivided attention and she was quite enjoying regaling him with the story.

George, on the other hand, was fretting. She wasn't telling him quickly enough and knowing Elaine, she would draw out the story for maximum effect. He gritted his teeth and smiled at her.

'Is that all? I would have thought it would have been a bit more than that.'

'Oh, it was. They took his fingerprints and asked him if he had been questioned by them regarding the murders. They asked to see his passport but he only had his driving licence, and then they wanted to know what kind of car he drove and what was the registration? Then after all that he finally had the blood test. He said the woman who took the blood was really rough and his arm was swollen where the needle went in.'

Elaine chattered on but she'd lost George now. He was quietly processing exactly what she had said and trying to turn it to his own advantage. He stood up abruptly.

'I'd better let you get on, dear, you're off out soon and if you don't get a move on, you'll be late.'

Elaine glanced at the clock by the bed and gave a little squeal, causing George to close his eyes. Acting like a teenager did not sit well on Elaine, but she couldn't see that herself. Jumping up, she rushed to the wardrobe and took down a bright blue dress that was hanging on the outside. So busy was she taking off the plastic film, she did not even notice George slip from the room.

Twenty-five minutes later, when she'd left, George went down to his shed and brought out all his clippings. He had a whole scrapbook now and lovingly read every word, over and over again. In one local paper was a picture of Kate Burrows, the Detective Inspector who was working on his case. Beside her was her Chief Inspector, a Kenneth Caitlin. He studied the blurred black and white photos and grinned.

They couldn't catch a cold, George thought.

He smiled at the witticism and went back to the pictures of his victims. As always when he saw Geraldine O'Leary, he felt a twinge of sadness. Her poor children, to have a mother like that! He sipped the last of his brandy and shook his head. They really were much better off without her.

Later, after he had read his fill, he put on a nice video and, pouring himself another brandy, settled down to watch it. For the time being at least he was happy to be just an onlooker while others perpetrated the deeds on screen. But he knew that before long the urge would come over him, and he would have to go out once more.

The girl on the screen had become Leonora Davidson and the most violent of the men himself . . .

George felt the stirrings of excitement.

Once Tony had taken his test for him he would be as safe as houses. In his mind, he toyed with the notion of getting rid of Tony Jones permanently and decided not to make a decision just yet. He would see how it went.

But if he tried to blackmail him? Threatened to tell the police? George smiled grimly this time. He would cross that bridge when he came to it. At the moment he needed Jones, and until that need had been answered he had to keep on good terms.

Tony Jones was worried. Very worried. The more he saw on the news and in the papers about the blood testing, the more convinced he was that he would be caught out.

If he was caught and they put him on remand, Patrick

Kelly would make sure he was dead within twenty-four hours. If he refused to help and George was caught, he would spill the beans and Tony would still be at the mercy of Patrick Kelly.

The news that Pat Kelly had sold off his massage parlours had rolled through London like a tidal wave. It was being said on the street that his daughter's death had made him chary of owning anything to do with sex. But at the same time, he had apparently begun to expand on his repo businesses.

Kelly was one of the hardest repomen in the country. It was rumoured he had even repossessed a jumbo jet for a British aircraft manufacturer who were owed hundreds of thousands of pounds by an African airline. Had repossessed it on the runway with all the passengers on board. Kelly had a reputation all right. He also knew all the right people, including the bird who was working on the murder inquiry. Barrow or whatever her name was. It was the talk of the town.

He looked out of the door of his shop again. George Markham was supposed to have been there an hour before. It was just after nine and he had closed the shop especially. Now there were men hanging around waiting for the doors to reopen and that bloody Markham was nowhere to be seen.

He had given Emmanuel the night off, with pay. He did not want anyone seeing or hearing his meet with Georgie. He was losing money hand over fist. It was Saturday night and all the nonces were out in force. Spending their cash on books, films and so-called marital aids. Tony Jones glanced at his watch again. It was nearly nine fifteen. Perhaps he wasn't coming? Had changed his mind? He felt relieved as he thought that.

A man banged on the window of the door and he went

to it, staring through the reinforced metal glass. It was not George but a man called Merve the Perve. He was well known in Soho and a good spender. Tony shook his head and pointed to the handwritten sign: Closed from 8 to 10.

The old man gave him a two-fingered sign and Tony gritted his teeth. There went a good fifty quids' worth of business. He watched Merve walk away and sighed.

Then he saw George and quickly unbolted the door and let him in. The shop was in semi-darkness as they made their way silently to the back. George sat down without being invited, which was not lost on Tony Jones. The quiet meek little man was slowly metamorphosing into a dangerous individual. He was even scaring Tony.

'I have a list here of the questions being asked and the answers you will give. I understand they want a passport if possible, something with a picture on.'

He passed the paper to Tony.

The man glanced at it. George's neat handwriting filled both sides of the paper.

'I can get a passport, but it will cost you. I'll need a photo of you as well, and your own passport number.'

'I brought a yearly one I had done this morning, just in case.'

He took it from his inside pocket and gave it to Tony.

'How much more will this cost?'

'Say three grand for the lot.'

'All right, the money will be paid afterwards. When I'm sure it's all OK. Don't get it into your head to try anything. It's a funny thing, you know. Once you've killed you lose your fear of it. Killing is easy. It's become a kind of hobby for me now.'

George watched Tony for a while until his words had sunk in then said, 'I want you to take the test on Monday the nineteenth at about six o'clock in the evening. They are coming to my place of work at nine o'clock on Thursday the twenty-second. I want my piece of paper ready for them then, to say that I had it done before. I will meet you on the Duggan Road, just outside Grantley itself, in a pub called the Lion Rampant at eight thirty, I will bring half the money with me then.'

'Why on Monday at six o'clock?'

'Because that is when the police are winding up to leave the unit. If you get there for about half past five you should get in at about sixish. Being one of the last of the day I think they'll just want to get you in and out as quickly as possible. Also, if you have a passport you're home and dry. It's the ones without a positive ID who are being given a hard time.'

Tony Jones nodded.

'All right. But I can't get there on Monday. I'll need a few days to get the passport sorted out.'

George was annoyed.

'Well, when can you meet me then?'

'Wednesday. On Wednesday. We'll stick to the same plan of where to meet and that, but I need time to get this thing sorted. It's Wednesday or not at all.'

'All right, but just make sure you get it sorted by then.'

George stood up. 'When you've memorised the answers, get rid of the paper.'

He walked out of the tiny room without a by your leave and Tony Jones stared at the paper until he heard the shop door close. Pushing it into his pocket, he left the room and switched on the lights to reopen for business. As he worked, one thought kept recurring.

It was of the day that Tippy had walked in battered and cut. He should have realised then that the bloke was two sandwiches short of a picnic. If he could rattle an old Tom like Tippy he was capable of anything.

How the hell had he got into all this?

George drove through London and out to Essex. He was listening to a talk show on Radio Essex as he hit the Dartford Tunnel. It was about the Grantley Ripper.

Women were phoning up, saying he should be castrated when he was caught, given a lethal injection, locked away in Rampton or Broadmoor.

George was enjoying listening to the silly suggestions. They would never catch him.

Kate had rung Patrick and told him about the meet with Dan at the Bull. She sat just inside the doorway, watching the people come and go, a feeling of dread on her. She had told Patrick that she would see Dan first, try and appeal to him. If that didn't work she would leave the pub and give Patrick a sign. He would be waiting with Willy, then he could have a word with Dan. One of his special words.

Kate hoped it would not come to that.

Dan came into the pub at ten past eight. He was wearing black trousers and a deep red sweater. He had taken his overcoat off as he walked in, and had it draped casually over his arm. Kate noticed more than one woman give him a second glance. Her big manly husband.

She felt like saying out loud, 'You couldn't afford him, girls. He wouldn't soil his hands on women from a backwater pub.'

It annoyed her that he could still make her feel inadequate.

He went to the bar without acknowledging her and came back with a spritzer for himself and a vodka and tonic for her.

'Hello, Kate.' He sat beside her, his voice smug. He knew just how much he had over her.

Kate nodded to him. 'Dan.'

She watched his mouth on the rim of the glass. Once he had been everything to her. Now she was amazed to find that she felt nothing, not even contempt for him.

'Why did you do it, Dan?'

He thought for a while, searching her face for some kind of indication of what she was actually thinking.

'Because, Kate,' he pointed a finger at her, 'you pushed me too far this time.'

'*I* pushed *you* too far?' Her voice was incredulous.

He nodded, warming to his theme.

'That's right. I came to you for solace, if you like. I've always taken you for a good woman, but what do I find? I find the mother of my child with a bloody villain! My God, Kate, I just couldn't believe it. You had the gall to pass me over for a thug.'

He took another long drink of his spritzer.

'It has nothing to do with you any more, Dan. My life's my own. I'm working on a big case . . .'

'Nothing to do with me? When my child is being neglected!'

Kate grabbed his hand and pushed it back on to the table with such force the glass he was holding spilt its contents over the red sweater.

'You listen to me, Danny Burrows. I put up with more than enough crap from you over the years, but this time, boy, it's over. It stops. If I lose my job, who's going to pay my mortgage? Not you, that's for certain. You couldn't pay your own way in a million years. That's why you fuck the Antheas of this world. You're a ponce, Dan, and I will not stand back and let you make a mockery of my life like you have of your own. I'm warning you . . .'

Kate was getting annoyed. She had known this was useless and now wondered why she had even tried to get him to see her side of it; he was incapable of real feeling. Intelligent feeling.

'You're warning me? That's a turn up for the book. You should be down on your bended knees, girl, because at this moment in time, I –' he poked himself in the chest – 'can make or break you, Kate Burrows. Your career is in the palm of my hand.'

He held his hand in front of her face and clenched it into a fist.

Kate saw how much he was enjoying himself, and was saddened. Once, a long time ago, this man had been the most important thing in her life. She had slept with him, cooked for him and had his child; he had walked out on her and she had held a torch for him for so long. Now, she was seeing him as her mother had seen him and she felt that her life had been wasted because she would not let go of her futile dreams for too long.

She stood and picked up her cigarettes and bag.

'Where do you thing you're going?'

'This is getting us nowhere. You make all these accusations about me yet you can prove nothing. You know something, Dan? You bore me. You bore the arse off of me. I only wish I'd realised it ten years ago.'

She walked from the pub and Dan followed her. Outside in the gravel car park he caught up with her and, grabbing her arm, swung her round to face him. He slapped her. Not hard, but a stinging slap.

It was then he saw Willy and Patrick.

Kate saw his face change in the gloomy light of the car park and turned to see Patrick running across the gravel towards them.

'You fucking bitch, you set me up!'

As Dan turned to make his way to his car, Willy caught up with him and Kate watched as Dan was dragged towards Patrick's BMW. A young couple pulled into the car park and got out of their car. They were watching Dan and Willy, a shocked look on their faces. Kate went to them and got out her ID. 'Grantley police, we're apprehending a known drug dealer. Did you happen to see anyone on the road as you drove here?'

Both shook their heads, not wanting to get involved. Patrick walked sedately to the BMW with Kate, taking her arm and nodding at the couple. Willy had already forced Dan inside. Kate felt as if she was caught up in a nightmare. She went to the car and got in the front, Patrick got in the back with Dan, Willy wheelspun out of the car park and on to the Grantley Road. Kate twisted in her seat and looked at Dan. He was terrified.

Willy slowed the car and Patrick lit a cigarette. He passed it to Kate in the front seat and then lit one for himself. He puffed on it until the end glowed bright red.

Kate watched him and he winked at her.

Then he grabbed Dan's hair and held the cigarette a fraction of an inch away from his eyeball.

'I could blind you, Danny boy, I could blind you without even thinking about it.' Kate went to say something and Willy put his hand on her leg to warn her to keep silent.

Patrick carried on talking in his sing-song voice and Kate watched, fascinated now, as Danny sat stock still. Not moving a muscle.

'You see, you've annoyed me, and when I get annoyed I do terrible things. I could even cripple someone if they annoyed me enough. And you have annoyed me, Danny boy, believe me.'

'Wh-Wh-What do you want?' Dan's voice was high as a schoolgirl's.

'I think you know what I want, I think you know what your wife wants. And I think you know we're going to get it. Because if needs be, I will hunt this country high and low for you, Danny, and I'll get you in the end. Like AIDS I am. You won't even know I'm there for years, but when I do show up the consequences will be devastating. Do you get my drift?'

Dan swallowed loudly. Kate heard it above the low drone of the car engine.

'Yes.'

'So you're going to be a good boy and tell the CIB that you gave them a load of old cod's, ain't you?'

'Yes.'

'Right. Willy, stop the car and let the man out.'

Patrick took the cigarette away from Danny's face and flicked the ash on the floor.

Willy stopped the car. Leaning over Dan, Patrick opened the door and pushed him out violently on to the road. He shut the door as they pulled away, leaving Dan lying in the road, so frightened he thought he was going to wet himself. He saw his overcoat being thrown out of the window and felt the sting of tears.

Kate had sat there and let it happen. He couldn't believe it.

But one thing was certain: he was going to do what Kelly said. As he had always admitted to himself, he was not the hero kind.

Kate stared out of the car, not sure if what she had witnessed had really happened.

'All right, Kate?' Patrick's voice was low.

She nodded.

He sighed. It was a shame they had had to do it in front of her.

493

'Look at it this way, Kate, if I hadn't've frightened him – and that's all I did, frighten him – you could kiss your job goodbye. He asked for that, girl. He damn' well asked for it.'

'Could you take me back to my car, please?'

'Turn the car round, Willy, Kate wants to get home.'

Patrick had a feeling of utter futility. He had been trying to help her, but maybe he had gone too far. Sometimes he forgot that she was from a different world. This night would make or break them, he knew that, but either way she still had her job and that, he knew, meant a lot to her. He had given her that much at least.

Kate was still shaking when she got home. She went upstairs and locked herself in the bathroom, running herself a hot bath. She stepped into it and lay there, trying to work out her troubled thoughts.

Tonight she had seen another side to Patrick Kelly. It had not endeared him to her. She was finally seeing exactly what she was taking on, and it was frightening.

But for all that, in a funny kind of way, she had enjoyed seeing Dan get his comeuppance. All those years of being hurt by him, of knowing that he had used her. Seeing the contempt he had for her tonight had hurt her more than she had thought possible. He had enjoyed having something over her. She had not enjoyed what Patrick had done to him, but she had enjoyed seeing Dan's fear, seeing him grovel like that.

It was these feelings that frightened her more than anything.

George had had an accident. He had dropped his hot chocolate all over the living-room carpet and had spent the best part of an hour cleaning it. He had gone to the shed and got the Bex Bissel, starting to clean the carpet. Then the patch where the stain had been looked cleaner than the rest and he had ended up cleaning the whole carpet. Now, three hours later, he was finally finished and he was wondering if he still had time to watch his film when he heard the low throb of a taxi. He looked through the curtains as Elaine paid the man clumsily. She was as drunk as a lord.

The bloody bitch!

He watched her lurch from the taxi, clutching her bag, and trying to walk up the cement pathway to the front door. He could hear her fumbling for her keys and trying to place them in the lock. Everything seemed magnified a thousand times. The front door banged open and he heard her heavy footfalls approaching the lounge. He sat on an armchair waiting for her to come into the room, but she passed by it and made her way into the kitchen.

He heard the click of the fluorescent lights and her heels clattering on the linoleum, then he grimaced as he heard her retch into the spotlessly clean sink.

He stood up slowly and followed her. Standing in the doorway, he watched her back and shoulders heaving as she brought up port and brandy into the white sink.

He walked to her.

He saw the deep red stains in the sink like clotted blood and turned on the cold tap. He watched mesmerised as the stain became a light pink before swirling around and down the plug into the sewer.

Picking up a tea towel, he soaked it in cold water and placed it on Elaine's forehead. Then, holding the back of her neck tightly as she tried to push him away, he brought the sopping wet cloth down over her nose and mouth and pushed with all his might.

Elaine breathed in and felt the tiny droplets of water enter her nasal canal and burn as she breathed them inside.

She tried to move her head and felt the vice-like grip of George's hand on the back of her neck.

She began to struggle as she realised through her drink-fuddled brain just what was going on.

George held the tea towel over her face, enjoying her panic, enjoying the pain and terror he was creating. This would teach her.

In her struggle Elaine knocked the mug rack by the sink flying on to the floor. The smashing mugs bounced and shattered, making a tremendous noise as the flying shards reached every corner of the kitchen.

George pushed her head down and under the rushing cold tap. The freezing water took the little breath she had left away. With one final surge of strength Elaine tried to bring her head up and felt the deadening pain as she came into contact with the stainless steel tap.

George heard the dull clang, and watched as red blood rapidly began to stain her orange hair. He felt her body relax as she lost consciousness, and held her for a few seconds. Then he slowly lowered her on to the floor, letting the tea towel drop from his hand into the sink.

Elaine lay on the floor amid the broken mugs. Her carefully applied make-up was streaked across her face. Mascara had come away from her lashes in lumps and now peppered the skin around her nose and cheeks. The deep red blood was running from the wound on her head and on to the pristine tiles into little red rivers that broke up and formed tiny map-like inlets.

George stared at her. Her orange hair was in wild disarray and her dress was soaked through. Her eyelids were flickering and when they opened he could see that she was unaware of what exactly had happened.

She closed her eyes again and groaned loudly. It was the groan that triggered him into action.

Going behind her, he lifted her bodily by linking his arms under her arms and across her enormous breasts, and dragged her through the chaos of broken mugs through to the lounge where he laid her on the carpet. Dragging one of the lace chair protectors off, he folded it up and placed it under her head to protect the carpet from the blood.

Then, rushing out to the kitchen, he got the first-aid box from under the sink and tenderly dressed the cut. He was gratified to see it was only a flesh wound; the blood made it look more serious than it was.

He worked quietly and quickly. When he had finished, he placed a cushion under her head and slipped off her sopping dress. Then he covered her with a blanket, warm from the airing cupboard. Satisfied that he had done all he could, he went and started on the kitchen.

Sweeping up the broken mugs, the broom spread bloody water around the kitchen like an abstract painting. The different shades mesmerised George as he worked. When he finally washed the floor clean he was sorry to see it go: he liked the patterns it made and the colours it created and the smell of it – the richly scented smell of fresh blood.

He went back in to Elaine and held her pudgy hand. He had nearly blown it, he knew that. If he'd killed Elaine, that would have been the end of him. She groaned again and opened her eyes. She had been unconscious for over an hour.

'Wha-What happened, George?' Her voice was still groggy with drink.

He smiled at her gently.

'I think you had too much to drink, my dear. You had an accident.'

Elaine stared at him with her compelling green eyes for

a few seconds and George went cold. It was as if the whole night's events were written in them for all to see. Then she closed them tightly.

If she remembered what had taken place she didn't say so. George was even more worried. Supposing she did? What then?

'Shall I make you a nice hot drink?'

Elaine nodded painfully, her hand going up to her bandaged head.

He got up from the floor and went to the kitchen, his eyes boring into every corner to make sure he had picked up every bit of evidence.

While he was gone, Elaine lay passively on the floor.

Then, unannounced, a fat tear pushed its way from underneath her eyelid.

George had tried to kill her. She remembered it all. He must know about Hector.

When he came back with the steaming tea, she was crying loudly, her ample shoulders heaving once more.

Putting the tea on the table, he pulled her into his arms.

She knew.

'I'm sorry, Elaine, I am so very sorry for what I did. I thought you had a boyfriend or something. I realise that's ridiculous. Forgive me for a moment of madness and jealousy.'

Elaine sniffed loudly, gratified in a way that George could be jealous, but not at all sure she liked the 'ridiculous' bit.

He did not know for certain about Hector yet he had physically attacked her. He had hurt her.

She would have to be very careful in the future.

George watched her face and knew everything she was thinking. It was like watching a television screen. Thank

God he hadn't killed her. For the Grantley Ripper to be caught like that!

But one thing he was sure of: he would have to play this one very carefully. Elaine was not going to forget this in a hurry.

She felt the change in George and shuddered. He was like before. When they had had the trouble. Only this time it was all her fault.

She closed her eyes. Poor George.

Chapter Twenty-Three

It was Monday morning and George brought Elaine breakfast in bed. She felt and looked dreadful. Her head had swollen where it had hit the tap and the scab that had formed had dried on to the surrounding hair, making it impossible for her even to touch her head lightly. Once the effect of the drink had worn off she was left with a violent headache and George's solicitous manner was not helping.

He got on her nerves.

After his attack – and it was an attack, she told herself – she did not really want anything to do with him. She needed time alone to think it all through.

'I made you some eggs and bacon, Elaine, with a couple of lightly grilled tomatoes.' George's voice was once more meek and mild. 'I poached the eggs for you because of your diet.' He placed the tray across her knees and smiled at her shyly.

Elaine glanced at the food on the plate, anything rather than look into his face.

'I think you'll feel better after a couple of days off work, don't you?'

She picked up a fork and began to push the food

501

around the plate, the livid blue of the willow pattern a focal point in her need to ignore George.

He hesitated for a few seconds, waiting for an answer. 'Well . . . I'll leave you to enjoy your breakfast then. I rang your manager and told him you had a bug. See you tonight. I'll cook you a lovely dinner.'

Please go, George, she thought.

He went and she felt a moment's lifting of her spirits as she heard the front door close.

Close, not slam, because George slamming a door would be like the Pope joining the Chippendales.

But he had attacked her.

She pushed the laden tray to the other side of the bed. George was capable of violence. He had attacked that poor girl on the train that time. The doctor had said that he was full of unhappiness and bitterness due to his childhood and his overbearing mother. That Elaine's condition and the impending birth had put a strain on him that had caused him to act out of character.

Why had she felt that it was all her fault?

Why had she stayed with him, stood by him?

Because she hadn't known what else to do, that's why. 'For richer for poorer, in sickness and in health.' Why hadn't it had anything about in prison or out of it in the ceremony?

Her head was aching. She closed her eyes and saw Hector. Good old Hector who had told her that he loved her. Hector who laughed all the time and wanted to have fun. Nothing more or less, just fun.

She smiled to herself slightly. And what fun they had had. She couldn't give Hector up! Hector was her life support. Her passport to a happier land.

She lay back against the pillows and surveyed her bedroom. It needed decorating. The whole house did. Years before George had been a handy DIY merchant. They had spent hours looking at paint charts and choosing colour schemes and papers. But that was before his trouble, as they referred to it – when it was ever referred to at all.

George had come out of prison a changed man. Never a gregarious person, he had nonetheless been a cheerful type once. But he had returned to her a sullen and unhappy individual, with a meekness that bordered on humility. Except she sometimes thought it was all a front. All he had been able to do was his gardening. It was as if the inside of the house was meaningless now, and that only the shell was to be maintained in any way.

She sometimes thought that was just like George himself. He had an outer shell that he wore day in and day out, but inside he was empty.

Empty and frightened.

When the murders had started in Grantley she had been inclined to think it was him, but she knew it couldn't be. George would never make a competent murderer. Everything he did just fell apart.

No, George was just a poor fool. But his outburst had proved to her that he did feel something. That he still looked on her as his wife.

The worst part of all the trouble that time had been the knowledge that he had been to a pornographic cinema. That, for some reason, had seemed worse to Elaine than the attack on the young girl.

A single fat tear careered from the corner of her right eye and snaked down her rounded cheek until she tasted the hot saltiness on her tongue.

Why had it all gone wrong? Where was the young girl who had waited so eagerly for her baby to arrive? When did she become a ridiculous middle-aged woman sneaking around to meet another man?

When, in God's name, would all this end?

*

Kate left her house at seven in the morning. It was foggy, the air laden with the smell of early spring. As she unlocked her car, she felt a man's presence and turned abruptly to face him. She thought it was Dan. Her mind had been so full of him all night, she had hardly slept. It was thinking about him and the lack of sleep that had driven her from home so early. She could not face Lizzy just yet.

She turned to look into the big moon face of Willy. She was startled, holding her hands to her chest instinctively.

'I'm sorry to scare you, I just wanted a word. I won't keep you long.'

He took Kate's arm and walked her along the road to Patrick's Rolls Royce. He opened the back and she sat inside. All her instincts told her not to be frightened, but she could not totally allay her fears. Willy started up the car and it rolled away noiselessly from the kerb. He put down the connecting window and began to speak.

'I know a little place where we can have a bit of breakfast if you like.'

Kate nodded to him, aware he was watching her in the mirror. 'A coffee would be nice, thanks, Willy.'

They drove in silence to a small transport cafe on the A13. He parked the Rolls where he could watch it from the window and took her inside. It was empty except for two women and one lone lorry driver, who gave Kate the once over as she sat down and Willy bought two coffees. Happier now she was within sight of people, she gradually relaxed. She lit a cigarette and sipped her coffee.

'I wanted to talk to you about last night, Kate. Can I call you Kate?'

She nodded. 'What about last night?'

'Well, after we dropped you off, Pat was really down. I

504

think he knew he had made a mistake, letting you see what was going to happen, but you must understand him, Kate – Patrick had your best interests at heart. He was trying to save your job and your relationship with him. He has a bit of sway with the big boys, as you probably guessed. Once that pra— I mean, once your ex-husband gives them the news he was just trying to stir up hag, they'll close the case there and then, and it will never be referred to again.'

Kate sipped her coffee and lit another cigarette from the butt of the previous one.

Willy sighed. 'Pat wouldn't have hurt him, I know that for a fact. Sometimes you have to use a bit of friendly persuasion . . .'

'If that's friendly persuasion, I'd hate to see you do it to someone you didn't like!'

'But that's just it – we only scared him, that's all. It was Pat seeing him slap you in the car park, it made him mad. Madder than hell. He was just trying to help you, that's all.'

Kate sucked on her cigarette and the smoke billowed around her head like a cloud.

'You got to understand Pat. He comes from an area that was poor, and I mean poor. We had nothing. He's worked his arse off to get what he's got. He ain't bothered about people like your old man. They're nothing to him, nothing at all. He did that last night for you.

'Pat hasn't put the frighteners on anyone before who wasn't directly involved in one of his businesses. In our game, someone gets out of order you threaten them with a bit of a slap. It's the law of the street and you live by it. I mean, it's not unknown for Old Bill to scare a suspect shitless until he's put his hand up for something he didn't commit. Look at them pub bombing blokes and that. The

Old Bill beat the crap out of them. Well, with us, we just threaten.'

God forgive me for lying, he thought.

Still Kate was silent, and Willy was getting exasperated now.

'He only wanted you to keep your bloody job! He was worried about the way he'd compounded you . . .'

'Compromised, Willy. That's the word you're looking for.'

'Yeah, well, that and all then. But you know what I mean, girl, you're not a silly bird. You know the score. Your old man won't be any more or any less hurt by what happened to him. He was asking for it. I know it must have seemed a little scary to you, 'cos you're not used to it, but believe me, Pat wouldn't have bothered but for you. You and your job. He knows how much it means to you.'

'Can you take me home now, Willy? I have to get my car for work.'

He nodded and they drove back to Kate's in silence. The traffic was thick now and she felt the stares of the other motorists wondering who was in the large Rolls Royce. As she stepped out at the bottom of her street, she patted Willy's arm.

'You're a good friend to Patrick, you know.'

'I worship that man, Kate. I know the good in him. I think you do too, otherwise I don't think you'd have got involved with him in the first place. Don't take what he did last night too much to heart. He loves you, I know he does, and he just wanted to help you. He's a bit cack-handed in the way he goes about it, that's all.'

Coming from Willy this made her smile. A smile she had not thought she had in her at the moment. It was definitely food for thought.

Willy drove back to Patrick's with a heavy heart. He had tried. If Pat had known where he had gone, he would kill him stone dead. But he'd had to try.

Kate and Patrick were good together.

George sat at work listening to Peter Renshaw's voice go on and on about the 'night out'. It was finally decided they would hold it on the Wednesday night, just two days away. George forced himself to smile as Peter regaled him with anecdotes on the leaving dos he had attended in the past. From what George could gather there were about twenty-five people going to his, most of whom he had never spoken to in his life.

Mrs Denham came into the office.

'May I see you for a moment, Mr Markham, in my office.'

George followed her and watched Renshaw's eyebrows rise rudely. George was glad of a respite from Renshaw's almost frenetic bonhomie. The anecdotes and jokes bored him no end. Once inside the office, Mrs Denham offered George a seat and closed the door behind him.

He sat down and watched her bustle to her own seat, the beige silk suit she wore whispering against her tights as she sat down.

George smiled warily.

Josephine Denham smiled back. Just as warily. She cleared her throat nervously.

'It's about your redundancy – I have a note here of the amount you will be receiving.' She passed a slip of paper across the desk to George and he glanced at it.

'If you would like to leave earlier than stated, we would do everything we can to accommodate you. Jones is leaving at the end of the week . . .' Her voice trailed off as she looked at his shocked face.

'Twelve thousand pounds? I thought it would be more than this.'

George's mind was whirling now. Elaine would go mad. He had told her about twenty or twenty-five thousand, which had softened the blow as far as she was concerned. Twelve thousand pounds. That would do nothing, nothing.

Josephine Denham watched the confusion on George's face and felt a moment of sympathy. She had never liked him. Like most of the women in the firm, she had felt uncomfortable around him. Not that he had ever done anything, of course. It was just his way of looking at you. Of staring at you from beneath lowered eyelids. She felt a prickling sensation on the back of her neck now as she watched his expression turn from confusion to fury.

'I need more than this! Much more than this.'

'Look, Mr Markham, it's all worked out on your wages. You're . . .'

George interrupted her. 'I know all that. I work in accounts, remember? It's just that I thought it would be more! Much more. I need more than that, for Christ's sake. Can't you understand, you stupid bitch!'

Josephine Denham's eyes widened to their utmost and she stood up with what dignity she could muster.

'I understand that you're upset, Mr Markham, but talking to me like that won't help matters. I think it would be better if you went now and we talked it over another day. When you're feeling . . .'

George was breathing heavily. Twelve thousand pounds. The words were flying around his head, banging and thumping against his skull. Twelve thousand lousy pounds. It was like a chant.

He stayed in his seat. Josephine Denham was gone

from his vision now. All he could see was the three thousand for the passport, and for Tony Jones to take his place in the testing.

The woman walked from the room and into the accounts offices. She pulled Peter Renshaw aside and after a hasty few words he followed her to her office.

It was empty. George had gone.

'I thought he was going to hit me!'

For once in his life Peter Renshaw looked at an attractive woman without seeing her breasts, eyes, hair, legs. He knew what was wrong with George. This place was his life. His refuge.

'Did it ever occur to you that maybe the man knows he's finished? That he'll never work again? That tens of young men and women are waiting to fill any job he might be eligible for? That he's got a wife and home?

'Of course it didn't, Mrs Denham, because you never think of anyone but yourself and this bloody firm. Well, when your turn comes – and it will, my love, make no mistake about that – I hope whoever axes you does it with a bit more tact.'

With that, he walked from the room and left Josephine Denham with her mouth agape.

On the table was the piece of paper she had handed to George. She picked it up and stared at it. Twelve thousand pounds. It wasn't much for fifteen years.

Elaine was fed up with lying in bed and had decided to get up. After making herself a cup of tea and reading the paper in the kitchen she decided she needed something to take her mind off things. She looked at the garden as she washed up her cup and a thought occurred to her. She could germinate the tomato seeds. Every year at this time George popped them into the airing cupboard ready to go into his greenhouse. Then all summer they would have big fat red juicy tomatoes.

She went upstairs and got dressed. Her aching head was feeling much better after a couple of aspirins. She pulled an old jumper carefully over her head and put on a pair of tracksuit bottoms. Elaine was a woman who needed to be doing something. That was why the house was so spotlessly clean. If she had five minutes to herself then her thoughts wandered to the way she lived and it made her depressed.

She made her way down to the garden shed. It smelt musty, like sheds should, and she looked around her. George had it quite cosy really. This was his little domain. His refuge. He spent a great deal of time here.

Suddenly, Elaine felt like an interloper. She shrugged. This was as much her shed as George's. He had the gardening sorted out like she did the house. His and hers.

Now, where were the seeds? She began by looking on the small shelves he had built. There were gladioli bulbs waiting to go into the ground. She would get him to put some by the front door this year, liven up the front of the house with a nice spray of colour. She was warming to her theme. Planning the garden would give her something else to think about. Once George was made redundant he would be spending a lot of time in the garden. He could replace the whole lot. Buy some nice rose bushes. She liked a nice rose and George was a good gardener. He was patient and thorough. There were never any weeds anywhere.

She began clearing the old desk of gardening debris, then opened it up to find his gardening magazines. She would flick through them and get some ideas. They could even have a bigger pond, with a nice rockery.

She pulled out the magazines and then went cold. She

stared down at the books as if not quite sure of what she was seeing.

A girl was looking at her, a Chinese girl, nearly naked and with a chain around her neck.

She was smiling.

Elaine picked up the magazine and stared at it, feeling the bile rising in her stomach.

Underneath there was another one. This had 'Nazi Torturers' emblazoned across it. On the front were two women in SS uniforms dragging a scantily clad girl between them.

Elaine closed her eyes tightly and opened them again. It was no good, they were still there.

Slowly she removed all the magazines. Her heart was heavy now. Underneath the magazines were some scrap books and she took these out. Sitting in George's comfortable chair, she opened one. It was full of newspaper clippings about the Yorkshire Ripper, yellowing with age now and brittle-looking.

There were the photographs of his victims. Headlines screamed out at her: I WAS CHOSEN TO KILL. HER EYES DROVE ME CRAZY. RIPPER IN THE WITNESS BOX.

She closed the scrapbook and opened another one.

This time the cuttings were newer, all about the Grantley Ripper, and suddenly Elaine knew what had happened. It was crystal clear.

It was George who had murdered all these women.

He was sick.

He had attacked her!

Elaine hastily began to put the scrapbooks and magazines back where she had found them. She had to get the police. She was fumbling in her haste and only half aware of the shadow that passed the shed window. She did not even hear the shed door opening. She turned around and came face to face with George. So great was her terror that instead of screaming she groaned, holding on to the desk for support lest she faint away completely.

George was staring at her. And he was smiling. The little smile that just showed his teeth.

'Come and have a cup of tea, dear, you look as white as a sheet. You've had a shock, I think.'

Kate was in the canteen having her lunch when she was told there was a phone call for her. She went to the phone on the wall by the door and picked it up.

'Burrows here.'

'Kate? It's me, Dan.'

She felt a surge of apprehension as she heard the desolate tone of his voice. She pushed herself against the wall to try and muffle their conversation.

'Look, Dan. About what happened. I swear I had no idea . . .'

He cut her off. 'I know that. Let's face it, Kate, I asked for it. Well, you can tell that . . . your friend, that it's done. The CIB are off your back. I've been round to see Lizzy and told her that I'm going back to Anthea's.'

'And are you?'

'Yeah. I rang her this morning. We're going to have another try.'

It was a lie. Dan was going as far away from Grantley as possible. He didn't want any reminders of Patrick Kelly.

'I hope it works out for you, Dan, really I do.'

The line crackled, Dan had muttered something inaudible and Kate said his name down the phone line a couple of times before hanging up. She went back to her table and lit a cigarette. The canteen was filling up but the babble of voices and laughter went unnoticed by her.

She was still thinking about Patrick and what he had

done. After Willy had dropped her off she had thought long and hard about Patrick and, much as she loved him, had admitted to herself he scared her.

The worst of it all was, scared of him, annoyed with him or anything else that she might feel, above all she wanted him. Desperately. It was this that scared her more than anything.

'Penny for them?'

Caitlin's voice was friendly.

'I wouldn't take money from an old man.'

He laughed in surprise. 'Is everything all right with the other business?'

She nodded and Caitlin grinned.

'Sure that Danny's an eejit. Imagine doing that. Still, the blood testing is going well, so that's something anyway.'

'It's certainly going better than anyone expected, that's for sure.'

'Did you hear about Spencer?'

Kate shook her head.

'Well, like all the male officers he got a letter, same as everyone else. He's doing his pieces! Thinks it's a deliberate slur on his character.'

Caitlin roared with laughter, bringing many eyes to rest on him and Kate.

'But it was what that Amanda said to him that's really caused the trouble.'

Kate was intrigued. She smiled at him. 'Go on then, tell me.'

Caitlin leant across the table and whispered: 'She said she had read a secret psychologist's report that stated the Grantley Ripper was a policeman in his late-twenties with a history of paranoia and violent and disruptive behaviour!'

Kate giggled. 'Well, if the cap fits!'

'My sentiments entirely!' Caitlin was roaring again. 'Sure she's a comical lass that one. So Kelly saw your old man then?'

He changed the subject so quickly he caught her offguard. 'Yes. It's all right.'

'That Patrick Kelly is a very astute man, you know. You just let him sort out everything. You're lucky to have such a good friend.'

She dropped her eyes.

'Come on, Kate, we've still got a good half an hour. Let me buy you a drink in the pub. My throat's as dry as a buzzard's crotch!'

Kate closed her eyes. 'You have a disgusting turn of phrase, you know.'

'Sure me wife, poor woman, used to say that. God rest her nagging soul.'

'You miss her, don't you?'

'I do, Katie, more every day. She had a tongue like an adder, but she was me wife. Come and have a drink, lass. This place gives me the heebie jeebies. All this youth makes me stomach turn.'

Kate stood up and followed him out of the canteen. She could do with a drink herself.

Elaine was sitting opposite George at the kitchen table. He had made her a cup of coffee and it stood in front of her, cold now, with a thick skin of milk floating on top. George had been silent, just smiling at her every now and then while he sipped his own coffee.

'Elaine.' His voice was so low she could barely hear him, but all the same she jumped in her seat.

'Don't be scared, Elaine. Would I hurt you? Now would I?'

She bit her lip.

'I didn't mean to murder anyone, believe me, my dear. It just happened.' He spread out his hands in front of him in a gesture of helplessness. 'I don't know what it is. I just see them – they're all whores, every last one of them.'

He was nodding to himself now and Elaine felt her nails bite into the flesh of her hands.

'Even that bitch O'Leary, with the children. They're much better off without her, believe me. You didn't see her like I did, Elaine. Sprawled out on the dirt. She had no tights on, you know, and the weather was freezing. She was a slut . . . a dirty stinking slut.'

Elaine put her hands over her ears to block out his voice. George stood up. Fear overtaking her, Elaine made a rush for the kitchen door. As she ran George grabbed at her hair. She shrieked as pain tore through her. Blood began to seep from her wounded head on to the vivid orange locks. George punched her to the ground, every movement calculated and controlled. He stood over her and shook his head.

'You've been a trial to me, Elaine, do you know that?'

Her lips were already swelling from his blows and she could taste the blood in her mouth.

'Why didn't you just divorce me? Why did you have to sit there all those years, a silent reminder of what I'd done?'

He gave her a vicious kick in the stomach and she gagged.

'Now I've got to kill you. You understand that, don't you? I couldn't possibly let you live now you know my little secret.'

He tutted a couple of times in exasperation. Elaine stared at her husband through watery eyes.

It dawned on her that George was as mad as a hatter

and she was never going to see Hector, her friends, or anyone ever again. She was as good as dead already.

He stepped over her cumbersome body and walked out into the hall. Elaine could hear him whistling between his teeth, a habit that had grated on her nerves over the years. She saw, from her vantage point, that he was opening the coat cupboard in the hall and lifting up the floorboards. She pulled herself painfully to her knees. Grabbing at the wall, she staggered upright. The floor was covered in blood, and as she swayed and tried to steady herself she felt droplets running down her chin and into the folds of her neck.

George pulled out his army knife and walked purposefully towards her. He was tutting again as if she was a recalcitrant child.

She heard him sigh and as she tried to run towards the back door felt the sharp slice as the knife went through the wool of her jumper and into her shoulder blade. She gathered up all her strength and tried to dodge around the kitchen table. The serrated edge of the knife was caught in the wool of her jumper and George watched in fascination as she staggered away, pumping out blood, the knife hanging half out of her back.

He shook his head. Elaine was always so difficult.

He watched her stagger for a few steps before she fell to her knees, her breaths coming in quick painful gasps.

He walked over to her and, pulling the knife gently from her jumper, raised it over his head. As he did so Elaine turned her head and looked into his face.

'George! Please . . . please, George . . . !'

She coughed and a trickle of blood seeped from the corner of her mouth. George planted the knife neatly into the middle of her shoulder blade, burying the blade up the hilt.

Elaine fell forward, and George watched her arms and legs twitch in the final throes of death. Finally he sighed.

Elaine was still, her cheek was pressed against the white tiles and her green eyes stared vacantly at the skirting board.

George knelt beside her body and tidied the orange hair, pushing it around her still face. Elaine had always been such a difficult woman but now she was at peace.

He made himself another cup of coffee and sat drinking it quietly, watching her body.

A little while later he began to whistle once more through his teeth. He had to make some plans now. He had to sort everything out.

At least this way he had saved her the knowledge of the pittance that had been offered to him. She would never have let him live it down.

He glanced at the clock. It was three fifteen. He wouldn't be able to do anything just yet. He made himself a sandwich and took it into the lounge. He'd watch one of his films and relax. It had been a very trying day.

Tony Jones watched the man sitting opposite him. Larry Steinberg could get anyone anything. He was nicknamed 'Harrods' among the villains he dealt with because of this. If you wanted a Nepalese yak Larry would find one, and at a reasonable price. Tony watched the tiny man push his pince-nez up along the bridge of his nose, settling them just below the large lump in it.

'I had a bit of trouble with this one, Tone, but I managed it for you as quick as I could. Needs must when the devil drives, eh? What did you say you wanted it for?'

'I didn't.'

'Oh, well, you obviously have your own reasons. My friends in the passport office are getting very expensive these days. But for you, a good friend, I do it for the old price.'

Tony took a brown envelope from his inside pocket and placed it on the desk. Larry opened it and counted the money carefully. One thousand pounds exactly. Not a bad day's work. He opened a drawer and passed a small burgundy-coloured passport across the desk.

'I even got you one of the new EEC ones.'

Tony opened it and looked at his photograph staring out of the page.

'Thanks, Larry. I owe you one, I think.'

He stood up, putting the passport into his top pocket. Larry watched him leave the office and then walked to the window. From there he watched Tony cross the road and hail a black cab.

Larry was intrigued.

The details in the passport were of a George Markham, from Grantley in Essex. The man already had a one-year tourist passport, as well as a ten-year passport with eighteen months on it. Larry knew that something not quite kosher was going down, but he was stumped as to what it was.

Something rang a warning bell in his head but he could not put his finger on it.

He went back to his desk and slipped the thousand pounds from the envelope into his wallet. At least he had been paid promptly. Nowadays that was something in itself.

Tony Jones walked into Sexplosion and poured himself a large Scotch. He drank it down, the alcohol biting into his throat and stomach, burning his ulcer.

The enormity of what he knew about George Markham was weighing him down. He felt sick every time he thought about it.

All his life Tony had lived among villains, pimps and prostitutes. He had dealt with most of the so-called gang bosses in his time. In his business it was inevitable you would stumble across them at some time or another.

He had always prided himself on his ability to work side by side with the most violent men, keeping his business going and his head above water. He never made their Christmas card lists but they had afforded him a modicum of respect.

His shop was one of the oldest in the West End. His father had run it for years, before handing it over to his only son. Tony wanted to hand it over to his son one day. It was a lucrative business now that porn was more socially acceptable. He had dealt with prostitutes who would give Frank Bruno food for thought before fighting them and with pimps who would carve you up as soon as look at you. Yet none of these people had ever frightened him like George Markham, the little man with the funny smile.

He poured himself another stiff drink and Emmanuel waltzed into the back of the shop, his heavily mascaraed eyelids fluttering.

'I need a bit of help out here, Tone, if you don't mind. I've been run off my feet.'

Tony glared at the boy.

'Emmanuel, piss off and don't come in here again today unless we get busted by the Filth or Joan Collins comes in to buy a vibrator. All right?'

The boy pursed his cherry red lips and stormed out of the room. He could be so bitchy, could Tony Jones. He noticed a new customer in a neat brown suit and immediately cheered up. He liked the newies.

He smiled at the man. His nicest smile. He had all day. By the looks of it Tony was going to drink himself stupid. He'd been doing that a lot lately.

'Can I help you?'

The man in the brown suit smiled sheepishly.

Emmanuel smiled back widely. He was worth a fifty at least.

George had watched his film and was now feeling relaxed and cheerful. He turned off the video and sat smiling to himself. No more Elaine. No more having to be polite.

His face darkened. No more alibi.

Then he brightened. His mind was working overtime. If he planned everything just right, he could get away with it all.

If he went away for a while and then came back he could say that Elaine had left him. If he went to Edith's in Florida he could say it had happened out there. And now that he was redundant he could sell this house and be free. The more he thought, the more viable it all seemed.

He felt absolutely wonderful. He was so clever! He patted himself on the back. Cleverer than a bag of monkeys.

But what was he going to do with Elaine? He would have to hide her away somewhere. He thought of burying her in the garden but dismissed the idea immediately.

He would put her right under everyone's nose, and still they wouldn't find her. All he had to do was have a good old think . . .

The phone rang and he jumped in his seat. The harsh tones echoed around the silent house, upsetting George. He crept out into the hallway and picked up the offending instrument.

'Hello, George. Margaret here. How's Elaine?'

He felt his heart begin to race.

'Oh, she's fine, Margaret, feeling a bit better . . . I doubt she'll be in this week though.'

'Can I have a word?'

'She's sleeping at the moment. I'll tell her you called though, Margaret, she'll be sorry to have missed you.'

'Okey doke then, I'll ring her later in the week. 'Bye.'

George replaced the receiver.

The whole conversation had taken less than two minutes, but to him it had seemed like a fortnight.

He stormed out to the kitchen, his temper flaring. Elaine was still sprawled on the kitchen floor, her sightless eyes staring at the skirting board.

'That was your friend Margaret. Checking up on you as usual. Are you listening to me?'

George knelt down and pulled her head up by her flame-coloured hair. He looked ferociously into her face.

'You're nothing but trouble, Elaine. That's all you've ever been.'

Then, as if the reality of events suddenly hit him, he cradled her head in his arms and began to cry.

Evelyn heard the door knocker and went out to the hall to answer it. She could hear loud music coming from Lizzy's room and smiled to herself as she wiped her hands on her apron. The child was like a young girl should be now, and that thought cheered her.

She opened the front door. Patrick Kelly was standing there.

'Oh, hello. Kate isn't here, but come away in anyhow. I was just going to have a coffee.'

He walked into the hall, hearing the loud music coming down the stairs. Evelyn laughed.

'That's Lizzy. You're forgiven for thinking she might be a bit deaf!'

They went through to the kitchen and Patrick undid his coat and sat at the breakfast bar.

'I'm just making a nice lamb casserole for dinner.'

'It smells delicious.'

She poured out two coffees.

'I like to cook. It relaxes me.'

He took the coffee from her and sipped it.

Sitting opposite him, Evelyn lit herself a cigarette and blew out the smoke loudly.

'So what can I do for you, or is this a social call?'

Patrick smiled slightly. She was a game old bird.

'It's a bit of both actually. It's about your trip to Australia.'

'What about it?'

'Well, the truth is, I don't think that Kate can really afford it, can she?'

Evelyn took another drag on her cigarette. She knew that Kate couldn't afford it really, that she was trying to get a bank loan to pay for it. But she had told Lizzy she was going and there was no way that she would let her down, even if it meant selling the car and every bit of jewellery she possessed.

Patrick could gauge what Evelyn was thinking. He sighed. Taking an envelope from his pocket he placed it on the table.

'What's this?'

'That, Mrs O'Dowd, is two first-class tickets to Sydney, with a four-day stop over in Singapore. It's a long old flight to Oz, you know, and you'll be glad of the break, believe me. I want you to take these tickets and tell Kate that you had some money left over from . . . well, whatever you like. Let her think you paid for them.'

Evelyn fingered the thick brown envelope and looked into Patrick's eyes.

'Something's happened between the two of you, hasn't it?'

He nodded. It was pointless lying. He told her about Dan. Evelyn did not bat an eyelid all the time he spoke.

'That would go against the grain with Kate. It goes against the grain with me to be honest. But I'm a bit more of a realist than my daughter. I know that desperate times mean desperate measures. I'll give you a bit of advice where Kate is concerned, shall I? Always remember that her job is the most important thing in her life. She fought hard to get to where she is and I think that the fact she allowed herself to get involved with you, knowing your reputation, speaks volumes. She's had only one man in her life, Danny Burrows. Now she has you. Or maybe I should say had you? I don't know. Only Kate knows that.

'If you care about my daughter, and I think you do, then you should remember these facts. They'll stand you in good stead for the future. Kate's as honest as the day is long.'

Patrick at least had the grace to look away from her, and Evelyn admired him for that. She knew that he loved her daughter, could hear it in the way he spoke her name, see it in the way that he tried in his own way to make things right for her. Like the tickets to Australia. An expensive way to make amends, but Evelyn knew that was what he was trying to do. She opened the envelope.

The tickets were for 4 March 1990, from Heathrow. She looked at him and frowned.

He held out his hand and took the envelope from her. He placed it back in his pocket.

'I never said I wasn't going to accept them, did I?'

Her voice was softer now. She held out her hand and he gave her back the envelope. He left a few minutes later, lighter of heart.

Evelyn let him out and as she closed the door looked

up the stairs. The thump-thump of Lizzy's music was still audible.

It was just as well the child had no idea he'd been here. Kate was astute enough to put two and two together. Evelyn only hoped she would believe her story about insurance money left over from her father's death.

She went into the kitchen and put the envelope into her apron pocket. It gave her a warm feeling knowing that it was there. She would see her other grandchildren and it would be thanks to Patrick Kelly.

No matter what anyone thought, she liked him. He was a product of the world they lived in and his lifestyle gave her not a smidgen of bad conscience.

As for what he had done to Dan . . . she shrugged. He'd been asking for that for years.

Her only regret was she hadn't been there to see it for herself.

Chapter Twenty-Four

George looked at the clock. It was five thirty-five and still dark. He rubbed at his eyes. They felt gritty and he could smell a funny smell on his hands. He leant out of bed and turned on the small bedside lamp. As the glaring brightness penetrated his eyes he grimaced.

His hands had rust-coloured stains on them. He held them up in front of him as if he had never seen them before and sat up in bed. He was fully dressed. He frowned.

Pulling back the covers, he slipped out of the sheets and stood uncertainly on the carpet.

His mouth felt dry and fluffy and he swallowed with difficulty. What he needed was a cup of coffee. He made his way downstairs humming to himself. He walked into the kitchen and turned on the fluorescent light. It flickered into life, illuminating Elaine's body. Ignoring her, he walked to the sink and filled the kettle. Stepping over her silent form, he made himself a strong, sweet coffee and took it to the kitchen table. Then he went into the lounge and brought back his Christmas cigars. He lit one and puffed on it for a few seconds to get it fully alight.

He sighed with happiness. Coffee and cigars. Cigars and coffee.

He grinned to himself. He was totally free now.

Finally he looked at Elaine.

Today she was going to disappear forever. He knew what he had to do. But first he needed a shower.

George had had his shower and was now in the process of putting Elaine into two large black bags. He covered her head and shoulders first. Her sightless eyes were getting on his nerves. Her head had stuck to the floor in a pool of blood that had congealed to a reddish-brown. It still had long strands of ginger-orange hair stuck in it. He would have to scrape it off the tiles. He finally had the bag over her head and tied it around her neck with string. Then he looked at her lower body. He had turned her over to make it easier for him and now her legs were wide open. He imagined her without her tracksuit bottoms and smiled to himself, feeling the familiar excitement. The blood everywhere was making him feel aroused.

He liked blood. He liked the sticky feel of it, like crimson semen. He pulled off her trainers and tracksuit bottoms, staring at her milky white legs as if fascinated. She had on a pair of white panties and her thick red pubic hair poked out of the sides with a jauntiness that pleased George immensely. Like this, Elaine was his perfect woman. Faceless, undemanding and completely available.

He poked a finger into her crotch, feeling the softness there. He ran his finger inside the silky material of her panties and round her pubic hair.

He licked his lips, feeling the sweat that was now beading them. He hooked his fingers into her panties and pulled them down her legs slowly, gently, revealing her most intimate parts.

He unzipped his trousers, locked in the almost sublime feelings of his fantasy world. He began to knead her thighs, feeling the cold strength of them. He tried to part her legs further to remove her panties, but they wouldn't budge! He pulled at them harder, trying to force them open.

George had not allowed for rigor mortis.

His breathing was laboured now, from his exertions and from his fantasies.

He frowned.

Elaine had always been the same: difficult. Even in death, she was still inaccessible.

He wiped a clammy hand over his face. Suddenly, the chaos around him registered. He had better get cleaned up. He had plenty of time for fun.

Real fun, with better women than Elaine.

He began to bundle her into the other black bag, his movements more urgent now. Finally he sat back on his heels and stared at his handiwork. Elaine was trussed up like a chicken.

Standing up, he zipped his trousers back up, carefully tucking in his shirt first. He would have a nice cup of tea, then he would start the second phase of his operation.

Kelly was waiting outside the pub where Kate and Caitlin had gone for lunch. As she saw his black BMW she felt a lurch in her breast. Caitlin grinned at her and said: 'I think you've got company, Kate. I'll see you later.'

He waltzed into the pub and left her standing alone on the pavement. She could see Patrick's face through the windscreen and against her better judgement walked over to the car and got inside.

'Hello, Kate.' Patrick's voice was normal and she swallowed hard.

'Patrick.' She let him drive. The closeness of him made her feel breathless. She could smell his aftershave. Despite herself she was glad to see him. This fact, admitted to and accepted, annoyed her.

Patrick drove to his house and she got out of the car and followed him inside. They had barely spoken a word. In his dining room the table was laid for two and the smell of a delicious roast assailed her nostrils.

He held her seat for her and she sat down.

'I'm sorry, Kate. I know that what I did to Dan was wrong. But I swear I was just trying to help you, that's all. I wanted the CIB off your back and that was the only way. I had no intention of hurting him, just scaring him.'

Kate could hear the desperate tone in his voice. Could see the absolute honesty in his face. But she also could feel the pull that this man had on her. She looked around the beautiful room: at the plush carpet, the watercolours on the walls, at the expensive linen and cutlery, and knew that she had missed all this but most of all had missed the man. Missed him with all her being, no matter what he had done. He was like the breath of life to her and she needed him. Whatever the attraction was between them, it was powerful enough to make her admit that what he had done to Dan didn't really matter when he was with her, when he was close to her, when she could reach out and touch his face.

She looked at Patrick and he looked at her. It was more than an exchange of glances: it was like a tangible force, there between them. Each knew the other intimately, each felt the attraction that had brought her here today. Each wanted the rift between them breached so that they could get on with their lives.

Kate's eyes were like dark pools of liquid light. Patrick searched them for some sign that she had relented. That he was forgiven. As she picked up her wine glass and smiled at him, he felt as if someone had given him an injection of pure happiness.

'Cheers, Pat.' She sipped the heavy red liquid and as she did so knew that there was no going back. She had accepted his way of living one hundred per cent. Dan would be forgotten, everything would be forgotten, except for their urgent desire.

Patrick opened the serving dish that had been placed on the table by Willy just as they had driven up and filled Kate's plate with slices of beef.

As she took the plate from him their fingers touched and the jolt that went between them was like a physical pain.

'How's Willy?'

Patrick filled his own plate and grinned. 'He's fine.'

'Good. I rather like Willy.'

And she did. She knew that Patrick would go mad if he knew that Willy had been to see her, but it was the talk she had had with him that had helped her sort out her own mind.

'Can I see you tonight, Kate?'

She smiled, taking a mouthful of juicy beef and wiping her lips with a napkin.

'I don't see why not.'

Putting down his own knife and fork he walked around the table and took her in his arms. They did not kiss, but as he rubbed his face in the softness of her hair, she felt as if she had indeed finally come home.

He was dangerous to her, she knew that. But she was determined to have him.

An hour later she was back at work, lighter of heart than she had been for days and raring to go. She looked and felt great, something which was noticed by just about everyone in the incident room.

DS Spencer, still smarting from Amanda Dawkins's practical joke, whispered into Willis's ear: 'Screwing a villain seems to cheer her up no end.'

Willis gave him a dirty look. Spencer got on his nerves. In fact, Spencer got on everyone's nerves.

'Why don't you piss off, Spencer?'

Willis walked away from him. Collating all the blood tests was much harder than anyone had thought, but it had given them an added impetus. It was a new avenue. It was their big chance to catch the Grantley Ripper.

When a man was blood tested his fingerprints were taken also. If he had a record then the fingerprints were matched. It was another way of confirming their alibis. If a man had no criminal file then his passport or some other form of identification was necessary. A driving licence was adequate, but something with a picture on was much more solid. This is what was taking all the time. Not enough manpower to keep abreast of the mounting names. Still, it was better than nothing and much better than they'd had before.

Willis picked up yet another file. He was dealing with the known sex offenders. Due to a delay in the computer system, they had only just received all the names of sex offenders in the area who had been tried and convicted in other parts of the country. These were known as 'floaters', passing through on their way to another prison sentence. They were the flotsam and jetsam of the criminal world, hated by police and villains alike. The pile was in alphabetical order and Willis picked up the first file.

Name: Desmond Addamson.

Willis flicked through the file: rape, arson and flashing, along with robbery with violence. He had turned up in

Grantley in the middle of January. Too late for the first murders. He picked up the phone. The man had better be checked out anyway. He would start with his probation officer. As he picked up the phone, he knocked the pile of files from his desk. He dropped the phone and tried to save them. Too late.

The files landed with a muted thud and papers were strewn everywhere. A small cheer went up from the others in the room and Willis smiled good-naturedly as he bent down to scoop up the papers. He would be there for ages putting all the papers back in their proper folders. He placed the last lot on the desk and there, staring up at him, was George Markham's face. Younger, with browner, thicker hair, but unmistakably George Markham.

Willis glanced at the photo without seeing it.

George had had a nice cup of tea and was now in the process of thinking how to get Elaine up into the loft. He had thought long and hard about where to put her and then it had come to him in a flash of inspiration. There was only one problem: Elaine was big. How was he to get her up there?

The answer was so cunning that he grinned with satisfaction. He was clever all right.

He stood up and looked at Elaine's body, wrapped in the incongruous plastic bags.

'I'm off out, dear, I won't be long.'

He went into the hall and put on his good overcoat. Then, carefully locking up, he drove to Grantley shopping centre, parked his car in the multi-storey car park and walked through the town centre to a small plant hire shop.

Stellman's Plant Hire had been in Grantley for twenty years. It was the first time George had ever been in there and he stood uncertainly among the debris of lawnmowers and wallpaper strippers. A young man came up and smiled at him.

'What can I do you for?'

'I beg your pardon?' George's voice was timid once more.

'A joke, mate.' The boy stared at George and shrugged. 'What can I do for you, sir?' He tacked the 'sir' on the end at the last second.

'I . . . er . . . want to lift an engine out of a car. A friend of mine is going to put a new engine into my car, you see.' George's voice trailed off. He should have prepared what he was going to say.

The boy was all the business now.

'I see. You want the Haltrac.' Seeing George's confusion, he grinned. 'The small block and tackle. It will lift about a ton, but it's lightweight. Not like the old ones of years ago. You just set it up and Bob's your uncle. Manual lift, the lot. How long would you want it for?'

George smiled now. This was easier than he'd thought.

'Oh, a couple of days at most.'

'All right. I'd have it for the week, though. If it pisses down with rain then you won't be doing much. It's cheaper that way anyhow. It's eight quid a day, but only sixteen quid for the week. Plus VAT of course. Mustn't forget Maggie's curse, must we?'

George was overwhelmed. The boy could sell, that much was obvious. But at that moment George would have paid any amount for the tool in question, and in fact was shocked that it was so cheap.

'Whatever you think is best. Can I take it now?'

''Course you can.'

The boy began to make out the paperwork and George paid him in cash. He left, the Haltrac held firmly in his hands. He drove back home feeling quite lighthearted.

Once indoors he began the serious work of the day. First he opened the loft hatch and, after cleaning it thoroughly, placed it on his bed. No need to make everything dirty. He hated mess of any kind. Then he brought the block and tackle up the stairs. He walked up the stainless steel, safety conscious steps that led to the square hole in the ceiling of the landing and began phase two of his operation.

Lifting himself into the loft, he looked around him critically. The roof sloped upwards and running parallel on each side were three sets of purlings, large pieces of wood that supported the roof joists. He went back down the ladder and returned with a length of half-inch-thick polyester rope in a lovely bright blue colour. He lashed this around the left-hand purling, tying it tightly, and did the same on the right-hand side, giving the rope a good hard tug to make sure it was secure. The purlings were eight feet from the floor and he balanced himself precariously on a large packing case to secure the rope.

He got off the packing case and jumped up, grabbing the centre of the rope to make sure it was secure. He held on to it for a few seconds, swaying, his feet off the ground. It was perfect.

He let go of the rope and dropped lightly on the balls of his feet. He felt quite gay. It was like when he was a child and they played on the bundle swings, hanging precariously above the ground, then that wonderful feeling of dropping on to terra firma. He smiled to himself and then repeated the whole process again, swinging for a few seconds more this time, swaying from side to side.

Then the significance of what he was doing penetrated his brain and he was businesslike once more. He went down the ladder and brought up the block and tackle. He placed the hook on the top of the tackle on to the rope, letting the tackle itself drop through the loft hole. He was ready.

He felt a thrill of anticipation course through his whole body. He went back to the kitchen. Holding Elaine's body through the plastic, underneath the arms, he began dragging her through the hall and up the stairs. Elaine's dead weight was more than he had bargained for and he had to leave her propped up on the middle of the stairs while he went for a cold drink. He was sweating like a pig. His euphoria was wearing off now and he was feeling positively disgruntled. Elaine always made everything so difficult. Every time he planned something, she messed it up.

He pursed his lips together into a hard line, the water forgotten in front of him as he brooded.

Half an hour later he was startled when the harsh trill of the telephone rang through the silent house. It was probably that nosy bitch again, Elaine's so-called friend. He pulled himself from his seat to answer the phone. The blood-spattered kitchen had not penetrated his consciousness yet.

'Hello.' His meek, humble voice was back.

'George?' His heart sank. It was Renshaw.

'You there, Georgie boy?'

'Yes. Hello, Peter.'

'Bad business that yesterday and I told that cow Denham what I thought about it as well. You're still on for tomorrow night though? Bugger the lot of them, we'll have a night to remember, what?'

'Tomorrow night?' George was puzzled.

'Your leaving do, of course.'

'Oh . . . Oh, yes. Yes, I'll be there.'

'Good. Meet you in the Fox Revived at eight thirty, OK?'

'Yes. That would be lovely.'

'I don't blame you for getting on your high horse, you know, George. That bitch needed taking down a peg or two. They all do in the end.'

'Quite.'

'See you tomorrow then?'

'Yes.'

The phone went dead and George replaced the receiver. Peter Renshaw was right. They did all need taking down a peg and he was the man to do it!

He walked up the stairs and stared at Elaine's grotesque form. She was another one. Ripping the top of the bag he watched, fascinated, as Elaine's orange hair tumbled into view. Then, taking the long hair in chunks, he wrapped it around his hands and dragged her bodily up the remaining stairs. The action forced her head from the bag and he laughed at her milky eyes. Glazed now and dry, they stared up at him passively.

With one final heave he had her on the landing. Then, pulling the tackle down, he hooked it into the rope that trussed her in the black bags. Satisfied, he went up the ladder and then, pulling the steps up behind him, picked up the slack rope that was attached to the pulley on top of the tackle and gradually pulled Elaine up into the loft.

It was easier than he'd expected. She lifted up as easy as pie and when she was dangling, her exposed head hanging sideways, staring at him as if in surprise, he tied the rope around one of the lower purlings and surveyed his handiwork. He felt almost gleeful again.

Elaine's body was swaying gently to and fro and he watched her in fascinated amusement. Her skin was a greeny-grey colour now and he thought she looked quite ill. He shrugged. The sooner he tucked her away the better.

But he had other things to do first. Placing the steps down once more, he climbed down and retrieved the loft hatch from the bed. Then he replaced it carefully, leaving Elaine dangling there in the dark loft. He took the steps and put them back in his shed then he walked purposefully into the kitchen. He looked around at the chaos and made little tutting noises before rolling up his sleeves and filling the sink with hot water.

He certainly had his work cut out for him today!

It took him all of three hours to clean the kitchen. The pristine white floor tiles would not come up to their usual standard. The blood left rust-coloured marks and finally he took out a bottle of Domestos and spread it liberally over the tiles. The thick liquid was then spread evenly, ammonia burning George's hands and eyes. Finally he was finished and the floor looked better. Much better. But the stains were still visible. He tutted again and shrugged. He had done his best.

He polished through the house and hoovered thoroughly. He changed the sheets on his bed, and the counterpane, then made himself an omelette. He glanced at the clock. It was seven fifteen.

Washing up his plate, he left it to drain. He went into the lounge, closed the curtains and put on the lamp. He turned on the television and put on channel 3, then page 251 on the Ceefax. He studied the holidays first, imagining himself in Thailand with some little Thai woman. He had read somewhere that you could pick up a bar girl for about two dollars a night. One day he would treat himself to that. It was a pity Elaine hadn't had a heart attack or something. He could have claimed the insurance money.

He flicked to the page of cheap flights. He saw what he wanted immediately: ORLANDO FLYDRIVE 21 NIGHTS 23 FEB.

Friday.

He would turn up at Edith's house, telling her how Elaine had left him for another man. In her delight at seeing him so unexpectedly, she would soon forget why he was actually there. He would have to box clever this end though, with Elaine's friends, but he would cross that bridge when he came to it. It's a shame her parents were dead. He could have said she was staying with them.

He picked up the phone by his side and dialled the number on the screen. People were there to take your calls until nine thirty. Within five minutes he was booked on a flight, had paid with his credit card and arranged to pick up his tickets and visa at Gatwick Airport.

He replaced the receiver and sat back in the chair. Tomorrow night he had his leaving do. He would go to that. That left tomorrow and Thursday to sort out the final details. He sighed with contentment.

Busy, busy, that was him. For the first time in his life he was at the centre of things and he loved it. He was in total control.

George phoned work at ten on Wednesday morning. He asked politely for Mrs Denham and waited nervously until her voice crackled over the line.

'Hello?'

'Mrs Denham, it's George Markham here.'

The line went quiet and he rushed on.

'I want to apologise about the other day. I'm afraid it all came as rather a shock . . .'

His voice was as sweet as honey.

'I understand. I think we had a communication break-down somewhere.' George could hear the smile in her voice. 'If you would prefer not to come back to work, I can arrange it for you.' Her voice was hesitant again now.

'Is that really possible? Only my wife is dreadfully ill . . .'

'Of course, I'll arrange it immediately.'

George sensed that she was glad to be rid of him and his mouth set in a grim line.

'About the money . . .'

'Oh, that will be paid into your bank account in about three weeks' time. That's the earliest I can manage it, I'm afraid.'

'That's fine. Lovely. Thank you very much.'

'You're welcome. And good luck.'

'Thank you, 'bye.'

Josephine Denham replaced the telephone and felt a moment of exquisite pleasure. What she was doing for George Markham was not strictly allowed, but to get rid of that man she would do anything. He gave her the creeps. She wanted him paid off and out as soon as possible.

Tony Jones was nervous. He had been in Grantley since ten thirty in the morning, acclimatising himself to the place. What a dump! In Tony's estimation, the Smoke was the only place to be. All these green fields disturbed him. Full of cow shit more than likely.

He sat in the Wimpy Bar in the town centre and watched people coming and going for the blood testing. He licked his lips again, his hand going nervously to the passport in his jacket pocket. He had paid out a good slice of wedge for it, and had yet to recoup the money from George Markham. He felt an insane urge to walk into the police vehicle nearby and tell them he knew who the Grantley Ripper was. He knew it was the decent thing to do. But Tony Jones loved money more than anything.

He wanted the three thousand from George and then he would go and see Kelly and do some kind of deal. He knew Pat Kelly well enough to know that if he found out Tony had had the Ripper's name and had not furnished him with it immediately, then Tony Jones was as good as dead. Besides, there was the money Kelly was offering . . .

He'd get this blood testing out of the way first, then he would approach Kelly.

It was lunchtime and Tony noticed that the line of men going in for blood testing was getting longer. In their lunch hour? Tony shook his head in wonder. If he was one of them he would use it as an excuse to skive off for an afternoon or morning.

People amazed him, they really did. They never had their eye on the main chance.

He ordered another coffee and watched. It was going to be a long day.

George had bathed and felt rosy and pink. That's what his mother used to say. Rosy and pink after a nice hot bath. He dressed himself in a pair of pyjamas that had seen better days, and putting on his slippers set about getting the ladder so he could go once more up into the loft.

Elaine was still hanging there and George smiled at her. Poor thing! She must be frozen. Then, going to the corner of the loft, he rubbed his hands together and stood staring at the water tank.

Elaine's final resting place.

The houses in George's street had been built before the war and still boasted the old sixty-gallon water tanks. Most of the houses in the road had been modernised, but George and Elaine had never really bothered with theirs. The water tanks were so big, they'd been put in before the roof of the house went on. Consequently, when people modernised, they had to leave the old galvanised water tank in the loft, as there was no way to remove it. In

George and Elaine's case, it still provided the water for the toilet and bath, and they had a small floor-mounted boiler in their kitchen to run the central heating. George lifted the lid off the tank and stared down into the water. A dead mouse floated on top. He picked it up by its tail and threw it into the corner, shuddering.

The tank was four feet by three feet and about three feet deep. George felt a moment of panic. Suppose she wouldn't fit?

Putting the hatch back, so he could move about more freely, George turned on the lights and began the job of getting Elaine's body down from the block and tackle. She dropped with a loud thud on to the dusty floor and he began the difficult task of dragging her to the tank.

The loft had been boarded out and around the sides were boxes of old photographs and clothes, old curtains, even an iron bedstead, unscrewed and leaning gently against the roof joists.

George dragged her body, his pyjamas already sweat-stained and covered in dust, over to the tank. Then, with a mighty heave, he pulled her up off the floor and pushed her head first inside. The water immediately overflowed from the tank and George cursed. The icy cold shock took his breath away. He lifted Elaine's legs and tried to push her into the tank. He tried to bend her in two but her fat belly would not allow this and still the water was spilling out everywhere. His slippers were soaked as were his pyjamas. The water was funnelling into the black sacks and making it even more difficult for him to grasp hold of her.

In the end, in sheer temper, he dragged her out of the tank and dumped her unceremoniously on to the soaked floor. His heart was crashing in his chest and he put his hand on it, feeling the thudding sensation of life with satisfaction.

Then he heard a low gurgling sound and his heart stopped dead. He flicked his head towards Elaine's body. Her face was on the floor, the skin squeezed up into grey wrinkles, and water was running out of the side of her mouth. All the gasses inside her and the trapped air were dislodged with the intake of water and she actually sounded as if she was groaning.

George felt a moment's sick apprehension before it dawned on him what was happening.

He prodded her with his slippered foot and she groaned again, accompanied this time by a loud breaking of wind.

He grinned, all the fear leaving him.

He had thought she was still alive!

He knew she would kill him for leaving her trussed up like a chicken overnight.

He began to laugh, a high cackling sound bordering on hysteria. She made the watery gurgle again and he had to sit on the edge of the water tank, tears streaming down his face. Oh, he hadn't had so much fun in ages.

He wiped his eyes with his hands and laughed himself hoarse. Then, finally, he calmed.

It was a quick change. From roaring good humour his face closed up and a cold calculating look appeared.

He knew what he had done wrong. He hadn't drained the water.

Picking up the ballcock in the water tank, he tied it with a piece of string so it was against the side of the tank. Then he opened the loft hatch and went down to the bathroom, opening the taps in the sink and bath. He did the same in the kitchen. He put the kettle on and had a coffee. His wet pyjamas were making him feel cold now and he slipped his overcoat over them to keep warm.

He drank hot coffee gratefully and then went back to

work. The tank was empty now. He dragged Elaine up the side and pushed her into it head first. Then he went around the other side and, dragging her under her oxters, sat her upright in it, forcing her legs inside. Then he pushed her head down between her knees and shoved with all his might. She stayed as she was.

In the process of dragging her inside, the ballcock was dislodged from where he had tied it on the joist and he placed it now at the small of Elaine's back. It was far enough away from the water line there.

Finally George picked up the lid and popped it on the tank. He was happy again.

He tidied up the loft as best he could and then dropped himself down on to the landing. He had better get himself cleaned up. He was going out tonight.

He put the water back on and ran himself another bath. George's mind was on the night ahead.

Elaine was forgotten now as the water tank began to fill slowly, very slowly, because the ballcock was trapped in the small of her back.

Tony Jones sat in the small Portacabin, nervously practising the answers to the questions he knew they would ask.

He was so nervous that when they asked him his name he nearly said 'Tony Jones'. Now they were calling for George Markham and he was sitting there wondering why no one answered. He stood up uncertainly.

'Sorry, I was miles away.' He smiled at the two men.

'This way, sir.'

He followed them into the tiny office next door and sat down.

'My name's Doctor Halliday and I will be taking your blood. Would you mind removing your jacket, please?'

Tony smiled widely.

She wasn't a bad-looking sort. Bit on the thin side, but then, educated women always were. Or so he'd found, anyway.

He removed his jacket and rolled up the sleeve of his shirt, sorry now that he had not put on a cleaner one. He was conscious of the smell of stale sweat under his arms. He saw the doctor wrinkle her nose and felt himself blush. The older of the two policemen smiled at him and sat carelessly on the desk. Tony guessed he was enjoying his discomfort and frowned.

Bloody Filth, they were all the same. He concentrated on the job in hand.

'Right, Mr Markham, where do you work?'

Tony took a deep breath and grimaced as the needle was plunged into his vein.

'I work at Kortone Separates.'

'Address?'

'Units 16 to 38, Grantley Industrial Estate.'

'Phone number?'

'04022 795670.'

Tony felt the doctor swab his arm and apply a small round plaster. He began to roll down his sleeve, glad to be putting his jacket on again. The other policeman came into the room. He smiled at the doctor, nodded at Tony and spoke to his colleague.

'He's the last one, we can shut up shop now.'

'Thank Christ. You going down the pub?'

'Yeah. Shall I get you a pint in?'

'All right, see you in about ten minutes.'

Tony was amazed as how easy it was.

The other man left and the policeman turned to Tony again. 'Got any identification please, sir?'

He produced the passport from his pocket and the man

glanced at it then took the passport number down.

'Would you sign this, sir, and then you can go.'

Tony signed the declaration and was outside the Portakabin within thirty seconds.

He couldn't believe it! No wonder they couldn't catch the Grantley Ripper. After what he had just witnessed, he would he amazed if they could catch the bus!

Shaking his head, he made his way to his car. He was meeting George at eight thirty. He looked at his watch. It was just after seven. Give him time to get a few drinks down him. He needed them.

George was ready. He checked himself over once more in the mirror and smiled.

Not bad. Not bad at all. He smoothed his scanty hair down with the palms of his hands and grinned. He was in the mood for an outing now. He was going on his holidays the day after tomorrow and the thought cheered him. Elaine was gone from his thoughts.

He imagined Edith's face when he knocked on her door. He felt a little jiggle of excitement inside his chest. It was going to be a wonderful holiday.

He locked the house up carefully before leaving and drove out to the Lion Rampant. He arrived there just after seven thirty and walked into the deserted bar. Tony Jones was sitting tucked away in the corner. George walked to him and sat down opposite.

'You're early.'

'So I am. Would you like another drink?' Tony nodded, nonplussed at the gaiety in George's voice.

'I'll have a large Scotch.'

George went up to the bar and got the drinks. When they were settled he smiled at Tony.

'Got the passport?'

'You got the money?' Tony's voice was hard and George pursed his lips.

'It's in the car.'

'Well, go and get it then.'

'Don't be silly, the barman's watching us like a hawk. People remember things, you know. He'll remember seeing us exchanging envelopes. No, we do the business outside.'

Tony screwed up his eyes and sipped his drink. It made sense.

'All right. I took the test. I tell you now it was difficult. They asked me lots of awkward questions . . .'

George was immediately alert.

'I hope you didn't muck it all up?'

Tony was aware of the underlying threat in his voice. 'They're due at my firm tomorrow. I don't want any worries, Tony.'

He realised his mistake. He was trying to impress on George that he had earned his money and all he had done was make him nervous. And George nervous made Tony nervous.

'Don't worry, I did a great job, I swear it. They never guessed a thing, honest.'

George visibly relaxed and so did Tony.

He kept forgetting that George was a murderer. A dangerous man. If only he didn't look so nondescript. All the murderers he had ever read about or known – and he had known a few in his time – had looked a few sandwiches short of a picnic. But this bloke here, he looked like a flasher. A weekend pervie. He looked like a lot of things – but not a murderer.

He didn't look dangerous. But he was.

'Drink up and we'll get going. I have an appointment.'

Tony tossed back his Scotch and they walked out into the cold air. He followed George to his car.

'Where's the money?'

George opened the door and motioned for him to get into the car. Tony sat in the passenger seat. The nervousness was back.

'Show me the passport, please.'

Tony slipped it from his pocket and George glanced at it in the dim glow of the car light.

'Where's the temporary one I gave you?'

Tony took that from his pocket. George put both passports into the glove compartment and then turned to face Tony.

'I'm not paying you a penny.'

'You what!'

'I said, I'm not paying you, Tony.' George grinned. 'Oh, come on, you never really thought I would, did you? I thought you were a man of the world.'

George chuckled. He was enjoying himself.

Tony's mind was reeling. He stared into George's eyes and realised he had been wrong earlier. George like this, with that horrible throaty chuckle and his feverish eyes, *did* look like a murderer. He looked diabolical.

Tony saw his mouth opening wider and the dark cavern that held his pink tongue seemed to draw him. He saw not only the money for the passport going down the Swanee, but also the blackmail money.

George held all the cards, because he knew Tony was frightened of him.

'Let's just say that we had a little misunderstanding regarding the money, shall we, Tony?'

He dropped his gaze and nodded.

George grinned to himself.

'Good man. Now if you don't mind, I have an important engagement.'

Tony slipped from the car and watched as George drove

away. Then he went back into the pub and ordered himself another large Scotch.

The barman looked at him curiously and Tony took his drink and went back to the corner table.

There was only one avenue left open to him: Patrick Kelly.

It wasn't just the money now, either. He wanted to see George get his comeuppance.

There was just one cloud on the horizon. How to give the name to Kelly without his own involvement being discovered. If Kelly found out that he had known the murderer of his daughter and had not told him . . . If he found out that he, Tony Jones, had taken the blood test for the man responsible . . . Tony felt faint with fright just thinking about it. How the hell had he got so embroiled?

A little voice in the back of his head said: 'Because you're greedy, Tony, that's why.'

He tossed back the drink and stayed sitting in the bar. There was a way to see Kelly and he would work it out, but it would take a bit of thinking about.

He was going to pay George Markham back a hundred-fold and save his own skin at the same time.

George walked into the smoky heat of the Fox Revived and there was Peter Renshaw and a crowd of other men standing at the bar. Peter saw him and shouted: 'Here he is, the man of the moment!'

George smiled. All the others smiled back. He had a drink thrust into his hand and smiled again. He didn't mind the warehouseman being there now. In his euphoric state of mind they were his bosom pals. He was pleased with the turnout. If only Elaine could see him now. Why, there must be twenty-five men here. For his leaving do. For him.

Renshaw slapped his back and brought his red beery face close.

'We'll have a few more here and then we'll make tracks to a nightclub. I know just the place. Drink up, man. We're a good few ahead of you!'

One of the warehousemen, a large, bulky man called Pearson, winked at George and then shouted to the barmaid: 'Another round here, love.'

He belched loudly and George felt his familiar distaste, but tonight he fought it down.

He was going to enjoy himself if it killed him.

He drank his brandy straight down and felt another being pushed into his hand almost immediately. The pub was filling up and the noise was getting louder. People were coming and going. George's crowd had taken over the right-hand side of the bar. He was in the midst of the crowd. For the first time in his life he felt he belonged. The men from the warehouse made him feel welcome. They patted him on the back and wished him good luck. They made dirty remarks about Mrs Denham's breasts and George felt a part of it all. When they left an hour later, in two minibuses, he was elated.

Renshaw certainly knew how to enjoy himself, by God. George regretted now not going on all the other dos Renshaw had planned.

The minibuses stopped outside a club in the seedier part of Grantley. They piled out on to the dirty pavement, then Renshaw produced a pile of tickets and they all walked boisterously past the dark-suited men on the door. George had heard of the Flamingo Club, indeed he had once wanted to join it, but the fear of Elaine finding out had put him off. Now here he was, sitting at a table with his friends and waiting for the pretty girls in their scanty outfits to serve them drinks.

The lights dimmed and a spotlight came on, illuminating the tiny dance floor. All the men cheered as a woman walked out into the bright light. She was wearing a schoolgirl outfit and her hair was in two long plaits that somehow stood out from her head like a St Trinian's girl. She had large freckles painted over her nose and her breasts strained against the tunic.

George's eyes were shining with excitement.

The strains of 'Daddy's Gonna Buy Me a Bow-Wow' crackled out of the speakers.

The woman bent over, showing navy blue school knickers, pulling them away from her body. The men all shouted in satisfaction as the pink slit was revealed. George looked around him in wonderment. He was surprised to see another drink in front of him and drank from it greedily, smacking his lips together as he had seen the warehouseman do.

His eyes never left the stage now as the woman began undressing, the men cat calling and whistling. She walked over to their tables and, grinning, sat on one of the warehousemen's laps, her legs spread. She gently rubbed herself up and down his legs. Then, undoing her side buttons, she let her tunic top fall to the floor. Her large baggy breasts sprang free and she pushed them into the man's face. George was enthralled.

Getting up, she pulled the navy knickers up her belly, so the lips of her vagina poked out of the sides, then gradually she began to pull them down, her eyes roaming over the men as she did this as if it was a personal show for each of them.

Then the music stopped, the lights went off and she was gone, amid clapping, whistling and stamping of feet.

Next was a female impersonator. A few tables away was a crowd of young men on a stag night. They had been served chicken and chips in baskets and the man on the stage, his face garishly made up under a deep red wig, walked to one of the young men and said: 'Here, love, do you know the difference between a big cock and a chicken leg?'

The boy went red and shook his head, his friends roaring with laughter. The man put his arm around him and said, 'Want to come on a picnic?'

George laughed as hard as the rest of them. He was amazed to find that he now had three separate drinks in front of him. Peter caught his eye and winked and George felt sudden affection for him, his usual annoyance forgotten. Peter had arranged this and George would remember that to his dying day. He was where he should be. Among men who liked what he liked. Who saw women for what they really were.

The female impersonator was finished and another stripper came on. Peter Renshaw called to the impersonator and he walked over to their table in a parody of a woman's wiggle.

'Hello, Peter, how are you?'

'All right, Davey. We're on a leaving do. How much for the live show?'

The impersonator grinned.

'Same as usual, Peter. You do the whip round and I'll sort out the girls. Don't forget my drink on top, will you?'

Renshaw grinned. 'Good man.'

The impersonator laughed. 'Do you mind?'

'Come on, lads, get your dosh out, we've got ourselves a live show.'

He turned to George. 'Ever seen one before?'

He shook his head, amazed.

'You'll love it, Georgie boy. Great fun.'

He got up from the table and went to the others. Men

were putting in money hand over fist. On his own table a pile of money now stood in the centre so George took out his wallet and put twenty pounds in the kitty. That was the average amount men were contributing.

Within minutes, Peter had arranged it all. George was impressed. The bouncers on the door had fifty each to lock up for the duration and the girls themselves had been paid. There was an air of expectancy in the club now.

George had removed his jacket. He licked a film of perspiration from his lips.

The spotlight was back on and two women were standing semi-naked, chatting together and smoking cigarettes while the floor was being set up. The young bridegroom-to-be and one of the warehousemen had been unanimously chosen to be the star performers and all the other men waited with bated breath for the real show to start.

The female impersonator came out with a microphone and announced that he would be the master of ceremonies. The young bridegroom and the warehouseman were stripped naked, the women put their cigarettes out and, plastering professional smiles on their faces, walked on to the stage area, smiling and waving at the audience.

George was mesmerised. The two women knelt down and took the men in their mouths. There were bets going on as to who would ejaculate first. The warehouseman was gripping the woman's hair and forcing his penis into her mouth. His cronies were shouting with excitement.

'Go on, my son!'

'Choke the fucking bitch!'

The warehouseman was making lewd faces and thrusting his hips around, loving the attention.

The young groom-to-be could not even get an erection. He was laughing and at the same time totally embarrassed. Finally, one of the other men at his table got up and, pulling off his trousers, lunged for the girl.

'Here you are, get hold of that.'

A loud cheer went up.

George watched, entranced, as the women were used by the men. Finally, the female impersonator called an end to everything and the men returned to their tables like conquering heroes.

The two women left the stage exhausted. Their elaborate hairdos were hanging in lank strands and their body make-up was patchy and running with sweat.

All the men were ragging the warehouseman who was now dressing himself amidst shouting and swearing.

George sat among them. The show had excited him. His eyes were red-rimmed now and feverish. He had shouted himself hoarse along with all the other men.

In his wildest dreams he had never envisaged anything quite like this. For the first time in his life George was sharing his pastime with others. Others who were enjoying themselves with him.

He felt an absurd feeling of happiness that made him want to cry. He felt the sting of tears and hastily blinked them away.

Peter Renshaw noticed and put his arm around his shoulder.

'Cheer up, Georgie boy. It's your leaving do.'

He faced Peter and said, 'This has been the best night of my life, Peter. Thank you. Thank you so very much.'

Peter Renshaw was gratified that George had had a good time. He had always felt a sadness in George, a strangeness that at times had bothered him. He smiled at him now. The drink was making them feel maudlin, he decided.

'Have another, Georgie boy, there's another stripper on in a minute.'

He nodded and picked up his drink.

Someone proposed a toast to George and, pink with happiness, he watched them all raise their glasses. Another round of drinks was delivered to the table and the men began some serious drinking.

A little while later the two women who had provided the show came to the table fully dressed for their money. The older of the two, a hard-faced blonde, held out her hand to Peter Renshaw.

'We want our money, mate, now.'

Her voice was weary.

'How about a please then, you old boot?'

This from the warehouseman who had taken part in the earlier proceedings.

The woman turned on him.

'Why don't you shut your mouth and give your arse a chance?'

All the men began laughing at this. The warehouseman picked up a pint of lager, gesturing to the other men at the table. They all did the same. Then, as if all of one mind, they threw the drinks over the two women, soaking them.

George's eyes were shining and he shouted, 'That'll teach you your manners, you piece of dirty scum!'

All the men laughed, mostly in amazement.

'That's right, Georgie, you tell 'em.'

'Smack her in the mouth.'

George heard the calls and preened himself.

The older woman wiped her face and held out her hand again. 'I want the money. Please.'

Peter, sorry for them now, handed it over. They walked back to their dressing room despondently. It was always the same after a live show. The men turned on you, because deep down they were ashamed of what they'd done. Once the excitement wore off, they blamed you for their own perversion. They'd go home now to their wives or their girlfriends, full of themselves. Tomorrow their night out would be the talk of their pub. But inside, deep down inside, they were ashamed of themselves. Ashamed of what they had done or witnessed.

The younger girl was in tears and the older woman put her arm around her.

'They're all wankers, darlin', don't let it get to you. We got ourselves a couple of ton, that's the main thing. My eldest boy wants a mountain bike, what you spending yours on?'

She tried to bring a bit of normality to the conversation. It was the only way to survive.

Chapter Twenty-Five

Tony Jones had lain awake all night. His tossing and turning so disturbed his wife Jeanette that at three thirty she got up and slipped into their daughter's old room, now the spare. Tony smiled despite himself. She liked her Sooty and Sweep did his Jeanette.

Finally, after many hours of restlessness, he had the glimmer of a plan. The main thing to bear in mind was that Patrick Kelly was not a man to cross. After the turn out with the rent boys, he knew without a shadow of a doubt that he would not make Kelly's Christmas card list. He shrugged mentally. He never had anyway. All the same Kelly would not forget his part in the rent boy business for a long time. If he went to the repoman with any old cock and bull story, Kelly would see to it that he did not live long enough to collect his reward. If Kelly even suspected that he knew the name of his daughter's murderer . . . Tony swallowed heavily.

But, and there was always a but, if he pretended that he had been going over his customer lists and happened to notice a George Markham from Grantley on it. Or better still on his mailing list. Yes, that sounded much better. As if he had never actually met the man.

He bounced the ideas around in his head for a while, finally convincing himself that if he played it just right, he would come out of it all with a good few quid and his neck intact. The latter being the most important.

He would put his plan into action first thing in the morning.

George woke up to a fine, crisp day and grinned to himself. The previous night's events bundled into his mind, crowding it with erotic images. George hugged himself in the warmth of his bed. All his life he had wanted to be part of the men's world, and always he had had to stand on the edge of it. Watching as an outsider. Last night it was as if a door had been opened and he had crept through it into the magic world of men together. He had been drunk on the mystery of it. At one point, he had experienced an ecstasy so acute he had felt tears sting his eyes.

He left the warmth of the bed and went into the bathroom. He had a long, leisurely bath as he dwelt on memories of the night before.

By nine he had finished packing, had ticked off everything on his carefully prepared list. He had everything from lightweight clothes to sunglasses. He had bought these a few years before. They were mirrored. He could watch and stare and no one knew what he was looking at. George kept them lovingly in a leather case.

He allowed himself the luxury of imagining himself on the golden beaches of Florida, watching all the girls and women. He'd watched the travel programmes, he knew what to expect. He felt a thrill of anticipation. He was flying out at seven thirty the following morning and had decided to stay overnight at the airport hotel. Start his holiday properly. He would have to check in to his flight at five thirty, so he would need a good night's rest, a good meal, and then he could get on the plane and relax.

He checked his passport, then the one Tony Jones had procured for him. He put them in his jacket pocket. Poor Tony Jones, he had been ripped off. But, he reflected, the pornographer had deserved it.

The house was beginning to feel claustrophobic. George bent his head to one side, a look of concentration on his face. He listened avidly. Nothing. He kept thinking he could hear Elaine calling.

He shrugged. Let her call, he just wouldn't listen. He took his bags out to his car and then had an idea. He could go and visit his mother. He would like to see her before he saw Edith. Give her a nice surprise.

He grinned. If she knew he was going out to Edith's it would kill her. Maybe he would mention it. But then she would know where he was going. He frowned. He'd see how it went. Happy now that he had a plan in mind, he began to make himself ready in earnest. It was nice, he thought, to be busy. To be in demand. To be a . . . what did the youngsters call it nowadays? A free agent. He smiled to himself in satisfaction, that's just what he was.

Up in the top of the house Elaine's body shifted slightly with the pressure of the rapidly filling tank. The ballcock that had been trapped at the small of her back shifted position with her and the tank began to fill up faster.

Patrick Kelly had kissed Kate goodbye at six thirty and was on his way to see a man who had some news for him. Important news by all accounts. He clenched his fists in agitation. It had better be something concrete or he was going to explode.

The traffic into London was heavy, and Patrick's Rolls

Royce was duly stared at and discussed. Every set of traffic lights had people trying to look inside, thinking it was someone famous. Patrick Kelly smiled to himself. He was famous to an extent, only not in the way these people thought. The Rolls drew up behind a funeral cortège and Patrick frowned. He felt, rather than saw, Willy shift gears and banged on the partition, sharply shouting: 'You bloody dare, Willy, and I'll murder you!'

Willy changed down again and sighed. They would be stuck here for ages now. Pat was like an old woman these days. Kelly shook his head in wonderment. He could just imagine the mourners' faces when a Rolls Royce wheelspun around them. Willy was an animal at times.

'Just take your time, we'll get there soon enough.'

'All right, Pat.' Kelly could hear the sullenness in Willy's voice and said, 'Show some respect. It's a funeral, for Christ's sake.'

Willy kept his own counsel, but deep inside hoped that Porsche would one day do a stretch limo so he could go to his own funeral in style, and with a bit of speed and panache. The first corpse to do a ton!

He didn't mention it to Pat though. He had a sneaky feeling he wouldn't laugh.

Kate sneaked into her house at seven, grateful that no one was up. As she showered she heard her mother get up and the distant clatter of breakfast being made. She went into her bedroom and messed up the bed, smiling as she did so. At her age she should not have to worry about spending the night with a man, but it was respect really. Respect for her mother and her daughter. She felt the glow that still surrounded her body. The night had been a long one. With Patrick sex was a labour of love, and she had missed him. Oh, how she had missed him. She relived in her mind the slow deliberate lovemaking. She knew she was undone and did not care.

Her mother had come up trumps over the Australia business. It was remarkable that she had kept that money secret for so long. Kate felt a great surge of affection for her, knowing that Evelyn was just trying to take the burden from her. Lizzy was like a dog with six lamp posts at the thought of going. It was as if after all the trouble they had been having, everything had finally come together. All Kate wanted now was the Grantley Ripper – and she would get him. And when she did, she would see him put away for ever. Then she could concentrate once more on her family and Patrick. She was looking forward to concentrating on him.

Lizzy knocked on her bedroom door and walked in. 'Oh, Mum, I just woke up and the first thing I thought was: This time next month, I'll be in Australia! I just can't believe it. A whole six weeks holiday in Oz! I can't wait.'

Kate smiled at her daughter in genuine happiness.

'Come here, poppet.' She put out her arms and Lizzy fitted herself into them.

'Were you with that man last night, Mum? That Patrick Kelly?'

Kate looked into her daughter's face, so much like her own, and sighed gently. She nodded.

'I think you should hang on to him, he's really sexy.'

Kate grinned. 'Oh, so you think that, do you?'

'Mmm, I do actually.' She kissed her mother's cheek and stood up, looking very young and innocent in her long white nightie that seemed to hide the womanly curves.

'I wouldn't mind going out with him myself!' She flounced from the room laughing. Kate laughed too, but uneasily. Knowing what she did about her daughter's sex life the remark hurt. Not because of Patrick, but as yet another reminder of the fact that her daughter was more experienced than she was sexually. Kate forced the thought from her mind. Lizzy was nearly a grown woman and she had had problems – ones that Kate blamed herself for.

She admitted to herself that she would be glad, in a way, to see her off at the airport. She needed space from Lizzy, as much as Lizzy needed space from her. The thought made her sad.

She comforted herself. She was looking forward to waking up with Patrick in the mornings. But, more than anything, she was looking forward to spending the nights with him.

Larry Steinberg ushered Patrick into his office and the two men shook hands. He had been here once before. Larry Steinberg dealt with the law, the unacceptable face of it. He was also a fixer, and had taken care of some things for Patrick that he had thought beyond the fixing stage. Patrick did not like him, but he had a grudging respect for him. And to Patrick, in business, respect was often preferable to liking.

He had called on Larry to defend a couple of his repomen a few years earlier. They had gone round a man's house to repossess his car and been met by a crowbar and a sawn-off shotgun. Not unusual in their game; people were often far from happy when repomen appeared. One of his men, however, had removed the crowbar from the punter's hand and then buried it in his skull, leaving the man scarred, semi-paralysed, and suffering from epilepsy.

Larry had arranged for the Attempted Murder charge to be quashed and for a pretty stiff out-of-court settlement that had guaranteed a satisfactory outcome for all concerned. The sawn-off shotgun had mysteriously disappeared from the armoury of the Metropolitan Police and had since been used on two different robberies, but that was not Patrick's business. One thing he knew for sure was that the man who had been hit with the crowbar was the man behind the robberies. He was a gas meter bandit gone big time, and with his pay-off from Patrick's insurance and his medical records he was as safe as proverbial houses.

Larry blew his nose and sniffed loudly. His bulbous eyes were watering and he wiped them with his fingers. Patrick disguised his distaste as best he could.

'Right then, Larry, let's not beat about the bush – what you got for me?'

'It's to do with Tony Jones. He came to me a while ago for a passport.'

'What's that got to do with me?'

'The passport wasn't for him, it was for someone else, a bloke from Grantley.'

Patrick's ears pricked up.

'Go on.'

Larry Steinberg wiped his nose once more with a grubby handkerchief. He knew that if you drew your story out, people became impatient and listened better.

'He didn't pay me much, Mr Kelly.' His voice had taken on a whining tone.

Patrick closed his eyes.

'Look, Larry, you'll get the money on the fucker's head as soon as I have a face. Now tell me the geezer's fucking name! I ain't in the mood for games.'

Larry hurriedly obeyed.

'It was Markham. A George Markham'.

'Did Tony say why the bloke wanted a passport?'

Save the best till last, that was Larry's motto.

'That was the funny thing about it all – the passport

had Tony Jones's photograph in it.' He watched Kelly's expression and gabbled on: 'Now be fair, Mr Kelly, I'm just a fixer. If you pay me enough I'll fix up anything, but I knew that there was something wrong with all this and that's why I'm telling you. At first I didn't think anything, you know yourself what it's like. Then I read about the blood testing in Grantley and it came to me like – well, like a vision from God . . .'

He shook his head for maximum effect. 'I've dealt with bank robbers who wanted to retire abroad, the scum of the criminal world. But my life, Mr Kelly, I would not cover for a sadistic murderer. I heard through the grapevine that you were looking for the man who took your young daughter's life and thought it was my duty to inform you of what I knew.'

Larry Steinberg himself actually believed this now, so good was his acting.

Patrick nodded.

'I hope I have been of some little help?'

'You'll get the money, Larry, if this is the man, I promise you that.'

He held out his hand and Larry shook it. Feeling the animal strength of Kelly, he shuddered inwardly.

Poor Tony Jones. Still, he reasoned, Kelly had shaken hands on it, and from him that was as good as a signed contract. Steinberg had to stop himself from rubbing his hands together with glee.

That would have been in bad taste, even for him.

Patrick left the office. Getting into his Rolls Royce, he shouted to Willy: 'Tony Jones's gaff, now!'

Willy started the car and Patrick filled him in on what had taken place as they drove. By the time they reached the sex shop, both were ready to commit murder.

Emmanuel had been on his own all morning and was

exhausted. Tony hadn't even bothered to ring him to say when he would arrive. The only high spot had been two definite dates for later that night from two rather well-dressed city gents. Tony hated him procuring from the shop, even though it brought in business. He heard rather than saw Kelly and Willy come in. The door flew open, sending a display of *Masochist Monthly* magazines flying all over the floor.

'Where is he?' Patrick Kelly's voice was low and Emmanuel felt his fury.

'Who?' The boy's voice was high and squeaky.

'Tony fucking Jones, that's who. Who else would we come in here for? Princess Diana?'

'I don't know where he is. He didn't come into work today.'

Willy grabbed Emmanuel round the throat and shook him. 'Where's he live? I want his address now.'

A big man in working clothes walked into the shop and Patrick grabbed the front of his overalls and threw him out on to the pavement with such force he careered into some passers-by. By now the other shopkeepers had noticed what was going down and were watching the action from strategic points.

Emmanuel wrote down the address with shaking hands. His mascara was running into his eyes and making them sting.

Patrick took the proffered paper and nodded at Willy, who promptly set about tearing the shop apart. Emmanuel watched in terror.

Whatever Tony had done it must have been bad. He wondered briefly if he should start looking for another job.

When Willy had finished the two men left. Emmanuel looked at the debris around him and began to cry again.

The other shop owners came in when the coast was clear and, under the guise of helping Emmanuel calm himself, tried to prise some gossip from him. He thought it was to do with the time Kelly came in looking for the rent boys and told them so. But it was obvious he didn't really know too much about anything.

The story hit the streets in Soho within the hour, it was the talking point of the day.

People nodded their heads sagely. Tony Jones had always courted trouble and now it had knocked on his door.

Tony himself heard the news ten minutes before Kelly and Willy arrived at his house. While they banged down his door, Tony and a very frightened Jeanette were on their way to their eldest daughter's in Brighton.

Nancy Markowitz, as she now liked to be called, sat drinking a cup of hot steaming tea. Her daughter-in-law Lilian was making the beds. Nancy scowled to herself. A cat's lick, that's what Lily gave the house. When she herself had been younger her house had shone out like a beacon, showing all the neighbours how a house should be cleaned. She passed a malevolent eye over the skirting boards in the front room. They could do with a good dusting. What she wouldn't have given then for a nice house like this!

She shook her head. Lily had always been lackadaisical, even her children had never looked right. Pasty-faced little buggers they'd been. Still were, in fact. Nancy sipped her tea. Like cat's piss, Lilian didn't even know how to make a decent cup of tea. More than likely poured water over tea bags. Real tea leaves would be too much of a chore for her . . .

She was taking her time making the beds. Nancy

glanced at the clock. It was nearly twelve. She shook her head again. Imagine not making the beds till lunchtime. Lazy bitch.

She sat sipping her tea, building up in her mind every little thing she could against Lily; all the things she'd done or failed to do, real and imagined.

Nancy Markham had a knack of putting other people in the wrong. It had been a major asset all her life. It was her power over people and she used it, along with bullying and cajoling, to her own best advantage.

Lilian was actually lying on her own bed reading a magazine and having a cup of tea and a biscuit herself. Savouring the half hour away from her mother-in-law. It was the only time of the day she had wholly to herself, where her mother-in-law's voice wasn't intruding on her thoughts, her bell wasn't stopping her from working and her presence could not be felt like a malign force. Sometimes Lily thought that Nancy was a witch. Fanciful as that seemed it was the only logical reason why everyone should hate her so. Her own children included. How many times had Joseph promised, under cover of darkness and the duvet, that he was going to put her away in a home? And how many times had he come face to face with her and backed down? Too many times.

Though Lily admitted to herself that she would not relish the task herself. Nancy frightened her. She frightened her grandchildren. She frightened her son. Her son whom Lily had loved once with all her heart and now despised for his weakness, a weakness that she had played on herself since learning all the tricks from her mother-in-law. Even Elaine and drippy George had balked at Nancy coming to live with them.

Lilian tried to concentrate on her *Best* magazine. It didn't do to dwell on things in this house. It was oppressive enough. Still, the Rabbi was due tomorrow. Even though Nancy's following her Jewish faith annoyed Lily, it also gave her a free afternoon a week when she could go out of the house in peace, knowing that the young Rabbi would be too frightened to leave Nancy alone until she came back. She suppressed a grin. The poor boy's face when she finally arrived was a picture. Nancy, self-righteous and actually being friendly, was more scary than when she was her usual overbearing and evil self.

Lily forced her mind back to her magazine just as the doorbell rang. She pushed herself up on the bed. Who could that be? She jumped up and hastily brushed her clothes to get rid of any tell-tale biscuit crumbs. The bell rang again and she rushed from the room.

By now her mother-in-law's bell was also ringing. It was an old-fashioned school bell and Lily sometimes fancied that it tolled her life away. She hurried to the front door.

'Hello, Lily.' George stood on the step smiling at her.

'Oh . . . This is a surprise.'

He walked into the spacious hall.

'Where's Elaine?'

George visiting was a shock, but George without Elaine was an even bigger one.

'Oh, she's at work. I had a bit of time and I thought, I know, I'll go and visit poor Mother.'

Lily's face froze. Who on earth in their right mind would visit Nancy Markham, correction Markowitz, if they didn't have to?

Nancy's voice thundered from the front room.

'Lily, who is it? Who's knocking the bloody door down?'

She wished that the caller had been the young Rabbi; she'd have loved Nancy to drop her guard in front of him.

The bell began to ring furiously and George gestured with his head to the door on his right.

'I take it she's in there?'

He walked into the room.

'Hello, Mother.' His voice was meek once more. His mother always had that effect on him.

Nancy recovered her equilibrium fast.

'Oh, it's you, is it?'

George dutifully kissed her cheek. He could smell her lavender perfume and face powder.

'I thought I'd give you a little visit, see how you were faring.'

She snorted. 'I'm not ready for the knacker's yard yet, me boy, if that's what you're thinking.'

She rang the bell furiously again. George watched her large hand grasping the wooden handle and lifting it up over her shoulder then swinging it down towards the floor.

'Lily, bring in a pot of fresh tea.' They heard her scuffling across the hall from the kitchen. 'And make sure it's stronger than that gnat's piss you made earlier,' Nancy called.

She settled herself once more into her chair. So her son had decided to visit her, had he? A nasty smile played on her lips.

'Where's Ten Ton Tessie today?'

George smirked. She could be cruel, could his mother.

'Elaine's working, Mother.'

He sat himself down on the settee and glanced around the room. It really was lovely; high-ceilinged, it still had the original ornamental cornice and ceiling roses.

'She wouldn't have come anyway.'

George dragged his eyes from the ceiling. 'Who?'

'Elaine, of course. Who'd you think?' Nancy patted her outrageous orange hair. 'So what brings you here anyway?'

'Mother, I only came to say hello.'

'Tripe. You've never visited me before. You're in some kind of trouble.'

'What kind of trouble could I be in?' George's voice was low.

Nancy shrugged. 'How should I know? Have you done something wrong, Georgie boy? You can always tell me, you know.' Her voice became confidential and wheedling.

George surveyed her and was surprised to find that his fear of her seemed to have diminished today. Normally her bullying voice would leave him a bundle of nerves, her malevolent expression would set his heart galloping in his chest, but today, all she did was make him want to laugh at her.

'Do you ever hear from Edith, Mother?'

He felt the temperature in the room drop to freezing point and continued, 'I hear from her sporadically. She's doing awfully well, you know.'

He watched his mother's mouth set in a grim line. He was enjoying himself.

'Why aren't you at work?' It was an accusation.

'I'm retiring.'

'Huh! Being made redundant more like. Elaine told Mouth Almighty and she told me.' She poked herself in the chest with a pudgy finger.

George felt his confidence waning.

'They didn't want you any more, that's the truth of it. How old are you now? Fifty-one . . . fifty-two. You're over the hill, my boy.'

George was getting upset. Why had he come here? He knew what would happen, what always happened. He clenched his fists. Nancy was warming to her theme.

'You've never had what it takes, Georgie. You never even had any friends . . .'

'I have got friends. Lots of friends, Mother. I was out with my friends last night. I do wish you wouldn't always try and upset me. You're such a bitter pill, Mother, no wonder no one ever visits you. How the hell Joseph and Lily put up with you I don't know.'

His sister-in-law was walking into the room with the tea tray when he said the last part and she nearly dropped the whole lot with fright.

'What did you say?' Nancy's voice was like granite.

But George was too far gone now.

'You heard me, Mother, you've got ears like an elephant's. Always flapping around, listening to everything.' He spied the white-faced Lilian with the tray and forced himself to smile.

'Here, let me help you with that, Lily.'

'Put it on the coffee table, please.' Her voice was breathless.

Nancy watched her son through narrowed eyes. She was shrewd enough to guess that if she carried on in her present vein he would leave, and she didn't want him to leave. He was the first of her children to visit willingly, out of the blue, without being summoned.

'Shall I pour?' George's voice was strong again.

The only sound in the room was the clinking of cups and spoons, and the heavy ticking of the long case clock.

Lily watched the two people in front of her. It was like some secret dance going on before her eyes. Her mother-in-law was subdued now, watching her son under lowered lids. Her yellowing skin had a grey tinge to it that had not been there earlier.

George, on the other hand, looked well. Great, in fact. She could not remember seeing him look better. He had an assurance about him that was at odds with his appearance. George even dressed humbly. It was an odd

569

thing, and if Lily had not seen it for herself she would have sworn it was impossible. How could someone dress in a humble manner? Well, George did. Only today his white shirt, grey tie and navy blue hand-knitted tank top looked almost jaunty. She took her tea in silence.

There was a subtle shifting of position here and Lily was not sure whether or not she liked it. If George upset his mother, she, Lily, would be the recipient of Nancy's bad humour when he left.

'I'll take my tea out to the kitchen if you don't mind, I have things to finish out there . . .' She was gabbling. Awkwardly she left the room. Whatever the upshot she wanted no part of it – but she left the kitchen door wide open.

'Now then, Mother, this is nice, isn't it?' George's voice was determined.

Then Nancy smiled, a rare genuine smile. As it softened the hard lines of her face, George felt a lump in his throat. For a few seconds she looked young again. He saw the softness that she had sometimes displayed, that she had occasionally allowed through her veneer of hardness. It was the smile of the girl she had once been, a long, long time ago, before her marriage and her children and her other life.

Before the men.

George wished fervently he had known her then.

He had his illusions about his mother, he needed them. He could not accept that she had been an evil force since childhood. That she had been using men to her own advantage from the onset of adolescence. That Nancy Markham had spent her whole life using and abusing people, none more so than her own children.

'Over there in the sideboard are my photo albums. Bring them to me, Georgie.'

He collected the bulky albums and put them on his mother's lap.

'Sit down at my feet and we'll reminisce.'

George did as he was told, like the old days when her word was law.

Nancy began to flip the pages, her eyes soft with nostalgia.

'Here, look at this one, Georgie. Remember this?'

He knelt up and looked at the picture. It was of him, aged about five with his mother. She was wearing a two-piece swimsuit that had been racy in those days and peering into the camera with a sultry look. Her hair was perfect; her long shapely legs partly obscured by a little boy holding a large candyfloss. George saw his baggy shorts with sticklike legs emerging from them, his close-cropped hair and serious elfin face.

It was a day that had stuck in his memory because it had been a good day. A happy day. A rare day. The moment caught in his chest like a trapped bird, fluttering against his ribcage. He could smell the heat and the sand and the people. The donkeys, the candyfloss and the aroma of melting margarine in the jam sandwiches. Could almost taste the strawberry jam, gritty with sand from grubby fingers. Could almost touch once more the saltiness of the blue sea. It had been such a good day, from the train ride early in the morning to the sleepiness and exhaustion of lying in his crisp cold sheets ready to sleep the sleep of the dead. He could remember Nancy kissing him good night. Smiling down on him from her soft peachy face.

'Camber Sands that was, Georgie boy. Lovely days those were. I was a picture then. Could gather the looks and all, them days.'

'You still look wonderful, Mother.'

It was a kindly lie, what she wanted, expected to hear.

'Well, maybe not as good as I used to look but not bad for my age, eh?'

Her voice was softer too, almost jocular. When Nancy was talking about herself she was animated and happy.

She turned the page. This time the picture was of her alone. A head and shoulders shot. Lips just parted to show her perfect white teeth. Her deep copper-coloured hair framed her face and she had on bright orange lipstick. The picture had been hand coloured by the photographer and he had caught the exact shade of her hair and skin.

Nancy stroked the page with wrinkled fingers, caressing the photograph.

'I can remember this as if it was yesterday. The man who took the photograph said I should have been a model. Said I had a perfect bone structure.'

And he should know, thought George. He moved in with us for a while if I remember rightly. He squeezed his eyes tight shut. He could see that day so clearly. They had all had their photos taken and afterwards his mother had sent them home. He could picture Edith in his mind shepherding them on to the bus, then making them something to eat at home. Later on his mother had come back with the man, a large gregarious type with a tiny pencil moustache and a Prince of Wales checked suit. He had brought back their mother, rather drunk, and a parcel of fish and chips, which had endeared him to Joseph and George immediately as he had not forgotten them. He had also brought them a large bottle of Tizer, then made them all laugh with stories of his time in the army. Telling the two avid-eyed little boys about shooting the Boche.

Then, later that night, much later, George had woken with a tummy ache from the fish and chips and the Tizer. On his way to the toilet he had heard groans coming from his mother's room. Opening the door quietly he had investigated. He had seen his mother kneeling on the bed with the man. His hands were in her long thick hair, fanning it around her head, pulling on it. He was groaning.

'That's it, Nance. Take the lot, Nance.'

He could see his mother's naked body in the dim firelight, could see her head and mouth moving up and down on the man. Then the man had spied him. Pulling Nancy up by the hair, he had dragged a sheet across himself to hide his nakedness. Too late George saw the fury on his mother's face.

'Get out, you nosy little bugger!'

Then she was scrambling from the bed, her face twisted in temper, her lipstick smudged around her chin. She was stalking towards him with her long-legged stride, her mouth like a big gaping cavern.

He had been three years old.

'Here, Georgie, look at this one.'

He was dragged back to the present.

'Look at my dress. I remember saving up for that dress for ages.'

George forced himself to look at the picture. He could feel the rapid beating of his heart subside.

'Who's the girl with you?'

'That, Georgie boy, is Ruth Ellis.'

He peered closely at the picture.

'I worked her club. It was called the Little Club, of all things. In Knightsbridge.'

Nancy looked at her son, a half smile on her face, enjoying the shock she was creating.

George peered at the photograph again.

'She ran a brothel.'

'Hardly a brothel, Georgie boy. More like a gentlemen's club.'

George looked into her face and saw the gleam in her eyes. She was using her past now, the past she would not have mentioned to a soul, to try and undermine him, intimidate him. From religious grandmother, the epitome of decency, she was reverting to the days of her whoring to bring him low. He knew her so well. How sanctimonious she could be. He remembered her berating Edith when she had fallen pregnant that time; remembered the false impression of genteel poverty she liked to give to the neighbours. Remembered how she had told all and sundry of Edith's fall from grace. Now her real life could be used to hurt one of her children, to wound, and she used it without a qualm. He felt an urge to strike her.

Nancy watched her son's face and guessed what he was thinking. The old malice was back in her now.

'Someone once said to me: "Nancy, you're sitting on a gold mine." How right they were. And do you know who said it? Your father's brother. I ran off with him. Your father hadn't died, Georgie. I dumped him.'

'You said he was dead! I believed . . .'

Nancy laughed again. 'He is dead now. He died about ten years ago. The police traced me and told me. He died in a bedsit in South London. He'd been dead ten days before they found him. Cheeky buggers wanted me to pay for the funeral! I told them where they could get off and all. He was useless, Georgie, bloody useless. Couldn't even die properly. Alone to the last.'

He felt himself rise from the floor, aware that his legs had gone dead at some point from kneeling – and then he slapped her. He knew he had slapped her because he heard the crack as his open palm met her baggy flesh, felt the force of her head snapping back and heard her scream of outrage.

Lily, outside the door, was hopping from one foot to the other in agitation.

'You evil slut! You dirty filthy slut!' George had balls of spittle at the corner of his lips. 'My father was alive. He could have saved me from you. Could have saved all of us from your men friends and your evil ways. You let men touch me for money . . . Touch me and use me!'

His mind was like a burst sore, all his hatred spilling out. He was dangerously close to tears and swallowed them back.

'You fucking filthy whore! You stinking tart!'

All his life she had taken pleasure in hurting him, while she gave pleasure to others for a price. He felt bile rising in his throat, burning him. He pursed his lips together to stop it spewing out on to the woman sitting in front of him with the old mocking grin.

'None of my children ever had any gumption. You were all like him, weak and sickly. I hated you all.'

Her voice was filled with malice and something else.

It was fear.

She was scared of him, of what she had caused. Of what the outcome might be.

George dropped back into a seat. Suddenly he was exhausted. It had been a mistake to come here. He should have known that. She had stolen his childhood, his innocence and his father.

The last he could never forgive.

The number of times he had run away from her, only to be brought back, when all the time he'd had a father he could have run to. A man to take care of him properly.

He looked at his mother as if for the first time. He finally hated her one hundred per cent. She disgusted him. She was a whore. They were all whores, every last one of them.

Suddenly he began to laugh, a high-pitched laugh bordering on hysteria, and it was that frightening sound that brought Lily bursting into the room.

The old bitch! All those years of her sanctimonious rambling, listening to Joseph pandering to her, coming second to the paragon of virtue who rang her bell like a demented school mistress and shouted, 'Get me this, get me that!' When in reality she had been a common prostitute!

'You lying old cow!' All Lily's hard-won refinement was gone now.

'You was on the bleeding bash!'

Nancy stared at her daughter-in-law, eyes like pieces of flint.

'You've driven us all up the bloody wall. Well, that's it now, my girl. It's a home for you. I don't care how much it costs. Wait till Joseph gets in! I'll give you Ruth Ellis! It's a pity they didn't bloody well hang *you*, you old bitch!'

George wiped his eyes with his handkerchief and with a final glance at his now terrified mother, walked from the room and out of the front door. Lily's shouting carried after him.

He started the car. On the back seat was his suitcase, packed and ready for his holidays.

Wait until he told Edith. George knew he would never see his mother again.

Patrick Kelly made his way to Brighton. It had not taken him long to find out the addresses of Tony Jones's family. If necessary he would take the elder daughter hostage until Jones came forward. It wouldn't take long for the whisper on the street to get back to him, Patrick knew that.

The Rolls Royce pulled up at an address in Steyning. Kelly nodded at Willy and they slipped from the car. Inside the small bungalow Tony Jones was drinking Scotch while his wife watched him. On his lap was his granddaughter Melanie.

She loved her grandad and cuddled into his big flabby frame. It was Tony's daughter who answered the door and she stood by silently as they walked in.

Patrick nodded at the girl. She was not part of this, he knew that.

'Where is he, love?'

She pointed to a door at the end of the passageway. 'In there. Look, Mr Kelly, my daughter's in there . . .'

He ignored her and walked into the room.

'Hello, Tone, long time no see. I've come to take you for a little drive. Have a chat like.'

Tony Jones blanched. The little girl on his lap sensed his fear and hugged him tighter.

Kelly looked at the long blond hair and enormous blue eyes. She could have been his Mandy as a child. He put out a hand and touched the soft downy head.

'Hello there, my darling. What's your name?'

The little girl looked up at the man and grinned, exposing tiny pearl-like teeth.

'Melanie Daniels and I'm three.'

'You're a big girl for your age, aren't you? Let Grandad get his coat, darlin', while me and you have a little chat.'

The child looked at her grandad and was glad when he nodded assent. She decided she liked the big man in the big coat. Willy watched fascinated as Patrick took the girl's tiny hand. He then accompanied Tony Jones while he got his coat. Tony opened his mouth to speak and Willy silenced him.

'You must have been barmy if you thought you could pull one over on Pat where that scumbag's concerned.'

Tony hung his head.

Melanie was sitting on Patrick's knee, regaling him with stories about her life.

'I've got a little cat called Sooty. Have you got a cat?' Patrick shook his head.

'How about a little doggie? You got a little doggie?'

Patrick smiled at her with genuine good humour. She was an enchanting child.

'Can I make you a coffee, Mr Kelly?' Jeanette's voice was flat. She knew enough about Patrick Kelly to know her granddaughter was safe. She had known Renée many years before. She knew that he would remember that.

'Why not?' Patrick looked into her eyes. 'I'm sorry about this, Jeanette, but you know the score.'

She couldn't meet his gaze so got up and went to the kitchen. Willy and Tony came back into the room.

'And I go to play school.' Melanie was still chatting and Patrick was enjoying the conversation.

'Really? What do you do there?'

Melanie bit her top lip in consternation as she thought.

'We do singin' and paintin', sometimes. I can sing "The Wheels on the Bus", all the way through.' This last bit of information was given with a toss of her long blond hair and Kelly laughed.

'You're a clever little girl, Melanie.'

'My grandad says I'm as pretty as a picture. And he sings me songs. Don't you, Grandad?'

Tony nodded his head, watching the scene in front of him.

Patrick looked at him as he spoke. 'And what songs does he sing you?'

'Can I sing one, Grandad? Please?'

Tony nodded again and she began to sing.

Patrick let Tony Jones sit stewing for another twenty minutes before he decided to leave. By this time Melanie had become so enamoured of him she screamed the place down because she wanted to go with them. Her cries followed them from the house.

She had insisted on a kiss from all three of them, and Willy had had to be scowled at severely by Patrick before he complied. Patrick, on the other hand, had stroked her hair and comforted her before leaving, enjoying the innocence and babyness of her; an innocence that had reminded him of another life, one where he had had a wife and a child.

In the car, he turned to Tony.

'A lovely child. You must be proud of her?'

Tony nodded, he couldn't answer.

'Wasn't she a lovely little thing, Willy?'

He half turned from his driving. 'Oh, yeah.'

Patrick continued conversationally.

'Imagine how you'd feel if someone took her, buggered her, and then left her for dead on a filthy floor. Half her skull battered away, hair stuck to the floor in a pool of blood. If you had to watch her die, slowly and painfully, in the hospital. Watch her fight for her life, after operations to cut her skull away bit by bit because her brain was so swollen inside her head. Makes you sick just thinking about it, don't it?'

Tony's nod was barely noticeable.

'Well, now maybe you'll understand why you're going to get the hiding of your fucking life, won't you? But first I want that cunt's address, phone number, post code. I want to know everything you know about him. All right?'

Tony nodded again.

At least Kelly hadn't said he was going to kill him. As far as Tony was concerned, that in itself was a result.

Book Two

'Hanging is too good for him,'
Said Mr Cruelty
             – John Bunyan, 1628–88

A rape! A rape!
Yes, you have ravish'd justice.
Forced her to do your pleasure
             – John Webster, 1580–1625

Life for life,
Eye for eye, tooth for tooth,
Hand for hand, foot for foot.
Burning for burning, wound for wound,
Stripe for stripe
                     – Exodus, 21:23

Chapter Twenty-Six

George booked himself into the Hilton Hotel at Gatwick. He was feeling upset. He knew he would not sleep.

He opened his suitcase. He had packed one of his favourite books and tonight he needed it. He needed the release from the real world. He opened the magazine at the centre pages. A girl was looking up at him. She had real auburn hair. George knew it was real because it was the same top and bottom.

He slipped off his clothes and hung them up neatly in the wardrobe, then relaxed on the bed in his underpants. This time tomorrow he would be in the USA. He allowed himself a grin. He'd be in Florida, starting a new life.

His tongue was just poking from the corner of his mouth now as he concentrated his energies, thinking up different situations and pastimes for the girl on the page.

George was beginning to feel better.

Patrick smiled at Tony Jones.

'So what you're saying is, Tony, you took the blood test for the bloke?'

He nodded, his eyes aimed at the floor.

'You actually went and took the blood test – the blood test that *I'm* paying for – so that piece of shite could walk free?'

'It wasn't like that, Mr Kelly. He had me by the bollocks . . .'

'I'll have you by them in a minute, mate.' Willy's voice was low and menacing.

Tony looked at Patrick in distress.

'I've been selling snuff movies. He bought them. Said he'd rope me into it . . .' His voice was desperate.

It was quiet for a while. Kelly and Willy both stared at the man in front of them with slitted eyes, as if trying to understand just what it was in front of them.

'Snuff movies? You sell snuff movies. You deal with scum who rent out little boys, you sell death, and you want me to be lenient with you? You want me to say, "Oh, don't worry, Tone, long as you make a good bit of bunce . . ."'

Patrick swung back his fist and began punching Tony Jones in the face and head. He could feel the bruising on his knuckles as they came into contact with the man's skull, felt the first trickle of blood as Jones's eyebrow split, and still he could not stop. Rage was inside his head, fuelled by the pictures of Mandy's broken face and body. The knowledge that she had been buggered, raped and humiliated by a sadist who had no more thought for her than he'd have had for a mad dog.

And it was all this man's fault! He pandered to him, was the means by which this George Markham fed his sick fantasies. Finally, spent, he walked to the corner of the lock-up garage. Outside he heard the scraping of the Rottweiler belonging to one of his repomen. It sniffed underneath the door, making tiny whining sounds. Every so often he heard Jimmy Danks quieten the beast. It occurred to Patrick that Tony could be dead soon.

He shrugged. He didn't really care at this moment. He blinked back tears; whether they were of rage or sadness he wasn't sure. All he could think about was his child. That took precedence over everything. There was nothing he could do to bring Mandy back. He accepted that, but he would find this George Markham and make him pay dearly for what he had done. Not just for Mandy but for all of them.

He heard a groan and turned to see Tony Jones regain consciousness. Patrick watched him pull himself up from the dirty floor and sit back on the broken-down chair. He opened the lock-up door and nodded at the man with the Rottweiler. Then he took one last look at Tony Jones and, gesturing for Willy to follow, walked from the lock-up.

The dog was straining on its leash now, scenting the air. Its huge jaws were clamping down, making snapping noises. Kelly stood by his car in the deserted block and watched as the man took off the lead and let the dog run into the garage, closing the door behind it.

By the time Tony Jones realised what was happening, one hundred and twenty pounds of muscle had already launched itself at him.

Kelly and Willy drove away to sounds of his anguished screams. The dog's owner was rolling himself a cigarette. He waved to them cheerfully as they drove off.

George had dressed and left the hotel at eight thirty-seven. He could not relax tonight. Even the book had done little to make him feel better. His mother had upset him so much. He drove around for a while, his head whirling with the things she had said.

His father had not been dead. He remembered only a tall thin man with dark blond hair and a smell of tobacco about him. George remembered sitting with the man on a large easy chair. Then one day he had gone.

His earliest memory of his mother was of her picking him up and kissing him on the mouth, holding him to her tightly even though he had wanted to get away. Her arms had been like steel bands around him.

He shuddered.

A car hooted its horn and he broke out of his reverie to find that he was at a roundabout. He pulled away and took the first turning. He looked at the signpost and saw that he was on the A26 going towards Maidstone. That was how upset he was. He had been driving, unaware even where he was going.

Only his mother could upset him like that.

He pulled off at the slip road that led to Nettlestead. It was half past nine. George drove along slowly, trying to gather his thoughts.

Then he saw a woman about thirty yards in front of him. She was standing by a large Range Rover, actually flagging him down!

George pulled up behind her and wound down his window. Cynthia Redcar rushed towards him, her large man's parka blowing open as she ran. She had been stranded there for thirty minutes.

'I say, I'm awfully sorry to trouble you, but my car's gone on the blink.'

George saw white teeth and abundant black hair. She had a long jawline and anyone looking at her would guess that she was a 'horsey' kind of person.

'Could you please take me to get some help? I must phone my husband, he'll be worried sick.' She smiled at him again.

'What seems to be the trouble?'

She pulled the parka around her slim frame and grimaced. 'I don't know a thing about cars, I'm afraid. It just cut out and died on me. Oh Christ, here we go again.' She ran back to the Range Rover at the sound of a child whimpering.

George got out of his car and ambled after her.

The woman was holding a boy of about eighteen months to her breast, stroking the dark head gently and crooning the way only mothers know how. She lifted her eyebrows at George. 'Poor little blighter's cold and hungry.' She picked up her bag from the back seat and set about locking the Range Rover. She stood in front of George ready and waiting, her eyebrows raised in query.

He really was an odd little man, she thought. Hardly said a word. She began to walk towards the Orion in a determined way. Opening the back doors, she placed the now quiet child across the back seat and slipped in beside him, talking softly and stroking his legs. George saw the child close his eyes and relax. He was entranced at the pretty picture it created.

The woman saw him looking and grinned. 'Another three like this at home, I'm afraid. I hope Dicky remembers to feed them! He can be so unreliable at times. I'll bet he fed the horses though, he'd never forget about them!' She laughed gaily. George stared at her and she felt the first prickle of unease.

'I say, I don't like to push, but if you could just drive me into the village?' Her eyebrows rose once more, this time in hope.

George was looking around him. The road was deserted. If she had been there for over half an hour then it was obviously rarely used. To the right-hand side were woods, to the left a cornfield. He could feel the familiar excitement mounting. He felt in the pocket of his coat and his hand grasped the handle of the knife. It felt cool to the touch. The road had lighting, but it was subdued, as if the planners knew that it would not be used very often.

'Do you live far?'

'No, about eight miles along the road. Trouble is the lighting packs up about a mile further on and I didn't fancy trekking along there in the dark.'

Her voice was so full of life. George imagined she would be a lot of fun to live with. Could see her playing games with her children, baking her own bread. She looked the type who worried about the ozone layer and tropical rain forests. Riding her horses.

He giggled.

'Are you all right? Only if I'm putting you to any trouble . . . ?' She sounded even more uncertain now and George saw her eyes scanning the road for any oncoming vehicles. His face set in a grim mask. The child began to snore gently and George grinned at her.

'Get out of the car.'

'I . . . I beg your pardon?'

He pulled her by the arm.

'I said, get out of the car.'

She went to pick up the child and George pulled the knife out. 'Leave him there.'

Cynthia Redcar stared at the man. The confusion in her dark eyes was apparent. George could practically smell her fear. She stumbled from the car.

'Take off your coat and cover him with it. He looks cold.'

Cynthia stood dumbstruck, staring at him.

George rolled his eyes. Why were women always so difficult?

He slapped her across the face, hard. 'Don't annoy me, I'm warning you. Just do as I say and everything will be fine.'

Cynthia took off her coat. The wind bit into her. She placed it gently over the child.

'Now shut the door and we'll go for a little walk.'

A minute later they were in the woods. In the dimness Cynthia felt his hand go to her breasts and instinctively she pushed it away.

'What's the little boy's name?' George's voice was low and menacing and Cynthia felt the threat like a physical blow.

'Please – please don't hurt James. I'll do anything, just don't touch my little boy.'

This was more like it.

'Take off your clothes.'

George watched her as she fumbled with the buttons on her jeans. As she pulled her jumper over her head. All the time her eyes were on him. He could see the shaking of her hands as she moved.

She had heavy baggy breasts. George guessed they were marked, could visualise the mauve veins in them from childbearing. Four children did she say she had? His mind was fuzzy again. It was the excitement from her fear. He loved the fear. He loved being in control. She was standing now in her bare feet, her hands across her breasts, trying to hide her nakedness.

'Lie down.'

'Please . . . whoever you are, don't do this.' Her voice was drenched with tears.

'Lie down.' He stepped towards her and she flinched as the blade of the knife neared her face.

She lay down on the damp cold ground, her hands between her legs. George surveyed her for a few seconds before he slipped off his overcoat and knelt in front of her, forcing her legs open with his knees.

'You're going to do some things for me, dear. And if, but only if, you do them very, very well, I'll let you go home.'

He unzipped his trousers.

Cynthia felt a wave of nausea wash over her.

George was happy again. Today had not been so bad after all.

Kate knocked at Patrick's door at nine thirty. He opened it to her himself.

'I got your message, Pat, is everything all right?'

'Yeah. I had a bit of business to attend to, that's all.'

They went into the drawing room and Patrick poured them both a drink. Kate slipped off her coat and placed it on a chair. She looked around the familiar room and felt a warm glow engulf her. She liked Patrick's house, liked it very much.

'Is it still cold out, Kate?'

'Yes, it's going to rain later by all accounts.'

She sat on the settee and sipped her drink. 'Are you sure you're all right, Pat?'

He jumped. He had been thinking about later, when he would finally get his hands on George Markham.

'Sure.' His voice was curt and he tried to calm himself.

'I had a bit of aggro with one of the repomen, that's all. It happens all the time.'

He should have left a message with her mother saying that he would see her tomorrow. He should not have arranged to see her tonight. They had been supposed to meet at eight and he had rung and told her mother to ask Kate to make it nine thirty instead. It was a mistake. If she knew what he was going to do tonight . . .

'What kind of trouble?' Her voice was concerned. He looked at her and loved her so much he felt an urge to cry.

'Nothing to worry about, Kate. How's things with you?'

His voice was softer now. She watched him lighting a cigarette. His hands were trembling.

'All right. The blood testing is going great guns.'

'I'm sure it is.' His voice was hard.

He felt like telling her that it was all a waste of time, that the Grantley Ripper, George Markham, had paid a man to take the test for him. It was a bloody mockery, the lot of it.

'We're doing all we can, you know.' Kate's voice was soft and Patrick felt a moment's fleeting guilt. Then it was replaced by apprehension. If she only knew what he was going to do . . . It would be the end for them. What he had done to Danny Burrows would be nothing to how she would feel when Markham was found murdered. Patrick didn't care if he was caught, as long as the man paid the price.

Kate was worried. He looked as taut as a bowstring. It was as if he knew a devastating secret but couldn't tell anyone.

'Have you eaten, Pat?'

Patrick could not help smiling. She sounded just like his mother: whenever there was a crisis or an upset she wanted to feed everyone.

Food was a woman's way of healing.

If only it was that easy.

'Come here.' It was a command.

She put down her drink and went to him. She stood in front of him, her hands on her hips.

'I'm not sure I like your tone!'

She was laughing and Patrick felt a feeling in his gut, like a hand gripping his entrails.

He knew what she was trying to do. She thought he was having a bad day over Mandy and was trying to cheer him up.

She was good. Kate was a good woman.

He pulled her on to his lap and put his hand up her jumper, rubbing at the soft skin of her breasts.

'Oh, Kate . . .' It was a heartfelt cry, and she felt it like a physical blow.

'Patrick, tell me what's wrong. I want to try and help you. Are you in some kind of trouble?'

'No. Nothing like that, I swear to you.'

'Then why are you like this? Is it Mandy? It's as if you're on tenterhooks for some reason.' Her voice lowered. 'It is Mandy, isn't it?'

He could tell her the truth about that anyway.

'Yeah . . . it's about Mandy.'

'You're missing her? It's perfectly natural, you know. It often hits people suddenly. I've seen it before.'

Her earnest face stared into his and he felt his heartbeat speeding up.

He wanted to tell her that he missed her every second of the day; that it was there with him when he opened his eyes in the morning and when he closed them at night. Even his dreams were no escape from the feelings of futility. But now he had the perpetrator within his grasp and tonight he was going to commit murder. And he couldn't wait!

But he knew Kate would not understand his need. The need to destroy the man who had ravaged the only decent thing he'd had. It would cleanse him. He knew he could lie to himself, say he was ridding the world of a piece of shite. That's what Willy had termed it. But deep inside he knew that that was only a small part of it. Revenge was what he wanted. Revenge, and the feeling of blood on his hands.

Kate watched the emotions cross his face and her heart went out to him.

Then, suddenly, they were on the floor.

Her clothes were being pulled off her and he was inside her, thrusting away as if his life depended on it.

She had never known a loving so brutal and so beautiful. They came together in a shuddering climax and then lay there, holding one another tightly.

Patrick stared at her dark eyes and wished he did not have to do what he was going to do. Because if this exquisite creature ever found out, he would once more lose everything he had.

But even Kate's love wasn't enough. Revenge had a bitter taste already, but there was no going back.

George was humming softly to himself. Cynthia was quiet and pliable. He arranged her limbs once more to his satisfaction. She had muscular thighs. All the horse riding, he guessed. She had passed out with fright, and that had annoyed him. Because tonight he wanted, needed, a woman to beg.

His mother should beg really. Beg him to forgive her. But she wouldn't.

He felt the rage coming again, then he heard the noise. It was a child's crying.

James was awake.

Cynthia stirred beneath him. The crying of her child was penetrating somewhere in her unconscious. She opened her eyes and, remembering what had happened, looked at George, terrified.

The crying was getting louder. The little hiccoughing sobs were like knife blades in her heart.

How long had she been out? Had the man hurt James? She tried to push herself up.

George tutted to himself. He felt the woman's hands on his chest and the force as she tried to push him from her. An animal strength seemed to fill her body. Her child needed her. Her child was in danger.

They were all the same.

Cynthia brought up her knee. Panic over her child galvanised her into action. She caught George in the groin and he groaned, a white hot pain shooting into his testes. Lashing out with the knife, he swiped it cleanly across her throat, slicing the skin and veins as neatly as a surgeon.

Cynthia put her hands to her neck in shock. Bringing them away covered in blood. She opened her mouth but only a strangled gurgle escaped.

George watched her head snap back as she shuddered to her last sleep, the gaping wound spurting blood.

Then she was still, her eyes fastened on him.

George wiped the blade on the dirt beside him, then he stood up and rearranged his clothes. Picking up his over-coat, he slipped off the white cotton gloves and pushed them into the pocket. He walked to his car.

James was crying hard. He had woken up in a strange car with a strange smell and his mother was gone. He huddled into her coat, trying to breathe in his mother's perfume.

George opened the door and scooped him up. Then he walked back to Cynthia with him.

The child struggled, and George held him tighter.

'Be quiet!'

James gulped in a large draught of air and screamed. George dropped him on to the leaf-covered ground. The child was stamping his feet and screaming and he watched, fascinated at the strength in the little body. At the determination to get whatever it was he wanted.

He watched him stumbling around on fat little legs, trying to find something familiar. Fear and panic were making him clumsy. Then George tried to grasp his hand but the child would not let him.

He pulled his arms away, screaming louder and louder until finally George began to hit him.

On his way to the hotel George started humming again.

Patrick and Willy pulled into Bychester Terrace at two fifteen. As Patrick walked up the path, he felt a loosening in his bowels. He would be facing the murderer of his daughter in next to no time. He felt a heat inside him as he thought about it. The few hours with Kate had been tinged with despair. Now she was gone from his mind. All he could think about, all he could see, was the future without Mandy. His child.

He knew as he walked to the front door that the house was empty. It had that deserted air. He knocked anyway and waited.

The anger was back. The burning anger that started in his chest and wormed its way through his body, seeping into sinew and bone. Maddening him.

He wanted George Markham. He wanted to strangle the life from him slowly. He wanted to castrate him. He wanted to hurt him more than he had ever wanted anything in his life.

This man had used his daughter as if she was a piece of dirt, and Patrick Kelly would see that justice was meted out.

He walked around the back of the house, Willy following. As they passed the overflow pipe a trickle of water splashed on to them.

'Bollocks! That water's bloody freezing.' Willy's voice was a whisper.

Taking a glass cutter from his pocket he cut a hole in the back door. Within seconds they were inside the house.

It was empty all right.

Patrick cursed under his breath.

Turning on their torches, they began the search for a clue to where their man might be. By tomorrow night latest they would know every move he made. Patrick Kelly had already arranged for that in case tonight's visit drew a blank.

Elaine's handbag was in the hall cupboard and Willy rifled through it. Taking a shabby brown address book from it, he put the bag back where he'd found it. Patrick motioned that they were leaving.

He felt as high as a kite. The adrenaline was coursing through him. He had not got this close for the man to evade him now.

If it took him the rest of his life, he'd find him. Especially now he had his name.

Nancy lay in her bed contemplating the evening's events. She knew that Lily had never liked her, the feeling had always been mutual. But she had never fully realised the extent of her dislike until tonight.

For the first time in her life, Nancy Markham was frightened. She realised that at eighty-one her life was nearly over and if what had been threatened tonight came to pass, she would finish it in a home.

A home!

How dare that stinking slut threaten her with a home? But she had.

And Joseph had agreed. Oh, not out loud, not in so many words. Her son was too much of a coward for that.

But he had agreed with his eyes. The eyes that were as grey and lifeless as his father's.

She clenched her fists in temper. When she thought of how she had fought to give them a decent life! And Nancy really believed that she had.

When she thought of the sacrifices she had made for them . . .

One of the things George had inherited from his mother was her capacity for fantasy.

Lily's voice was at full throttle in the room next door.

'She goes this time, Joseph. She should have been put away years ago. You know that and I know that.'

Joseph stared up at the ceiling.

'She's as nutty as a bloody fruit cake. But she's cute.' Lily wagged her finger at him.

'Oh, she's cute all right. Well, I'm telling you now, Joseph Markham, I've had enough. I've had to put up with her all these years. It's all right for you, you're out all bloody day. Have you any idea what it's like, having to listen to that sodding bell, day in day out? Well, have you?'

He closed his eyes tightly.

'Even the children hate her. I never see them any more. She's driven them from the house.'

Suddenly, it was all too much for her and her voice quavered. She swallowed back her tears. Joseph turned to her and hesitantly took her in his arms. The display of affection was too much for her and the dam broke. Sobs were shaking her whole body and Joseph held her to him, seeing in his mind's eyes the girl she had been.

'Hush now. Hush now, Lily. Everything's going to be all right. I'll sort out somewhere for her tomorrow.'

She pulled away from him.

'Pr-Promise?'

'I promise.'

Now he had actually said it out loud, it was true. He'd see the doctor first thing in the morning. If he could, he'd get her put in council care. If he couldn't, then he'd pay for it. The time had come to let go. He had done all he could for her. Anything he owed her had been repaid in full. Over and over again.

It was funny, but after all that he had heard tonight, he had no fear of her any more.

It was as his wife had told her: she had finally fouled her nest.

He stroked Lily's hair and smiled to himself. It'd be nice to see the children more often.

In the Mile End Hospital two nurses stood over Tony Jones. He was heavily sedated. Jeanette had left the hospital ten minutes earlier.

'Poor man! He'll be scarred for life.'

'Those bloody dogs should be put down, all of them. To think it could be wandering around now. Imagine if it attacked a child!'

'Yeah. Didn't you think his wife was a bit funny?'

'In what way?'

'Well . . .' The other nurse lowered her voice confidentially.

'It's as if she knew he was going to be bad. She didn't seem surprised or shocked when she saw him.'

'Can't say I noticed really.'

'Oh, well, maybe it was just me.'

'Come and have a cuppa before we start the turns.'

Tony groaned in his drug-induced sleep and the two women watched him for a second. He settled down once more.

'Poor little thing. He'll know all about it when those stitches on his face begin to tighten.'

'Let's get that cuppa while we've still got the chance.'

Chapter Twenty-Seven

George had just had his meal on the plane and was now watching a hilarious episode of *Some Mothers Do 'Ave 'Em*. Frank Spencer was a motorbike messenger for a firm called Demon King and was inadvertently delivering pornographic pictures instead of letters and parcels. Everyone on the plane was screaming with laughter and adjusting their headphones. George laughed more than any of them. He was really enjoying himself.

He had eaten all his meal, discovering he had a ravenous appetite when he had seen the Beef Stroganoff, Duchesse potatoes and peas. He had also had a small bottle of red wine.

He sat in a window seat looking down at the cottony clouds and felt a moment of euphoria. He was going to Florida; he was going to see Edith. His Edith. He was going to enjoy himself.

He thought about the night before and his happy expression faded for a second.

The memory of the child was troubling him.

Then he shrugged. All children got beaten at some point, by parents or by teachers. He knew this for a fact.

Satisfied again that he had not done anything really wrong, he savoured once more the delights of the woman's body. He could feel his own excitement and forced those thoughts from his mind, concentrating on the clouds and the blueness of the sea that peeped through the whiteness every so often, reminding him that he was leaving England. England, Elaine, his mother . . . mustn't forget his mother . . . and all his troubles.

He would start again in Florida, he had decided. He would sell the house. It was all his now. He experienced a small feeling of annoyance, just a flicker really, that Elaine had had to die like she did. Not because he felt any guilt, but because it had stopped him claiming the insurance money.

He had it all worked out. When he went back to sell the house he would say that Elaine had run off with someone. He gave his little grin. That would immediately win him sympathy. He would put the house up for sale and then return to Florida and Edith.

He would remove Elaine from her watery grave and bury her somewhere. He'd put her out with the garden rubbish in black bags and then dump her on the tip.

This made him want to laugh again. Elaine on the tip! Better than she deserved, maybe. He'd cross that bridge when he came to it. Either way, she was gone.

Beside him sat a little girl. She was sandwiched between George and her mother. Her mother was still laughing at Frank Spencer, showing pearly white teeth.

George decided he approved of her. She looked like a mother should. Flat-chested, clean and wholesome-looking. No make-up or jewellery. The programme ended and Desmond Lynam came on the screen to talk about the next feature. George pulled off the headphones and relaxed. The little girl did the same. She smiled at him shyly. George smiled back, smelling the sweetness of the little body. He noticed she had a pack of cards and leant towards her.

'Would you like a game of snap?'

The child flicked back her long blond hair disdainfully.

'I don't play snap. I play poker, pontoon or five-card stud.' She saw the dismay on George's face and hurried on, 'I also play rummy and trumps.'

George smiled once more.

'How about a game of rummy, then?'

'All right.' She began to shuffle the cards expertly and he sighed.

Nothing and no one was ever what they seemed.

Five-card stud indeed!

Kate looked down at the two bodies and felt sickness wash over her. The woman was lying spreadeagled on the dirt floor, her neck a gaping wound. Blood had dried on her shoulders and breasts. Her mouth was in a perfect O. That was bad enough, but it was the child's body that affected her.

His little face was crushed completely, nose and cheeks collapsed in towards his brain. His tiny plump baby fingers were curled in his palms. He was lying huddled into his mother's body.

The pathologist shook his head.

'She's been dead longer than the child. My guess is he crawled to her for comfort then suffocated in his own blood.'

He pointed with his pen at the child's face. 'See here and here? Well, the blow caused the blood to flow down the back of his throat. His nose couldn't release it, no way. He practically drowned in his own blood. Poor little fucker.'

Kate wanted to cry. She wanted to cry desperately. But not here. She refused to though she guessed shrewdly that more than a few of the men around her were feeling the same.

Murdered people were bad enough, but murdered children? They were the worst.

When they had received the call that the Grantley Ripper had decided to expand his area, they had all felt a sense of shame. They hadn't stopped him and the man was on the move.

And the case had a new dimension. He killed little children now. Christ alone knew where he would strike next.

Kate heard the sound of sobbing and turned to the left. In a clump of yew trees stood DS Willis, head bent. Caitlin was patting him on the shoulder and lighting him a cigarette. It was the boy's first child corpse.

Kate felt a surge of affection for the young man. And for Caitlin. Much as he tried to be the hardfaced know-all, Kate was realising he was in fact quite a soft-hearted man. She looked at the two bodies and pictured the tiny child trying to find his mother's warmth. Crying, in acute pain, he had dragged himself to her. Believing, as all children believed, that she would protect him. Make him better. Only Mummy was already dead and the child's time was running out.

Dicky Redcar had alerted the police to his wife's disappearance at eleven fifteen.

Two patrolmen had found the Range Rover at eleven forty-nine and assumed she had tried to walk and maybe gone to a friend's. There was no reason to suspect foul play. At one twenty-five they had begun a search; the bodies had been found just after two.

Kate had been alerted at five thirty that the Grantley

Ripper had decided to extend his operations. The DNA on the woman had been conclusive. It was the same man, and the only clue they had were his tyre tracks.

As Caitlin· had remarked, unless they had a definite make on the car the tyre tracks were a piss in the ocean. How many dark-coloured saloons were there, for heaven's sake?

Kate saw Frederick Flowers arrive and heaved a sigh. The heavy mob was here. That meant the newspapers were already on to it.

Dicky Redcar was in shock. His three remaining children had been taken by relatives. His sister had wanted to stay with him, but he needed to be alone.

He sat in his study with a photograph of Cynthia and James on his lap. He could hear Major, one of his horses, whinnying outside the window.

The photograph showed Cynthia holding young James on a pony. He'd had a natural seat. All their children did. Rosie, nearly eleven, was already a name on the children's eventing circuit. Jeremy, aged nine, was following in her footsteps. Even Sarah was a natural at five. It was what they had lived for. The horses, the children and each other.

Since returning from the Falklands, he had given up his army career and they had settled down to their 'real life', as they referred to it. He had seen enough death and carnage out there. He'd never expected to see it at home.

There was a knock at the door and he closed his eyes.

He felt a shadow cross the window at his side and glanced up. Two men were standing there, smiling at him. Who the hell were they?

He rose from his seat and opened the window, putting the photograph on the sill.

'What do you want?'

'Hello.' The man was tall and slim with a ready smile. 'I wondered if we could have a word?'

The second man brought up a camera and the flash made Dicky Redcar reel.

Damned reporters!

'Go away! Leave me alone. I have nothing to say to you.'

'Come on now, sir, this is news. Five minutes and we'll be gone.'

Dicky stepped away from them as if they were the plague. He side stepped his chair and stumbled from the room. The two men watched him bolt and shrugged their shoulders at each other. The tall man put his hand inside the open window and picked up the photograph.

'Look what I've found.' He raised his eyebrows in delight. 'Not a bad-looking piece. Bit flat-chested, but you can't have everything. Shame about the kid. His face is a bit blurred. Come on, let's talk to the neighbours, see what we can gather. I hope he was a war hero, that always makes great copy.'

The two men slunk away.

Major whinnied again, wondering where his mistress was with his morning carrot.

Patrick was on a high. He had not slept from when he had left George Markham's, his energies set on finding out everything about him.

He was now sitting outside Kortone Separates, waiting for people to arrive for work. The address and phone number had been in Elaine's phone book.

A large man, slightly balding, drew up in the car park in a Granada and Patrick stepped from his Rolls-Royce. The early morning cold hit him, sending his breath into the sky life puffs of smoke.

'Excuse me. Can I have a word?'

Peter Renshaw turned to look at the man. His eyebrows rose at the sight of the Rolls Royce. What could he want?

'Yes? Can I help you?'

'Do you work there?' Patrick flicked his head in the direction of the factory opposite.

'Yes?' It was a question, coming out in a bewildered fashion.

'Do you happen to know a George Markham?' Patrick's voice was friendly, friendly and neutral.

The man's face relaxed.

'Old Georgie? Know him well.'

Patrick gave him a big smile.

He opened the door of the Rolls and got inside, motioning for Peter Renshaw to follow him.

Peter clambered in, without a trace of fear. He could smell the pure luxury of the car and relaxed into the leather upholstery with glee.

'Lovely motor.'

'Thanks. Can I get you a drink?' Patrick opened the small mini bar. It never failed to impress people, especially those in C-reg Granadas.

'Bit early for me, it's only eight twenty!'

'Fair enough.' Patrick poured himself a brandy and swirled it around the glass.

'I'm Patrick Kelly, I don't know if you've heard of me?' He watched the man's face drop. 'Don't worry, I've no grievance with you. It's George Markham I'm interested in. "Old Georgie" as you just referred to him, Mr . . .'

Peter Renshaw wished he'd taken the drink now. Patrick Kelly was serious trouble. What on earth could he want George for?

'Renshaw. Peter Renshaw. I don't really know George that well . . .'

He was babbling.

Patrick poured out another brandy and handed it to him. 'I think me and you need to have a little chat, Peter. I can call you Peter?'

Renshaw nodded. As far as he was concerned, Patrick Kelly could call him anything he liked!

The car purred to life.

'Where . . . Where are you taking me?'

'Just for a little drive. Now calm down. I think you're a sensible man. I think I can trust you.' The threat was there as plain as daylight. 'I can, can't I?'

Peter drained the brandy at a gulp.

'Yes. You can trust me, Mr Kelly.'

'Call me Pat. All my friends do, and I want us to be friends, Peter. Now, starting from the beginning, I want you to tell me all you know about George Markham.'

'But what for?' It was out before he realised what he was saying.

'Because, Peter, I asked you. And as far as I'm concerned, that's reason enough. OK?'

He took a deep breath.

'I only know him as a colleague at work. He's a quiet little man. I suppose you could say I've always felt a bit sorry for him.'

Patrick's eyebrows rose.

A quiet little man? He wouldn't be quiet when he got his hands on him. He'd be screaming his head off.

He already had the make and reg of Markham's car. That had been the easy bit. The hard bit was finding out where the hell the little bastard was. But if he could locate the car, he could locate George Markham.

Until then, he would hound everyone he could. Use force if necessary.

All his men had the description and details of George

Markham's car. He had been on to some friends in the Met and they were looking for it as well. Something had to give eventually.

Then he would have him in the palm of his hand.

Twenty minutes later, he dropped off Peter Renshaw outside Kortone Separates. It had been obvious he knew nothing of importance. Except that George was not coming back to work.

There was something going on here. Where was the wife? Was she with him? If so, they were looking for a couple.

In that case, Patrick would either have to get rid of her, or abduct George off the street.

Either way he'd get him.

Then the news of the murders came on the radio. Willy turned it up and put it over the intercom. Patrick listened as the newscaster's voice droned on. He felt a coldness in his bowels. At the mention of the child he locked eyes with Willy in the mirror on the windscreen.

The filthy bastard!

It only added incentive.

Patrick felt Willy put his foot down and settled himself back in his seat. He stared at the passing scenery and then pulled the address book from his pocket.

'I think the brother's house next, Willy. We'll drag him out if necessary, and fuck the consequences. No more pussy footing around.'

Willy nodded. Those were his thoughts entirely.

Joseph had been ringing around all morning. Yellow Pages was choc-a-bloc with nursing homes. Like all good businessmen he was finding out the rates before committing himself. Eighty-one his mother might be, but she could live for a good while yet. The council had informed him that she was not their responsibility and he had wondered briefly if they had ever met her. Once people had they generally kept well away.

She was shouting at Lily at the moment and the sound went through his skull. His wife had taken the school bell from her and now Nancy was demanding its return.

Lily had changed overnight. It was as if knowledge of his mother's past had wiped away all fear of her.

He picked up the phone and began to dial the number of the Twilight Home for the Elderly.

Then there was a banging at his door.

'I'll get it, dear.' Putting down the phone, he opened the front door and saw two men.

One was large with a bald head and a toothless grin. The other was tall, athletically built and very well dressed.

'Joseph Markham?'

'Yes. Can I help you?'

'Would it be possible for us to talk in the house, Mr Markham? It's about George.'

Without stopping to think, Joseph stepped out of the way so the two men could enter.

'Who's that at the bloody door?'

Nancy's voice was at fever pitch. She was convinced the men would be coming to take her away at any moment.

'My mother. She's . . . not very well.'

Willy frowned.

'She sounds all right.'

Patrick was having trouble controlling himself.

'Look, about George. We wondered if you knew where he might be? He's not at home. We really need to find him quite urgently.'

Joseph frowned.

'Not at home? He was here yesterday. He came to visit Mother.'

'Did he? Was he alone?'

'Oh, yes, Elaine was working. Look, what's all this about?'

Patrick walked towards the voice. He pushed the door open and walked inside.

Nancy saw him and immediately calmed herself.

Patrick watched her. It was as if a new skin grew over her in a matter of seconds. The wrinkles evened out and her face took on a sublime expression.

'How do you do? Won't you take a seat? Lily, make some tea.'

He smiled at the woman, a wide friendly smile. So this was the scumbag's mother.

Lily looked at the two men and her eyebrows rose in a question. Joseph, in the doorway, shrugged in bewilderment. But if they shut his mother up, they could stay all day as far as he was concerned.

'Make the tea, Lily.' His voice was low.

She went from the room.

Patrick and Willy sat down.

'We're friends of George's, Mrs Markham. We wondered if anyone knew where we could find him?'

Nancy Markham patted her outrageous hair and smirked. 'I think there must be some mistake.'

'Sorry?' Patrick smiled again.

The woman's face hardened.

'My son hasn't got any friends.'

Willy and Patrick exchanged glances.

No wonder the bloke was a nutter. The whole family seemed a few paving slabs short of a patio.

Out in the kitchen, Lily and Joseph made the tea.

'Who the hell are they?' hissed Lily.

'I don't know.'

'Well, don't you think you ought to find out then?

After all, they are ensconced in our living room with your mother.'

Joseph allowed himself a small grin.

'I think she can look after herself, Lily, don't you?'

He put a few biscuits on a plate and added them to the tray. He would sit in and listen to the conversation. For some reason he didn't fancy confronting the two men. They looked as if they could take good care of themselves.

George got off the plane and smiled at the hostesses. He walked down the flight of stairs and lifted his face to the bright Florida sun. He was in America. Before he knew what was going on he had collected his luggage, changed some money and was on a courtesy bus to Lindo's car rental on Sandlake Road.

The driver of the bus was a large man in a leather baseball hat with 'Chicago Bulls' in blood red lettering across the front. His voice had a slow southern drawl and George was enjoying listening to it. It was so American.

'Orlando Airport is one of only three airstrips that is capable of landing the Space Shuttle in an emergency. As y'all know, Kennedy Space Centre is only twenty minutes' drive from here, so if ever the shuttle missed its target, we could land it here, safe and sound.' He paused for maximum effect then continued, 'If you look out of your window on the left you will see a B52 bomber. This was used in the Vietnam War and is now here purely for ornamental purposes.'

George stared enthralled at the bomber, as did most of the little boys on the bus.

'In England I understand you see dead cats and rabbits on your highways. Well, here in Florida, don't be surprised to find baby 'gators flattened in the middle of the road. The 'gators are night creatures by nature and are very rarely seen during the daylight hours. They provide a natural security for the Space Centre, as you can imagine.' He paused again and everyone laughed nervously.

'But if you go to Gatorland you can have your photo taken with them and see the 'gator wrestlin'. Refreshments are provided there and you can even eat 'gator burgers.'

George listened enraptured. Oh, why hadn't he come here before?

The journey from Orlando Airport to Lindo's took only ten minutes and he and the other passengers were soon standing on a large lot, with their cases at their feet, waiting for their designated cars. George gave his papers to a tall slim black man and gasped with surprise when he returned driving a Chevrolet Caprice. In America this was a small compact car; to George it was on a par with a Porsche or a Ferrari.

The black man in his Lindo's overalls showed him how to open the boot, or trunk as he called it, how to put the car on automatic cruising, how the lights worked and where the fuel tank was.

George listened raptly, smiling incessantly. The man stowed his case in the trunk and shook his head at George's obvious pleasure.

He thanked the man and promptly opened the door and sat in the passenger seat.

The black man grinned at him.

'Y'all better git used to drivin' on the left, boy. Lessen' you end up havin' an accident.'

George got out of the car sheepishly and walked around to the driver's side. He slipped a crisp five-dollar bill into the man's hand.

George was elated. He had his car hire agreement tucked away safely in his pocket, he had a map of Orlando from the car hire company and a wad of dollars in his pocket. He felt like a millionaire.

He studied the map to find Edith's address. It was on Apopka Vineland Road, Windermere, Orange County.

It was only a few miles from where he was!

He relaxed and started the car. As he drove carefully away, the little girl from the plane waved to him from her mother's Dodge. George gave her a little wave back. She had won three pounds fifty off him eventually.

He pulled out on to Sandlake Road and started the journey to his sister's, full of excitement.

The sights and sounds around him astounded his eyes and ears. Big billboards proclaimed the delights of 'Wet'n'Wild', 'Disney World', 'Universal Studios' and 'Gatorland', which he already knew about.

George drank it all in.

He drove past large shopping malls that put English shopping centres to shame. He saw tanned, healthy-looking people, milling around car parks, either getting in or out of cars. Someone on the plane had said that no one walked anywhere out here and George now understood why.

It was much too big.

He turned on his radio and caught the lunchtime news. He shook his head in wonder.

It was five o'clock in England now. The wonder of the aeroplane! In eight and a half hours he had travelled thousands of miles to another time zone.

He pulled into a large car park and studied his map. He was nearly there. Unlike in England, American roads had large signs going across them with the place names written in black lettering. It was almost impossible to get lost. No straining the eyes to find the road sign as you passed the corner of the road here. Oh, no. The name of the road was emblazoned across it!

He had only two more sets of traffic lights to go and then he was there.

He drove out of the car park and resumed his journey. Americans seeing the 'Dollar' sign on the car made allowances for him and waved good naturedly.

George beamed back at them, full of camaraderie. He liked Americans.

He drove into Apopka Vineland Road. It was clearly residential, but not what he'd imagined. The houses were large and beautiful. Edith lived at number 22620. George could not imagine a house number so big. He drove along the quiet road slowly, taking in his surroundings.

Edith and Joss must have done very well indeed to be able to afford to live here. He thought of Joseph's large house back in England. It looked like a shack compared to the properties here. The numbers were in the 22600s now and George felt excitement pound within him.

Then he saw it.

He stopped the car and stared at Edith's house. It was large, like all the others, and set well back from the road. It had a long, sweeping drive that led up to a whitewood house that positively sprawled. It had to be at least eighty feet across. It had a deep cherry red roof from the centre of which rose a turret with windows round it, like an observatory. The windows all over the house had cherry red shutters and the double front door was cherry red as well. The gardens alongside the drive sloped down to the road and were a riot of shrubs and trees. George could see a lemon tree with a white seat beneath it. The lawns were cut to perfection and he could hear the faint sounds of the sprinklers as they watered the ground.

He wished his mother was sitting in the back, so she could see how well Edith had done for herself. But only for a second. If his mother had been here, the day would have been ruined.

She ruined everything.

He would send her a photograph of the house, though, to annoy her. He drove cautiously up the drive to the front door and stopped the car.

Then pandemonium broke out.

Two large Dobermans appeared around the side of the house as if by magic. George saw two sets of teeth coming towards him and immediately set about closing the electric windows, the dogs' ferocious barking sending chills of fear through him.

Then he heard a female voice. 'Dante . . . Inferno . . . Here, boys.' The two dogs immediately stopped in their tracks and ran towards the sound, their small stumpy tails like lather brushes wagging as they made their way to the woman standing by the side of the house. It was Edith.

A changed Edith.

She was wearing a white dress with a thick black belt around her waist and black high-heeled shoes. She was slim and curvaceous. George was amazed. Edith had never had breasts. She looked better now than she had twenty years ago. He watched her put up her hand to shield her eyes as she tried to see who was in the car.

He opened the door and stepped out.

The bigger of the two dogs made as if to run at him and Edith called it back.

'Hello, Edith. Long time no see.'

He watched happily as her eyes opened wide and her mouth curved into a grin.

'George?' Her voice was husky with emotion.

He nodded and then she was running towards him and into his arms, the dogs following, sensing that he was a friend.

'Oh, George . . . George! It's so good to see you. Why didn't you ring me and let me know you were coming? Where's Elaine? How's everything back home?'

The words were tumbling out, tripping over each other as Edith led him into her house. Her heart was bursting with happiness. She had experienced so much with George, he was her closest relative. Her childhood confidant. The only part of life in England that she regretted leaving. Now he was here with her, her happiness knew no bounds.

George held her arm tightly as they walked into the beautiful house, a lump of emotion in his throat.

There was nothing like family.

Patrick and Willy were driving back to Grantley.

'I'm telling you, Pat, she was nuttier than a squirrel's posing pouch. And that bloke Joseph weren't much better.'

Patrick nodded absently. It had been a waste of time. They had known nothing.

But the man had to be somewhere. If he used his credit card then Patrick would be on to him. Oh, he knew all the faces that could help him. He wasn't a repoman for nothing. He could find just about anyone, given time.

But time was something he didn't have.

If Kate found out who the Ripper was, then the police would be looking for Markham as well. He could still get to him in prison, but it wouldn't have the personal touch. And Pat wanted to do this job himself.

Chapter Twenty-Eight

Patrick answered the telephone. A female voice came down the line.

'Mr Kelly?'

He yawned. 'Speaking.'

'I'm Louella Parker from Colmby Credit. I have some information regarding a Mr George Markham.'

Patrick felt a surge of excitement.

'Go on.'

'Subject to the usual terms, of course.' The woman's voice was crisp. 'I do rather put myself out for these things.'

'All right, all right, don't make a meal of it. If you tell me what I want to know you'll get the dosh.'

The woman cleared her throat delicately and he was glad for a moment that she was on the other end of a phone line, otherwise he would have grabbed her throat and shaken the information out of her.

'George Markham booked a flight to Orlando by credit card on the twentieth of this month. He was due to leave on the twenty-third. The company he travelled with was Tropical Tours.'

Patrick was stunned.

The dirty bastard had outwitted him!

'Mr Kelly, are you still there?'

'What? Oh, yeah. Sorry.'

'I trust that's what you wanted to know?'

'Oh . . . yes. Yes. You'll get the money, Miss Parker, in the usual way.'

While the woman thanked him, he put the phone down gently and stared out of the library window.

He'd gone to the States?

Patrick began looking through the phone book for the number of Tropical Tours. Once he had established the flight number and whether or not George Markham had been aboard, he would plan his next move.

Frederick Flowers scanned the sea of faces in front of him. He always felt nervous when addressing the press. You never quite knew what you would be asked.

'Is this the work of the Grantley Ripper?' The scruffy, bearded man stared into Flowers's face.

'I really cannot divulge that sort of information, as well you know. At the moment we are liaising with the Kent Constabulary to ascertain whether it is the same person.'

'Why is Detective Inspector Kate Burrows here, then? Do you think that a female officer might handle the case differently? Better?'

Flowers made a conscious effort not to screw up his eyes in annoyance.

'Detective Inspector Burrows is a very capable police woman, she is respected by her colleagues and myself. Her sex has nothing to do with it.'

The female reporter pressed on, undeterred. 'Nevertheless, it is unusual for a female DI to be on a case of this size.'

'My dear girl, I assume you are writing with a feminist slant? Well, can I go on record as saying that we are here to trap a cold-blooded callous murderer, not to discuss sexual politics.' He turned from the woman and looked around. 'Who's next?'

The reporters laughed.

'Have you any idea at all who the man is? Any leads?' a booming voice called from the back.

'Was the child molested at all?' called another.

Kate followed Caitlin out of the building and to their car. Caitlin lit one of his cigars.

'It's funny you know, Kate, but why would the man come here?'

'I thought that, Kenny. I wondered if maybe he was visiting over this way. Could he work here maybe? Has he family in the area? The murders in Grantley were obviously done by someone who knows the neighbourhood. Maybe he lives here now but was brought up in Grantley? Why kill the child so brutally?'

Caitlin shook his head.

'The blood testing is backlogged, did you hear?'

Kate nodded. 'I heard. We need more manpower on it.'

'It's the results that are taking all the time. Still, we'll keep at it. Time's the one thing we haven't got, but it's also all we've got, if you get my meaning.'

Kate smiled wanly.

'I keep thinking of that child. How can we not have anything to go on? Jesus Christ!'

'Look, girl, Peter Sutcliffe took years to find. Then there was Dennis Nilsen. He was even cooking the poor fuckers' heads and no one would have found him if he hadn't blocked up his drains with human flesh. Murderers like this only get caught quickly in books and on TV. Real life is a different thing altogether. This man is probably discussing the murders with his family, friends, workmates, acting like he's as shocked as them. But underneath it all he's laughing at them and us. Oh, yes, especially us. He'll read the papers and grin all over his face.

'But you mark my words, he'll do something wrong and when he does make a mistake, we'll be waiting for him. And do you know the first thing I'm going to do?'

'What?'

Caitlin leaned towards her and grinned.

'I'm going to smack him once for every corpse that I've seen with his handiwork on it and twice as hard and as long for the child. It's what will keep me going.'

Kate turned from him. Before she could answer the reporters began filtering out of police headquarters and she started the car. The last thing she wanted was to get caught by them.

Caitlin's words troubled her though. More than she cared to admit. She was aware that any suspect they had now could be in great danger. James Redcar had put a different light on this inquiry altogether. Everyone knew that even criminals had their own code of conduct when it came to a child murderer. As soon as the Grantley Ripper was identified, there'd be more than just the police out to get him. She just hoped they could get to him first.

As she drove back towards the Dartford Tunnel she saw a plane taking off from Gatwick and sighed.

How she wished she was on it.

Patrick went back through Elaine's address book and grinned. Willy grinned back.

'He's gone to his sister's. Well, we can soon put a stop to his gallop. Get me Shaun O'Grady on the blower, I've just had a great idea.'

While Willy dialled, Patrick poured out a fresh cup of

coffee. He had the man now. He was convinced of it.

He thought fleetingly of Kate. If she ever found out what he was going to do, she would never forgive him.

His mouth hardened. This had nothing to do with Kate, this was family business.

He sipped the hot coffee and lit a cigarette. Willy handed the phone to him.

'Shaun? It's me, Patrick, how are you?'

Shaun O'Grady sat in his luxurious home in Miami and whooped with delight.

'Hiya, Pat. How's tricks?'

'I've got some trouble, Shaun, family trouble.'

Shaun O'Grady pushed the woman beside him away. He pulled himself up to a sitting position and gestured to her to light him a cigarette.

'What kind of family trouble?'

'It's Mandy. My Mandy. She's dead.'

'Dead?' O'Grady's gravelly voice was disbelieving. 'What happened? Was it an illness, what?'

He took the proffered cigarette and pulled on it deeply, his eyes travelling around the large room without seeing anything. He had been dealing with Patrick Kelly for over fifteen years. Although the two men had met face to face only twice, they had built up a mutual respect and friendship over the long-distance telephone line.

Shaun O'Grady was an American version of Patrick Kelly. Except Shaun O'Grady had branched out into other areas that Kelly knew about only through word of mouth. One of which was a service providing professional hits.

As Kelly spoke, the woman watched O'Grady's face. Sighing heavily, she pulled on a negligee and left the room. She switched on the thirty-six-inch television in the bedroom and, sprawling on the bed, began watching *I Love Lucy*.

She knew Shaun well and when his face had that look, it was best to keep out of his way.

'Pat, Pat, I'm heart sore for you.' O'Grady thought of his own three daughters ensconced in a large house in Palm Springs with his ex-wife. He might not spend much time with them, he was a busy man, but they were his children, his flesh and blood. He felt a moment's guilt as he recalled he hadn't seen any of them since the Christmas holidays.

'What can I do to help you? You name it.'

'Our man is at this moment in Florida. That's why I've called you, Shaun. I want him removed from the earth. I want him dead.'

'It's as good as done, Pat. Give me the details and I'll see to it at once.'

'I'll send the money within a few days . . .'

'There's no need for money.'

'Fair dos, Shaun, I'll pay. I'll ring through the details in a couple of hours.'

If it was one of his daughters . . . O'Grady closed his eyes. It did not bear thinking about. He began to jot down Edith's address and after a short exchange both men rang off.

O'Grady sat on his white leather Italian settee and stared at the Salvador Dali on his wall. He was fifty-eight, with a bald head, long baggy jowels and a large belly that nothing would get rid of. He had short stubby legs and arms.

He caught his reflection in the mirror and wiped his hand across the stubble on his jaw.

He thought of his ex-wife's house, with its comfortable battered furniture and his three young daughters. He heard Lucille Ball's voice coming from the bedroom and winced.

He had exchanged all that for a bimbo and a two million dollar bachelor pad.

The joke was that Noreen, his ex-wife, had never tried to stop his affairs, so why the hell had he dumped her?

He picked up the telephone again and dialled her number.

The phone was answered by his youngest daughter, Rosaleen.

'Hello, Daddy!' He heard her put the phone on the table with a clunk and call to her mother.

'Mommy, Mommy, Daddy's on the phone!'

O'Grady tried to ignore the sound of surprise in the child's voice.

Noreen's gently New England twang came on the line. Noreen had class, he admitted that to himself. He should never have divorced her.

'Hello, Shaun, this is a surprise.'

As he began to answer, the woman came out of the bedroom. She still had on the negligee and her impossibly long brown legs were visible through it. She pushed back thick black hair and lit a cigarette with natural grace.

O'Grady watched her, fascinated, then spoke into the phone. 'I'm coming up at the weekend to see the children. OK?'

'Fine. Let me know when you'll be picking them up and I'll make sure they're ready. They do miss you, you know.'

'I'll call back with the details, Noreen.'

'Fine.'

She put the phone down.

He immediately began dialling again, his eyes on the woman's buttocks, shimmering beneath the thin silk. He smiled at her and she half smiled back, retreating once more into the bedroom.

'Hello, Duane? Get yourself over here now, I have a job for you.'

He put down the phone and stubbed out his cigarette. He could hear Ricky Ricardo's laugh and guessed that the programme was coming to an end.

Tasha loved the old programmes: *I Love Lucy*, *The Three Stooges*. He had bought her the Marx Brothers collection. She was twenty-five.

How old was Noreen now? Thirty-eight? Thirty-nine?

He would see more of the girls, he was determined on that. Christ, what Pat had told him made you think! Who said the screwballs were only in America.

George was the centre of attention and loving every second of it. Edith looked fantastic and he couldn't take his eyes off her. Her hair was perfectly coiffeured. He knew it must be dyed, but it was dyed a natural colour and it suited her. She did not look like a woman in her fifties. Joss, on the other hand, looked every bit of his sixty-five years. His face was deep brown and leathery. Both of them had American twangs which George found exciting and attractive.

Edith was talking nineteen to the dozen.

'I've been in touch with the children and they're both coming tomorrow. Joss Junior, as we call him, is flying from Denver – that's in Colorado. He works for a big drug company. And Natalie is driving up from Miami, she works for a cosmetics company there. She's a buyer, you know. Wait until you see them, George. They're beautiful.'

'I wish Elaine and I had been blessed with children, but after the boy died . . .' His voice trailed off and Edith looked at him with ready tears gathering in her eyes.

How could Elaine have left him? After all this time too. The woman was a heartless bitch and if she ever saw her again, which she admitted was unlikely, she would say so to her face. Poor George. He had no luck with women. First their tramp of a mother and now Elaine. She pursed her perfectly painted coral lips.

Joss's loud, booming voice broke into her thoughts. 'How about we take Georgie here into Orlando for a slap-up meal? We could go to the Mercado on International Drive.'

Edith smiled widely, displaying all her expensive dentistry. 'Oh, let's. George, they have thirty-two ounce steaks there.'

George was worried. 'I don't think I could eat all that, Edith.'

'You old silly, we share it! Come on, let's get ready.'

In the back of her mind, she hoped George had a decent suit with him. He looked so damned touristy.

Still, she reasoned, it was lovely to see him. She fought down the impulse to squeeze him to her again. She was so damned pleased to see him, she could take a big bite out of him. Instead she put her arm around him and kissed him lightly on the cheek.

'It sure is good to see you, George. So good.'

'And you, Edith, my dear. It's been far too long.'

She accompanied him to the spacious guest room. She was amazed that her brother, whom she had honestly thought she would never see again, was actually in her home. Her beautiful home that she hoped he told their mother all about when he went back. That would be one in the eye for the old bitch!

'How's Mother, George?' She sat on his bed, her face troubled now. Every time she thought of her mother, she thought of the child.

George sat beside her and took her hand. 'The same as always, Edith. Spiteful, nasty. She hasn't changed.'

'I bet.' Her voice was vehement. 'Does she know about Elaine? Leaving you, I mean?'

George shook his head vigorously. 'No. I was going to tell her, I visited her just before I flew out here, but we got into a bit of an argument.'

Edith's eyebrows arched.

'Don't you mean she argued with you?' The playfulness was back now.

George grinned. 'No. Actually, I told her what I thought of her. I only wish I hadn't left it so long.' He rubbed a hand over his eyes. 'Edith, did you know that mother . . . was . . . well, a good-time girl?' He found it difficult to form the words. He found it even more difficult to understand Edith's laughter.

'What's so funny?' He was getting annoyed now.

'Oh, George, you always were the eternal innocent. I sometimes think that's why she picked on you so much. Don't you remember all the men she used to have around? Remember her fights with them and her drunken ramblings?'

'Of course I do, but I never thought she was . . . well, charging them.'

Edith sighed.

'You get changed, George, and we'll go out and have a big juicy steak and a really good time. Mother's thousands of miles away. She couldn't harm us now, even if she wanted to.'

George smiled his assent, but inside his head a little voice said: 'Can't she?' He would have been surprised to know that Edith was thinking exactly the same thing.

Alone in his room, he looked around at the blues and greens of the furnishings. On the hardwood floor, Indian rugs were placed at strategic points and the cover on the bed matched them perfectly. It really was a lovely room and a far cry from the house they had been brought up in.

He opened the wardrobe door and was surprised to find a bathroom in there. He filled the bath and poured in some bath salts he found on the window sill.

He was in America, in Florida with his Edith, Mother was not going to spoil it. He sank back in the water and let his mind wander on to other, more relaxing things.

Edith, more disturbed than she cared to admit, went to her own room and, opening her wardrobe, took down from the top shelf a little box. Placing it on her large oval bed, she opened it and took out the old black and white pictures.

There was George, in his short trousers and long grey school socks. There was Joseph and herself. She peered at each picture for a long while. In each and every photo, not one of the children was smiling.

Patrick was ecstatic. He had George Markham! He was disappointed that he could not put the man away himself, but he accepted that. He was grateful that he had done something. It was the frustration of knowing the man was somewhere safe, laughing up his sleeve, that had really got to him.

Now, though, he had him. Shaun O'Grady was going to see that he was no more. Just thinking about it gave Patrick a thrill.

If Kate knew what he had arranged today . . . He closed his eyes. Kate was good. Kate was everything that was right and decent and he loved her for those very qualities. Until they intruded on his concerns, that is.

He knew that if she had even an inkling that he knew the Grantley Ripper's name and whereabouts, she would create havoc. She wanted to bring the man to justice. Her justice.

Well, the man was getting Patrick's kind of justice and it had a much sweeter taste to it so far as he was concerned.

He clenched his fists. George Markham would soon be dead.

Dead, dead, dead!

He looked at Mandy's photograph on the mantelpiece and his face sobered. What he wouldn't give to have her back. Sometimes, late at night, when the house was quiet, he imagined he heard her voice.

He awoke, covered in sweat, hearing her crying. Calling out for him in distress. He would put his hands over his ears to blot out the noise.

It was then he imagined her terror.

The acute fear that must have enveloped her as the man began to pound her face with his fists. The thought of her lying there, on that dirty floor, while the bastard raped her . . .

He could still see her face, battered beyond recognition, as she lay in the hospital. He still heard the low buzz of the life support machine as it failed in its job. Saw her bruised body as it jerked with the electric shocks they'd used to try to resuscitate her heart.

Oh, George Markham had a big payout coming to him.

The telephone rang and he jumped.

'Hello?'

'Hello, Pat? It's me, Jerry. The fight's at the old hat factory near the Roman Road. I've faxed the directions through to you, OK? It's a nine thirty start.'

Patrick closed his eyes, he had forgotten about the fight.

'Look, Jerry, I might not be able to make it. I've got a lot on here.'

'Okey doke. It's gonna be a good one though. If I see you, I see you then. Ta rah.'

He replaced the receiver and sighed. He had been looking forward to the fight. He liked illegal boxing matches. It was like the old-style bare knuckle fighting of years ago. No one knew where the matches were to be held until a couple of hours in advance. That way the Old Bill, by the time they did find out where the venue was, were too late to do anything about it. The crowd and the fighters were long gone.

Patrick poured himself another generous measure of whisky and glanced at his watch. He wished O'Grady would ring with the details so he could really relax. He took a large sip of his drink.

A little while later the phone rang again and Kelly picked it up. He was gratified to hear the distant whirring and clicking of a long-distance call.

'Hi, Pat. Can you hear me OK?'

'I can hear you, clear as a bell.'

'It's arranged. Your man will be out of the way in the next three days. It'll cost fifty thou – dollars that is. I have one of my best men working on it. He's already setting it all up.'

'I'll have the money with you in twenty-four hours. Thanks, Shaun, I won't forget what you've done for me.'

'Hey, what are friends for? I'll keep you posted, OK? You just try and get over your loss, Pat. I'll sort out everything this end.'

'Thanks, Shaun. 'Bye.'

'No problem. Talk to you soon.'

The line was dead.

He had George's address and now he knew when he was to die. Patrick smiled to himself. It wasn't too late to go to the boxing match after all. Might take his mind off everything for a while.

*

Willy pulled up outside the hat factory and Patrick helped Kate from the car. There were people everywhere. She was aware that their arrival had caused a stir and instinctively stayed close to Patrick. He pushed his way towards the entrance, greeting people here and there. Then they were inside. A haze of cigarette smoke hit them both full in the face and a little grizzled man ran towards them, a large grin splitting his face.

'Pat! Pat! You made it. Hello, my dear.'

'Jerry, this is Kate, a special friend of mine. Kate, Jerry. An old reprobate.'

Kate smiled and took the tiny hand in hers.

'How do you do?'

Jerry sized her up expertly. Not the usual tit and bum that Kelly saddled himself with, but not bad for her age.

'I do very well, my dear. Come, I've saved you some front row seats.'

Patrick held on to her arm as they moved through the crowd. Loud soul music was coming from speakers and everyone was shouting to be heard above it. The place was filled to capacity already and Kate was amazed at the sights and sounds around her. Touts were openly taking bets and when the large boxing ring came into view she was even more puzzled. Surely he hadn't brought her to an illegal boxing match?

Jerry ushered them to their seats. Kate looked at Patrick sternly.

'Is this what I think it is?'

He laughed. 'Yes. Quick, Kate, over there!'

He pointed. Sitting on the opposite side of the ring was Chief Constable Frederick Flowers and what looked to Kate like half the Serious Crime Squad. She waved weakly as Flowers whistled and called over to them, obviously the worse for drink. Patrick was laughing his head off and Kate turned on him.

'You brought me here deliberately, didn't you?' He saw the confusion in her eyes and was sorry he'd laughed.

'I didn't know they'd be here, Katie, I promise you. I was coming here on me own account and then I thought you'd enjoy it. I just wanted to be with you.' He smiled and put his hand to his heart like a schoolboy. 'Scout's honour.'

'Well . . . you said it would be an experience.'

'It will. Now then, how much shall we bet?'

Kate frowned. 'How about a fiver?'

'Listen, darlin', if I bet a fiver here my reputation would go down quicker than free Bushmill's at an Irish wake! I'm putting a ton on Rankin Rasta Dave, my love. He'll piss it.'

As he spoke, the *2001 Space Odyssey* theme came over the speakers and a large Rastafarian walked from the make-shift dressing rooms. Kate gasped with surprise. The man was huge, with enormous arms and legs. His hair was tied back in a ponytail of big fat dreadlocks like sausages. He had a handsome, proud face. The crowd was cheering or jeering depending on whether they had a bet on him.

Pat got up and said, 'You keep looking at him with love in your eyes while I go and put the bets on, all right?'

Kate grinned despite herself. She had never seen such a big man. He stood in the ring, jumping around, shadow boxing and flexing his oiled muscles. A woman nearby tapped Kate on the arm and shouted: 'He could put his boots under my bed any day of the week.'

Kate put her hand to her mouth with shock and then laughed outright. Then the music changed and she heard Dana singing 'All Kinds of Everything' and a mighty cheer went up.

Another large man climbed into the ring. He held

enormous arms above his head in an arrogant stance. He had a big, finely chiselled face surrounded by shaggy red hair. Little blue eyes like pieces of flint surveyed his opponent and, to the satisfaction of his supporters, obviously found him lacking. He held up a large gloved hand at the Rasta and spat on the floor aggressively.

Patrick slipped back into his seat. His voice startled her. 'That, Katie, is Big Bad Seamus. He's come over from Dublin especially to fight the Londoner, Rasta Dave. There's an awful lot of money riding here tonight.'

Kate looked at him, her eyes troubled.

'I can't believe I'm here. I've never seen anything like this in my life. They're going to batter each other's brains out, aren't they?'

Kelly grinned. 'I bloody hope so, girl. If they don't the crowd will tear them apart themselves.'

A small man in a dinner suit climbed into the ring and began announcing the rules of the fight which to Kate seemed to mean only one thing: anything was allowed bar sawn-off shotguns or knives. Then both men sat in their corners while a half-naked young girl walked around the ring to whistling and cat calling, holding up a piece of cardboard with 'Round 1' on it. A bell went and the two men came at each other like bulls in the proverbial china shop.

Kate watched, amazed, as they began to fight. The Rasta took the initiative from the first punch. He delivered pounding blows to the Irishman's head again and again. Kate watched in morbid fascination. The Irishman was up now. He lunged at the Rastafarian, head butting him sickeningly just below his eye. She watched the swelling rise and put her hand to her mouth. She closed her eyes tightly. This was barbaric. Two grown men pummelling the life out of one another. The atmosphere in the warehouse was charged and Kate glanced around her. She saw women standing up screaming at the two men; now that the fight was getting really violent it was as if they had been waiting for the real beating to begin. Kate's eyes were dragged towards Frederick Flowers, who had also leapt from his seat and was shouting advice into the ring.

'Nut the bastard back! Don't let the Irish ponce get away with that!'

The black man in the ring seemed to heed the advice and was once more hammering the life out of the Irishman.

Kate watched Flowers as if she had never seen him before. He had made press statements about illegal boxing matches, as he had on many subjects over the years. It was one of the things he was supposed to be stamping out. Out of uniform and with too much drink in him, he looked what he was, a cheap shyster. Gone was the aura of respectability, the wise demeanour he assumed all day as the Chief Constable. In its place was just another assumed persona. The 'I'm one of the lads really' character. There wasn't much to separate him and Patrick.

A dark-haired woman in her twenties brought Flowers a drink and he took it from her without acknowledging her presence. She sat in his vacated seat and pulled her skirt down ineffectively. She was definitely not Mrs Flowers. Kate had met Flowers's wife on two separate occasions. She was a very refined woman, given to wearing sombre plaids and sensible shoes.

Why had Patrick brought her here, anyway?

Somewhere in her mind, Kate heard a bell. She looked at the ring and saw the two men swaggering back to their respective corners.

'All right, girl?' Patrick's voice was concerned.

Kate stared at him. Despite all the noise and confusion around them, he seemed to sense her feelings.

'Katie?' He raised his eyebrows a fraction and Kate looked away. Flowers now had his hand halfway up the bimbo's skirt. Patrick followed her gaze. Kate saw him grin and felt a tightening around her heart. He looked at her again.

'He's a right old slag is Freddie. That's not his bird as such, Kate. She charges about two ton a night. She's on the bash.'

His eyes went back to the ring. Another girl, black this time, was walking around the ring swinging her skinny hips, holding a piece of cardboard with 'Round 2' written on it. The Irishman grabbed her as she passed and put her over his shoulder, pretending to bite her buttocks. The girl squealed with delight, loving all the extra attention.

Kate watched the Rasta put his whole head into a bucket of water and come up shaking his hair like a shaggy dog, sending droplets of water everywhere.

Patrick lit two cigarettes and passed one to Kate. She took it gratefully.

'Patrick . . .'

She was going to tell him she wanted to leave but the bell had gone again and it was too late. His whole attention was on the ring.

Kate watched, sickened, as the hammering and pounding started again, even harder this time. About two minutes into the round the atmosphere changed again, becoming charged with malice. The black man was different somehow. His punches were landing heavily on the Irishman's face. Kate saw the lumps form around his eyes and mouth. Then the crowd surged forward in their seats. The Irishman was down on one knee. The black fighter saw his chance and took it. Swinging back his enormous arm he began pounding it into the other man's face and head.

The crowd were ecstatic. Women as well as men were screaming out advice to the two fighters. Kate watched terrified as the black man dragged the Irishman up from the floor and, holding him up, began to pummel his face and body. The Irishman was out on his feet and still the merciless hammering went on. Finally, after what seemed an age, the Rasta threw the man on to the canvas, delivering a swift kick to the groin as his last shot.

The Irishman lay there as if crucified, his arms spread out on either side of him.

The crowd were going wild. In the back small fights had broken out among rival fans. In the ring the Rasta was walking round, arms held up in the air like a conquering hero. His dreadlocks had freed themselves and now flew this way and that around his face as he moved. A tall, good-looking white woman of about thirty climbed into the ring and threw herself into his arms, landing a smacking kiss on his swollen and bruised lips.

Patrick turned to face Kate. 'That's Veronica Campella, otherwise known as violent Veronica . . . She's his manager. Veronica's got one of the biggest stables in England and she knows her job all right. She got him a twenty grand purse for tonight. Not bad for two rounds, is it? She even takes her boys as far as China and the States for fights.' Kelly's voice was admiring.

Kate was silent as she saw the Irishman being helped from the ring. The Rasta went to him and they embraced like old friends. The Irishman was obviously a good loser.

'Can we go now, Pat, please?'

'There's another couple of fights on yet, Kate.' He looked at her closely. 'What's the matter?' His voice was genuinely puzzled.

'I just want to get out of here. It's horrible. All this,' she spread her arms out, 'makes me feel sick to my stomach.'

For a fleeting second she saw a flicker of annoyance cross Patrick's features. Then he seemed to remember who she was, because he smiled at her sadly.

'Not a very good idea this, was it?'

Kate picked up her bag from the floor and shook her head.

'Not really. I don't like legal boxing, Patrick. I can't stand any form of violence.'

'Then we'd better go, hadn't we?'

She knew that she had annoyed him for real this time. His voice was flat and he walked through the crowd ahead of her, nodding here and shaking hands as he went. As they left the heat and excitement of the hall and walked out into the cold air, Willy appeared as if by magic.

'How did you fare, Pat?'

'Not quite as well as I expected, Willy. You?'

Kate heard the tone of voice and gritted her teeth.

'Won meself a quick grand. I knew the soot could take him, Pat. I just knew it. That boy can fight!'

Patrick smiled at him. 'You stay and watch the rest of the action, Willy.'

'What about you two?'

Patrick sighed. 'I'm quite capable of driving me own car, Willy.'

Willy knew something was up. Kate looked like a wet weekend in Brighton and Patrick didn't look much better. He handed over the keys.

'Well . . . If you're sure . . .'

He didn't like Pat driving the Roller, she was his baby.

'Well, don't gun her, right? She ain't really used to you driving her. You have to know how to handle her . . .'

636

'Willy!' Patrick's voice was clipped.

'What?'

Patrick pushed his face close to the other man's and said, 'Goodbye.'

With that he opened the passenger door for Kate and walked round to the driving seat. Kate got into the car in dead silence. Willy watched them closely all the time, shaking his head. Patrick started the engine and wheelspun the car out of the car park, sending stones showering everywhere. On the main road he settled down to sixty miles an hour and in the darkness Kate heard him laugh bitterly.

'What's the big joke?' Her voice was flat.

'That bloody Willy, sometimes I wonder why I've kept him on so long. He's more like me mother than me minder.'

'He's a good friend to you, that's why.' Kelly's criticism added to Kate's annoyance.

Patrick pulled the car into a layby and cut the engine.

'Listen here, I don't need this crap, Kate. From the moment you saw Freddie Flowers you've had the bleeding hump . . .'

Kate interrupted him.

'That's not true! You had the audacity to take me to an illegal boxing match, Patrick. Just because my Chief Constable was there and having the time of his life doesn't mean to say I had to. I thought it was barbaric, cruel and degrading, not just to the two men who fought, but to the people who paid money to see it.'

'What this boils down to, Kate, is this. We come from different worlds. I ain't apologising for taking you there, no matter what you say. I am what I am, Kate, you take me as you find me.'

'And the same goes for me, Pat, I'm not apologising either.'

They looked at each other in the dimness of the car, the atmosphere thick and pungent. Kate felt her heart hammering; she had to let him know what she was feeling. Suddenly, this wasn't about boxing any more, it was about them, the two of them as people. The differences between them.

Patrick lit them both another cigarette.

'What do you want from me, Kate?' It was a plea.

Kate paused.

'I want a bit of respect. I want to be cared for. But most of all, I want to feel that I am not compromising myself in any way by being with you. That . . . that . . . spectacle tonight made me feel physically ill. When they began to really pummel one another, it scared me.'

Kate heard the whirr of the electric window being lowered.

Patrick stared out on to the road. Cars whizzed by, their engines intruding now into their world. A cold breeze settled around them. Patrick sighed. It was the sigh of an old man.

'I'm sorry, Kate. You're right. What else can I say? I know we're different, but most of the time we're on the same wavelength. I've had to rethink a lot of life in the last few months. Like when I sold the massage parlours . . .' He paused to pull on his cigarette. 'I should never have taken you there tonight, I see that now. Even if you wasn't an Old – I mean a DI – you're not geared up for that type of thing. Renée wasn't, either. All I can say in my defence is . . .' He turned to face her. 'It's been a long time since I had a woman who didn't just go along with whatever I wanted to do.'

Kate searched his face in the darkness, she could make out his features, and her eyes caressed them one by one. He kissed her lightly on the lips and it was like an electric shock going through her body. 'I'm not sorry for being what I am, Kate, let's get that straight now. I'm apologising for not thinking about you and what you must be feeling. Does that make sense?'

Kate nodded.

'Well then, give us a proper kiss.'

He pulled Kate into his arms and kissed her hard on the mouth.

As they broke apart, Kate saw a head look in at the window.

'Is everything all right, sir?'

Neither of them had noticed the Panda car pull up behind them.

'Yes, thank you, officer, everything's fine. We're just going.'

Kate smiled at the officer and as Patrick pulled out of the layby she put her hand over his on the steering wheel.

'I don't want us to fight, Pat.'

'Let's just forget abut all this. Now, how about some food? What do you fancy? Italian, French, Spanish, chinky, what?'

Kate laughed. 'How about an Indian?'

'Trust you to say the one food I missed out! Tell you what, how about we skip the meal and just go home to bed?'

'No way.'

Patrick sighed. 'It was worth a try.'

Kate squeezed his hand gently. 'I never go to bed on an empty stomach.'

Suddenly she wanted him so badly she could taste it. She felt him put his foot down on the accelerator.

'Willy told you not to gun the car.'

He glanced at her and smiled.

'Willy didn't say anything about emergencies.'

*

Much later, as she lay beside him, the smell of him in her nostrils and the laziness that rough lovemaking brings enveloping her, she pondered her situation.

The warm loving individual beside her would murder the Grantley Ripper at the drop of a hat. He was capable of murder, she knew that. He had never made any secret of it.

Yet still she wanted him.

He stood for everything she disagreed with. The bed she was lying in was paid for through one or other of his borderline businesses, and he had taken her to an illegal boxing match. Yet one look at his handsome face and she could forgive him anything.

Anything? she asked herself again, and couldn't answer. Not honestly anyway.

She snuggled down deeper into his arms. She felt his flaccid penis against her leg, moist and soft, and felt the thrill of him again. He woke momentarily and drew her towards him as if surprised to find her there. She kissed him on the mouth hungrily, trying desperately to empty her mind. He rubbed her breasts roughly and she responded by kissing him harder.

'Kate?'

'What?'

'You can deny this if you want, but I think that big Rasta turned you on.'

'Oh, you!'

He grabbed hold of her and kissed her again, slipping on top of her as if they were made to fit. She was glad of it.

Neither had mentioned the murders or the fight. It was as if they had an unspoken agreement to drop the subject. But even in the throes of orgasm, it was in the back of both their minds.

Eventually, it would all come up again. Their differences, their divided opinions on right and wrong, these would bring them into conflict.

And it would bring them grief.

Chapter Twenty-Nine

Duane Portillo watched number 22620 Apopka Vineland Road. He sat opposite the house eating a sandwich and waiting for his quarry to show himself. He had been furnished with a description that fitted the man he had seen earlier perfectly. All he needed to establish now was that the guy was English. He bit into his sandwich, savouring the taste of moist chicken and crisp salad. He had been there over two hours and the two Dobermans had been watching him from the gates with beady eyes.

Duane approved of the dogs. If he had a house like that he would have had two similar dogs. He knew exactly what could happen to you if someone decided to rob you. He knew because he had been a robber himself for a while. Now he enjoyed the good life. He just let loose a few bits of lead and was paid a great deal of money. It was an arrangement that suited him. He would give this guy another thirty-six hours before he wasted him, Mr O'Grady's orders.

Duane guessed in his shrewd way that he was waiting for the money to arrive before committing himself. Mr O'Grady was one clever guy. Duane blessed the day he had met up with him.

Duane caressed the gun case on the passenger seat. It held his favourite weapon, a Ruger mini 14. It had an accurate range of four to five hundred yards and he used the .223 bullets that had been used in Vietnam. They could blow a man's brains out while sounding no louder than a whisper.

He finished his sandwich and started his car. He drove a few hundred yards down the road, turned the car around and watched the house from a different angle.

Sure enough, he saw what he was looking for.

He picked up his binoculars and watched the man through them. He didn't look like someone with fifty thousand dollars on his head. Duane shrugged mentally. Well, whatever the man looked like, it didn't matter. What did matter was that he had annoyed someone in England enough to merit his head being blown off. And Duane would do just that.

George had got up early and was enjoying the sunshine in the garden. He could not help looking at the swimming pool. Its water shone, blue and cool, and he wished he had the guts to jump in it. But George couldn't swim.

His niece and nephew were due later in the day and he was excited at the prospect of seeing them. Especially Natalie. He had seen photographs of her and she really was a good-looking girl.

Edith had informed him that she never rose before ten so he had the early morning to himself. Edith's housekeeper, a pretty Mexican woman, told him that he should go and explore and he thought he might just take her advice. He fetched his car keys and made his way from the house. The two Dobermans growled at him as he passed them and George hurriedly opened the gates and drove through. Then, shutting them carefully, he began to drive.

He was completely unaware of the large Buick trailing him. George drove towards Orlando itself, enjoying the clean sunshine of Florida. He had rolled up the sleeves of his shirt and now, with the sunroof open and a light breeze playing through his hair, he relaxed. After a while he found what he was looking for: the Orange Blossom Trail.

Last night at dinner, Edith and Joss had told him about the Orange Blossom Trail, saying its lovely name belied its function. It was downtown Orlando, where the tourists who flocked to Disney only went by accident. It was the Orlando version of Soho and George couldn't wait to get there.

He drove along enthralled. It was full of sleazy hotels advertising blue movies and waterbeds. Women of every shape, colour and description stood around dressed in tiny bikinis, their bodies tanned to a leathery mahogany. Some of the women lounged against their own trailers, mobile homes that they used to entertain their customers, thereby saving on hotel bills. George drank it all in like a man dying of thirst. He smiled at different women and was pleased when they smiled back. He came across a place called the Doll's House which promised delights such as topless dancers and drinking partners.

George carried on driving, until he came to the heart of the Orange Blossom Trail. Gone now were the big hotels of International Drive and the shopping malls. Gone were the pleasant-faced people wishing you 'Have a nice day now'. Here were the shanties, with people slumped outside them in various states of drunkenness or drug-induced lethargy. Here, shoeless children watched vacant-eyed as an obviously strange car drove by. Here, dirty-looking men pushed themselves from walls and lurched towards George's car, causing him to put down his foot on the accelerator. Here was the last stop for the poor, the addicted and the criminal.

George looked around him now in dismay. Turning the car, he drove back to the Doll's House and parked. Within seconds, women and men were propositioning him. George stepped from the car, locking it, and began to stroll along. A young girl waved at him and began to walk leisurely towards him. George stopped to feast his eyes on her.

'Hi.'

'Hello, dear.'

'Why, yo' English. Are you from London?'

George smiled. 'Originally. I don't live there any more.'

The girl looked disappointed. She thought London was England. 'What you lookin' for? Maybe I kin' help you.'

George stood in the dirty, dusty street, in the hot sunshine, and felt a thrill of expectation.

'I'm looking for a little fun.'

The girl smiled, displaying crooked teeth. 'Well, you certainly came to the right place. My name's Loretta.'

'George.'

'Well, George, how about you and me go for a little walk? My trailer's just down the road a mite.'

George walked with her, listening to her chatter. She greeted people as she passed them. Her soft southern drawl was captivating, he decided. She was no more than eighteen. George climbed into the trailer behind her and she shut the door, turning to smile at him.

'Would you like a drink. I ain't got no icebox, but the beer's usually cold enough.'

He nodded at her and she bent over to open the cupboard under the tiny sink. George watched her bikini bottom ride up into the cleft of her buttocks. As she straightened up with the can of beer, a little smile on her face, she saw the man staring at her strangely.

Englishmen were so cold. Maybe it was the climate. She had heard that it rained all the time there.

'You OK?'

George smiled, his little smile that just showed his teeth. 'Perfectly.'

Duane sat watching in his Buick. He lit himself a cigarette and settled down to wait for the Englishman to do his business.

Jack Fenton was a retired Army corporal who had lived in Bychester Terrace for ten years. He was not a man to mix very much with his neighbours, but he knew their comings and goings. His wife Daisy said he was nosy, but as far as Jack was concerned he was just observant.

Like the other night when he'd heard a car pull up late in the night, a Rolls-Royce no less, and two men going into the Markhams' next door. That had thrown him, he admitted. The Markhams kept themselves to themselves, and in Jack's book that was how it should be. But all the same he would have liked to know who the men were. It was a lovely car. In the end he had put it down to rich relations.

Now their overflow pipe was another matter. He had noticed when he had gone down to get his newspaper and his Woodbines that their overflow was causing a bit of distress. There was a large puddle around the side of the house. He had knocked but got no answer. So after a strong cup of tea he had informed his wife that he was just going next door for a recce. He still used army slang to the annoyance of Daisy, who hated the armed forces with all her heart.

Pulling on his wellingtons Jack went next door. It was a fine crisp morning and he took a few deep lungfuls of air, feeling the burn as it went down his throat. Then he began to cough dangerously so took out his Woodbines, puffing on one until it controlled the tickle. He surveyed the offending overflow pipe, the Woodbine clamped firmly between his teeth.

A blockage somewhere, he would lay money on it. He opened the back gate and walked into the garden, ducking to avoid the falling water. If George and Elaine weren't careful they'd end up with damp in their walls.

Then he saw the Markhams' back door.

He walked purposefully towards it and shook his head. There was a perfect round hole cut in the glass by the door handle.

He himself still had the original wire-reinforced glass in his door. The Markhams had a hardwood back door with four glass panels in the top.

Jack wasn't surprised when the door opened. He walked into the kitchen, his nose quivering like a blood-hound's.

The place was spotless.

He walked into the lounge and found the same. Nothing had been touched.

There was something strange afoot here or his name wasn't Jack Fenton. Picking up the telephone he dialled the police. Then he sat at the kitchen table and waited patiently for them to arrive.

A Panda car finally came over an hour later. Jack opened the door and showed them the evidence in silence. The two young PCs dutifully looked around and declared him right. There had been some kind of break in.

'Do you know where the occupants of the house are?'

Jack looked at them as if they were imbeciles. They didn't total his age between them.

'They're at work, of course.'

'Where do they work? Do you know?'

''Course I know. I'm their neighbour, aren't I?'

The elder of the two PCs took a deep breath.

'Well, if you'd be so kind as to tell us?'

'Her, that's the wife, Elaine, she works at the super-market in town. What's it called? Lowprice or whatever. As for George, he works on the Industrial Estate at Kortone Separates.'

'Thank you. Did you notice anything suspicious at all, before you saw the window?'

'Well, I don't know if this means anything, but I saw a Rolls Royce here the other night. Two men got out of it and knocked here.'

'Are you sure it was a Rolls Royce?'

''Course I'm sure. I just said so, didn't I?' His strident voice was beginning to get on the PCs' nerves.

'You want to get a plumber in, boys, that overflow's going to do some damage, I tell you. Well, I'm off home. I only live next door if you need me.'

He left the house, shaking his head sadly. He had expected detectives at least.

PC Dendy radioed the break-in to the information room. The duty officer sent a constable to Lowprice to speak to Mrs Markham and was told she had been off sick for a week. The constable had then gone to Kortone Separates and been told Mr Markham had recently retired.

Puzzled, he radioed both messages in, and the desk sergeant, being a suspicious man, had a talk with plain clothes. There was more going on here than met the eye. Rolls Royces turning up in the middle of the night? Holes cut in windows and the video still in the front room? Neither occupant of the house to be found? One sick and one retired? It didn't add up.

Caitlin was told about the mysterious case in his coffee break and would have laughed if it hadn't been for one thing: the Rolls Royce. A deep red Rolls Royce, Kelly's car.

He got the address from the desk sergeant and drove around to Bychester Road himself. The PCs were surprised to see him.

'Has anyone been back yet?'

'No, sir. It doesn't look as if anything's been taken.'

'I want you to search this place thoroughly. The house and the shed and the garage. Thoroughly, mind.'

'What are we looking for, sir?'

Caitlin smiled. 'That's just it, lads. I don't really know.'

He was outside in his car smoking one of his cigars when a PC came outside and tapped on the window.

'I think you'd better have a look at this, sir, I don't know if it means anything.'

Caitlin followed him through the house and up the garden to the shed. There were all George's magazines and scrapbooks.

Caitlin nodded to himself. His hunch has been right. There was only one thing wrong: it seemed Patrick Kelly had found the Grantley Ripper first.

He went out to his car and radioed in.

Kate was there within ten minutes with her squad. They began systematically to tear the house apart. No one was really sure what they were looking for until DS Willis and DS Spencer went up into the loft.

'Cor! What's that bloody awful smell?'

Spencer turned on the light as he spoke and Willis pulled the lid off the water tank.

Spencer watched as he staggered backwards, his hands over his mouth, until he dropped out of sight through the loft entrance.

The other detective sergeant went to the tank and put his handkerchief over his nose.

Elaine was lying on her side, her head at an impossible angle. Her eyes were milky white and bulbous. Her waterlogged skin was purple-grey and swollen.

He fainted just as Kate and Caitlin climbed into the loft. Kate called through the hatch: 'Someone get up here and remove Spencer, please, and call the pathologist.'

Kate and Caitlin took one glance at Elaine and then looked at each other. This was the Grantley Ripper's home all right, complete with dead wife.

The only question was, where was George Markham?

In Caitlin's mind there was another question. Where the hell was Kelly?

He made a mental note to have the Rolls Royce part omitted from the next-door neighbour's statement. Until he knew more, anyway.

He stared at Kate, a look of sadness on his face. She instinctively put her hand on his arm, assuming that he was sad for the poor woman in front of them.

It never occurred to her that the sympathy could have been for her.

The mood in the incident room was one of pure elation. They had the Grantley Ripper.

Kate allowed Caitlin to give her a glass of whisky. Everyone was patting themselves on the back, laughing and joking.

She picked up her phone as it rang. It was Frederick Flowers, and Kate held her arms up for hush as she put the phone on to the intercom.

'Well done, one and all. I knew you'd catch him. I'm releasing the news to the press in a couple of hours. You can all be very proud of yourselves.'

As he rang off, an almighty cheer erupted from everyone. Caitlin kissed Kate on the cheek and she hugged him. It was over. All they had to do was find him, and now they had his name, that was a formality.

Then Amanda Dawkins tapped Kate on the shoulder. The girl's serious expression made her frown.

'What's up?'

'I think you'd better put a stop to the party, ma'am. George Markham was blood tested. It was a negative.'

'What!'

Kate's shout cut through the noise around her and gradually it died down. She took the piece of paper from Amanda and read the results wearily.

George Markham had tested negatively.

They had been celebrating too soon.

She passed the paper to Caitlin, who stared at it for a long time.

'Shit . . .' The word was drawn out from between his lips.

'I can't believe it. I just can't believe it.' Kate's voice was low. She clenched her fist. 'I thought we had him there!'

The policemen and women began to whisper amongst themselves as the news penetrated them. The atmosphere in the room went flat in a matter of seconds.

Kate took a swig of her Scotch, she needed it now. 'So if he's not the Grantley Ripper, he's murdered his wife and gone on the trot. It's a different case entirely?'

'That's about the strength of it, yeah.' Caitlin's voice was low. 'Those videos and books, though. Jasus, I would have laid money on him being our man.'

Then another thought occurred to him.

Patrick Kelly also thought he was the man.

Kate watched him as he rushed from the room. If she had not been so disturbed by the news of George's negative test, she might have wondered what was wrong with him.

She was more annoyed that he had left it to her to break the news to Flowers.

How could they have assumed so much before confirming it? She finished the scotch in one gulp and picked up the phone. She did not relish this job one bit.

Patrick Kelly had spoken to Caitlin and assured him that he knew nothing about a George Markham. The next-door neighbour was probably half asleep and had made a mistake. He listened to Caitlin tell him about the negative blood test and made the appropriate noises of dismay at their mistake. Then he put the phone down and smiled to himself. George Markham's little plan had paid off.

He knew, and Tony Jones knew, that George's blood test would have been positive. Now Tony Jones was in hospital and George Markham was about to meet his maker. All in all this hadn't been a bad day.

Kate arrived at his house by cab two hours later.

'Hello, Patrick. I've had a terrible day. Pay the silly cabman before I arrest him!'

'Are you drunk?' Kelly's voice was shocked.

'A bit. And if I have my way, I'll be drunker.'

He took her arm and helped her across the hall and up the stairs.

'Where are we going?' Her voice had taken on an aggressive tone.

'I'm going to put you in the shower, my girl. Now get up them stairs.'

Willy walked out into the hall and Kelly snapped at him, 'She's pissed. Pay the cab, then get her some coffee.'

Willy nodded and watched Patrick half carry and half drag a drunken Kate up the stairs.

In the bedroom, he let her flop on to the bed and began to pull her clothes off. She was compliant now. The aggression had turned to a weary resignation.

'We thought we had him, Pat, but we didn't. We didn't . . . All we had was another murderer. He'd murdered his wife . . .'

'All right, all right, calm down.'

He hoisted her naked off the bed and walked her into the en-suite bathroom. Turning on the cold tap, he held her under the shower. The freezing water made her gasp for breath and she tried to leap out of the shower tray. Patrick held her in there with difficulty, the white silk shirt he was wearing getting soaked.

'Let the water run over you, Kate, it'll make you feel better.'

'You bloody bastard! Let me out of this shower now! It's fr-fr-freezing.'

Kelly watched the goose bumps appearing all over her skin as if by magic and stifled a grin. Her nipples were enormous!

He was still holding her under the flowing water when, about five minutes later, he heard Willy bring the coffee into the bedroom. Turning off the shower, Patrick wrapped her in a large bath towel.

'Come on then, into the bedroom.'

'Flowers told me off good and proper today. Not Kenneth Caitlin, though. Oh, no. Only me.'

He poured out a strong coffee, but when he took it over to the bed she was already asleep.

Her long hair was plastered across her body. Droplets of water made her skin look pearly. The bath towel barely covered her. Never had she looked so vulnerable or so desirable. For a fleeting second, looking down at her, he was sorry for what he had done. He knew, without a shadow of a doubt, that George Markham was her man. But he could never tell her.

There was something he could do, though, and that was put Frederick Flowers in his place. The thought consoled him for a while.

Kate finally opened her eyes three hours later. She looked around her, trying to get her bearings. Then she saw Patrick.

'Hello, love, feeling better?'

She pulled herself up on the bed.

'I feel rough actually.'

'I'll ring down for some fresh coffee.'

While he called the kitchen Kate pulled the damp towel around her more tightly, catching sight of herself in the mirror opposite the bed. She frowned. She looked terrible. Patrick sat beside her on the bed.

'I'm sorry about that Markham bloke.'

'Oh, don't remind me about it, please.'

He kissed her bare shoulder.

'If only we'd checked the blood tests before we put the finger on him, Pat. I feel such a bloody fool, but I would have sworn on a stack of bibles he was our man. The snuff movies, the books. It all fitted in. He'd even been in prison for attempted rape and battery. We found that out too late as well.'

'Well, he murdered his wife.'

Kate cut him off. 'But did he? For all we know someone else murdered her and Markham, dumping his body elsewhere. Until we find him or his body we don't know anything.'

Willy knocked on the door and brought in the coffee. 'Phone call from the States, Pat.'

He leapt off the bed and out of the room. 'Shall I pour, ma'am?'

'Yes please, Willy. I don't feel very steady at the moment.'

'I paid your cab for you. You was very drunk, you know.'

'I know.'

She took the cup from him.

'You look like you've been done and left!'

Kate couldn't help smiling. 'I feel like it, Willy.'

He pointed a short fat finger at her. 'Then let that be a lesson to you. Never have liked to see a woman in drink, it's horrible.'

'I'll bear that in mind in future.'

Willy left the room and Kate sipped at her coffee. God knows how the others must be feeling, they had been even drunker than her. Once the initial shock had worn off they had all started in on some serious drinking. The last she remembered was Caitlin slipping off his chair. One and all they'd been blotto.

But, by Christ, why not? After the news they'd had, they damned well needed something.

She closed her eyes as frustration assailed her again. All day the picture of James Redcar's tiny body had haunted her.

Patrick came back into the room, sat down beside her and slipped the towel from her breasts, caressing them.

'I think me and you could do with cheering up a bit. I know a little game you might like to play. Take your mind off your troubles for a bit.'

'What's that?'

'It's called lorries and garages. I don't know if you've ever played it before?'

Kate looked at him with one eyebrow raised.

'I can't say I have, no.'

'Well, do you see this?' He put her hand on his erect member. 'This is my lorry, right. And I have to find somewhere to park it. Get my drift?'

Kate roared with laughter.

'Oh, Patrick, I need you tonight. I need you so much.'

He looked down into her brown eyes. The lashes were glistening with tears and he felt an overwhelming sadness. Kate was hurting, and he could stop the hurt with a few words. The solving of this case was everything to her, and he could tell her everything she wanted to know.

Instead he began to kiss her, losing himself in her sweet-smelling body as he felt her respond to him. Felt her tongue slip between his lips. Her nails travel down his back and under his body to cup his testicles.

Then she was shuddering beneath him. He watched her face as she thrust her hips into him and he loved her then. Loved her to death.

Soon it would be all over, and Kate would never be any the wiser.

At least, that was his prayer.

Amanda Dawkins had stayed relatively sober. She sat on in the incident room collating everything she had about George Markham. She stared at the picture of him from his file. He had attacked a young girl on a train eighteen years earlier. It had been a vicious assault, and he had been sent to Broadmoor. He had been in and out in three years. His wife had given birth to a stillborn son, and that had helped with his release.

Amanda shook her head as she read his statement: 'The girl was asking for it, she was smiling at me. Egging me on.'

How many times did a policeman hear that?

She looked at his picture again. At the nondescript man staring out at her. He had lifeless grey eyes and a weak, almost non-existent chin. He did not look like a sexual pervert at all. He looked like someone's uncle.

She poured another Scotch into the paper cup by her side. They'd really thought they had him.

Her eyes travelled to the pictures on the wall. Cynthia Redcar and her young son were now added to them. The picture of the little boy's battered face seemed to be imprinted on her mind. Who the hell could hurt a child like that?

She dragged her eyes back to the file in front of her. There had been ructions earlier over this. Caitlin and Kate had wanted to know why George Markham had not been brought to their attention. Amanda had been sorry for Willis then. He had knocked over a whole stack of files and got them all mixed up together. He had then shoved them into a filing cabinet and promptly forgotten them. It was only when they had tapped into the central computer that they had found out they had already been sent a copy of Markham's file, along with many others. Caitlin's swearing could be heard all over the building.

Amanda sipped her Scotch and looked at the statement again. George Markham's handwriting was spidery, barely legible. Then she sat forward in her seat with a jolt. As she scrambled through the paperwork in front of her, her heart began to pound.

Then she found what she was looking for: George Markham's blood testing statement. He had signed it in a large childish script.

She held the two signatures together, her hands shaking. Then she downed the Scotch in one gulp and picked up the telephone. Kate's mother answered. Leaving her home number, Amanda told Evelyn that Kate was to ring her as soon as she got in.

Kate was home at one thirty, the day's events a blur, except for Patrick's lovemaking. She walked into the house and straight up the stairs to her bedroom. The note on the table by the phone went unnoticed.

She heard the alarm go off at six and pulled herself from bed. Her mouth felt dry, as if it was full of cotton wool. She pulled on her dressing gown and padded into the bathroom. She needed a good hot shower and at least one pot of coffee to get herself set up for the day ahead. After yesterday's fiasco, she knew that today was not going to be a good one.

In the shower she soaped her body absentmindedly. Patrick had made her feel good. He had held her and told her he loved her, and she had needed that so much. He had been so understanding with her that she felt almost as if he knew what she was going through, as if he had an affinity with her, a special knowledge.

She was so lucky to have him.

She wrapped herself in a large bath towel and, pushing on her slippers, walked down the stairs to make her coffee. It was six fifteen.

As she walked past the telephone she saw the piece of paper that her mother had left for her and picked it up and read in the hallway light.

She dialled the number.

'Hello, Amanda?'

'Oh, Kate, I've been worried out of my mind! Look, I think George Markham *is* our man . . .'

'What!' Kate's voice rose.

'I went back through his files. The signatures on his statements are different. He must have had someone take the test for him.'

As the enormity of what Amanda was saying penetrated, Kate felt a surge of excitement.

'Who else have you told?'

'No one.'

'Oh, Amanda, you're brilliant! I'll see you in about twenty minutes, OK?'

'OK.'

'And, Amanda . . . thanks a million.'

'Any time. Oh, and one last thing. I put a call out for his car again. I told them to concentrate on the Kent area. That's obviously the last place he was.'

'Great, Amanda. You'll make DI yet, my girl.'

The two women laughed and said goodbye. Kate put down the phone and did a little jig. She had known he was the man. She had known it in her heart. He was wily. He must have a very good friend if he would take a blood test for him. Especially a blood test on a murder case. A man who could arrange a bluff like that was obviously not lacking in imagination.

She threw on her clothes, pulled on her coat and picked up her bag, her coffee left by the phone to go cold. Forgotten now.

She would find George Markham wherever he was. Find him and put him away.

The earlier depression had disappeared. Kate felt wonderful.

Chapter Thirty

Ratchette and Caitlin were both looking at her expectantly.

'I have proof that George Markham is our man.'

She watched their eyes widen.

'Last night, Amanda Dawkins checked through George Markham's file. It seems the signatures on his statements for the blood testing and his previous arrest differ. I can only assume he had someone else take the blood test for him. He's definitely our man.'

Caitlin's face lit up.

'I knew he was the bugger we were after. I just knew it in me guts.'

'Well, we have Amanda Dawkins to thank for this. She saw what was under everyone else's nose. I think she deserves to take full credit.'

Ratchette smiled gently.

'Another good woman coming up in the ranks, eh, Kate? This is excellent news. I'll get on to Flowers immediately.'

'Make sure he knows it was Dawkins. I think she did an exceptional job.'

'I will. So where will you go from here?'

'Amanda Dawkins put another call out on Markham's car. This time she asked them to concentrate on the Kent area. That was obviously his last port of call. I can only guess his wife was on to him, he murdered her, and now he's trying to disappear. At some point someone would have wanted to know where she was. She'd been dead a few days so he has a head start on us. My guess is he picked on Cynthia Redcar while in Kent. God knows where he'll strike next.'

'Well, you follow up any avenues you have to. And tell Dawkins well done. I'll see her myself later. Now I think you'd better tell all the officers on the case. A bit of morale boosting wouldn't go amiss today.'

Caitlin left the office with Kate and put his arm around her shoulders. 'Sure you women like to stick together. If it had been me and Ratchette you'd have accused us of pushing you out.'

Kate grinned at him.

'Kenny?'

'What?'

'Up yours. That's how you would have answered me if I'd accused you of pushing me out!'

Caitlin laughed out loud. 'You're learning, Katie, and that young Amanda did good. It'll be one in the eye for Spencer anyway.'

They walked into the incident room and Caitlin called for silence.

'I have an announcement for you all that I think will take the sour expression off your faces.'

Everyone stood staring at him.

'Thanks to a certain young lady,' he pointed to Amanda Dawkins, who went red with embarrassment, 'we have reason to believe that George Markham *is* our man.'

There was a murmur of surprise.

'It seems he got someone to take the blood test for him. The signatures on his statements don't match. We must concentrate on finding out who that was, and on looking for George Markham. One can only lead to the other.'

The telephone rang and Amanda Dawkins picked it up, glad of something to do. Everyone was grinning at her.

'Today we will concentrate on people who knew the Markhams: workmates, friends, relatives. Anyone at all. Let's get going!'

The excitement was back in the air. Cigarettes were being lit with a flourish, the disappointment of the night before evaporated. Kate watched the change in her team and felt the adrenaline in her own veins.

They would find George Markham. She was convinced of it.

Patrick ate a hearty breakfast and went into work. He had managed to shrug off his feelings of despondency over Kate. Had convinced himself that what she didn't know couldn't hurt her. Once George Markham was out of the way, he would be able to relax once more. His debt to his daughter would be paid in full. He could live again.

He smiled at the men in his office and they smiled back, wondering who had put the smile on his face in the first place.

'Gentlemen,' he announced, 'I am officially calling off the hunt for the murderer of my daughter. The man who gave me the information will be paid in full in a few days.'

He saw the men's faces drop.

'Now then, down to business. Larry, I want you to go down to Colchester today and repossess a Jag. The owner is a Paki and he ain't paid more than one instalment on it.

The credit company think he may have ringed it. I want you to find out.

'There's also a large warehouse in Surrey that needs to be cleared out, mainly colour tellies and video equipment. The whole lot is to be moved from there and impounded. I'm saying this only once, so listen good. Only a telly or a video apiece can go astray. If I hear that any of the stuff's being sold on the side there'll be trouble. Right, Jimmy?'

He hung his head. Pat sussed all right. Everyone laughed.

'Now we've got a lot of furniture snatchbacks today, you know the score. Council flats with leather settee suites and solid oak dining tables, mainly catalogue collection, so look after the gear right. There's a list outside for each of you, with a route map. Take the big removal vans. It's the after Christmas rush at the moment so there's plenty of work. Don't hassle the occupants of the places unless you have to. I heard through the grapevine that Dinny Morris's lot slapped a young bird the other week, I don't like that kind of behaviour. You'd throw a paddy if someone came to take your furniture away, try and remember that. Have a bit of sympathy for them.'

The men looked at Jimmy again.

'I don't know why you're all looking at me! I'd never slap a bird.'

'Not unless you was living with her anyway.'

Ronald Baker's voice was hard and the men looked uneasy. Jimmy lived with Ronald's youngest sister.

'All right, keep your family feuds outside this office and this company. Lastly, I want you to tell your teams that when they are debt collecting I want all the money paid in pronto. I keep hearing how the men are keeping the Saturday collections at home until the Monday morning. That's got to stop from now on. I know every scam in the book, and a couple of the collectors have pissed money up the wall by Monday then sworn black was blue they never collected it. Any more stories like that and they're out, along with their team leader which will be one of you.'

He lit himself a cigarette slowly to let his words sink in. 'Other than that, I don't think I've got anything else to say.'

The men stood up and began making their way to the door.

'Can you stay behind for a minute, Ronnie?'

He resumed his seat and waited for the room to empty.

'I've got a special job for you.'

'What kind of job?' Ronnie's voice was neutral.

'A very lucrative job. Are you game?'

Ronnie nodded his head. His thin-lipped mouth had a tight roll-up stuck in the corner. It moved up and down as he spoke. Kelly could never remember seeing it lit.

'In Spain there's a certain old lag who owes a considerable amount of money to a friend of mine. He wants the debt collected this week.'

Ronnie nodded again. 'How much is my bunce?'

'Your take will be ten per cent as is usual in these cases. The amount to be collected is eighty grand.'

Ronnie nodded again.

'Who's the lag?'

Patrick took a deep breath. 'William Carlton.'

Ronnie's taciturn expression never wavered. 'Tell the bloke I want twenty per cent and he supplies the shooter. I'll bring the money back by boat.'

'That can all be arranged. You're to go tomorrow morning.'

'Fair enough.'

Ronnie stood up. 'One more thing, Pat. Jimmy will be

out of work for a good few months soon. I thought I'd let you know so you could replace him.'

Patrick nodded. 'What's the rub?'

'He gave me sister a kicking Saturday, thinks no one knows about it, but she phoned me mum. I can't swallow no more, Pat. She's only twenty-two and five months pregnant. The slag won't even marry her.'

'What about your sister, can't she leave him?'

'She won't. Thinks the sun shines out of his arse. She's only a kid, Pat. Don't know what's good for her yet.'

Patrick stood up and shook the man's hand.

'Thanks for letting me know. I'm sorry to hear about Clare, she's a good kid.'

'Thanks, Pat. I'm glad you found the scumbag who done your Mandy. Fucking real, ain't it? The shite that's knocking about these days. No one's safe.'

Patrick saw him to the door and sat back at his desk. Well, the piece of scum who'd killed his Mandy had had his card marked for sure. His days were numbered.

Patrick began to whistle through his teeth as he studied his books.

Hector Henderson was worried. Very worried. He had not heard from Elaine for over a week. He had gone round to Margaret Forrester's house and been informed that Elaine was off work ill. Some kind of flu. Except she'd had all day to ring him while George was out at work, and nothing. Nothing at all.

He chewed on his thumbnail, his big fat face shining with a film of sweat. Suppose she didn't want to see him any more? He chewed harder at the thought, causing his ill-fitting teeth to make tiny popping noises as they rattled against his gums. Since the New Year he had become fond of Elaine. More than fond in fact. He would even go so far as to say he loved her.

Yes, it was no use denying it, he thought the bally world of her.

She was a good handful was old Elaine, a good laugh, and a very accommodating woman. Bet she could cook too. Stood to reason, the size of her. If only she wasn't married to that George chap.

He sighed. Elaine might leave him, though. The only thing was, how was he going to convince her to throw the man out? He looked around his little bedsit. They couldn't live here. Perhaps if Elaine sold her house they could buy a nice flat. He nodded to himself. That would be the best bet. After all, he didn't want to see her husband with nothing. The last time he had seen her she had been like a ripe plum, ready for the picking, and he had picked her all right. He smiled to himself. Surpassed himself in fact. She did like the old one-eyed snake did Elaine! That was another of her attractions.

He settled himself back in the large armchair. He was worrying over nothing. Elaine had told him in no uncertain terms that she loved him. She was probably lying in bed at this very moment, half dead with flu and a raging temperature. He pictured this in his mind. That was why she hadn't been in touch, bless her heart. He scolded himself for his earlier, unworthy thoughts. His Elaine was a diamond, a 24-carat diamond. She would see him all right. She would get him out of this dump.

She had to. He was depending on it.

He was startled by a knock on the door. He sat quietly for a few minutes. If it was that old bitch for her rent money she usually gave a warning shout. Nothing. He felt his panic subside. Perhaps it was Elaine?

He leapt from his chair as the knocking began again, his

eyes taking in the chaos of the room. He could have kicked himself, he should have tidied up a bit. He glanced in the piece of broken mirror on his mantelpiece. Hurriedly tidying his hair, he opened the door with a flourish, a big smile on his large round face.

'Mr Henderson?'

Hector nodded cagily, racking his brains to think if he was in any kind of debt.

'I'm Detective Inspector Burrows and this is my colleague, Chief Inspector Caitlin. We would like to have a few words with you.'

Hector stared at the tiny cards in their hands.

'What about?'

'Elaine Markham. We understand from Margaret Forrester that you were close friends.'

Hector stood aside to let them in. Caitlin's nose wrinkled at the sour smell.

'I'm afraid we have some bad news for you, Mr Henderson. Elaine Markham has been murdered.'

Kate watched the shock and disbelief on the man's face and felt sorry for him.

'No . . . No, it can't be true. Not Elaine.'

His voice was a distraught whisper. All his dreams were dissolving in front of his eyes. A proper home, a wife, a companion for his old age. Hector knew as sure as eggs were eggs that Elaine Markham was his last chance.

'Murdered, you say?'

Caitlin nodded.

'Well, it wasn't me. I haven't seen her for over a week.'

Hector was now out to save his skin. Maybe they thought he had done it?

'We have a good idea who murdered her, Mr Henderson, you're not a suspect. We just want you to tell us all you know about Elaine Markham and anything she might have told you about her husband.'

Hector Henderson nodded slowly. He looked around the grubby room and sighed. It had all been too good to be true. His dancing clothes hung from the picture rails around the room, mocking him, and he felt an urge to cry.

Elaine had been a good egg. She would have seen him all right.

Inside the trailer it was hot. Loretta lay on the bed, watching the Englishman. As he brought his arm up to run his hand through his hair she flinched.

'Don't worry, my dear, I wouldn't hurt you.'

He smiled at her, displaying his tiny teeth.

Loretta took a large swallow. She put a hand between her legs to try and ease the burning.

'Let me drink my beer, and then we'll get back down to business.'

Loretta closed her eyes. She ached all over.

The Englishman was cold, as she had first thought. Cold and callous. Never before had she had to endure the things he wanted from her, and she had done them all, she'd had to do them. This man was frightening in his intensity. He took his sex seriously. He had lain on top of her and pounded into her, as if he knew exactly what would hurt most.

Luckily for Loretta, she lay passively, letting him do just what he wanted; some inbred cunning told her that this was not a man to fight with. Even when he dug his fingers hard and spitefully into her genitals, she had just whimpered, biting down the scream that was trying to emerge.

She did not want to upset this guy.

George looked into the young fresh face. A trickle of blood ran down from her swollen lip.

She really was quite a pretty little thing.

'Turn over on your stomach, dear.'

Loretta did as he asked and as she felt him straddle her she bit down once more on her bottom lip. Big fat tears squeezed out from beneath her closed lids. As she felt the sharp pain of George's penis entering her anal passage she began to beg him to stop, her words becoming incoherent as the pain engulfed her again.

George looked down at the long tanned body and smiled.

Outside in the Florida sunshine, Duane yawned and settled himself more comfortably in his seat.

This guy certainly liked his money's worth.

Kate came back into the station at two thirty. She had just got herself a coffee when Amanda came to her desk.

'His car's been found. In Gatwick Airport car park. Caitlin's on his way down now, he'll wait for you outside.'

Kate picked up her bag and rushed from the room. They made their way to Gatwick in record time, barely exchanging a word.

Both were filled with the same thought: He'd left the country. Either that or someone had left his car here for him. They already knew they were dealing with a clever man.

The flights were being checked, as were the ferries. He did not know yet that his wife's body had been found. George Markham was still in the clear so far as he knew. The press hadn't got so much as a whiff of this one.

In the car park George's car was opened. In the back was Cynthia Redcar's parka. It had a little plastic toy in the pocket. Looking at it, Kate felt a wave of sadness.

Later, the car had just arrived at the forensics workshop and Kate and Caitlin were watching it being dusted for prints, before being stripped, when the call came through.

George Markham had gone to Orlando on a charter flight three days previously.

Cynthia Redcar had been his last little fling before boarding. He was due back on 16 March. He was on a fly drive holiday. That meant he could be anywhere.

But they were interviewing his brother soon. Maybe he could shed some light on the trip. There had been no address books in the Markham house. Joseph Markham's address had been found on an old letter.

First though, they were going to Kortone Separates.

George arrived back at Edith's happy and relaxed, and full of good-natured bonhomie as he embraced his nephew, Joss Junior.

'Natalie is just coming down now, George. She's so excited.'

George heard her footsteps on the stairs and turned in their direction, a large smile on his face. When she walked into the room his face froze.

In the flesh, Natalie was the living image of his mother. She looked nothing like the photograph he'd seen the day before. Her hair was the same deep red, her eyes the same greeny-blue. George felt his heartbeat quicken. He half expected her to say something cutting as Nancy would have. Instead she ran towards him and embraced him, enveloping him a cloud of Giorgio perfume. George automatically put his arms around her slim waist. He could smell the slightly musky smell of her sweat. Not unpleasant, he decided, but womanly.

'Oh, Uncle George, I've heard so much about you. I feel as if I know you already!'

671

Her voice was pure American, as was Joss's, and the reminder of Nancy evaporated. George caught Edith's eye and realised she knew what he was thinking.

Joss Senior came into the room with a jug of martinis. 'Who wants a drink?' he boomed.

Everyone moved outside to the sunshine and George listened to all the family chit chat. Joss Junior, unlike his namesake, was very subdued. In fact he reminded George of himself when younger. George smiled at him now and then and the boy coloured slightly and nodded back.

Edith thought her heart would burst.

She had all the important people in her life around her, something she was sure she would never experience again.

'Where did you go today, George?'

He blanched. 'Oh, I just drove around, you know. Had a little look about.'

Natalie squealed, 'I know, let's take him to MGM tomorrow. Oh, Uncle George, you'll just love the studios.'

George beamed. He liked Florida right enough. It really brought him out of himself. An hour later he was half listening to Joss, Joss Junior and Edith chatting while he watched Natalie swimming in the pool.

She was Nancy Markham all over again, from the big fat breasts to the jutting hip bones. George watched her closely and nodded to himself. She had her grandmother's lust for sex too. That was evident in every move she made. A flicker of repugnance crossed his features. He watched her pull herself from the pool and dry herself, rubbing hard at her skin with the towel, causing her breasts to shimmy in their tiny top.

They were all the same. Every last one of them. Abruptly he got up and went to his room.

Edith, Joss and their children all gave one another puzzled looks.

'I think the flight probably caught up with him,' said Edith. It sounded lame even to her own ears.

George locked himself into his bathroom. He sat on the toilet seat, his mind filled with thoughts of his niece's body and presence. Erotic visions played in front of his eyes. He felt the familiar urge rising in him. He would show them. He would show them all. They were all bloody whores!

His mother, Edith, Elaine . . . he pictured all the women he had murdered, and then somewhere, tacked right on the end, was his niece Natalie. In his mind's eyes he saw her beneath him, begging for him to stop hurting her, and he smiled.

Downstairs Natalie sat with her family, feeling safe and secure. Happy to be with them and part of their lives.

George heard her tinkling laughter; it wafted up to him on the heavy Florida air, and somewhere in his mind he decided she was laughing at him.

Well, he would teach her a lesson she would not forget.

Edith watched her children with pride. She had spent a lifetime protecting them. She did not even guess that the biggest threat her daughter had ever faced was sitting upstairs in her own home.

Peter Renshaw was nervous. Kate could sense the sweat coming from his pores.

'I understand you were quite friendly with Mr Markham?'

'I knew him as a workmate, that was all.'

Kate frowned. He was hiding something.

'Look, Mr Renshaw, I understand you arranged his leaving party for him. I got the impression that you were one of the few people who was actually close to George Markham.'

'Look, why is everyone interested in George all of a sudden? What's he supposed to have done?'

Renshaw's voice was high and uneasy.

'What do you mean by everyone? Who else has been looking for him?'

'No one. No one at all. Why would anyone want him?'

Kate watched him chew his fingernail.

'Listen here, Mr Renshaw.' She stressed the 'Mr'. 'You can either chat to me here or I can haul your fat arse into the station. It's up to you. But I warn you now – I don't like people holding out on me. Now who else was looking for George Markham?'

'If I tell you, do you promise me you'll keep it to yourself?' His bulbous eyes were pleading.

Kate nodded.

'It was a local hard man . . . Patrick Kelly. He pulled me up a few days ago.' He looked at Kate and stood up. 'Here, are you all right?'

'Patrick Kelly?' she whispered.

Renshaw nodded. Then watched as she stormed from the room. He shook his head. He hoped to Christ she kept her promise.

Kate drove back to Grantley at record speed. Patrick had already seen Renshaw. He already knew who they were looking for. George Markham was in America and Patrick had taken a call from the States . . . She felt icy fingers at the back of her neck. Hadn't he told her he would pay his daughter's murderer out? Hadn't he told her that?

He had known where George Markham was all along. He had made love to her knowing that. Knowing he had murder planned.

Patrick must have thought she was the most stupid bimbo he had ever come across in his life. He'd been laughing at her. If he knew where Markham was then Markham was a dead man – unless she did something about it.

She drove as fast as she could to Grantley Police Station and went in search of Caitlin. By this time she was in a fury so passionate it was making her shake.

Patrick Kelly had a lesson to learn: never to mug off Kate Burrows again!

Caitlin was in the incident room, thick grey cigar smoke curling around his weather-beaten face. He took one glance at Kate's expression and hurriedly bundled her from the room, much to the chagrin of the other officers present, who could smell a rat before it was stinking.

Spencer glanced at Amanda Dawkins. 'She looked fit to do murder. I wonder what's going on?'

Amanda shrugged. 'How the hell should I know?'

Caitlin had taken Kate to an empty interview room. Now she stood facing him. It was all as clear as day. Even Caitlin had known what was going on. She could have cried with temper.

'You know, don't you?'

He was nonchalant. 'Know what, Katie?'

'Don't you bloody "Katie" me, Kenneth Caitlin. You know what I'm going to say, don't you? By Christ, I must be some kind of dunce. I should change my name to Detective Inspector Thicko.'

Caitlin sat down at the table and puffed on his cigar. 'Sit down, woman, and tell me what's on your mind.'

Kate placed both hands on the table and looked into Caitlin's face.

'Last night I was at Kelly's when he had a call from the States. This morning I find out that that's where George Markham has gone. Now I don't know about you, but that tells me that George Markham is a dead man.'

'It could be a coincidence.'

'Coincidence my arse! When I think of all the work that's gone into this case. The blood testing, the man hours . . . And all the time we were working for Patrick fucking Kelly!'

Caitlin's eyes widened to their utmost. Two swear words in one sentence from Kate Burrows told him just how annoyed she was. 'Well, he won't get away with it, matey. I'm going to see Flowers. I want some answers, and I want them now!'

She slammed out of the interview room and Caitlin followed her as fast as he could. He finally caught up with her in the car park where he banged on the window of her car and motioned for her to unlock the passenger side.

'Bugger off!'

Caitlin watched the small car drive away, and sighed. Then he went to his own car and began following her. She'd need all the help she could get when she saw Frederick Flowers.

The episode in the car park had been witnessed by the occupants of the incident room.

Spencer shook his head.

'That's why women should never have been allowed in the police force. They're too emotional. Look at the way she was carrying on.'

The others allowed their eyes to peruse the ceiling.

Frederick Flowers was sitting in his office nursing a hangover when his secretary's chirpy tones informed him that Detective Inspector Kate Burrows was demanding to see him. He winced. That bloody woman got on his nerves. Before he could put her off, Kate herself stood in front of him, sending his office door crashing against the wall. The noise whiplashed in his aching head. The door opened again and Flowers relaxed slightly at the sight of Caitlin.

Kate was firing on all cylinders.

'You listen to me now! George Markham, whatever he's done, is in mortal danger and we must do something about it. Patrick Kelly has sworn he's going to kill him and I know he will. He is aware of George Markham's whereabouts, and we have a duty to protect that man so he can stand trial.'

Her chest was heaving and Flowers took a crafty peek at it before answering. Like this, with two red temper marks on her cheeks and her face glowing, he could see what Kelly saw in her. Her dark silky hair had been hastily pinned up in a French pleat and shone in the weak February sun.

'You have no proof of this, Burrows, it's all conjecture on your part. From information I have received, Markham is on a fly drive holiday to his sister's. The finding of his wife's body will not be in the newspapers and Markham will fly back to England none the wiser that we have tumbled him. As he steps off the plane on to British soil he will be arrested.'

'But that's just it! He'll be coming back to England in a bloody coffin.' Kate clenched her fists. 'I have every reason to believe that Patrick Kelly has put a price on his head.'

Caitlin closed his eyes. Oh, Katie, he thought, you stupid woman.

'Look, Burrows, I think you're overwrought. I think you should go home and have a good think about all you've just said. They're very serious allegations and unless you have concrete evidence I would advise you to keep your thoughts to yourself. Patrick Kelly is not above suing us for defamation of character. I might add that after listening to your hysterical ramblings, I wouldn't blame him.'

Kate opened her mouth to speak. Flowers held up his hand for silence, but she ignored him.

'You're all in on it, aren't you?' Her voice was low and bitter. 'Oh, I know that no one could actually put your faces in the frame, no more than they'll be able to put Kelly's. But you all know the score, don't you? You're all quite willing to let him collect his debt, aren't you?'

Her voice was disgusted and Caitlin at least had the grace to look away.

'I must have been living in some kind of fools' paradise. I honestly believed in my work. You must all think I'm a cretin.' She poked a finger at Flowers and he flinched as it came within an inch of his face. 'Well, I'll settle you lot if it's the last thing I do.'

Flowers found his voice.

'Are you threatening me? Because if you are, you listen to me and listen good, Burrows. I know that you, a Detective Inspector, have been seen with Patrick Kelly on more than one occasion. Now I'd say that constitutes a slur on your integrity, don't you?'

She was dumbstruck.

'You've known him a lot longer than I have, Flowers,' she said at last.

Flowers grinned.

'Sure I know Kelly, he's a well-known figure, but think about this very carefully, Burrows. I'm not sleeping with him, am I? My husband has not made a statement to the CIB to that effect.'

Kate felt an anger born of futility engulf her. 'You dirty stinking bastard!'

'As from now, Burrows, you're off this case and suspended from duties. Caitlin, take her away, for goodness' sake.'

He flapped his hand in a gesture of dismissal and Kate found her eyes filled with tears of frustration.

'Shall I tell you something, Flowers? For the first time in my life I realise just what you are. You're quite willing to let a man be murdered in cold blood, aren't you? It means nothing to you, does it? You're even willing to sacrifice my career so your friend Kelly can get even with Markham.'

Caitlin pulled her by the arm. He had stood silently all through the exchange, but now he realised he had to get her home and talk some sense into her. He owed her that at least.

'Come on, Katie, before you say some more things you'll regret.'

'Regret?' She laughed out loud. 'The only regret I have is getting mixed up with you lot.'

Caitlin's voice was firmer now.

'Shut your bloody mouth up and give me your keys. I'll drive.

In the car, neither of them spoke until Caitlin turned off the dual carriageway and down a country lane, stopping at a small public house.

'Come on, Kate, we're going to have something to eat and drink, and a talk.'

She followed him, her shoulders slumped inside her jacket. She knew she was beaten. Nothing in all her experience had prepared her for something like this.

Sitting in the comfortable bar, Caitlin ordered two roast dinners and a bottle of Chianti. Then he added two large Scotches.

Absentmindedly Kate said, 'We'll be over the limit.'

'Let me worry about that.'

Finally, with her drink untouched in front of her, Caitlin began to talk to her.

Martina Cole

'Look, I know how you're feeling, believe me. I've experienced the same thing myself. What you seem to have forgotten is that George Markham was a murderer of the worst kind. He took seven lives, Katie, and God Himself only knows how many more he would have taken. He raped and murdered innocent girls and women. He was a sadist.'

She interrupted him.

'You just said he *was* a murderer. You used the past tense, Kenny. Is he already dead then?'

'Oh, that was just a slip of the tongue, Kate. What I'm trying to say is that, noble as your sentiments are, they're wasted on him.'

'Flowers has sewn me up nice and tightly, hasn't he? You all have. You, Flowers, and let's not forget Kelly, shall we?'

'Kelly's daughter was brutally murdered, Kate. Even if he does have Markham taken out, think of the alternative. All the money it would cost to keep him locked up for the rest of his life, because that's what would happen.

'You disappoint me, Kate. I always thought you were a sensible woman. You're putting your career on the line for a piece of filth. If he was put in prison in the morning all he could look forward to is years of abuse from prisoners and staff alike. Years ago he attacked a young girl on a train and beat the frigging crap out of her. His wife gave birth to a dead child over it. We're not dealing with a blagger here now, Kate, we're dealing with a sadistic rapist.'

'That's just it, though. I know what we're dealing with, and no matter how you, Flowers, Kelly or bloody King Street Charlie dress it up, it's still condoning murder!'

Caitlin shook his shaggy head. His hair was sticking up in all directions where he had run his hands through it.

680

'Kelly was the one who paid for the blood testing, Kate. It was him who got it okayed. He tried hard to help find the killer.'

'I know he paid for the blood testing.' Her voice was bitter. 'How good of him. Just so he could find out who did it for his own ends!'

'You still don't know for certain if he has put a price on the man's head. Like Flowers said, it's all conjecture on your part.'

She sneered, 'Oh, grow up, Kenny, for Christ's sake. You know as well as I do that Markham's a dead man. But just to be on the safe side, I'm going to see the Golden Boy myself.'

Kate stood up. Snatching her keys off the table, she stormed from the pub. Caitlin did not attempt to follow her this time. Instead he poured her drink into his glass and cancelled one of the dinners.

He had done his bit. Now it was up to her.

Kelly was like a cat on hot bricks. He had arranged the payment of the fifty thousand dollars, a minuscule amount for what he wanted done. Now all he wanted was confirmation of the hit. Every time the telephone rang he rushed to answer it, a feeling of excitement in his breast.

He couldn't relax until that piece of scum was dead. His eyes went automatically to Mandy's photograph. The familiar lump came to his throat.

He saw her as she had been when she was eleven. Her hair a mass of blonde around a tiny heart-shaped face.

'Mummy won't be coming home any more, Princess.' The feel of her little skinny sobbing body had helped to allay his own grief. He had had to pick himself up and brush himself down for Mandy's sake. He had comforted her through the inevitable nightmares and depressions. He had tried his hardest to be a good father to her. To be there for her always. To protect her.

And for what? For that ponce to batter her brains out on a filthy floor while he raped her. It would have been better if she had been in the car with his wife. At least that way she would have died without all the shame and fear. It would all have been over in seconds.

Willy knocked softly on the door and stepped into the room. 'Any news yet, Pat?'

He shook his head.

'Never mind, no news is good news. Can I get you a coffee or anything?'

Kelly looked at Willy's big moon face and felt a surge of affection.

'I love you, Willy, you know that?' The words were quietly spoken and the minder knew their significance. Together they had been through the worst life has to offer.

Willy smiled. 'I never had you down as a shirtlifter, Pat.'

Kelly laughed painfully.

'Oh, Willy, only you could get away with that.'

'Have a nice cup of coffee, Pat, it'll settle your nerves.'

'All right. Shove a drop of brandy in it, would you?'

Willy opened the door. Looking back over his shoulder, he said in his best man-to-man voice. 'I recipcreat your sentiments entirely.'

'It's reciprocate, Willy.'

'Oh, who gives a toss, Pat? You know what I mean.'

Kelly smiled to himself. Kate had been right: Willy was the best friend he had. Sometimes he thought he was the only friend he had. The only genuine one anyway.

As if his thoughts had conjured her up, Kate's car screeched to a halt outside.

One look at her dark expression told him everything

and he braced himself for the onslaught he knew was to come. A brief of his had once told him: 'Deny, deny, and deny again.' Well, he'd need to use that tack now.

Kate pushed past Willy and into the entrance hall of Patrick's house.

'Where is he?'

Willy was so shocked he just pointed to the library door. She stormed in there to see Patrick sitting behind his desk, casually smoking a cigarette.

'Hello, Kate.' He stood up, smiling at her widely.

'Don't you bloody "hello" me! I've just had the Third World War with Frederick Flowers over you. I've sussed you out, Patrick Kelly.'

'I don't know what you're talking about.'

'Oh, don't you? Well, let me enlighten you then. When I was here yesterday you had a call from the States. And George Markham, the man we want for our inquiries into the Grantley Ripper murders, is in the States. Florida to be exact.'

He butted in, 'What's this got to do with me?'

Kate pushed her face towards his.

'You swore to me that you would get him for what he did to Mandy.'

'Can you blame me? Well, can you? How would you feel if it had happened to Lizzy?

'All that aside, Kate, I have many business dealings in America and Europe. Don't you come round here reading the riot act to me over a fucking phone call!'

'You're just like Dan, do you know that? Attack as the best form of defence. Well, the minute I hear that George Markham has been hurt, I'm going to the newspapers, Pat. I mean it. I'll scream it from the bloody roof tops.'

He shook his head sadly.

'I don't know what you're talking about, Kate.' His soft voice belied his eyes, which were like granite.

'You're disgusting, do you know that? What did I ever see in you? Maybe it was pity because of your daughter, I don't know. But one thing I do know – the thought of you touching me now makes me sick to my stomach.'

She spoke through clenched teeth and the vehemence of her voice cut Patrick to the bone.

'I think you'd better go, Kate. Before we both say things we'll regret.'

'Oh, don't worry, I'm going. The sight of you makes me want to spew. But remember what I said, Pat. As soon as I hear Markham's dead, I open my mouth. You can tell Flowers that and all, when you speak to him. I'll go as high as the DPP or the Chief Justice. I'll even go to the blasted Queen.'

The phone on his desk rang shrilly and he looked at it for a second before answering. O'Grady's American twang wafted over the distance.

'One moment, please.' Putting his hand over the mouthpiece he looked into Kate's eyes.

'I think you had better go, before I throw you out.'

Giving him one last look she walked from the room. Patrick waited until she had slammed the door before he spoke to the man on the other end of the phone.

'Sorry about the delay. What's the score?'

He watched through the window as Kate got into her car and drove away. He felt as if a crucial part of himself had gone with her.

'It's all set up for tomorrow morning. As soon as the deed is done I'll be in touch.'

'Can't it be done today?'

'No can do, Pat. Stop worrying. The man will be well

out of the ball game tomorrow. A professional job like this takes planning. That's what you pay for.'

'Tomorrow it is then.'

He replaced the receiver and Willy walked in with the tray of coffee.

'It's tomorrow, Willy.'

He nodded and poured, adding a liberal amount of brandy. Then, sighing, he said, 'I take it you're not seeing Kate any more then?'

Kate drove home and let herself into her house. It was quiet. Too quiet. She went into the kitchen and made herself a cup of tea. She sat at the table drinking it, still with her coat on. She could not take in the events of the last few hours. Everything had gone wrong. Terribly wrong.

Her job was on the line, she was finished with Patrick, everything she believed in was being trampled underfoot. She put her arms on the kitchen table and cried.

Last night she had slept with a murderer. A man who could pay money for the ending of another man's life. The logical part of her brain told her that Patrick was settling the score for his daughter's death in the only way he knew how. To him there was only black and white. You destroy something of mine, I destroy something of yours.

But inside herself, Kate knew this thinking went against the grain of her profession, her beliefs. Patrick Kelly still lived by the old adage: 'An eye for an eye'. And that was wrong. It had to be wrong. Otherwise all she had instilled in her own child, all she had lived and worked for, counted for nothing.

Yet still a tiny nagging doubt burned into her. Supposing he was right?

If her child was murdered could she honestly say she

could forgive? Would she be happy knowing the perpetrator of the deed was alive, locked up maybe but alive, while her child was dead? She remembered reading somewhere that the mother of one of Myra Hindley's victims had even found out when Hindley's mother had died and had turned up at the funeral to berate her.

As a mother herself, she could understand that feeling of hatred.

But murder?

She licked away the salt tears from her mouth.

Flowers was quite willing to use her association with Patrick Kelly for his own ends. He had dropped her from the case, and despite all her shouting about the DPP and the Lord Chief Justice she knew that she was finished. If she went to the papers it would cause a stink for a few days, but that would be all. Because Patrick Kelly would look like a hero to everyone. A vigilante who had taken the law into his own hands. Were there many men who would not sympathise with him?

He would be like a modern day Robin Hood while she would come out of it as the bitter mistress who had been dumped and was trying to get her own back.

Between them, Kelly, Flowers and Caitlin had her right where they wanted her. But the worst of it was that, for all Patrick had done and was going to do, she still wanted him.

Chapter Thirty-One

Edith was worried – about what she was not really sure. Since George's weird reaction to Natalie, she had felt a shiver of apprehension go through her every time they were together. It was nonsense, of course. George was her closest living relative. Her child was like his child.

She shrugged. He had just been overcome, that was all. The flight, the excitement, they had taken their toll.

Today, at lunch, he seemed a bit more relaxed. Edith watched him as he stared across the table at her daughter. It seemed to her, though, that he stared at Natalie for too long. She had to force herself to look away from George and concentrate on Joss when he was talking.

George, like herself, had obviously noticed Natalie's startling resemblance to their mother. Over the years it had distressed her too, so she could guess how he was feeling. But inside Natalie was the antithesis of their mother. She was kind, considerate, caring; she had a lot of friends, real friends, that bore evidence to this. She was a beautiful person inside and out. And if the talks they had had were to be believed, she was still a virgin.

No, Natalie had none of her grandmother's

licentiousness. A deeply religious girl, she lived a good, clean, wholesome life. They would never have to worry about Natalie.

Unaware of the stir she was creating, Natalie was listening to her father telling one of his long boring golf stories. She was a good daughter who laughed in all the right places and Joss loved her for this alone. His son on the other hand looked bored, as did George and Edith. He brought the story to a premature ending and concentrated on his steak.

George still watched Natalie closely, unaware that Edith was watching him.

Every movement the girl made was his mother's, even the way she brushed her hair from her face. Her shoulders in the lightweight dress were his mother's. They looked too fragile to hold up the enormous breasts.

George cut into his steak so hard he scraped his knife across the plate, causing more than one set of teeth to be set on edge.

'How long are you staying, Uncle George?' Joss Junior was not really interested but felt the question was expected from him.

'For a couple of weeks. If I like it I might sell up and move out here. I have nothing at home any more.'

Edith's heart immediately went out to him. Poor George. No wonder he was acting so strangely. Elaine leaving him must have been a bitter blow.

'Well, you're welcome to stay here as long as you want, until you find a place of your own.'

George smiled at her gratefully and Joss Senior chewed harder on his steak.

Edith's brother troubled him. He was too damn' meek and mild. His eyes went to his son and he swallowed hard. He had often wondered who the boy took after; now he knew. Try as he might he could not really love his only son. There was something disturbing about him. He felt the same about George Markham. But he was Edith's brother, her closest family, and he would accommodate him.

There was something funny about Edith's family. About the set up. The mother had been as mad as a hatter, the other children like scared mice. The eldest, Joseph, had seemed to him more like his mother's lover than her son. From the bits and pieces that Edith had let drop over the years he knew they'd all had a terrible upbringing. He remembered when he had gone to tell Nancy Markham he was marrying Edith. Her malice as she'd told him about her daughter's illegitimate child had shocked him.

She was sick in the head, Nancy Markham. No wonder the children all turned out weird. Except for Edith. She had been the sweetest girl he had ever known, and even though over the years he had systematically cheated on her with everyone and anyone, he still loved her. He still thought of her as that same sweet girl he married. But Edith had a distaste for sex, touching, even kissing. Oh, she had tried to hide it, but he knew. You always know when your attentions are welcome and when they're not. But she was a damn' fine wife and mother and that was the main thing.

Natalie watched her uncle eating and smiled at him. She had heard stories about her Uncle George all her life. He was her mother's closest living relative. She knew her grandmother was alive. They heard from her only occasionally, and after a communication her mother was always jumpy for a few weeks.

Her greeny-blue eyes surveyed the room around her. She loved this house. She loved being inside it with her family. One day, when she met the right man, she would own a house just like it and she'd fill it with children and laughter. She smiled to herself at the thought.

Until then she had her job and her dogs. It was Natalie who had named the Dobermans. She had read Dante's *Inferno* and it had made a great impression on her. Dobermans to her were devil dogs. But she loved them, as she loved all animals.

George watched his niece. When she had smiled at him then he had been convinced that it was his mother sitting opposite him. George felt the strangeness that came over him at times. As if he was hand in hand with reality one minute and left out, floating in limbo, the next. The room had taken on smoky edges. Nothing looked solid any more. His mind was filled with thoughts, crowded with them as if they didn't have enough room to manoeuvre. Flickering pictures entered this brimming morass. He saw Geraldine O'Leary with her long beautiful hair lying beneath him. He saw Mandy Kelly and he saw Elaine. They all drifted in and out of his mind, and after every vision this girl was before him. He felt an urge to take his steak knife and push it through her throat. Let the blood bubble from the wound, strangling his mother's voice.

He could hear her now: 'Who's Mummy's little soldier, Georgie?'

He could smell the sheets on the bed, scented with Lux flakes. He could hear the dreadful ack-ack of the anti-aircraft fire. The bombs were going to land on their house but Mother made them stay in bed while she drank tea and smoked. He could feel the ache in his bowels and the red rawness of his rectum where the tubing had been forced past his sphincter. Sweat was pouring from his brow. He could feel it running on to the pillows with his frightened tears. Why didn't she come? Why didn't she comfort him? He was Mummy's little soldier, wasn't he?

'George . . . George. Joss is talking to you, dear.'

He was dragged back to the present and looked around the table, bewildered.

'Are you feeling all right, George?' Edith's voice was concerned.

Joss Junior glanced at his watch. 'I really have to go soon, Mother, if I'm to catch my plane.'

Edith was immediately concerned. George took the opportunity to try and pull himself together.

'Natalie's company gave her the week to see her uncle. I wish yours had done the same.'

Joss Junior smiled. 'Well, Ma, I'm doing an important job. They can't afford to let me have too much time off.'

Edith was gratified to hear this.

'Your father and I will run you to the airport. Finish your meal.'

Natalie stretched in her chair, pushing her long tapering fingers through her hair in a completely feminine gesture. Edith and Joss Senior watched her with pride. George watched her with hatred. Joss Junior took no notice of her whatsoever.

'Do you want to drive to the airport with us, George?'

'No. I think I'll just relax, Edith. I feel so tired.'

'Do you want me to stay here with Uncle George?' Natalie's voice was concerned.

'No. You leave your uncle, let him have a rest, Natalie. Come with us and see your brother off at the airport.'

For some reason, Edith did not want George and her daughter left alone.

George smiled at them as he waved them off a little later. Then, climbing into his car, he made his way to the Orange Blossom Trail.

Duane Portillo watched the little family climbing into

the large Lincoln Continental. A few minutes later he followed George Markham out towards the Orange Blossom Trail.

Linette Du Bouverie was what was known on the trail as an 'ornery' whore. She was petite and a natural redhead. But she sure was 'ornery'. She was known as the loudest, most foul-mouthed and argumentative woman on the Trail. Her vicious mouth was hated by other whores, pimps and police, in that order. She was a heroin addict and needed her daily fixes desperately. Linette would take a man on for a measly five dollars if necessary.

Today she was banging on the door of the little one-roomed apartment of Elvis Carmody.

Elvis was a pusher of uncertain creed. He had black wiry hair and the reddish skin colour of a Mexican. His mother, a hooker, used to joke that he was her Heinz 57. She never knew who fathered him. Elvis had built himself a business of sorts. He supplied heroin, crack, dope, uppers, downers . . . anything, in fact, that he could lay his hands on. He opened the apartment door to Linette and whistled at her through his teeth.

'You look terrible, baby!'

She walked into the room on her high heels. She was having trouble focusing properly in the dim light. Somewhere in the room she heard the rustle of bedclothes and, peering through the dimness, made out the shape and face of a little Puerto Rican hooker named Marigold. She swore under her breath. If Elvis had just had some ass he was not going to come across to her and give her a little bit on account.

'What can I do for you, Linette?' Already Elvis wanted rid of her.

'I need a fix. I'll pay you in about an hour, man, there's

nothing going down in the street just yet. Once it's dark the place will be buzzing.'

Elvis lit a Marlboro and blew out the smoke noisily. 'No way, baby, you still owe me twenty bucks from yesterday.'

Linette felt her famous temper rising. Going to the bed, she grabbed Marigold's hair.

'You'd give her some, though, wouldn't you, you motherfucking creep? I'll pay you the goddam' money, but first I need me a little bit on account.'

Elvis walked to her and untangled her fingers from the girl's hair. Marigold had not batted an eyelid.

Taking Linette by the scruff of her neck, he ran her to the doorway and threw her on to the dirty floor outside.

'Why don't you quit annoying people, Linette? If you didn't have such a bad attitude, people might be more inclined to help you.'

He shut the door on her. Dragging herself up, she threw herself at the wood, kicking and pummelling the door. There were tears of frustration in her dark green eyes.

'I'll cut your motherfucking throat, you stinking creep!'

There was no answer from the room. Feeling sorry for herself, Linette walked from the building into the bright sunlight outside.

George saw a tiny, slim girl of about twenty-five lounging against a wall. Her red hair was catching the rays of the sun and she was dressed in a green suede hot pants suit. Her ample breasts practically spilled out of the material and he smiled at her. His secret smile that just showed his teeth.

Linette, knowing a punter when she saw one, smiled back. Her sweetest smile.

George opened the window of his car. Linette ambled over to him.

'Hello there.'

George smiled again, wider this time. 'Hello, dear.'

'How would you like some company?'

'Get in.'

Linette walked round and got inside the car. 'Drive to the Lazy Q. We can get a room there, movies, anything you want.'

George was already on his way. Linette lit a cigarette and smiled to herself as they neared the motel. He knew where he was going so he wasn't that green. She wondered how much she should hit him for. She could already feel the sweating that told her she needed a fix. And soon.

The man who gave them the key was now watching an episode of *Married with Children*. George wondered briefly if he ever left the TV set. Up in the room, Linette picked up the phone and ordered a bottle of bourbon. It would ease her nerves till she could score some smack.

While she waited for it to come she slipped off her clothes. George watched her, fascinated. It was as if she did not even realise he was there. She had not attempted to make conversation. He sat on the bed and took out some small change. Putting two fifty cents into the meter on the television, he turned the knob and a porno film flickered into life on the screen. Linette answered the door to the boy with the bourbon, naked except for her shoes. Linette never removed her shoes. Ever.

She looked at George. 'I need ten dollars.'

He calmly peeled the money off a large roll and gave it to her. The young black boy watched her in total fascination as she swayed towards him in her high heels.

'Here you are, boy. Take a good look. And when you get paid, child, you come and see Linette.'

'Yes, ma'am.' This was said with every bit of manliness the fourteen year old could muster.

Linette shut the door and laughed. She cracked the top and drank the whisky from the bottle.

'That's a lot of money you got there, honey.'

George took off his clothes and folded them neatly on a chair.

'How much do you want?'

She liked his meekness. 'I charge sixty dollars, the best lay you're ever gonna get.'

George handed three twenty-dollar bills to her.

He watched the film for a moment. It was of a woman, a dog and a large black man.

Linette sat beside him on the bed. Pushing her breasts against his arm she stroked his flaccid penis. She wanted this over with as quickly as possible.

'Come on, baby, Linette ain't got all night.'

George could smell her sweat. Her hair was lying across his arm and he could see her rosy nipples. Her hand on his penis had deep red-painted nails. She looked just like his mother. She even smelt like his mother. He pushed her hand away from him impatiently.

'Don't touch me like that.'

George's voice was hard. Linette fell backwards with the force of his push.

'Who the hell you think you're pushing, you little shit!' Her natural antagonism was surfacing.

George faced her. She was standing now, the whiskey bottle still in her hand. Her legs were long and shapely in the green high heels. She took another long pull of the Jim Beam. George stood up and faced her.

She was just like his mother. Just like Natalie. They were all whores, every last one of them. Give themselves to anyone who had a couple of pounds. All women were the same. They were whores. Well, he knew what to do with whores, didn't he? Hadn't he shown them in Grantley? Grabbing her hair, he punched her in the face, putting all his weight behind the blow. He watched, a smile on his face, as Linette staggered backwards and fell against the wall. The blow had hit her in the mouth and she leant against the wall, her breasts heaving. She poked a little pink tongue out of her mouth and tasted the blood that was seeping from her lip. She watched warily as he walked towards her. He was naked and his stomach wobbled as he walked.

As he lifted his fist again Linette kicked out. George felt a stinging sensation and when he looked down he had a cut across his stomach.

Linette Du Bouverie kept a blade in the toe of each shoe, a trick she'd learned in prison.

That's why Linette never took her shoes off. George watched the blood begin to run and looked at the woman in astonishment. He lurched at her, putting up his hands to seize her hair, and grabbed empty space.

Linette kicked out at him again. This time she caught his back. A long searing pain engulfed him. She had ripped the skin right across the kidney. It was a deep cut of half an inch. As he dropped to his knees Linette took another long pull of whiskey, then smashed the bottle against the chest of drawers by the bed. His back was bleeding profusely now.

Using all the strength that he could muster, George slammed his fist into her solar plexus. Linette doubled up as she tried to breathe. George pulled himself up to his feet; his hands were covered in blood.

On the screen, the black man, the woman and the dog careered around, impervious to what was going on.

'You friggin' creep, nobody hits me, nobody. Not you,

not anyone.' Her mouth was a twisted gash. This time the blade caught him across his thighs, the blood spurted out in crimson droplets, the skin opening slowly, as if shy about revealing the flesh beneath. George dropped to his knees once more, for the first time realising he was up against a will much stronger than his own. This woman was of the same calibre as his mother. Pulling his head back by his hair, Linette grinned at him as she brought the jagged edge of the Jim Beam bottle across his throat.

George dropped to the floor, his face turned towards the television. His last sight was of the woman grunting as the black man pushed his impossibly large member inside her, the little dog yapping as it ran around their bodies.

Linette sat on the bed, dropping the bottle on to the carpet. She placed a bloody hand on to her breast to stem the beating of her heart. Looking down at George, she drew her lips back from her teeth in disgust.

Linette had been physically and mentally abused all her short life. Her father had been the main offender, her brothers had followed his example. Her mother had turned a blind eye. When Linette had left home at fifteen, she had been thrust into a world where only her looks and her sex had been her saving graces. She had taken her first fix and turned her first trick within thirty-six hours of hitting the streets. Selling her body was all she could do. Allowing men a free licence with it was all she had ever known. But once she'd left home, Linette had always balked at being beaten. It was the thing she hated most. Sexually, she'd do anything for money. Anything. But a man or woman beating up on her was an admission of failure. If she could keep herself protected then she still had a certain amount of self respect. It was important to her. Her violent reputation had stood her in good stead over the last few years. A violent whore was not wanted by a pimp, a violent whore would not get robbed by another whore. The law of the streets was strength, and even though she was tiny, she was strong and she could look after herself. The man on the floor was nothing to Linette, he was a trick, a John, a means to an end. Without looking at him again she got up from the bed and went to the shower. She washed the blood from her body, then calmly got dressed, brushed her hair and repaired her make-up, feeling the slight swelling already around her eye. She took all George's cash and traveller's cheques. She left the credit cards; she'd quickly become a suspect if she tried to use them. Taking one last look at herself in the mirror, she left the room, shutting the door quietly behind her. Ten minutes later she was at Elvis's, George's eight hundred dollars assuring her of a very warm welcome. As she pushed the needle into her arm, she felt the first waves of euphoria rushing to her brain; she breathed in deeply and let the good feelings flow.

George Markham was already gone from her mind.

Duane Portillo watched Linette walk from the hotel. He sat up in his seat and waited for George to emerge. But George did not come out.

George still lay on the floor of the motel room, still staring, vacant eyed, at the blue movie. The blood had long ceased pumping. The girl on the film seemed to be staring back at him, her face a mask of pretended pleasure.

But George couldn't see her. It was a shame really. He would have loved it.

Edith was getting worried. They had got back from the airport and George was nowhere to be seen. Every time she heard a car she rushed to the window to see if it was him.

'Oh, for Christ's sake, Edith, he's a grown man,' Joss told her. 'He's probably gone out for a beer and got talking to someone.'

She did not bother to answer. She tutted. Imagine thinking George would get talking to someone. Sometimes she didn't think that Joss realised just what was going on around him. George talking to strangers indeed!

Natalie kissed them good night and went up to bed. Edith watched her walk up the stairs and felt the pride she always felt in her children.

She had done well for them. She had always looked after them and protected them.

The police answered the call at eleven thirty. The hotel manager had dragged his eyes away from the television set at eleven twenty to go and rout out room number 14. They had been in there for over five hours. He now had another couple who wanted the room. He asked them to wait and went up and knocked on the door.

It was deathly quiet.

He unlocked the room with his master key. He was not too shocked at what he found. He told the couple to come back another time, and hid George's credit cards before he phoned the police.

Edith was informed at twelve ten precisely.

Duane Portillo watched the proceedings before he left the scene. He went straight to Shaun O'Grady with his story. Shaun scratched his head in bewilderment.

'You mean the guy you was gonna kill has been killed! By a goddam whore, for Chrissakes!'

Duane nodded. He couldn't quite believe it himself.

Shaun O'Grady saw the funny side.

'Well, who the hell would credit that?'

Duane Portillo laughed too. It sure had been a weird day.

Kate was helping Lizzy sort out what clothes she was taking. Since she had been dropped from the Grantley Ripper case, she had tried to assume an air of nonchalance but it had gradually been slipping away from her.

'Mum?'

'What, love?'

Lizzy turned her mother to face her.

'What's wrong really? Have you had a tiff with Patrick?'

Kate felt an urge to cry and laugh at the same time. A tiff? Lizzy sat on her bed and looked at her mother.

'Please tell me what's wrong with you, Mum. I can't stand seeing you so unhappy.'

Kate looked into the dark eyes so like her own and felt a rush of love for her daughter.

As she tried to speak her voice broke and Lizzy pulled her into her arms. Kate sobbed her heart out on her daughter's shoulder.

Somewhere a little voice was saying that this was wrong. That it was she who should be comforting her daughter. But it felt so good to have someone to hold her, and kiss her hair, and tell her everything was going to be all right. Even though she knew in her heart that nothing would ever be all right again. That all she had wanted and held dear was destroyed. That she had been used by a man she loved so desperately that she would still have him now, if he came to her.

Lizzy stroked her mother's hair and sighed gently. It felt good to be able to help her for once; to feel that she was in control of the situation. That her mother could let down her defences and admit that she was not Wonder Woman, that she had problems too.

It made her seem more human somehow.

Lizzy knew with the awareness of womankind that she could help her mother by holding her and loving her. For the first time ever, they were equals. They had healed a breach that spanned fifteen years. In spite of all her heartache, it felt good to Kate. It felt very good.

Later on, in her lounge with her mother and Lizzy, Kate heard the shock statement on News at Ten. She was drinking a bacardi and coke, having just got out of the bath. Lizzy had run it for her, filling it with the fragrance of lavender to make her feel calmer.

She had needed all her calm when Sandy Gall started speaking.

'A British tourist was murdered today in Florida by a prostitute. George Markham was savagely slashed to death and his throat cut. From the reports we have had in so far, Mr Markham, who was fifty-one years old, had been wanted by the British police in connection with the murders of six women and a child. He is believed to have been the Grantley Rapist. The police here have confirmed that they wanted to interview him on his return from Florida.

'In the Lebanon today . . .'

'Jesus suffering Christ!' Evelyn's voice was shocked and low.

Kate stared at Sandy Gall's face for a moment. Then, jumping from her seat, she went to the hall and phoned Caitlin's home number. It was answered on the second ring.

'I take it you've heard the news, Katie?'

'It's true then?'

'Oh, it's true all right. It seems he got his come-uppance. He was murdered by a known prostitute called Linette something or other. She told police that he attacked her and it was self-defence.'

701

Kate nodded into the phone, forgetting Caitlin couldn't see her.

'Are you still there, Kate?'

'Yes. Oh, Kenny, I feel such a fool.'

She heard the smile in his voice as he answered. 'I told you not to jump in at the deep end, but you wouldn't listen, would you?'

'No.'

'Look, Katie, have another few days off. I'll speak to Flowers for you. You're a good policewoman and I know he doesn't want to lose you. Now this Ripper thing is over, I think we can all relax.'

Kate said goodbye and hung up.

She felt such a blasted fool. She had accused Patrick Kelly of trying to murder the man. She had gone to his house and shouted her mouth off. She could hear everything she'd said and her face burned with humiliation.

He must feel disgusted with her. And who in their right mind could blame him?

She put her head against the coolness of the wall and sighed. Everything had gone wrong and it had been her fault. She was suspended from work, but more importantly to her she had botched up the only chance of real happiness she'd had.

As Patrick would say, she was a 24-carat fool.

Her mind was filled with thoughts of the nights she had spent with him. The excitement. The closeness. The shared love.

He had told her he loved her, and how had she repaid him?

Patrick took the call at seven fifteen.

Willy watched him exclaim: 'You're joking!'

O'Grady's voice crackled over the line.

'No, Pat, it was a classic, I tell you. I waited until I could get the full facts before phoning you. The man picked up a prostitute on the Orange Blossom Trail. That's Florida's answer to Soho, you know. Well, it seems things got a bit out of hand and he attacked her. That's always a whore's defence, of course: The man attacked me, so I pulled a knife, a gun, whatever.

'By all accounts she said she never reported it to the police because she knew that they wouldn't believe her. When it came on CNN today that the man was wanted in England as a serial killer, this place went wild. The woman's a frigging national heroine, for Chrissakes.'

'Jesus, I can't believe what you're telling me. Markham murdered my daughter. I would have followed him to the ends of the earth. But to have that happen to him . . . I mean, it's just unbelievable.'

O'Grady's voice was quiet.

'Believe it, buddy. He's dead. Now you just go on living your life. I'll see that the money's returned to you tomorrow. I've got to give my guy something though. He still trailed him, you know.'

'Anything you say, Shaun.'

Kelly replaced the receiver and stared at it for a few seconds as if not sure he had really had the call.

He stared at Willy. 'You're not going to believe this.'

'Try me.'

Edith looked down at George's body and felt the sting of tears.

'Is this your brother, ma'am?' The policeman's voice was low and reassuring.

She nodded.

She looked at the man as he gestured to the mortuary

703

assistant to cover George's face again. Suddenly she felt very old and frightened.

'Ma'am, I have some more distressing news for you.'

'What? What could be worse than this?'

'We have been notified by the British police that your brother had murdered seven people, including his own wife and a young child. It seems the British cops were waiting for him to return to Britain to arrest him.'

Edith realised she had known this inside all along. She still read the English papers, knew all about this Grantley Ripper. Deep down in her heart she had known it was her brother. She looked into the policeman's sympathetic face.

'Joss, please take me home.'

He pulled himself wearily from his seat and took his wife's arm. In their car Edith spoke.

'I know what George did was wrong and I'll regret his coming here for the rest of my life. But, Joss, only I know why he was like he was. And knowing what I know, all I can do is pity him.'

Her husband said nothing.

If the whore who had done it would come forward, Joss would shake her by the hand.

Joseph Markham and his wife watched the news in stunned silence. Both looked over to Nancy and saw that her face was grey and drawn.

Lily was the first of the three to come to herself. 'How will we ever live this down?' she shrieked. 'Your brother, the Grantley Ripper!'

'Oh, be quiet, Lily. George was always a stupid fool. All my children were useless,' snapped Nancy. 'Look at him.' She flicked her head at Joseph. 'He sits there like a big lummock. His brother is a murdering rapist and he just sits there. At least George had some life in him.'

'We'll have to sell the house, I can't live here now. The neighbours will be laughing up their sleeves. Every time we leave the house people will be pointing at us, talking about us.'

'I knew there was something wrong with George, I told the policeman that the other day. My sons are spineless nobodies. All my children are. Not one of them inherited a thing from me. They're all like their father. He was just the same.'

Joseph Markham listened to his wife's high-pitched voice and his mother's deep-throated tirade and finally, after thirty years, he spoke up.

'SHUT UP, THE PAIR OF YOU!'

Nancy and Lily both stared at him in shock.

'You,' he pointed to his mother, 'are going in to that home, first thing in the morning. I can't wait another week to get shot of you.'

She opened her mouth to speak and Joseph raised his hand menacingly.

'I told you to shut up, woman.'

His wife's mouth dropped open.

'The house is being sold, Lily, and you will get half the money. I am buying myself a flat and neither of you two will have the address. I've spent all my life listening; first to you, Mother, then to Lily, and finally to the blasted pair of you. I must be the only man in Christendom nagged in stereo.

'Well, the buck stops here. George murdered all those people, including Elaine, and neither of you two even care. You're worried about the neighbours. Fuck the neighbours! I couldn't care less about them. My brother is dead, six women and a child have been murdered by him. So why don't you two just shut your bloody stupid mouths up and think about other people for once?'

He began to walk from the room.

'Where are you going?' Lily's voice was frightened.

'Where the hell do you think? I'm going to phone poor Edith. She must be in a terrible state. Then I'm going to get my coat and go to a hotel. I'll be back tomorrow to arrange for her to be put away – as far away as possible, I might add – and to sort this lot.' He gestured around him with his hands.

Ten minutes later, they heard his car splutter to life and drive away.

'This is all your fault!' Lily turned on her mother-in-law.

'Why don't you piss off?' Nancy's voice was bored-sounding.

Lily pursed her lips. There had been too much swearing tonight for her liking. Just as she and Joseph were getting on a good footing, this had to happen!

As he drove along Joseph tried to piece together the night's events in his mind.

George had finally gone over the top. Why hadn't anyone noticed? He had been left too much to his own devices, Joseph supposed. They rarely visited except for Christmas. He was George's elder brother and should have looked out for him more.

Well, his mother had gone too far this time. He must have been mad to put up with her all these years. His threat to Lily was shallow, he wouldn't leave her, but he had a sneaky feeling that letting her think he would might augur better for their future.

Edith was in a terrible state, she was barely coherent. And deep down inside Edith knew, as he did, that it was their mother's fault. He remembered shamefully how they had held George down while he was a child. How she had gradually strangled every natural instinct in them.

Joseph pulled the car over and sat for a few minutes. His hands were shaking on the steering wheel.

Into his mind came a picture of George when he was a small boy, in his National Health glasses and long grey socks. They had been playing hide and seek while their mother was out working and George was laughing his head off. Real, robust, childish laughter. Joseph remembered it clearly because it had happened so rarely.

The Markowitz children had had nothing to laugh about most of the time.

Joseph wept.

He wept for the George he had known. The little boy he should have protected more. The little boy who used to cry every night, who was frightened of his mother and yet loved her so much. No matter what she did to him.

Patrick Kelly slept heavily that night, a long blissful sleep, the first since his daughter had been murdered.

His last thought as he drifted off was of Kate. He wished she was beside him, but after what she had said, he knew the gulf between them was too wide.

Kate Burrows was a luxury he couldn't afford. Tomorrow he would get out his little black book. Go back to the women who understood him. Who wanted nothing more from him than a good time.

He didn't need Kate Burrows. She was a forty-year-old woman while he could have any gorgeous girl he wanted. And have them he would. He would become a playboy again.

He smiled to himself at the thought. That would please Willy. He had always enjoyed observing his boss's affairs.

Kate Burrows could get stuffed.

Happy he had sorted his life out, Patrick slept.

*

Kate lay awake, her mind in a turmoil, her body aching to be touched. To be comforted by Patrick Kelly's lovemaking.

Chapter Thirty-Two

4 March 1990

Kate was in the airport lounge watching Lizzy and her mother checking in for their flight. She stood by as their baggage was tagged and taken from them. A feeling of desolation assailed her. She would be alone for six weeks.

All she had was her work, and she was not happy with that, she admitted to herself. She wished she was getting on the plane with them. That she was going somewhere where she could forget the last few months.

Lizzy and Evelyn approached her. Kate watched the tall slim girl, who caught more than a few male eyes, and the stooped little woman beside her.

When had her mother developed a stoop? When had she become old?

She walked with them towards passport control, chatting about nothing. She was dreading saying goodbye, but knew that they had to go. Her mother would see her other child and the grandchildren whom she had only seen in photos and spoken to rarely, when funds allowed. She still had all their letters and had chronicled their ages from lovingly preserved school photos.

Dear Grandma . . . Now she would see them for herself. Kate was glad for her really. It was only selfishness that wanted her to stay at home.

They were at passport control now. Kate pulled her mother into her arms and kissed her hard.

'Have a good time, Mum. Look after my baby for me.'

Evelyn looked into Kate's face and said seriously, 'Haven't I always? You look after yourself.'

Lizzy was crying and Kate smiled at her, a single tear escaping from the corner of her own eye.

'Goodbye, baby.'

Lizzy threw herself into her mother's arms and hugged her.

'Oh, Mum, I wish you were coming with us. Will you be all right on your own?'

Kate kissed her again.

'You just go and have a good time. Enjoy it. Before you know it, you'll be back home.'

Evelyn stroked Kate's face. 'You ring that Patrick Kelly, you hear?'

'Oh, Mum! Get yourselves through and send me a card from Singapore.'

'It was him who paid for this, you know. I didn't have any money at all. If I had done, I'd have spent it years ago. You know that. Did you know we're going first class? He did this to try and help you when Lizzy was bad.'

Kate stared at her mother for a few seconds then Evelyn took Lizzy's arm and they walked through to the departure lounge.

Kate's head was whirling. Patrick had paid for the holiday.

It was the final humiliation. She had accused him of everything heinous under the sun and he had spent a fortune on airplane tickets and hotels for her mother and child.

Oh, the generosity of him. The concern for her. And she had taken what he had offered and thrown it back in his face.

She watched them till they were out of sight, then drove home to her empty house. As she put her key in the lock she felt it was mocking her.

At five fifty-five she poured herself the first drink. At seven she was in a drunken sleep.

Oprah Winfrey stared into the camera and smiled. Her studio audience was finishing its applause and the opening credits had been rolled.

'Thank you.' She looked around at her audience. 'Five weeks ago in Windermere, Florida, a man attacked a prostitute. The woman, Ms Linette Du Bouverie, fought the man off, killing him. She left the scene of the crime because she was frightened of the consequences. She was later identified by a young man who worked at the hotel who had delivered a bottle of Jim Beam to the room. It turned out that Ms Du Bouverie had in fact killed a vicious serial killer from England. Tonight we hear from women who have killed the men who attacked them. Let us start by giving a big hand to Linette Du Bouverie.'

The audience went wild.

Linette walked out on to the stage and smiled. She was pretty and petite and looked like everybody's next-door neighbour.

Elvis watched her smile at the camera and laughed out loud. That Linette was some bad dude.

Kate came home from work and made herself a coffee. In the month that Lizzy and her mother had been away, her routine had not changed at all. The empty house seemed to mock her and she put the radio on as she did every night to fill up the hollowness with sound. What she would not give to have Lizzy's music blaring out now!

The phone rang and she picked it up. It was Amanda Dawkins.

'Hello, love.'

'I wondered if it was all right if me and Phil popped round tonight, Kate? We've got a great video and a bottle of wine.'

She smiled into the phone.

Amanda did this every so often, came around with her boyfriend as if she knew that Kate was lonely and needed a bit of company.

'That would be lovely, Amanda, as long as you're sure you haven't got anything better to do?'

'We'll see you about half past eight.'

'What's the video?'

'*Beaches* with Bette Midler.'

'I bet Phil didn't pick that one!'

'You guessed exactly right! If he'd have chosen it, we would have watched *Nightmare on Elm Street* or *Hallowe'en*!'

'See you later then.'

She had a sandwich and went upstairs for a bath.

Patrick Kelly glanced at the girl beside him. Leona had the biggest blue eyes he had ever seen in his life, and the biggest breasts. She faced him and smiled, displaying white teeth. 'Would you like another glass of wine?'

'Please.'

She had a little lisp that had sounded enchanting when he first met her. Now it was beginning to get on his nerves.

Leona was one of a series of women he had been dating since his break up with Kate. Patrick was hoping against hope that one of the bevy of lovelies would take his mind off her once and for all. He had hoped Leona would be the one to pull him out of himself.

He poured her a glass of white wine. It was cheap Liebfraumilch. There was no way he was going to give her expensive wine. She drank it down in two gulps. He watched her do it, leaving a thick red line on the rim of the glass.

'How old are you, Leona?'

'Twenty-one, why?'

'I just wondered, that's all.'

Kelly sipped his own wine and racked his brains for something to talk about.

Leona watched his troubled face. This was their third date and he hadn't tried it on once. This was a novelty to Leona and she wasn't sure if she was glad or not. He was a damn' sight better looking than most of the men she dated.

She made a golden rule of going to places where the clientèle were men who were rich, getting on, and not too fussy. She was astute enough to know that with her looks and body she could have her pick of them.

She drove a brand new Golf Gti, had her own flat, bought and paid for, and relied heavily on men like Patrick Kelly to supplement her lifestyle. Leaving school with no qualifications, and nothing going for her except a pretty face and a double D bra size, she had quickly assessed her position and cashed in on her only assets.

So far, along with the flat and the car, they had taken her around the world.

She could like this Kelly, though. He was a good-looking man with an air about him that she liked. She was quite looking forward to getting into bed with him. He seemed very generous as well, which to Leona was the most important thing.

She watched him struggling to find something to talk about. 'Tell me all about yourself, Patrick.'

She relaxed into her chair. Someone had told her once that the secret of keeping a man happy was to get him started on his favourite subject: himself. This had been proved correct over and over again; it kept them occupied for hours. Leaving Leona to think about *her* favourite subject: herself.

Patrick still struggled while he told her bits and pieces. He didn't want to share any part of his personal business with her. He didn't really want her there at all.

He couldn't be bothered to make the effort to chat. He took the bull by the horns.

'Want to come to bed?'

Leona shrugged.

'OK.'

She followed him up the stairs, pricing everything she saw on the way.

He was rich all right.

Phil studied Kate and Amanda as they watched the film. He smiled to himself. Women loved nothing more in a film than a good death. It amazed him. He had sat through *Terms of Endearment* and *Who Will Love My Children?*. Both films Amanda had loved while he had hated them. Deathbed scenes weren't his favourite subject. He would much rather be watching *Predator*, there was plenty of death in that, but it was not slow and lingering enough for Amanda. Or Kate for that matter. Women liked a good bout of cancer or someone coughing up a lung. That appealed to them.

He cracked open another lager and poured out more wine for the two women. Kate and Amanda had a box of Kleenex on the settee between them and every so often a little hiccough could be heard.

Kate gazed at the screen and sniffed. She loved a good weepy, and it was nice to cry in company. Bette Midler was on the beach with her best friend's daughter, trying to make friends with her before her mother died.

She sipped her wine and wiped her eyes again. She felt so lonely. So very, very lonely.

She got up from the settee and went out to the kitchen. She had made some sandwiches earlier and now took the cling film off them and brought them into the lounge.

Phil, his bright copper-coloured hair shining in the light from the television screen, grinned at her as he took the plate and started to eat.

Kate hoped they wouldn't stay too late tonight. She liked to go to bed and read for a while until she dropped off. Amanda had really come up trumps for her since the Grantley Ripper inquiry, and Kate appreciated that. But sometimes you can be lonely even when you're in a crowd, and that was just how Kate was feeling. For the first time ever she had more than enough time to devote to herself and every second of it was a form of torture.

She knew what was wrong with her, and knew who could cure it. But she could not bring herself to dial his number or go to his house.

Patrick was lying on his bed naked, smoking a cigarette. Leona was still undressing. He noticed she was hanging her clothes in his wardrobe and grinned ruefully to himself. She obviously thought she was set for a good few months. He watched her as she turned to face him with her incredible breasts, a half smile on her face, waiting for the effect they always had on men.

Especially older men.

Patrick took one look at her and his heart sank down to his boots.

What was he trying to prove?

Like the others he had had in recent weeks, Leona did nothing for him whatsoever. He saw her mouth twitch with disappointment and felt a moment's sympathy for her.

She walked timidly towards him. 'Don't you like me?' Her voice was small.

'Of course I like you, you're beautiful.'

She pouted prettily and rubbed his flaccid penis. 'Leona wants to play!'

Patrick sighed. What he wouldn't give for a pack of cards or a draughts board!

She pulled his foreskin back, slowly and expertly, and Patrick felt the first stirrings inside him. He closed his eyes. When he felt the wet heat of her mouth enveloping him he groaned.

Leona sucked away as if her life depended on it. For the first time ever she had to take the initiative, and she didn't like it at all. One look at her boobs generally had them champing at the bit. She felt him stiffening in her mouth and fought down the urge to heave.

Leona hated oral sex. She usually saved it for when the man was getting tired of her. It normally gave her the edge then.

Her dark blond hair fell over her face and she cupped his testicles as gently as possible. Then, satisfied he was hard enough, she climbed on top.

She was as dry as a bone, but nevertheless forced him inside her. As she moved up and down, her breasts brushing against his chest, Patrick opened his eyes.

Instead of long, silky dark hair there was thick blond hair. Instead of Kate's small pointed breasts with their cherry red nipples there was an enormous pair, hanging over his face. Instead of dark brown eyes looking into his there was a pair of startled-looking blue ones.

Patrick Kelly lost his erection in record time.

Leona felt him deflate inside her and leapt off him in temper. How dare he? After all she had done!

She sat on the side of the bed, her arms crossed over her breasts and a frown on her pretty face.

'I'm sorry, love, I'm tired that's all.'

Leona glared at him. One thing Leona was sure of: her body was the best thing this creep had ever seen in his life. He must be a homosexual or something. She shuddered, wishing now she'd made him use a Durex.

She looked at him through slitted eyes.

'Are you a poofta, Mr Kelly?'

Patrick stared at the girl as the words penetrated. Then, to the amazement of both of them, he began to laugh. He laughed so loudly that Willy, who was in the library downstairs enjoying a brandy while he read the racing paper, looked up at the ceiling, pleased that Patrick was having such a good time.

He laughed so much that big fat tears rolled down his face.

As far as Leona was concerned, enough was enough. She dressed herself as quickly as possible. Standing over the bed, her dignity back now, along with her clothes, she poked a perfectly manicured fingernail into his chest.

'I've heard about men like you. You should come out into the open. It's not a crime any more. They call it coming out of the wardrobe. I'll bill you for my time in the morning.'

With that she went down the stairs to call a cab.

Patrick lay against the pillows. He could still smell her perfume.

He began to laugh again at her words. Then, abruptly, he stopped laughing.

In reality, she could have been his Mandy. Mandy had had a lot more savvy, he knew that, but she was the same age. What would he have thought if he had found out his daughter was sleeping with a man over twenty years her senior? And not for love either, but for a few quid and a good time.

He closed his eyes and rubbed his fingers against them, trying to blot out the image of those breasts. He felt the loneliness as it welled up inside. He should have Kate beside him. But after what had happened between them? He knew that she had thought the worst of him and admitted to himself that he was glad now that Markham had died through another's means. He was glad that he was not the cause of the man's death.

He had hoped against hope that Kate would have rung him up when she heard the news and said she was sorry. Then they could have got back on their old footing. But nothing. Not a word. And being the kind of man he was, he had had too much pride to get in touch with her.

What she had said to him had hurt because it was true. She had sussed him out all right. It was only after he knew Markham was dead, when the euphoria had worn off, that he'd realised that revenge is not as sweet as you first imagine. It had come out in all the papers about the man's terrible childhood. His sister in America had spilled the beans. Wanting to set the record straight, she said.

Kelly had read the stories and felt a funny kind of sorrow for the man. He was sick in the head. But he had already known that, hadn't he? When he was planning to kill him.

He shifted uneasily in the bed. Kate had been right. The man had needed help. He wished that she was here beside him. He had wanted Kate beside him from the minute he had seen her. He admitted that to himself now.

What was it his old mum used to say?

'God pays back debts without money.'

Well, both he and George Markham had more than paid the price.

Kate and Amanda looked at each other as the film ended and both started to laugh through their tears. Phil stood up and put on the overhead light.

'You women amaze me. Imagine watching something that makes you sad!'

'Oh, Phil! That was a lovely film.'

He walked out to the hall and was just at the bottom of the stairs, going up to the bathroom, when the phone rang. Without thinking, he picked it up.

'Hello?'

The line was quiet and he spoke again.

'Hello, who is this?' He heard the noise as the connection was broken.

Kate came out to the hall.

'Who's that?'

Phil shrugged. 'Wrong number.' He carried on walking up the stairs to the bathroom and Kate went back to make some coffee.

Patrick Kelly lay in bed with the phone in one hand and his fingers on the receiver rest.

He was fuming. It hadn't taken her long to get someone else!

He glanced at the clock. It was just after eleven fifteen. Probably interrupted their lovemaking. The snidey bitch!

To think he had thrown out a perfectly good woman because of her. Because he was silly enough to fancy himself in love with her.

Well, that was the finish as far as he was concerned. That would teach him to think that he could ever replace Renée.

Face it, boy, he told himself, you're on your Jack Jones and the sooner you realise that, the better.

Downstairs, Willy helped himself to another brandy. The girl had gone and Patrick had tried to use the phone. Willy had heard the bell as he'd picked it up, and then again as he'd put it down.

He shook his head sagely.

Patrick Kelly's trouble was he didn't know when he was well off. And he had been well off with that Burrows piece. Willy had liked her himself. She wasn't that well stacked but she'd had class.

He sipped some more of his boss's brandy and went back to reading his paper.

Kate was at work on a series of burglaries that had been happening over a two-year period. They all had the same MO. It was a lone man and he broke in while the woman was sleeping, sexually assaulting his victim before he trashed the bedroom, taking money and jewellery. It was the assaults that bothered her. He used the burglary as a blind. He was working up to a full-scale rape, she would lay money on that.

The phone rang.

'Burrows.'

'Hello, Kate.'

She took the phone from her ear and stared into the mouthpiece before answering.

'Is that you, Willy?'

'Yes.'

The line went quiet.

'Well, what can I do for you?'

'I wondered if I could see you, like?'

'What about?'

'Well, I don't like to talk about it over the phone. Can we meet, please?'

Kate licked dry lips.

'Where do you want us to meet?'

'How about the Cartella restaurant? Tonight at eight thirty?'

'Is this something to do with Patrick?'

Willy swallowed deeply and she heard the sound over the phone.

'Oh, no. He'd kill me if he thought I'd rung you up.'

Kate felt her heart sink down to her boots. So he didn't even want her name mentioned. Well, she couldn't blame him.

'See you at eight thirty then.' Before Kate could answer, the phone went dead.

Meet Willy for a meal? She pushed the thought from her mind and went back to the papers in front of her. She'd decide later what she was going to do.

Patrick walked into the drawing room and grinned. 'Where you going, all poshed up?'

Willy had on a dinner jacket and smelt like a poke of devils.

'I've got a date, actually.'

'A what! You ain't been out on a date for years.'

'Well, there's always a first time, ain't there? I got meself a right classy bird for the evening.'

Patrick laughed out loud.

'Good bleeding luck to you and all. How much is she rushing you?'

Willy looked annoyed.

'If you don't mind, Pat, just 'cos you spend most of your time with bimbos don't mean we all have to. This is a very respectable woman. Got a good job and everything. In fact, if you saw her you'd fancy her.'

Patrick looked at him and smiled. Willy usually went out with women who made a Japanese Tosa look good. But he kept his own counsel.

'Well, you use the Rolls, Willy, that'll impress her.'

'Thanks, Pat. What time's your table booked for?'

'A quarter to eight. Don't worry about driving me, I'm quite capable of taking one of the motors.'

'Okey doke then, Pat.'

Willy watched Patrick leave the house and then sat down for a minute. He hoped Kate turned up.

Kate decided she would meet Willy. If nothing else at least she could find out how Patrick was. The thought of being seen with him in public worried her, though. He looked like a bad accident, did old Willy, lovely as he was inside.

She had bought herself a new trouser suit. It was deep red and showed off her dark hair perfectly. She slipped it on with a white camisole top underneath, then stepped back from the mirror and admired herself.

Not bad.

She pulled up in the car park of Cartella at eight twenty and there, waiting for her in Patrick's Rolls Royce, was Willy. As she locked her car he walked over to her.

'You look lovely, Kate.'

She grinned at him, the overpowering smell of his aftershave making her cough. He looked almost presentable in his dinner jacket and she felt an enormous surge of affection for him. As they walked into the restaurant she took his arm. He patted her hand and smiled at her.

Patrick smiled at the girl opposite him. She really was very lovely. Since he had phoned Kate's house that night and a man answered, he had gone all out to have a good time.

He had met Michelle three days before. She was stunning, and he had watched every pair of male eyes assess her as they walked to their table. She was five foot ten, slim, and like her predecessors had enormous breasts. In the white sheath dress she was wearing, though ostensibly covered up, her breasts were actually in full view of everyone because of the way the dress moulded her tanned and healthy body. She had long blond hair and violet eyes.

For the first time in months Patrick felt he might actually get to like a girl. Michelle was a career woman. She was personal secretary to the managing director of an export firm and Patrick had met her by accident in the man's office. Unlike her predecessors, she had a brain in her head and her talk stimulated him.

She chose her own food and Patrick was gratified at her appetite. He hated women who picked at their dinner, worried that every mouthful would be an extra pound in weight. Especially when the meal cost a small fortune.

But Michelle was the kind of woman who lived life to the full.

'I've never been here before. Do you use this restaurant a lot? The maître d' seemed to know you.'

Patrick had the grace to blush.

The maître d' also knew how many women he had brought here. At one time they had run a book in the kitchen on how long a particular girl would last. Michelle deserved better than that. It was the reason he had never brought Kate here.

'It's local, you know. I don't always fancy driving into the Smoke.'

She chatted on and Patrick watched her, fascinated. She really was a lovely girl.

As Willy and Kate walked into the restaurant, arm in arm, the maître d' walked towards them with a happy smile on his face. It was Friday night, the place was packed, and he could hear the cash tills ringing. Pierre, real name Albert Diggins, had a part ownership of the Cartella, and now it was really paying its way, he was a happy man. He walked towards Kate and Willy, wondering briefly what such an attractive woman was doing with such an ugly man.

'Name, monsieur?'

'It's Gabney. Mr William Gabney. I reserved a table for two.'

'Ah, the special table. I remember the booking, I took it myself.'

He smiled widely enough to encompass them both and any strangers in the vicinity. Gabney's was the champagne table that was costing the man a hundred pounds already.

'Please, follow me.'

He swept out his arm. Kate, stifling a smile, followed with Willy. She was still holding his arm when Patrick Kelly looked up from his steak and saw them. He nearly choked.

Kate looked into his face and saw her own shock mirrored there. She watched the blonde goddess sitting opposite him get up out of her seat and playfully pat him on the back while he coughed. The action caused the girl's breasts to shimmy in such a way they caught the eye not only of Willy and every other male diner in the place but also of Pierre, who walked into a chair, doing himself a painful injury.

Kate didn't know how she kept her head. Clutching her arm tighter, Willy followed a practically cross-legged Pierre to their table.

It was only about six feet from Patrick's and the champagne was already there on ice.

Pierre made a big deal out of opening it, hoping to entice some of the other diners into ordering the same thing. It was Cristal and Kate sipped the bubbling liquid nervously. She was sitting opposite Patrick and they glanced at one another surreptitiously.

Michelle knew something was up and looked behind her.

'Do you know that woman or something?'

Patrick coloured. 'I know her slightly.'

Michelle laughed. 'I think you know her a bit better than slightly, don't you?'

He nodded.

Willy sipped his champagne and watched Kate's face. He was sorry now he'd brought her here. Kate looked at him and shook her head.

'I'm sorry, Willy, I have to go.'

She stood up and walked out of the restaurant. In the foyer she went straight into the ladies' room. She leant against the sink, her face burning with humiliation. She looked at herself in the mirror.

She looked good, she knew that, but no one could compete with the girl Patrick was sitting opposite. Poor Willy. She had walked out on him in front of everyone.

Why on earth had she decided to come?

She splashed some cold water on to her face to try and calm herself down. She put on a film of red lipstick and walked from the ladies' room.

Patrick was waiting for her.

She looked straight into his eyes.

'Hello, Kate.'

'Patrick.'

She felt as if a hot mist was gradually filling her head. His closeness was making her feel physically ill. She had to use all her willpower not to reach out and touch his hair, the lines of his face.

She looked down at the floor, unable to face him.

'How are you?'

'Fine. And you?' Kate marvelled at how normal her voice sounded.

'All the better for seeing you.'

Her eyes dragged themselves to his face of their own volition.

'I've missed you, Kate.'

Patrick was doing what he'd sworn he would never do. If she walked away now, he would feel humbled and humiliated for the rest of his life.

Kate looked into his face.

'Really?'

'Really. I love you, Kate.'

'What about Titsalina in there then?' She gestured with her head towards the dining hall. 'Do you love her as well?'

Patrick felt a moment's euphoria.

She was jealous.

Kate saw his smile and regretted the words immediately.

'No, actually, Kate, I don't. It's you I want. I can't eat, I can't sleep, I can't even bonk since we split up, if you must know.'

Kate laughed. Patrick could be so comical. Here he was begging her to have him once more, and it had been her fault they had split up in the first place!

'So what are we going to do?'

'We're going to walk out of this restaurant and go home. Home to my house, Kate.'

'But what about Willy and that . . . girl.'

'I'll sort Willy out. As for Michelle, she told me to come out here. A clever girl that, she'll go far.'

Kate looked into the blue depths of Patrick's eyes and admitted the truth to herself. She needed this man. When he was there she felt alive, really alive, and she wanted that feeling for the rest of her life.

'I've missed you, Patrick.'

As they stood there Willy came out to them.

'I'll drop Michelle off home in the Roller.'

'Thanks, Willy.' Patrick and the big man shook hands, each grasping the other's wrists.

Willy went red. 'I knew that if you two just saw each other you'd be all right.'

Kate smiled at him and he went back into the restaurant.

'Right then, shall we go home?'

Kate took the proffered arm.

'Yes, let's go home, Pat.'

In the car park they stopped by Kelly's BMW. He took her in his arms and kissed her.

Willy watched them through the window of the restaurant. They fitted together perfectly, like two pieces of a jigsaw. He held up his glass in a silent toast: To Pat and Kate.

'They thought I'd be a one-hit wonder...'

MARTINA COLE was just 18 when she got pregnant with her son. Living in a council flat with no TV and no money to go out, she started writing to entertain herself.

It would be ten years before she did anything with what she wrote.

She chose her agent for his name – Darley Anderson – and sent him the manuscript, thinking he was a woman. That was on a Friday. Monday night, she was doing the vacuuming when she took the call: a man's voice said 'Martina Cole, you are going to be a big star'.

The rest is history: *Dangerous Lady* caused a sensation when it was published, and launched one of the best selling fiction writers of her generation. Martina has gone on to have more No. 1 original fiction bestsellers than any other author.

She won the British Book Award for Crime Thriller of the Year with *The Take*, which then went on to be a hit TV series for Sky 1. Four of her novels have made it to the screen, with more in production, and three have been adapted as stage plays.

She is proud to be an Ambassador for charities including Reading Ahead and Gingerbread, the council for one-parent families. In 2013, she was inducted to the Crime Writer's Association Hall of Fame, and in 2014 received a *Variety* Legends of Industry Award.

Her son is a grown man now, and she lives in Kent with her daughter – except when she chases the sun to Cyprus, where she has two bookshops.

Her unique, powerful storytelling is acclaimed for its hard-hitting, true-to-life style – there is no one else who writes like Martina Cole.

To find out more about Martina Cole and for a Q&A with Martina on writing her DI Kate Burrows books, visit www.martinacole.co.uk.